CHAINS
OF THE
EARTH

The Ascension Cycle:
Book Three

DAVID
MEALING

orbit

orbitbooks.net

Copyright © 2023 by David Mealing

Cover design by Lisa Marie Pompilio
Cover illustrations by Arcangel and Shutterstock
Cover copyright © 2023 by Hachette Book Group, Inc.
Map by Tim Paul
Author photograph by Vakker Portraits

Orbit
Hachette Book Group
1290 Avenue of the Americas
New York, NY 10104
orbitbooks.net

First Edition: December 2023
Simultaneously published in Great Britain by Orbit

Orbit is an imprint of Hachette Book Group.
The Orbit name and logo are trademarks of Little, Brown Book Group Limited.

The publisher is not responsible for websites (or their content) that are not owned by the publisher.

The Hachette Speakers Bureau provides a wide range of authors for speaking events. To find out more, go to hachettespeakersbureau.com or email HachetteSpeakers@hbgusa.com.

Orbit books may be purchased in bulk for business, educational, or promotional use. For information, please contact your local bookseller or the Hachette Book Group Special Markets Department at special.markets@hbgusa.com.

Library of Congress Cataloging-in-Publication Data
Names: Mealing, David, 1982– author.
Title: Chains of the Earth / David Mealing.
Description: First edition. | New York, NY : Orbit, 2023. | Series: The Ascension Cycle ; book 3
Identifiers: LCCN 2023000579 | ISBN 9780316552370 (trade paperback) | ISBN 9780316552387 (ebook)
Subjects: LCGFT: Fantasy fiction. | Novels.
Classification: LCC PS3613.E157 C53 2023 | DDC 813/.6—dc23/eng/20230109
LC record available at https://lccn.loc.gov/2023000579

ISBNs: 9780316552370 (trade paperback), 9780316552387 (ebook)

Printed in the United States of America

LSC-C

Printing 1, 2023

For Jamie and Evangeline

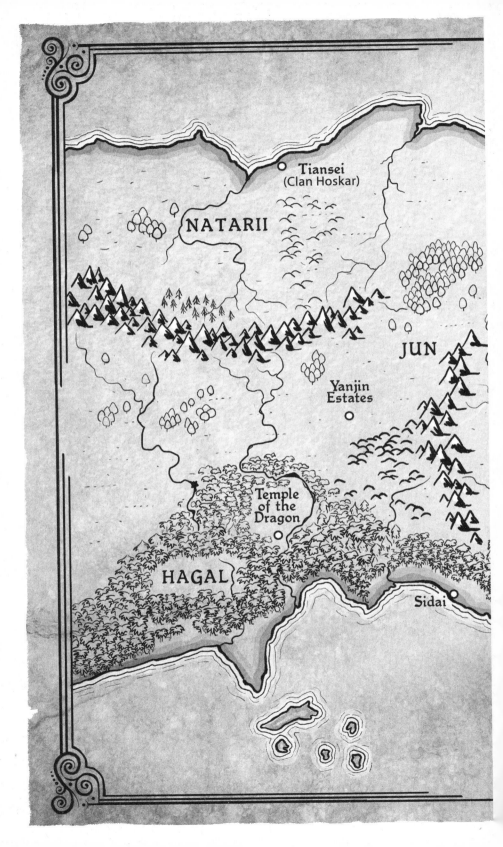

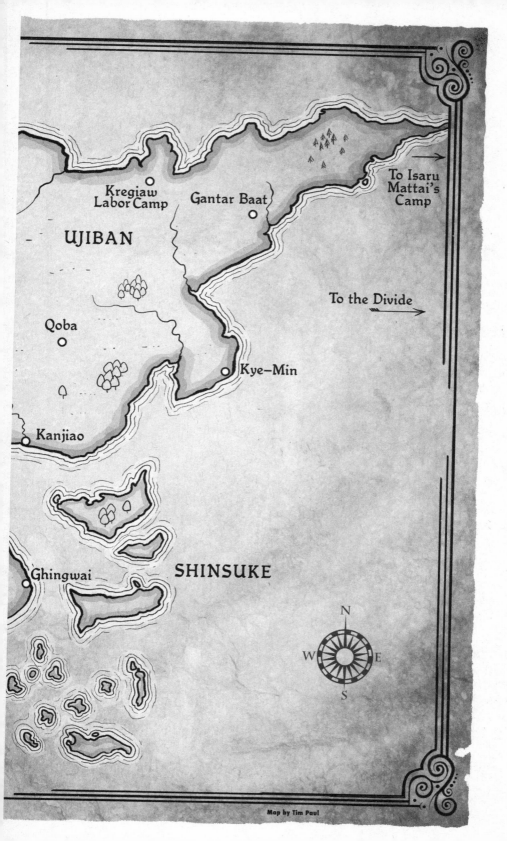

PART 1: SPRING

THE SISTER'S STOLEN GRACE

1

SARINE

Library
The Gods' Seat

The air shimmered in front of her, and the pages of the book in her lap turned without being touched.

She sat cross-legged on the cold stone floor. Shelves of books lined the walls, tomes more ancient than the oldest, most decrepit scrolls in the best-preserved libraries in the world. She'd chosen a stack that lay piled beside her, books written in long-dead languages covering metaphysics, strategy, religion; anything that might touch, however obliquely, on the coming war between her and her enemy, between Regnant and Veil. The selections had been hers, but today's reading was prompted by the shimmering man-shape rippling the air in front of her. She sat, waiting, as the pages turned, seemingly of their own accord, while the Watcher thumbed through the volume, seeking whatever it was he wanted her to see.

He's frustrated, Anati thought to her. Her *kaas* lay perched atop another stack of books, the ones she'd pulled aside yesterday that had yet to be reshelved. Anati's scales seemed to shine, as though reflecting an unseen light of purple and soft blue. *He's looking for something he can't find.*

"I thought this was his library," she said. "And he's been here for what, tens of thousands of years? You'd think he'd know it all by now."

"The ghost giving you trouble today, sister?" Yuli asked. The Natarii clanswoman sat on the opposite side of the chamber, in a chair that seemed designed to match the tattoos on her face, hides stretched over sharply pointed bone. A massive tome of Jun Imperial history lay open on her lap, each of its pages illustrated in rich color.

"I'm not sure," she said. "This is the third book he's had me stare at while he flicks the pages. Anati says he's looking for something."

"That's positive, then, isn't it?" Yuli said. "You're close to something he considers important."

"Maybe," she said. "How about you? Learning anything about our enemies?"

"Not really," Yuli said. "Except did you know Tigai was born under the sign of the Rooster, according to their sky-scholars? Supposedly it means he is hardworking and industrious, though that fits him about as well as gloves on a falcon."

"Well, if it says anything about their armies, or weaknesses in their strategic thinking," she said. "Let me know so we can add it to Erris's lists."

Yuli folded the tome delicately closed atop her lap. "Armies?" she said. "I thought this was going to be decided by champions, ours against theirs, once the Divide comes down."

"It is," she said. "Or, it should be. I don't know. Some of the Watcher's reading is making me ask questions. All of the more recent books only talk about champions, but some of the earliest ones go on and on about armies and battles, wars that cover every continent. He seems to want me to read those especially. I'm not sure why."

There, Anati thought. *He's found it.*

She turned her attention back to the book lying open in her lap. Suddenly the pages had stopped turning, and the left page was depressed, as the Watcher pushed an invisible finger into the second paragraph.

The script was one of the ancient ones; the characters blurred and became readable in her mind without her needing to think or study them too closely. One of many benefits to her bond with Anati, and an especially useful one in a library as old as this. She started reading where the Watcher's finger dented the page.

"See, this is another one," she said. "It says here they 'could devise a game to control for the chaos of war, where a champion might'...wait."

"A champion might wait?" Yuli said. "What does that mean?"

"No, I mean...wait," she said. She read the passage again. "Anati, who wrote this?"

Doesn't it say on the spine? Anati thought to her. *Or inside the cover? That's how your books are usually made, isn't it?*

"Yes," she said, inserting a finger to hold the place. "This book is *Meditations on Light and Shadow*, written by a man who calls himself Dominus. But people have other names. I've read three books I'm sure were written by Axerian now, using three different names, and this is in a similar style...only it's older. I'm sure of it. The way this writer talks, it's as though all of this, all of the champions and the war between Regnant and Veil...it's as though..."

"As though what?" Yuli said. "What does it say?"

She scanned it again, starting from the place where the Watcher's finger had indented the page.

"It's as though it hadn't happened yet, when this was written," she said. "Listen to this: *'We could divide the world in two in the regenerative stages, isolating the systems bound to her, and to him. Using champions as proxies, a game structure for power transitions minimizes risk of interference from the apex lines of emergent strains not bound to either master.'* It sounds like whoever is writing this is talking about instituting the whole thing. The champions, control over the Soul, all of it."

"That sounds like a stretch," Yuli said. "Are you sure it couldn't mean something else?"

"No," she said. "Here, it actually calls them by name: *'Absent direct interference by Regnant or Veil, the proposed Divide-based game structure ensures retention of control by isolating powers that might theoretically contest the champions at the fulcrum point of each transition.'* Anati, where did this book come from?"

What? Anati thought. *You plucked it from the shelf, over there.*

"No, I mean, ask him," she said. "Who wrote this, and how did it get into this library?"

The Watcher sat still and unmoving, an unseen finger still firmly planted in the page. Then slowly the air rippled in the shape of a head nodding.

He says it was written by who it says on the spine. "Dominus." "The Master."

"The Master," she said. "One who came before the Regnant and Veil?"

The air rippled again.

She slid the book out from under his finger, closing it gingerly and saving the place.

"Erris has to see this," she said, rising to her feet. "I have to *study* this. This could change everything. It talks about the whole thing, the champions, the Divide, the struggle for control of the bloody *world*, as though it were a game. Something they devised to keep outsiders from interfering."

Yuli joined her on her feet, falling into step with her as they left the library behind.

"How could they devise anything together?" Yuli asked as they walked. The cold stone from the library floor extended through the passages, spiraling outward toward where the Gods' Seat had made rooms for her, and each of her champions. They'd been here since the last ascensions, her and Yuli, Erris and Arak'Jur and Reyne and Tigai. Trapped, or at least in stasis, with only the map room and Erris's *Need* bindings for contact with the outside world. "Aren't the Regnant and Veil mortal enemies?"

"As far as I know," she said. "Maybe they were, and this 'Master' devised his game to keep their conflicts in check? I don't know. I've only read a few pages. We need to study it to know for sure."

"But why would it be printed and published?" Yuli said. "Did this 'Master' have an audience for his thoughts on how to devise systems to control the world?"

"I have no idea," she said. "You're right, though: It's not like the Veil's journals. This was printed and bound."

"I'm only asking because I want to be sure we're not misinterpreting," Yuli said. "Maybe this was fiction, and it only sounds like it does because that's what you want to find."

"I agree, we need to be cautious, but it referred to them by name," she said. "It sounds clear to me. We'll see what Erris thinks."

"It mentioned 'others,' too," Yuli said. "Others…peers of the Regnant and Veil? I wonder who it might mean."

She left that part unanswered, ignoring the chill she felt at Yuli's words. It was only a few paragraphs, but already the book threatened to shake her understanding of where they were, and why. A game? If the Regnant and Veil were playing a game, she was entirely ignorant of the rules. And rules could be broken. Games could be set aside. Too many had died already; how many more might die with them if all of it up to now had been a game?

She and Yuli took familiar passages spiraling outward from the Soul. The library room was one of the closest to the burning light at this place's heart. Their private chambers lined the halls leading outward, toward the map room and a handful of other, emptier chambers whose purposes she hadn't yet been able to discern. The strange art and sculpture here was slowly being replaced by the familiar, the longer they stayed: Sarresant paintings had begun to appear on the walls in place of the smeared inks and wrought iron, at least near her, Erris's, and Reyne's chambers, whereas Tigai's hall had murals of Jun soldiers, and Yuli's had plinths with limestone sculptures of fearsome warrior-women as marked and tattooed as she was. None of them, so far as she knew, had asked the Watcher to change the décor, yet it had changed all the same. More mysteries of this place, and always too many for her to unravel.

A rap on the carved white door was met by silence from within. She opened it anyway, and stepped inside.

Erris's desk was covered with papers. Loose parchments and three separate inkwells had been pushed to the edges, while maps spread out across most of its surface. More maps and parchments scrawled with notes lay on the low table between two of her couches, marked with blue bars and lines to denote the current disposition of the Imperial armies of New Sarresant, Thellan, and Gand. The Empress herself sat behind her desk, slumped against her ornately carved chair, both eyes rolled up into her head so only the whites gazed out over her papers and maps. For anyone else she might have panicked, rushed to offer aid in the form of *Life* and *Body*. For Erris, it meant her consciousness was elsewhere, sent to attend meetings or deliberations through one of her vessels, through the power of *Need*.

"May as well sit comfortably while we wait," Yuli said. "I wonder if the Watcher will have anticipated us coming...mmm, and there it is."

A tray of tea sat atop one of Erris's cabinets, piping hot, with a plate divided between Sarresant biscuits and what Yuli had called Natarii dipping cakes. Yuli fetched the tray, carefully folding one of Erris's maps to clear space on the low table.

"There are some parts of this place I'm going to miss," Yuli said. "Hot tea ready and waiting before you even know you want it. Like having an army of Jun palace servants watching over you, and not one of them inclined to sell your secrets to your enemies."

She sat across from Yuli, tucking both legs under her atop the cushions and reopening the Watcher's book to where she'd saved the place. Erris would return from her *Need* connections soon enough. Until then, she might as well make good use of the time.

The virtues of a game-structure would be twofold in principle: First, to ensure a regulated transition with minimal oversight between the Regnant and Veil while inuring their systems from influence from the outside; second, to select for refined genetic stock to be bred among survivors into each of the program's next phases.

Most of the words made sense as she read them, though the broader picture eluded her. Yuli was right to be cautious. But this was describing the Regnant and Veil, it said so in specific terms. And something else, these "outsiders" and "others" the text made mention of. She thumbed ahead looking for the word, and found it again three paragraphs down:

On exceptions to the point of non-interference: The rival claimants would of necessity need to be rebuffed by the principals; both Regnant and Veil must be free to respond to the threat of the others imbuing champions of their own to contest each cycle's victory.

Champions of their own rang in her ears as she read it. There were champions bound to her, and champions bound to him. That was supposed to be the end of it; whichever side killed the others would gain control of the Soul of the World.

"Yuli," she said, rereading the passage again to be sure she'd gotten it right. "Take a look at this. I think it says there could be other champions. Here, and here."

She pointed, turning the book around to face the opposite couch.

The couch was empty.

She hadn't heard Yuli get up to leave, and it wasn't like Yuli to go without saying anything, no matter how absorbed she was in whatever books or scrolls she was studying. She frowned, glancing toward the door. Still closed, and she hadn't heard the hinges or the latch. Even Yuli's tea was still there, sitting on a stand beside the couch, with a half-eaten dipping cake lying beside the cup.

"Sister?" she called toward the door. Erris wouldn't hear or notice anything while her senses were wrapped up in *Need*. "Yuli?"

Nothing.

She closed the book, turning to face Erris's desk.

Erris was gone, too.

All the maps were still there, the ornate desk chair still as it had been when the Empress sat in it. Impossible for Erris to have returned from her *Need* binding and left with Yuli without either of them making a sound. She'd been studying the Watcher's book for no more than a minute or two. A few cautious steps toward the desk gave her a view of Erris's sleeping room, adjoined to her workspace. Nothing.

"Erris!" she shouted, hearing agitation creep into her voice as she left Erris's chambers and returned to the stone hallway. "Yuli!" When nothing came she added the others: "Arak'Jur! Tigai!" And even finally, "Reyne!"

No response, other than the echo of her own voice as it rebounded through the stone.

She ran through the twisting halls, still calling for her champions. Tigai's chambers were as empty as Erris's had been. Arak'Jur's were silent. The Gods' Seat had never been welcoming, or familiar, whatever comforts had been put here on their behalf, but at least she hadn't been alone. She'd spent many late hours studying in the library, knowing that only Erris was likely to still be awake in her chambers. The silence was different now, the silence of empty halls instead of quiet ones.

She checked every room as the halls spiraled outward. Empty. Finally she reached the last, the room they'd arrived in, farthest from the light of the Soul burning at the Gods' Seat's core. It had been decorated with crude wall drawings and wrought iron sculpture then; those were gone now, leaving the space empty save for the device that gave the room its name.

A map of the world spread atop a table more akin to a stone altar, covering the back half of the room. Details sculpted onto the map made it come alive; it was as though every mountain, every tree of every forest had been replicated atop its table in all their textured contours, as though you were a God reaching down to touch the world whenever you stood over it. No sign of her champions here either. But something on the map had changed. Lights shone from either side, beams of pure white rising from the map's edges.

She stepped into the chamber, and a voice thundered in her head the instant her footstep touched the stone.

IT BEGINS.

The sound came from everywhere, and nowhere, reverberating in her ears as though her head were an orchestral hall.

She froze, waiting. Nothing changed. The lights on either side of the map pulsed. She went to the device, feeling her heart thundering as though Anati had pumped her full of *Red*.

The continents and textures were all the same. There were still thick forests covering the westernmost continent, where New Sarresant nestled on the ocean's shore. Broad mountains rose on the eastern landmass, burning deserts in the South, deep jungles near Jun cities, rolling arctic plains in the North near Yuli's home. But the Divide was gone.

Always before when she'd looked down on the map, a searing black line had separated east from west, running directly down its center. She'd stood in the towering shadows that line had represented, crossed through them, felt the screaming in her ears as the shadows closed around her and her companions. Seeing it here had never done it justice, but now it was gone. The land ran unbroken from east to west, the Bhakal continent undivided as it had been by the line of shadow cutting across its sands, jungles, and rolling plains.

Five lights rose from the western edge of the map. Eight from the east. She braced against the tabletop, studying them. Five. Yuli. Arak'Jur. Erris. Tigai. Reyne. Her champions had vanished, but perhaps...

She studied one of the western lights. It gave no indicator where its source was on the map; all thirteen of the beams rose from the outer edge, beyond the surfaces depicted in the center. But they seemed to call to her, too. The more she focused, the more the light drew her in, pulling her senses. Her eyes focused on the beam, and her skin, too, feeling its warmth and heat, her tongue and nose tasting the smells on the air, her ears filled with the sounds of... birds?

Suddenly she was there. Watching from above.

A clearing in a forest. A decrepit log cabin, long abandoned. Wild grasses grew over and through a broken fence. Cracked glass decorated its windows.

Erris stood next to a stone well, in full military uniform, as she'd been dressed sitting behind her desk in the Gods' Seat. Her champion seemed to be in a daze, disoriented, as though she'd only now come to, as shocked as Sarine to find out where she'd gone. Sarine tried to call to her, tried to say something, and heard only the sound of her voice echoing in the map room. Erris gave no sign she'd heard. Yet, after no more than a few moments of surprise, Erris pivoted toward the house, searching for something. Sarine tried to call out again, and once again heard only her own voice.

She leaned back, pulling away from the light, and her senses returned to the map room.

Erris was alive. All her champions were; those five lights were her people, wherever they'd been scattered across the world. She looked in on another to confirm it, and found Arak'Jur running through a thick forest. She tried another, and saw Reyne laughing to himself on a street corner she didn't recognize. The other eight had to be the Regnant's. She peered to look at one of those, and saw a woman in red silk robes kneeling in the middle of some kind of ceremony, surrounded by what looked like monks dabbing her with a cloth. Another, and she saw a man in white retrieving a sword mounted on a wall, fastening its scabbard to his belt.

It begins, the voice had said, still echoing in her ears. Was the Regnant in a room like this somewhere, looking down on her champions? No way to tell precisely where they were unless she already knew their surroundings, but who could say what the Regnant would be able to discern from a forest, a street corner, an old log cabin. She had to reach her people and warn them.

She blinked, searching for the starfield and the strands. For weeks she'd been kept here, unable to leave the Gods' Seat. Neither she nor Tigai had been able to sense the strands. Now the waiting was over. Her champions were down there, in danger, but alive. For the first time since their ascensions, she could sense the stars, and the blue sparks of Life, offering her a way to leave the Seat. Whether all of this was a game or no, whatever else the Watcher's strange book promised to reveal, the voice had been right: This was a beginning, and she meant to find a way to see it all through to its end.

2

YULI

Village of Verkhon
Clan Hoskar Land

*I*T *BEGINS.*

Yuli heard the voice in two places. One in Erris's chambers in the Gods' Seat, where she sat atop too-soft cushions enjoying a delicious cake of honey and flaky dough with her tea, watching Sarine engrossed in her latest find from the Watcher's library. But by the time she understood the words sounding in her ears, she was somewhere else.

A dark room lit by early-morning sunlight, with hexagonal walls, a low table stocked with hard bread and cheese, and a man, a woman, and their child, suddenly frozen and staring at her.

The woman screamed, staggering back from the table, while the man moved to protect their child, a girl of no more than five. The Twin Fangs rumbled inside her, a stirring of predator scenting prey. For a moment her emotions mirrored the Twin Fangs': This was wrong. She wasn't supposed to be here. She was supposed to be with Sarine, safe and waiting in the Gods' Seat for the true war with the Regnant to begin.

But she recognized these people's tattoos. A black mark like a falcon's wings was inked on the man's cheekbones. A wolf's paw covered the woman's cheeks and the bridge of her nose. Two small dots were inked on either side of the girl child's face, markings that would grow fuller when it was clear who she was meant to be. Hoskar tattoos. The Gods' Seat had begun to feel like home, especially in Sarine's company, and in Tigai's. But this was her true home. This was Hoskar territory.

"Forgive me, good mother," she said, bowing where she sat, on the opposite side of their table. "I'm not sure how I came to be here, but I've intruded, and spoiled your morning meal."

The woman fixed her with a look of distrust, but her words, spoken in the Hoskar tongue, softened the feeling between them. The Twin Fangs still stirred in her belly, but it relaxed as the mother did, and the man followed her lead, though the child still stared at her in wonder.

"*Magi* trickery?" the woman asked.

Yuli nodded. "Has to be."

"Share bread with us, then," the woman said, making a ward with her fingers, quickly repeated by the man, and their child. "You are in Gornat Hard Paw's house, in the village of Verkhon."

"My mother was from Verkhon," she said. "It's my honor to return. I'm Yuli Twin Fangs, daughter of Vannar Long Stride Khan Hoskar."

The woman made another sign with her fingers, this one to honor the dead.

It seized her heart. No Hoskar would make that sign unless the one they spoke of was laid to rest, dead and mourned. Her father was dead. If not for the bond she shared with Sarine, strengthening her control, the sight might have sent the Twin Fangs into a frenzy.

"You must have been long away, Yuli Khansdaughter," Gornat said. "Hyman Three Winds leads us now. Your father returned to the earth some months past."

Tears formed in her eyes, and the Twin Fangs rose in her blood. She longed to let it come, to howl and run and find an animal to kill.

"Are you a warrior?"

The child's voice pricked through the haze of the Twin Fangs' rage. Gornat's husband *tsk*ed at the rudeness of the question, but Yuli wiped her eyes and turned to face the girl.

"Yes, little daughter," Yuli said. "I am."

The girl stared up at her, and Yuli leaned forward over the table.

"You may touch my tattoos, if your mother allows it," she said.

The girl glanced at Gornat for permission, before turning back to Yuli, reaching up to run tiny fingers over the Twin Fangs tattoos. A sacred thing, and she remembered well the first time she'd seen the elaborate lines of a warrior's markings on her mother's sister's face, when she'd been no older than this little girl.

"Where are our warriors called to assemble?" she asked, keeping her face low enough for the girl to trace the lines of the claw marks on her forehead.

Gornat and her husband exchanged a look. "Hyman Three Winds has issued no call to war," Gornat said.

Yuli leaned back. "He must have. When I left with Isaru Mattai, the Empire was already on the brink. Now..." She left the rest unsaid, but in the weeks she'd spent with Sarine and the rest at the Gods' Seat there had been talk of little else. It was never the way of Clan Hoskar to sit out, or let others fight their battles.

"No," Gornat said quietly. "We've heard rumors. But our Khan has said nothing, nor issued any summons."

A moment of quiet passed between them. War was nothing to be looked for; she'd seen enough of blood and death already to know it. But this was no time to be sitting idly, leaving soldiers harvesting fields and warriors attending the Khans at court. Somehow she'd come here from the Gods' Seat. It had to mean that the true war, between Regnant and Veil, would soon start in earnest, if it hadn't already. Not a time to leave the clan's warriors without direction. She was far from the most senior among her sisters, no matter her father's standing as Khan. But she was bound as champion to Sarine. She had to lead, or, failing that, to push them to be ready.

"Where is he?" she asked. "Hyman Three Winds?"

"The Khan makes his seat in Tiansei," Gornat said.

"Thank you for your bread, then, good mother," she said, rising from the table and offering them a bow.

"You will need horses, and supplies," Gornat's husband said. "My brother will see you provisioned, as soon as we can rouse him."

She shook her head. "Thank you, but no. I must go at once."

"But it's a week's journey to Tiansei," Gornat's husband said.

"Not for the Twin Fangs."

She bowed again, and left.

Snow crunched beneath its feet as the Twin Fangs loped through the trees. It longed to be in control always, to seize the muscles and bone and tissue of this body and change them to reflect its true form. When Yuli had control they were smaller, pale-skinned, narrow-faced, long-haired, with only the tattoos on her face and upper arms to suggest the majesty stirring under her skin. When the Twin Fangs ruled their form they towered over others of her kind, head and shoulders taller than any human, thickly muscled and hairless, with a properly elongated snout, honed and full of sharpened teeth for their enemies. Its limbs surged with power as they ran, bounding on all fours, claws retracted as they pounded through the snow.

Yuli's emotions stirred deep inside the Twin Fangs' belly. Fear. Relief. Sadness.

Grief. Love. The Twin Fangs felt only hunger; it had been too long since it had been sated. But the two were one now, and had been since the pairing of their souls. Some part of Yuli bled into its emotions as it ran. So the Twin Fangs howled, for its hunger, and for Yuli's father, and the forest shook with the force of its grief.

The sun had reached its apex when the Twin Fangs scented a man.

A half league distant, but they were well enough away from any Hoskar village. Yuli cautioned it to be careful, to make certain its prey was not a traveler, trader, or fellow clansman under her people's protection. But no; the scent coursed through its senses as they tracked toward its source. A Jun smell. The Twin Fangs ran in a low crouch, careful to plant its paws in deep snow to mask the sound of its approach. The wind was good. It could hear the Jun man's heartbeat now. Soon it would eat.

The Twin Fangs roared in frustration as Yuli seized control. Its claws receded. Its jaw shortened, framing a human face, with human skin as she wrenched their body from its grasp.

"Tigai?" Yuli said.

The Jun nobleman stood out against the taiga, wearing the same yellow coat he'd worn to visit her chambers the night before. He was clumsy, with none of a clansman's grace, and he nearly fell as he staggered away from her, the pistols slung from his belt burning wisps of smoke where they touched the snow.

"Bloody fuck," Tigai cursed as he recovered his footing. "That creature... I'll never see that thing as you, *aryu* fuck my eyes if you didn't have me bloody pissing myself. I almost hooked myself to Gantar Baat."

She covered the distance between them and wrapped him in her arms. They almost fell together, but she kept them upright. Tigai was well-muscled, and pretty to look at when she could get him out of his coat and silks, but he was a Jun lord, short-statured and soft compared to Hoskar men. She would have wagered on herself in a wrestling match between them, and the Twin Fangs could crush him and never notice he'd been in the way. But he had other gifts, not least where their mutual nakedness was concerned. He loved like a wolf, loyal beyond life and death to his pack, rather than the tiger he tried to pretend he was on the outside. With the burden of her father's death on her shoulders, she needed that love now, and she took it, holding him close as her tears returned.

"All right, all right," Tigai said, trying to pull away. "What's happened? I heard that...voice...and I woke up in Yanjin Palace, in Dao's chambers, before I came here."

"The same for me," she said. "I heard the voice, '*it begins*,' then I was in Verkhon, my mother's birth village. I received news of my father's death there. But how did you get here?"

"Your father?" Tigai said. "I'm sorry. I didn't…I mean, I'm sorry, for your loss."

"Wait a moment," she said. "How *did* you get here?" They were well away from any settlement, another hour even at the Twin Fangs' pace to reach the town of Tiansei.

"I could sense the strand connecting us together. It was near enough to an anchor I'd set before, and I figured—"

"You bastard!" she shouted. "You set an anchor outside Tiansei so you could move your pirates to attack the town. You've raided here, on Hoskar lands!"

"It was years ago!" Tigai shouted back. "How was I to know it was your people? I didn't even know who the fuck you were at the time."

"And count yourself lucky for that," she said, her eyes narrowing. The Twin Fangs' rage resurfaced; she fought to keep it in check.

"Look, I came here to get you. I can sense Sarine's half of the world now, through the starfield and the strands. Do you realize what that means? We've got bigger problems than some raids I might or might not have done several years ago. The Divide is down; it has to be. We need to find Sarine and Erris d'Arrent and figure out what we're supposed to be doing."

"I know what I'm supposed to be doing," she said.

She left him with a confused look, though she refrained from letting the Twin Fangs return. It meant traveling at a tenth the speed, but between grief for her father and rage for Tigai's piracy, she couldn't have guaranteed the Twin Fangs wouldn't tear him to shreds if she gave it control. A blessing, that her bond with Sarine let her decide when they would change. If she hadn't been bonded, the Twin Fangs would have seized their body whether she willed it or no.

"Yuli," Tigai said, tromping after her through the snow. "Please, be reasonable."

"I find out my lover has the blood of my clan on his hands," she said. "I learn this on the same day I learn of my father's death, and you think it's unreasonable that I feel emotion? Am I a stone?"

He missed a step. She noticed. It wasn't right for her to be angry at him for something he'd done years before. He could as well have been furious at her for the Jun soldiers she'd killed in wars long since settled. But she had every right to feel *something*, and she meant to hold to it for as long as she pleased.

"All right," Tigai said. "Look, I'm sorry."

She said nothing, though a small smile slipped through her façade, kept well hidden as they walked.

"Where are we anyhow?" Tigai continued. "Somewhere in Hoskar lands, clearly, far to the north. Shouldn't I take us to New Sarresant, or somewhere we can meet with the others?"

"As I said, I know what I'm supposed to be doing," she said. "My clan's Khan is in Tiansei. I want my sisters, the Hoskar warriors on our side in this war. You can come along, if only to bring us to New Sarresant when I've finished."

"Ah," Tigai said. "Tiansei."

She took another few steps before rounding on him.

"You have an anchor there, too, don't you?" she said.

"I didn't know!" Tigai said. "It's not as if there's a sign in front of the town saying, 'Watch out: The girl you love is going to be from here!'"

"You are a fucking *bastard*, Yanjin Tigai," she said.

"I know," he said. "I'm sorry."

"Just take us," she said, and she moved to stand near him as he closed his eyes.

The sounds of civilization filled her ears, an abrupt shift from weeks spent in contemplation at the Gods' Seat. They were standing on a broad thoroughfare, where farmers and traders pulled carts to travel to or from market. Hexagonal buildings like the ones in Verkhon lined the streets as tobacconists, taverns, clothier's shops, and fur traders. But the largest of all stood in front of them, a palace of wood and stone built low to the ground, wide enough to swallow three blocks' worth of space: the clan chiefs' meeting hall.

Tigai followed her in silence as she mounted the steps. Hyman Three Winds had been her father's closest advisor. A fine choice for Khan, in the wake of his death, but she knew the sight of Hyman wearing the albino bear's mantle of his station would send her renewed tears. She'd loved her father. It was a cruel world that would take him without letting her say goodbye.

Two guards stood on either side of the door to the hall. Both men, carrying pistols and swords, which made them soldiers, not warriors. They bowed at the sight of her Twin Fangs tattoos, then straightened as Tigai attempted to follow behind.

"This is no place for an unmarked Jun man," one of the guards said. "He stays."

"He is bound to me by blood and magic," Yuli said. "He comes, on my honor, at my side."

Both guards bowed again. "Peace and health, warrior," the two men said together.

They went inside.

The smells of wood and smoke greeted them as they crossed the threshold, and she led them toward where her father had kept his chambers, deep within the second building on the grounds. Little had changed since she'd last walked these halls. Attendants and bureaucrats bowed and made proper deference as she passed, though none were faces she recognized, even as they drew closer to the Khan's rooms near the palace's heart.

"Yuli," Tigai whispered. "Hold a moment. I've been thinking."

She turned to face him. "Yes?" she asked.

"Well, you said you intended to convince your Khan to call his warriors, to take a side in the war."

"We're not *his* warriors," she said. "If he calls us, it will be for all of us to decide what's best for our people."

"All right, well, you said you meant to have them fighting for Sarine."

"Of course."

"It might be better to have them pledge to the Jun, and the *magi*. A deception, to allow us to get closer to the heart of what they're planning. The Great and Noble Houses will expect your people's service, and if—"

"Yuli Twin Fangs Khansdaughter," a new voice said. She turned and bowed at once.

"Alka Nine Tails," she said. "Hyman Three Winds Khan Hoskar."

As she'd expected, the sight of Hyman wearing her father's mantle brought tears to her eyes. She let them come. He stood in the far doorway of the chamber they'd been passing through, empty save for a long table and a hearth burning beside bearskin carpets over the stone. Alka stood beside him, a weathered, gray-haired woman with the markings of the Nine Tails tattooed across her face. Four similarly marked women trailed behind. Her sisters, each of their spirits bound to their warrior-forms, as hers was to the Twin Fangs. The Hoskar warriors: Juni Flame Scale, Imyan Iron Bark, Namkat Wind Song, and Kitian Blood Claw.

"So you've heard the news at last," Hyman said. "I'm sorry, Yuli. Your father was a good man."

"How is it you arrive here in Tiansei unannounced?" Alka asked. "To say nothing of being here, inside the Khan's palace."

She saw tension in Alka's stance, as though the elder warrior was a heartbeat away from summoning the Nine Tails. The same unease was reflected among the other four, women who had been her sisters, once, and now looked at her as though she were an adder in their midst. Suddenly her impression of her standing shifted.

"Why do you have so many warriors at your side, Hyman Three Winds?" she asked. "I was told you hadn't summoned our people for war."

"We did what had to be done," Hyman said. "Your father had fallen under a spell of *magi* trickery. You must understand, what we did, we did for the good of our clan."

Rage flooded her veins.

"You...murdered him?" Yuli's voice, but the Twin Fangs already stirred, changing her limbs, strengthening her body, elongating her fingernails into claws.

"He was already dead," Alka said. "Yuli, stop. The *magi* had hold of him, if it was even him at all. He'd never have sent you south, otherwise."

The Twin Fangs heard their words, but cared nothing for such deception. Already two of the other women were changing, too, a form of smoke and cinders where Juni stood, and a flowing shape of dark crimson around Kitian.

"Don't," Hyman said, stepping in front of the others. "Kill me, if you must. But our clan has need of our warriors' strength, not to spend it on misunderstandings and heated blood."

"Why," Yuli managed through the haze of the Twin Fangs' control.

"War," Hyman said. "It's come at last. The Jun have an army headed by *magi* marching for clan territory, and I need our warriors to meet them."

3

ARAK'JUR

The Alliance Village
North of New Sarresant

*I*T BEGINS.

The words sent him away from the Gods' Seat. He'd been sleeping when the voice rang in his head like trees cracking in a storm. Then he opened his eyes, and he was somewhere else: an overgrown clearing, with places for tents occupied by overgrown saplings, brush, and grass.

The words rang again, this time in memory. *It begins.* Duty demanded he go at once to New Sarresant, to meet with Erris d'Arrent, to fight the Goddess's enemies on behalf of all the light and life in the world. But none could object if he took a longer route toward New Sarresant, to first travel to the Alliance village, to see Corenna, and his son.

He called on *mareh'et*, the Great Cat, and ran. He knew these woods, the pines, furs, and spruce, and he knew the site where the voice had taken him. Sinari land, which meant the Alliance village was to the east. Calling on *lakiri'in* when *mareh'et*'s gift faded kept him moving, then *astahg*, *ipek'a*, and a half-dozen more. What an ordinary man might have covered in an hour's time flew past in minutes, until he saw smoke on the horizon. White columns rising from stone chimneys, half-finished buildings decorating the outskirts, stretching west. As he'd run, he'd half expected a great gathering waiting for him as he drew close. Instead there was only one man, reclining against a wood frame that would become a house large enough to swallow five tents, when it was finished being built.

He crossed the grass in silence, until he drew close enough for Ka'Hannat to see him clearly, and raise a hand in welcome.

"Arak'Jur," Ka'Hannat called. "Past time you return. I've been waiting all morning."

The Nanerat shaman wore traveling clothes, a thick fur coat with a pack slung from his shoulder, pouches hung from his belt, and a gnarled oak walking stick in his hand.

"Honored shaman," he said. "Do you mean to leave in my place, now that I've returned?"

"We go together, guardian. And you're already late."

"I came to the Alliance village to see—"

"Your son, yes," Ka'Hannat said. "Ghella has his keeping. We can stop to see her before we go south."

"South?" he said. "Why does Ghella have Kar'Doren? Where is Corenna?"

Ka'Hannat frowned at him, eyes narrowing in what looked like anger. He'd expected to find Corenna wearing that sort of expression, but among a sea of welcoming faces, celebrating their guardian's return. Instead it seemed as though the shaman hadn't bothered to tell them.

"Corenna has more to do than pine for you, Arak'Jur," Ka'Hannat said. "She's north of here, scouting sites for new villages before the fair-skin priests expand their barrier. We are not an idle people, and we have better things to do than feast the return of one man, however important he believes himself to be."

"There's a war coming," he said.

"And what of it?" Ka'Hannat said. "Does war mean we no longer have crops to plant, houses to build? The spirits of things-to-come have spoken to me about this war, and so here I am, ready to journey with you, to meet with Erris d'Arrent and plan for how best we can fight it. But there is more to us, to who we are, than our warriors."

He fell quiet. In all his dealings with the shamans, he'd never been rebuked with such disdain. Ka'Vos would never have spoken to a guardian so, nor would Ka'Inari. But then, it made no difference. The mantle of protecting their people still fell to him, whether the Nanerat shaman approved or no.

"Take me to my son, then," he said, and Ka'Hannat nodded, turning swiftly to lead him along the outskirts of the village.

The sounds of work being done carried through the buildings. After only a few months away, he felt a distance that had never been there before. They were seeking sites for new villages, Ka'Hannat had said, to the north, where the fair-skins would expand their barrier. And with the fair-skins' magic to protect them, then they would have no need of guardians to drive away the great beasts of the wild.

It gave him pride, imagining Corenna's place in securing their people's future. But he feared that the ice between them could too easily become stone, if left to sit too long. Ascension was finished; perhaps the compulsions that had driven her to hunt him would be gone, too.

"Here," Ka'Hannat said, and led him toward one of the newer houses, constructed on the southern edge of the town. "Inside."

The shaman leaned against his walking stick, making no move to accompany him.

Arak'Jur went, ducking beneath a low doorway. Ghella sat on a pile of blankets beside a stone hearth, weaving thread in a tangle between her fingers.

"Ah," Ghella said, taking a moment to recognize him in the firelight. "Our guardian returns."

He bowed his head. "I'm here for Kar'Doren," he said.

"Here for him?" Ghella asked. "Do you mean to take him with you, into the wild?"

His eyes went to another pile of blankets, where a tiny form rested, wrapped tight for warmth. His son. Kar'Doren. *It begins*, the voice had said, but he longed for nothing more than to do precisely as Ghella said: to abandon his duty, to take Kar'Doren and raise him in the Sinari way. Instead he said, "No."

Ghella seemed to relax as she gestured toward his son. "He sleeps. But he will be delighted to see his father."

She rose to unwrap Kar'Doren as Arak'Jur came to stand beside his blankets. His son's face was wrought in miniature, a tranquil, sleeping treasure, with red patches on his skin and tiny fingers startled into grasping the air. Ghella passed Kar'Doren into his arms, and for a moment, all the cares of the world melted into nothing.

"His mother wishes it were her, you know," Ghella said. "In your place, answering the spirits' call."

"How is she?" he asked quietly.

"Angry," Ghella said. "Restless. She is far from the first mother to feel shackled by her babe, for all she loves him. These are heavy, difficult times, and Corenna feels the weight as strongly as you do, or Ka'Hannat, or any of us."

"Worse is coming," he said. "But thank you, for caring for our son." Kar'Doren stirred enough to open his eyes, startled again. It caught Arak'Jur's heart, but the boy drifted back to sleep as quick as he'd awakened.

"He belongs to all of us," Ghella said. "A boy of the Sinari. Son of a guardian, and a great woman. He will be a great man, in his time. And his mother will be sad, to have missed you."

Ghella reached for the boy, and he could have as easily surrendered a limb as let Kar'Doren go. But he did, and Ghella tucked him back into his blankets.

"Thank you, Ghella," he said.

"Go with our blessing, Arak'Jur. You're no less a son of this tribe than your boy."

He left the warmth of Ghella's hearth behind, reemerging into the cold wind.

"Good," Ka'Hannat said. "I was afraid you'd try to stay. We have much ground to cover, and I can't travel at your pace."

Arak'Jur paused, looking back at the town. A hundred buildings like this one, and a permanence to it he'd never felt in all his years among the Sinari tents. Yet the shadow threatened it all, a vision of poison wind and blackened skies stronger than any dream of what his people might become. He had a war to fight. And Ghella's words had sealed his course, more than any sending of the spirits.

"Go on south," he said. "As you said, you travel slower than I do. I'll catch you before you reach New Sarresant."

The shaman scowled. "Your boy is a child. Ghella can look after him. The spirits chose you for a greater duty, and it is my place to see you fulfill it."

"I don't mean to stay here with my son," Arak'Jur said.

"What then? You can't—"

"I mean to find his mother. I need her at my side, when we face the shadow."

Ka'Hannat began another protest, but Arak'Jur had already started moving. *Munat'ap* could find her, and *mareh'et*, *lakiri'in*, *kirighra*, *ipek'a*, and *astahg* would see him to Ranasi land before sunset. Whatever visions drove the shaman would keep. Arak'Jur was a guardian, meant to protect his people, but Corenna was a warrior. No matter the enmity between them, her place was at the front of the wars to come.

———————

Munat'ap's gift surrounded him with a nimbus of the Great Timber Wolf, and his senses sharpened, until the forest came alive in his ears, his nose, his eyes, and tongue.

The Ranasi woods had always been full of life, but they blossomed now. He felt a caterpillar crawling across a tree branch as though it were crawling on his own skin. He smelled elm and oak on the wind, felt each leaf as it stirred against the cold. He could have tracked a single rabbit from among a score within reach of his senses, projected outward farther than he could see. But it was Corenna's scent that filled his nose. She was close, and he ran through the trees toward her.

The forest had grown thick in recent years, though he was near where the Ranasi village had stood, before the tribe had been destroyed. Corenna's home. She wasn't alone. He scented five others as he passed through the outer edge of the ruins, where tents still stood, left open to be claimed by raccoons, squirrels, and nesting birds. A surprise, to think she'd want to resettle in the ruins of her people's village, where so much pain had been dealt to her. But she was here, seated alone on a fallen log while her companions searched the tents.

Her hair was braided, a thick rope of black hanging farther down her back than he'd remembered. She wore a tan cotton dress, a fair-skin cut, but decorated with red designs almost like *echtaka* paint. Even from behind she was beautiful; she sat with a still grace, and her figure had returned to its normal shape, the last vestiges of pregnancy gone with the coming of spring.

He slowed his approach, suddenly unsure what to say.

She turned, and held his eyes.

"Arak'Jur," she said. "I thought you'd gone."

"I..." he began, finding his mouth too dry to continue. He'd left her, and their son, to follow the spirits' will. It had seemed right when he'd done it, but then, he'd been as driven as she was, to follow the spirits' promptings, to hunt his quarry, and ascend. But where she had refused the drive to kill him, he'd given in, and followed his quarry across the sea.

"Honored sister," one of Corenna's fellows called through the ruins. "The old steam tent still stands. We could salvage it, as a shelter against..." The man trailed off, coming to a halt facing Arak'Jur and Corenna both. A Nanerat man, by his shaved head and the thick otter pelts sewn to make his coat.

"See it done," Corenna said. "And leave us, if you will. Tell the others. The Sinari guardian has returned to us, and I would speak with him alone."

"As you wish, honored sister," her companion said, sparing an eye for Arak'Jur before he turned to go.

"Ka'Hannat told me you'd be here," Arak'Jur said. "Scouting sites for new villages. Important work."

She kept emotion from her eyes. "The shaman told me nothing of your coming," she said. "Thinking to protect me, I'm sure. Just as you did."

"Corenna..."

"I don't need protecting. I've had enough of elders thinking they need to restrain me, of taboos and traditions and all of it."

"Corenna, I'm sorry."

"For what?"

She said it with ice in her voice. It struck him harder than the anger he'd expected to find.

"For leaving," he said firmly. "For pursuing ascension, when you chose to hold back."

"Did you find it?" she asked.

"Yes."

She nodded as though there could have been no other way. "I thought it meant you'd be taken away. When *kirighra* spoke to me, it was of far-off places: ascension to a seat of a Goddess, of being chosen to present myself to fight for her."

"I was," he said quietly.

"And is it over? You've fought for this Goddess, and won, and now you return to reclaim what was yours?"

"Corenna, you were never *mine*."

"Yes, I was," she said, scarcely above a whisper, and for the first time, he heard a thread of hurt behind her words.

"The fighting isn't over," he said. "It hasn't yet begun. I came north to make sure you had a place, before I travel south to—"

"And you mean to give me this place, is that it? Is that your right as chosen, where I was deemed too weak?"

"You're the strongest warrior in any tribe," he snapped back. "I don't mean to give you anything you haven't earned."

"You don't know the tenth part of it," she shouted, and suddenly a nimbus of *mareh'et* enveloped her. "Ka'Hannat tried to hold me back, too, cautioned me against ranging too far in winter. He told me I didn't know the guardians' ways, but I hunted the Great Cat and brought it down. *Kirighra* opened the way for me to hunt guardian spirits, and I've collected more in the passing of one season than any guardian alive. More than Arak'Doren had. More than you."

"I'm sorry, Corenna," he said. "I never meant to wrong you."

"Sorry changes nothing," she said, and for a moment he saw all the Great Cat's ferocity in her, the rage behind its fiery eyes. Then it dimmed, and she looked down at her feet.

"I'm sorry, too," she said. "I thought you were gone forever, and now here you are. I need time. I'd already tried to put myself past it, to begin to—"

They'd been alone in the ruins, speaking beside a rock and a ruined tent. Then suddenly shapes were there, materialized from nothing. Shapes carrying steel.

He shouted a warning, *lakiri'in* granted his blessing, and he dove forward as a sword bit the air where he'd been standing. Corenna had already impaled one of their attackers with *mareh'et*'s spectral claws, throwing the body into the slush, and then she blurred, moving away from him. Arak'Jur rolled to his feet, pivoting back toward the tents. Ten of them, or more; too many to count at a glance, every one dressed head to toe in black. He called on the Swamp spirits as he moved, surrounding himself with tendrils of black smoke. The enemies in black rounded on him, calling out orders as they attacked.

One woman came toward him and touched the smoke, immediately falling to her knees in a fit of coughing. The others twisted around it, weaving with impossible speed as they struck toward him with their steel. *Una're* gave his blessing with a thunderous roar, and he parried a hard cut with his forearm, sending electric shocks coursing up the blade where it struck. He felt his bone crack where the sword hit, but called on *astahg* before another could land a blow, blinking through space to reappear behind them. He slammed into one with *una're*'s claws, tearing a man's shoulder from his chest with a roar and sending the body down into the dirt.

The others spun, keeping their blades level with their waists as they fanned out once more, surrounding him.

Mountain gave its gift, and this time he attacked, charging before they could move away. Gouts of fire blasted toward them, but each attacker dodged, bending their bodies like reeds in the wind. He reached one of them, a man, switching to *mareh'et*'s claws as quick as the Great Cat could have sprung, slashing in a flurry of blows, every strike met by a clang of steel. The man moved like a tempest, flicking his blade up to turn every strike, though he made no attacks of his own, only held Arak'Jur in place while his companions repositioned behind him, out of his sight.

A shove connected with the man's steel, pushing him back in time for Arak'Jur to spin and engage the attackers at his flank. Only they weren't there. All of them had fallen back, barking commands as they grouped together among the ruined tents.

They vanished.

Arak'Jur drew on *munat'ap* to bolster his senses, willing the Timber Wolf's gift to project outward and discern where they'd gone. He smelled nothing; only the birds scattering at the sound of violence, the squirrels hiding, trembling in fear, and Corenna, along with the five tribesfolk who had been with her before. Their enemies were gone.

"Arak'Jur," Corenna called. "I'm unharmed. Are you well?"

He rose, his blood still thundering, his senses still searching for any sign of the unfamiliar.

"A broken arm," he said. "It will heal."

Corenna emerged from behind a fallen tent, holding a sword with a severed hand and forearm still wrapped around the hilt.

"The man I struck, the man whose sword this was," Corenna said. "I swear I saw him healed in an instant; one moment he was lying on the ground, the next he stood where he'd been moments before, still holding his weapon with two good arms. How is that possible?"

"Tigai," he said. "Or, not Tigai, but his magic. The Dragons' gift. Those are our enemies, Corenna. I need your help to fight them."

She held his eyes for a moment, then cast the sword and forearm both into the dirt. "Yes. Of course."

Relief coursed through him. "You said you'd been hunting great beasts while I was away. How many have you slain?"

"Eleven," she said.

"Good," he said, suppressing the instinct to wince at the taboo. Eleven! No guardian in any tribe had hunted so many, so quickly. "We'll need every gift to catch up with Ka'Hannat and reach New Sarresant by morning."

4

SARINE

A Private Meeting Room
Rasailles Palace

Her escort bowed stiffly, remaining outside as the door closed behind her. Once, the palace of Rasailles had been the stuff of idle dreams, the seat of the hand-picked representative of the de l'Arraignon Kings in the New World; now it was clean, bare, and functional. The room her escort had brought her to was a simple chamber dominated by a long table, five chairs, and a small mountain of paperwork. Essily, the Empress's chief of staff, sat at its head, drafting hasty notes in a flowing, precise hand. A wide-eyed young woman with a lieutenant's pin on her collar sat quietly on his right. The rest of the seats were empty.

"Sarine," Essily said without pausing his writing or looking up to greet her. "Good. You're expected. Please sit and attend the Empress's pleasure."

She took the chair opposite the lieutenant. For a moment the only sound in the room was Essily's pen. A map of what appeared to be the lower Thellan colonies lay open on the far end of the table. The rest of its surface was covered with papers, small stacks and taller ones, in neat columns and rows.

"Hi," she said, breaking the silence. "I'm Sarine. You're Erris's vessel?"

The lieutenant opened her mouth to reply, and Essily spoke over her.

"It's easier for Her Majesty if those on duty maintain a focused, calm demeanor. If you will please sit and wait, the Empress will make an appearance shortly."

The lieutenant shrugged, half mouthing an apology. Apparently Erris had done more than change the rugs here at Rasailles. Did she have an army of vessels like this young woman, sitting idly and waiting for a *Need* connection for Erris to step inside their senses and give orders anywhere in her empire? They hadn't spoken of it during their time at the Gods' Seat, only that Erris was making preparations for the coming war. She hadn't thought to pry into what those preparations meant.

Light flashed, and Essily set down his pen.

Suddenly the young lieutenant's demeanor changed. She sat forward, leaning into the table. Both her eyes were flooded with beams of golden light.

"Your Majesty," Essily began, cut short as Erris took over her vessel's body midsentence.

"—first sightings reported in Wiedlaska, in the Old World," Erris said in the lieutenant's voice. The pitch was lower, the timbre softer, but she recognized her champion's intensity at once. "It might be Jun scouts, a contingent delivered by Dragon-*magi*; the reports are unconfirmed. I'll need to shift to the council hall for strategic planning to make sense of it."

"Erris," she said, drawing the lieutenant's golden eyes toward her.

"Very good, Majesty," Essily said. "I can summarize today's briefings and have them delivered to New Sarresant if you expect to be occupied by military affairs."

"Yes, that will serve," Erris said. "And Sarine. Good. You've made your way here, I hope without putting Dragon anchors in my palace. Are the others accounted for?"

"I'm not a fool," she said. "I came here directly from the Gods' Seat. I heard a voice there. '*It—*'"

"'—*It begins,*'" Erris finished for her. "I heard the same. I expect it means precisely what it says. If there are Jun scouts in Skova, then the Divide is down and our war has already started. Which means I need your champions accounted for."

"It put you somewhere on a farm, right?" she said.

"Yes," Erris said. "How did you know?"

"I saw you, and the others, through the map device in the Gods' Seat," she said. "The others are safe, near as I could tell. There were lights, and when I looked closely it was like seeing them from just overhead. Five for us, eight for the Regnant. I couldn't see any details, but—"

"You saw the enemy's champions?" Erris interrupted.

"Yes, the map showed both," she said. "Like I said, I couldn't see much more than their immediate surroundings. Arak'Jur was in a forest, Reyne was on a city block. Not of much use if I didn't already know the places."

"I'll need vessels in the Gods' Seat immediately," Erris said. "Along with a team to decipher the locations we see there. Cartographers, to study the topography. Architects, naturalists."

"Tailors, perhaps, for clues in dress and styles," Essily offered.

"And anything else you deem might be useful. Have them prepared at once."

"Yes, Your Majesty," Essily said. "I'll have the first summons executed and ready by sundown."

"I could hardly see anything to give away the champions' locations," she said. "It was like seeing them from a bird perched directly overhead."

"You knew I was on a farm," Erris said. "If you knew implements, crops, seasonal rotations, and soil, you could perhaps have narrowed it to a few dozen plots in southern l'Euillard. The smallest details could reveal more than you imagine. And we have to assume our enemy possesses the same capability. Damn. That's a bloody fine thing to exist in wartime, a mirror showing the enemy's most prized assets and materiel. Like lighting signal fires from your supply trains. I need the rest of the champions informed at once. This has serious implications for our planning."

"Fine," she said. "I can try and bring your people to the Seat, if you think it will help. But—"

"I need to adjourn this meeting," Erris interrupted. "Essily, see to it the day's papers are sent into the city. I'll need to repurpose your couriers to deliver orders to Royens's command, so be sure you don't send anyone essential to operations here."

"No, wait," she said. "Erris. There was something I needed to show you; I brought it to your room in the Seat before the champions left, before the voice."

"Another time," Erris said. "Be sure the couriers bring fresh maps of the Skovan reaches, too; the ones at high command are outdated by—"

"No!" she cut in, and produced the Watcher's book, setting it down harder than she meant to on the table in front of her. It tipped a stack of papers into another, and stilled the room to a sudden silence.

"My time is too precious for tantrums, girl," Erris said.

"I know," she said. "I'm sorry, I didn't mean to knock anything over. But you need to see this. It's important, for all of us."

"As we speak I have over two hundred vessels focusing on me," Erris said. "Those from among the several thousand I have available in all corners of this Empire. Even with bureaucrats and delegates to handle the daily affairs, there are still dozens who believe whatever matter is pressing on them is worthy of my attention, right at this moment. Do you understand how *Need* works?

My vessels' lights shine more brightly when they believe whatever they're dealing with requires my intervention. That means more than ten score of my people all simultaneously believe their issue should be at or near the top of my priorities, and six of those are burning bright enough to be certain of it. Four of those six, at this precise moment, all happen to be in the same place: the council hall in New Sarresant, my high command and military headquarters for the New World. So I ask you, are you quite certain your need is strong enough to outweigh them all?"

The lecture put heat in her ears. Conviction outweighed it.

"Yes," she said firmly. "This book could change everything. I got it from the Watcher in the Gods' Seat, not an hour before '*it begins*.'"

"One minute," Erris said. "Then I'm gone. I'm already overdue to respond to my people in the hall."

Her mind spun, framing the arguments from what she'd already studied from the Watcher's *Meditations*. Erris said one minute, and her champion meant it; she'd seen and been a part of enough meetings cut short to know it.

"It's a feeling, mostly, from what I'm reading in the text. This book was written before all of this. It refers to the Regnant and Veil by name, but it's as though they were allies instead of enemies, working together. It talks about the champions and the Soul of the World as though it were all a game."

"A game," Erris repeated.

"It doesn't come out and say the game doesn't matter," she said. "Or even what the rules might be. But it's written from a perspective that assumes the Regnant and Veil are working together, not against each other. I don't know what to take from it, except that the Watcher was insistent I find this passage."

"And you trust this…Watcher?" Erris said. "Do you even know what manner of being it is?"

"I don't know," she said. "But he's helped me before. He showed me the Veil's journal, he's helped me to piece together most of what I've come to understand about all of this. And now this book is shaking it all loose. If the Regnant and Veil aren't truly enemies, if the contest of champions is nothing more than a game, it might mean all of our strategies are wrong. So far we think it's going to be his champions against mine, but what if it isn't? What if the voice, all the '*it begins*' and all of it is just a distraction from something else?"

"Such as?" Erris said. "Does the book suggest what their true aims might be?"

"I haven't studied it enough yet to know for sure. It mentions 'others.' I think it might mean rivals, maybe the ones the Regnant and Veil are allied against. I know the champions matter, and control of the Soul, but maybe—"

"Two of my vessels…" Erris said, and suddenly the lieutenant's eyes went wider still, mirroring the Empress's emotions. "I have to go at once."

As quickly as it came, the light vanished from the lieutenant's eyes.

Sarine thumped the book on the table, this time not caring when a stack of papers went sideways. It drew a sidelong look from Essily, without slowing his pen.

"Can you get her back?" she asked the lieutenant. "Whatever's demanding Erris's attention elsewhere, it isn't more important than this."

"I think not, Lady Sarine," Essily said. "You'd do better to compose yourself before you see Her Majesty again."

"What?" she said. "This isn't some matter of logistics or bureaucracy. This is the core of what we're fighting for. I need Erris's help to make sense of it."

"As I heard it, you brought Her Majesty little more than conjecture and speculation," Essily said. "Whatever the contents of your book, you would be well served to read and study it on your own before you waste the Empress's time again."

"Waste her time?" she said. "I'm talking about the nature of—"

"Good day, Lady Sarine," Essily said. "I'm certain you can find the way out on your own."

He went back to his pen as though she'd vanished from view.

Anger surged, watching him return to his note-taking. A score of gifts burned under her skin: the storm spirits, the spirits of beasts and land, Anati's colors, every tether of the leylines running under the palace, to say nothing of the blue sparks, her bond with the Soul of the World, her place as a Goddess at the heart of the conflict between Regnant and Veil. Not that she was about to use magic to lash out at anyone. But he'd treated her as though she were some unimportant child, when he was what? A note-taker? A bureaucrat? Whatever service he provided Erris in managing bloody grain shipments or wool and cotton yields or whatever else, he mattered less than a single word on a single page of the Watcher's book, when it came to deciding what to do next.

The thought helped to calm her. His rejection didn't matter. She needed Erris, however half-formed her understanding of what they were dealing with. All the soldiers in Erris's Empire counted for nothing if they couldn't anticipate the Regnant's next move. She had to make her champion see, had to harness the power of Erris's strategic mind if it bloody killed her trying to get and keep the Empress's attention. And that meant following her champion to New Sarresant.

She closed her eyes, searching for the starfield and the strands. A bare handful of stars glistened in the darkness on this side of the world, each one a beacon if she used it while enemy Dragon-*magi* were watching. She had to be careful. A few flashes and strand-tethers shone from lights close enough to be inside New Sarresant. Strange, for there to be such strong activity inside the city, but then, she hadn't had Tigai's years of practice in understanding how to read the strands. Memories and ties to a place could cloud the lights around any anchor; cities swirled with eddies of thousands of individuals' strands and connections, but she didn't need to spend the time sussing out what was what to choose a star close enough to the Southgate district to suit her needs. She cinched the tethers into place, and left the palace, and the scratching of Essily's pen, behind.

Suddenly cool air blew over her skin. She blinked again to clear her vision and orient herself. Good. She knew this place, four blocks from the council hall that Erris had remade into her military headquarters. Signs of rebuilding still permeated the city, scars Reyne d'Agarre had left, and fresher wounds, from Erris's soldiers seizing the capital. Scaffolding and building materials decorated the street corners, lumber and iron pipes still exposed to the air, all signs of work being done, signs that New Sarresant would revive itself in time, whatever the world threw at its gates. A comforting thought, that her city would endure.

The green surrounding the former seat of the colonial Assembly was expansive, though the statues of the de l'Arraignon Kings had long since been torn down. Blissfully no one drew near her, and she had the green to herself. She reached the broad stone steps leading to what used to be the Lords' chambers, since repurposed to be Erris's high command.

It wasn't until she broached the doors, pushing one open to reveal an empty hallway, that she remembered there should have been guards on duty in front of the Hall. *Life* snapped in place almost without thinking, sharpening her senses enough to fill her nose with the smell of blood.

Anati pulsed *Red* in her veins. Her steps quickened as her heart thundered in her chest. A stench of iron hung in the hallway, growing stronger as she raced toward what used to be the assembly's main forum. There should have been aides coming and going, generals and their staff overrunning the place, wrapped up in Erris's planning for wars and contingencies in the Old World and the New. Instead the way was quiet. Empty.

She reached the main doors, where she should have been greeted by a second set of armed guards. No sounds came from within. Only the smell of blood, steadily rising as she walked the halls, that now threatened to snuff out the rest of her senses. *Life* would have revealed the sounds of fighting inside the chambers, had there been anyone alive to fight. But the double doors swung inward, and her eyes confirmed what her nose already knew would be waiting.

Bodies, cut and torn, littered the chamber. Military uniforms had been cut cleanly with limbs still inside. A leg lay seeping on the carpet in front of her. Arms, heads, torsos decorated the raised levels of the hall, all severed clean through, cut precisely with sharpened blades. She might have expected survivors, the wounded gathering what was left of themselves, moaning in pain, recovering what they could with their attackers nowhere in sight. But there was no sound at all. Whoever had done this had been thorough enough to leave no one wounded and still alive. With *Red* coursing through her blood she would have noticed any movement, any sign of life or threat from an attacker waiting behind in ambush. But there was nothing. Only stillness, quiet, and the overwhelming smell of blood.

5

TIGAI

Ulnak River Crossing
Border of Hoskar Territory and Vimar Province

A speck in the distance seemed to dance as it dipped beneath the clouds. There weren't any other birds in the sky, as far as he could see. Bloody smart creatures, to fly south instead of enduring the cold. It called into question why he was here, sitting atop a shaggy, stunted, half-breed of a pony on the far bank of a river frozen solid into ice, when he could be in Qoba, or even Sarresant, with an eyeblink and a simple tether to the starfield and the strands.

"Namkat's sighted them," one of Yuli's sisters said. Imyan, the one with an old woman's iron-gray hair, though she otherwise looked to be no more than twenty.

"You're sure that bird is her?" he asked.

"That's her," Yuli said. She'd taken a place among the other women with an easy confidence, riding the last two leagues from his anchor point as though she were a lady returned to court. "The Wind Song doesn't need to fly beneath the clouds. She could see them where she was; coming into view was for our benefit, not hers."

"You're certain you don't know why they're here?" Alka asked him. She was the elder, a woman with gray hair in truth, and the wrinkled skin to back it up. Nine Tails, they called her, and he could see every one tattooed across her face.

He shrugged. "*Magi* business," he said. "Who knows why they do anything."

"Not only *magi*," Kitian, the red-haired one, said. "An army, according to Hyman Three Winds. Soldiers, from Gantar Baat."

"The Jun know better than to attack us," Yuli said.

"I wouldn't count on the *magi* knowing anything," Tigai said. "Especially where their humility is concerned."

"Yet you think you can settle this with words?" Alka asked.

"I think it's worth a try," he said. "They'll send out riders to parley when they see us here. Just follow my lead. If it comes to fighting, you'll know it."

Kitian and the other of Yuli's sisters, Juni, said something he couldn't quite hear, a rapid exchange back and forth between them.

"Yes," Yuli said. "We can trust him. Lord Tigai is good with his tongue. Very good."

It turned his cheeks red, and they laughed. Bloody foreigners.

The speck in the distance dipped below the clouds again, this time circling in a wide arc, slowly moving toward the river. Not a hawk or a falcon, not if it tracked an army's movements that precisely, and the soldiers would question it, too, all the more so with *magi* among their ranks. With the Divide coming down *magi* would be everywhere, putting *magi* plots into action. Yuli had agreed with his plan of trying to fool them into thinking they were on the same side. Now he just had to puzzle out how to do it.

He'd formed the better part of an idea when the army came into view, flying red and gold, a full company at least, marking ten thousand soldiers scurrying over the hillside onto the flat plain. A group of riders split from the main body almost at once, pushing hard toward where he and the Natarii sat beside the riverbank.

The riders counted six: four men and two women, judging by their dress. Three in lamellar plate, two in what appeared to be court riding dresses, and one in boiled leather, dyed black, all mounted on horses that towered over Hoskar ponies. They rode straight for the river, and made no attempt to slow when they reached its banks. *Magi* confidence; he was sure of it now. They rode over the ice, and came to a halt less than a stone's throw from where he, Yuli, and her sisters sat, waiting.

He said nothing, waiting for them to be the first to speak.

"Who is this, who stands in our way?" one of the men demanded. A gruff Ujibari voice, speaking accented Jun.

Again he said nothing. Alka stirred beside him, and he gave a subtle hiss to silence her.

One of the women in blue nudged her horse forward.

"Warriors of the clans," the woman said. "We come on behalf of the Everlasting Emperor of the Jun, may his light shine forever. To whom do we have the honor of speaking?"

"These warriors are sworn to no clan," Tigai replied. "They are sworn to me. You will declare who heads this army, and explain why the Emperor's hand, may his light shine forever, reaches twice for the same fruit."

Murmuring sounded from among their line, too soft for him to hear as they conversed. The same disharmony threatened within Yuli's ranks, as she and her sisters craned to look at him. *Aryu* send they had sense enough to play along.

"I am Tancha Mirin ni Surawong, of the Great and Noble House of the Owl," the woman said. "With me is Captain Rashin, of the Company of the Fighting Lion, and my sister, Sasha ni Surawong, also sworn to the Great and Noble House of the Owl. We've traveled a hundred leagues to be here, and, your forgiveness, good master, but our superiors said nothing of any other expedition to pacify the clan rebels."

"Rebels?" Yuli said. "We haven't—"

"Be silent, Hoskar dog," Tigai snapped. She obeyed, but gave him a look that promised he'd hear the rest of it, when next they were alone. "I've already been given, and performed your task. I am Wen Xijiang, sworn to the Great and Noble House of the Crane, and *my* orders are to take these creatures to the nearest of the hundred cities with all haste, now that I have them in hand."

"What? Your forgiveness, Master Wen, but we cannot stand down without some proof of your words."

"You require proof? Very well. I can at least show you I've succeeded in subduing the rebels. Yuli Twin Fangs, kill this woman."

A gamble, but Yuli played into it beautifully, her back arching as it lengthened, her jaw elongating into a snout as her fingers slowly grew into claws. A slow, horrifying transformation, and she'd only taken one step before the Lady Tancha and her retinue shied their horses back.

"No, good master, please," the Lady Tancha said. "Owl's gift is for medicine. We are no warriors."

He held up a hand, and, wind spirits bless her, Yuli stopped her advance.

"You are no warriors," he said. "And yet you are set against a clan renowned for fielding women such as these."

"Our orders were to march on their settlements in force, to demand their warriors pay the tribute owed in service to the Emperor, may his light shine forever."

"And do you not have what you came for? I, and my pets, will ride with you for Gantar Baat. A successful assignment for both of us, it seems to me, and an unexpected delight, to enjoy the pleasure of the Fighting Lion's hospitality on the road."

The Lady Tancha eyed Yuli, who remained halfway through her transformation, long metallic claws pointed upward, toward where the woman sat her horse.

"Yes," Tancha said. "Very well. We are honored to have you as our guest, Master Wen, and look forward to the pleasure of introducing you, and your pets, to the masters of our order."

Wheeling the company around took the better part of an hour, and he endured sidelong looks from the Hoskar warriors throughout. Thankfully the Ladies Tancha and Sasha stayed by his side, and he fielded questions enough to keep them talking while the spears, crossbows, arquebuses, and cannon were turned to march in reverse. It would be a week to Gantar Baat, provided no last gasps of winter came to drench them on the road. He intended to pry loose every scrap of information in the meantime. And, if he could help it, to never be alone near Yuli after how he'd had to treat her for the sake of his charade.

The last held until suppertime, after Captain Rashin's personal guard set up two tents, one for him, and one for all six Hoskar women. The guards had no sooner bowed and given him the space than Yuli barged in, glaring at him as though her eyes were coals, and he was kindling.

"Yuli, look," he said. "I'm sorry. I didn't think any other approach would work."

"Sorry for what?" she said. She'd stripped off her coat before he was sure she didn't mean to strike him. "That was bloody brilliant."

"I didn't think they'd—wait, what?"

In answer she removed her shirt, then worked to unfasten her belt, showing him the same fire in her eyes as her fingers undid the clasp.

"You're not angry?" he asked.

It served to halt her undressing. "No, Yanjin Tigai," she said. "Why would I be angry? You turned aside a company of soldiers with no more than words and empty promises."

"Well, yes, but—"

"Do you imagine my sisters are so prideful we can't submit ourselves to turn away our enemies? We'll play our parts until this Jun army is safely out of our lands. I'll be your pet, even." She said the last with a grin that creased the lines of her tattoo. "If you'll have me."

This time his fingers flew faster than hers, undoing the buttons on his shirt and coat.

When it was done, they lay together atop Jun blankets, and for the first time since following the strands to Yuli's homeland, he was finally warm.

"Did you learn anything from the *magi*?" Yuli asked. She was still naked, the full extent of her tattoos trailing from her face down the sides of her shoulders and collarbone. It gave her an exotic look, the paleness of her skin contrasted against the inks in the dim light coming through the canvas.

"Not much I didn't already suspect," he said. "The masters of their orders have them running errands throughout the Empire, gathering soldiers, exercising old claims, calling in debts. It seems Erris d'Arrent was right."

"A great war," Yuli said. "Sarine warned of it, too. I hoped it would be champions against champions. Not this."

"It'll take them time to marshal all their armies. There will be a few raids with *magi* using Dragon magic, I'm sure, but the real battles are a season away, maybe more."

"Why not use the Dragon gift to move them all?" Yuli asked.

"Oh, they'll use it for sure," he said. "But the Empire has too many soldiers."

"It's going to be a terrible thing," Yuli said. "All of this."

He nodded, letting the moment sit between them. It would be; even in wars between noble houses, thousands would die, and this was far, far worse. A *magi* war, with soldiers from two entirely different worlds. Even the oldest histories said nothing about this sort of fighting.

"It's easy enough for me and my sisters to fight against the Empire," Yuli said. "But these are your countrymen. Are you sure you've chosen the right side?"

"You heard the shadow, in the Gods' Seat," he said. "It promised ruin on both sides of the Divide. Sarine might be half a fool sometimes, but she's fighting for life, and light, and preserving the world the way we know it."

"Perhaps some among the Jun could be convinced," Yuli said. "If they knew it. The stories Sarine told, and Arak'Jur...it makes me wonder why anyone would fight for that thing."

"Thousands will," he said. "Millions." He took a breath, remembering the exchange he'd had after Voren stabbed him in the chest. "I never told any of you this, but that wasn't the first time I'd spoken with the shadow creature."

"I know," Yuli said. "In the Tower."

"No. After we went across the sea, one of his *magi* knifed me in the chest. It brought me to him—the old man behind the shadow. He promised me my heart's desire, if only I would betray Sarine. He'll have made the same promises to the *magi*, and they drive this war."

"A terrible thing, then," Yuli said, and once more quiet fell between them.

At least Dao was safe, and Mei, and Remarin. Erris d'Arrent had seen to it Dao was given a military posting, a *kaas*-mage to translate for him, and Remarin to drill his soldiers. Mei was ensconced in the Sarresant palace, twisting the ears of half the court by now, he was sure. At least they were free of *magi* influence, fighting to make a place for their family.

"Master Wen," one of Yuli's sisters said, from outside the tent. "Visitors for you."

He could have kissed whichever one of them it was, for a proper deference without a hint of glibness or humor. Yuli had snatched up a blanket, half covering herself before he could cut her short with a dismissive *tsk*.

"Admit them," he said lazily, affecting a bored nobleman's tone.

The tent flap rose, and the Lady Sasha knelt, poking through the canvas. Her cheeks colored immediately, seeing him naked, and Yuli beside him, though he made no attempt to hide or cover himself.

"Yes, Lady Sasha?" he asked. "Is there something more you require?"

"My sister wishes to invite you to dine with us," Lady Sasha said. She was young, barely of an age to come to court, with features that were almost Jun, but clearly too southern to be properly noble. Tigai embraced the difference in their status, reclining against his blankets as she spoke.

"Tell the Lady Tancha I must respectfully decline her invitation," he said. "I've already had my fill, of a sweeter fruit than any I'm like to find in your stores."

Lady Sasha mumbled something, finally lowering her eyes, though her cheeks were now bright red.

"I'll join you both for the morning meal," Tigai said. "And see to it I'm not disturbed again before sunrise. I've a mind for another round of supper."

The lady nodded quickly, withdrawing with a proper bow and an improper lack of grace, nearly falling back through the canvas.

"Was that necessary?" Yuli said when she was gone.

"Very much so," Tigai said. "I was sure they'd come back to make the offer, and I needed to be certain we'd be undisturbed."

"So you do have a renewed appetite, then?" Yuli said, grinning.

"No," he said, then paused. "Not yet. I've set an anchor here. We need to visit Sarresant—Old and New—and see if we can track down Sarine and Erris before morning."

Yuli showed him a look of disappointment as she extended a hand.

"Let's be quick about it, then," she said.

He nodded, closing his eyes to search the starfield and the strands. The connections were plentiful on this side of the world, a shining sea of lights and colored haze between them. On Sarine's side, the stars were few, and scattered, with the clearest anchors set where he and Sarine had already used the Dragons' gift to move between them. A set of fresh connections hovered around a star at the heart of New Sarresant, and he lashed them both to it, tightening the connection until the tent vanished, and they stood together on a street corner he recognized, a few blocks from Erris's high command.

6

SARINE

Anati watched her from atop a wood railing, scales flushed as *Red* pulsed in her heart.

So many dead, Anati thought. *Why?*

She carried a body as delicately as she could, dried blood smearing her clothes as she hefted it across the main chamber. With Anati's help she could have carried more, two or three at once, but it seemed wrong. These soldiers had died because of her, because her enemies were trying to strike at her, or her champions. They deserved dignity in being laid to rest.

"I don't know," she said. "I don't know what he gains from this sort of attack."

They don't even harvest the Red, *or the* Black, Anati thought. *They leave it here to go to waste.*

She carried the corpse through the main door, to where Erris had ordered a team of wagons and soldiers to help dispose of the bodies. Anati blinked atop the walls of the wagon bed, looking down as she and two men hefted the latest corpse into a neat row with its fellows. White sheets had been laid in the wagon bed, now stained crimson. She stepped back when the body was in place, making way for the next one, carried by a team of two to lay it alongside the others.

Erris's vessel, Marie, approached her as she reentered the main hall. The woman's eyes had been flush with golden light before. They were empty now, indicating the Empress had turned her attentions elsewhere.

"Lady Sarine," Marie said. "Will you help me with these next ones?"

She nodded without words, following as Marie led her around the elevated edges of the room. A heap of tangled limbs greeted her at the base of a long table, all stained red. Marie had tried to separate them, and order them by which torso they belonged to, but the sight churned vomit in her stomach, and she fell to her knees, retching out air from a long-since empty belly. Marie stood by, waiting quietly until she was done.

"I'm sorry," Sarine said.

"No need to apologize," Marie said. "Though you should try to find some time to sleep soon."

"When it's done."

Marie nodded, and they set to work, moving pieces of each body onto linen sheets so they could be transported together.

"Empress d'Arrent thinks highly of you, you know," Marie said while they worked. "I've never felt her have such strong reactions. I know it's to be expected, given... this. But when she brought me here, and we saw you, she felt hope. A powerful hope, strong enough for it to linger in me."

"I didn't know the Empress's vessels felt her emotions."

"We do," Marie said. "She's a great woman. I hope you're worthy of the faith she has in you."

Dragon.

Anati's thought resounded through her mind.

"What do you mean?" she said. "Is that a warning?"

Marie frowned. "Only inasmuch as I hope—"

"No, no," Sarine said. "Anati?"

Yes. Dragon magic, used nearby.

"Where?"

Before Anati could answer, raised voices sounded from the hall.

She moved, drawing instinctively on Anati's *Red*. The voices had turned to shouting, and her heart thrummed as she crossed the main chamber. If the Jun Dragons had returned to resume the horrors they'd already inflicted here, they'd find far less vulnerable prey waiting this time.

Body tethers joined Anati's *Red* as she came within sight of the main doors, where two figures were engaged in a shouting match with Erris's freshly posted guards. Relief melted away the anger as suddenly as it had come.

"Stand down," she called to the soldiers. "I know them both. Friends, and allies."

"Thank the wind spirits," Tigai said. "Sarine. But what the bloody fuck happened here? Is that... is that a body?"

"They attacked Erris's high command, here in New Sarresant," she said. "At least a hundred dead. Maybe more."

"Oh, sister," Yuli said. "I'm sorry. These are your people, your city, are they not?"

She nodded, feeling another wrench in her gut as the soldiers resumed their work, carrying remains from the hall.

"So it's started, then," Tigai said. "Fuck me in the eyes. It won't be the last attack like this. Dragon magic?"

"It had to be," Sarine said. "Erris and I searched the chambers for sign of whoever carried out the attack. We found nothing. It was done with swords, no guns discharged that we could see."

"Empress d'Arrent is here?" Yuli asked.

"After a fashion," she said. "Come."

She led them down the hall, back into the main chamber, where the excitement of the shouting around their arrival had already faded into reverent silence as the soldiers carried on with their work. Even with the horrors surrounding them, there was comfort in having two of her champions at hand again.

"Yanjin Tigai, Yuli Twin Fangs Clan Hoskar, this is Marie d'Oreste. One of Empress d'Arrent's vessels."

Marie bowed to both of them in turn.

"Can d'Arrent be summoned?" Tigai asked.

"I was about to ask the same," Sarine said.

"No," Marie said. "Not directly. If I focus on a feeling of need, great need, sometimes she comes."

"A reunion with Tigai and Yuli is cause enough," Sarine said. "Can you try?"

Marie nodded, and Sarine went back to the bodies. Too much needed doing to be idle. Yuli joined her without her asking, while Tigai hovered nearby, pale-faced, watching them work.

"You were both sent to the far side of the Divide?" she asked.

"Yes," Yuli said. "To Hoskar lands. Tigai came there to meet me."

"Do we have any sense of what the Regnant is doing there?"

"He's called half the Jun Empire to arms," Tigai said. "Building armies, with *magi* at the head, as Erris believed he would. We answered one of those calls ourselves, pledging Yuli's clan sisters to one of the Great and Noble Houses. So far, no talk of anyone that might be a champion yet, though that may change when we reach Gantar Baat."

"Good," she said. The talk helped distract from the bloody work. On a swift count, Yuli helped lift the sheet when it was ready, and they made way toward the main door. "I know the champions are important, on both sides, but I've been questioning all of it, in light of the Watcher's book."

"The book you took to Erris's rooms," Yuli said. "Before we left the Seat."

"Yes," she said. "It has me doubting whether any of us understands what's going on."

"You said all of this would be decided by us killing their champions," Tigai said. "Or them killing ours. It stands to reason that's what they were doing here, right? Trying to catch Erris at her high command?"

"That seems likely," she said, veering toward one of the empty wagons with Yuli's help. Fresh white linens had been laid across the bed, immediately stained red as they hoisted the bundle they carried between them into the cart. She tried to lay it as gingerly as she could, then stepped away as another pair of guardsmen came behind with more dead to set in place. "I only wish we had more answers."

"My brother would remind us there is a time for seeking understanding, and a time to act," Tigai said. "It seems to me our enemy has decided which it is, for him."

"I know," she said. "And I think you're right about him trying to reach Erris with this attack. Clearly killing the champions is important, even to him. But there's more going on here. The book Yuli and I found suggests the Regnant and Veil were allies, once. I wish I understood why, and what they were allied against."

"Well," Tigai said. "We have to be in our tent when morning comes in Vimar if we want to maintain our charade, but with the bonding, the strands hardly take any effort now. Yuli and I can return nightly, if we need to."

"That might be wise," she said. "If you can wait until Erris comes back, she can tell you where and when to meet with her. Even if I can't puzzle all of this out, Erris will have orders for you I'm sure."

"Is that...Arak'Jur?" Yuli asked.

It turned all three of their heads down the green. Three figures moved across the grass surrounding the council hall. Two she didn't recognize, a man and a woman, and a third that cut the same figure as her champion, head and shoulders taller than the others. Last she'd seen him through the Gods' Seat's map he'd been in a thick forest. If the voice had put him in Sinari territory he'd have had to be moving since they'd left the Seat to be here already.

"It is," Yuli said, just as she was sure, too. They drew closer, and she recognized Corenna, the mother of Arak'Jur's child, at his side.

"What's happened here?" Arak'Jur asked. The bloodstained carts gave off the smells of death; *Life* would amplify her senses, just as the beast gifts amplified his.

"A terrible thing," she said. "As good as it is to see you here, we all arrived too late to stop it."

"An attack?" Arak'Jur asked.

"Dragons," Tigai said. "*Magi* with my gift, moving other *magi* here. It was over fast enough for the Sarresant soldiers not to be able to fire a shot."

Arak'Jur and Corenna exchanged a look.

"It must be," Corenna said.

"What is it?" Sarine asked.

"We can't be sure," Arak'Jur said. "But I believe we encountered the same thing. Warriors in black appeared at the Ranasi village. We drove them away, and thank the spirits there were no other tribesfolk close enough to be harmed."

"The Ranasi village," Sarine said. "That was where we stopped, on our way back from Kye-Min, wasn't it?"

"Yes," Arak'Jur said. "It was Corenna's home, before it was destroyed."

"There was a star there, wasn't there?" she asked Tigai. "A strong one. And we traveled from there, to make it stronger."

"I think so," Tigai said.

"And here at the council hall," she continued. "There was another star, where you traveled to the Old World."

"You think the enemy is sending *magi* to wherever we've placed stars on your side of the Divide?" Tigai asked.

"He has to be," she said. "On your side there are millions of stars, too many to count. But on ours, only a handful, mostly made by you and me before ascension. It stands to reason he would try attacks there."

"We could try setting traps," Tigai offered, and she nodded quickly.

"He might not attack again using the same method, but perhaps if we all traveled together to one of the other stars, one he hasn't used yet."

"Should we consult with Erris d'Arrent first?" Yuli asked.

"There might not be time," she said. "Erris can take hours to respond to *Need*. By then, the assassins might have killed again."

"We'll go," Corenna said. "Ka'Hannat can remain behind, to treat with Erris d'Arrent, if she returns here. I mean to go, and fight."

"We're with you, too," Tigai said, and Yuli nodded. "There are few enough stars here I can see which ones have fresh strands, and which don't. If we go to one without any recent connections, it might mean it's due for an attack."

"Good," Sarine said. "Ka'Hannat, find Marie d'Oreste in the council hall. Marie is one of Erris's vessels. If she returns, tell her we're coming back, and to check in every hour. We'll be back here soon, and hopefully with these bastards' blood on our hands."

7

SARINE

Coastal Bluffs
Old Sarresant

Adistant crash of waves heralded their arrival atop the hillside. Otherwise it was dark, with a blanket of stars overhead, thicker and brighter than she was used to, in the city. It still took getting used to, that they could use the Dragon gift to go from seeing sunset on one side of the world to its noonday apex on the other. Empty hills surrounded them, with long grass and sparse trees and brush, and no sign of the blood and death they'd left behind at high command.

"I'll see to a fire," Yuli said.

"Are you sure that's wise?" Tigai asked.

"We could be here until morning, no?" Yuli said.

"Just be on your guard," she said. "We won't have any notice, if they come."

"I can watch the starfield," Tigai said. "It won't be much, but there might be some warning."

The rest of them fanned out, arrayed to watch the crest of the hill where they'd appeared. The Regnant's *magi* would appear there, too, if they were coming. Tigai had assured her there were no recent strands here; she couldn't see it as clearly, when she looked at the starfield, but then, Tigai had a lifetime of practice whereas she was new to the art.

"This is where Erris d'Arrent made her camp," Arak'Jur said. "Two seasons ago, when she first landed with her armies, across the sea. Is that why there are stars here?"

"Yes," she said. "Though the soldiers have since moved south, near the capital at Sarresant. I don't think it will matter. The Regnant's *magi* went to the Ranasi village even though it was empty, right? I expect they'll check every star."

Arak'Jur nodded and returned to a place near Corenna, a few paces away from her and Tigai. She blinked to check the leylines, searching for the ink-clouds of *Death* that might signify the *magi* had been here already, though it appeared to be no more than an empty hilltop. There was trampled grass, wagon ruts, patches of missing earth where tents had been, but there hadn't been soldiers here in weeks.

Tension held in the air, though it could have been an ordinary night by any other measure. A calm, quiet breeze blew under a clear sky.

"Did the voice take you to New Sarresant, then?" Tigai asked.

She shook her head. "No. I heard it where I was, in the Gods' Seat map room. But Erris told me it took her to l'Euillard, where she was born. She's been riding through the night to reach New Sarresant."

"It was like that for me. Yanjin Palace, in my mother's old chambers. I was eating a bowl of soup in my room in the Seat, when suddenly a bloody voice boomed in my ear like it was shouting at me over my shoulder. '*It begins,*' and the next I know I was sitting on Lady Yanjin's favorite carpet."

"And Yuli?"

"She heard it, too. I met up with her outside Tiansei, the Hoskars' largest town."

"A shame we didn't know where the Regnant's champions were born, then," she said.

Tigai frowned. "I hadn't considered that. What if they'd had *magi* waiting in Yanjin Palace?"

"I've been wondering how much they know about us. The Regnant was there, when I bonded you. I'd think he would know who my champions are. But I don't have a clue about his."

"That's right," Tigai said. "He called us by name, in the Tower in Kye-Min. Maybe it's some ability you have yet to discover?"

"Maybe."

A hollow thought, if it was true. She'd spent every free minute in the Gods' Seat trying to learn, to test the limits of the Veil's powers, devouring her journal and conversing, such as she could, with the Watcher. She knew the Regnant had a more complete understanding than she could hope to. It didn't change that she had to fight him.

"Well," Tigai said, "Yuli and I will go as far as we can, within their ranks. Maybe we can learn something once we get to Gantar Baat. And even if we can't, her sisters are...well, they are something to behold."

"What's this about my sisters?" Yuli asked. She let go of an armful of kindling and dry wood behind them, kneeling to strike flint in a sharp, practiced motion.

"I was only expressing my admiration for Hoskar clan gifts," Tigai said.

Yuli showed him a knowing smile as she moved to kindle the first sparks. "If there were more of us, we'd be free of Jun masters," she said.

"Will you tell me more about your magic?" Sarine asked.

"A lorekeeper could do it better than I," Yuli said. The first flames rose from the wood, casting shadows on her face as she spoke. "But there are twelve." She blew on the fire. "Twelve souls, ancient creatures that came to us when all the clans were young. They choose women among the clans to bond with, and we become more than we were without them. I am Yuli, but I am also the Twin Fangs. When I die, the Twin Fangs' soul will pass to another."

"And your sisters hold the other bonds?"

"Not blood sisters. Sisters-in-arms. And yes. Six for Hoskar, six for Gorin. Though sometimes it takes time for a soul to manifest, and sometimes souls switch clans, or even break off to form new ones."

"Do the souls always choose women?"

Yuli nodded. "Some loremasters claim there are male souls, somewhere. Others claim all the male souls were slain long ago, by a woman in a veil, and a man cloaked in shadow."

The meaning was clear. "Yuli, I didn't..."

"Of course," Yuli said. "I know you're new to your station, as I was new to the Twin Fangs, when I was a girl. And they're only stories."

She fell quiet, coming closer to the fire. She didn't need the warmth with the guardian's gift, but it served to focus her thoughts. Yuli's story was only another example of the long legacy for which she lacked any experience or understanding. Then again, Axerian, Paendurion, and Ad-Shi hadn't known the depths of the Veil's secrets either, and they'd managed to succeed against the Regnant for tens of thousands of years.

Arak'Jur and Corenna joined them by the fire, and shared what they could about their attackers, the black-clothed swordsmen who had appeared in the Ranasi village. Between Yuli and Tigai they pieced together the composition: at least one Dragon-*magi*, to take them there, but the rest had to be Cranes, sword-wielders gifted with a combination of perfect technique and unnatural speed. No way to tell whether any of them was one of the Regnant's champions, but she would be satisfied so long as they could be stopped before any more mass killings.

"We'll need to use *Black*," she said for Anati's benefit. Her *kaas* had appeared sitting in the fire, coiled around a log positioned over top of the rest of the kindling.

We have enough, Anati thought. *Do you want me to drain the Cranes, since you already have the Dragon?*

"Focus on their Dragon," she said. "I want to stop them from escaping."

"Are you sure?" Yuli asked. "Remove a warrior's path to escape, and you only make her fight twice as hard."

"It's that, or watch them flee as soon as they realize what they're up against," she said.

"Best hope they come within the hour," Tigai said. "And so much for any hope of sleep, for us. The camp will be stirring soon, in Vimar."

Sarine nodded. Too much to hope the enemy would act exactly as she'd predicted.

"You've fought them already," she said to Arak'Jur and Corenna. "Could you two handle them, with my help, if Tigai and Yuli had to go back to—"

"Wait," Tigai said. "Something is—"

Dragon. Anati pushed the thought into her mind along with a surge of *Red* in her blood.

Ten figures appeared in an instant, each wrapped head-to-toe in black cloth. Before she could see them clearly, Arak'Jur leapt into them, a roaring sound echoing through the hills, accompanied by the nimbus of a bear shimmering around him. Corenna followed, scarce more than a heartbeat behind, surrounded by the image of a winged serpent. Yuli had been replaced by the creature she called the Twin Fangs, all sinew, muscle, and metallic claws. Then the hillside devolved into chaos.

The lead swordsman rushed toward her, leaping at her through the fire, and she bound *Body* and *Entropy* together, one strand through herself, boosting her speed and reflexes, while the other exploded in the swordsman's path. He should have been incinerated; instead her attacker wove, his form blurring too fast even for *Body* and *Red* to see as he jumped back, avoiding her *Entropy* but halted in his attack. Yuli took the man instead, the Twin Fangs rushing at him in a flurry of claws and snapping teeth. Again his form blurred as he whipped his sword to block the strikes, a perfect sequence of defense as Yuli rained savage cuts toward his head and limbs.

"Use *Black*!" Sarine shouted, moving around where Yuli and the lead swordsman grappled their sword and claws together. The rest of the hilltop had scattered, figures in black leaping away as Arak'Jur and Corenna became a whirlwind of roars, hisses, ice, and fire.

A haze surrounded her vision, though she felt nothing out of the ordinary.

Enough that the swordsmen were still here; if Anati had drained their Dragon-*magi*'s gift with *Black*, they would have no path to retreat, save trying to run away into the Sarresant hills. Thought fled as two of the enemy *magi* charged her. *Shelter* put a barrier of blue-white energy between them, while *Faith* tethered a cloak of invisibility around her, hiding her from view.

Lakiri'in granted his blessing to speed her up further, and this time she added *mareh'et*, striking before the swordsmen could scan the area where she'd been standing. One of them still managed a parry, swatting aside her attack and leaping backward to collide with her *Shelter* in a hiss of smoke. The other raised his sword a fraction of a moment too late, and *mareh'et*'s spectral claw ripped a hole in his chest.

White ribs and red pulp flew as she jerked her hand back, a font of bone and blood spewing out of the man's torso. His sword fell to the grass as he slumped forward, and a pulse of golden light burned inside her, a tingle running from the base of her spine as the *Black* from the swordsman's death threatened to overwhelm her senses. The light flared, but she fought it down as the other *magi* attacked, leaping toward her as fast as the first one had died.

With *Red*, *Body*, *lakiri'in*, and *mareh'et* the *magi*'s attacks finally slowed to a manageable tempo. Even so, when she rounded on him his blade snapped into place to turn her strikes: a high cut to match her sweeping attack, a warding thrust to drive her back as she tried to rake him across the shoulder. He pushed her away, and she countered, forcing the man to pivot his sword in whirling cuts, as though a bubble of steel hovered around him, woven by the speed of his blocks and parries. They traded blows until Corenna emerged around the edge of her *Shelter*, surveying the battle and locking frost-covered eyes on her duel. Sarine struck again, putting all her effort into her attacks; the swordsman parried one, then another, before Corenna put an icicle through his heart.

Her opponent collapsed into the grass, but Corenna had already moved away. She followed, dismissing her first *Shelter* barrier and preparing another shield as they advanced back toward the fighting.

Tigai appeared atop the hill, getting close to one of the swordsmen before they both vanished. Arak'Jur held against four, gouts of fire erupting from his hands where a great bear's claws shimmered. Yuli faced off against a single swordsman, this one in white where the others wore black, near where their fire had burned, now trampled into smoldering coals. The Twin Fangs seemed covered in blood, trails leaking from a score of cuts on her arms and shoulders, though she held her ground, swiping at the white-clad swordsman's strikes as quick as he made them.

Sarine approached quickly, letting Yuli see her before she wove another cloak of *Faith* and vanished. Yuli's opponent attacked in a flurry, whereas most of his fellows seemed content to rely on their skills for defense; not so this one, who landed a jarring *thunk* into Yuli's forearm where she missed a parry with her claws. The Twin Fangs howled, but struck back, pushing the white-clad swordsman down the hill a step, toward Sarine's approach. Sarine opted for the Storm spirit, channeling the gift of Tanir'Ras'Tyat into an arcing bolt of lightning. She discharged it toward the swordsman's back, breaking the cover of *Faith* as her bolt leapt to where the man had been standing.

Motion blurred, and the white-clad swordsman moved.

Lightning cracked the earth where her bolt struck, sending a fountain of dirt and grass into the air. The swordsman was already gone, whirling from where he'd stood facing Yuli into a flying leap down the hill toward her instead.

His blade flicked toward her, and then before she could react, he switched stance and drove a thrust into her belly.

White flared around her as Anati pulsed her shield. The Crane-*magi*'s eyes widened before he flew backward, narrowly ducking beneath a swipe from Yuli's claws.

"Use the rest of our *Black*," Sarine called to Anati. "It doesn't matter if we risk their Dragon getting away. We have to drain him."

In answer a black haze formed at the edge of her vision, but the white-clad swordsman attacked with the same speed, a furious driving cut as he swatted Yuli's attack away, with no sign of slowing.

It isn't working, Anati thought to her. *Why isn't it working?*

Yuli snapped her jaws to keep the Crane back, but he stepped through her guard, landing a swift punch with his free hand that cracked Yuli's neck upward while his sword cut into her upper arm, drawing a thick gash across the Twin Fangs' flesh. Yuli pushed him off with her other hand, but the damage had been done; her wounded arm dangled limply as she reset her stance, leaving her exposed on her weak side.

Dragon. Anati's warning sounded in her thoughts, and for a moment she felt relief: The enemy's Dragon-*magi* was no longer drained with *Black*, wherever they were hiding. Perhaps it meant they intended to escape. But no; Yuli's opponent was still there, still lashing his sword like a snake's tongue as the Twin Fangs swatted it away. She prepared a wave of *Entropy* paired with the blue sparks. A risk, that her fire would scorch Yuli, but better than leaving her to the swordsman's cuts.

Before she could release it, Tigai came running down the hill. The white-clad swordsman pivoted toward him, and just before he struck both the Crane and Tigai vanished.

Suddenly the hillside was quiet.

"They're gone," Arak'Jur shouted from the other end of the hilltop.

"Where are they?" she said. "Anati?"

I stopped draining their Dragon, Anati thought. *They must have left.*

"What about Tigai?" she asked. "He was just here. He didn't follow them, did he?"

Corenna and Arak'Jur both came running before Anati could reply, and Corenna dropped to her knees at Yuli's side, where the Twin Fangs had slumped to the ground. Yuli's claws were receding, her skin and jawline returning to her human form.

"I'm fine," Yuli said as she waved them away. "The Twin Fangs isn't about to be brought down by some Jun lordling with a steel prick."

"The hillside is clear on this side as well," Arak'Jur said, hovering over them. "It seems they're gone."

"Almost," Tigai said from behind, though he hadn't been there a moment before. "I saw Yuli in danger and tethered us both upward, into the sky. You may want to put up one of those barrier things you do."

Sarine frowned. "What do you mean?"

Tigai pointed upward. "Over our heads. A barrier. Just in case he—"

A hollering sound came from above, and all four of them turned upward as a figure in white came rushing toward the ground. Before she could trace its path the man crashed down with a sickening crunch, the sound of bone cracking as it thudded into the dirt.

FOR THIS ONE, IT ENDS.

The voice thundered in her ears, an ancient echo, as though the words had first been spoken on the far side of the world.

"The voice again," Tigai said, frowning.

"I heard it, too," Sarine said. "It must mean…" she paused. "That Crane-*magi* was one of the Regnant's champions. He had to be."

"A champion?" Corenna said. "And what voice? I heard nothing."

"We should return to New Sarresant," Sarine said. "We can piece it together there. Yuli, can you stand?"

Yuli nodded, leaning on Corenna and Tigai for support as she rose to her feet. "Yes," Yuli said, "though we should return to our camp in Vimar. It will be daylight soon."

"New Sarresant first," Sarine said. "Erris will connect with Marie soon if she hasn't already. We need her help to plan what we do next."

8

ERRIS

A slightly curved sword lay at the center of her conference table. A foreign design: It lacked a crossguard above its hilt, while its steel was rippled like woodgrain, swirls of dark iron mixed with gray steel along the edge and a series of strange characters imprinted on the blade. Proof enough they faced a foreign enemy, if every report and even her own witness in the Skovan highlands wasn't enough to confirm it.

"This sword belonged to one of the Regnant's champions," Sarine said, seated to her left. Arak'Jur and Corenna flanked her on that side of the long table, while Tigai and a wounded Yuli sat opposite them to her right. She sat at the table's head, though her physical body was still lashed to a farm-horse, making a snail's time on the l'Euillard roads. Her senses were here by way of Marie d'Oreste, and the power of *Need*. "We all heard the voice, when he died. You had to have heard it, too."

She nodded slowly, giving nothing away. "I did," she said. "'*FOR THIS ONE, IT ENDS.*'"

"That's right," Sarine said. "I'm not sure precisely how the voice works, but it has to be part of the 'game' I mentioned, from the Watcher's book. The one the Regnant and Veil devised to settle control over the Soul."

"Did you consider what might have happened if the enemy had intended for you to set your trap?"

She put it harshly, as she might have done in a rebuke to a junior officer. Sarine took it without flinching.

"We were strong enough to face whatever the Regnant could throw at us," Sarine said. "Now, if I can return to the Gods' Seat, I can—"

"You can't possibly have known that," she interrupted. "Yuli almost fell, to what you claim was one of our enemy's champions. What if there had been more?"

"It was a small squad, meant to do exactly as they did here in the council hall: Kill, and get out with Dragon magic."

She slammed the table, cutting Sarine short. "You don't bloody well know that either. For all you know, they could have planned to strike once or twice with a probing force, then set a trap with all their strength. What if every champion the enemy had was waiting for you in those hills? What if the Regnant himself was there?"

"We could have retreated," Tigai said. "With Sarine's bonding, I can work the strands almost without rest. We could have gone as easily as we came."

"Could you have?" Erris said. "Sarine said she used her *Black* to suppress the enemy's ability to leave. Are you so sure the enemy has no corollary gifts, to do the same to you?"

"We won an important victory," Sarine said. "I don't see the point of raking ourselves over what might have been."

"You got lucky," Erris said. "Any lucky fool can win a battle. No amount of luck can win a war."

"One of the Regnant's champions is dead," Sarine said. "Dead because we acted, where it sounds like you would have had us weighing every possibility until the sun rose, and the moment was gone."

"One death," Erris said. "A price I would have willingly paid, to find out my enemy is a rash fool prone to risking far more materiel than the prize is worth. And you are a fool, Sarine Thibeaux, make no mistake, where military matters are concerned."

Sarine stared ice at her, but said nothing. The others fell just as quiet.

"What do you propose?" Yuli asked.

"All of you are weapons," she said. "Powerful weapons, each worth a company of binders or more. But I don't turn over command of my divisions to muskets and cannons, nor to the soldiers who wield them. The best minds win victories, not the best tools."

"This conflict isn't about armies against armies," Sarine said. "There's magic at work here, an older, deeper magic than any of us understand. It's champions against champions, and even that might only be the beginning."

"All the more reason to be conservative," she said. "If this conflict hinges on killing the enemy's champions, on '*FOR THIS ONE, IT ENDS,*' then every one of you is a liability as much as you're a weapon. If there are more unknowns, we need answers and a path to find them. Above all we need a coherent strategy, and a clear chain of command."

"You intend to put yourself in command, then?" Sarine asked. It was the sort of petulance she was used to seeing in civilians exposed to military discipline, for all she'd expected better from the girl.

"I don't command five individuals," she said. "I command five million. You might well be right that decisive action was required of you here, today, but we needed intelligence on the enemy's capabilities before we could be certain it was a risk worth taking. That means we need roles, we need assignments, and we need to leverage our resources. This is not a squad of magically gifted assassins. This is the foundation of the most powerful military the world has ever seen. I intend to see us integrated with every unit and resource at my disposal, in furtherance of a grand strategy that ends in victory. I have to know each of us shares this goal. Can I count on you? On each of you?"

Tigai and Yuli shared a glance before nodding. Arak'Jur did the same with Corenna, and said, "Yes. For both of us. Yes."

Sarine looked at her in silence.

"We need to know more," Sarine said finally. "We need to understand the nature of this war, of the Regnant, of my place as the heir to the Veil."

"I agree," she said. "Without question, we need to return to the Gods' Seat and see what we can discern from the map, from the texts there, from the Watcher. Tigai and Yuli are well positioned to learn what they can of the enemy's capabilities from the inside. Arak'Jur and Corenna are needed to rally others of their people, to recruit them into our ranks. The point is we have options to consider, and intelligence to obtain. Sarine, you have a place at the head of this army. But we have nothing if you won't work with us, to allow us each to leverage our strengths. I ask again: Can I count on you?"

She's the Goddess, not some frontline soldier. The thought materialized directly in her mind, as Sarine's crystal serpent became visible, standing atop the sword at the center of the table.

"No, Anati," Sarine said. "She's right. We each have a part to play. Yes. You can count on me to do mine."

"Good," Erris said. "Then we have planning to do."

―――――――

She hoisted herself into the mare's saddle as the sun broke the horizon in the east. She hadn't slept a minute since the voice had put her in l'Euillard. Leather cords bound her legs and hips in place in the saddle, and she heeled her mare north as she reached out for *Need*. The best thing to come of her bond with

Sarine was an endless supply of the golden light. That had been Paendurion's trick, to tether the strands a thousand times and never grow tired, or at least, not to tire from that. Now it was hers.

The connection snapped into place, and once more her senses jumped a hundred leagues away.

"Good morning, Your Majesty," Essily said. Essily had moved her briefings to Rasailles Palace, though *Need* rendered the fact of where she put her seat of government irrelevant. He'd argued that the symbolism mattered, and she'd given in without a fight. "I hope you passed the night well, with at least an hour or two of sleep."

"As it happens, I didn't," she said. "You'll have had news of the incidents at the council hall in New Sarresant. And I could do without the sarcasm, Essily. It was a hard night."

"As Your Majesty commands, of course," Essily said. "The council hall was the first matter for discussion, as you said, of course, but there are several other pertinent issues in need of Your Majesty's attention."

She gestured for him to continue, only half listening as he relayed news of the Gods' Seat map team he'd assembled for Sarine, followed by a grain shortage in Lorrine, a dispute between her admiralty and a merchant's company over shipping lanes between Cadobal and Covendon, the armed seizure of a newspaper's offices in Villecours, and a half-dozen other points of news or interest throughout the colonies. She'd started her day with these sorts of briefings for weeks now, even while she was sequestered in the Gods' Seat.

"Very good," she said when Essily was finished. "I'll tether *Need* to the Gods' Seat as soon as the team arrives, and provide updates here as I can. In addition, I have a few requirements that must be met, from our deliberations last night."

"Deliberations, Your Majesty?" Essily said.

"I met with Sarine, and the other champions."

"Ah," Essily said.

"They'll be needing accommodations," she said. "A warehouse in the city, a wing of the palace at Rasailles perhaps. Somewhere they won't be disturbed, as secluded from civilians as feasible. If we're to make a cohesive team of her and her champions, they'll require space to live, practice, and plan together."

"Of course, Your Majesty. Is there more?"

"Yes. Sarine is preparing a map for me, marking every location of one of her and Tigai's 'stars.' We must evacuate them, and post a vessel to observe them, day and night. Have new scouts prepared and trained to travel to new postings, too. Sarine is certain our enemy intends to create their own stars as quickly as possible."

"Stars, Your Majesty?"

"The Dragon magic," she said. "'Stars' are Tigai's vernacular for the anchor points where their *magi* can travel without a pre-existing connection. Just make certain Sarine has whatever she requests."

Essily nodded, and she continued.

"I may be a day or so delayed in reaching New Sarresant," she said. "I intend to stop first in Villecours, when I reach the city."

"The unrest there, Your Majesty?"

"What?" she asked.

"From my report, Your Majesty, your forgiveness if I didn't deliver it clearly. There has been news of increasing disturbances in Villecours over the past week. A newspaper office seizure was the latest, but not the least. The port has reported trouble with armed folk accosting customs officers, and a granary was robbed just yesterday."

"No," she said. "I only intended to find Reyne d'Agarre. There hasn't been word from him, since we heard the voice."

"Reyne d'Agarre, Your Majesty?" Essily said. "The rebel?"

"The same man. One of us now, one of Sarine's champions."

"And you suspect he's behind these disturbances?"

"No, I…" she began, then stopped. Bloody fool of a man. That was precisely the sort of thing Reyne d'Agarre would do. "Regardless of what he's been up to, I intend to find him and bring him to New Sarresant. That's all. See to it the relevant ministers are given authority to suppress any other dissent in Villecours."

"Very good, Your Majesty."

"That's all for now, then," she said. "Until tomorrow."

He bowed, and she let go of *Need*.

Sleep pulled on her body as she rode north. Another hour before they turned east toward Villecours. She heeled the mare again to be sure it felt her presence, and reached out again, this time to the admiralty. An exchange there gave four more connections to make, and she made them, each in turn, to the decks of four men-of-war, then another to the admiralty to report the captains' latest positions. A Skovan vessel gave a firsthand account of strange ships sighted in the Old World's southern seas, and then a Sardian one confirmed it, adding reports of Bhakal ships seen veering outside the sanctioned trading lanes.

She missed the eastern road by half an hour, and cursed when she had to turn back. If she'd had any sense she would have commandeered a carriage, and attendants to drive it. Not too late to book one in Villecours, or to make Reyne her footman.

Instead a fresh *Need* connection took her to Old Sarresant, across the sea, to Field-Marshal de Tourvalle's billiard room.

"Your Majesty," one of de Tourvalle's aides said as soon as her senses slid into place. They had the room to themselves; the tables were empty, save for the one her vessel and this aide stood over, a pair of cigars laid on the edge alongside the cues.

"I need Marquand," she said. "I need to know where the field-marshal has him." She could have connected to him herself, to find out, but she needed him alert, not spewing curses at her as soon as she severed the link.

"Of course, Your Majesty. Colonel Marquand is here, at the palace. Shall I bring him here?"

"No, take me to him at once."

The aide made a swift bow, setting down his cue stick hastily and leading the way from the billiard room. She followed behind, earning swift snaps to attention from the soldiers posted outside the chambers they passed. Private rooms and offices, from the look of it. De Tourvalle kept an orderly command; it was why she'd selected him for promotion to command the 2nd Corps, in spite of his noble blood. Every soldier wore full uniform, immaculately cleaned and pressed, given the resources available here in the city. She followed de Tourvalle's aide up a flight of stairs, pausing for her guide to salute and ask directions from a sergeant on duty guarding the sleeping quarters. It took them back down the stairs, to a meeting room where she could hear shouting even through the closed oak doors.

Her guide entered first, cracking the door to let loose a tide of angry invective.

"...bloody fucking stupid, if you think horse can maneuver fast enough to make use of *Shelter*. I might trust a handful of your best riders. But no bloody company ever made could—"

"You forget your place, *Colonel*," a woman's voice shouted back. "You are here to support my strategy, not to dictate the composition of my units, nor to make any demands whatsoever."

Erris pushed through the door, not waiting for de Tourvalle's aide to calm the exchange. Gods knew Marquand and Vassail weren't likely to stop for one junior officer's pleas, no matter who he heralded waiting outside their room.

"General, Colonel, if you please," the aide was trying to say. Both ignored him.

"Attention!" Erris shouted, letting a roar echo from her vessel's lungs. It quelled the room immediately. Both Marquand and Vassail turned to her with anger on their faces, calmed when they saw her vessel's golden eyes.

General Vassail stood at once, snapping to with a crisp precision. Marquand was only a heartbeat late, thumping his leg against the table and wincing as he stood, trying to affect a similar poise.

"Whatever it is you were arguing about, it ceases now," Erris said. "Am I understood? We save our fire for the enemy in this army."

"Yes, Your Majesty," Vassail said, echoed by Marquand with a shade less enthusiasm.

"Colonel Marquand, who would you propose should command the Second Corps binders in your place?"

His face went red. "Am I being demoted? For speaking my mind? What the fuck is this?"

"Decorum, Colonel. Answer the question."

"It bloody depends," Marquand said. "Are we talking infantry action, artillery, a scouting expedition, reconnaissance of a known enemy, movement through hostile country, what?"

"General Vassail?" Erris asked.

"Cavalry maneuvers, Your Majesty," Vassail said. "The field-marshal has instructed us to be ready to deploy at a hard ride, to counter small squads of enemy binders—or, *magi*, Your Majesty. But my first concern is speed."

She raised an eyebrow back to Marquand.

"The general's first concern ought to be deploying worthwhile defenses against an unknown force," Marquand said. "Not who can best sit a saddle. And for that, I'd recommend Corporal Jessain Orrin have the command."

"A corporal? Are you trying to insult me, Colonel?" Vassail said.

"She's the best bloody *Shelter* binder in the army. You can handle whatever logistics are needed to get them into the field. But you'd bloody well better let Orrin have the final say for your defense, or you're more of a fool than I—"

"Enough!" Erris snapped. "I expect better, from both of you."

"Yes, Your Majesty," they said again.

"Give this corporal the command, then, as your second, General Vassail," Erris said. "Marquand, you're being reassigned, effective immediately. Take one of the *kaas*-mages and ride north, for the star along the coastal bluffs. Sarine will take you to New Sarresant to meet with the rest of your command."

"My command, Your Majesty? I know the binders of the Second Corps better than anyone alive. Why would you reassign me?"

"Because, Colonel, you're the best I have, when it comes to binders, and the use of magic in the field. I need you commanding the best mages. Five of them, to be precise. Six, if I can get Reyne bloody d'Agarre out of Villecours."

9

REYNE

Colonial Times *Offices*
Seaside District, Villecours

The crank lurched as the pressman released it, a quick jerk as the pressure released inside the machine. Reyne held his breath as the men finished their work. The pressman pulled the plate out, and his apprentice lifted the upper piece away to reveal the sheet, still blank on the backside, before the master lifted it carefully, holding it for all of them to see.

The Codex
A Chronicle of the True Words of God
Vol. 1
Translated by Reyne d'Agarre

A miracle, to see the beginnings of what would be his masterwork. Tears came to his eyes as the pressman handed him the sheet with a delicate touch.

"Careful, Master d'Agarre," the pressman said. "It needs to dry."

The rest of the people in the shop all looked to him, waiting on his pronouncement. The compositors and typesetters had fear in their eyes, a product of the slight prods of *Green* and *Yellow* that Xeraxet wielded with a master's touch. His militia looked to him with expectation, an eagerness in their faces, each one awaiting the fulfillment of their task.

"Perfect," he said, scanning through the words on the rest of the opening page. "You've done fine work. Important work. These will change the lives of millions, when they're done."

The shop erupted into applause, and more than a few relieved sighs, as he handed the sheet back to the pressman.

"A book," Victoire said, thumping his shoulder as soon as the sheet was clear of his hands. "Who would have guessed a book would herald your return."

"More than just a book," he said. "And this will bring down more than a prince, when it spreads."

"A prince, and a Duc-Governor," Victoire said. "I believe that's the score you set, last we played at revolution."

Reyne smiled. After so long away in the Gods' Seat, it felt strange to be around so many friends again. He couldn't suppress the second part of his sight, the part that saw *Black* behind their movements, behind their breath, the part that craved the sweetness that spilling their blood would bring. A horrible thought.

"I'll settle for the Church," he said, dispelling the craving from his thoughts. "Their lies have persisted long enough. It's time for the world to hear the truth."

"You'll find a willing congregation here, if you mean to preach," Victoire said.

"Later," he said, and Victoire nodded.

"The city watch, then," Victoire said. "They'll be coming again soon."

"Leave them to me."

He passed through the newspaper's offices, surrounded by militia and workers, each of them offering congratulations or engaged in the work of setting type for the second page. There would be hundreds more before it was done, but the pressman assured him they could work swiftly. He expected the first copies printed in a matter of days. Easier, perhaps, if he had acquired the money to buy the paper outright, and avoid the guards' attention, but he needed speed. The Truth had lain fallow too long while he sat in the Gods' Seat. The people of New Sarresant—his people, and he'd never relinquish them to Erris d'Arrent or her so-called Empire—deserved to know what they faced, and why.

He emerged in front of the shop, on the bottom floor, where stacks of yesterday's *Times* lay unsold in the lobby. There would be no edition today, or tomorrow, or any of the next days, until his Codex was finished. Only the words of his book. And the pamphlet, already circulating in the city, heralding his return, and promising the rest of the Truth to come.

Another craving struck him as he stepped onto the street. He could feel the tableau of emotions from the lookers-on peering at him through shuttered windows. Doubt, fear, curiosity, pride. Xeraxet's *Green* could handle them, at his urging, and he nudged the latter two, curiosity and pride, while mollifying fear and doubt. He scanned the streets as he worked, using his eyes and Xeraxet's senses, seeking the city watch Victoire had been right to assume were on their way. He found them, found their emotions: a knot of fear, anger, worry, resolve, coming toward the printer's shop. He could have used *Yellow* to push fear, and keep them away. Instead he stroked anger, and resolve. Let the guardsmen come and face him. Let them believe they did their duty with every step.

You mean to kill them? Xeraxet sounded in his mind. Saruk had always been firm and direct, at least as direct as any *kaas* could be. Xeraxet's tone was never anything other than toying or amused.

"Yes," he said quietly.

It will send a message to your fellows as much as your enemies, Xeraxet thought. *And with a bond in place, I have no need to collect deaths to feed you* Black.

"I don't care," he said. When the cravings struck, it was as though someone else controlled his voice. In the Gods' Seat, there had been no means to slake his thirst. There was, here.

As you wish, then.

"The streets seem quiet, Reyne," Victoire's voice sounded from behind. "Our runners will give warning if the watch are coming. Come join us. Aliel's group brought wine from Lorrine."

"No," he said. "They're coming now. Keep the others inside."

"You're sure?"

"I'm sure."

A door closed, and he was alone on the street. Villecours was a week's ride south of New Sarresant, but the city clung to winter's chill this early in spring. It made him doubly grateful he'd kept his red coat, as much a symbol for who he was and what the revolution stood for as a means to keep warm in unpleasant weather. The city watch were coming, and they'd see him here, standing alone against a full squad of their best. If his thirst allowed him to leave one alive to tell the tale, the red coat would remove all doubt that Reyne d'Agarre was back.

He held his ground as they appeared, a full squad marching purposefully down the street. What little traffic there was gave way to their blue-and-white uniforms, making a clear path between them. He held to their emotions like a tavern player, plucking the strings of aggression as he urged them forward. Violence was coming, and with it, *Black*. He could feel the watching eyes of the citizens around him, pressed against glass windows from two- and three-story buildings, and the newspaper offices at his back.

"Stand aside, citizen," the lead watchman said. Absent Xeraxet's influence, the man might have been cool, calm. Instead his tone was harsh, the voice of a man pushed too far, needing only the slightest provocation for violence.

"For what cause?" he said softly. "I have a right as a citizen of New Sarresant to stand where I please."

"We have reports of an armed group seizing control of the offices behind you," the watchman said. "Comply with my order, or face arrest."

"Arrest me?" he said. "Do you know who I am?"

On its own, he felt their fear rising. He let it grow, but pulled aggression along with it. Fight, not flight.

"Don't much care if you're the Empress's own nephew," the watchman said. "This is your final warning."

In reply, he let his coat fall open, revealing the long knife on his belt. A red haze blurred the edges of his vision as his heart pumped double, Xeraxet's gift surging in his veins.

One of the watchman's fellows fumbled a pistol from his belt, but Reyne had already moved.

Quick knife thrusts took the man in the belly, his pistol clattering into the street. The man's eyes widened in shock as he worked, stabbing six times in the stomach, once more beneath the ribs, then again through the heart. With *Red* he could kill before the others turned to react, and he did, keeping his face level with the watchman as life snuffed from the eyes, the blood meant for the man's brain instead leaking through knife holes into his coat.

Shouts sounded as the first wave of *Black* washed through him. Golden waves pulsed across his spine, sending tingling shocks through his senses. A pistol discharged in a cloud of smoke, but *White* flared around him, shielding him and deflecting the shot into a nearby building. He moved, the cravings now in full control after tasting their fruit, and struck again, violent slashes instead of thrusts, striking a young man across the face, his blade biting deep enough to spill more *Black* into his veins. Blood spattered on the stone, and a shimmering barrier sprang into place around him, a wall between him and the rest of his prey.

The cravings demanded that Xeraxet dispel it, and his *kaas* reacted, spinning threads of *Black* to rip the gift away from the young woman who'd woven *Shelter* to try and stop him. She looked at him with horror in her eyes, the marks on the backs of her hands quivering as she continued trying to use the gift he'd stolen away. He stabbed one of her fellows, grabbing the lead watchman from behind as he impaled him, scraping his knife along the man's spine.

He let the lead watchman's body fall, and turned on the woman who'd tried to bind him. She remained frozen, shaking from fear. Xeraxet's *Yellow* wouldn't work on a binder, but his display had served well enough to root her in place. A dark stain appeared where the woman had pissed herself, but he held back, keeping his knife steady. He was in control. The cravings shuddered inside him, gnawing at the pearl of gold that *Black* had delivered into his senses. He was in control. He was powerful. He was satisfied, for now.

"Hear this, citizens of Villecours," he said, making his voice a thundering bellow, echoing up the street. "Reyne d'Agarre has returned, and he will not suffer tyrants, whether they be born of Kings or made by their own hand. Those who love liberty know they need never fear from me. But those who serve evil deserve death, and I call it justice." He raised his knife to point at the young woman's throat. "Go and tell your masters. Lady Guillotine has returned. And this time she will not rest until the blood of every false King and priest soaks the soil of this country with the nectar of *égalité*."

The woman stayed frozen in place, and he held his knife steady. "Go," he said.

She took a step back. Then froze again as golden light spilled from her eyes.

"Reyne?" the woman said, all sign of fear gone from her voice. "What in the Nameless's twisted mind are you doing here?" She scanned the street, her eyes widening as she saw the bodies, then narrowing just as quickly as she rounded on him. "You bloody fucking bastard. Sarine trusted you. We need you to fight the Regnant, not to—"

He lunged, ramming his knife through the woman's throat and withdrawing it with a sharp yank. The golden light flickered behind her eyes, then vanished, and fear returned to her face, mixed with disbelief as she raised her hands to the bloody wound. She slumped forward, then fell face-first into the street, and *Black* came again, this time bitter as much as sweet.

Erris d'Arrent. It had to be. The golden light, and her *Need*. A piece of rotten fruit in an otherwise delicious morning.

"Fine work," Victoire's voice sounded from behind. "A message the d'Arrent tyrant won't soon forget."

"We have to move," he said. "Get your people to pack the plates, and the press, too, if we have wagons to carry it."

"You think they'll send more to stop us, after that?" Victoire asked.

"D'Arrent knows we're here," he said. "She'll be coming in force, and we can't let her stop production of the Codex. The book is everything. The rest of the revolution will flow from its words. We need citizens everywhere reading it, as fast as we can turn them out."

"I'll get our people moving, then," Victoire said. "You want us to conscript the newspaper workers, too?"

"Bring them. We'll need them all."

Victoire gave a grim nod, sparing a look for the bodies in the street, before he went back inside.

Xeraxet hummed a new mix of emotions from the streets: fear, shock, doubt, hope. Reyne flared *Green* to bolster hope, as strongly as Xeraxet could give it. Word would spread, and with Xeraxet's help, his message would be carried from Seaside to the Hilltop district, to Lorrine and New Sarresant and beyond. Sarine and Erris d'Arrent and the rest of them wanted to fight a war against some shadow in the East—well and good. But victory meant nothing without revolution. If the *kaas'* gifts made him a soldier, he would fight for the rights of all, and champion others to take up the cause at his side. That was his calling. The rest counted for nothing without *égalité*.

10

SARINE

A Disused Hunting Lodge
On the Outskirts of Rasailles

The smell of leather and firewood cut through layers of dust as they stepped inside the lodge. White sheets lay draped over what furniture remained, though the antlered trophies had been left exposed, a full herd of deer's heads severed and staring down from above. If the decision had been left to her, she might have picked a dockside warehouse, a Southgate workers' hall, a converted church, even a repurposed guardsman's barracks before she dreamed of putting them here. But Colonel Marquand beamed as he took it in, nodding to himself as he looked around the room.

"Perfect," Marquand said. "Bloody perfect."

"Wasteful," Arak'Jur said from behind them. "And ugly."

She found a look of disgust on Arak'Jur's face that mirrored hers. Plenty of taverns had deer's or boar's heads mounted as trophies, but she'd never seen so many in one place. It was as though the entire sloping ceiling had been covered in bone, easily four armspans of animal heads staring blankly with black glass for eyes.

"What?" Marquand said. "Oh, the trophies. Fuck them all, burn them for all I care. I meant the room. It's perfect. Space enough for all of us, and secluded enough there'll be no danger to civilians if a bloody kill squad springs out of the bloody air."

"We don't have to put a star here," Sarine said, still eyeing the sea of empty deer's eyes above them. They seemed to be full of pain, as though the taxidermist had captured the moment of each animal's death. Perhaps that had been the point. "We're close enough to Rasailles to walk, if this is truly where you want to have us meet."

"No helping it," Marquand said. "This place is meant as a training ground, for all of us. That includes your Dragon stars and anchors. Besides, I doubt our enemy will try the same trick twice, after his hand was burned the first time. One of you get started with the antlers, if you want them taken down, and the other give me a hand with these."

He tugged a sheet free of one of the room's creased leather couches, spilling a sea of dust into the air. She opted for the furniture, letting Arak'Jur see to the dead creatures on the walls.

"So what are you aiming for us to do?" she asked as they worked. A lampshade similarly covered with dust came loose in her hands, caking her forearms as she tried to clean it.

"Study," Marquand replied. "First ourselves, and each other. Then an accounting of what we know of our enemies. We'll have to work as a team, and we have to know what we're up against."

"The Regnant's champions aren't sitting around in hunting lodges studying magic," she said. "They're out there, acting. Setting traps. Looking for us."

"More fool them," Marquand said. "Preparation wins battles. Knowledge wins wars. As I understand it we're at something of a disadvantage on both fronts. So unless you want to rush headlong into defeat after defeat, you slow down, follow my orders, and act when I'm satisfied we know what we're dealing with, not before. Am I understood?"

"You are speaking to the Goddess of this world," Arak'Jur said midway through dislodging the first of the deer's heads, leaving antlers protruding from his hands. "Her bonds are what makes us champions, what extends and empowers our gifts."

"I don't bloody care if she's Empress of the fucking nine seas," Marquand said. "If we gave command to those who are best at magic then I'd have been a bloody field-marshal before I had a beard worth shaving. The best minds give the orders; the best soldiers carry them out. That's our duty. That's *your* duty, if you give even half a shit for victory. Given the stakes of this war, I'd say every one of us ought to give a whole ass's worth of shits, but if I'm wrong, you feel free to go your own way and leave the rest of us to it."

"We're here," she said. "And we're with you. Of course we want to win."

"Bloody right," Marquand said. He tugged a sheet loose from a cabinet, spilling more dust into the sunlight.

"If we're going to plan for victory, though," she continued, "we need to know precisely what winning means."

"Your book," Marquand said. "The one you got from your invisible bloody man in your Gods' Seat. The Empress told me. She says it has you doubting this whole exercise, of our champions against theirs. Have you had more time to study it?"

"Some," she said, wishing it was more than a half-truth. "I've been able to glean something of the relationship between him and her, between Regnant and Veil. They were allies, once, and all of this is their design."

"But we know whichever side's champions wins, they control your Soul of the World, right?" Marquand said. "We know it's happened before, with Paendurion, and the rest of your predecessors."

"Yes and no," she said. "The Veil was still the Veil, then. She's dead now, Anati cut her out of my head."

"And now?" Marquand said.

"Now I don't know," she said. "I'm playing her part, and I don't know what it means. There are rules, and some magic in place to govern them—that's where the voices, the '*it begins*' comes from. Some force in place to govern this whole thing. But the book made it sound like it was a game, a system put in place to keep outsiders from interfering with the Regnant and Veil's alliance."

"Outsiders?" Marquand said. "Such as who?"

"I don't know," she said. "There's so bloody much I don't know."

"I've planned operations in the Thellan marshlands," Marquand said. "Fog so thick you couldn't see your pecker to piss with. You could travel half the day and end up where you started, sure you'd never taken a turn east or west. Sometimes not having a fucking clue what's going on can be liberating; if you don't know what you're doing, the enemy can't anticipate your plans."

"How is that supposed to be helpful?" she said.

"It tells us where to start," he said, unfurling a tablecloth draped over a thick wooden table set inside a nook surrounded by tall glass windows. "Here. Sit. Imagine the surface of this table is the world. The whole bloody world. That's our battlefield, yes? What do we know of the terrain?"

"What?" she said.

"The terrain," Marquand said. "The ground we're fighting on. The first rule of any engagement is to know the ground."

"The world is much the same on both our sides, is it not?" Arak'Jur asked. "Forests, plains, hills, mountains, jungles, deserts."

"So far as we know, it is," Marquand said. "But there's one clear difference we've already observed, with the attacks by the enemy's assassins."

"The stars," she said, understanding Marquand's intent. "The Dragon gift. I've seen it myself. On the Eastern side of the world, the strands run between thousands, maybe millions of them. Anchor points where Dragon-*magi* have tethered themselves, made anchors that became permanent, dozens in every city, even the smallest villages, the most remote forests and towns. But on our side of the world, it's clear. All but empty, save for a small handful of points *we* made, using Tigai's gift to move around."

"Precisely," Marquand said. "So we know the enemy's terrain is navigable, while ours is like a sea without safe harbors. That's an advantage."

"What does that have to do with the Watcher's book?" she asked. "With how to learn what we're fighting over?"

"I don't have a bloody clue," Marquand said. "But that's the point. My squads didn't go into the Thellan marshes knowing what we were going to set on fire. We were there to cut into supply lines, to disrupt trade, and more than anything to instill the fear of the fucking Gods into our enemies. We know who we're fighting, and we have an advantage over the ground. That's enough to start sowing some bloody chaos. For now, a change of plans. You sit here. Study your book while we work. I'll be back in an hour and we can start making some sense of this."

He got up, leaving her sitting at the tableside. "Wait," she said. "I'm not even sure what I'm looking for. What kind of information would be helpful?"

"Whatever you think is worthy of our attention," Marquand said. "I've had a version from the Empress; I want a fuller version from you. Sit. Take the time to read, and think. Then we'll sit and think together. After the tribesman and I burn these bloody de l'Arraignon antlers."

With that he left her, returning with Arak'Jur to the lodge's main room.

Anati appeared on the tabletop almost as soon as Marquand left, coiling in the sunlight. It left her alone for the first time since the voice had thundered in her ears at the Gods' Seat. She'd been wary of Marquand being put in charge of her and her champions, whatever sense it had seemed to make in Erris's meeting room. But if he had sense enough to give her time to study and think before acting, perhaps he wouldn't be such a bad commander.

She produced the Watcher's book again, cracking it open to where she'd creased the page. The first few passages were the same as they'd been when the Watcher's unseen finger pointed them out. The Regnant and Veil had worked together, once. Rereading it made it clear. They'd been allies in control of the Soul of the World, which meant they'd shaped the world together. But the Veil's memories had shown her what the Regnant sought to do now, if he gained control on his own: the skies blackened, the water made poison, all life forced underground, when it survived at all. Had the Regnant and Veil drifted apart, and become enemies? But the Watcher's book made mention of the "game" they'd designed, with champions against champions, there from the start.

Perhaps it was a mechanism to hand over control of the Soul of the World. Maybe it was a compromise, something they did to share power, in spite of their different visions of how the world ought to be structured. She thumbed forward, scanning more nearby passages. The book was titled *Meditations on Light and Shadow*; originally she'd thought the Veil was meant to be Light, and the Regnant Shadow. But the more she read, the more it became clear both of them contributed to each side. They'd divided the world to ensure that champions came forward to face each other, and they agreed to be bound by the outcome of those contests. Bound. That implied rules for Regnant and Veil, over and above whatever forces compelled the champions to fight each other to the death.

She read the passages on the Regnant and Veil being "bound" again, then skipped ahead, searching chapter headers and opening paragraphs for any new instances of the word.

Not the most powerful of Gods, are they? Anati thought into her mind as she read. *If they have to obey these rules.*

"How do you mean?" she asked, stopping at a page that made more references to their "game."

A God should be able to do what they want, Anati thought to her. *If I were a God, I wouldn't let the outcome of someone else's fight decide what I got to do with my power.*

"Well, it sounds like they designed the system," she said. "Whatever they were trying to do, maybe it required this kind of compromise."

Why? Anati thought.

"I don't know," she said. "That's what I'm trying to learn."

No, I mean, why? Anati thought. *If they were Gods, they wouldn't give up power unless they had to. Right? So, they had to, no matter the reason, which means they did give something up. It seemed like a useful thought.*

She paused. "I think I understand what you're saying," she said. "It's not necessarily important what compromise they made, it's that they had to compromise at all. Meaning whatever rules they submitted to, the key is that they submitted."

Right, Anati thought. *They're bound by something, even if it was something they put in place.*

She read the rest of the page she'd stopped on, letting Anati's words echo in her mind. Her *kaas* would follow along even without it being spoken aloud. The Regnant and Veil had bound themselves by the rules of their game. It meant killing the Regnant's champions still mattered, was still a path to victory, even if...

A thought crystallized in her mind. Anati gave it voice before she could.

He's trying to get out of it. The rules.

"Because circumstances have changed," she said, finishing the thought. "Because I was never meant to exist. I wasn't meant to be the Veil. So now, instead of a partner..."

He has an enemy, Anati thought.

"And he might still be bound by the old rules," she said. "By the game he and the Veil designed. Now if only I understood what exactly it meant, for both of us."

You know the champions matter, Anati thought. *If one side is victorious, it means control over the Soul, right?*

"Right," she said. "But what does that mean?"

The right to remake the world, isn't it? Anati thought. *I thought that's what you were fighting for from the beginning.*

"That's the goal," she said. "But I need to know the means to achieve it. Let's say our champions manage to defeat his. What changes? What power do I suddenly have that I was missing before?"

Anati went quiet, coiling back toward the book lying open on the table. She had to be close to understanding. It felt right. But she had no more answers than her *kaas.* If the game bound her, the same as it bound the Regnant, then what dormant power was waiting there, ready to be unlocked? She could already travel to and from the Gods' Seat at will. A double meaning lay in front of her: that the contest of champions was essential, binding both Gods by its outcome. And yet there was a second truth, that whatever game the Regnant was playing, it had another layer underneath the first. The "others" mentioned in the book might hold the clues. Equals of the Regnant and Veil, perhaps? Rival claimants to the Soul of the World. Everything she'd read suggested the Regnant and Veil had held sway for hundreds of cycles, hundreds of millennia where the world was born, reborn, made and remade. Perhaps there had been something else before.

She closed the book, standing to stretch her legs.

Done already? Anati thought. *But we don't have all the truths yet.*

She almost laughed. "Do we ever have all the truths?" she asked.

We could study more, Anati thought. *I don't like not having all the answers.*

"If you have ideas, I'd love to hear them," she said. "But I think we have enough to take to Marquand. If the champions matter, and I think they do, then we have enough to act on for now."

Marquand and Arak'Jur had made a pile of antlers in the clearing surrounding the lodge. She'd watched them build it, one deer's head at a time, as she read the Watcher's book. Only now they seemed to be gesturing at each other, both of them with backs turned toward her window. No; not toward each other. Someone else was there. Two someones: Yuli and Tigai.

She snatched her book up as Anati faded from view and headed for the lodge's main door. As soon as she rounded the lodge's corner she heard the shouting she'd seen gesticulated through the windows. Tigai and Marquand faced each other on opposite sides of the pile of bone, Yuli and Arak'Jur at either's side.

"It could be a bloody trap," Marquand snapped. "It bloody well has to be. They'd never be so blatant otherwise."

"The hells they wouldn't," Tigai snapped back. "I was there at the council hall. Were you?"

"Those were *my* countrymen," Marquand said. "Don't presume to lecture me about what happened at the Hall."

"Your countrymen died to Dragon-*magi* using stars as plain as the noonday sun," Tigai said. "If you don't think they'd do it, you don't understand *magi* arrogance."

"Welcome, sister," Yuli said to her. "Would you care to join in, or stand with me and watch the boys fight?"

"What's this about?" she asked.

"Sarine," Tigai said. "Thank the wind spirits, we'll have some bloody sense. You must've seen it, too?"

"Seen what?" she asked.

"The stars," Tigai said. "Here on your side of the world."

"Lord Tigai believes our enemies have deployed their *magi* with a network of new stars and anchor points," Marquand said.

"It's not a bloody question of *belief*," Tigai said. "I can see it, as sure as you can see me standing in front of you."

"And they'll know you could," Marquand said. "Which meant they wanted you to see what they were doing."

"Wait," she said. "Hold on. You mean there are Dragons here? Near the city?" Her thoughts went to her uncle, for all the Regnant's soldiers should have little reason to attack a church.

"No," Tigai said. "Not here. On the far side of this continent, near where the Divide used to stand. You haven't sensed it?"

She shook her head. "I've been studying. Not watching the stars."

"Try," Tigai said. "Focus on the West—far to the west. You'll see what I'm talking about."

She'd already closed her eyes. The starfield was mostly empty here. Black space with filaments of color pulsing across the void. She could sense the stars nearby, one at Rasailles, another to the north, at the Ranasi village, another within New Sarresant. A handful more anchor points, all crisscrossed with the strands' colored lines.

"It's all darkness to the west," she said. "I don't know what I'm looking for."

"Farther," Tigai said. "Almost to the other side of the world."

She pushed her awareness. Strands ran the length of the world's curvature, the memories, loyalties, and bonds connecting people to each other, to places and objects of close affection. On the Regnant's side of the world stars were numerous, a thousand more at every turn, and so far away they blurred together. But the strands traced the lines anywhere there were people, even without the stars' brightness. The contours of land gave way to lakes, rivers, then finally the sea. If she focused, even new to the gift as she was, she could sense the lay of the land itself. The map room's device conjured what it should look like in her memory, where the lines of each continent should be. And sure enough, along the far western edge of the continent she'd learned to call the New World, lights pulsed along the shore's edge, too distant to be sure of their number or the strands connected between them. But they were there, where no stars at all had been before the Divide fell.

"I think…" she said, pausing to focus on the lights. "I think I see them. A handful, right? No more than five or six."

"There," Tigai said. "You see? Dragon-*magi*, sure as sunrise."

"Can you tell what they're doing?" Marquand said. "Any indications of why they're there?"

"It doesn't work like that," Tigai said. "We can tell they've set anchors, enough to bundle the nearby strands, which means they've been moving back and forth quickly. Usually anchors take more time to form into stars. More than that…we have to go and see for ourselves."

"Out of the question," Marquand said. "It's far too likely to be a trap."

"I don't like the idea of letting them move with impunity on our side of the world," Tigai said. "If every star they make is a trap, they can go anywhere, do anything, without our looking on. We'd squander one of our greatest advantages, surely you can see it?"

Marquand frowned. She closed her eyes again, pushing her awareness back to the western shore. The contours of the land suggested it was far to the northwest, as far as it was possible to go. She'd visited that coast before, what seemed a lifetime ago, with Axerian at her side. And now stars were there. It suggested the enemy had Dragon-*magi* close at hand. Maybe even a champion, if they dared to risk moving so boldly. Marquand was right; it could be a trap. But so was Tigai. Letting the enemy move unhindered meant a repeat of the council hall, bodies piled and broken when they could have acted to meet the attacks.

"Let me and Yuli go," Tigai said. "We can move with stealth, and take every precaution."

"You wouldn't have a bloody clue what precautions to take," Marquand said. "It could be two Dragon-*magi* with a squad of riflemen trained on their stars. It could be a squad fifty strong with Crabs, Cranes, Herons, and more. What manner of stealth is going to keep you hidden when you don't know what you're bloody hiding from?"

"This kind," she said, drawing their eyes. It would be a risk. But the Regnant's champions had already shown the lengths to which they would go for victory. She had to be willing to meet them, to spring their traps if it meant a chance to stop them.

She found a pool of *Faith* beneath Rasailles. A tether tightened into place; in an ordinary crowd it would have drawn gasps of surprise as she suddenly vanished from view. Here, Marquand's eyebrow raised, while Tigai grinned.

"There, you see?" Tigai said. "*Faith*. Sarine can keep us hidden no matter how many bloody *magi* they have set to watch their stars."

"I don't like it," Marquand said slowly. "But you're right. We can't let them move unchecked. Only, Sarine will go without you. Far too risky to commit both our Dragons to the same maneuver. Arak'Jur will go with her, and you'll both report back as soon as you have a sense of what the enemy is doing. Scouting only, no engagements, no matter how tempting the bait. Am I understood?"

"I know the stars far better than she does," Tigai began. "It would be better if—"

"Corenna will be here soon," Arak'Jur said as Tigai spoke. "She won't be pleased to find me gone, whatever the—"

"Enough," Marquand said. "If this team is going to function at all, you need to get the idea of arguing with my orders out of your bloody skulls."

"You're well understood, Colonel," Sarine said. "We're to go, and scout the new stars, see what the enemy is doing, and return home."

"Good," Marquand said. "I trust whatever you found in your book, it can keep until then?"

"It can," she said. "And it points me toward staying ahead of whatever the

Regnant is doing. Whatever alliance existed between him and the Veil, I'm not her. He's my enemy—*our* enemy. That's enough, for now."

"Bloody right, then," Marquand said. "Both of you stay safe. Learn what you can. And come back whole. That's a bloody damned order I expect to be obeyed."

11

ARAK'JUR

A Warcamp
Chappanak Land

*S**he wants you to stay close.*

Sarine's serpent whispered the thought into his mind, while she held a finger to her lips for silence. He gave a slight nod, and kept behind. Corenna had bidden him to go with Marquand and Sarine while she oversaw preparations with Erris d'Arrent's aides. She'd never forgive him for leaving her again, however briefly. This was supposed to be a quick glance into the enemy's plans, and yet they'd already scouted a sprawling army, filling his sight in every direction. Yanjin Tigai claimed there were no more than a handful of stars here, but for every star there seemed to be ten thousand soldiers, swarming and working and preparing their camps.

They moved through a sea of their enemies, the canvas tents arranged in rows covering the bluffs from the shoreline as far inland as he could see. Everywhere he looked, they worked or drilled, with orders being shouted to conduct the camp as it stirred. Sarine wove around them, careful to leave a wide enough berth for him to follow, and he did, trying not to marvel at how they managed to pass through the camp unseen.

Faith, Sarine had called it, combined with the Veil's magic—what Sarine called the "blue sparks" of *Life*—to make him vanish, a more thorough camouflage than even *juna'ren* could have managed. They came within an armslength of soldiers marching down the paths, scurried aside to let them pass, and continued on until Sarine peered into a tent, then nodded, gesturing for him to follow her inside.

"Careful," she whispered as soon as he was clear of the entry flap. "We're visible now. I just need a moment to tether to a leyline here. My Gods, though, did you see it? I'd never imagined so many in one place."

"The Regnant's army?" he asked. "They're many, but Empress d'Arrent can surely field an equal host."

"No," she said. "No I mean...of course you can't see it. The leylines. It must be him...he's tethering so many. A million strands of *Body*, everywhere, as far as I can see. Bloody insane. What should we do? Tigai showed me the stars, but I never imagined it would be like this. Should we head back to New Sarresant? I don't have enough *Faith* here for more than fifteen minutes, at most."

He lifted the tent flap and peered back out into the camp. Thousands of soldiers moved with purpose, setting up new tents or striking old ones.

"Enough time to move through their camp?" he asked. "We should see as much as we can before we go."

"It's dangerous," Sarine said. "Anati is giving me warnings: *Lotus, Crab, Heron*. There are *magi* here. And the leylines...Gods, I never expected this. I thought we'd find another squad of *magi* with Dragon magic, and us hidden behind *Faith*. There must be fifty thousand of them here."

"This is the western coast, yes?" he said. "Of our land, the continent of the Sinari, and New Sarresant?"

"Yes, it is," Sarine said. "How long do you think it would take them to cross the continent and reach—?"

He hissed for silence, falling back against the tent wall as a soldier in lamellar plate pushed through the entryway. The tent Sarine had chosen was large by the camp's standards, but still no more than three or four armspans in any direction. The soldier paid them no mind, discarding his helmet on the floor of the tent and unfastening his belt, letting his scabbards fall with it to the ground as he worked to loosen his epaulets and breastplate, but he was within touching distance, if Arak'Jur had a mind to strike. Instead he gestured silently to Sarine, edging around where the soldier worked, and withdrew from the tent.

Sarine followed with more agility than he'd expected, sidestepping the man, then gesturing in an eastward motion. He shook his head firmly. They needed a full accounting of what they faced here. From where he could see the enemy's tents extended far enough to go past the horizon, but the horizon was limited by sharp bluffs and hillsides. From a higher vantage they would have a clearer view, and a better sense of the enemy's strength.

They moved again, this time with him leading the way. A cart full of rolled canvas cleared the path, and they ducked around it, avoiding soldiers and horses as they climbed toward the ridge overlooking the shore. If what Tigai had told them of his limits was true, it wasn't possible for so many soldiers to have come here with the Dragon's gift. There had to be a crossing overland, a narrow channel for ferries, even a bridge.

He had to suppress his instinct to stay low, avoiding the horizon line. They stood exposed to the whole camp, yet not a single pair of eyes looked up toward them. *Faith*. A powerful magic, and frightening to think what it might mean in an enemy's hands.

"Gods," Sarine whispered. "There are so many. And...what's that?"

He followed her gaze northward, where the tents stretched all the way to another ridge, dim on the horizon and easily a half day's journey away, but the camp didn't stop there, only wound around the foothills to extend even farther north. Sarine's focus was closer to the shore, where a greatfire had been built, twenty armslengths in diameter, belching smoke through a pyre assembled from what looked like boats cut from great trees, hoisted together to form a conical tower of smoke and ash.

"An offering of some kind?" Sarine asked.

He squinted, and saw what looked like two men carrying a third between them approaching the pyre. They threw the man they carried into the blaze, belching cinders where the body landed.

"A means to keep their dead," he said.

"Their dead?" Sarine said. "But, was there a battle here?"

In answer he called on *gai'ti*, the Great Mountain Goat, who made its home far to the south of Sinari land. A beast he'd never slain, but the spirit had nonetheless answered his call since Sarine's bond. A nimbus of the Goat surrounded him, and suddenly he could feel the heat on his skin, taste the charred meat from the bodies within the flames. Not a lone corpse, or even a handful—soldiers who might have died from disease or cold. He'd expected those, and instead he saw hundreds. The pyre was made from them, from piles of bodies heaped at its center, where the fire burned hottest. Soldiers, animal carcasses, but innocents too. Elders, and children.

"What are you doing?" Sarine hissed. "Stop! Let go of whatever magic you're using, now!"

He let *gai'ti*'s gift fade. "What is it? Why?"

"*Faith*," Sarine said. "It drains ten times faster if it's combined with any other gifts." She blinked, and cursed. "It's all but gone now. We have to go. Stand close."

"No," he said. "Leave me behind."

He thought of Corenna. She would hate this. But he had to hope she would understand, in time. Whatever distance separated the tribes of these eastern shores, they were his people. His charge, as champion. If they died at the hands of the Regnant's armies, the blood was on his hands.

"What?" Sarine said, her expression mirroring the shock he imagined on Corenna's face. "No, you're coming back to New Sarresant."

"That pyre is made from bodies, not wood," he said. "Bodies of tribesfolk, those who lived here before this army arrived. There will be other tribes nearby. I mean to run ahead, and warn them."

"But...wait. How would we find you? And without *Faith*, how can you move through their camp?"

"Tell Corenna I love her, and promise to return," he said. "And I'm not without my own gifts. This is an army of our enemies. I'm sure our paths will bring us together again."

"Don't," Sarine said. "We need you. Marquand was right. This is too much of a risk, for an unknown."

"This is my path," he said. "I am a guardian. I can't let these tribes die without knowledge of what's to come. Go. Bring Erris d'Arrent and her armies. You will find me facing this enemy, an army of guardians and spirit-touched women at my back."

She looked to him with doubt in her eyes.

"*Go*," he said again, and called on *juna'ren* to blend his skin into the dirt and smoke behind him.

Sarine shook her head, but she went, leaving behind a puff of wind as she disappeared from view.

Juna'ren made the passage slower, but the amphibian spirit's gift held as he moved from tent to tent, wagon to wagon, a shimmering concealment hiding him from all but the most adept of eyes. He moved east, away from the sun, where troops of soldiers were already gathering to march. He'd been in the thick of Erris d'Arrent's armies, among divisions of her troops flooding through hills and valleys, and nothing he'd seen from her came close to rivaling the mass of soldiers here, with more still waiting beyond the northern horizon. It filled him with awe, and envy. All the tribes from every corner of their continent couldn't have produced so many soldiers.

He waited to draw on *mareh'et*'s speed until he was clear of the camp, where the first units of soldiers were beginning their march into open country. He kept *juna'ren*'s concealment with *mareh'et*, becoming a streaking blur as he ran parallel to their path. If they saw him, he heard no alarm, and so he shadowed them, outpacing their march with the Great Cat's speed until they vanished over the western horizon.

Soon *mareh'et* tired and he called on *ipek'a*, then *astahg, rin'ji, lakiri'in*, and *mareh'et* again, using each beast's powers of swift movement to cover vast stretches of ground. The land here was as different as Old Sarresant and Thellan had been; thick pines and hemlocks covered every surface, with an overcast gray sky and a light drizzle of rain, whereas spring showers would be heavier in the east. The people would be strange, too, with foreign traditions and ways as different from Sinari traditions as the Lhakani, the Nanerat, and all the other distant tribes. They were still his people, bound by the land they held sacred, the spirits that watched over it. Mountain had spoken to him, named him champion. He meant to honor that calling.

Munat'ap's gift scented a village after the sun reached its apex, and he changed course, still cycling through the gifts that granted speed. He raced from hilltops through forested valleys, leaving a trail of trampled brush and claw-marked trees. The Timber Wolf aided his senses, but he saw nothing as he approached, only a thick canopy of evergreens. Still the smell of people filled his nose: cooking meat, fresh-harvested vegetables and fruits, sweat and dirt, all the efforts of a small village, wafting toward him on the wind. He followed it until he emerged into a clearing, and the scent shifted from the harmony of a village to a sharper, deadlier smell: a man, standing opposite him, clothed in a sewn-hide vest, with a single black stripe painted across his eyes.

Arak'Jur raised both hands, ceasing *lakiri'in*'s gift as he came to an immediate halt.

"Greetings," he said in a slow, clear tone. "I come as a friend, bearing news of grave importance for your people."

The man stared at him, unmoving. He carried no weapon, but stood as though he were threatening Arak'Jur, trailing every movement with his eyes.

"Who are you?" the man asked. "How do you speak our tongue?"

"My name is Arak'Jur, of the Sinari," he replied. "A people of the far distant east. I understand your tongue by means of a blessing of the spirits. And I come with a warning of great danger. I must speak to your shaman at once."

"A blessing of tongues," the man said. "You are a seer yourself then? But you named yourself *Arak*."

"I'm a guardian," he said. "Not a shaman, not a seer. I saw this danger with my eyes, coming toward your village from the west."

The tribesman eyed him with uncertainty. Even with the Gods' Seat's gift of tongues, there would still be differences in custom, and tradition. The man had known the word *Arak*. But perhaps they hadn't understood each other's meaning.

Arak'Jur closed his eyes, keeping his hands still as he called on the Great Cat spirit. Its nimbus surrounded him, and he slowly opened his eyes.

"*Arak*," the tribesman said, suddenly nodding. "Brother."

In mirror, the tribesman summoned a spirit of a black bear, surrounding himself with its image as a deep roar seemed to echo around him.

"Brother," he said, affirming it.

"I am called Riosan," the tribesman said. "*Arak* of the Tilannak people."

"Riosan," he repeated. "Will you take me to your shaman? Your *Ka*? Your people are in great danger. I came here to warn, and save as many as I can."

"Our *Ka*," Riosan said with sudden understanding. "Yes. Seer Shimmash. Come. This way."

With that, Riosan turned, beckoning him to follow, and they passed under the evergreen canopy, emerging into a village both strange and not-strange, together at once. Children laughed and pointed at him, and a young boy ran to touch his leg, then ran away again in a mad dash accompanied by cheers and whoops from his peers. Women hung hides outside large, slant-roofed houses, massive structures painted and carved with unfamiliar shapes and figures. Riosan led him toward its center, past carved poles three and four times the height of the houses that had to have been hewn from the trunks of ancient trees. A house stood alone at the center of the poles, painted pure white whereas the others were marked with reds, yellows, blues, and greens.

"Wait here," Riosan said when they reached it, and he did, bowing his head in a gesture of respect.

Riosan went inside. It left him alone on the threshold, surrounded by a foreign people. Clearly they were accustomed to visitors, as his passage had occasioned little more than curious looks, though he saw no sign of horses, powder weapons, or steel that would have indicated an eastern trade. Groups of women talked and laughed in the paths between the houses, pointing at him openly, and groups of men did the same. He looked them over as openly, taking in the strangeness.

"You may enter, Arak'Jur," Riosan said, appearing in the doorway and holding it open for him. "Seer Shimmash awaits."

He ducked low to enter the house. The interior was warm, with a fire burning in a stone hearth, and solid cedar for walls, painted brown and red. Woven carpets decorated the floor of the main room, and two mats lay opposite the doorway. But where he'd expected the shaman there to greet him, instead two figures sat cross-legged on the mats: a man, white-haired and leather-skinned, with pruned lips wrapped around a long-stem pipe, and a woman, half the man's age but still some years Arak'Jur's elder, with hair of mixed black and gray and eyes that burned red, all traces of black in her pupils gone, replaced by fire.

"Sit," the white-haired man said, pointing to an empty mat in front of the door.

Arak'Jur eyed all three of them as he sat, lowering himself slowly to be certain it was their intent to welcome him. It seemed it was, though the white-haired man studied him, inhaling and breathing out deep puffs of white smoke from his pipe.

"I am Arak'Jur," he said. "Guardian of the Sinari. Chosen of the Wild. I bring dire news for your people."

The woman and Riosan fell quiet as soon as he started speaking, while the white-haired man continued puffing his pipe.

"Arak'Jur," the white-haired man repeated. "Arak'Jur."

Suddenly the man's eyes glazed white. "You are a man of great power," the white-haired man said, suddenly speaking perfectly accented Sinari. "I am Shimmash, High Seer of the Tilannak Nation. This is my granddaughter Herumi, chieftess of this village. And my great-grandson, Riosan, a guardian of the second rank."

"Arak'Jur," Herumi said. "What rank is this man, to take the guardian's mantle for his own name?" Her words, too, had changed from their tongue to his, a perfect transition from their language to Sinari.

"He is second rank, too, mother," Riosan said. "Second rank, or greater. He has *mareh'et*. He must be."

"How is it you speak my tongue?" Arak'Jur asked. He'd witnessed shamans speaking other languages in the throes of the spirits' will, but never while retaining knowledge of themselves, and never granting the gift to others in their presence. Yet Herumi and Riosan had both done it, and seemed to understand his words as well as the shaman had.

"You speak our tongue with the spirits' gift, do you not?" Herumi asked. "Do you not have High Seers among your people?"

"We can speak on gifts of magic later," Shimmash said. "Enough to say this man, Arak'Jur, is far beyond the second rank. The Truth Spirits know him. They believe his words. They whisper to me that I should believe his warnings. And yet their whispers are faint, almost as if..."

The shaman trailed off, his eyes suddenly distant.

"High Seer," Arak'Jur said. "There is a great army marching east, toward your people. I have come to rally this village, and others in their path, to send as many as you can to safety, and to give me warriors to stand against them."

The old man dropped his pipe.

"How..." Shimmash said. "How did I not see?"

"Grandfather?" Herumi said. "What is he talking about?"

"This army," Shimmash said. "They are not marching toward us. They are already here."

Silence and confusion hung in the air, split by a thundering boom in the distance.

"Already here?" Herumi said. "What? Grandfather? Should I summon our warriors? Are the Truth Spirits certain of this?"

Another boom rattled the walls.

"A great evil," Shimmash said, his voice suddenly croaking and hoarse. "An evil capable of hiding itself from the Truth Spirits. And now it's too late."

"It's not too late," Arak'Jur said. "Summon your guardians, the spirit-touched among your women. I intend to rally the eastern tribes, and stand against them. If not here, then with another people. Another village. But we must move swiftly, and take all the strength we can."

Shimmash blinked. "Yes," the old man said, then turned to Herumi. "I'm sorry, granddaughter. I've failed as seer. Disperse our people. Run. Now. Save what you can."

She stared at him in horror, frozen in place.

"Did the spirits put flax seeds in your ears?" Shimmash roared. "Go!"

Herumi scrambled to her feet. Shimmash sprang to his, belying a strength that shouldn't have been possible for his aged, leathered frame. But a nimbus of *mareh'et* shimmered into place around the shaman's body.

"Perhaps I will succeed as guardian, where my seer's eyes failed," Shimmash said. "My great-grandson and I are with you, Arak'Jur of the Sinari."

"What?" Riosan said. "Great-grandfather, no. We have to stand and fight!"

"I came too late," Arak'Jur said, feeling the pain his words would carry among this people. "The enemy now approaching is tens of thousands strong, with *magi* at their head. For now, we must run, and gather what strength we can."

"With me, great-grandson," Shimmash said. "And with Arak'Jur. Our people are at the mercy of this enemy. But our strength will run with the champion of the Wild." The shaman turned to him. "The Sananesh tribe is closest. Four days by foot. With guardians' gifts we can reach them by nightfall."

12

YULI

Fortress of the Owl
Gantar Baat

The *magi* seneschal wielded her quill like a kitchen knife, darting jabs of ink across her paper with no more than a glance for the characters as she formed them.

"I expect nothing short of your finest guest rooms," Tigai was saying. "With a parlor, and adjoining rooms for my pets." He looked Yuli and the rest of them over. "Three servant's chambers will do. Note it down. And hot water for a bath. One immediately and another each morning."

"Yes, Master Wen, of course," the seneschal said. "It shall be as you say. But, forgive this servant for her rudeness, won't you be joining the other Crane-*magi* inside the city soon?"

"I forgive nothing, you insolent dog," Tigai snapped, then paused and fingered a coin from his purse. "But of course, no dog would have gotten a posting to your position without intending to sell information of your House's comings and goings to interested buyers."

The seneschal blanched. "Master Wen, I would never—"

Tigai struck her across the cheek with his fingertips. Yuli had to suppress the instinct to start forward and intervene, and saw the same lurch among her sisters. Thankfully none followed through.

"Do not presume to speak to me as though we are equals," Tigai said, dropping his coin to the floor with a clink as it struck the tile. "Pick up your bribe, and forget you found us rooms. There will be ten more coins of the same weight if I am satisfied you have kept faith during our stay. Am I understood?"

The seneschal lowered her eyes, showing two droplets of blood on her cheeks. "Yes, Master Wen. This one understands perfectly."

"Good," Tigai said. "Fetch us tea while your people prepare the rooms. We'll wait here."

The seneschal bowed, and Tigai took the lead, guiding Yuli, Alka, and the rest of her sisters toward couches in the sitting room.

"Was that truly necessary, *Master Wen*?" Alka asked when they were alone, putting emphasis on Tigai's chosen pseudonym.

Tigai affected a bored, nobleman's pose, reclining into the cushions and putting his mud-covered boots atop the couch without a care for where they smeared stains.

"I wasn't wrong," Tigai said. "She'll sell the information of our comings and goings no matter how much I pay her. At least now she knows not to sell it cheaply."

Kitian and Namkat shook their heads with rueful grins. Imyan wore the same look, directed at Yuli. "I hope you're making him pay for all of this, sister," Imyan said. "His private hours would be full of penitence, if he were mine."

"He pays well enough," she said, enjoying the discomfort warring with aloofness on Tigai's face. He was a pretty man, almost too pretty, though days spent on the road had left him travel-stained and in desperate need of a razor.

"It's a risk, bringing us here," Alka said. "And doing violence in front of us. I've held the Nine Tails back, but it will need sating soon. A Jun city is no place for clan warriors. We should discuss when it will be time for us to go home."

Her sisters murmured agreement, but Yuli spoke, sitting straighter on her couch. "We're here for more than distracting an army," she said. "This war is more important than one threat to our people. We must stay until we see it through."

"I never agreed to that," Alka said. "Hyman Three Winds never agreed to it. Lord Tigai used words to scatter a great enemy, and I honor him for it. But Clan Hoskar is what matters, not *magi* wars for *magi* empires. We're going home, as soon as we're sure the threat has passed."

Alka stared at her, her back as rigid as Yuli's had been. One on point, Alka was right: The Nine Tails hadn't been sated in too long. She could see in her sister's face the Nine Tails was near the surface, burning for a challenge, for an excuse to seize control. With Sarine's bond she had near-perfect control over the Twin Fangs. But her sisters had no such protection. This would come to violence, if she pressed the point.

She lowered her eyes, and Alka nodded with a reluctant satisfaction.

"Wait," Tigai said. "That can't be the end of it. We're in Gantar Baat to get closer to the seat of *magi* power. That was the whole fucking point. We need to find their champions, and learn what we can of their plans."

"This is of no concern to you," Alka said. "This is Clan Hoskar business, between warrior and warrior."

"Like hells it doesn't concern me," Tigai said. "If you leave, this whole façade is finished. I'm not about to let one woman's ignorance damn this exercise, not least when she doesn't have a fucking clue what—"

Alka rose to her feet, glaring at Tigai. The Nine Tails was on the verge of taking control.

"Tigai, no," Yuli said. The Twin Fangs burned inside her, aching to meet Alka's Nine Tails and let both forms erupt to the surface. She fought it down. "Alka is wise. This is neither the time nor place for a challenge."

"A challenge?" Tigai said. "You're bloody mad. I don't want to bloody fight her. I want her to listen to reason. At least to come with me, to meet Sarine in person. You're the one who's bloody bonded to her, Yuli. Make them understand."

All her sisters turned to her with expressions between curiosity and surprise, and her cheeks colored as red as her ears had been.

"There will be time to discuss this later," Alka said. "For now, we—"

Footsteps in the hall cut her short, and Tigai instantly snapped back to his languid, reclining pose. The others followed his lead, relaxing to be seated on their couches, though Yuli felt the heat behind Alka's eyes, carrying a promise that not only was there time to discuss Tigai's words later, the discussions would be painful, and at length.

"Past time you bring our bloody tea," Tigai said loudly, though when the door opened it was no servant holding a tray. A man loomed in the doorway, tall and thick enough for his head to brush the ceiling. He wore black from head to toe, a pair of scabbards hanging from his belt.

"No son of Crane would bring any man tea," the newcomer said. His voice was deep and dark, with a threat of violence in every word. It stirred the Twin Fangs, and she saw the same in her sisters; after her exchange with Alka their forms would already be hovering near the surface, waiting for a reason to seize control. But Tigai reacted with a relaxed surprise, springing to his feet.

"I see our Lady of Owl works swiftly," Tigai said. "Not a quarter hour and she's already sold word of my coming, and to a brother no less."

The storm cloud in the newcomer's expression melted into a half smile. "I had it from Captain Rashin and his Fighting Lion, as soon as you broached the city walls."

"Never enough coin to bribe them all for silence, is there?" Tigai said. "And too many so-called friends to keep them silent with the blade."

The newcomer gave a gruff laugh, and the tension in the room subsided.

"I am Dhanan Naranjani," the newcomer said. "Acolyte of the temple at Radaban."

"Wen Xijiang," Tigai said, offering him a formal bow. "Of the temple at Jin-So. These are my pets, the warriors of Clan Hoskar, sworn to my service: Alka Nine Tails, Kitian Blood Claw, Yuli Twin Fangs, Namkat Wind Song, Imyan Iron Bark, and Juni Flame Scale."

"Jin-So," Dhanan said. "A Heron city, is it not?"

Tigai waved a hand dismissively. "Heron are allies. Mine was a small monastery, an offshoot of the temple at Ghingwai, and temporary, while I conducted the business of our order. What brings you to Gantar Baat? A long way from Radaban, by any reckoning."

Tigai wove his lies so quickly Yuli almost believed it, and she saw the same on Dhanan Naranjani's face, a mix of curiosity and doubt, though he seemed to go along with Tigai's story as he spoke.

"The summons," Dhanan said. "The order came to assemble, and so we did. Master Indra of the Dragons brought us with his gift."

"Ah," Tigai said, a sudden fire in his eyes. "Master Indra. He's here in the city?"

"I believe he is," Dhanan said. "You have business with the Dragons?"

"No," Tigai said. "Nothing pressing. An old debt I owe the bastard, and I'd as soon avoid the Dragons' holdings here, if you can show me where they're hiding out. I assume you're here to fetch me on behalf of Crane? I intend to take lodging with the Owls, for my pets' sake, but it would do well to show me the lay of the city, otherwise."

Dhanan frowned. "The masters promised we would be marching with the next companies. My instruction, once I learned you were here, was to fetch you and bring you before them for assignment."

"Of course," Tigai said. "But between now and then, business can be done. I'd hoped for a hot bath first, but if the masters insist, we best not keep them waiting."

Dhanan turned, and Tigai made to follow, almost reaching the door before Yuli stopped him.

"Master Wen," she said. "Ought we not accompany you into the city?"

"Nonsense, dog," Tigai said. "Owl will see to your accommodations. Bathe yourselves, and attend my return."

Yuli tried to think of something more to say, some coded means to signal her concern over him going into the city alone, but found nothing. Tigai gave her a lingering look, disdain and impatience writ in his expression as though he truly were Master Wen Xijiang, and not the man she'd been bedding down with for months. She let him go, laughter ringing in the hall between him and Dhanan Naranjani as they left.

Alka rose to shut the door behind them.

"That one is a viper," Juni said. "You're sure you want to lay with him, sister? I worry he'd have me convinced I was someone else, before we were through."

"And that," Alka said, "is precisely what we will now discuss."

Yuli's cheeks flushed. "I know who I am," she said.

"Bonded," Alka said. "Tigai said you were bonded to this woman, this Sarine you and he have been visiting these nights. What did he mean? A common cause? Some pledge you made without consulting your sisters, or your Khan?"

The others fell quiet, their eyes boring into her with the same question, though they were soft silk where Alka was iron.

"I never asked for my father to send me away," she said. "I couldn't have consulted any of you in Kye-Min, or Sarresant. I did what I judged best, for me, and for our people."

"Far-off places, with troubles of no concern to our clan," Alka said. "As to your judgment, I suspect you are in need of reminding that you are a warrior, not a lorekeeper or sage. Your judgment is best limited to how the Twin Fangs should rend our enemies, not to pledge yourself to foreign armies, or foreign wars."

Yuli held her tongue, lowering her eyes to the floor. She'd never had her father's fire with words, to shout down opponents in the political sphere. Once again she could see the stirrings of the Nine Tails on Alka's face. Anger risked giving in to the form, and it was a testament to Alka's will for her to hold it back. Without her bond with Sarine, Yuli would doubtlessly have already lost control to the Twin Fangs; her sisters would see her restraint as a point of pride, perhaps, if she was lucky. But Alka and the others had no such bond. Any moment, the chamber could erupt into violence.

"I beg your forgiveness," Yuli said. "Though I ask you to consider my reasoning, before you pass judgment."

"That is a matter for Hyman Three Winds," Alka said. "Our purpose here was to turn aside a threat to our people, and we've done that. As I said before, it's past time we return home."

"But Tigai," Yuli said. "If he returns to find us gone, he will—"

"He will handle himself, as he seems quite capable of doing," Alka said.

Once more she held her tongue. Rage boiled inside, from the Twin Fangs as much as her own emotions. She wanted to shout Alka down, demand she listen, rage at her sisters and fight them all, if their forms demanded it. Instead she kept calm.

"Tigai can take us home without a week's journey, if we wait for him to return," she said. "I humbly ask we stay here, until we can request the use of his gift."

Alka looked at her dubiously.

"Please, sister," Yuli said.

"Agreed," Alka said finally. "If only because staying means a hot bath. The lot of you smell as though you've been rutting with pigs."

"We couldn't all have a Jun Lordling to keep us up nights," Kitian said. "A woman makes do with what she has at hand."

The rest laughed, though a thread held between Yuli and Alka, a promise of unsettled tension between Nine Tails and Twin Fangs. Soon, she would have a chance to explain, to persuade her sisters to join Sarine in fighting against the shadow's promise of ruin. And she meant to do it, whatever the difference in standing between her and her eldest sister, even if it took Tigai taking them to Sarresant instead of Tiansei.

13

TIGAI

A Winding Street
Gantar Baat

The Hagali swordsman all but blocked his view as they made way toward the city center. Whatever his supposed standing here in Gantar Baat, one didn't use a swordsman the size of a cow as a messenger unless one wanted to send a message. Wen Xijiang's time as an honorable *magi* of the Great and Noble House of the Crane was about to come to an end. If he was going to gather something for Marquand and Sarine and the rest to act on, he had to do it fast.

"How many of us did the Dragons ferry from Radaban?" he asked as Dhanan guided him left, down a broad thoroughfare. The city hummed with enough activity for even a man of Dhanan's size to garner no special attention, as carts, wagons, sheep, horses, and merchants flooded the roads, and soldiers pushed past each other to get at their wares. Impromptu stalls had been set up in the backs of wagons, where they hawked foodstuffs, brass jewelry, half-naked bed slaves, and even weapons for ten times the usual prices in gold and *qian*.

"All of us, Master Wen," Dhanan said, barking it back over his shoulder loud enough to be heard over the throng.

"All of you?" he shouted back. "Radaban is a large temple, is it not?" An utter fabrication, but so far the man had seemed willing to accept foreignness, and Jun arrogance, as a substitute for knowledge.

"The largest in Hagal," Dhanan said. "Fifty acolytes, and ten times as many men-at-arms."

"And Indra took all of you?"

"Did you not receive the same order, in Jin-So?" Dhanan asked. "Every acolyte, every master, every pair of hands capable of wielding sword or spear."

"I've been away, on temple business," he replied. "I only just received the order, in the field." Blessedly, Dhanan seemed content to let it lie. Even so, *every magi* had been ordered here to Gantar Baat? There must be a thousand of them in the city, and a score or more of mercenary companies, each with ten thousand soldiers or more sworn to their banners. Half the bloody empire was here, it seemed, and more than half the *magi*. There had to be a champion or two behind this. If he played it right he would sniff them out before they sniffed him first.

"This way," Dhanan said, turning toward a troop of soldiers in mail with white paint streaked across the links. Others on the street bowed and made way for the soldiers; Dhanan marched straight through.

"Why do you suppose the masters have us massed here, so far north?" he asked Dhanan as they moved.

"War," Dhanan said. "Beyond that is the province of the masters, and the Red Lady."

"The Red Lady?"

"You *have* been away from the monasteries, haven't you?" Dhanan said. "She's been coordinating all this. She was with the Dragons, when they came to Radaban."

"No, no, of course," he said, trying for a clean recovery. "I only meant I was surprised to hear she's here, in Gantar Baat."

"She comes and goes. Here." Dhanan stopped in front of a three-story building, a large square of white brick beneath a two-tiered pagoda. "The seat of our order in the city."

Dhanan led the way up the steps, past spearmen posted at either side of the main door. Inside the building it was chaos, a miniature storm to mirror the bustle in the streets. People of importance in black garb similar to Dhanan's crossed the floors with retinues in tow, servants and fighters trailing after them, while others packed and loaded crates, making way for those of higher rank.

"Busy," Tigai said.

"As I told you, Master Wen," Dhanan said. "The Red Lady has summoned us to war."

They climbed a set of steps, then took another flight, leaving behind a second floor as hurried as the first. A sentry greeted them on the third level, this one garbed in the same blacks as Dhanan himself. Words were exchanged, then bows, and the man moved aside to let them climb again.

The top floor was sparser, a straw mat covering the length of the main chamber, with sword racks on either wall beneath glass windows, but its people were no less hurried. A man in long robes barked orders to two servants, while an elderly woman paused midway through directing a maid to weigh Tigai and Dhanan as soon as they appeared atop the stairs.

"Grandmaster Arisaya," Dhanan said, bowing deep enough to satisfy any noble. Tigai muttered the same as he bowed still deeper.

"Master Naranjani," the woman, Arisaya, said. "You've returned. And this is…?"

Dhanan bowed again. "Master Wen Xijiang, of Jin-So."

Tigai repeated his gesture as the woman covered the ground between them. She wore a courtly dress of blue silk, and carried a pair of swords at her hip in spite of it. She came to a stop in front of him, and reached a gloved hand to touch his chin, standing close enough he could smell rose liquor on her breath.

"Master Wen Xijiang, of Jin-So," Grandmaster Arisaya repeated. Tigai tensed, and tried not to let it show, maintaining a firm hold on his anchor among the starfield and the strands. The barest threatening motion and he'd cinch it tight, transporting himself back to the room where he'd left Yuli and her sisters. Instead she let her fingers fall, as though the air were as delicate as his skin.

"You are no acolyte known to me, Master Wen," Arisaya said. "And yet to hear it told, you've arrived at Gantar Baat with claim on the service of all six Hoskar warriors. An impressive feat, for a man too young for me to know his name."

"This acolyte only did his duty, Grandmaster Arisaya," Tigai said, adopting a posture appropriate for what she'd labeled him: an ambitious man seeking to rise above his station, showing humility in his moment of pride.

"His duty," Arisaya said. "And which master assigned him this duty, I wonder?"

Once more he fought to keep the tension from showing in his face. Here it was. The question that would unravel his lies. A woman of power might have no knowledge of a junior acolyte, but she would never accept an invented name for a master. Still, Dhanan had given him a thread to grasp for. If it failed, he would use the strands and revert to his anchor, but as long as there was hope, he meant to seize it.

"It was no master of our order, Grandmaster," he said. "I received my orders from the Red Lady herself, when she came to our temple at Jin-So."

Dhanan's features creased with surprise, and Arisaya froze for the barest moment—an equal tell, considering her station. She recovered quickly, and Tigai tried to avoid giving shame by revealing that he'd noticed the pause.

"The Red Lady," Arisaya said. "She must have chosen well, for you to have succeeded in the task."

Tigai bowed, less steeply this time. "Thank you, Grandmaster," he said. "The Hoskar are wild, but wild things can be tamed. They await my pleasure at the Fortress of the Owl."

"An excellent turn," Arisaya said. "And fortuitously timed. You will want to make the report to the Red Lady in person, I expect?"

"Of course," Tigai said smoothly, concealing the sudden spike in his heart. Any woman in command of a thousand or more *magi* and their attendant mercenary companies was a woman of significance, to be sure, but there was a chance—a damn good chance—that she was more. One of the Regnant's champions. She had to be.

"Then we go," Arisaya said. "At once. Dhanan, fetch Master Hilo and his retainers. Three masters will suffice for an honor guard, I think, in light of Master Wen's success."

"Three?" Tigai said. "Shouldn't we fetch the Hoskar women, to make it nine?"

The Grandmaster's eyes narrowed, only the slightest fraction, but enough to be a shouted measure of suspicion, to trained eyes.

"The Red Lady gave you the task, Master Wen, did she not?" Arisaya said. "I'd as soon bring your word before her, and not six uncivilized barbarians."

"Yes, Grandmaster," Tigai said, making a point of lowering his eyes to the floor. "It shall be as you say."

Silence passed between them, and wind spirits send she read it for no more than shame at being rebuked when he'd expected favor. Damn but it would have been bloody nice to have Yuli and her sisters at his side, in case the Red Lady did indeed turn out to be one of their enemies.

"You've been away, Master Wen," Arisaya said. "For that, I can forgive some ignorance of our house's standing in the Empire. There will be time later to educate you. It is enough for now to say swiftness is imperative, in restoring the Red Lady's confidence, and absolute propriety. In her presence, you will follow my lead, and speak only if prompted. Am I understood?"

"Yes, Grandmaster," Tigai said, keeping his eyes low and his features smooth. "I will do as you say, and hope my service proves worthy of your blessings."

With that, Dhanan, six soldiers, and another man in black returned, each bowing to Arisaya as they arrived.

"I hope the same, Master Wen," Arisaya said. "Now, we go."

———————

Ten horses draped with red blankets stood waiting in the street, and Arisaya, Dhanan, and the rest climbed into their saddles smoothly. As soon as he was seated, Arisaya shouted a command, and they set off at a gallop toward the city's eastern edge.

If he'd been surprised to see the mercenaries give way to Dhanan before, it paled against the throng's reaction to a squad of mounted riders bolting through their midst. The streets swarmed with soldiers, traders, farmers, and more, but Arisaya made no move to avoid them, and their procession stormed through the crowd without slowing. Shouted cries went up ahead of them, and the path was clear for every stretch of road, until they crossed half the city in the time he would have taken to move down one street.

They slowed only once they reached the edge of the city. A man in white-painted armor trotted forward, exchanged words with Arisaya, then beckoned to admit them to the camp beyond the city's streets. They followed behind Arisaya's horse at a walk, and in a hundred paces, they left the chaos and disorder of the city behind.

The paths in front of them were clean and precise, and it was all Tigai could do not to gape. Every soldier outside the city was assembled as though preparing to stage a parade, crisp ranks and stiff postures instead of the lax discipline that he expected to prevail in a warcamp. Even his brother hadn't maintained such rigid order. And this wasn't a single unit assembled for review; endless ranks and formations extended from the city to the horizon, all of them assembled as though they were one command away from marching onto a battlefield.

"Impressive, no?" Dhanan said from atop the horse next to him in their line.

Tigai kept his features calm. "A great army," he said carefully, and Dhanan and one of the other swordsmen exchanged grins.

"I almost pissed myself when I saw it for the first time," the swordsman said.

"And he's only seeing it now," Dhanan said. "It was twice this size a week ago."

"How...?" Tigai said, stumbling, and recovering from his awe. "That is, how can we feed so many soldiers in one place?"

Dhanan shrugged. "They aren't here for long. The Red Lady's gift is impressive, to say the least."

A prod, or a boast, designed to get him to ask for more. But he'd already claimed dealings with this Red Lady. Speaking might give away more than he intended. Instead he put on a knowing smile, while his thoughts roiled.

So bloody *many*. Erris d'Arrent couldn't field a tenth so many soldiers, and if this Red Lady had a gift that could sustain them, that alone would justify an attempt to kill her before the fighting began in earnest. An Ox-*magi*, maybe, though most Oxen he knew of had the gift to transmute dirt to stone, glass to iron, or something similar in kind. A gift to transmute snow to grain might explain why they were gathered here in Gantar Baat, the northernmost, and frozen-most, of the hundred cities. So far as he knew, Gantar Baat was a staging ground for invading a heap of frozen tundra and not much else.

They'd tracked past a square of soldiers in green armor with yellow tassels on their spears before he remembered Isaru's warcamp.

Two hundred leagues east, the towering shadows of the Divide had blanketed a frozen stretch of seawater, a narrow bridge across the ice. Gantar Baat was closest to it, of all the hundred cities, and now with the Divide gone they could march across its shores and reach the land on the other side. Sarine's land, if the maps he'd seen were accurate. But it was still two hundred leagues of tundra to the crossing. It would have taken all the supply wagons in the Empire to feed an army as it crossed the ice and snow, to say nothing of how many leagues of waste lay on the other side.

Arisaya led them toward the heart of the camp, where a pavilion of tents had been put up on open ground. The assembled soldiers parted before Arisaya's horse, just as the crowd had done in the city, and the Cranes made their approach, coming to a halt outside the main tent.

"Grandmaster Arisaya," an attendant in a red sash said, greeting them with a bow. "No Cranes are slated to be part of today's departures. To what do we owe the honor of your visit?"

Arisaya slid from her horse, offering him a bow deep enough to show respect. "We bring news of a small victory. A minor thing, but suitable for the lady's ears, if she can spare time to hear it."

The attendant looked them over, as though he were counting the horses and Crane-*magi* before replying. "Yes," he said finally. "Wait here."

The attendant ducked into the main tent as Dhanan, the other *magi*, and their guards followed Arisaya in dismounting. Tigai did the same, waiting beside his horse and trying not to stare at the assembled mass of soldiers all around them. A land invasion; it had to be, and this Red Lady's gift had to be tied to somehow feeding or transporting these soldiers across the strait. With luck his deception would last long enough to learn how she was doing it, but he'd already seen enough to warn Erris and Sarine and the rest. All he needed was a few more moments, a chance to see—

The tent flap swung upward, and Arisaya dropped to a knee beside her horse, followed by Dhanan and the rest of their party. Tigai remained standing.

The other Cranes noticed, hissing at him to show proper respect. He heard nothing.

In the tent entrance, the man in the red sash held the flap open for a woman, clothed all in red. She wore a soldier's uniform, red ribbons binding her hair and a trim of gold tracing patterns on her sleeves and cuffs. He'd seen her wear the same sort of fare before, though her captain's uniform had been far plainer when he'd first captured her on the battlements of the Kregiaw fortress.

The Red Lady was Captain Lin Qishan.

The woman who had taken Mei, Dao, and Remarin captive, and used them to force him into the Dragons' service. The woman who Sarine had sworn killed herself, stepping into the light in the Gods' Seat after she attacked Paendurion from behind.

She met his eyes, and he saw recognition there. Recognition, and hate.

He blinked to find the starfield as an image shimmered around her, a Great Cat roaring with spectral claws and eyes of fire. She moved in a blur as he made the tether to the Fortress of the Owl, cinching the strand around himself. She raised a hand, unleashing a bolt of lightning that streaked toward his chest as he stepped between the stars.

He shifted.

Something hit him in the ribs as his anchor slid into place, and he coughed, tasting smoke and burnt cloth.

Yuli was on her feet as he slumped to the ground, the rest of her sisters rising as she rushed to his side.

"I'm fine," he said, coughing again and waving her off. "Close, bloody fucking close, but I'm fine."

"What happened?" Yuli asked, still hovering over him.

"I met someone I bloody well thought was dead," he said. "And she apparently wanted me bloody well dead, too."

"She?" Yuli asked, a sudden intonation in her voice.

"No, no," he said. "Nothing like that. And...wait, why are you all still here in the waiting room? Shouldn't the Owls have prepared rooms by now?"

Yuli's back stiffened. "Alka Nine Tails has decided it is time for us to return home. We waited here for you to take us."

"Fuck that," he said. "It was Lin Qishan, Yuli. You saw her die, didn't you? And whatever she's doing here, she's found a way to mobilize an army ten times the size of anything Erris d'Arrent has in the field. We have to reach Sarine to warn them, and figure out what in the hells is going on."

"Lord Yanjin, we have endured enough," Alka said. "You have done us a great service, but Clan Hoskar's strength must be used to fight clan battles, not foreign wars."

He met her eyes. Rage stared back at him. He saw the signs of Hoskar magic, familiar now after all the months he'd spent with Yuli. But he needed Yuli by his side, not least for her being one of Sarine's champions, too.

"Sorry," he said. "I can't leave you here. They know Wen Xijiang was a lie. And that means you're coming with me, at least for now."

He found the strands before Alka could protest again, and snapped the tether into place.

14

SARINE

A Makeshift Training Yard
The Hunting Lodge, Rasailles

She held the sparks of *Life* tightly. Blue energy coursed through her, yearning to obey her command, as though it meant to guess what she wanted, to leap to take action before the thoughts could fully form. It was like trying to grasp fire. Life magic split, and ran, and arced a hundred directions at once. Not more than a handful of sparks wrapped around the red motes of *Body* before streaking off, dissipating into the void.

She let it go.

"I can't," she said. "It's like trying to weave a blanket with lamp oil."

Marquand paced between her and the tree line, forty paces off. Room enough for practice, Marquand had said, but so far she'd only practiced failure.

"Try again," Marquand said. "You said the Regnant's soldiers were infused with *Body*. It had to come from somewhere. Not a chance every soldier in their army suddenly gained access to our leylines."

"They didn't," she said. "It was coming from far away, over the western horizon. I think it was *Body*; I saw it when I went to tether *Faith*. But this is impossible. You're asking me to channel ten thousand tethers at once. I can hook regular tethers to the blue sparks without thinking. I can't do it ten thousand times over."

"Paendurion could," Marquand said. "Empress d'Arrent told me he could work a hundred strands of *Need* all at the same time. Half their bloody commanders had the golden eyes, all at once."

"That's different," she said. "Paendurion never did it with *Body*, and *Need* works differently. This has to be something else. Some gift the Regnant gave his champions. Maybe the Regnant himself is behind it, I don't know. But this is beyond me."

"Just try," Marquand said. "We need to know what precisely you saw on those shores."

She closed her eyes. Life magic was there, waiting as it always was. A deep reserve of blue sparks, jumping and fighting for her attention. It was bloody maddening. She *should* be able to do this. It nagged at her, the energy desperately wanting to obey her will, to bend and flow where she wanted it to go. But every attempt ended the same way: with the blue sparks dissipating as she strained to entwine with the leylines. She'd seen the blanket of *Body* tethers in the Regnant's camp, itself enough of a shock, finding familiar magic in use by the enemy. It had to be something else. Half of her wanted to give up this exercise and hook back to those stars, just to see it again. Instead she concentrated on the blue sparks.

Hardly any *Body* lingered under the forest clearing or the hunting lodge, but it couldn't matter for this. There was no chance that enough *Body* to power ten thousand soldiers' bindings would be found on those western beaches, even with the horrific pyre that had spurred Arak'Jur to remain behind. The strands had come from far away, over the horizon. She reached out with the blue sparks, projecting her awareness beyond the palace grounds, to New Sarresant in the east, the forests in the north and west, the trade roads and cities to the south.

Perhaps if she relaxed, and let the energy come on its own. An awareness of *Body* drifted outward, seeking the red energy wherever it hovered on the leylines. The blue sparks crackled and surged in her mind. This was *her* power. The rest was...borrowed. The thought came up amid the void of patience. She didn't have to think. The sparks would sense what she wanted. Erris's soldiers were camped outside the city, to the northwest. The red motes would drift toward them, carried on the blue sparks' backs. Not tethers, then. More of a net. No, her first analogy had been right: a blanket, laid gently rather than tied in place. A blanket, that could...the sparks slipped. Blue energy leaked away, first into the leylines, stirring colors wherever she touched, and then into nothing. Into the void. She refocused. She should be able to do this. All she had to do was grasp it by...The sparks faded. The blanket unraveled, as quickly as she'd made it, and leaked out into the void.

"Gods damn it!" she said, blinking as the clearing came back into focus. "It was close, so bloody close, but...Marquand?"

He wasn't there. She swiveled around, between the trees, the empty grass, and the lodge. The sound of conversation rose from the side of the building. She blinked again, then went to find him. She should have been able to do it. Perhaps if she tried again, she might puzzle it out. She was close. And it meant they were right: The Regnant himself was behind those tethers on the western shore, or a champion imbued with the leylines. After all, she'd bound Tigai and Yuli, both from the Regnant's side of the Divide. Perhaps he'd found a way to make a champion out of one of her leyline binders in return.

"…newly promoted, by virtue of being assigned to this very unit," a familiar voice said, beaming with pride. "By the Empress's own hand."

"A bloody major, at what, twenty-five?" Marquand said. "Nameless stick me from behind, Her Majesty must be truly desperate."

Laughter took the sting out of Marquand's words, and she rounded the building to find half of what she expected: Captain—no, Major, now—Rosline Acherre, a gold leaf pinned to her collar, one heavy bag slung over her shoulder while another dropped at her feet. She would have rushed to greet Acherre with both arms wide, military decorum be damned, but for the other woman at Acherre's side: Corenna. Arak'Jur's companion, already glaring at her with frost in her eyes the moment she rounded the lodge.

"Sarine," Acherre said. "You're looking well. I hope Colonel Marquand doesn't have you breaking too many rocks in this prison detail."

"I never meant for him to stay behind," she said at once. "Corenna, I'm sorry."

"Arak'Jur had orders to return with Sarine," Marquand said. "He disobeyed those orders."

Corenna said nothing, weighing them both.

"Ah," Acherre said.

"We saw a pyre, made from the bodies of dead tribesfolk," Sarine said. "He stayed to warn nearby villages. He promised to return, with their guardians and shamans at his side. He said to tell you he loved you. I'm sorry. I should have made him come back."

Frost held in Corenna's eyes a moment longer before it cracked.

"No," Corenna said. "He makes his own choices. Forgive me, for harboring anger toward you. It was no fault of yours. We remain sisters-in-arms, if you will have me."

"Yes," Marquand said. "Well. I'd intended for us to begin with trials and testing as soon as you'd arrived, but if you both need time to settle in, you'll find empty rooms inside the lodge. Food, too, bless the Empress and her quartermasters. Sausages, salted pork, oranges and figs shipped up from the Thellan isles."

"I don't need time to rest or to settle in," Corenna said. "If we're meant to work, let's begin."

"You're sure?" Marquand asked, but Corenna had already moved past him, on her way to the open field.

She took the moment to give Acherre the hug she'd intended, eliciting a laugh as she squeezed the woman's freshly pressed uniform.

"There's the Sarine I remember," Acherre said. "It's bloody good to see you again."

"Same for you," she replied. "And Marquand isn't working us too hard. Not when our goal is saving the whole Gods-damned world."

"Sounds like an appropriately scoped mission, then," Acherre said. "When the Empress summoned me for this posting, I thought for sure she was having a joke at my expense. A squad of Gods and Goddesses, she called it, meant to fight the same among our enemies."

"It doesn't sound much like Erris to have a joke at all, much less at anyone's expense," she said.

"True enough, that," Acherre said, grinning broadly.

"All right," Marquand was saying, already back to his pacing, gesturing for them to take places on the green. "For starters, I need a better understanding of what everyone can do. Empress d'Arrent gave me a written briefing. I need to see it in person."

"You already know my work with the leylines," Acherre said. "Best to start with Corenna, since part of her gift overlaps Sarine's?"

Marquand nodded, turning to Corenna.

"What do you wish to see?" Corenna asked.

"D'Arrent says you can channel beast spirits," Marquand said. "How many, and to what effect?"

"Eleven," Corenna said. "Do you wish a demonstration? The spirits will find it vulgar, but I am willing."

Acherre and Marquand watched with rapt interest as Corenna went ahead, speaking a beast's name before surrounding herself with a shimmering image of the creature itself, then showing what its gift could do. Sarine recognized *mareh'et*, the Great Cat, when Corenna chose it first, and grew spectral claws from her fingertips before she leapt at a nearby rock with a rush of speed, cleaving it in two as easily as she might have torn a sheet of paper. The next was foreign: *rin'ji*, a winged serpent, by which Corenna leapt into the air, then spit hissing acid in a puddle that sank deep into the dirt. *Juna'ren* followed, then *ipek'a*, *eli'ko*, *astahg*, *anahret*, *munat'ap*, *wana'tai*, and *lakiri'in*. Of those only *lakiri'in* was familiar to her, the Great Crocodile's furious burst of speed that had Corenna racing the whole length of the clearing before returning to where they stood in front of the lodge.

"The eleventh has refused me, though I earned the right to call upon its gift," Corenna said. "*Kirighra*, who stalks its prey through shadows and kills with elongated, razor fangs." She mimicked the fangs' size, tracing a line in the air from her teeth down to her belly. "Its spirit grants the same: a cloak of shadows to hide movement, and a bite of great strength and power."

She went quiet as she finished, leaving Marquand staring at Corenna in silence.

"Exarch's balls for an omelet," Marquand said finally. "You can do all that? Bloody skewer me if I didn't see it for myself."

"She can do more than that," Sarine said, feeling a touch of pride on Corenna's behalf. "The war spirits."

Corenna bowed her head, then began a second demonstration. This time her eyes pooled with color, shifting hue as she moved from one spirit to another. A gray film for Air, from Hanet'Li'Tyat, and blue for Ice. A bright green fire for Growth as she brought a year's worth of weeds out of the dirt, then a darker green for Rot as they withered and flaked away on the wind. She finished with her eyes going pure black for Death, conjuring inky tendrils that she dismissed almost at once into puffs of smoke.

"What would happen if we came into contact with that smoke?" Marquand asked.

"Sickness," Corenna replied, touching her forearm to demonstrate. "Boils, rashes, itching, vomit. Death, if the contact lasts too long."

"She could hold a charge by herself," Acherre said. "No bloody regiment ever made would keep ranks into that."

"What about attack?" Marquand said. "We could use her as one prong of a pincer, even with the enemy's back against a fortification."

"A double envelopment around one woman," Acherre said. "My Gods. And with Sarine and Tigai to reposition..."

The thoughts soured on her tongue, even as Acherre and Marquand swapped ideas for their gifts' use. War was war, but all of them working together would mean slaughter by the thousands. It had to be done, but the thought made it no easier to face.

And Black, Anati thought to her. *It would mean a great pool of* Black. *More than you could handle.*

"I know," she said to herself as much as her *kaas*.

"What do you know, sister?" Corenna asked.

She tried to relax as Corenna approached. "I was replying to Anati," she said. "I truly am sorry, Corenna. I didn't mean for Arak'Jur to remain behind."

"Don't think of it," Corenna said. "As I said before, he is his own man. What did your *kaas* say?"

"She says I couldn't handle killing so many, and she's right," she said. "All of us, working together, would be a fearsome, terrible thing."

"All killing is terrible," Corenna said. "It is a great taboo among my people, for a woman to seek out war magic as I have. But it is no evil, to be able to visit death on one's enemies, if the enemies are chosen well."

Life and Death, Anati thought. *Love and Hate. Enmity and Loyalty. Choice doesn't matter, when—Dragon.*

Sarine frowned. "What does that mean?" she asked. Then she saw them. A group suddenly standing beside the lodge, where there had been only grass and shrubberies a moment before. Six—no, seven, fanning out at once, facing each other and scanning the area as though they meant to fight.

She bolted to her feet, snapping a call to the others and shifting her vision to the strands.

"Sarine?" Tigai called. "Are you here?"

She let the strands go. "Tigai?" she called back. "What are you doing here?"

"Thank the fucking wind spirits," Tigai said. "Sorry for the unscheduled arrival. There were...complications in Gantar Baat."

"What is the meaning of this, Lord Yanjin?" one of Tigai's companions snapped at him. A tall woman with iron-gray hair, who seemed to be growing taller as she spoke.

Corenna relaxed at mention of Tigai's name, while Marquand and Acherre bounded toward them.

"No, Alka," Yuli said from among the pack of Tigai's companions, who she could see now were six women, each tattooed across the face as Yuli was. "You mustn't let the Nine Tails—"

"Be silent, child!" the first companion, Alka, said. Alka's voice had grown harder, echoing with a deep resonance as her features shifted. She'd been a woman when they arrived, and now she seemed to have fur growing to cover her skin. "He will not keep us hostage for the price of one good deed."

"Now, hold on a bloody minute," Tigai said. "We had to get out of there, and I figured we might as well come to the lodge and talk this through before bringing it to the Empress."

"Bringing what to Erris?" she said. "What is this, Tigai? What's going on?"

"All of you, stop!" Yuli shouted. "Tigai is mine, and I will stand for his intentions. He isn't trying to keep us hostage."

Alka turned to glare at Yuli, but any semblance of the woman with iron-gray hair was gone, replaced by a creature more than half again the woman's height.

Long limbs covered in fur extended toward Yuli, while the iron gray in Alka's hair had been replicated in streaks from a narrow fox's snout down the length of her back, to where nine separate tails flicked, each one quivering in anger.

Yuli's transformation followed, instantaneous where Alka's had been a gradual change. She'd seen Yuli's Twin Fangs form before: not as tall as Alka, and hairless, but with claws twice as long and thick, like butcher's cleavers where Alka's were needle points extending from the tips of her fingers.

The tattooed women around them backed away, while Tigai stood next to them, gaping. Marquand barked an order to stop at once, an order both ignored.

Before any more could be said, the two forms rushed each other.

They moved faster than she could follow without *Body* or *Red*. She reached for her gifts without thinking, and the mêlée seemed to slow, the whirling torrent of claws and fangs becoming a dance instead. Alka slashed for Yuli's chest, and Yuli lowered a shoulder, avoiding the attack and turning it into a rushing charge. The two connected and staggered back, each of Alka's nine tails elongating into a whip, cracking to make space between them. Yuli snapped her jaws at the tails, connecting with one and yanking her neck to drag Alka off her feet. Only instead of falling, Alka spun a kick into Yuli's cheek, red claw marks from her toes spraying blood up the side of Yuli's head.

"Stop!" she and Tigai shouted together. Neither of the women obeyed. Yuli raked Alka's shoulder with her claws, deep cuts running rivulets of blood down her chest, while Alka's tails wrapped around Yuli's waist, covering her back in welts and gashes where they struck a flurry of whipping cuts.

"Give me *Black*," Sarine shouted. "Drain them both."

Of course, Anati thought. *But Yuli is a champion.* Black *won't—*

Yuli howled as Alka's tails closed around her throat, a cry mangled into a choking gasp as each successive tail whipped a coil around her neck.

"Now, Anati!" she shouted. "Make them stop!"

An inky haze appeared at the edge of her vision as Anati granted her *Black*, the *kaas*'s gift to rip away power. It struck both women, but only Alka's tails dissolved, her fur receding, her body returning to its weathered skin and iron-gray hair. Yuli had been raking Alka's belly, a succession of darting jabs to push the woman off her throat. Now Alka's form was gone, Yuli's claws impaled pink, human flesh in place of fur. Blood spattered on the grass, and claws the length of a forearm protruded through Alka's spine.

Yuli changed in an instant, suddenly cradling Alka's body as a woman instead of savaging her as a beast. Shock whitened Yuli's face, while blood leaked from Alka's mouth, and the older woman coughed.

"No," Yuli said. "No, eldest sister, no. I only meant to meet your challenge."

A somber quiet descended on them all.

Should we release it? Anati asked.

Tears rose in Sarine's eyes. It was her fault. Anati had tried to warn her. *Black* would have no effect on Yuli, with the champion's bond, while the other woman...Alka...would be left defenseless. The other tattooed women had moved to gather around Yuli, a silent ring separating Alka's body from the rest of them.

Sarine?

"What?" she said. "What does that mean, to 'release it'?"

The Nine Tails. Black *is holding it here, keeping it from going to be reborn.*

Sobs and cries came from the ring of women around Yuli. They put arms across each other's shoulders, kneeling together in the grass.

"I...I'm sorry," she said. But as she said it, foreign emotion flared inside her. A sense of pride in death, satisfaction in a long and gloried life, and hunger for rebirth. It seemed to know it was dead, and risked dying further, unless it found a host.

"Sarine?" Tigai said. "What in the hells are you doing?"

The women kneeling in the grass turned, and Yuli rose to her feet. Yuli seemed shorter than she'd been a moment before. And a glance down revealed that Sarine's forearms had grown longer, and sprouted the first tufts of fur.

"The Nine Tails," Yuli said. "How is this possible?"

"I don't..." Sarine said. "I didn't...Anati, what's happening?"

The form, Anati thought to her. *It likes you. It thinks you're worthy.*

A searing pain shot through her legs as she grew taller, her spine stretching as it fractured above her tailbone. The form sent feelings of warmth, and assurance. It would be a good partner. She would be a good host.

Life magic flooded through her. Her vision shifted to the Infinite Plane, where a torrent of blue sparks made a column that she knew instinctively was her. Another torrent had wrapped itself around hers, black and red sparks where hers were blue. It crawled up the base of her column, entwining itself with the eddies of her consciousness, blending into her like water mixed with blood.

No. Her thought, not Anati's.

The word reverberated through the Plane, a shock wave of force emanating from the blue sparks.

It isn't sure what you want, Anati thought. *It isn't like us. I don't think it understands.*

I know, she thought back. *But I am Sarine. I am the Goddess. I've shared this body before. I won't do it again.*

The presence inside her recoiled, wounded.

Tell it to go, Sarine thought.

The red and black sparks diminished, shrinking back to a pool at the base of her column.

I don't think it can, Anati thought. *It's already bonded itself to you.*

Anger flared. Her anger. She saw it manifest in the blue sparks, as some changed from blue to red. The black sparks shrank further.

It obeys me, then, she thought. *It comes when I call, and does nothing I don't want.*

The black sparks shuddered with relief. They grew again, this time keeping a distance from the blue as they coiled around the base of the torrent that was *her*, here on the Infinite Plane.

She gasped, and her vision snapped back to the clearing. Yuli knelt over her; she must have fallen, lying down in the grass.

"Is it possible?" Yuli said, barely above a whisper. "Has the Nine Tails chosen you? Are you to be our new pack leader?"

"I'm sorry, Yuli," she said. "It was my fault. I tore her gift away trying to stop her from hurting you."

"Alka lived a long life," Yuli said. "The Nine Tails wouldn't have left her if it wasn't ready for her to die."

"You don't understand. I did it, with *Black*."

Yuli went quiet. Then she went to her knees, offering a hand to help her rise.

"Fate is cruel, then," Yuli said. "For my newest sister to have wronged my eldest. But we are sisters now, sisters in truth, and if you are the Nine Tails' new host, then we will mourn Alka together."

15

ARAK'JUR

A Narrow Canyon
Quanang Land

He remained still and silent, moving only with the rustling of the wind. The canyon walls were steep, too steep to climb, though he could descend with the spirits' gifts. He, and the others who had hidden at his command. Guardians, and spirit-touched women, and a *Ka*, gathered from the remnants of half a dozen tribes. They ringed the canyon walls, nestled in thick bushes, hiding. Waiting.

The first Jun soldiers appeared, running too fast for any man to move.

They came pouring into the canyon, scanning and searching the heights. Ranks of macemen, spearmen, arquebusiers, marching beneath flags of foreign design. Red banners, or white, bearing stars and the lines of strange characters. Officers in decorated uniforms walked among them, and *magi* in red and saffron robes.

The main body. He'd already evaded their scouts, in setting this trap.

He waited until a thousand soldiers had filtered into the canyon. It should have taken an hour to move so many. Running should have tired them; running at their pace should have winded them in minutes. Yet they came on without slowing, and filled the canyon end-to-end.

He cupped his hands and made an osprey's call, two long, high-pitched cries, then four quick chirps. It drew eyes toward his side of the ridge, and for ten heartbeats he kept still, willing the others to do the same.

The attack came from the opposite side. Beast images shimmered around the guardians as they leapt down the steep inclines. *Mareh'et. Una're. Cantaguar.*

Astahg. Wielded by the spirit-touched from the Tilannak, Sananesh, Nuxailak, Chaikum, and Ilingit tribes, the tribes he and Shimmash had visited so far, carrying warning of this Jun army.

The soldiers whirled around to face their attackers, officers shouting orders over the warcries as they pivoted with the same speed that had carried them into his trap. Spears raised in a palisade as the first guardians collided with their line. Wood cracked, and bone. Steel pierced flesh, and spirit-claws cut men down in a rain of earth and blood.

Arak'Jur bellowed his own cry. *Kirighra's* triumphant howl paired with *ipek'a's* thundering screech. He pushed off from the bush, *ipek'a's* leap propelling him halfway across the canyon, directly over the Jun soldiers' heads. The rest of the guardians and women on his side of the ridge followed, racing down the walls as their fellows on the opposite side had done. The Jun soldiers whirled, caught between two screaming forces, and split their ranks, facing both sides with weapons raised.

Kirighra's gift shimmered around his skin as Arak'Jur fell, blurring his body with shadow. *Ipek'a* absorbed the shock of his landing, ripping apart an officer next to a red banner with his scything claw. Blood and tissue scattered in chunks, and the soldiers around him whirled, looking for him and finding only the blurred motion of *kirighra's* gift, no matter their speed. One man stabbed the air with a spear; another swung a mace toward where the officer had been standing. Arak'Jur moved around both, calling on Mountain's gift to unleash fire into their ranks.

The sounds of battle rose around him, screams and cries, whimpering and rage. Smoke blinded him as Mountain's fire bellowed in a circle, erupting from his hands as he spun. Twenty died in an instant, making a wreath of fire and a column of black smoke at the heart of the Jun line.

A creature came through the smoke. He was ready. Fire scorched glass, but the hulking figure gave no sign of slowing.

Magi.

Glass shards shattered as he met the Ox-*magi* atop a pile of charred corpses. *Una're's* claws delivered a massive blow to the glass-hulk's shoulder, twisting the *magi's* torso and coursing lightning over the rest of its body. It swung back, peppering the air with shards of glass that drove him to the side, stinging wounds covering his forearm.

Soldiers closed around him, leveling spears to force him back toward the glass-hulk. He charged the spears instead, ducking beneath them as another salvo of glass soared over his head, sinking into the soldiers' chests and arms. They howled, and he struck, this time bolstered by *lakiri'in's* speed and *kirighra*'s spectral bite. He tore them to pieces, the Great Crocodile's speed eclipsing whatever magic had bolstered the Jun.

The glass-hulk stepped toward him, then collapsed into the dirt as a ringing explosion took it from behind.

The crunch of cracking glass shook the earth, and one of the Tilannak spirit-touched women emerged behind it, weaving shields of earth to turn aside thrown spears as she moved. The glass-hulk pushed itself back to its feet, spinning toward the woman. Another explosion of earth threatened to throw them both off their feet, and instead he charged the hulk from behind, wrapping his arms around its torso to drive it to the ground.

Una're gave his gift again, and he sat astride the hulk's chest, pounding the *magi*'s glass until finally it broke, revealing unprotected flesh. He struck again, turning the woman inside the armor to pulp and gore.

A maceman's blow struck his back before he could rise, and he howled. *Mareh'et* gave its blessing, and he ran the opposite direction, to where a line of arquebusiers leveled their firing tubes toward a mêlée, prepared to fire into their own to hit some of his. He sprang into them with the Great Cat's grace, catching one of them through the neck and severing another's arm before he could fire. A few managed to press their matches to the firing pans, and discharged bellowing roars of smoke and powder. Another guardian—Riosan of the Tilannak— charged into them at the same moment, wielding *mareh'et*'s gift as Arak'Jur did, and together they brought the soldiers down in a flurry of raking claws.

A mass of soldiers tried to flee, clustering near the mouth of the canyon, at the narrow choke that marked its entrance. Guardians attacked, weaving between the spears of the outer ranks, and women hurled ice, earth, wind, and fire, throwing bodies into the air. He ran toward them, trusting Riosan to follow.

A dome rose behind the soldiers' front ranks.

Shimmering force cut the canyon off from the valley behind, cutting his guardians and women from the remainder of the Jun army. The soldiers trapped on the wrong side panicked, screaming, throwing down weapons, hammering their fists against the dome. His spirit-touched women sent blasts of fire and wind into their ranks, ripping them apart.

"Back," he shouted. "With me."

The guardians and women obeyed, retreating from the dome. Blood drenched the canyon floor, painting bushes red, making small rivers where it ran together, pooling and bubbling against the dome's shimmering force. Through its haze he could see Jun soldiers retreating, and a single *magi*, veiled in a saffron robe colored pink by the wall between them. The Heron met his eyes, full of shock and hate.

He called on *lakiri'in*, and ran, the rest of his people trailing behind.

"Two dead," his *Ka*, Shimmash of the Tilannak, said. "Kian'Arak of the Nuxailak, and Sindal of the Chaikum. Nine more wounded, and recovering."

"More of them than us," he said. "A great many more."

"There are a great many more of them than us," Shimmash replied. The words brought a chill wind in spite of the desert heat.

"They'll leave the mountains soon," Ilanna Great Oak said. She'd come from the Hurusi, sent by a great gathering of plains tribes, following the spirits' visions to find him and Shimmash recruiting among the Ilingit. "We'll need new tactics to surprise them when they reach the plain."

Silence fell between them, and the cracking of the fire. The tribes he'd visited so far had given him all the strength they could, and scattered before the rushing wildfire of the Jun army. He'd saved thousands. And still he needed more.

"The Quanang live among these mountains," Shimmash said. "We should visit them, and bring their guardians, before we reach the great plain."

He nodded. "What of the Hurusi?" he asked. "Can your people spare more than they've sent already?"

"Perhaps," Ilanna Great Oak said. "Most of us followed the Vision spirits' call. But even the mightiest of our *Ka* couldn't foresee the Jun army advancing so quickly across this land. They are like locusts." She spat. "The Erhapi will fight, too, if we can reach them. They have more heart than any Quanang, and more spirit-touched among their warriors."

"We should divide our numbers, then," he said. "Send one party to the Quanang, another to the Erhapi, another to the Hurusi."

Shimmash and Ilanna Great Oak nodded together.

"Do the spirits speak of any more tribes in danger?" he asked. "And of Erris d'Arrent. We must find one of her vessels. What she knows will come from Sarine; she must be told of the speed with which the Jun cross these lands. She must be told they are coming."

Shimmash bowed his head. "The Truth Spirits give what they give. But I can ask."

"We must find one of Erris d'Arrent's vessels," he said. "Whichever is closest. Tell them of the woman who dances between forms, sharing her senses with her golden light. The spirits will know her."

"I will ask, guardian," Shimmash said. "More than that, I cannot promise."

He rose to his feet, and Ilanna Great Oak followed, leaving Shimmash alone at the fire.

More fires would be burning in the canyons and valleys of these mountains. Thousands of fires. The trains of the Jun army extended for days, maybe for weeks, all the way to the western sea. Companies moving, one or two together as they trailed across the land with *magi* at their head. A terrible shadow, greater than any omen any shaman had seen before. They'd annihilated one company with their ambush, brought down a handful of *magi*, and he might as well have thrown a pebble in the way of *una're*.

"Erris d'Arrent," Illanna Great Oak said. "A strange name. And a strange magic, of stepping into another's skin. You claim she is our salvation, far to the east. Will we ever reach her, I wonder?"

"It is truth," he said. "You have heard of the fair-skins, of the lands they settled, the cities they built? We travel toward them. We have allies, waiting for us there. Great allies, with powers beyond the spirits' gifts."

"A sweet dream," Ilanna said. "Or a sweet lie. Perhaps this land goes on forever, instead, and we are meant to watch as these Jun destroy us."

"Among the Sinari, it is a grave insult to accuse a man of lying."

"Among the Hurusi too. But I will speak my mind, with these Jun sweeping across our lands. Decorum can burn, and the spirits too. All of this is ash."

Rage seeped from her, like heat from a fire. He stepped away, closer to the cliff's edge, looking out toward the mountains on the horizon.

"There is still hope," he said. "Why follow me if you don't believe it?"

"I never imagined there were so many people in all the world," Ilanna Great Oak said. "And now we fight them, single ants standing against a great horde. You promise us allies, and my *Ka* sent us to you, but I worry for the Hurusi. I worry my people will be lost in the storms of things to come. How can the spirits see us, with so many souls to cloud their sight?"

"They see us," he said. "They saw you, to send you here. They saw me."

"Perhaps they did," she said. "Rest well, Arak'Jur. There may be more blood to be spilled in the morning."

He let her go. They'd crossed half the continent in the time it should have taken to walk from Sinari lands to Vhurasi, from New Sarresant to Gand. The Jun had done the same, keeping pace with guardians' gifts. Too many had died already; villages and peoples in the army's path. He'd meant to do no more than scout the western stars. Instead he'd discovered the front lines of the war to come, Jun soldiers racing across the land faster than they could have managed without some dark magic to aid them. Sarine would give Erris d'Arrent warning of soldiers on the western shore; it fell to him to find her, to warn her of the tide of steel rushing across the land. Corenna should have been with him. He'd failed her, however many he'd managed to save.

Sleep came as soon as he lay in the dirt to find it.

16

ERRIS

Private Chambers
Rasailles Palace

Deep cushions seemed to massage every muscle in her body at once. Comfort on the road meant a patch of thick grass to sleep in, a clean-running stream to wet her feet and wash her clothes. Returning to the palace had been a shock, enough to almost lose herself to the groomers, the comfort of a fresh-pressed uniform, the luxury of pillows on a couch.

"Reports from Villecours, Your Majesty," Essily said, reading from a pile of papers spread across the table between them. "They corroborate accounts of the militias operating there. A constabulary put to the torch, and a grain silo slated for military disbursal seized and, so far, held by these militias."

She reclined, staring up at the carved and painted ceiling. A scene from the Trithetic myths: the Exarch leading a march against an army of demon-soldiers, with the Nameless at their head, wielding a curved black scythe. If only the world could be so simple, the armies of light and truth, fated to conquer their enemies.

"Reyne d'Agarre," she said.

"Majesty?" Essily said. "Some number of the reports do mention d'Agarre, but surely it's a claim meant to invoke revolutionary fervor. I can't imagine they've recruited a *kaas*-mage, or we'd—"

"It's him," she said. "Him, in person. I haven't a bloody clue what he's after, but I can't spare the binders to march on the city. A problem for another day. What else, Captain?"

"Yes, Your Majesty," Essily said, shuffling papers on the table. "You're certain it's him? There would be no small amount of discontent, even here in New Sarresant, if rumors of his return were true."

"They're true," she said. "I saw him through a vessel. I bloody lived alongside the man for weeks, in the Gods' Seat. It's of no consequence. He's a *kaas*-mage. It'll take another *kaas*-mage, or a full company of binders, to deal with him, and I can spare neither."

"Of course, then," Essily said. "As Your Majesty commands."

She sighed, returning to studying the painting on the ceiling. Whatever Reyne d'Agarre was doing, it would end up being Sarine's problem. She had a thousand other matters to attend to. Unless d'Agarre started driving half of Villecours mad, and then it would be doubly Sarine's problem. At least now Sarine was working with Acherre and Marquand. The beginnings of discipline, perhaps, if Sarine and her champions could follow orders.

"General Yanjin Dao and the Lady Yanjin-Zhang Mei are your next appointments, Your Majesty," Essily said. "Shall I have them sent here, or would you prefer to meet them in the state rooms?"

"Here is fine. Thank you, Essily."

Her aide bowed and withdrew, gathering his papers with a minimum of noise. Scarce more than a day back in New Sarresant, and already a ten-stone weight on her shoulders. Not that the weight had ever truly left.

"General Yanjin, and his wife, the Lady Mei," Essily said, bowing to admit both of them into her receiving room. Both entered with stiff-backed grace. General Yanjin shared the better part of Tigai's features, fitting given they were brothers, while Mei's eyes burned with a cool intensity, the sort of look she knew from officers expecting to climb quickly through the ranks.

She rose from the couch, accepting their formal bows with a nod and a gesture to be seated.

"Empress d'Arrent," Mei said, speaking the Sarresant tongue cleanly. "We were pleased to receive your summons. Anything we can do to be of service, you have but to ask."

"How are you settling in with the Ninth?" she asked. She'd been surprised to learn that Field-Marshal Royens had promoted Tigai's brother to a division command, but from the reports the Jun lord had already proven himself with an impeccable eye for discipline, organization, and logistics. An unusual arrangement, given the man required his wife to translate for him among their soldiers, but evidently the pairing had worked; she'd heard more than one officer remark that the Lady Mei had earned a colonel's commission in her own right, for all she professed to know nothing of soldiering.

"Very well, thank you, Your Majesty," Dao said, his stilting, accented speech a heavy contrast to Mei's fluency.

"Our soldiers obey with passion and zeal," Mei said. "It speaks well of your leadership, that your people conduct themselves as though you paid them six thousand *qian* instead of six silvers a week."

"Jun soldiers are mercenaries, isn't that right?" she asked.

"Yes, Majesty," Mei said. "It was a great surprise, coming here, to find standing armies without a share of plunder or spoils. In our home lands, lords raise their banners to maintain their treasuries. And private companies bid themselves to any cause deemed martial by the courts, the same as the lords do."

"The courts?" she said. "Your judges have a role in war?"

Mei translated it for Dao's sake, speaking quickly as her husband nodded along.

"Yes, Majesty," Dao said. "The Emperor gives his say, both sides bid, and then... war."

"A conflict must be sanctioned," Mei added. "By an Imperial... magistrate, I think, is the word you would use?"

Erris shook her head. "It's a bloody strange system, your pardon for saying it." Both bowed their heads as though they were embarrassed. Right. She was an Empress now. "At any rate that's why I asked you both to be summoned here. I need to know what I'm fighting. If they're mercenaries, can their companies be bought off with counteroffers? How loyal will their soldiers be? Can they be counted on to hold their lines under duress?"

Mei turned to Dao, both of them exchanging quick words in the Jun tongue, before Dao spoke. "Not impossible to buy loyalty, Majesty," he said. "But... price is steep."

"The *shēnghuó jiàgé*, is our word for it," Mei said. "Life price. Enough for the company and all its soldiers to retire, when the fighting is done. It is similar, for holding their lines in battle. None would hire a company with a reputation for breaking ranks, to say nothing of the cost in social standing at court. So, in order to buy loyalty, one must buy the livelihood of every soldier."

She tried to imagine such an army, and failed, beyond a basic reckoning of mores and social structures far different from anything in the Old World or the New. The New Sarresant army used mercenaries, of course, troops of red-capped Skovan, Sardians, Gandsmen, or Thellans. But they were never given real responsibility in a battle plan.

"How many?" she asked. "What numbers will we face, assuming your Emperor summons every available company?"

"*Every* company, Majesty?" Dao asked.

"There are always holdouts," Mei said. "Those who abstain, or who find the price below their operating costs."

"Say every company, for my curiosity."

They exchanged quick words again, and Mei translated.

"Even the Emperor could not command the loyalty of every trained soldier in the Empire, Your Majesty," Mei said.

"I need a number," she said. "Any plan must begin with the worst possible scenario. The Regnant is not your Emperor. Best if we assume he can do what a mortal King cannot."

Mei and Dao conferred again, only this time a flash of golden light crept through at the edge of her vision as they did. Two flashes; somewhere far distant, grown in importance enough to bleed past the need to look to the leylines to find them.

"Seven," Mei said finally. "Perhaps eight or nine. But my husband prefers the conservative figure."

"Seven, then," she said, still watching the globes of *Need*. She'd have to attend to both, whatever else was slated for her schedule. "And each company is what, ten thousand? So seventy thousand all together? I can field a force of equal strength here and in the Old World, if it comes to—"

"So sorry, Your Majesty," Mei said. "We must beg forgiveness. Not seven companies. Seven million soldiers. Perhaps a thousand companies, though most would not be at full strength."

"Seven *million*?" she said. The number was impossible. There weren't seven million people in all of New Sarresant.

"Million, yes," Mei said. "That is the word, is it not? One, ten, hundred, thousand, ten thousand, hundred thousand, million. That is your system of mathematics?"

She nodded numbly. Seven million. According to Acherre's reports from her and Sarine's operations on the far side of the Divide, Jun soldiers were equipped in a fashion roughly similar to what Sarresant soldiers would have used two hundred years before: matchlock firing tubes and rudimentary cannon, coupled with maces, spears, and swords. But with seven million they could be armed with sticks and rocks to throw at her lines. Seven million.

"My husband assures me this number is more than any Emperor has commanded," Mei said. "Forgive us if we misspoke, or offended Your Majesty."

"No," she said. "You gave me what I asked for: the truth, nothing less. Now if you will forgive me, there are matters to which I must attend. You've given me great insight, and much to consider before we speak again."

"Yes, Majesty," Mei and Dao said together, rising to match her. Both bowed deeply.

"We will speak again," Erris said. "Soon." She paused, then added, "I wonder if both of you would prepare a report. Cover everything you think I need to know about the Jun military. Their organization, customs, methods of fighting. Even prominent generals. Major battles. Histories. Everything."

"Yes," Dao said. "Of course, Majesty."

"We'll spare no detail," Mei said. "And have it as quickly as it can be written."

Erris collapsed back into the cushions as soon as they left the room.

Seven *million*.

Her first instinct was to doubt it, to weigh the possibility that Dao and Mei were traitors sent to seed discontent. Royens was as fine a judge of character as any officer in her army, but perhaps he'd misjudged, owing to Dao's foreignness. But then, they were Tigai's family. She'd heard the story of their capture and abuse by Jun *magi*. She'd accepted the reasons for their emigration then. Doubting it now when faced with numbers she found unsettling was the worst sort of paranoia. A novice commander's mistake, to explain away unpleasantness until the reality of a battlefield stared you in the face, bare of anything but the naked truth.

The two globes of *Need* still flickered at the edge of her vision. A welcome distraction. She needed time to process what Mei and Dao had said. She had to learn more, and consider her own thoughts, before reacting.

She reached for the eastern globe, allowing herself to feel the vessel it connected to: a young woman, thirteen, terrified but sure of her duty, pining for her Empress's attention.

Need slid into place, and her senses shifted.

The briny air of a ship at sea assaulted her nose, paired with open water in front of its bow, an expanse of sea far away from sight of land.

"Empress," a voice said from behind her. "Thank the Gods. I feared we weren't scheduled for an update for another week."

She turned and recognized the voice as she recognized the man. Admiral Pranton, commander of her eastern fleet, which made this ship the *Grand Kestrel*. Last she'd checked in with the admiral, the *Kestrel* and the fourteen ships of the line that sailed with her were south of the Old World, scouting trade routes near Bhakal country.

"*Need* can attract my attention, if circumstances are dire enough," she said. "Is that the situation here?"

"I think so, Your Majesty, your pardon for asking the girl to invoke your bond. Here."

He handed her a spyglass, pointing off the ship's forward prow.

"What am I looking at, Admiral?" she asked.

He steadied her shoulders, repositioning her aim with the glass until she sighted five black boxes along the horizon line. So distant, they must have been towering hulks of wood and sail. She wasn't accustomed to judging distance on the ocean, but on land she would have marked them at least three leagues away.

"I believe it's them, Your Majesty," Pranton said. "The Jun Armada, or a piece of it at any rate. Those ships are like nothing I've seen on our seas."

"*Magi* aboard?"

"You'd know their capabilities better than I, but it cost me a three-decker trying to test their range. There are five in the squadron we can see, but I swear we caught sight of more beyond the first."

"And your position? You were scouting Bhakal shipping lanes when last I was here."

"That's right, Your Majesty. I'd bet my commission that's where they're landing."

"The Bhakal continent?"

"Yes, Majesty."

She turned back to the sea, staring out at the miniature dots on the horizon. The Bhakal. It made little sense. The people of their nations were unwelcoming at best, trading in sanctioned ports and hostile to any attempt at landings elsewhere. More importantly, they were part of no army she had in the field. A mostly insular people, trading in raw ores, fruits, spices, and animal skins. A handful of wars had pushed back the Old World powers' attempts to settle there, beyond the foothold of the trade cities. And this was meant to be the Jun's first line of attack?

"How far are we from their coast?" she asked.

"Two days' sail, under favorable winds, to reach Domakar," Pranton replied. "That's the nearest trade city on this heading. Do you have orders? I've kept my ships in tight formation, and the enemy at maximum range, but we've stayed with them for four days now."

"You haven't been able to discern whether there are more than those five ships?"

"Five bloody dreadnoughts, beg pardon, Your Majesty. Each one is twice the height of one of my three-deckers. And yes, I'm sure there are more. They might be landing already."

She closed her eyes, picturing maps of the Bhakal coast. "Domakar," she said. "Making the next nearest city..."

"Abakra, Majesty, on the Iron Coast."

"That's your destination, then, Admiral. I need diplomatic contact. If the

Bhakal are under attack, we need to know it. Get this woman, this vessel, into the court of the nearest Bhakal prince. We decide the rest from there."

"Yes, Majesty, though if you'll permit me, I'd as soon keep a pair of frigates on the tail of those lumbering beasts. They're frightening in battle, but slow as pigs in mud. The *Goshawk* and *Pride of Victory* can keep pace with any ship on these seas, I'd swear it on the Veil herself."

"Very well. See to it they have *Need* vessels posted aboard before you send them off."

"Yes, Majesty," Pranton said. "It will be three days to Abakra under full sail."

She nodded, sparing one last look through her spyglass at the boxes lingering on the horizon. A puzzle, and one she intended to unravel with all possible haste.

She released *Need*, lurching her senses back to her receiving room.

Seven million, and a landing on Bhakal shores. Two tangled knots to solve, with Reyne d'Agarre sharpening a thorn in her back and another sphere of golden light pulsing at the edge of her vision, bleeding through the leylines with urgency and need. Those five ships couldn't be the full strength of the Jun fleet. An invasion force, or worse, a diplomatic one. What did they offer that the Jun wouldn't already have on their own continent?

Three days for Pranton to reach Abakra. She could let it keep, and ponder what it meant with her admirals, generals, and aides while they sailed.

The other sphere of *Need* pulsed brighter than when she'd left it. She gave it her attention, and frowned. It was coming from far to the west, as far from Thellan as she was sitting in Rasailles Palace.

She made the connection, slipping her senses into the vessel's body through *Need*.

She stood on a flat plain of red dirt and sparse brush, surrounded by people in disparate dress. Some wore woven tunics of wool or dyed linen, some went bare-chested, others covered their torsos and faces in paint. All were tribesfolk. No sign of soldiers, Thellan or Gand.

"What is this?" she demanded. "Where am I? What's going on here?"

"She's here!" a man said, an old, white-haired, leather-skinned man standing beside her vessel. "Fetch Arak'Jur! She's here!"

Hearing the familiar name turned her attention along with the tribesfolk around her, to a group of their fellows standing near a yellow tangle of brush. Arak'Jur stood among them, half a head taller than any of the rest, his expression coming alive as he met her vessel's eyes.

"Erris d'Arrent," Arak'Jur said. "At last."

"What's happening here?" she said. "Why is my vessel away from his unit?"

"We found the man here, alone," Arak'Jur said. "Guided by a vision from Shimmash, the Tilannak *Ka*, searching for the nearest of your vessels."

"This man is a deserter, then?" she said.

Arak'Jur shrugged. "It's of no concern to me. Only, the man was traveling west. If he'd kept on another day he would have reached the main force of the Jun army."

His words rang in her ears. "Say that again?" she said.

"The Jun are crossing this continent," Arak'Jur said. "Aided by a gift of their *magi* to move swift as any horse. They run, from dawn to twilight, and again the next morning. Those with me here have used the guardians' gifts to keep a step ahead of the Jun advance. We've bled them when we could, but they've bled our peoples in return. Entire tribes slain or scattered, and still the Jun come."

She swallowed, tasting the dust on her vessel's tongue.

"How many?" she asked.

"A thousand thousand," Arak'Jur replied. "Enough to spread their companies from here to the western sea. At their pace, they'll reach your cities within a quarter-turning of the moon."

17

TIGAI

The Hunting Lodge
Outside Rasailles

I t was her," he said, halting his pacing in front of the table. "It was bloody
her. You said she was dead. You said she was bloody dead!"

Yuli, Sarine, Acherre, Marquand, and some infantryman with bloody
golden eyes stared at him with the same expression, as though they'd
choreographed it, all five of them ringing the dining table as though they were
sitting down for a midmorning brunch.

"I didn't *know* she was dead," Sarine said. "But Lin touched the light in the
Gods' Seat. You saw what it did to the room: It melted bloody stone."

Lin Qishan should have been dead, Anati thought to them all. Sarine's *kaas*
had materialized atop the table, standing upright as though the lizard were a
soldier at attention. *Without my* White, *you wouldn't survive touching the light
for long, if you survived at all.*

"Well, she's alive," Tigai said. "I saw her in Gantar Baat, the bloody 'Red
Lady,' they called her, at the center of the biggest fucking military operation
I've ever bloody seen."

"Calm yourself, Lord Tigai," the infantryman said, speaking Erris
d'Arrent's words if not her voice. "Cool heads are needed now. First, I need
answers as to how the Jun are moving so quickly. And second, a means to stop
or slow them, if we can."

"It's *Body*," Sarine said. "I saw it. That means Lin Qishan can't be the one
behind it, or at least, not by herself. She's an Ox-*magi*, with a gift of turning
dirt to glass. That's not going to hasten anyone to run across a continent."

"I agree," Yuli said. "I don't know of any *magi* gift that could allow an army of that size to run across a continent, let alone to feed itself."

"Dragon-*magi* could handle the feeding at least," Tigai said. "I could move enough food by myself to supply a hundred thousand or more. A few wagons at a time."

"It has to be a gift from the Regnant," Sarine said. "Maybe even the Regnant himself. I've been working on it, trying to channel *Body* through the blue sparks. It hasn't worked yet, but it might, if I keep at it. As to how to slow them down, I don't know. *Black*, or *Death*, but on that scale...I don't think it could be done."

"Forgive me, but I need to leave these deliberations to you," Erris said. "Whatever the cause, we have planning to do."

"Wait," Sarine said. "I can help. You'll need me for planning a defense. I can counter numbers with *Yellow*, and Reyne, too, if we can—"

"Reyne d'Agarre is back to sowing discord on the streets of Villecours," Erris cut in. "If you can rally him, all the better. But we're not planning a defense. There isn't time. Even half of Arak'Jur's estimate gives the enemy ten times the number of my soldiers in the field. They stole a march on us, no matter how they did it. We have to accept it, and plan our response."

"But you said you're not planning a defense," Sarine said. "What else is there?"

"An evacuation," Erris said. "Between you, Tigai, and every merchant and military ship I can sail into a harbor. We're going to get our people away to safety, as many as we can."

"No!" Sarine said. "We have to fight. We can't let them take a whole continent unopposed. What about the tribesfolk and the colonies in the west. What about New Sarresant!"

"Speculation as to the enemy's methods might help us mount a countereffort in the Old World," Erris said. "I invite you to continue this discussion, but I'm needed elsewhere."

With that the infantryman's eyes winked out, the golden light replaced by normal brown irises and a stunned look on the man's face.

Sarine rattled the table, jolting to her feet, then narrowed her features in a scowl.

Before anyone else could speak, Sarine vanished, and Anati with her, leaving an empty chair, a bare tabletop, and Marquand, Yuli, and the stunned infantryman exchanging glances in silence.

"Well," Tigai said finally. "I suppose that's that."

Acherre and Marquand began to exchange heated words. He didn't bother listening. Yuli joined him on her feet, leaning against the table.

"You're angry," Yuli said.

"I'm a bloody pack mule," he said. "Pack mules don't get angry."

"I think I prefer arrogance on you, to petulance," Yuli said. "You're more attractive as a man than a spoiled child."

"You know I'm right," he said. "They're going to use me to ferry people, supplies, cannon, powder, whatever else. I'm not a person to them, I'm a bloody mule."

"You're being a bloody mule right now," Yuli said. "We all have our gifts. Did you stop to think that your muling is going to save hundreds—thousands—of innocents, before the Jun soldiers arrive?"

"They're not going to butcher innocents," he said. "They'll spare anyone that doesn't take up arms against them. More likely they bring food and gold to dole out, appoint local leaders to positions of power and authority. All the same tricks the Empire has used to conquer and rule elsewhere."

"Right," Yuli said. "Then, after they have control, they lop the heads off anyone who speaks even a whiff of dissent."

"I'm not trying to make excuses for them," he said. "The point is, it works, it's been used a thousand times before, and it means the people here aren't in any danger they don't bring on themselves. The Jun army isn't campaigning to conquer these lands, anyway. They're coming for *us*. Remember the shadow, in the Gods' Seat? We're what matters, us and our counterparts on the other side. Ferrying people to safety is as good as shining a stage light on where I am, and where Sarine is. It's going to draw another of those bloody *magi* death squads eventually. The only reason it hasn't yet I'm sure is because of the trap we sprang on them before. But this isn't a conventional war. Empress d'Arrent is losing sight of what matters, because she's used to moving soldiers against soldiers, or staring at a bloody map. *We're* the battlefield now, you and me and the others, wherever we're standing. All the rest counts for nothing if we lose us."

"There he is," Yuli said. "The man, instead of the child."

"Yuli, I'm bloody serious."

"I know," she said. "So tell them. Sarine will listen, even if the Empress won't."

"Tell them what? They're being foolish pigheaded idiots, trying to save their own people? No Empress in the world would tolerate an insult like that, not from me."

"Now you're the one losing sight of what matters," Yuli said. "You're one of Sarine's champions. You, me, Erris, Reyne, Arak'Jur. The five most important people in the world, right?"

"Don't mock me."

"I wasn't."

He glowered at her, and saw only softness and affection in return, the lines of the fangs tattooed on her cheeks contorted by the expression. Maybe she was right, but in his experience nobles and generals weren't apt to listen to anyone's judgment but their own.

"The colonel and I both agree," Acherre said from behind them. "About what you said. About what matters."

"We need a new plan," Marquand said. "The Empress is concerned with saving her people, as she bloody well should be. But Sarine was right: There isn't enough *Death* in the world to disrupt so many *Body* bindings. That means we hit them at the source. That means we attack."

"What do you mean?" Yuli asked. "What sort of attack?"

"For starters, we shouldn't use Sarine or Tigai during the evacuation," Marquand said. "Tigai is right—it will draw their *magi*, as it did in the council hall. Instead we can use the Dragon gifts for an assault on the city where you saw her."

"Gantar Baat?" he asked.

"Yes," Marquand said. "Gantar Baat. Sarine is worried the Regnant himself might be there; well and good. We'll bring Sarine and be as bloody well prepared as we can be. But if it's not him, we know Lin Qishan is likely one of the Regnant's champions if she's still alive. It might be a trap, but I don't bloody well think it is. We can strike there, in their city, when they're expecting us to defend."

"Empress d'Arrent will sanction that?" he asked. "You think we can convince her?"

"This is my command," Marquand said. "I don't need to convince her."

"Sometimes it's better not to ask," Acherre said with a wicked grin. "Act first, ask forgiveness later."

18

REYNE

Harbor
Villecours

Ayellow haze flared at the edge of his vision, and the city watchmen ran. Victoire and the others reacted with cool efficiency, fanning out as they'd planned. Teams of two made for each ship. Xeraxet pulsed between *Green* and *Yellow*, calming the dockworkers and stirring the city watch into a panic. Erris d'Arrent had given orders for an evacuation, to begin with all possible speed and secrecy. His people had intercepted the details before the wax was pressed to paper. He meant to sink those orders, as surely as he put her ships on the bottom of the harbor today.

"Shall we?" Victoire asked, making it an invitation. They stood near a two-masted merchant's ship moored in the berth closest to the shore. Teams of his people had already moved farther up the pier, or taken rowboats toward those anchored in the bay.

He led the way toward the merchant ship, climbing rope ladders to reach its main deck. Sailors stared at him with empty, glassed-over looks in their eyes, watching him and Victoire without reaction.

"Sailors," Victoire shouted, his voice booming loud enough to carry. "Travelers, merchants, traders, and anyone else aboard this vessel. It is imperative you disembark at once, and clear a safe distance between yourselves and the harbor. Move at once; there will be time to understand later."

Xeraxet's *Green* had already stilled them to complacence; he pushed his *kaas* to use more *Green* now, smothering any signs of confusion, wonder, doubt, uncertainty. He focused on obedience, and calm.

Everywhere through the harbor, sailors climbed down from their ships, or took smaller rowboats toward the shore. The same scene would be repeating on the deck of every ship that had his people aboard. His *kaas*'s power was enough for Villecours, but they had more *kaas*-mages in New Sarresant, Cadobal, Fullington, and Leventry. All the main port cities of the New World. Erris d'Arrent had shown her hand in sending out her orders to evacuate. Reyne d'Agarre would stand for no such order, nor would any true son or daughter of liberty. These were their homes. This was where they would fight.

"There will be powder below," Victoire said. "Best to get the worst of it over with, yes?"

"Yes," he said. "Harm as few innocents as possible."

He ignored the nagging pull of *Black*, following as Victoire led the way belowdecks, where two gun ports hosted a pair of nine-pound cannon. They'd all agreed: The goal was to block d'Arrent's evacuation order, not to sow more chaos or injury—to persons or property—than was required for the cause. Still, the prospect of deaths enticed him, stuck in his nose like the scent of sweet wine. Some would die; it couldn't be helped. There would be *Black*, before they were done.

They found the cannons' powder in barrels behind a lock easily broken with a thump from Victoire's cudgel. Reyne kept his focus on *Green* to keep the harbor docile, but he lent a hand, steadying the barrel as they poured a trail leading from the powder room back past the cannon, up the wood stairs, and onto the deck.

"So die the dreams of tyrants," Victoire said, grinning as he quoted Fantiere.

"Only a first step," he said. "But a necessary one. I'm glad you're here at my side for this. This will be the day we remember as the first day of resistance, the first day of our second revol—"

An explosion erupted across the harbor.

One of the tall ships, a thirty-gun frigate lying at anchor a hundred feet from the shore, was suddenly engulfed in a fireball, tendrils of smoke expanding outward like a hedgehog's quills. Wood and ash flew away from the fire, tumbling in a dome of wreckage that seemed suspended in the air.

"Now that's a sight," Victoire said. "By the bloody Veil herself, that's as fine a sight as I've ever seen."

Smaller fires had started on a handful of other ships, miniature orange splotches dwarfed by the lingering clouds of the frigate's explosion. It put heat in Reyne's blood. The old kind of heat, before he'd learned the delicacies of *Black*, but no less sweet for it. The heat of zeal, of passion for the cause. Erris d'Arrent was no better than the de l'Arraignons who had come before her. His turn to remember Fantiere: True liberty, true *egalité*, would come only when the last tyrant was interred beside the last priest.

He moved closer to Victoire, pulling the man toward him with an arm around his waist, and Victoire grinned again, reflecting the same passion. They kissed, and he tasted powder mixed with sweat, felt the familiar bristles of his oldest companion's unshaved cheeks.

"For the Republic," he said when they separated. "For *égalité*."

"For our dream," Victoire said.

Victoire withdrew a slow-burning match from a pouch on his belt, one of a dozen each team had prepared before they'd descended on the harbor, and dropped it into the trail of powder.

It hissed, sparking and igniting, and both men scrambled, laughing as they swung down the rope ladder back onto the pier.

They ran, toward where a hundred or more sailors and tradesfolk already congregated, milling about under the influence of *Green*, staring at the fires now raging through the ships.

The merchant ship exploded. Not as mightily as the frigate had done; only a distended burst that shattered the rearward cabins, but enough to lift the vessel's prow out of the water before it smacked back down and the rest of it began to burn.

It was enough. Enough to be sure the ship would never sail again, it and the dozens—hundreds—of others his people would destroy today. It would cripple the colonies' trade for some time, a massive economic blow, but given the circumstances it couldn't be helped. If they hadn't done it, Erris d'Arrent would have ordered her armies to flee. Now she had no choice. Now she had to stand and fight, and the people would see her for the tyrant she was, even as they stood together, back to back and arm in arm, against these Jun invaders.

"A victory," he said, raising a wineglass. "A great victory, for the Republic. To you—to each of you, who had the courage to make it happen."

He drank, and the rest of his captains followed his lead. They were in a salon almost as finely appointed as his manse had been, before the first revolution. Rows of books lined the walls, decorating the room with knowledge rather than tapestries or art, though two marble sculptures stood opposite the main door, winged muses instead of the Oracle or the Veil.

"We'll have word from New Sarresant by the morning," one of his people said, a woman who had charge of recruitment in Villecours's western districts. "From Gand's colonies in two more, and Thellan's two days after that."

"The tyrant's great advantage," Victoire said. "She'll know what we've done at once, and be planning some further act of cowardice to thwart us."

"All the more reason we planned as thoroughly as we did," he said. "And we're not without advantages of our own."

It earned another wave of toasts, this time toward Xeraxet and his fellow *kaas*, four of them materialized atop a wide ottoman at the center of the room.

"Drink," he said, making it a command. "Feast, celebrate. We struck a great blow for our people today. Let's enjoy it before we worry over the challenges ahead."

A wave of cheers rose, and he retreated onto a pair of chaises with Victoire as the room dissolved into chittering conversation. Servants wove through his people carrying trays of freshly filled wineglasses, cheeses, nuts, and fruits. A well-deserved celebration, for a plan executed to perfection. They'd stormed the harbor with a minimum of collateral damage. They'd come for the ships, and burned them, and if she'd managed even a brigade's worth of soldiers fleeing, he'd have wagered against any more.

Victoire made room for them to lie beside each other, with a plate of dates and cheeses between them.

"This is your victory," Victoire said. "We ought to be toasting you, and your return."

"You've celebrated me enough," he said.

"Who would have imagined it," Victoire said. "Two boys from the streets of Villecours, at the head of an organization fit to topple Empires."

He smiled, remembering their first meetings, two decades before. Even before Saruk had revealed himself, even before he'd first read a copy of the Codex, he and Victoire had gotten drunk on the prose of men like Fantiere, Gallemond, Duchain, and a dozen others as often as they'd gotten drunk on wine, or on each other.

"None of it would have been possible, if you hadn't maintained our organization's meetings while I was gone."

"I knew you'd come back. For me, if not for the Republic."

"And here I am," he said. "A God, in the flesh."

Victoire laughed. "A God indeed. But then, who better to have cause for arrogance? *Let your leaders be beautiful, for if they be not wise—*"

"*—at least one might enjoy the sights, on the path to ruin,*" he finished for him. That was Duchain, from his satire on noble etiquette and costumery.

"Try another," Victoire said. "*The wise man knows he dies twice…*"

"*Once of body, and once when those who preach his wisdom twist it into vanity,*" he said. "Fantiere, from the *Masquerade*."

Both men fell quiet, sharing smiles as they sipped their wine. Ah, but he'd missed this. The roar of conversation around them, the heat of debate and intellect mixed with passion and fire. This was the crucible where he'd been forged for greatness, and who could deny he'd attained it? This was the future, here, in this room. Men like him, like Victoire, who understood the natural rights and freedoms of every human being born into this world.

"What happens next?" Victoire asked quietly. "Today was a victory, but also a beginning."

"We'll fight," he replied. "All our people, all our militias, and as many as we can recruit from Thellan and Gand."

"To depose the tyrant, d'Arrent?"

"In time, of course," he said. "But first we must deal with these invaders. That was the plan all along, Victoire. These Jun are coming; securing our homeland means fighting them, driving them back. You said it yourself: We burned the ships to force d'Arrent to stand and fight for our people."

"And you believe her reports, that these foreign armies are so great in number? I'd as soon believe those numbers were concocted to solidify her power—the oldest trick in any tyrant's repertoire, to conjure an external threat to justify domestic control. We've seen d'Arrent fight three wars now: the Gand, then the Thellan. Now this. And each time, her authority has grown."

"I lived alongside her, Victoire. I know what she is."

"Do you?" Victoire asked. "Were you there, when my agents among her magistracy were brought before her for her oaths of *Need*, and found wanting? Were you there to watch them thrown in prison as traitors, for the audacity of believing in *égalité* over Empire?"

"Her time will come," he said. "I swear it. I swear, I will stand beside you and help you cut the rope when we introduce her to Lady Guillotine. But for now, this threat is real, and our people must rise to meet it. *The price of freedom's fire is—*"

"*—is vigilance against those who would snuff it out,*" Victoire finished for him. "I'm not afraid to bleed for liberty, and neither is any of those sworn to our cause. But bleeding alongside that monster turns my stomach, Reyne. She's as terrible as any de l'Arraignon King."

"I know," he said. "But we must have patience. Change comes slower than we would wish, even with the winds of history at its back."

Victoire frowned. "You have me there. I don't recognize it. Is that Gallemond? Or de Frees?"

"That one's mine," he said. "And it's truth, as sure as any other philosophy or dogma. We have to be patient, and we have to fight. Are our people ready?"

Green, Xeraxet thought to him.

"They're ready," Victoire said. "We still have muskets and powder from the campaign we'd planned against Louis-Sallet."

"Good," he said. "Past time they be put to use."

Green, Xeraxet thought again, a touch of irritation in his tone.

"Of course there's *Green* at work here," he said. "Why should it matter?"

"*Green* at work?" Victoire asked. "Is there a problem?"

Not one of us, Xeraxet thought. *My youngest sister. She's here.*

He sat up, scanning the room. "Your sister? Which of us has the bond? You never told me you had a sibling among our number."

Victoire relaxed, a sign that he'd recognized Reyne switching to speak to his *kaas*. Victoire had never found the gift in all the hours they'd spent studying the Codex together, but Reyne had explained as many of the *kaas'* secrets as Saruk had allowed.

She isn't sworn to one of yours.

A commotion sounded from one of the entrances, a clatter and a thud, and suddenly Sarine stood beside one of the statues of a muse. The Goddess herself, her *kaas* wrapped around her forearm. Fury shone in her eyes as she swept the room, settling on him.

"You're behind it, aren't you?" Sarine said. "You burned the ships in the harbor."

The other four *kaas*-mages in attendance each looked toward him, and conversation throughout the room stilled to quiet.

"Sarine," he said. "Good of you to join us. As always, I would rather have had you with us from the beginning."

"The Nameless take your courtesies," Sarine snapped. "Did you do it? I thought you understood what was at stake here, but Erris was right. You're a rabid dog."

He forced himself to maintain a veneer of calm. "Join me, please. We can speak in private, and I will explain."

"Answer me first. Confirm everything Erris fears you've done, everything I've always known you are."

"Yes," he said. "We burned the ships in every port from here to the Thellan isles. It's done, and no amount of rage or wrath will bring them back. So perhaps, instead of whatever display you imagined you'd put on here, you'd care to come with me and hear the reason why."

She glared at him, the righteous stare she'd fixed on him since their first meetings turned sour. A great regret, that he'd never managed to turn her to their cause. For all her failings, Sarine was a woman who understood justice and rightness in the world, the sort of instincts that had driven him and Victoire and all the rest. A sister-in-arms, for all she'd never admit it, even to herself.

He gestured toward a side room adjoining the main chamber, and she followed. Victoire came along, too, rising to accompany them and simultaneously reassuring the rest of the room that all was well, that they should return to their debates and revelry.

"Well?" Sarine said as soon as Victoire closed the door behind them. "I'm here, and I'm listening. Though what possible reason you think you could have for destroying dozens of ships, I can't begin to imagine."

"Hundreds, I think," he said, smiling. He meant it as a lighthearted comment, to soften the mood between them, but she took it with ice. "You know d'Arrent meant to use them to evacuate her armies. She meant to abandon our people; the very crime Louis-Sallet intended to perpetuate, the crime that earned him a knife in his back."

"*Your* knife in his back," Sarine said. "I remember; I was there."

"And I'd do it again," he said. "Have you been watching her, Sarine? Have you witnessed her descent from common general to tyrant?"

"Erris? She's fighting to do what's best for our people."

"She's all but enslaved our people, or hadn't you noticed she's been using her *Need* to force oaths of fealty from every priest, every magistrate, every officer in her army? Personal oaths, loyalty to her, not to the state."

Sarine frowned. "I'm sure she's using it to put vessels in place wherever she might need them."

"And what of those who refuse the oath, or those with whom *Need* doesn't work, for whatever reason? She's had them imprisoned. Hundreds of them. Imprisoned, replaced, and forgotten. Branded traitors, and never mind what it's done to their families, to their children, to the communities who had supported them and put them in place. Now we have loyalists to d'Arrent in every avenue of power. She doesn't give a damn about our people, or their will. She doesn't give a damn about *égalité*. She has to be put down, and if there was time to revolt against her before these Jun armies arrive, we'd already be rallying our people in the streets. As it is, we had to burn the ships to keep her armies here, but her time will come as soon as our homeland is secure, make no mistake."

Sarine fell quiet, looking between him and Victoire, her righteous anger softened, though it still smoldered underneath.

"There's a larger war going on here," she said finally. "We don't have time or energy to spend fighting with each other. You hurt us today, Reyne. Whatever Erris's failings, we needed those ships."

"Reyne has told me about you," Victoire said. "You're the one who can use the leylines and the *kaas*, aren't you?"

"Yes," Sarine said. "But that doesn't—"

"You're one of us," Victoire said. "Properly you always should have been. You understand that sometimes, doing what's right means sacrifice. From all I've heard of you, you should be the first to believe that our people must be empowered to fight for themselves, for their homes. The ships are burned; we saw to it. It's done. But I wager when we make our stand here, defending New Sarresant, you'll be standing at the front lines, shoulder to shoulder with every citizen who will take up arms beside you."

Once again she fell quiet, this time studying Victoire as though she'd met him before, but couldn't quite place the face.

"She will," Reyne said. "Sarine has always shared our ends, for all we've disagreed on methods to attain them. And I hope, my dear, that you will carry a message from us to Erris d'Arrent. Our militias stand ready to defend these colonies, and our *kaas*-mages, too. We are at her service, for now, until these Jun invaders are turned back. Politics will follow, when the time is right. For now, we fight, together, as the trueborn children of the New World."

Sarine turned to him. It was a gamble; he knew firsthand what she was capable of, if she decided to turn this salon into a slaughterhouse. But that had never been her way. He'd bet on it again and again, just as he bet his life on it now.

"You'll fight?" she said finally. "You and all your people?"

"We will," he said. "When the hour arrives, our militias will make common cause with the tyrant's soldiers. And then again I hope, when the time comes to put her head on a spike."

"Fine," Sarine said. "See to it they're ready. You're a Gods-damned fool, Reyne d'Agarre, and you always have been. But I'll tell Erris your people will be there for the fight."

"Count on it," he said, smiling. Another victory, if this was all the tyrant meant to send at him today. The rest would come, with patience and diligence. He'd long since learned there was nothing inevitable about this path, however right the cause. Only blood could buy the future. A phrase he needed to remember, when next he found time to write. Then young men would quote him, too, alongside the rest. That thought did as much as anything else to broaden his smile, and spread the flush of victory.

19

SARINE

Verrain River
Riverways District, New Sarresant

She crossed the Louis-Toullard Bridge at a brisk pace. Since she'd learned the secrets of Tigai's gift the world had grown smaller. What had once been an afternoon's walk through the Riverways, the Gardens, or Southgate was now a hurried rush. New Sarresant had been all she'd ever known; now it was a single point of glowing light, among a field of countless others. And all of them had demands on her, every star and vortex of blue sparks, every leyline, every spirit, every colored emotion through her *kaas*.

You're being melodramatic today, Anati thought.

"I am not either being melodramatic," she said. "Or didn't you notice I just had to deal with one of the most pigheaded idiots on this side of the Divide?"

Reyne d'Agarre, Anati thought, as though they hadn't left his salon only moments before. *A powerful soul, the sort that twists events around him.*

"I don't need you singing his praises," she said, keeping her head down as she crossed the iron gate that marked the entrance to the Maw. A fellow pedestrian eyed her as they crossed paths, keeping a wary distance for all the man was twice her size.

I'm not singing. I don't think kaas *can sing, can we?*

"I'm not in the mood," she said. "You know what I meant."

Come to think on it, I don't believe I've ever tried singing. What was the song we heard the other night? "I knew a lad with skin like cream, lips as soft as silk; tried to give him home and hearth; all he gave me was his milk."

Her cheeks flushed. "That's *not* the sort of song you should be singing. Where did you hear that?"

At the Pig's Roost, night before last, in Villecours, before we went looking for Reyne. You were busy making faces at the man in the dark green trousers.

"I wasn't making faces!"

You looked like this. Anati lowered the slope of her head, fluttering her eyelids and flushing the scales over her nose a bright shade of pink.

It earned a snorting laugh, and a second glare from the man passing her on the otherwise empty street.

I wasn't trying to be humorous, Anati thought to her.

"Yes you were."

Maybe a bit.

She shook her head, trying to fight down the smile Anati had managed to coax through the fog of her mood. There wasn't time for humor; the quiet on the city's streets attested to it, with no small measure of real fog besides. Thick clouds hung low over the Gardens and Southgate, leaving the southern side of the Verrain cloaked in mist. It felt as though her last glances of the city were being stolen. Battle was coming here again. She might not see the city again, or at least, not as it was, not as she remembered it. It brought a wave of sadness, as quick as Anati's levity had dredged a smile.

Sulking now? Anati asked.

"Stop it," she said. "I just… there isn't time to sketch the city, is there?"

No. Probably not.

She kept walking. For a moment she could almost feel her world as it had been, what felt like so many years before: the straps of her pack, the weight of fresh paper and charcoal and nothing else in the world on her shoulders. Her and Zi and untapped stores of *Faith* on the leylines. She hadn't needed anything else.

The last streets of the Maw at least still felt like home. Her feet knew the way without thought, past broad thoroughfares of warehouses, three- and four-story housing blocks packed so tight it seemed one building ran into the next. The little garden surrounding her uncle's chapel, the rows of gravestones in the yard. The main steps and the Sacre-Lin's ornate wood doors, the stained-glass windows set in rows facing the street, and the side entrances no one but her, her uncle, and the occasional peddler ever used.

"Uncle?" she called, pushing open the service door that let straight into the kitchens. She'd have known at once if Father Thibeaux had been conducting a sermon, silhouettes and activity visible through the chapel's stained glass. Though now she heard the sound of laughter coming from the main hall.

A cauldron of soup had been put on, filling the kitchens with the scent of bubbling carrots, poultry, spices, and broth.

"Sarine, my child, is that you?" her uncle called back. It put more warmth in her belly than any soup or hearth to hear his voice. "Come, help me greet our guests."

She pushed through the kitchen doors into the chapel, emerging behind the dais where her uncle conducted his services. Rows of pews stretched into the main hall, empty save for where a small group rose to their feet. Her uncle, Father Thibeaux, in familiar brown robes, though his gray mustaches had sprouted growth to cover his jaw and cheeks in the beginnings of a full beard. Behind him Rosline Acherre stood, Colonel Marquand behind her, and Tigai, Yuli, and all four of her Natarii sisters.

"Uncle," she said again, and he met her with open arms, engulfing her in a tight embrace. "You seem to have lost your razor."

Her uncle smiled, fingering the growth on his jaw. "Do you like it? I thought it time for a change."

"It's lovely," she said. "Or it will be, when it's grown. When it stops looking like a patch of weeds in need of tending."

He laughed, his eyes shining. "You know Major Acherre and Colonel Marquand," her uncle said. "And the rest. Quite the company you've been keeping since you've been away."

She turned to them, giving Acherre the same embrace she gave her uncle, and Yuli. "What are you doing here?" she asked.

"We came for the sermons, of course," Acherre said. "Word around the district is no one preaches the Chronicles of Wrath and Mercy quite so well as Father Thibeaux."

"We're here for you, sister," Yuli said. "We've been planning a great attack, and we need you at our head."

"An attack?" she said. "How did you know I'd be here? I haven't been back since we left the Gods' Seat."

Tigai shrugged. "Seemed the likeliest place to find you, given you weren't at the hunting lodge. It was this or hop around the stars, and risk drawing attention from their Dragons. We'd have started doing that if you hadn't shown up by nightfall."

"I figured Erris would have you taking soldiers across the ocean," she said.

"I figured the same," Tigai replied. "But Marquand impressed on her the danger, and he'll do the same for you. We can't risk using the Dragons' gift with their armies so close. May as well hang a sign around our necks telling them where we are."

"Is that what this is about?" she asked. "Assassins?"

"After a manner of speaking," Acherre said. "By which I mean we're going to be the assassins this time. Seems right bloody proper, given we've got the reincarnated Veil on our side and so far we've done little more than spring their traps."

"All right," she said. "But you know the Jun are almost here. I'd intended to help Erris and Reyne defend the city."

"What's this about the Veil?" her uncle said, still smiling as though waiting for them to explain the joke. "I'll not tolerate blasphemy in my church."

"It's . . . it's nothing, uncle," she said. "I'll explain later."

"Last reports have the Jun armies two, maybe three days out," Marquand said. "There's time. And with bloody Dragons on our enemy's side, there's no guarantee two days will stay two days for long. We have to strike soon. Tomorrow, while the soldiers on both sides are forming up. Gods damn us all if they've moved already."

Her uncle harrumphed, eyeing Marquand with a glare. "I meant what I said about blasphemy in these halls, Colonel."

"Err . . . sorry, Father," Marquand said.

"Who is 'they'?" she asked. "The target of your assassination?"

"We're attacking Lin Qishan," Tigai said. "She has to be one of the Regnant's champions, to have survived what she did, and to be at the head of their army. Whatever else is going on with her, or with the Regnant's armies, that's our plan."

"You said Lin was in Gantar Baat," she said. "On the Regnant's side of the world."

"Gantar Baat," Tigai said. "Yes."

"We need you at our side, sister," Yuli said. "Come with us."

She glanced back at her uncle. She longed for all of them to go away, to leave her alone for even a few minutes with the man who had raised her.

"What does Erris think of this plan?" she asked. "I was with her this morning, not six hours ago. She didn't say anything about an attack."

"She doesn't know about it," Acherre said. "But she put Marquand in command. It's his prerogative to deploy us. And this is how we're going to win this war. Not with armies, and not by defending our cities and people. We find their champions and kill them, before they find ours. It's ugly, but this is how it has to be. You said it all yourself."

Tigai and Yuli and her sisters nodded along as Acherre spoke.

"I just met with Reyne," she said. "He's gathering *kaas*-mages and rallying his militias. If we're going to do this, I need time to see to his people first. With Tigai's help we could ferry most of them into action in a matter of hours, before the Jun armies arrive."

Acherre grinned. "So you're with us?"

"I'm with you," she said. "I agree; Lin has to be a champion. Let's grab some bowls and help my uncle serve soup and you can explain the rest of this plan."

Sitting on a bench in the main hall eating soup brought memories of better times. She'd watched her uncle serving food to the district's worst-off for years, brewing giant kettles of steaming chicken broth, vegetables, and meat. He was in his element, passing between them with kind words as Marquand outlined his plan. By the time the colonel was finished, all had emptied their bowls of soup, and returned for second or third helpings. A warm glow seemed to settle in her belly as she ate, as much for the soup as for being home.

"You bring interesting company these days," her uncle said, taking a seat next to her in the pews. The others were discussing something: a finer point of tactics between Tigai, Marquand, and Acherre.

"I know, uncle," she said. "I'm sorry for not being here more often."

He waved a hand dismissively. "You have great matters on your shoulders, from the sound of it. I'm blessed to have you here at all."

"How have things been here in the city?"

"Hard, but when are things ever easy?" He cleared his throat. "*Life is a trial, made to find our limitations by demanding we exceed them.*"

"That's from the Exarch, isn't it? From the epistles during the Kylian exodus."

"Just so," her uncle said. "A dark time for the Gods. Yet they survived, and went on to greater things." He paused, glancing back to where Marquand and Acherre exchanged heated words. "You know, I'd always hoped you would become a priest. You would have done well here, tending this church."

"Uncle?" she said. He'd never mentioned anything of the kind before.

"I know, I know," he said. "We kept you from the binder's tests. A vain hope from an old man. But you have a kind heart, for all your fire. You would have made a good priest."

She let the sentiment lie, feeling a mix of embarrassment and pride. When she was a child she'd tried hard to memorize the scriptures he'd given her to read, eager for his praise as much as practice with her letters. Yet the priesthood had always seemed distant, a thing for others, in spite of all the good it brought the people around her. Certainly her uncle could have pushed her, molded her in that direction. Or at least he could have tried. It brought a smile, imagining how she would have resisted, if he had.

"You know you can't stay here, uncle," she said. "I know you love this church, but the city is in danger."

"No," he said firmly.

"You can't," she said. "I mean it this time. You have to let me take you to safety."

"My child," he said. "I hoped I'd see you, after I heard the news of these invaders. And I knew if I did you'd try to convince me to leave. But my answer is the same as it's ever been. No. I stay here, with my church and my congregation."

"Uncle, this isn't some Gandsmen, or revolutionaries, or even the tribesfolk. This army that's coming are our enemies, on a deeper level than some dispute over land or *égalité*. They don't share our faith. If they take the city, they might well kill you just for being a priest."

"Then I'll die for being what I am," he said. "And count it a good life well lived. This is my home. These are my people. No matter who sits a throne or rules us. The poor still need soup. The weak and lonely need an ear to listen, a hand to help them back to their feet. If these Jun or whatever they're called come and conquer us, some among them will be in need of succor, too. Perhaps they'll even listen when I preach."

"You don't understand," she said. "My gifts have grown stronger. I can take you across the sea in an eyeblink, faster than you could walk to the kitchen."

"Don't you dare," he said, and for the first time in years she saw signs of anger in his face. "If you did such a thing, I'd be on the first ship back across the sea. This is my home, Sarine."

"I'm not going to let you risk your life for pride, uncle. You won't be safe here. You have to let me take you away."

"*This* is my life," he snapped back. By now the others had gone quiet, turning to watch their exchange. "Take me away from this chapel and you'll be the one who's killed me. What good is blood in my limbs and air in my lungs? That isn't life. Life is what I've built here, the meaning behind what I've chosen to be. Remember the Veil: *Love sustains us. Love binds. Love is all that endures, through the vagaries of death and the distance of time.* As I've loved you, my child, and as you love me, you must understand, this work is what I've loved most. This is who I am. Leave me to it, if you care for me at all."

"It means leaving you here to die," she said. "When I had the power to save you."

"It means accepting that there are limits to power, even for someone with all your gifts. Go, go with all your friends. Change the world in your way. Leave me here to change it in mine."

Tears came, and she closed her eyes. Even a single nod felt like a betrayal, but she gave it, and felt her anger turn to worry, and fear.

20

ARAK'JUR

2nd Corps Encampment
Sinari Land

Corenna stood beside the fair-skin generals, watching him and his guardians approach. In a half-turning of the moon he'd run across the continent, from one sea to the shores of another. His muscles ached, and dried blood and dirt caked his body. Erris d'Arrent had given the order for him and his guardians to approach the command tents unmolested, and so they had. But all of his people bore the marks of their journey, blood and fatigue making the crudest sort of war paint as three score guardians, *Ka*, and spirit-touched women presented themselves to the leaders of the New Sarresant Army.

"Arak'Jur," an officer in a blue uniform said. "Be welcome. I am Major Savac, translator for Field-Marshal Royens." She spoke the Sinari tongue well, but Arak'Jur only had eyes for Corenna.

"Tell the field-marshal he can speak for himself," he said. "The champion's bond includes a powerful gift for tongues."

"I understood that," Field-Marshal Royens said, his voice touched with awe. "A powerful gift indeed."

"My people are weary," he said. "And the Jun companies are close behind."

"No need for formality, then," Royens said. "We'll see you fed and given tents. The Empress sent word ahead of your coming. Can we count on you, when our enemy arrives?"

"We'll fight," he said. He locked eyes with Corenna, who hadn't spoken. She wore her usual Ranasi woman's dress, white with hems of blue. "Rest first. The first companies of Jun will arrive by morning."

"The Empress said you were keeping pace with a company at the head of their march," Royens said. "One bearing sigils of a white cat."

"The White Tiger," he said. "Those men are dead."

Royens frowned. "The Empress said they were eight thousand strong, marching north from—"

"They're dead."

It earned a moment of quiet from among the generals. He seized it to end the conversation, nodding to Shimmash to lead the rest of his people into the camp.

He went to Corenna.

"I'm sorry," he said. "Sarine took me to the west. I meant to scout the Jun with her. But the Tilannak were in danger, then the Sananesh. I followed the Jun army's path from there. I never meant to leave you behind."

"Didn't you?" Corenna said.

It hurt. "Corenna," he said. "I swear, I never meant—"

"You did, though," she said. "I chose to live with a compulsion to kill you, the man I loved. You chose to leave me, to leave our son. Then or now, what does it matter? You made your choice. I don't expect it to change."

"What of our son?" he asked quietly.

"Kar'Doren is with Ghella and the rest of our Alliance. You uprooted them again. New houses, left behind for the safety of fair-skin walls."

"I'm sorry," he said again. It sounded hollow as he said it, but he hadn't thought of anything better, even knowing their reunion would come.

"You know, I don't even feel the compulsion anymore. *Kirighra* knows I failed. He knows I am less than I was meant to be, and so do I. So do you. But I hope I've at least earned a place among your guardians tomorrow, when the fighting begins. I hope you can give me that."

"Corenna..."

"Can you? Can you at least let me fight?"

"You never needed my permission to fight for our people."

"I know," she said. "I was asking for permission to fight at your side. But you can't even give me that much."

"Of course you can fight with us. I can give you that, and more. Corenna, I'm sorry."

She waved him away, turning her back on him.

He let her go, feeling a pull on his heart with every step.

Shimmash waited for him atop a rise leading into the rest of the camp. The old man had proven hardy on their journey, his sinewy muscle belying the lines of age traced on his skin. No few of their companions, some two generations younger or more, had faltered during the run, while Shimmash had never dragged, never uttered a word of complaint.

"Your woman?" Shimmash asked as he drew near.

"I don't know," he said. "The mother of my child. But I don't think she wants anything from me now."

"Good," Shimmash said. "There will be fighting in the morning. Nothing makes a man crazier in battle than troubles of the heart. Come. Let's get what rest we can before the killing resumes."

———————

Bells woke him from sleep. Ringing bells, and brass horns.

He emerged from his tent to find the camp in a flurry. His guardians had slept near the field-marshal's tent, at the base of a high, forested hill. Soldiers scrambled west, some half-dressed, others trying to load their muskets as they ran. The guardians seemed to share a single mind, each one leaving their tent with weary, ready looks.

"Arak'Jur!" a woman shouted, racing down the hill. It took another glance to realize she had golden light shining from her eyes. Erris d'Arrent.

"Empress," he said. "I take it from the horns the enemy is close."

The woman came to a quick halt. "Your attaché managed to sneak off in the night. This woman is your new connection to me. Keep her with you, and keep her safe. And yes. Bloody yes. The Jun marched two companies through the night. They've crossed the Verrain—the river you call the *anakhrai*. They'll be on the first regiments of Royens's Corps within the quarter hour. I need you there, if you can move quickly."

"We can. Are you sure it was only two companies? The White Tigers were in the lead, but there were many more behind them."

"I don't know," Erris said. "These Jun march too fast for my scouts to be sure how many are behind the leaders. I need you and your people there at the point of first impact, to give me time to assess the field before I deploy the rest of our troops."

"Which direction?"

"West, near the river. This vessel is a scout. She can guide you toward the Eighty-First."

He nodded grimly. By now all his guardians had surrounded him and d'Arrent's vessel. They'd heard. No need to repeat the order.

"Gods be with you, guardian," Erris said. "A shame they didn't give us another hour. I'm on my way to Royens's field command in person. We could have broken bread together before the day began."

"Then we may yet meet on the field," he said. "If the spirits will us to victory."

"Keep yourself safe," she said. "And move in all haste." With that the light behind her eyes winked out, returning her irises to a pale blue.

"What's your name, soldier?" he asked the woman.

"Lance-Lieutenant Ralle, sir," she replied, looking shaken, and all the more so as the guardians manifested their gifts, a chorus of howls, snarls, and roars as *una're, mareh'et, lakiri'in*, and the rest empowered his guardians to move as quickly as the Empress had asked. Arak'Jur called on *mareh'et* himself, surrounding his body with a nimbus of the Great Cat.

"Can you wield the fair-skin leylines, Lance-Lieutenant Ralle?"

She shook her head. "No. I can't."

"Climb on my back, then," he said. "It will serve, until we can find you a horse."

Order prevailed the closer they got to the frontline regiments. Royens's tents had been a flurry of activity; the soldiers they passed on the way to the 81st's commander were calm, with the tension of a bowstring drawn but not yet fired. They knelt in ranks behind makeshift fences of piled rocks and fallen branches, their muskets leveled to point deeper into the forest.

Ralle led the way, her blue uniform the only sign that Arak'Jur's company belonged on this side of the soldiers' line.

"Lance-Lieutenant," a man wearing a captain's star said as they approached the regiment's flag. "What are these tribesfolk doing here?"

"Orders to report to Colonel Calvert," Ralle replied. "These tribesfolk are their versions of binders. They're here to reinforce your line."

The captain eyed him before returning to Ralle. "Colonel Calvert is with the southern part of the regiment, seeing to integrating the...whatever it bloody was, the *kaas*-mages?...the girl brought. I have temporary command here with the main body."

"The Empress made no mention of additional reinforcements," Ralle said. "And her orders were thorough. She intends for Arak'Jur and these tribesfolk to be part of a counterattack, sallying out from your line as soon as the Jun arrive. Did you not receive copies of the order?"

"Colonel Calvert might have seen it," the captain replied. "I didn't. I don't know what to make of this, Lieutenant. I'm told the enemy will attack at any moment—that we're to be ready for immediate action. Yet we get here and our scouts haven't seen a bloody whiff of any enemy army. Then the girl shows up as though she'd been here waiting for us, with five hundred ragtag militiamen and a metal lizard on her forearm, insisting they be part of our defense. It's all highly irregular. Most unlike Her Majesty's usual battle plans, if you'll pardon my saying so."

"A girl," he said. "With a metal serpent on her forearm. Sarine?"

The captain gave him a second look, and this time stayed fixed on him. "That's right. The girl said her name was Sarine. You know of this, tribesman?"

"I do, fair-skin," he said, putting bite in it to mirror the captain's rudeness. "Where is she now?"

"She's gone. Bloody vanished. I saw it with my own eyes. Highly irregular, all of this."

"Keep your soldiers ready for fighting, Captain," he said. "The Jun will arrive faster than your scouts could deliver the report. They move like wind across a plain."

"Now," Shimmash said from behind. "They arrive now."

The captain frowned, but before he could speak, the roar of musket shots rang out from the front line, accompanied by battle cries in two different tongues, and the blurred shapes of soldiers charging through the trees.

Mareh'et's gift sang in his blood as he fought.

Jun spearmen ran ahead of their muskets, screaming as they raced forward, their spears held high, decorated with streamers and flags of red, white, and orange. He used the trees for cover, bolstered by *juna'ren*'s shimmering aura to blend his skin into their colors. He took a squad of spearmen from behind as another of his guardians attacked from the front. Three men were sliced in half before the rest knew there was a predator behind them; the rest fell before they could raise their spears, chopped to bloody meat by his claws, and his fellow guardian's.

Blasts of fire erupted around him, tree bark chipping as shells exploded. Muskets, and artillery. He ran west, toward another squad of spearmen. The spearmen moved with the frenetic speed of all the Jun soldiers, but they were men at their core. Some would make mad charges, confronted with *mareh'et*'s savagery in battle. Others would run. This group froze, every one of them, staring at him as he left behind the bloody ruin of their fellows and came for them. He gored a man through the belly, severed another's head at the shoulders with a roaring swipe, and only then did the others react, throwing down their spears as they ran.

He let them go. Two of his guardians, twin brother and sister from the

Chamassat tribe, danced with a single Jun swordsman in a thick copse of trees nearby. The swordsman slapped away an attack with *una're*'s claws by the Chamassat brother, while his sister let loose a caustic wind, searing the air where the swordsman had stood. An ordinary man would have burned; the swordsman rolled away, twice as fast as any of the other soldiers could move.

Magi, and he knew the kind: Crane, the masters of the sword.

Arak'Jur called on *ipek'a*, leaping overhead into a bough of branches, and then he leapt again, angled toward where the swordsman would step to meet the Chamassat twins' next attack. He judged it wrong, and came crashing down into brush and loose leaves as the swordsman spun, whirling his steel to ward away Arak'Jur's attack. This time the sister called on *astahg* and shifted, appearing behind the Crane, her eyes glowing red as she prepared another sheet of fire. The *magi* leapt sideways, letting go of his sword in midair to reverse the grip, slamming it backward to impale the sister through the ribs.

Bone cracked, and the sister howled with her brother. Arak'Jur sprang again, leaping with *ipek'a* and calling on *kirighra* to cloak him in shadows for the attack. The Crane withdrew his sword with a jerk, swinging it into place to impale Arak'Jur as he dove. He welcomed the steel, letting it pierce through his shoulder as he came within reach for *ipek'a*'s claw and *kirighra*'s bite. He anchored himself with *ipek'a*'s claw in the man's chest as he bit across the bridge of the swordsman's nose, rending pieces of bone from his skull as his eye sockets collapsed into the gash.

The *magi* shrieked and let go of his blade, leaving it lodged in Arak'Jur's shoulder. He shoved the man to the ground, then stamped a foot on the ruin of his face, silencing his cries.

The Chamassat sister dropped to her knees, clutching the hole torn in her lung and leaking trails of blood from her mouth. He withdrew the blade from his shoulder, letting it fall beside the *magi*'s corpse.

"Carry her back to the tents," he said.

"Are... are you sure?" the Chamassat brother said. "You don't need me...?"

Vanity, to ask. He made no further reply. The order had been given, and the man would make his choice.

He turned back toward the fighting. Brown banners and gray paint streaks decorated the mail shirts and breastplates of these Jun. No signs yet of any others, but they would come. Erris d'Arrent's plan was to strike hard enough to shatter the point of their attack, blunting their advance and giving her time to field the rest of her soldiers. His place was at the foremost point of their attack. So far the Jun had died by the score, but their lines held, and more soldiers advanced into the carnage.

"Arak'Jur!" Lieutenant Ralle shouted from behind. She'd found a horse, and rode behind him, shadowing his movements as best she could. But this time it wasn't Ralle; her eyes shone with golden light, her saber drawn and waving in her hand.

"Empress," he said. "What orders?"

"I need you and as many of your guardians as you can to attack. North of here, a quarter league directly north. There's a new company in red and blue, with a third behind them in white. We have to break them before they can deploy. Go! Now!"

The golden light winked out, leaving Ralle breathing hard, reining her horse to a stop beside Arak'Jur.

"Follow," he said, and she nodded.

Ipek'a's gift still surged in his veins. He cupped his hands to his mouth and remembered what it was to be the alpha female, her blood-soaked feathers decorating her leathery hide. His screech thundered through the forest, unmistakable and clear, cutting through the roar of battle. Every guardian knew the sound; all that still lived would move toward him, and follow him north.

Fifty-four guardians assembled with him, screening their movements through the trees. Four were missing, fallen to the Jun soldiers or the *magi* among them. A small fraction of the damage they'd inflicted on the Jun, but a heavy loss, for even one of the spirits' chosen to fall.

The red and blue company had massed ranks of spears ahead of arquebusiers, broken into smaller companies separated by the foliage. On an open field they might have made a line as long as any village, but here the forest necessitated their splitting into smaller groups, disjointed and separated from each other by thick trees and brush. Perfect for being hunted.

He moved among the guardians, assigning smaller groups to move and work together, with a handful left in reserve, meant to shadow the rest in case Jun *magi* presented themselves. He kept himself in reserve, too, and gave the order for the rest to move.

Spirits' forms shimmered around his people as they crept forward, *juna'ren* and *astahg* and *kirighra* granting camouflage or cloaks of shadows to those who had earned their blessings. When the first Jun soldiers began screaming, even he couldn't see the strikes that brought them down, but soon the smaller squads he could see were moving, drawing ranks together, closing gaps in their lines.

He kept low as he moved forward, darting from tree to tree. The growth here was thick, too thick for him to see past what had been the Jun's front ranks, but their attention had turned inward, to where his guardians were falling on them from behind. Gunshots rang in the air, and the clash of metal, but he saw none of the telltale signs of *magi*; nothing unnatural, save for the speed behind every Jun soldier's movements.

Lieutenant Ralle approached, dismounted, having left her horse behind. Once again, her eyes shone with golden light.

"Your people are in place?" Erris d'Arrent asked through her vessel.

"Already attacking," he said.

Her eyes flashed a brighter shade of gold. "Good. Damn good. This is it. This is where the Jun intend to mass their attack. I'm leading a countercharge myself. Hold them here, the red-and-blue and the white. You'll be the anvil, and my cavalry the hammer. We'll shatter them and turn back their advance, at least for today."

He nodded, a sharp jerk, keeping his eyes focused on the red and blue soldiers ahead. Ralle's eyes dimmed, returning to normal. He still saw no sign of *magi*. It felt wrong, as though his people had cornered a single wolf, forgetting that the pack would use a lone wolf for bait while the rest encircled their prey. But he had to trust Erris d'Arrent. She had eyes for more than the battle in front of him, an eagle's view of the enemy's movements in her mind. His place was to attack; better if he did so. And if he was meant to serve as a distraction, he had no need for stealth.

Una're and *lakiri'in* gave their gifts together, the surging speed of the crocodile with the thundering power of the great bear. Lightning coursed over his hands and feet, leaving hissing trails of smoke among the leaves as he ran. He roared, shaking the trees with the force of it, and he drew a hundred men's attention at once, three separate companies along their front line each turning to him with terror in their eyes.

Spears rose to block his path. He tore through them with a blast of Mountain's fire, falling on the gap in their line with swipes of *una're*'s claws. He sheared spears in half, and men with them, sending thundering jolts into the metal breastplates of any soldier unlucky enough to touch him while he was energized with *una're*'s blessing. The Jun moved with a strength and speed beyond the limits of any normal soldier, but none among them had communed with *lakiri'in*'s spirit. None among them knew what it was to drink the sun's gift, to feel its energy coursing through their limbs as they exploded in a fury. He became *lakiri'in*, the Swamp, the Bear, the Cat, and more. Red and blue soldiers mixed with white as another company reinforced the first, swelling numbers threatening to swallow him as they encircled his position. Still he fought, chaining the spirits' gifts without rest, ignoring the gashes, cuts, and bruises where their weapons found his skin.

A brass horn from the east signaled Erris d'Arrent's arrival.

Pockets of Jun fought him and his guardians, swirling masses centered on the predators in their midst. The outer ranks turned, leaving their backs exposed as Erris's cavalry blew the signal for their charge. He swiped a man down the spine, splitting him in two, and scattered the squad of spearmen around him as the first horses came into view. They thundered through the trees, weaving and dodging, the leaders among them moving as fast as the Jun, aided by fair-skin leylines to give their horses unnatural agility and grace. Erris herself rode at their head—six copies of her, each seated atop copies of her monstrous white horse, leveling the point of her saber at the Jun as though she meant to cut them down personally, to a man.

The Jun soldiers broke, turning to run, but the horses outpaced the men, and Arak'Jur fell on them, cutting down their backs as they tried to flee. Erris crashed into them, her copies colliding with soldiers and shimmering, while the real woman brought down steel and fire, striking men left and right as her horse raced into the shattered remnants of their line. He followed, and only belatedly noticed the whirling gusts of wind from beside Erris's lead horses. Corenna ran with them, and he ran with her, channeling Mountain as she channeled Wind and Earth and Ice. A thousand horses came charging behind their vanguard, an endless tide of blue uniforms sweeping over the Jun soldiers' painted armor, firing pistols and carbines as the Jun lines inverted, then collapsed, sending men scattering into the trees.

"How many of yours dead?" Erris asked him. He'd grown used to speaking to her through a vessel's eyes; the sight of the woman herself, still mounted on her white horse's back, was strange, as though between Erris and Lance-Lieutenant Ralle he saw her twice, duplicated like one of her leyline copies.

"Six," he said. "And eight more seriously wounded, in need of time to heal."

"Only forty-one, among my cavalry. We're still awaiting final tallies from the Seventh Division in the south, and from the Jun, but they claim their companies numbered twenty-two thousand here today. Damn good odds for us. The sort we'll need if we intend to win this war."

A troop of captured soldiers marched nearby, prodded by bayonets. His skin was caked in blood and dust, and he felt the sting of a score of wounds, gashes, and burns on his body. They would heal in time; not so the guardians who had fallen. Every death weighed on him. Erris commanded thousands—tens of thousands. He wasn't sure how she bore it.

"What of their *magi*?" he asked. "We brought down one, a Crane swordsman. Are the rest accounted for?"

Erris reined her horse to a stop, letting another column of captured Jun march past.

"What do you mean?" she asked. "I'd assumed your guardians dealt with them, if there were any. My cavalry reported no encounters with *magi*, beyond whatever power is enhancing these soldiers' strength and speed."

"No," he said. "We met no *magi* from the red-and-blue, and none from the white."

"That's damned odd," Erris said. "No *magi*? You're sure? My scout's reports had at least two score *magi*, closer to fifty, between these companies."

"I'm sure," he said. "We faced only one. The rest must have pulled back from the fight."

Erris shifted in her seat, staring past the captured soldiers as though weighing his words. "We can't be certain," she said. "Though we'll ask it of the prisoners. If you can spare your man, Shimmash, the one with the gift of tongues, to help us interrogate them, I'd be even further in your debt."

"Of course."

"See to your people, then," she said. "We'll regroup and fall back toward the city once we have the situation here in hand. More will be coming, but even if the enemy *magi* managed to retreat, this was a victory, and no small part of it belongs to you and your guardians. Be sure they know of my gratitude, on behalf of all of New Sarresant, Thellan, and Gand."

He bowed his head, and she nudged her horse away, leaving him behind. A victory, yet it felt hollow. So much death and killing, with so much more to come.

He would need to speak to Shimmash, to consult the visions of things-to-come and ask the aid Erris d'Arrent had requested. But first he went to find Corenna. She'd been right that he had made his choice, but as he saw it, there was room for love and duty, side by side. In the wake of so much death, he had to hope she would feel the same.

21

SARINE

The Red Lady's Pavilion
Outside Gantar Baat

Nerves made a lump in the back of her throat as they waited. Even with all she'd seen and been through, she wasn't a warrior. Yuli and her sisters seemed composed, Acherre and Marquand seemed eager, and Tigai wary and ready to get them out as quickly as he'd gotten them here. None of them had to worry what *Black* might make them do, when the killing began. It would be easier if the fight just started, without the waiting. Easier if she didn't have to think.

She blinked to check the leylines again, finding the same mammoth weave of *Body* tethers extending out over the eastern horizon. Too many to trace them all, and this was the source. Terrifying, that the Regnant might be behind it. But she didn't think so. An old memory, perhaps, something dredged from when the Veil still resided in her head: He had always remained in his place, never strayed into control over the leylines, or the spirits, or the *kaas*. This had to be something else. A champion drawn from her side of the world, or—

She was still piecing the thought together in her mind when Lin Qishan appeared.

Lin was dressed in red, as she had been when they'd first met her in Kye-Min. It was unmistakably the same woman, tall, sure of herself, shoulder-length black hair pulled back and tied in a knot behind her head. She came striding out from the nearest tent behind the officer who had served as their guide, turned to look toward where she and the rest stood, and the world seemed to shift as she met Lin's eyes.

Marquand shouted.

Yuli's skin changed with a piercing howl.

Kitian's body erupted into flowing blood; great wings burst from Namkat's back; Juni's skin turned to blackened scales; Imyan's body was covered in thick iron bark. Tigai raised a pistol. Acherre spun a wave of *Entropy's* fire, the first to attack, a searing knife cutting across the space between them.

Lin blinked, and the blue sparks swarmed around her.

Shelter slammed into place around all of them, a weave of expert precision, white pearls folded into honeycombed prisons, hexagonal walls trapping them on all sides. At the same moment, Anati whispered *Red*, *White*, and *Black*, all three words at once, and Sarine reacted by instinct, channeling her own surge of blue sparks around Lin's, flaring Anati's *White* as Lin's attack threatened to snuff out all nine of them, a mix of *Black* and *White* she barely saw, woven into the fabric of each *Shelter* prison.

Suddenly her mind shifted. She wasn't here, at the foot of a pavilion of tents outside Gantar Baat. She was on the Infinite Plane, watching as Lin Qishan ensnared the torrents of a hundred different columns of energy, warping and twisting them as she flared power to alter the fabric of what was real, and what was about to be. The image blurred with the scene in front of her eyes: She saw it from above, looking down, her and her companions trapped within Lin's honeycomb prison as their torrents, the energy that represented *them* on the Infinite Plane, were bent, obeying Lin's will as they flared red and blue and green.

"You aren't Lin Qishan," she said, hearing the words echo from her lips in the physical world as they vibrated through the columns of energy.

The woman across from her laughed. Again, the gesture was replicated in both worlds, the physical and the infinite. Lin Qishan's body shook, standing in front of the tents outside Gantar Baat while the presence that was *her* emanated disdain across the Plane.

"No, you idiot girl," Lin said. "I never imagined you would be so stupid as to show yourself. To come to me! You are arrogant, for someone never meant to be more than a host to keep my new body warm while I finished dying."

She drew blue sparks to match Lin's movements, and they answered her call as swiftly as they answered Lin's. Whatever the other woman was doing, she could match it. Counter it. The torrents that marked each of her companions crackled and surged with light, shifting from blue to red to pink to yellow to gray. She channeled the blue sparks on the Infinite Plane while her physical body wove *Death* through Lin's *Entropy*, and Anati flared *White* to counter the other woman's *Black* and *Red*. She didn't understand the barest part of what she was doing, only that Lin's attacks were meant to do more than kill. She meant to unmake them, to revoke their existence. The slightest falter would see her companions reduced to nothingness, and her with them.

Tigai was shouting. Marquand, too. A feeble strand of *Death* attacked Lin's *Shelter*, then another; Marquand and Acherre, biting like ants at the feet of a giant.

"Run," she shouted. "Tigai, take them and go!"

Yuli smashed into the walls of her enclosure, savage cuts and rips doing more to bruise her limbs than dent her prison.

"Do you imagine I will let you leave?" Lin said.

"We can't!" Tigai shouted. "My magic—it isn't working!"

Something twisted in Lin's grip on the torrents in the Infinite Plane. She felt it as a subtle shift, like a tingle in a limb gone to sleep.

"Two," Lin was saying. "You've brought two of my champions here. Where are the others? And how many did you bond? Tell me so we can end this quickly. The Regnant may yet forgive, if you submit."

She only half heard the words, fixated on the tangle of threads being woven into the torrents on the Infinite Plane. New colors had appeared—black and orange, interspersed with the rest, but in tiny knots swirling around the centers. She picked at one of the knots, and found it tight, but pliable. She pulled, and another strand came loose. Grabbing hold there led to another slip, and she gave it a tender touch, sliding the black through the orange until it came undone.

Acherre screamed as a wave of *Death* and *Entropy* descended on her. Sarine shifted her focus away from the knots, forming *Death* webs of her own, barely slicing through the *Entropy*. But she had no answer to the Storm spirits' gift. A crackle of lightning surged within Acherre's prison, reflecting off the walls as the major's screaming peaked, then fell quiet, her skin continuing to burn and pop in the violence of the storm.

"Poor fool," Lin said. "How many more will die for following you, thinking you are more than an echo of the true power in this world?"

Marquand roared, flinging *Death* of his own at a second web of *Entropy* enveloping his prison.

The black and orange knots had to be the key; the *Entropy* and spirits' gifts no more than a distraction. She sent *Death* to bolster Marquand's defense, but turned the bulk of her attention back to the Plane, unraveling another set of knots as quick as she'd unmade the first. They came apart, dissipating black and orange energy into the void, snapping one by one as she ripped them away.

Marquand screamed as Mountain's gift of fire rained down into his prison.

Then suddenly the prisons of *Shelter* vanished, and her people with them.

She was alone, kneeling in the dirt in front of the tents, the smoldering ruin of Acherre's body the only sign she'd been accompanied by anyone at all. The orange and black knots must have suppressed Tigai's gift. She'd picked them loose, and let him escape.

Lin howled a curse, rounding on her with a fresh wave of *Entropy*, Storm magic, and *Black*.

Anati flared *White*, shielding her as Lin's attacks struck her body. She turned her attention to herself, to the torrent that represented her. Sure enough, the black and orange knots were there, too. She ripped them apart, with none of the delicacy she'd used before. They obeyed, falling loose and fading into the void.

"Don't think of running," Lin said. "I'll follow, wherever you—"

She blinked, tethering herself to the strands, and shifted.

Sweet air filled her nose, the tang of salt and grass mixed together. She stood in a field overlooking the sea, the quiet thrum of waves crashing against rocks below a gentle counterpoint to the chaos she'd left behind.

She stayed still, breathing hard, letting adrenaline course through her body. Acherre was dead. Because of her. The others had managed to escape, but—

Lin appeared in front of her.

Faith came by reflex, met by a scornful snap of the other woman's fingers, conjuring a *Death* binding to sever her tether.

"Did you forget I was still bound inside your head, when you stole the Dragon's gift?" Lin said. "I can follow wherever you run."

Once again she switched focus to the Infinite Plane, anticipating more attacks from the blue sparks. Instead she sensed only another torrent, stalking around the torrent that represented her.

"You're the Veil," she said, hearing it echoed between the physical and the infinite.

"Yes," Lin said. "Good. Better, if you drop any pretense to claim what's mine."

"How?" she said. She still watched every space available to her: the Infinite Plane, the leylines, the physical world, guarding against an attack she knew would come.

"We never imagined you would come to me in person," Lin said. "This whole plan, all of it, the Regnant's attack on your home city, all of it was designed to flush you out. And here you are."

"You were gone, and Lin was dead," she said. "I saw her incinerated at the Gods' Seat. And I cut you out of me."

"You set my consciousness adrift in the Plane," Lin said. "And Lin, this woman who provided me her body, I encountered her floating there. A fortunate accident. And now that you and I are together again, you can surrender the keys to the Soul to me. We can still settle this war, maybe even preserve the better part of our plans, before all of this goes too far."

She tensed, still watching every vector of attack. But Lin—the Veil—seemed content to stay still, watching her.

"You know better than to think I'd ever surrender," she said.

"What choice do you think you have?" Lin asked. "The world needs its torpor. After sixteen cycles of Life, it hungers for Death. You must have sensed it on the Plane. All creation is frayed, close to unraveling. Another cycle and it might have crumbled to dust. I've fought harder than you—harder than anyone—to preserve Life as long as it could be preserved, to keep us strong, in case the Regnant ever tried to seize the full mantle of the Master's power. But even I know there are limits."

"Axerian explained all of this," she said. "The shifts between Life and Death; the world as it was before they took it back from the Regnant's control."

"Axerian knew less than a child. If he was your teacher, you've been sorely misinformed."

"He told me of a world kept in shadow," she said. "Of poison clouds and ash, people hiding underground in caves, eating fungus to survive."

"And what of it? The world has been ruled by Death a thousand times since the Master's fall. Rebirth into Life is always waiting, one cycle away, or two."

"I'm not going to let you destroy the world."

"Not destruction. Rebirth. The Master thought as you do, before we became the Regnant and the Veil. He was drunk enough with power to try and maintain the balance between Life and Death alone. He tried, and almost ruined the world. The Regnant and I took power from him before his failure would have let others step in to seize control. We put safeguards in place to prevent his brand of madness, even from each other."

"Your game," she said. "The champions, set against each other to prevent outsiders from seizing control of the Soul of the World."

Her understanding seemed to catch Lin by surprise.

"That's right," Lin said. "But don't imagine we bound ourselves in ignorance. We knew the risks. When my champions imprisoned me, we feared all our work would be lost. You represent a greater threat, greater than you know, but you also hold the possibility for our salvation. You worry over a few million lives, when the keys you hold could be turned to doom us all."

"A few *million* lives?" she asked. "That's meaningless to you?"

"Yes!" Lin snapped. "Rocks and pebbles, when the mountain is about to erupt. One life—a million lives—is nothing. I would have sacrificed ten million; I would have burned half the world just to have you in front of me. You would have done the same, if you understood the tenth part of what's at stake."

"You're wrong," she said. "You speak of sacrificing millions—tens of millions—and I know you believe it, you and the Regnant both. That's why I'm fighting you. I may not understand all of this, but I know right and wrong, good and evil. You say I have power. Good. I intend to use it to protect the innocent from people like you."

Lin fell quiet, watching her as the waves crashed behind them.

"There's still a chance to stop this," Lin said finally. "Surrender the keys to the Soul to me. Let the Regnant change the world."

"No," she said.

"Sarine," Lin said. "I was you, once. Naïve. Full of justice. If you force us to break the compact, you risk damnation as sure as if you refuse the world its rebirth. The Others could appoint champions, or God forbid, try and seize the Soul themselves. At least the Regnant and I are fighting to make the world better; our counterparts have only ever sought power, with all the ruin it implies. Please listen. It doesn't have to end this way."

"If you mean to slaughter innocent people, you'll have to kill me first."

"Was I ever such a fool?" Lin said.

Death tethers snapped into place by reflex, cutting through *Shelter* and *Entropy* before she noticed Lin's attack. Anati sounded a warning in her head, and she ducked in the physical world as she drew the blue sparks on the Infinite Plane. Fire spouted around her, an unnatural torrent conjured into place by Lin's will; she unmade it as quick as Lin had set it there, picking apart the sparks and letting them dissipate into the void.

Lightning blasted into her, shielded by Anati's *White*, but maintaining an arc of pure energy between them as Lin channeled the Storm spirits' gift. Lightning answered her call in return, and she sent a second arcing blast crackling between them. *White* sprang up around Lin the same as it made a shell around her.

Heat surged around them both, burning and blistering her skin. She ignored it. On the Infinite Plane, their wills danced, drawing closer as the torrents that represented their lightnings connected them there, too. Lin attacked again, willing a cloud of poison gas into being around her, and she unmade it before she drew a breath, scattering it into mist. Another attack came, frozen shards of ice threatening to impale her from above, melted to harmless vapor before they could fall.

Lin stepped closer. Her skin was blistered, too, a sheen of sweat slicking her forehead as the lightning coursed between them.

"Let me go," Sarine said. "We're evenly matched, and I'm not going to surrender."

A gale of wind struck, knocking her to the ground. She scrambled back to her knees, maintaining the channel of lightning, adding a two-pronged attack with *Entropy* and a conjured torrent of fire through the blue sparks. Lin warded both away, glaring at her as she unmade them into smoke.

"You are far from my equal," Lin said. "And if you think the use of my magic makes it so, then I will help you see the truth."

In the physical world, nothing changed. Lin stood over her, twin bolts of lightning surging as they enveloped her and Lin and their *kaas'* shields of *White*. But on the Infinite Plane, the torrent that was Lin jolted forward, until it touched her, and they merged into one.

She screamed; or Lin did. In the same moment she heard Lin's voice whisper: *This magic exists because I wrapped its chains around the Soul of the World. All of this is my doing. I made these keys. They belong to me. I alone know their secrets. I alone can deny their use.*

Fingers seemed to reach inside her. She tried to unmake them, to force them out. Swirls of color blurred her vision in both planes, until she felt the fingers grab hold of something inside her. A net. A woven fabric of seven shapes and colors, held together by a gray mesh stuck between them. *Body, Life, Death, Shelter, Mind, Entropy,* and *Need*, bound together by *Faith.* The fingers ripped it out of her. A wrenching pain tore through her gut, flashing through her as each seam of the net popped and scattered from her grip. She saw the net come loose from her, set adrift in the Infinite Plane, and reached for it to put it back in place, only to watch it dissipate into nothing before she could claw it back.

A prison of *Shelter* closed around her in physical space, and she blinked by reflex to find *Death* to disrupt it. She saw nothing. The leylines that had always been there, her refuge from the world behind the gray clouds of *Faith*, were gone.

She sobbed from the pain.

"Are we evenly matched now?" Lin said, at the same moment the whisper on the Infinite Plane said, *You are nothing but my shadow. You are only what I have allowed you to be.*

The fingers clawed into her again, this time reaching for a lucid dream, the memory of what it was to be the great hunter, the basking crocodile, the spirit of the storm. She fought. All her will pushed against the torrent that was Lin, forcing her back, trying to drive her out. The fingers grabbed hold of the dream, swirling through it like shapes cutting through fog. She screamed a wordless scream, but Lin jerked her hand, and the images of beasts, winds, mountains, lakes, and rivers came loose, dissipating as they drifted into the void.

The lightning surge coming from her stopped, leaving only Lin's torrent blasting into Anati's shield. The nature spirits—the beasts, the spirits of the land—fell silent in her mind.

"No," she whispered through her tears. She was doubled over in the grass now, devoting all her energy to pushing Lin away on the Infinite Plane. "Leave me the *kaas*. Don't take Anati away. Don't take Zi."

Lin said nothing in the physical world, only wore a look of condescension mixed with pity. On the Infinite Plane, she whispered, *I leave you nothing. I will unweave the Soul of the World from you if it takes stripping away every gift, every sense, every memory, every tongue.*

The fingers clawed into her, reaching for the darkest places, where she was naked and alone. Anati snapped at Lin's hand, her miniature jaws sinking into the torrent that was Lin's flesh, drawing blood even on the Infinite Plane. She pushed back, pouring all her will into protecting this place, this part of her. Anati stood beside her, her scales flushed white, as pure as untouched snow.

I'm sorry, Sarine thought. *I can't stop her.*

You can, Anati thought back. *Hold on to the Soul. Hold on to Life. She can't force you to give it up.*

She's going to take you away from me, she thought.

Yes, Anati thought. *But I've loved you, as much as my father did. If you loved me back, don't let her win. Don't give in.*

I did, she thought. *I do.*

Then that's enough. Goodbye, Sarine.

Lin's fingers returned, harder, forcibly grabbing the space around Anati. The shadows seemed to shake, trembling as Anati bit again, snapping at the hand until blood mixed with her anguish, coating the torrent in streaks of red and blue. Lin yanked her hand back, and Anati seemed to blur, her scales translucent, dimming as the shadows loosened their hold.

Another presence came awake.

It had been locked away by the *kaas*'s power. But the serpent called Anati was under attack now, and the *kaas*'s focus had shifted to protecting itself, to keeping itself anchored to their mutual host. The presence remembered the host. Sarine. She was a mighty warrior, worthy of the bond she had earned in battle, when its last host, the clanswoman called Alka, had fallen. The *kaas*'s seals came free, and for a moment the Nine Tails and Sarine blurred together, each remembering the other. Each calling to the other for help.

The Nine Tails seized control, and Sarine's body transformed.

It was enclosed in a barrier of blue-white haze, with a shield of flickering white energy guttering around the Nine Tails' body. It moved, attacking the blue-white barrier with two of its tails, whipping them with force enough to send cracks rippling through the energy. It struck again with a third tail and the barrier shattered, leaving it facing a woman looming over them. A woman in red, the source of the lightning, whose eyes were misted over with a far-off look. Lin Qishan. The Veil. Her attention was elsewhere. The Nine Tails would demand her attention here.

It sprang at her, wrapping her body with four tails while five more raked the Veil's skin with lashing strikes. Blood soaked its fur as the Veil's eyes returned, bulging from fear and surprise. The host—Sarine—cried out for Anati, and the serpent answered her call, professing love, reassuring the host that she was still here. More importantly, the serpent gave the Nine Tails its magic: a thundering *Red*, redoubling the Nine Tails' strength and speed. A white shield swirled around the Veil. With *Red* in its blood, the Nine Tails constricted its tails around her, and energy hissed and burned against its power. On the Infinite Plane the Veil's sparks swirled, orange and red and black, as the Veil lashed out, first desperately trying to unmake the Nine Tails, then to use the Dragon gift to escape. Sarine picked the Veil's sparks apart before they could take form.

They held together, locked in place, a tide of sparks dissipating while the Nine Tails lashed itself around the Veil's body. Then the white shield broke.

In an instant, the body of Lin Qishan was reduced to a burst of blood, tissue, organs, and bone.

Sarine wept, lying in the grass.

The Nine Tails was gone; it had served honorably, and now returned control to its host. Grief ran through her. Lin's body had been shattered and broken into a mess of yellow and red and brown. Lin was dead. The Veil was dead, and Sarine had survived.

I'm still here, Anati thought. *I didn't expect that.*

She cried, her body shaking with tears. No words came, but Anati would be able to read her thoughts, and feel her love without them.

22

REYNE

They needed uniforms.

He would put a company of his colonial militia against the best regiment in Erris d'Arrent's army, especially with the backing of his *kaas-mages*. But d'Arrent's people had uniforms, neatly sewn blue coats with brass buttons for the regulars, while the officers wore knots of rank and had buttons made of gold. His people wore civilian clothes—wool breeches or skirts, linen shirts, cotton and silk coats, with a plain mix of browns, grays, and whites.

Here outside the city the presentation left something to be desired. They'd formed ranks within a stone's throw of the city, delivered in strength by Sarine's magic from Villecours, Lorrine, Mantres, even a few companies from Ansfield and Derrickshire. Erris d'Arrent's lines were farther west, in old Sinari territory, but even without uniforms, his were the ones that mattered. If d'Arrent faltered, it fell to him to defend the city. And the people of New Sarresant would know it. A political victory. Between his *Green* and the sight of thousands of militia arrayed in defense of their homes, these people would know who their true saviors were, no matter what happened between d'Arrent and the Jun.

"Master d'Agarre," a young woman said, offering him a salute in a facsimile of a military style. She wore a too-small white linen dress, the sort worn by children, though she was clearly in the beginning of her teenage years. The brace of pistols at her side made clear she was one of his. He smiled and returned the salute.

"What is it, my child?" he asked. "Has there been news from the west?"

The girl shook her head. "No," she said. "I've come from Master Duwayne, with the fifth Southgate company. He asked me to find you as quick as I could."

"Out with it, then," he said. "What news from Master Duwayne?"

"Jun riders," she said. "His scouts saw a pack of them, coming toward the city."

"A pack? Did he say how many?"

The girl frowned. "No. But he asks for help. As many companies as you can spare."

Outwardly he maintained a veneer of cool confidence. Better for all around him to see him in good spirits, with a firm hand on their deployment. But he could have used some proper scouts to go with his companies. A "pack" of riders? And nothing to indicate the difference between five cavalrymen out foraging and a full armed brigade. He made a mental note: some proper training for the scouts, to go with the uniforms.

"Did you hear that?" he said loudly, enough for the militia around him to hear. "D'Arrent's lines have proven as weak as the woman herself. Little surprise there." He paused for polite laughter among his people, nudged along by *Green* to overcome their nerves. "I'll ride north myself. Master Duwayne need not fear—he asks for companies to reinforce him. I'm worth two at least. Lead the way, my child."

"Master d'Agarre," one of his people with these militia said. "Who has the command here, while you're away?"

"Victoire," he said. "Treat a word from him as a word from me."

The Villecours militia exchanged looks with each other. "No one's seen him."

"Find him, then," he said. "Send word to all nearby companies; Victoire is in command until I return."

The militia made a mix of bows and salutes, and he returned them with a nod and confident smile.

"I assume Master Duwayne provided you with a horse," he said to the girl.

"Yes, Master d'Agarre," she replied.

"Lead on, then," he said. "To wherever you left it. They'll furnish me an animal to go with yours. And what's your name, girl? I assume you're with the Southgaters, from here in the city."

"I'm called Reed," she said. "And yes, from Southgate."

"Reed, eh?" he said. He could see why; the girl was as thin as the barrels of her pistols.

"I killed the man that first called me it," the girl said. "A house cook. Kept the name to remind me after we stuck the fat bastard with his own knives, and did the same for the master of the house."

"*Égalité* the only way that counts," he said solemnly. "From the point of a knife, or the barrel of a gun."

The girl stayed quiet, saying nothing else in reply. No surprise a street girl wouldn't recognize Gallemond's *Rights of Commoners* when she heard it quoted, but then, that was always the point of the revolution: Justice was meant to count for all, whether they'd been given an education in salons and universities or by poverty and life on the street. A life was worth the same, whether commoner, noble, or King.

The horse Reed had been provided was too fine by half—a chestnut stallion as thick and strong as Reed was suited to her name. He took a roan and they set off north, riding in front of the militia's line where he could be seen by all. His red coat earned cheers, and he waved back, letting Xeraxet do the bulk of the rallying with *Green*.

The fifth Southgate company had the northern turn in the line, where the militia bent like an elbow to turn east. Reed led the way, handling her too-fine stallion with determination instead of grace. They passed companies from Lorrine and other districts of New Sarresant, until Reed pointed toward a makeshift flag that looked like what it was: a painted bedsheet, bearing a crest of blue and white for the Republic.

"There," Reed said. "Master Duwayne."

The militia greeted him with belated cheers, though the officers wore sour looks, not least the heavyset man in factory worker's clothes standing beneath the flag.

"Master d'Agarre," the man who had to be Duwayne said. "Good of you to come. How many soldiers are behind you?"

"Just me, my good man," he said, sliding from his roan's back as Reed did the same for her stallion. "Your messenger said you'd scouted some Jun riders heading this way."

"Just you?" Duwayne said. "I asked for as many companies as you could spare. Those aren't just any riders. My scout said they're done up like priests. *Magi* was the term the army's soldiers used. Fifty of them at least."

He smiled, still making every effort to project confidence. "Where's your scout? You'll find my gifts to be worth some number of companies all by themselves. Have your scout saddle a horse and take me to them. I'd as soon see the threat for myself."

"There isn't time for another bloody sortie," Duwayne said. "My man had them riding toward this very spot. By the time you found them they'd be upon us. Nameless only know how they got past d'Arrent's lines."

"Humor me, good master," he said. "My *kaas* serves me well for tracking *magi.* If that's what these riders are, I'll know it. And if not, your militia here will be more than suited for the task."

Duwayne gave him a dour look, but nodded, and a boy not much older than Reed stepped forward.

"I'm the scout," the boy said. "Therry's the name. They was to the west, two leagues or so. Between us and the Empress's army."

"Saddle up, then, lad," he said. "We'll ride hard to find them."

"I'm coming, too," Reed said, swinging back up into her stallion's saddle.

Reyne shot an eye toward Duwayne, but the factory man shrugged. Prudence suggested leaving the girl behind if they were riding into danger, but who was he to tell her how to spend her life? She hadn't gotten in the way on the ride from the Villecours companies. Another pair of eyes could be welcome.

He climbed back into his roan's saddle. "Lead the way, then, Therry," he said. "And Master Duwayne, see to it your people are ready for a fight. If d'Arrent has failed to stop these *magi*, all hope for our city is going to rest on us."

Therry proved a competent horseman, weaving them through tracks in the wood between New Sarresant and Rasailles. No need to ask where the lad had come by his skill with woodcraft; judging from his commoner's clothes and his clear knowledge of the terrain around Rasailles Palace, the boy had made his living as a poacher. Neither he nor Reed had the skill to keep up, though neither held the other back, and they cut through the woods as quick as their horsemanship allowed, heading north-northeast, judging by the angles of the sun.

"Can you really tell whether they're *magi*?" Therry asked when their horses came together, side by side. "They wore orange robes, with veils covering their faces, if that helps."

"I really can," he said. "And it does. How many were they? Master Duwayne said fifty?"

" 'Bout that," Therry said. "Fifty or so. Most wearing those orange robes, a few in other dress. One wore white, from head to toe, and another was an old man, barely able to keep his saddle, from what I saw."

"You got a good look at them, then," he said.

"I did," Therry said. "They rode slow, on account of the old man. I didn't think he was wounded, just old."

"Anything else you can remember? Did you see them using magic, or anything that looked like it?"

"Naw," Therry said. "It was just, the veils, and the robes. They looked like priests. I figured, since our priests are trained with the leylines, theirs would be, too."

"You did well."

"We should be on them soon, if they kept moving at the same pace."

"You can track where they'll be?"

"Sure," Therry said. "At least, I can make a guess of it. Only way of knowing for sure is to find their trail."

"Keep at it, then," he said, and fell in behind Therry as they tracked along a narrow in the path. Reed rode in silence behind, watching him as intently as Therry watched the trees. Xeraxet flashed *Green* as soon as he willed it, and he felt the tableau of his companions' emotions: anger, resolve, anxiety, lust for blood. A strange mix. But he also felt a second set, at a distance: weariness, anticipation, resignation, majesty. It could have belonged to soldiers, or merchants, part of d'Arrent's supply train. But the foreignness of the second set marked them for what they were. Jun emotions.

He leaned on their weariness with *Yellow*, and felt nothing. No change.

"They're nearby," he said. "And you were right, boy. They're *magi*. Fifty of them, you said?"

Therry looked back over his shoulder, his face suddenly pale. *Green* bolstered his resolve before Reyne could even form the thought, and the boy nodded. "Yeah, that's right," Therry said. "Give or take."

Fifty. And every one a *magi*, if *Yellow's* inability to affect them counted for proof. He should retreat, rally his *kaas*-mages, and get his militia ready. But then, retreating meant sharing the *Black*, when the killing began. And he was a God. He could stand against fifty, even where Erris d'Arrent's people had failed. He'd been right: Saving the city would fall to him, one way or another.

He pointed toward the knot of emotions. "That way," he said. "Take us close, as quietly as you can."

Green pushed resolve and duty even harder, smothering a wave of fear in the boy. He saw the effects at once: Therry gritted his teeth, his knuckles tight on the reins, lowering himself close to his horse as he moved them in the direction Reyne had pointed.

The trees grew dense as they rode west. There would be a battle raging farther in this direction, between the Jun armies and Erris d'Arrent's, but here in the Rasailles woods there was no indication of it, only quiet, birds chirping in trees and a stillness hanging in the air.

"We should dismount," Therry said as they reached the lip of a valley, though all sides were still covered by trees and foliage. "If you want to get any closer."

"You think they're nearby?" he asked. *Green* still painted their emotions clearly, but he couldn't tell precisely how close.

Therry pointed. "They're here. There."

He slid from the saddle, edging toward the top of the decline. Sure enough, better than two score figures rode slowly along the valley floor, most dressed in orange robes, arrayed in a loose-formed square with what appeared to be an old man at their center. The man was bald save for wisps of white hair, with a long white beard visible even at the top of the valley.

Reed appeared beside him, having dismounted without a sound. "Those are them," she said, her voice scarcely above a whisper. "Those are the invaders. Come to rape us. And kill us."

"Those are them," he whispered back. With *Red* he could close the gap before most of them noticed. *White* would protect him from the worst of their attacks, while his knife evened the odds. He'd need to see their magic in action before he chose what to steal with *Black*. A gamble, not knowing precisely what gifts he could count on stealing, but with a little luck, he could chain their deaths together, riding a wave of *Black* from one *magi* to the next. Not all that different from slaughtering priests, or soldiers. All he had to do was—

A thunderclap sounded, loud enough to have come from right beside him.

He recoiled, and only belatedly realized it had indeed come from right beside him. Reed held one of her pistols level, bracing with her off hand as she aimed it into the *magi* below. She fired again, then again, three shots faster than he could react. Clouds of hot smoke and powder rose around her, and finally he cursed.

"What in the Nameless's bloody eyes do you think you're doing?" he roared.

Shouts and bellows came from the valley floor, where two domes of shimmering energy had enveloped the riders like soap bubbles drawn around the trees.

"I hit him," Reed said, smiling. It was the first time he'd seen her show anything but a dour expression. "I shot him, the old fucking pig."

Red coursed through his veins, as Xeraxet prompted him about a host of unfamiliar magicks: *Heron. Lotus. Ox. Crab.*

He cursed again, and leapt forward down the side of the incline. The *magi* stirred like a kicked anthill, some pointing toward the ridge while others collapsed inward, dismounting their horses and swarming around where the old man stood at their center. Four of them changed forms: He could have sworn they were ordinary before, but now they were statues come to life, one made of glass, another iron, and two of stone. They sighted him as one, charging forward through the soap bubble dome.

Gods but he could have used more knowledge of their gifts. Still, *Black* was waiting, calling to him, trapped inside the shells of each of their bodies, and he was close, so close to tasting it.

He drew his knife and met their charge. *Red* bolstered his speed so each living statue seemed to be mired in tar. One threw glass shards at him; he wove to the side, drawing on *Black* as he moved toward the first of them, the one hewn from iron. He tore the gift away, and the woman who had become the statue suddenly reappeared, the iron she'd worn for a skin drained by his gift. He stabbed her through the chest, wrapping a hand around her back to draw her close, wrenching the blade through the heart.

Golden ecstasy flowed into him as she gasped, coughing blood into his face. He twisted the knife again, letting her corpse fall, and felt the pull of her gift. *Ox*. The dirt called to him, and he let it cover him as he ran toward the next statue, conjuring its power from the ground beneath his feet. Suddenly he was coated in iron, just as the woman had been, but with none of her plodding slowness. *Red* sang in his veins alongside the joy of *Black*, and he moved as though the iron were his skin, rather than a suit of armor.

He chained the *Black* from the woman's death, stripping one of the hulks of stone, revealing a thin, wiry man in an orange robe hiding underneath. This time he had no need for the knife. He smashed an iron fist into the man's head, exploding it in a rain of blood, caking his iron armor and the leaves and grass around them in gore. *Black* came again, flowing through him. He could have gone to his knees, weeping with the joy of it. Instead he channeled its power, tearing away the gifts of the other two Ox-*magi* at the same time, leaving them frozen, standing in shock and terror as their second skins gave way to orange robes with no protection from his attacks.

One of the soap bubbles vanished before he could smash the last two Oxen, and suddenly he was knocked off his feet, a wave of force strong enough to lift him and his iron armor, throwing him skidding into the dirt.

Heron, Xeraxet prompted. Then a moment later: *Lotus*.

He let out a wordless snarl. These *magi* wouldn't come between him and another sip of *Black*. Iron clanked as he jerked himself upright, racing toward the last two Ox-*magi*. He caught one of them with a crushing grip around the man's waist, snapping the *magi*'s spine as he drew him in, flattening the body against his chestplate. *Black* flooded his senses as another unseen force cracked down from above, sending him sprawling to the ground. He could have laughed. He did laugh. The sweetness of *Black* overpowered any pain from the Heron-*magi*'s strike. He would find the Herons and drain them, too. He was a God. Lesser magicks were nothing against the power of the *kaas*.

"I can't stop him," a voice shouted. The man in white. "How can this be? Master, he is immune to Lotus's power."

He rose to his feet again. A shimmering dome had been conjured around him this time, a new soap bubble, made to imprison him, if he guessed aright. He set his feet above the smashed ruin of the last Ox-*magi* he'd killed, watching the fourth run back toward the safety of their horses. Most of them were still gathered around the center, kneeling beside a slumped figure that had to be the old man. The man in white stood beside them, gesturing frantically. Three more fixed eyes on Reyne. Those had to be the Herons, responsible for these soap bubble shields, and the strikes that had knocked him to the ground.

He tested it, reaching out with an invisible tendril of *Black*, and wrenched the magic from one of the three, leaving her gasping as he stole her power, and consumed it. A small portion of his *Black*, and an investment. With new magic came new opportunities for killing.

He felt a new sense. An awareness of Force. The dome around him had been conjured by it, set in place to reverse any action taken to strike, or pass through. Simple if he set an equal and opposite Force against it. He tried it, and the dome exploded.

A shock wave rippled through the valley floor, shaking boughs of the thickest trees and slamming saplings and bushes into the ground. Horses screamed and bolted in all directions. The *magi* shouted, too, covering their faces and ducking. But Reyne was already moving. *Red* made him faster than any of them. He reached one of the Herons and bull-rushed over her, shoving her to the ground and making sure to place a foot to crush her skull before he thundered onward to the next. This one tried to turn and run, screaming the scream he'd come to associate with *Black*'s sweetest moments. He leapt after her.

And froze.

He'd been suspended midmotion. The Heron-*magi* he'd been chasing tripped and fell, sprawling a few paces in front of him. He should have had her. He should have smashed her brain, crushed her rib cage, something, anything to release the sweet *Black* hiding inside her bones. But he couldn't move. He tried to snarl and laugh at the same time, sweeping a look over the rest of the *magi* to find whatever gift had frozen him.

Death, Xeraxet prompted, though without more knowledge the name alone wouldn't help him find it.

The old man stood at the center of the orange-robed figures. He'd risen to his feet, and the others backed away, bowing to him. Blood streaked the tattered rags the old man wore as clothes, two crimson splotches where Reed's pistol must have struck home.

"He's one of her champions," the old man said. "That is why your Lotus cannot touch him, Lord Isaru. But it's curious that I can reach him, even if you cannot."

"Master?" the one he'd called Isaru said.

"The Veil must have fallen," the old man said. "She was the one who bound this man, her champion of the *kaas*, not the girl. For my *Death* to affect him so..."

"Let me kill him, Master," Isaru said.

The old man raised a hand. A feeble, slow gesture. Reyne wanted to howl, to shout, to curse, but still couldn't move.

"No," the old man said. "If the Veil is dead, then I will speak with him first, and find out what he knows."

The world wrenched away from his senses.

He was falling. Shadow surrounded him, dotted with points of light shining like the night sky. Vomit rose in his belly, and he doubled over, letting it loose. He could move again. He called on *Red*, and on *Ox* and *Heron*. Nothing came.

The old man stood close, watching him. He was here, writ exactly as he was on the valley floor, down to the bloodstains on his shirt, though everything around them was blackness, or stars.

"Champion of the *kaas*," the old man said. "I came here seeking the girl, the one called Sarine. You know her, yes? And where I might find her?"

"Who are you?" he managed. Shock was passing through his system; he'd seen it enough in others to know the signs. "What is this place?"

"This is my place," the old man said. "And you may call me by my birthright. Death. I am the end of all things. Regnant to the torpid half of the Master's throne."

"Death?" he said. "A children's tale, come to life?"

"Even children die, champion," the old man said. "They are wise if they haven't forgotten me, in so many cycles of Life. And you will be wise to tell me what I wish to know."

Reyne laughed. He was dead, then, or soon to be dying. He'd never been afraid of death. Death was *Black*; perhaps dying meant living in that state of bliss forever, one with the power of his *kaas*.

"It's of no consequence," the old man said. "I can take what I need, whether you wish it or no."

His body spasmed. Vomit came again, this time purged onto his coat.

Memory flowed. A dark haze, settling over his thoughts. He was standing in the New Sarresant harbor, frowning as he scanned the docks, looking for sign of the one he hadn't managed to scatter with *Yellow*. He was in his salon, laughing with Victoire as they debated a point of epistemology over wine. He exulted in *Black*, cutting down a pair of whores, leaving their bodies in the street. He was here, outside New Sarresant, watching the last of his soldiers appear before Sarine vanished, bidding him do his best to defend the city while she was away.

He collapsed, coughing as he rested in the blackness.

"She isn't here," the old man said. "Unfortunate. And your attack wounded me, in the physical world. I'd hoped for a more subtle approach, but alas, this will have to do."

He fought to return to his knees. His head swam, burning hot, feverish, glistening with sweat.

"Tell me, champion," the old man said. "You know the girl, Sarine, well. Will she respond to this sort of gesture?"

"What gesture?" he said.

"Perhaps you are unaware of what my magic can do. See these lines, between the stars? These are strands, connecting the torrents of Life to the souls that animate them, to the places they know, to the core of their memories." The Regnant gestured to soft light, glowing around each star in the distance. Before, he might have said the stars glowed, no different than a bright night in the sky. But now he could see they were made up of individual strands, thousands of them surrounding each star.

"At a great distance, the strands are difficult to make out. But consider this one." The old man pointed to a star directly overhead, a bright, pulsing light surrounded by a patchwork of strands like tiny strings, vibrating as they collided and danced around each other. "These are all the souls in your city. New Sarresant. I'd hoped to be closer, to divine the strands most tightly connected to your Goddess and draw her out that way. But I believe this will serve. Do you agree?"

"You believe what will serve?" he asked.

Suddenly the light the old man had called New Sarresant winked out. No, not one light. A million, all at once. All the souls in the city, the old man had said. The strands around it seemed to writhe, jerking frantically before each one burned, a brilliant spark of light flashing, before going dead.

"This," the old man said. "A blunt approach. But if something has happened to the Veil...if Sarine is behind it...this will draw her into the open. She cared for this city, in your memories. This will provoke her to action, if your assessment of Sarine proves accurate."

Reyne hardly heard him. A wave of *Black* broke around him, washing his senses with raptured bliss. Ordinarily he had to do the killing himself; he'd stood on battlefields and felt no more than a tingling sensation when soldiers died by others' hands. This was that same tingling, writ a thousandfold. A millionfold. *Black* so strong it blinded him, pounded blood in his ears, left his muscles quivering and raw. A million dead, all at once. A tidal wave. A surge of power deeper than any he'd imagined in the world.

The old man sighed. "Ah, yes. A *kaas*-mage in truth. One of the more unfortunate consequences of their bonds. I thank you, champion. Without your memories, I might have pressed on in spite of my wounds. Now I can withdraw, and she will come to me."

He wasn't listening. *Black* poured over him, drenching his senses with pure joy. A sensation of golden, perfect euphoria. He could live a hundred lives and never feel its equal.

"You can't hear me, through your *Black*, can you?" the Regnant said. "I suppose it's a gift. You've served your purpose. Now you can die contented. A luxury few who touch the Soul's chains are afforded. Goodbye, Master d'Agarre."

A fire burned inside him. Memories flashed, all his connections to every place, every person, every lesson, every book, every word he'd spoken, every lie, every truth, every moment of love and passion, of hate, anger, or greed. They ignited, all at once, and the person who had been Reyne d'Agarre was dead.

The shell of his body heard a voice as its consciousness faded.

FOR THIS ONE, IT ENDS.

ELSEWHERE

INTERLUDE

KOA

In the Boughs of a Baobab Tree
Near Dooralalong Town, Tarzal

He held still, as quiet as he could be. The trick to finding the Moon was to try and notice movement. It would've been easier if she showed herself in daytime. But then, Koa's grandmother often told him anything worth having was worth having worked for.

The rest of the Dooralalong delegation waited at the base of the tree. His mother was there, with the Head Dreamer and the Head Man of the town, along with the two silk-dressed foreigners. They'd chosen him because he was the Moon's friend. He'd tried to warn them that Orana didn't always show herself. Sometimes he came here and spent hours waiting in silence, only to leave and go home when it was clear she wasn't going to let him find her. They didn't listen. It was of the utmost importance he bring the foreigners to her, so his mother had said. The Head Man had repeated it. The Head Dreamer said nothing, only looked at him with the unnerving look the dreamers had in their eyes, and somehow he'd known she too desperately needed him to find Orana today. So here he was, in the highest boughs of the biggest baobab tree in three days' walk from Dooralalong Town, with no guarantee Orana would let herself be found.

He froze when a branch wavered in the wind. Movement. He'd seen something. He kept his head still, swiveling only his eyes. The delegation was a stone's throw under his feet; this baobab tree was an ancient elder, a thousand years planted when any other tree near the town first sprang from its seed. A hundred birds made their nests here, feasting on the lizards that in turn feasted on the ants that feasted on the sap. He'd fallen in love with this grandfather tree long before Orana had ever shown herself to him. He was a climber, so his mother said. He knew the sounds and smells of the baobab better than he knew the Dooralalong streets. He knew when something was out of place.

There.

He turned his head, slowly, upward, and he couldn't help from breaking into a broad grin.

She sat perched high above him, her skin caked with dirt and dried sap, making it nearly impossible to tell her apart from the star-filled skies. He'd never have found her if she hadn't shined moonlight through the branches. It limned her tiny body in a soft white light. She'd first appeared to him when he had eight years of dreamings; now he'd had sixteen, but Orana hadn't aged a day. She was still the eight-year-old girl she'd been the first time they met, naked and covered in dust. Her skin was pale, unlike anyone else's, and her eyes were red, like the albino *kahla* bear his mother had found last summer. She stared down at him through the branches, her eyes as full as the fullest moons, sitting as still as he was, waiting for him to approach. Some days she would scurry away if he tried to draw too near too quickly. He had to be patient, and calm.

He climbed toward her, slowly, trying to make his approach seem nonchalant, nonthreatening.

A bird chirped to warn him when he drew close to its nest. He froze. Orana was still there, waiting. She was close enough he could have leapt from his branch and landed next to her on hers. He kept still. Perhaps this was close enough. But he'd learned in his years of visiting this tree it was best to let her decide when he'd come close enough to speak. He moved again, and before he could find his footing, Orana gestured for him to sit.

"Hello, Koa," Orana said. Her voice was small, like any eight-year-old child, but he'd learned to hear the weight of eons behind it. She was wise, wiser than the wisest Dreamers. "Do you have anything to eat?"

"Hello, Orana," he replied. "I will bring some dried fruits, if it will please you."

Her eyes shone brighter, though she didn't move. He was close enough to reach her, if he stretched. He fished through his belt-bag, finding a handful of dried quandong slices.

She snatched them with the quickness of a feral animal. He glanced downward while she chewed them. The delegation was far out of sight beneath the boughs, but they were waiting for him. Thank the dream Orana had shown herself without an hours-long wait. But he'd been preoccupied with whether she would appear. Now that he had to lure her down to meet with them, he wasn't quite sure what to say.

"I…" he started to say, while Orana was still chewing. "I…ah…I will dance with Allia at the next gathering."

"The head scribe's daughter?" Orana asked. "The pretty one?"

"I think so," he said. "My friends will say she is too dour, unsmiling, that she will prefer books and scrolls to company. But she will smile for me."

"Allia," Orana said. "It's a good fit. Thank you for bringing me this news."

He could never tell what parts of his life Orana would find interesting, but he was delighted to have guessed aright this once. Sometimes he brought her news of other towns, of merchants' comings and goings, even of the battles fought between Dooralalong men and the men of Yitarong and Kindumu, and she seemed utterly indifferent, while she might beam and thank him for telling her of a painting he'd made with his fingers, of a meal he'd learned to cook, or a dance he'd learned to impress a girl.

Now he waited. It was her turn to share.

"Would you like to see what I've been seeing, these past nights?" Orana asked.

His heart surged. Sharing her sight was a rare, rare thing. He nodded vigorously before he could help himself. It had to bode well, if she was in such a mood.

She reached a hand to him, and he grasped it.

The world soared beneath him.

He was an eagle, flying straight up into the night sky. Orana's baobab tree shrank to the size of an insect, then smaller, as his sight expanded. He saw the Dooralalong plain and coastline, the town itself, perched at the mouth of the bay. He saw the wisps of clouds as their sight rushed ever upward, past the westward hills and the rivers that fed into the sea. Even the mountains, where Kindumu Town dotted the foothills, shrank and became no more than a rough texture on the land. He saw all of Tarzal, with its hundreds of towns and villages, its deep forests and dry, arid deserts. Then their sight shifted to the north.

He was the Moon now, the same as Orana was, looking down from the heavens. He saw the curvature of the whole world. They sped past archipelagoes and the northern coastline, past mountains and jungles, to a land of ice and snow. Then suddenly, the eagle of their vision dove toward the earth. The ice and snow settled into the contours of a foreign land, covered with hills. The hills seemed to be swarming with insects, moving and writhing in a great mass. No, not insects; men. Soldiers. They dove closer, closer, and he saw men in steel and iron armor. Spears and maces and other stranger weapons he didn't recognize. Wheeled tubes and horses and carts and tents seemed to litter the landscape between the men. Suddenly a host of the men, a hundred or more, all vanished at the same moment, leaving a bare spot on one of the hilltops. Then it happened again, atop another hillside.

Orana let go of his arm, and his sight returned to their baobab tree.

A whistling sound rose in his ears, coming from far away, and Orana looked sad.

"That is…incredible!" he said. "Thank you, Orana. I will never imagine the world to be so large, so full of different places and people."

"Do you understand what you saw?" Orana asked.

"Soldiers," he said. He knew the look; the men of Dooralalong had girded themselves with metals, too, before they went to fight. "But so many! I will never imagine there would be so many willing to go to a battle. There must be ten towns' worth of soldiers."

"Ten thousand towns' worth," Orana said. "More. All the towns on his part of the world."

"His?" Koa asked. "Whose? One man will control all those soldiers?"

"Yes," Orana said. "The Regnant. But did you see where his soldiers went?"

He shook his head. He still could hardly fathom one Head Man in charge of so many.

The whistling noise was growing louder. He couldn't tell where it was, or what it was. But even so! His heart still raced from what Orana had shown him, from the mysteries she was ready to reveal.

"He should be sending his armies to her part of the world," Orana said. "To find the Veil's champions. Instead he sends them to Bhakal. To Skova. To Rabaquim, to Nikkon. Even here, to Tarzal."

"Those soldiers have come here, to us?" he asked. Suddenly he worried for Dooralalong. The men of Dooralalong were no more than two hundred, perhaps twice so many if they let elders and boys like him take up arms. He'd seen thousands in those frozen hills.

"They are here already," Orana said, with what sounded like sorrow in her voice. "You brought them to me, Koa."

The delegation. His heart raced. Of course, she would have seen them, if she'd been watching.

The whistling was loud now. Ringing in his ears.

"Those are only two foreigners," he said. "They will meet with the Head Man, and the Head Dreamer. They will ask me to come to you, to see if you will meet them. I will be sorry, Orana, if I should not have brought them."

"Two foreigners," Orana said. "Two Dragons. They set their anchors, and a thousand more arrive. My sister and I knew this day would come, when the Regnant and Veil tired of playing their game. But they will find the Sun and Moon no easy prey. I'm sorry, Koa. You were a good friend. You should have become a good man, dancing with your Allia, making good, strong, Tarzali babies."

"Orana?" he asked. Fear passed through him at her words. "What will you mean?"

"Come to me," Orana said. "Before your soul passes beyond my reach. Come to the Moon. I will try to find you, and see that you are reborn. But I will not meet with your Dragons. I will show them, and show their master, what comes of playing games with the powers of the sky."

He frowned, about to ask again what she meant, when the first meteors crashed into the upper boughs of the baobab tree.

His last sight was fire, flaming rock, and sadness in the Moon's eyes as she whispered goodbye.

INTERLUDE

VICTOIRE

Private Chambers
Rasailles Palace

T he palace stank of death. Not a smell, in the proper sense, though there
would be scores of bodies rotting in the city, where Empress d'Arrent's
crews had yet to complete their searches. No, the palace had an air of the
soon-to-be-dead waiting to join their friends and families, of empty eyes
resigned to defeat at the hands of a foe too great and terrible for them to accept
what had happened.

The steward who escorted Victoire through the halls wore a mask of stupor,
and deposited him with no more than a word. It was a finely appointed
chamber, suited to the likes of the Duc-Governor's loftiest servants, perhaps
even to the Duc himself, before the revolution had put the man to death. A
new painting hung on the wall, of Erris d'Arrent in full military dress, with
a gold crown on her head and the scepter of royal office in her hand. Soon
enough she'd join the Duc-Governor in dying. A pity the terror that had swept
through New Sarresant hadn't taken her as well.

"Master Victoire," a man said from the opposite doors, closing them behind
himself as he entered the room. "You've arrived at last."

Victoire stood, offering a proper bow returned in haste by his host. "Of
course, Captain Essily," he said. "I wouldn't think to refuse an Imperial
summons."

Essily nodded along as though there were no hint of irony in Victoire's
words. Never mind that he'd spent the better part of the last season at Reyne
d'Agarre's side, rallying Republican loyalists and burning half the ships in the

New Sarresant Navy. He'd prepared a whole host of potential lines of logic to explain his presence here in the palace. It seemed he wouldn't need them.

"Sit, please," Essily said, joining him atop two of the man's cushioned couches. "I'm told you were d'Agarre's second, and head of his operations in Villecours."

"That's right," he said, and no point denying it. Perhaps he'd need some of his prepared logic after all. "We were persuaded by the Lady Sarine Thibeaux to ally ourselves with the Empress, and came north to dispose ourselves for battle under her command."

Essily waved him off. "Yes, of course. We're in no place now to address weeks-old affairs and grievances. I'm certain you'll agree the tragedy that has befallen us here in New Sarresant outweighs all other concerns."

"Of course," Victoire said.

"And I'm certain you'll agree that, for our military to continue to resist the Jun forces, the city's factories must run, day and night. We need munitions, arms, food, to say nothing of clothing, livestock, even paper, metalworks, refined ores, and textiles. How many of d'Agarre's militia survived the event in the city?"

He almost sneered, but held it in. The "event" in the city? Every living thing, animal or human, in New Sarresant had dropped dead without a mark on their skin, without sign of poison or disease. If that qualified as no more than an "event," he was Head Vicar of a Trithetic Order.

"All of the militia survived, Captain," he replied. "We were outside the city walls. Evidently it made all the difference."

"Do you have a count, then?"

He shrugged. "Twelve thousand of us, perhaps. Most from New Sarresant itself, save those Sarine Thibeaux brought from Villecours, Lorrine, and the rest of the colonies."

"Twelve thousand," Essily said. "Good. A fine start. And these were tradesmen, yes? Cityfolk trained for factory work, not farmers?"

"The bulk of them, yes," he replied. "Am I to understand it's your intent to have d'Agarre's militia work the factories in New Sarresant?"

Essily nodded absently, consulting a sheaf of papers he'd moved from a nearby table into his lap. "Yes, that's right. With attendant grants of property, raw materials, and whatever else is needed to establish them in the city. We managed to slaughter most of the animals affected by the event, but we'll need help in preserving their meat, and in skinning and..." He sighed. "You can imagine, the work required to reestablish a suitable base of operations, and that's only the beginning. Once we have the core industries functioning again, there are matters of trade: exchanges of necessary inputs for each market, food and outputs to support industries in the South."

It was all Victoire could do not to stare at the man. Tens, no, *hundreds* of thousands had died, and his only apparent concern was restarting the city's businesses and trade. Was Essily a machine himself? A good note, to remember that the man valued numbers in his ledgers over the human cost of what the numbers meant.

"Of course," he said. "You'll have the militia's support, in whatever capacity required."

Essily nodded, taking a quill to one of his papers, his scribbling filling the sudden silence between them.

"How is the Empress handling this?" Victoire asked after a moment. "Have you met with her, since the 'event'?"

"Empress d'Arrent is preoccupied with military matters," Essily said. "She entrusts the recovery to me and the rest of our staff here at the palace." He paused, then added, "Of course, she is deeply saddened and aggrieved. Once the military supply lines are reestablished the Empress will preside in person over a mass ceremony, after the new investiture of clerics is finished."

"She hasn't been here to the palace in person?"

"I'm sure you are aware of her magic of *Need*," Essily said. "The Empress can be wherever she needs to be, regardless of her physical presence."

"She connects to you, then?"

Essily frowned, setting down his ledgers and looking up at Victoire. "You'll forgive me, sir, but I can't divulge the Empress's routines."

"Ah," Victoire said, rising from his seat and making as though he intended to pace the room. "Yes. I understand. More likely for you to brief her anyway, I suppose."

"Better if we turn our conversation to the logistics of moving your people into the city. As I understand it, Reyne d'Agarre has been missing since the battle. True? You'll be our primary liaison, if so. I'll need an accounting as soon as you can give it, of the trades and talents of your people. If you can index their skills against—"

Essily kept talking for almost a full breath before he looked down at the knife Victoire had plunged into his chest. A hand's length of steel, delivered expertly and adroitly. One of the first skills he'd learned as a youth.

Essily's eyes widened, and a choking noise rose first from his throat, then a cough, threatening to spray blood across the cushions. Victoire was ready for it, raising a hand to block the captain's mouth.

"Shh," Victoire said. "Easier for us both if you die quietly."

Essily struggled. They always struggled. Victoire moved to wrap arms around him, hauling him from his seat as they slumped together quietly to the floor. His knife had pierced the captain's heart. Death would come swiftly, in the time it took for blood to fail to reach the man's brain. Essily wasn't a small man, but Victoire had the advantage of a firm grip and clear expectations for what was to follow. Essily thrashed in shock, and Victoire held tight. Another beat. Two. A muffled scream. Writhing. Then stillness.

Victoire withdrew his hand from Essily's mouth, coated in blood and spit. He wiped it on the captain's shirt. No hiding the blood there, but if he was careful he could avoid needing to replace the coat and breeches. He worked quickly, unlacing the front of the shirt and using it to soak up as much of the blood as he could. The coat came off with a few shakes of the corpse, and he set it aside. They'd been quiet enough that he wasn't afraid of sentries or aides coming to investigate the noise, but they were still in a place of governance. No telling when a man as important as Empress d'Arrent's chief aide might be interrupted, even in a private meeting. He had to be quick.

His mind relaxed. The first exercises of his House, taught when he was no more than a child. He let go the image of himself as Victoire, the confidant, the revolutionary, the lover, the poet, the philosopher, the man. His features changed, reverting for a brief moment to his true skin, though he fought to suppress that sense of self, too. Easier if he changed from one to the next as quickly as possible. He was Fei Zan, Grandmaster of the Great and Noble House of the Fox, only for an instant. A taste of the dead man's blood helped refocus his thoughts toward the change, and his skin shifted again. He became Essily, chief of staff to the most powerful general and monarch in the western world, a meticulous man, obsessed with order and detail, who valued numbers, figures, and propriety over compassion, empathy, and even justice. He could serve a tyrant, and care only for whether her schedules and orders were carried out to their fullest.

A shape of the dead man's memory settled into his mind. He wouldn't have perfect recall, of course; such mastery eluded him, even as Grandmaster. But the shape of Essily's experiences would be there. The facsimile of the truth. It helped that Fei Zan had known Essily when he'd worn the skin of Anselm Voren, but that man had died when the Lord of Death severed the *Need* binding that had connected him to Erris d'Arrent during his ascension. He wouldn't have the *Need* binding now, either, but if he'd guessed aright, d'Arrent wouldn't attempt a connection to Essily directly. The man was far too important to be no more than a vessel. It would serve. He would serve.

Already he'd engineered the destruction of the New Sarresant Navy, and prodded Reyne d'Agarre to the meeting that had ended in his death. Now his focus would turn to bringing about the ruin of the rest of the New Sarresant military machine. Warriors like the champions of Crab, Crane, Heron, or Ox served the Great Lord in their way, but true destruction, true power, required the perfect trust of one's enemies. He had that now, wearing Aide-Captain Essily's skin.

He balled the shirt into a wad of blood and cotton, using Victoire's old clothes to tie a bandage around the corpse's wound, then set to hiding the body.

INTERLUDE

AMANISHIAKNE

Prince Massik's Palace
Abakra, Western Bhakal

The air shimmered with an image of her sister's face. She kept her composure; only the most attentive would notice that their Queen's focus had shifted. In front of her, her nine thousand, three hundred and eighty-sixth son held court in his city, atop a throne adorned with gold leaf and polished stone. Her throne was raised higher, as befitted the Queen, removed a few paces from the others, but lacking the gold and jewels Prince Massik had ordered carved into his seat. A New Sarresant admiral's daughter knelt at the chamber's heart, while five more of her sons and a full score of advisors stood in attendance, facing the foreigners and thrones together.

Her attention was elsewhere. Her son could handle the business of the day.

You should return to Konghom.

The thought rose in her mind, as though she'd been the one to think it. She knew better. Thoughts transmitted over such a distance were difficult, but she and her sister had long ago learned to do the difficult as a matter of routine.

In reply she formed an image of the future. A foreign army on Bhakal soil. Faceless, shapeless figures marching under a colorless flag. Blurred terrain swept under their feet, until they stood on a hill overlooking one of her cities. A coastal city, with its ports open to foreign trade. It could have been any of a dozen such that occupied her western shores; the gold-plated spire made clear it was this one, Abakra, where Prince Massik reigned in her name. An enemy was coming. When, she couldn't say. Visions of the future were always clouded, even under the clearest of circumstances.

I know this, Sakhefete thought back to her. *I've seen it, too. But it could be a cycle away, and you fear for nothing. You should return to Konghom. There are matters to discuss, between us and our enemies.*

This time Sakhefete sent a vision back: a coastal bluff, where two women fought. One draped in red, the other burnt and broken, struggling to rise from the ground. The woman in red lashed out, and the other cried in pain.

The Veil, fighting against the Veil reborn, she thought to her sister. *But which of them survived? I saw only the beginning of the fight. Not the end. And what does it mean for us?*

There are Jun emissaries, come to treat with you, Sakhefete thought to her. *They will explain.*

In Konghom? she asked.

No, Sakhefete replied. *I had them travel to meet with you there, in your son's city. This is too important. Meet with them, and tell me your answer at once.*

My answer? To what question?

Silence greeted her where it mattered. In the throne room, Prince Massik had risen from his seat, giving a grand pronouncement of friendship between the Bhakal Empire and the newly founded Empire of New Sarresant, Thellan, and Gand, declaring their willingness to trade. All eyes in the chamber were fixed on the prince, save one pair. Her nine thousand, four hundred and nineteenth son, Omera, newly returned from sojourn in the far west. Omera looked to her, his brow furrowed in concern, or with a question.

Unprompted, a new vision came.

Omera stood alone in a river of blood. No, not alone: Another figure stood at his side, its features cloaked in shadow. Gold from a melting crown leaked down from his head, mixing with the currents of the river at his feet. A woman lay dead in front of him, a woman wearing a copy of her face. Suddenly she knew: He would be a King. Not a prince. And the price would be dear, paid in honor, and pride.

She gasped in spite of herself.

The room fell silent. Even Prince Massik turned to her with worry in his eyes.

She rose. Best to salvage this, and move on. Speculate as they would, the rest had no need to know what her vision had shown.

"The Bhakal affirm our friendship with New Sarresant," she said in her Queen's voice. "But the time for this audience is at an end. Go now. All of you, and be at peace."

She remained standing, her neck held stiff, her head raised as though to look beyond the horizon. As one, the attendants and sons made for the room's exits: a wide, gilded double door inlaid with ivory carvings, and two other side doors that led to advisors' quarters, rooms where negotiations conducted in the presence of the throne would be put to paper and made binding.

Prince Massik turned to her as his people were leaving the room.

"Mother," Massik said. "Are you well? I assure you, my doctors are among the best in the Empire. Speak, and I will have them fetched at once."

"You, too, my son," she said, keeping her eyes above the horizon. "Go. Leave me the room." She finally broke her pose, lowering her sight to find Omera among those leaving through the double door, his eyes still turned to her with concern. "Tell your brother to bring the Jun emissaries when they arrive."

"My brother?" Massik said, following her line of sight. "Prince Bikawan? Or Prince Omera? And Jun emissaries?" He lowered his voice. "Is that why you terminated our audience so abruptly?"

"All will be made clear," she said. "Have Omera bring the Jun when they arrive. That is all, my son."

Massik scrunched his face, hesitating to obey, before he relented, taking the steps smoothly enough that few would question whether the order to leave the throne had come from him, or from her. Always a challenge, when her sons let princedom inflate their sense of station in the world. Her Empire was run by a hundred Massiks, spread in cities from Abakra to Ruhadan, with fifty more waiting to inherit when their brothers passed on, or stepped down. Her concerns had always been higher. Between her sister's warnings and the vision she'd just had, they could be no higher than they were today.

The room fell quiet as the doors slid shut, and she was alone.

She sealed off the vision she'd had of Omera, shifting it to a secret corner of her mind. Sakhefete kept secrets from her, too; a necessary thing, when their minds were connected always. Her sister would be watching, probing her for whatever emotion she hoped would come from this audience with their enemies. What she showed would be her choice, and her choice would come from careful study and consideration.

She let the vision come, this time prepared for what she would see.

The river of blood assaulted her senses again. It pulsed with life energy, reflecting a dark-colored sky. Its currents ran ankle-deep, lapping at her son's calves and shins. It was Omera, she was sure of it now. He stood, facing a host of what he saw as his enemies, and once again she saw the woman lying at his feet, the woman wearing her face. Desperation coursed through her in the vision. His sword was out, and herbs burned fire in his blood. But the woman he'd killed wasn't her. It was her sister. Her twin.

Omera was a prince, in his mind.

Behind him, she saw the truth.

An ancient host gathered as a million souls encircled him, watching his deeds. She knew the host. She'd seen it as a girl, when she'd first raised the banners of the Bhakal. They had smiled on her then, all the gathered souls of all her people, living, dead, or yet to be born, and they had smiled on her sister. Together, Amanishiakne and Sakhefete had secured the future of this continent, of the people who dwelt on it.

Now that future rested in Omera's hands. Would it mean her own soul would be part of that host, finally put to rest after so many centuries of cheating death? And Sakhefete, too, would be part of the host, even while her body was freshly dead at her son's feet. Tears clouded her eyes. The vision showed what it showed; divination was never precise, however she willed it.

She calmed her heart, and wiped her cheeks, and waited. There would be time to watch the vision again, a hundred times more if she needed it. Until she was certain what course to take, she would watch, and wait, and consider. Omera had always been one of her favorites. She could do worse, if she had to choose an heir. But she wasn't ready to die. Perhaps that was the message the Jun brought, something tied to her death, something to set Omera on the path to kill her sister, even if they were unaware of what they carried. Perhaps that was why Sakhefete needed her answer. Perhaps she and Sakhefete could face even death together, arm in arm, as they had faced all their challenges in life.

The double doors swung open, finding her seated calmly atop her throne.

Omera came at their head, and the vision flashed again as she saw him. He was strong, well-built, and powerful, a curved *shotel* blade at his left hip and three pouches of herbs fastened to his right. The future King of the Bhakal, if her divinations didn't err.

Two figures came behind him, both clad in eastern silk. She saw what they were before they emerged into the throne room. Mantis, one who wielded flame, and Dragon, one who danced along the edges of space and time. A man and a woman. Both had already met with Sakhefete, if her sister's sendings were true, though she'd sensed neither in their shared thoughts.

Omera knelt, pressing his head to the floor. The Jun followed his lead, and did the same.

She said nothing, letting silence prevail. All three figures stayed bowed in position on the ornately woven rugs that dominated Massik's throne room.

"My sister sent you here," she said abruptly. "Speak, and explain why."

Both Jun had the good sense to stay kneeling, their faces hidden, while Omera rose to his feet.

"Great Queen," the Mantis, the man, spoke in perfectly accented Bhakal. "We come bearing tidings from our lord."

"Your lord," she said coldly. In ordinary times it would mean the Jun Emperor. Today it meant something else.

"The Lord of Death," the Mantis said. "Regnant to the Master's Throne. He Who Reigns—"

"He Who Reigns over Half the World," she interrupted. "But he does not reign here. Why have you come?"

Finally the emissaries lifted their heads from Massik's rugs, facing her throne, but daring only to look at her feet, not to meet her eyes.

"The Veil is dead," the Dragon, the woman, said. "The Regnant desires an equal, to take her place at his side."

At her words, the second part of Sakhefete's vision intruded into her mind.

Two women, fighting on a coastal bluff. The one in red lashed out, invading the other woman's mind, ripping her magicks free and casting them into the void. This much, she'd seen on her own. But the vision continued. The other woman transformed, shifting her body into an old shape, a shape of the distant north. Nine tails lashed out as one, wrapping like whipcords around the woman in red. *Kaas* magic pulsed through the Nine Tails' body, swatting away the attempts of the woman in red to fend off its attacks. The woman in red broke, her spine snapping as her rib cage cracked and collapsed. Magic leaked from her corpse. For a long moment the woman who had been the Nine Tails wept in pain, lying alongside the broken body of her enemy. Then Dragon magic enveloped her, and she vanished from the hillside.

The vision came with a sending of words: *You see, sister? Everything has changed.*

She formed a thought in response, and forced it down without sending it.

"What does your master know of equals?" she said.

"He is prepared to set aside the laws that have bound him, and his partner," the Dragon said. "New laws can be put in place, once the Soul is secure."

"How?" she asked. She needed them talking. Distracted.

"Forgiveness, Your Majesty," the Dragon said. "I am a simple servant, and know little of the workings of the great magicks. My lord bade us to tell you it would be a matter of reconstruction, of rebuilding what the Veil knew. He wishes us to assure you it is possible, with your and your sister's cooperation. He spoke of opening a door long thought to be sealed. If you wish, I can bring you to him through my gifts to walk the starfield and the strands. He will explain the fullness of what he plans, if it pleases Your Majesty."

Reconstruction. The word vibrated in her skull as soon as the Dragon said it. *Oh, sister.* Once again the thought formed, but went unsent. *What have you done?*

Both Dragon and Mantis bowed again.

She worked quickly. Her mind had a dozen compartments, secret places for her deepest thoughts, her darkest memories. She moved the weight of her consciousness into them now. She'd long ago imagined the possibility of what this Dragon had proposed. Reconstruction. Rebuilding the Veil's memories, or the Regnant's, into hers. She'd imagined it as something her and Sakhefete could have done together: one of them ensnaring the Regnant's secrets while the other trapped the Veil's. They could have become Queens in truth, each inheriting half the world instead of half an Empire. Power. But with the risk of losing what she was, who she was, as the memories of her enemy festered in her mind.

And it was impossible, unless both sisters acquiesced. Their minds were too deeply connected, even as she fought to move her consciousness behind her seals. If Sakhefete let him in, it would mean the Regnant would be able to freely access Amanishiakne's mind. Perhaps he already had.

"I accept," she said loudly. Calmly. A pronouncement from her throne. "Bring me to your lord."

She studied the Dragon and Mantis as both figures rose. The success of their mission would momentarily disarm them both, the flush of victory relaxing the natural barriers of a diplomat.

And there. The Dragon's lip curled into the faintest suggestion of a smile.

She struck.

Her mind invaded both Mantis's and Dragon's simultaneously. With care and time she might have sent them back to their master, each believing that Amanishiakne had been subdued, though neither would have been able to say how, or to what she'd agreed. Instead she sliced through shields of identity, self, memory, and belief with a surgeon's precision and none of a surgeon's care. She severed every connection, cutting away the core of who these *magi* believed themselves to be.

As one, both Jun emissaries dropped to the floor in a crumpled heap.

Omera let out a startled yelp. She was already racing down the steps.

"My son," she said, grasping him by the shoulders. As she touched him the vision played again. He stood facing a great enemy, the host of all Bhakal souls watching and praying for their King. She fought it down. "Omera."

"Mother," Omera replied, still wide-eyed and staring at the bodies of the Jun emissaries.

"My sister will be coming for you, and your brothers," she said. "I will shield as many of you as I can reach, before she strikes, but you must trust no one. Assume Sakhefete has turned them all, no matter what they claim. Omera!"

His name startled him back to focusing on her.

"You will return to Konghom," she said forcefully as she worked to protect his mind. "You will reach her, before the Regnant can complete his reconstruction. And you will kill her. Do you understand? As you love me, as you love our people, do you understand what I'm asking you to do?"

Omera shook his head. His eyes were glazed, half in shock, half from the work she'd been forced to rush inside his head. No helping it. So long as he could be made to understand.

"I...I don't..." he began. She cut him short.

"Reach my sister," she said. "Queen of the Eastern Empire. Sakhefete. Reach her, and kill her. As fast as you can ride. Do this, and..." She hesitated. "...and you will be King. Are you hearing this, my son? Do you understand?"

He nodded slowly. Once more her vision flashed. He would wear a gemstone crown on his head, and pay a terrible price for every stone. Sakhefete would die at his hand. Of this she was certain. The other costs would be settled when they came due.

She let him go, testing the shield a final time before withdrawing from his mind. He held her eyes, and the glaze over his pupils faded, replaced with strength, and resolve.

PART 2: SUMMER

THE SISTER'S FADING LIGHT

23

SARINE

Sacre-Lin Cemetery
Maw District, New Sarresant

The ground was cold under her legs. She sat still, feeling the chill. As a child she'd hated the cemetery, the one part of the chapel grounds that had been off-limits to her. Now it was all that remained. Now all of it was a cemetery: the Sacre-Lin, the Maw, the city itself.

The headstone had been carved from granite. Most of the markers in the yard were cast iron, and the larger burial sites outside the city used wood, both considered more fashionable, for all it mattered now. But granite would endure. This was his place. A hundred years from now, another lost child might come to visit the yard. They should see his name. They should remember.

Jean-Henri Thibeaux
Father. Uncle. Caretaker of the Grounds.
Died 15 Apollinaire, AC 1796. Aged 52.

She reached out, tracing the word *Uncle*. It was the only name she'd called him since her earliest memories. He'd been Father to his parishioners, Brother to his fellow priests. He was more than any of that to her.

"I should have taken him," she said, feeling the hoarseness in her throat, though her tears were long since dry. "It's my fault. I should have taken him away."

He wanted you to let him stay. Anati remained unseen, though her voice sounded clearly in Sarine's thoughts.

"I wanted to play with the kitchen fire when I was a child," she said.

"He scolded me and sent me running to my loft with a sore backside. This time I knew better than he did. I knew the danger, and I let him stay. It's my fault."

No, it isn't, Anati thought. *You have the power to prevent all sorts of harm, to all sorts of people. Is it your fault every time something happens you might have prevented, had you been there?*

"I *was* here. I was in this chapel two days before the battle. I could have taken him across the sea. I could have saved him."

He wouldn't have wanted you to grieve by blaming yourself.

"How do you know?" she said. "You hardly knew him."

It wasn't fair, and she regretted it before she sensed the pain from her *kaas*. But in the moment, grief outweighed regret. The loss ached deep inside her, the hollowness where she'd lost the leyline magic, and the spirits' touch. It hurt, red and raw, where the Veil had reached into her and torn two of her gifts away. She could still sense the red wires, burning cinders that left her incomplete, a shell of what she was born to be. All of it paled against the pain of sitting here, atop the plot of land where they'd buried her uncle. Tradition dictated respect for the dead by avoiding the ground in front of the headstone, but tradition counted for nothing anymore. This was as close as she could get to him, so this was where she sat.

"He tried to teach me to sing, once," she said when her anger cooled. "Before we discovered my talent for sketching. He insisted everyone needs some form of art in their lives."

Tavern songs? Anati thought. *Like the one I tried?*

"No," she said. "Hymns. He ran me through two complete hymnals before we mutually concluded I wasn't ever going to carry a tune. I did my first drawings in those hymn books, using coals from one of the chapel hearths to trace lines between the notation. He was furious—the books had cost him four silver pennies each—but the next morning, he went out and bought me a proper set of charcoal pens and paper."

Did he sing? Anati asked. *Was that his art?*

She shook her head, smiling through fresh tears. "He wasn't any better with a tune than I was. His art was cooking. Probably why he accepted the posting here at the Sacre-Lin: so he could make soup for the poor all day."

Anati appeared, her coils draped over top of the headstone, forward claws clutching to the edge of the stone.

That was Green, Anati thought. *The first time you've made it since his body was put in the ground.*

She wiped her cheeks, smearing moisture on her fingers.

It was her fault, no matter what Anati said. And it was his fault, too, damnably stubborn man that he was. Patient, merciful, kind, and so full of charity it seemed he spent every waking minute either serving people or preparing to. No one else lived that way. The city was full of selfish, greed-driven, indolent, angry people; she'd seen it all, felt the tableau of their emotions through her *kaas*. Father Thibeaux was different. He'd taken in a street girl, fed her, educated her, taught her the virtues and the arts and all he knew of the world. He'd sheltered her from the priests' tests, kept her hidden and safe. He'd given her a life. She'd given him all the love she had. He would have said it was enough. But it wasn't. And now he was gone.

Somewhere inside her the Nine Tails stirred, echoing her grief. A loved one's passing deserved to be mourned. A gentle touch, pawing the corpse. A howl, picked up and carried by all the members of the pack. The host mourned inwardly, directing sadness inside herself where the Nine Tails would have called out, but perhaps the two could meet, one surging into the other, and mix with the serpent's curiosity with the best of both its colors, green and yellow. A bitter joy in remembering. A sweet sadness in letting go.

She rose to her feet.

"I don't know how to fight him," she said to Anati, still perched atop the headstone. "How can I stand against someone who can do this?"

The Regnant, Anati thought to her. *You're sure this was his work?*

"It had to be. What else? But I couldn't even strike back. I don't know anything about him. He knew this city was my home; I wouldn't do this to one of his cities even if I knew it was his."

You think he did this to hurt you?

"I can't think of another reason. The Veil...Lin...she told me they would sacrifice millions just to flush me into the open. He did this to goad me, or maybe to show me it's hopeless to fight."

But it isn't, is it? I still feel hope in you.

"You're right," she said. "It isn't hopeless. But he did this to try and draw my attention, and he's got it."

The threat in her words hung in the air, followed quickly by a return to emptiness. She didn't know where the Regnant was, or how to reach him. And she'd been gutted by the Veil, half her magic ripped away and thrown into the void. Closing her eyes since the city's fall had revealed nothing, only blackness where there should have been leyline energy waiting for her to touch it. The spirits were silent in her mind. She was crippled, sure as the malformed children and old soldiers begging for coin on market streets in hotter months. She was half what she should be, and even at her full strength she could never match a power that could kill every living thing in a great city. She couldn't—

That isn't true, Anati thought, interrupting her thoughts before she'd formed them into words. *Even without the leylines or the spirits, the Veil had the power of creation, and you're all that's left of her now. They were equals, her and the Regnant. That means you have that potential, too.*

"I don't want to have the potential to do this," she said. "I wouldn't do this, even if I could. All I want is to stop him from repeating this horror ever again. I feel like he wants me to show myself, to join the battles openly, or he'll keep murdering innocents until I do."

And you mean to do it, to keep him from killing?

"I..." she began, then stopped herself. Part of her felt obliged to do exactly that, to do whatever it took to stop him from murdering any more people, any more cities. The Regnant seemed to want a confrontation with her directly. But if she gave it before she understood the balance between them, the reason why he and the Veil had shared power, the truth behind their being equals, as Anati had said... she risked everything with ignorance. She risked worse than her city's destruction, and her uncle's death.

"I don't know," she finished instead. "I wish I had more time, to learn my place in all this. I wish—"

A loud thump from within the chapel drew her and Anati's attention.

People, Anati thought. *And emotions.*

A sense of them came through their bond: determination, hope, despair, fatigue.

"That doesn't feel like soldiers," she said. "Maybe looters, come to see to the Sacre-Lin."

A second thump sounded, this time with raised voices inside the chapel walls.

She brushed dirt from her trousers, then rounded on the service entrance, bounding up the steps and pushing into the kitchens to investigate.

"Slower next time," a man's voice echoed from the main chamber. "You'll crack the tile, or rattle the windows, and do you know what stained glass costs to repair? More than the prelate intends to pay, and the difference will come from your wages, Oracle strike me if they don't."

She emerged into the ambulatory behind the pulpit and saw the chamber flooded with sunlight, both of the main doors propped open, while a team of two oxen pulled a cart into the central nave. Two pallets had already been lowered onto the floor, each stacked high with boxes, crates, and barrels, with ropes fixed to let two large men handle the load. A third stood by, the one

CHAINS OF THE EARTH

who'd barked out orders, directing their work, while a fourth, a woman in a brown robe, looked on.

"What's going on here?" she demanded, drawing weary looks from the workers, annoyance from the foreman, and surprise from the priest.

"Who in the bloody Nameless's arms are you, girl?" the foreman snapped. "If you're looking for looting, you'll find better pickings elsewhere."

"This is my chapel," she said. "What do you think you're doing?"

"Her chapel," the foreman said to his men. "Bloody fucking rats, already marking territory and thinking they own the city."

"Hold, Master Huwain," the priestess said. The woman was young, not more than a few years her elder, though she spoke with authority that went along with the brown robes and scars on the backs of her hands. "Were you one of this chapel's parishioners, my child?"

"I live here," she replied. "This is my uncle's chapel. I've lived here since I was a girl. What are you doing here?"

The priestess raised an eyebrow. "I wasn't told my predecessor kept an orphanage. Though, from the look of you, you should be well enough on your own by your age. And this isn't your uncle's chapel, child. This chapel belongs to the Church. My name is Sister Marisse. I've been assigned here, to see to its upkeep during the restoration of the city."

She shook her head. They couldn't. Her uncle was dead; it stood to reason they'd replace him. But the Sacre-Lin had never had anything to do with the Church. It was her uncle's place. She'd never seen another priest come up their steps in all the years she'd lived there, not a visitor, nor a messenger, traveler, or guest.

A spark of yellow light flashed at the edge of her vision.

That had to be because my father kept them away, Anati thought to her. *Don't you think? It would be easy to do, if you wanted me to get rid of them.*

Sister Marisse was looking up at her with a mix of compassion and stern authority; the foreman had already turned his attention back to unloading the cart. It *would* be easy to get rid of them. *Yellow* would send them running. She could even set a warding with Life around the chapel; it had been her first lesson, when Axerian showed her how to use its power. She could anchor a wave of *Yellow* so strong no one would ever come near the Sacre-Lin again.

"No," she said instead. "I'm sorry. I was only grieving, visiting my uncle's headstone. I didn't realize they'd be sending a replacement so soon."

The priestess's expression softened. "Not a replacement, my child," Sister Marisse said. "No one can replace our loved ones in our hearts. But remember the lesson of the Veil's first martyrs. *Every thought of grief is homage to its source. We feel love most strongly—*"

"*. . . most strongly in the pain of remembering those we've lost*," Sarine finished for her. "From the Grand Betrayal, seventh parable, second verse."

"Just so," Sister Marisse said. "Your uncle taught you well."

Fresh tears threatened to well over, and she let them come. "He did," she said. "I should get my things. I still have them in the loft. I can move them if you need the space."

"They'll keep, my child," Sister Marisse said. "I'll be some time settling in. Leave your things, for now. Perhaps you'll come back and share stories with me, next time you pay respects."

She nodded, stifling another surge of grief.

"Thank you," she said. "Take care of this church, please. It's more than a chapel to me. It was more to the people of this district, too."

"I will," Sister Marisse said. "I promise; my services will honor their memories."

She spared a last look around the nave. Her loft hung beneath the main reliefs, where she'd sketched the stained glass and parishioners both. Some benches had been displaced for the sake of the ox cart, but most still stood in rows facing the chancel, where her uncle had preached and offered comfort to the people of the Maw. The Exarch's wing extended behind it, with the Oracle's and the Veil's on either side, making a cross atop the main chamber. She'd prayed to each, more times than she could count. Somehow she couldn't see the men and women behind them in the images etched in glass. Paendurion, the Exarch. Ad-Shi, the Oracle. Lin Qishan, the Veil. The Gods were more than any of them. The Gods had given her uncle purpose in life, and they weren't dead, even if Paendurion had been run through the heart, Ad-Shi had fallen from a clifftop, and Lin Qishan had been broken by the Nine Tails. The Gods lived on in her memory. Her uncle would, too.

She pushed past the foreman, the workers, and their cart, though they'd already returned to unloading their crates, ignoring her as she left through the main doors.

Sure you don't want me to scatter them? Anati thought to her. *It feels wrong. This isn't their place.*

"It is now," she said. "And we're already late." She glanced up at the sun, now well past midday. Erris and the rest of her champions could wait for her; she wasn't about to return to the hunting lodge without visiting her uncle's grave. But as much as she might have enjoyed watching the foreman and his workers race through the streets in panic, there was no malice in Sister Marisse.

She walked the familiar streets through the Maw toward the district boundary. She would come back and walk these streets again—how could she not, when her uncle was buried at the Sacre-Lin? But it would never be the same. The thought caught in her throat, and she crossed the rest of the city with tears threatening to blur the way.

24

ERRIS

The Hunting Lodge
Outside Rasailles

Jiri snorted as they drew closer to the de l'Arraignons' former lodge. It was smaller on the outside than it appeared from within, a construction of logs and thatch meant to look rustic, while preserving every comfort for its noble occupants. Yuli raised a hand to acknowledge her and Jiri's approach. Arak'Jur stood beside her, alongside a third she didn't recognize, a girl in white, each gathered in the yard in front of the lodge's main entrance. A covered cart had been set down on the grass in front of them. Jiri sensed her nerves, and quickened their pace toward the cart. She'd always tethered *Need* to arrive here directly, before. Today she came in person. She needed to see Yuli's finding with her own eyes.

"Empress," Yuli said with a deep bow.

She slid off Jiri's back, dropping the reins and trusting to her horse to graze without straying away from the lodge.

"Show me" was all she needed to say.

The girl in white climbed atop the cart, where a white sheet had been spread across its bed, and pulled the top aside, revealing what she'd been promised she would find.

Reyne d'Agarre.

Dead.

His skin was ashen and tight, his lips cracked and dry. He still wore his red coat, spattered with dried blood. Both eyes were closed, more peaceful than she'd ever seen him in life.

"We found him outside the city," Yuli said. "Reed led us to his body. Dead in the same way the city's denizens were: dropped to the ground, without any obvious sign of injury."

"It confirms why we heard the voice again," Arak'Jur said. "'*For this one, it ends.*' It had to be Reyne d'Agarre."

She nodded, studying the body. Poor, stupid fool. He'd been a thorn in her Empire's foot since they'd returned from the Gods' Seat. But he was still one of Sarine's champions. Losing him was a blow, alongside far worse damage done to her capital city.

"Where is Marquand?" she asked. "And have Sarine and Tigai returned yet?"

"We expected both around midday," Yuli said. "But we haven't seen Marquand since...since the battle. I was worried we'd find his body, too, while searching the graves for Reyne."

This time she cursed. If Marquand had finally gotten himself killed it would be ten times as dear a loss as Reyne bloody d'Agarre.

"He fought better than anyone I've seen," the girl in white said, perched over the body in the cart bed. "Never saw a man handle a knife like him. But then the old man snapped his fingers and he fell down, dead, same as the rest of the city, I guess."

"Who is this girl?" she asked. "You called her Reed?"

"That's right," Yuli said. "Reed. A survivor of the battle."

The girl glowered at both of them, still hovering over Reyne's body as though it were a holy relic.

"You fought alongside Master d'Agarre?" she asked the girl. "You were there when he died?"

"I was, and I did," Reed said. "Rode with d'Agarre into the woods. Saw it all. Even shot the old man twice before he snapped his fingers. Then I ran, and hid."

She exchanged a look with Arak'Jur and Yuli. Gods damn Marquand if he'd gotten himself killed. She needed his mind right now. So far as she knew there were no *magi* among the enemy that could kill with a look, or a snap of the fingers, though it was all too possible the girl was fabricating stories, even if she claimed to have been there.

"Describe it for me, girl," she said. "Now, and spare no detail. How, exactly, did Reyne die?"

"Who made you the bloody fucking Empress?" Reed said.

"She *is* the Empress, Reed," Yuli said. "It would be a great help if you could..."

She turned her head midsentence toward the cleared green behind the lodge. A figure had appeared there without warning—a man, and Erris's nerves spiked until she recognized Tigai. "If you could tell us what you saw," Yuli finished.

"Get what you can from her," Erris said, already striding toward the green. "As much detail as she can remember."

She crossed the yard, leaving the girl, the cart, and Reyne's body behind.

"Empress," Tigai said as she approached. "Unexpected, to have you here in person."

"I came to see d'Agarre's body," she said.

"They found him?" Tigai asked.

She nodded, letting the loss settle between them.

"What do you have to report?" she asked. "Any news from the Jun lines?"

Tigai shook his head. "They've tightened security since their Red Lady's death. The leylines are still active enough, but I have to be careful when I move between their camps."

"Take due care, of course," she said. "But I need to understand their deployments. A hundred field scouts mapping their positions could be worth less than a single document, a single conversation you might overhear. And find out who's been promoted to the command, with Lin Qishan dead."

"So far it's all rumors," Tigai said. "Companies are being relocated by their Dragon-*magi*, though no one knows to where. The only standing orders are to take up defensive positions and wait. No orders to prepare for an attack."

"My scouts report the same," she said. "What I need from you is why. Even with the victory we won against their vanguard, they should have triple my numbers deployed here in the North already. I need to understand why they're digging in instead of maneuvering. It defies sense. There's nothing of value to hold in the Sinari forests."

"Their advance got cut off when I killed the Veil," Sarine said from behind them. Erris spun, her heart all but seizing in her throat.

"Nameless bloody take me, girl," Erris snapped. "Announce yourself before you speak."

Sarine shrugged. "I saw activity on the strands," she said. "Figured it would be safe if Tigai had just arrived. And I think that's why the Jun aren't attacking. When the Veil died, they lost their tethers of *Body*, so their armies will be spread out across the continent, stuck where they were. They're weeks or maybe months away now, instead of days."

"My scouts confirmed that already, and we've already accounted for it," Erris said. "It doesn't explain why the units they have here in New Sarresant haven't maneuvered around my armies. A command of seven or eight million wouldn't be mired by indecision with one loss at the top. There would be redundancies, corps and division commanders able to operate independently of their commanding general."

"You think their objectives have changed," Tigai said.

"I know it," she said. "But so far as I can tell, they aren't threatening me anywhere along our lines. Which suggests their eyes have turned elsewhere."

"They already murdered the whole bloody city," Sarine said. "How much more threatening are they supposed to be?"

She shook her head. Arguing with Sarine was fruitless on the best of days.

"On that point," she said. "What I need from you is—"

"Is that…oh Gods, that's Reyne," Sarine interrupted, leaving them both midsentence as she stormed toward Yuli and the cart.

"She's never been one for proper decorum, has she?" Tigai said.

"As much of a thorn as Reyne d'Agarre ever was," Erris said. "And doubly so for her still breathing while d'Agarre lies in that cart."

"I'll do my best in the Jun camps, Your Majesty," Tigai said with a slight bow. "I have Kitian, one of Yuli's sisters, with me. I've studied their Dragons' movements along the leylines. We should have access to their command tents soon, within a few days' time."

"Good," she said. "Get me what you can on their commander at least. And take care of yourself. No unnecessary risks."

Tigai bowed again, and they moved together toward the front of the lodge. Sarine had climbed up into the cart alongside the girl, Reed, kneeling beside the body. How much simpler it all might have been if Sarine's gifts had been given to someone with military training. And Marquand. His absence stung. With so many dead in New Sarresant, it was all too possible he'd been among them. She'd need to appoint a new commander for Sarine and her champions as soon as a suitable replacement could be found; until then, their reins would sit squarely in her hands. Another burden she didn't need.

"He's really dead," Sarine said. "I didn't want to believe it."

"It speaks to what I need from you, girl," Erris said. "With the Veil dead and the Regnant attacking our cities directly, we need a plan. My council of advisors is assembling to review our situation, but I need insight from you on what to expect from our enemies."

"What do you mean?" Sarine asked. "The Watcher's book? I told you already I went over it with Marquand, we agreed the contest between champions was at the heart of—"

"Not the bloody book," she snapped in reply. "Go to your Watcher himself if you have to. I need answers, not speculation. I need to know *before* the Regnant slaughters one of my cities, if that's something of which he's capable and intending to do."

"You think New Sarresant is my fault?" Sarine said. "How was I supposed to know what he was planning? You're the strategist, not me."

"Strategy is only as good as our intelligence," she said. "I need more. I need you to understand what the Regnant is aiming at, and to what lengths he'll go to get it. His tactics have shifted, and I need to know before they shift again."

"Fine," Sarine said. "It's my fault, then. I'll go to the Seat and see what I can get you."

"Sister, wait," Yuli said. "That's not what the Empress meant."

"Yes it was," Sarine said. Cold anger shone on her face. Erris kept her features smooth and cool. Anger could be useful, if it motivated action. She hadn't laid the blame for New Sarresant at Sarine's feet; that responsibility was hers, and no one else's. But perhaps shame and guilt might push Sarine to get her the answers she needed.

"Step back unless you're coming, too," Sarine said to Yuli. Yuli stepped closer rather than replying. No surprise there, but she hadn't anticipated the girl in white, Reed, rushing to stay at Yuli's side. Sarine spared her a last glare before all three of them vanished.

"Well," Tigai said. "That was something."

"I don't know how Marquand dealt with her," Erris said. "But we need whatever answers she can bring."

"You have vessels in the Gods' Seat, right?" Tigai said. "You can speak with her there if she learns something?"

"I do," she replied. "They're overdue for a report. And there's been no unexpected activity on the strands here around Rasailles?"

"None," Tigai said. "Which is fucking bizarre in its own right. I was sure Marquand meant this place as a trap for them."

"He did," she said idly. Her thoughts remained with Sarine. If there was knowledge at the Gods' Seat, she had to hope Sarine could find it. Something had changed in their conflict with the Regnant. He'd marched the entirety of his armies across a continent, then all but abandoned them after one minor defeat at her hands. Perhaps Lin Qishan's—the Veil's—death had realigned his efforts, but to what end? She needed to know, before another city's population fell dead.

"Give me a hand with this?" Tigai asked, untying a pick and shovel lashed to the cart's side. Arak'Jur moved quietly to help him.

They were finished here. Confirming Reyne's body was enough without dirtying her hands putting him in the ground. She clicked her teeth for Jiri, who came trotting with long grass half-chewed in her mouth.

She ran through her vessels without thinking, brushing *Need* across the thousands of connections that ran from her at their center. Tigai's reminder focused her thoughts on her vessels in the Gods' Seat, studying the map device and seeking connections to help find the enemy's champions. If they'd had anything to report with urgency, she would have felt it through their bond of *Need*. So far they hadn't.

Better, then, for her to focus elsewhere. Two lights shone from the South, in the Thellan colonies. But something was off. She retraced her thoughts. Something was missing. Out of place.

"Empress?" Arak'Jur said. "Are you well?"

Jiri snorted at her impatiently. She ran through her *Need* connections again. And suddenly she knew.

"They're missing," she said. "Gone."

"Gone?" Tigai said. "Who?"

"My vessels in the Gods' Seat," she said. "The ones I sent to track the Regnant's champions through the maps. They hadn't requested my attention since their arrival. I assumed it was for want of anything to report."

"Wait," Tigai said. "You're sure? If they're missing, that means…"

"It means my vessels are dead," she said.

"Dead," Tigai repeated. "And Yuli and Sarine just went to the Gods' Seat. Bloody fuck me. What if the Regnant is bloody well sitting there waiting for them?"

"No point in idle speculation," she said, swinging her legs up over Jiri's saddle. "See to d'Agarre's body, and to your posting. We'll know soon enough if the worst is waiting in the Seat."

"What?" Tigai demanded. "How will we know?"

"The voice," Arak'Jur said. " '*For this one, it ends.*' "

"Fuck me," Tigai said.

She clicked her teeth and Jiri moved forward.

Arak'Jur was right, painful as it was to think it. Speculation was pointless. Whatever was waiting for Sarine in the Gods' Seat, she had wars to fight here. Sarine was one ploy to suss out her enemy's intentions, but she had scouts and reports waiting on both sides of the ocean. The pieces were there. It fell to her to find the way to join them together.

25

OMERA

A Pilgrims' Hostel
City of Domakar, the Western Empire

He kept his head down over his plate. Fresh fish, tomatoes, and rice made for a fine comfort after hard days on the road, but it had been a risk to enter Domakar, no matter that he needed supplies to cross the open sands. The woman now pushing through the beaded doorway, drawing the eyes of half the travelers gathered in the common hall, was the reason why.

Her clothes were fine, and free of the dust clinging to the rest of them. She wore gold bangles on either wrist and a shawl of purple silk wrapped across her shoulders. The color alone marked her as out of place, though her demeanor did for the rest. She scanned the room with piercing clarity as she strode toward the kitchen's proprietor, expecting deference from those in line to eat, and getting it without needing to ask.

"Now what do you suppose a woman like that wants with us," one of the two men seated next to him asked. Caravan guards, the first touched with gray hair in his beard, the other younger, chest and arm muscles worthy of being sculpted from marble, both with leather scabbards slung from their belts. He'd chosen to sit beside them in hopes they'd draw attention away from him as he ate.

"Maybe she's lonely, eh?" The younger guard grinned. "With a fat husband who cannot satisfy her like Meeshok of Sabadou."

"Hope for her sake you handle your rod better than your sword, boy," the first one said.

"Twice as good," the second, Meeshok, said, still grinning. "Ask your sister, eh?"

Omera ignored their banter, keeping his eyes focused on the woman while one hand slipped down to his pack. He'd been a fool to stow his blade. At least he'd kept his herb pouches fastened to his belt. A dab of *tisa irinti* calmed his nerves as his other hand unfastened the stays. He was the weary traveler, stopped for food and fresh canteens before the long journey west. Nothing more than the twenty or so others who had come here for a midday meal.

The woman's gaze shifted back to the commons after exchanging words with the kitchen-master. She scanned the room with precision, pausing as though she took the time to memorize every face. He took a bite of his fish when she came to him, relying on *tisa irinti* to keep his pulse calm. He'd found his sword, the hilt now sticking up at the top of his pack. Easy to draw if he needed to. Her eyes bored through him as he chewed. She lingered on him, longer than she'd spent on the others, and she frowned, pushing his heart to surge even with the herbs calming his blood.

He could announce what she was, and send the room into a panic. Some might have guessed already, though their fears wouldn't settle until after she was gone. Seers, they were called in some cities. The Queen's Hand in others. Mindhunters, in the sorts of tales that spread in the aftermath of what they could do. Scores of princes controlled cities in their mother's name, throughout the Bhakal Empire. The Mindhunters controlled the princes, wielding slivers of his mother's magic to keep them bent to her will. His mother's personal agents should have found no fault with his passage through Domakar. But the Queen had told him to trust no one. "No one" would include even the agents of her Hand.

"I told you, eh, Orbon?" the caravan guard Meeshok said, rising from his seat as the woman drew close to their table. "She is come for love, and like to find it here. Come, pretty lady, let Meeshok of Sabadou show you—"

Meeshok froze midsentence, hovering halfway between sitting and standing, his arm extended in a gesture to invite the woman to sit.

Tisa irinti burned in his veins, keeping his nerves calm and cool.

The woman stopped across the table in front of him, her eyes still focused on his. The rest of the room fell silent.

"Prince Omera," she said. "I am called Jahi, a servant of the Queen. You will come with me."

He held her gaze.

His mother had done something to him, in their last meeting in Abakra. A shield, she'd called it. A shield against the sort of Mindhunter magic that would otherwise have had him blubbering and falling over himself to comply with a Hand agent's order. The Queen also gave him a charge: reach Konghom.

Kill her sister, Sakhefete, before the Empire could be plunged into chaos. Let nothing stand between him and the fulfillment of her command.

His hand gripped his sword from within his pack. The Mindhunter's eyes widened. Then the room erupted into madness.

He drew his *shotel*, his other hand dabbing a pinch of *ubax aragti* from his belt pouch and smearing it across his gums. Instinct told him to spin and parry as he drew the blade; he followed his training without question.

A clang of metal sounded where his head had been. The first caravan guard, Orbon, had slashed without warning from his seat, rising and drawing as fast as Omera could without his herbs. The second, Meeshok, roared and drew his blade, too, suddenly unfrozen and fighting for his new mistress as though he'd been in her service all along. Four more men drew blades in unison from across the common room, directed by the same call stirring in their minds. This was the dread Mindhunter magic, a pale echo of his mother the Queen's power, but no less fearsome for it: domination of the will, to make ordinary people dance like marionettes to the will of their puppetmaster. The rest of the travelers in the common room rose quietly, all directed by the same mind, as though they were a procession filing away from a prayer service, and not a room full of travelers suddenly plunged into the heart of a mêlée.

He jumped backward as Meeshok swung a sword in a two-handed grip, smashing his fish and rice as the plate split atop the table. Orbon followed in a cautious stance, holding back with a veteran's instincts for defense. With *ubax aragti* igniting as it spread through Omera's veins, neither swordsman could match him. But he had to be decisive and quick, or the four other swords now approaching would entrap him before he could break away.

He feinted into Meeshok's reach before shifting his feet and lunging at Orbon. The elder sellsword already had his blade set for a parry, clanging the two swords together. But *ubax aragti* gave him speed unmatched by any man. He turned the elder's blade and struck again, landing a deep cut into the sellsword's upper torso. Orbon went down in a heap, crashing forward with the momentum of Omera ripping his *shotel* free from the older man's flesh.

Meeshok was already on him, swinging wildly, and two of the newcomers advanced from either side. He'd be cut off if he didn't commit to a move. The Mindhunter herself drew back, hovering near the beaded doorway. She'd sent the remaining two of her thralls to block the way back to the kitchens, where the stables offered a second exit behind the cookfires and pots of rice. A numbers game, then, and the Mindhunter appeared to be armed only with a belt knife, whereas the other thralls carried curved long swords in the western

Imperial style. He slashed the air to his left to force Meeshok and the other thrall away, then ran for the beaded door.

The rest of her thralls converged as soon as he moved. He upended a table to block the ones behind him, clattering porcelain, brass, rice, and tomatoes to the floor. One of the men reached him with an overhand swing; he parried it and whipped his sword into the man's gut in a spray of blood. The body crumpling to the ground bought him space, and he took it, racing for the exit. The Mindhunter stared at him, brandishing her dagger as an afterthought, as though her eyes were her true weapon, and perhaps they were. He danced around her as her thralls leapt over the obstacles he'd set in their way, and made it through the beads.

A canvas awning stretched over top of the exit, and he was on the street. Left would take him inward, toward the city center. Right was toward the gates. A nagging thought made him hesitate: He still needed supplies, and he'd left his pack behind with his meal. His steps carried him away from the hostel, but he glanced left as the Mindhunter and her three remaining thralls emerged onto the street behind him.

He took an alleyway heading deeper into the city. Domakar was full of life today, as merchants prepared to make their final crossings before the open sands turned murderous with the summer heat. Camels, goats, and sheep filled the streets as much as people stopped to trade, gossip, run their errands, or see to their goods. He raced around a pair of women stopped to chat in front of a doorway, avoiding a child playing in the alley with a wooden horse. He could turn to the right where the alley met the street, then double back as he crossed between more buildings, hopefully evading the Mindhunter without the need to spill any more—

Without warning two men stepped into the alley. Neither was armed, and both had glassed-over eyes as they stared at him, their bodies blocking the way. He collided into them, and they grappled and clung to his clothing as all three went down in a heap.

Screams echoed from nearby, and he shoved the two men as they tried to grab hold of his chest and legs. A rush of footsteps sounded as the people on the street ahead pushed to get away from the commotion. More footsteps echoed from the alley behind. The Mindhunter, and her thralls. He still held his *shotel*, but disdained the thought of using it on unarmed men. Then again, her first thralls carried swords, and who could say how many more she would snare to slow him down.

"Stop," the Mindhunter, Jahi, said. "Prince Omera. Don't. There's no need for further violence. Let these men live."

He hesitated. A moment longer than he should have done; even with *ubax aragti*, one of his attackers grabbed hold of his hand, wrenching his sword free to clatter into the alley.

"Rise, Your Highness," Jahi said. "And please, do not run."

Without a verbal command her thralls let go of his limbs at the same moment, though both men moved to block the alley from the street. The other three, Meeshok and two other swordsmen, trotted to a halt in unison behind her, their weapons still drawn.

"Two men died for you," he said, finding venom in the words. Mindhunter magic was a thing all men feared, rare as they were.

"It was your blade that took their lives," Jahi said. "I ordered you to follow, not to fight."

"Why?" he asked, craning to see the street. His scuffle with her thralls would account for a few shouts, maybe a few hurried footsteps as onlookers rushed to get out of the way, but the commotion hadn't abated. This was more. Shouts and screams rose, and footsteps, too. It drew his attention, even with her two thralls blocking the way.

"One of my sisters shielded you," Jahi said. "Why? Are you under her protection? Why have you come to Domakar?"

"I meant to be gone by tomorrow," he said. "Bad luck, for you to find me when you did."

"And I take it you are unaware of your mother the Queen's decree?" Jahi said.

"What decree?" he asked. By now he could see something in the distance, at the far end of the street. Something moving together, almost like...

"For all princes to submit themselves to the nearest of my sisters at once," Jahi said. "For safekeeping and protection. Not a thing my order takes lightly. For Her Majesty to give such a command, high treason must be suspected, yes? So you can understand why you were apprehended."

He hardly heard.

At the end of the street, marching toward the city center, a foreign army raised its banner.

Rows of soldiers in gray paneled armor unlike anything he'd seen in New Sarresant, unlike anything used by soldiers of the Bhakal. They carried spears and primitive firing tubes, some with what looked like crossbows slung at their hips.

"Treason," he said. "How are they here, within the city walls?"

"Yes, treason," Jahi repeated. "One, or more, of your brothers and the Queen directed us to—"

"No," he interrupted. "Them."

By now the foreign soldiers were within a stone's throw of the alley's entrance, marching up the street. Jahi looked at him warily, and suddenly two of her thralls moved closer to him, both with swords drawn to check any movement he might make toward their mistress. She stepped to the corner to look, and her eyes went wide.

"This is your doing," he said. "This is why you came for me."

"You accuse the Queen's Hand?" Jahi said. "When Her Majesty's own command has us looking to you, and your brothers?"

"No," he said. "No time for this." His mother's words repeated in his head: *Reach my sister. Kill her. Trust no one.* He knelt to fetch his sword, sheathing it in a swift motion, bolstered by the herbs coursing through his veins.

"Prince Omera," Jahi said. "You must come with me. If your mother suspects treason, and there are foreign soldiers within Domakar's walls, I cannot allow you to wander free."

To punctuate her words, all three of her armed thralls leveled their swords toward him at once. The *thrum* of soldiers marching up the street grew louder.

He whirled to face her. No time.

"My mother," he said. "The Queen herself."

"What?" the Mindhunter said. "What of Her Majesty?" Signs of fear now showed on her face. The foreign soldiers would arrive at the alley's entrance any moment.

"That's who shielded my mind," he said. "She bade me act on her personal orders. She saw...whatever this is...she saw it coming. Now either you get out of my way and let me flee this city or you come with me."

He didn't wait for her to decide. *Ubax aragti* would give him speed enough to draw and parry any attacks from her thralls. He ran back the way he'd come, praying there wouldn't be a second column of foreigners marching up the hostel's street to meet them.

Jahi uttered a curse, and suddenly six pairs of footsteps sounded, all five of her thralls running as fast as she could push them. His nerves remained on a razor edge until the sounds of their swords being sheathed echoed from the walls, and then they only dimmed to a knifepoint. This had to be what he'd been sent to stop. A foreign army on Bhakal soil, and his mother's sister at the heart of it. And now he had a Mindhunter and five thralls for traveling companions, when the Queen had bidden him to travel alone, and trust no one but himself.

A fine mess. But for now he had to escape the city, and reach Konghom. He could worry over the Mindhunter once the sands and the city were behind him.

26

YULI

Sarine coughed, sagging almost to her knees before Yuli tightened her grip on her sister's hand. The trip from the hunting lodge to the Gods' Seat was never more than an eyeblink for her, but Sarine carried it harder. She made sure they both had steady footing before she let go.

"What is this place?" Reed asked. Her eyes were wide. "Are those...dead bodies?"

Yuli turned to look where Reed was facing, and her stomach lurched. They'd arrived in the map room, as she'd expected, with the strange, crude paintings that seemed to be hand-drawn on the walls and the twisted metal sculptures arranged across the floor, but her attention was focused where Reed had put it. Five corpses lay slumped between the sculptures' stands, scattered around the room. Three men, two women. All wearing Sarresanter clothes.

She went to them, while the Twin Fangs' senses projected its awareness outward through the halls. She turned one over, met with dried, taut skin and open, glassed-over, dead eyes. She moved to the next and found the same. Open eyes, almost peaceful, their jaws slack and their skin dead and gray. She closed both, pressing her fingertips to the eyelids.

"No sign of fighting," she said, moving to the third. "No blood."

"This was Erris's map team," Sarine said. "All five. I brought them here, not a few weeks ago."

"Well, now they're dead," Reed said. "Dead like the people in the city. Where in fuck did you take me? What is this? How are we even here?"

Yuli ignored them while Sarine tried to explain Dragon magic and the Gods' Seat and whatever else to calm the street girl's nerves. The Twin Fangs' senses resonated through the halls, attuned by the sight of death. It had no desire to taste these ones' flesh. They'd been dead too long, long enough for their hearts to have tightened, all the blood in their veins turned slow and thick. The Twin Fangs was no carrion-eater, even in the direst of times. But it knew these halls. Knew this place. Something had changed, like the scent of a den after a predator had found it and cleared away the pack's young. Yuli knelt quietly over the dead, and the Twin Fangs listened and felt the change on the air.

"He was here," she said after the Twin Fangs was sure.

Reed had gone sullen and silent, listening to Sarine's explanations, but Yuli's words stopped her sister midsentence.

"Yuli?" Sarine said. "What do you mean, 'he was here'?"

"The Regnant," she said. "It's the same smells as it was in the city. Reed was right—the Empress's people died the same way the people of New Sarresant did. But the Twin Fangs doesn't scent any danger now. He was here, but now he's gone."

"I didn't think he could come here," Sarine said quietly. "I didn't know, or I'd never have brought Erris's people."

"They knew what they were doing," Yuli said. "They served the Empress, in their way."

Sarine turned away, her face full of grief. Yuli finished closing all five pairs of eyelids. Without dirt for a proper burial she could do no more. Perhaps they'd take the bodies when they left.

"Let's head to the Soul," Sarine said. "I need to make sure...I don't feel anything different, but if the Regnant was here, he might have done something."

Yuli nodded, taking the lead. Reed trotted behind, wearing an empty, angry expression.

The halls were the same cold stone. Nothing else had changed, so far as she could see, until they passed by the residence halls, where her and Tigai's and Erris's rooms had been. The décor that had adorned the walls was missing. Outside Tigai's room there had been plinths with Jun sculptures; outside hers, woven rugs and furs in the Natarii style. Now the walls were bare.

"Hold here," she said when they reached the door to her chamber. She pushed it open slowly, cautiously. "It's gone. Changed."

"Your furniture?" Sarine said, and she nodded. New designs had replaced the traditional Natarii furnishings she'd had before. She'd never asked for any of them; whatever forces controlled this place had seemingly plucked the decorations from her mind. Now it was bare, replaced by simple, utilitarian furnishings without style or ornamentation.

"What does this mean?" she asked. "Is it only that we've left the Seat?"

"I don't know," Sarine said. "It might be no more than that. I'd be more worried if the rooms had changed to the Regnant's style, or to his champions'. Maybe this is only the Watcher preparing for whatever comes next."

"What's a Watcher?" Reed asked.

"The caretaker of this place," Sarine replied. "I don't sense him nearby, but I have to hope this is his work. Let's continue toward the Soul?"

Yuli nodded, resuming her place at their head. Nothing else had changed about the Seat, but she felt uneasy now. Always before there had been a place for her here, a place deliberately designed to feel like home when so little else had since Isaru Mattai had first come to Tiansei. To have it stripped away made the Seat's already foreign chambers feel all the more distant. And if the Soul itself had been touched, or changed...

They continued inward, spiraling through smooth stone passageways wide enough for all three of them to walk abreast.

As it had been before, the central chamber of the Gods' Seat was a massive, circular room, dominated by a pillar of light burning at its center. So far as she could tell, the light itself remained as it had been, a stream of pure white energy running from floor to ceiling, both cut away from its edge. The rest of the room was the same polished, smooth stone as the passageways, precisely as it had been the first time she'd come here, before Sarine had touched the column of light and melted half the room to slag and jagged stone. All that damage seemed to have been erased, leaving the room quiet and calm, filled with a soft, flickering light emanating from the pillar at its heart.

"The chamber's been repaired," Sarine said, walking slowly toward the light. "But I don't...I'm not sure..."

Yuli reached to stop Reed from following Sarine. The last time they'd used this chamber the light had exploded, burning and twisting the now-repaired stone. Better if they stayed back and let her sister work alone.

"What *is* this place?" Reed asked.

"The Soul of the World," Yuli replied. "The heart of everything. A dangerous, and powerful place."

"And you're scared the old man, the one who murdered Reyne d'Agarre, he came here?" Reed asked.

"He's called the Regnant, and yes," she said. "He did. We aren't sure why. This is what he and Sarine are fighting over: control over this place. It means control over the world."

Sarine had almost reached the light, walking in a daze, staring through the column as though her eyes saw past it.

"It looks the same," Sarine called out. "But I'm not sure I would know if he touched it, if he did something."

"Control over the whole bloody world?" Reed asked. "Who's going to do what you say because you own a stupid light?"

"There's more to the world than the people in it," Yuli said. "The Soul gives you the power to make the world what it is. Sarine has control now, so the world is green and full of light. The Regnant wants to blacken the skies, to spread poison and drive people underground to hide."

"That seems like a bloody stupid thing to do with the world," Reed said. "Why would he do that?"

Sarine raised a hand, almost brushing against the column. Yuli stepped back, ready to flee into the halls. Then Sarine's hand jerked to a halt, almost like something grabbed hold of her wrist. The Watcher.

He doesn't want you to touch the light, a voice thought into her mind. Anati, Sarine's *kaas*.

"I wondered where he was hiding," Sarine said. "Ask him whether he stopped the Regnant like he just stopped me."

"Ask him what he did to my couches," Yuli said.

He says the Regnant never left the map room, Anati thought to them.

Sarine and Yuli exchanged a look across the chamber. The silhouetted man-shape of the Watcher burned against the backdrop of the Soul's light, imposing itself between Sarine and the column.

"If the Regnant never left the map room, then he came here to kill the Empress's scouts," Yuli said. "And maybe to scout us in return."

He doesn't like that you're here, Anati thought. *He keeps saying "It isn't time," and that you "don't have all the keys." I'm not sure what he means.*

"Let's go back," Sarine said. "Anati, can you ask the Watcher if what Yuli said is true? Did he see what the Regnant did with the maps?"

Yuli wheeled around, retracing their steps. She'd never been comfortable with the Watcher, though the Twin Fangs didn't seem to mind the creature's presence. Relief enough if Sarine couldn't detect any changes to the Soul. They'd come here looking for answers as to the Regnant's next steps after the battle at New Sarresant. Maybe there was a clue with the map, though Sarine had already studied it at length, and Erris, too. It showed a view of each champion, on either side. The Empress had hoped she could use it to find the Regnant's people, to lead them to their enemies. Frightening, to think it might work for the Regnant in reverse.

They came here, killed Erris's people, and left, Anati thought. *He says they talked about "promises" and something called "reconstruction," but I don't know what that is.*

"Wait," Sarine said as they walked the halls. "Who is 'they'?"

Silence held as the *kaas* put the question to the silhouette walking beside them. They retraced their steps past the now-redecorated residence chambers, back toward the maps.

The Regnant for sure, Anati thought. *He called the other "the Queen."*

"Wasn't the Veil the Queen?" Yuli asked. "And you killed her, in Lin Qishan's body. Maybe they came before Gantar Baat?"

"I don't think so," Sarine said. "Erris would have noticed her *Need* connections missing for that long. At least I think she would."

They reached the map room, with the five dead bodies still lying on the floor, their eyes gently shut in a more peaceful facsimile of sleep.

"So we know the Regnant is working with someone else," Sarine said. "That's progress."

Yuli went to the altar, stepping gently around the dead as she crossed the room. "What if this 'Queen' is one of his champions?" she asked. "That might be why he came and killed the Empress's scouts. They were traveling together, and he didn't want us to be able to watch his movements."

"That makes sense," Sarine said. "Try the map while I question the Watcher further?"

She nodded, stepping to the altar's sides and bracing herself against the stone. The map was as fluid and beautiful as it had ever been, a lush, green-and-blue depiction of the entire world, as though they were looking down on it in perfectly replicated miniature. Even the clouds floated over top of the rugged contours of forests, mountains, hills, jungles, and plains. Six great land masses spread out across its surface: the sprawling, jungle- and desert-covered continent of the Jun; the jagged coasts and fjords of what Sarine referred to as the Old World; the Bhakal lands, largest of the six, split down the middle by where the Divide had once stood; the thickly forested New World, where New Sarresant stood on the eastern shore; a southern continent underneath the New World, unnamed and so far as she knew undiscovered by Sarine's people; and finally an overgrown island south of the Jun Empire, joined by a long archipelago of what looked like thousands of tiny islands jutting out from the eastern sea.

Framing the map were the lights, five on the western edge and eight to the east. One of the five was dark: That had to represent Reyne d'Agarre, slain by the Regnant's hand. But her attention turned to the east, where seven of the eight lights shone brightly and one was dead and dark. That had to be the Crane swordsman they'd killed in their coastal ambush. No way to be certain which of the Regnant's champions remained, between the Great and Noble Houses of the Jun: Ox, Crab, Heron, Mantis, Owl. Perhaps Dragon, if the Regnant and Sarine could both bind champions of the same line. The last remained a mystery.

She focused on one of the eastern lights, and let herself be drawn in.

She was looking down on a military camp. Three soldiers stood around a table with a paper map unrolled atop it, each nodding along as the man at their center gave orders. She recognized the maps: They depicted the contours of the forests, rivers, and hills around New Sarresant, for all the surrounding vegetation suggested this camp was somewhere deep in the jungle.

Her view shifted as the man strode around the table, gesturing as though to make a point. She got a clear look at his face.

"Impossible," she said. "That's…" The name died on her tongue as she stared. The man who'd come to Tiansei, who'd beguiled her father into swearing her into a foreigner's service. The man who had led her and fifty others through the Divide, promising dreams of fulfillment in service to a greater lord. The man Tigai had taken away and abandoned in the middle of a desert, left to die without water or shade.

"Yuli?" Sarine asked. "Do you see something you recognize?"

She stared a moment longer.

"Isaru," she said at last. "Isaru Mattai. He lives, and I think he's at the Jun high command. I think he has command of her armies in the New World."

"Wasn't Isaru the rebel leader? The man Tigai killed?"

"The man Tigai stranded in the desert, yes," she replied. "He should have been dead. Sister, this is unmistakable. He must be one of the Regnant's champions. And if we knew where their high command was located, we could strike him today."

"That's news at least," Sarine said. "I can pass word to Erris when we get back."

"I don't understand this," she said. "It can't be this easy to find his champions using the map. Why hasn't the Regnant struck at all of us if he could come here? We've hardly bothered to hide at all, using the hunting lodge as our gathering place. Surely he could find us if he wanted to."

"I've tried to look in on champions before," Sarine said. "I think you got lucky. Most of the time I saw nothing I recognized—trees, sometimes buildings or houses. And Erris had her people here, experts in architecture, geography, natural science. If there were something to find, they'd have found it."

"The Empress's people are dead," she said. "The Regnant killed them, precisely to stop them from using the maps."

"So what are you saying?" Sarine said. "If he could find us anytime he wants to, then—"

Then he doesn't want to find you, Anati finished for her. *He wants something else.*

Yuli let the map's focus fade, getting a last lingering look at Isaru Mattai as he gave commands to the assembled officers.

"Something else..." Sarine said. "What? What does the Watcher think? Did the Regnant use the maps at all, when he came here?"

Anati's words echoed in her ears as Sarine continued asking questions. Something else. The Twin Fangs stirred within her. It felt vulnerable, like prey caught in open grass. The map device was too simple; they should have been able to find every enemy champion as soon as they stepped out of hiding. But the thing had always existed, hadn't it? It meant the Regnant and Veil could have interceded to kill the other's champions a thousand times before. Her memory flashed back to Sarine's insistence over the past weeks that Regnant and Veil were allies. Here was proof. And now, with Sarine playing the Veil's part, the Regnant's goals had changed. The champions were no more than a distraction.

She braced herself against the map device as her mind worked the problem.

There had to be a reason. He came here to stop the Empress from using the map device to scout his champions; that was enough to confirm their first thoughts, that killing the champions was still a point of vulnerability for them both. But if he didn't try to strike at Sarine's champions, it meant either he feared them or he wanted them alive. He wanted to keep this conflict going. But to what end?

Her gaze shifted across the contours of the map. Then one of the eastern lights flashed, and she was drawn in.

She hadn't meant to stare too long. Her senses followed the familiar lurch, plummeting into the map's scenery, but she could break them again as easily by moving away from the altar. She prepared to, then froze as her vision cleared.

She was in a city. No, not a city; *her* city. She knew these streets, knew the hexagonal architecture, the thatched roofs burning plumes of smoke through their chimneys even while summer heat gripped the southern parts of the world.

The map's vision focused on a single shape amid the familiar buildings and streets.

A woman, but not a woman, just as she was Yuli and the Twin Fangs together, separate and one. One of the Clan Gorin forms, not the more familiar Hoskar: a creature of shadow, human-shaped, but with wisps of black rising from its skin. It stood on Tiansei's market street, shouting something, though she had no ears here, and saw only motion without sound. The Gorin warrior's stance suggested she was bellowing whatever was said, delivering a proclamation meant to be heard many streets away.

She wrenched her vision back, panning her view above the market square, and almost gagged.

Ten armspans from where the shadow-woman made her speech a cart had been overturned, spilling apples across the street. Two oxen were dead, leaking blood across the fruit. A man lay dead between them, and a woman, and a small boy, their bodies cut with long, deep gashes. Five armspans from them four more bodies lay together. Two spans from that, the upper half of another man lay twisted around a street-pole. At the mouth of the street a city watchman knelt, holding his own entrails into his stomach as he made quiet sobs she couldn't hear.

She refocused back to the Gorin warrior, zooming her vision in as tight as it had been before.

Mileva, that was her name. The woman who bore the Far Sight form, as Yuli bore the Twin Fangs. Mileva Far Sight Clan Gorin.

The Twin Fangs smoldered its anger, growing its claws. The map-vision wasn't real, wasn't truly here in the map room, but the Twin Fangs could mourn the Far Sight's victims with rage. It gripped the sides of the altar as it changed, scratching fissures in the stone. Yuli had never met Mileva; encounters between the clans' warriors too often ended in blood. This one would. If their warrior acted with the Gorin chief's blessing, the Twin Fangs would return the horror a dozenfold, running to Askara's gates as soon as Mileva Far Sight's body was cold. If not, well, that would be a matter for Yuli to decide. Vengeance belonged to both, but each half knew which was best suited for killing, and which for speech.

"Yuli?"

Sarine's voice. Sister, not prey.

Yuli resumed control of their body, feeling her heart quickening along with her breath.

"Yuli, what's wrong?" Sarine asked. "What did you see?"

"Sister," Yuli said. Her own voice felt almost foreign in her ears. She expected to hear the Twin Fangs' growl and snarl. "We must go to Tiansei at once."

"The Hoskar city, right?" Sarine said. "Why? Did you see something through the map?"

"One of his champions," she said. "There. Now. Killing my people."

Sarine's expression softened, then hardened again.

The shimmering man-shape beside her seemed to grab hold of Sarine's upper arm while shaking its head.

He doesn't want you to go, Anati thought to them. *He says you need to focus on the "keys," not... not what he calls "chasing a shadow." I'm not sure I understood that part.*

The Twin Fangs understood enough. The shimmering man-shape stood in its way. A growl built in Yuli's throat as the Twin Fangs hovered on the edge of control.

"No," Sarine said. "No, of course not. We're not staying here while Yuli's people are dying. Stand close, all of you."

He says it's a mistake to go, Anati thought.

"I don't care," Sarine said.

The Twin Fangs' rage cooled, turning to ice as Yuli moved them closer to her sister. Sarine understood. Its legs seethed with energy, ready to run toward the market square, wherever her sister's Dragon gift put them. Then, without further warning the stone vanished, and they were standing in a forest, surrounded by trees still dusted with late-season snow. She knew this place. Outside Tiansei. Her place. Her home.

The Twin Fangs seized control, and Yuli gave it, and they ran.

27

TIGAI

A Storage Tent
Silver Beetles Encampment

He clamped a hand over the quartermaster's mouth as Kitian's knife did its work. The man writhed, his eyes wide as the realization set in. Never a pleasant thing to see. It still gave him nightmares, some nights, remembering the faces of the dead, however sweet the spoils or necessary the cause.

He kept his hand in place during the final spasms, pressed tight enough to suffocate any screams. There weren't any; Kitian had aimed her blade true, angling the strike upward through the lungs into the heart. Blood bubbled up through Tigai's fingers, but he didn't let go until the man's eyes were full white and the tent had fallen silent. The camp around them stirred, but they should have a few hours, wind spirits willing, undisturbed. By the time the twilight shift of logistics officers came to take the dead man's place he and Kitian would be long gone, one step closer to finding the location of the Jun high command as they traced the patterns of the Dragons' strands.

"Is it safe?" Kitian asked in a low voice.

He went to the tent flaps in response, poking his head out to quickly survey the camp. They were directly across from the tent marked for the Dragons' use—kept permanently empty, to avoid any accidents when the *magi* made their arrivals. Lucky. He'd tethered his strands almost exactly matching the ones the most recent Dragon detachment had used, only slightly offset to avoid actually appearing in the same room with them. It had put them here, in this quartermaster's tent, more unlucky for the poor fool who'd been assigned to work it. More than once he'd tried the trick and ended up in plain view of dozens of Jun soldiers; those were hasty aborts, retreating back across the strands quick enough to leave the soldiers wondering whether they had actually seen what they saw. This one was more promising.

"It's clear," he said, hastily grabbing the ropes tied to either tent flap and beginning a knot to close the tent to outsiders. "Clear, and I have a damned good feeling this is the one. They have to report back eventually."

Kitian said nothing in response. Her skin was already melting into deep crimson sludge. He averted his eyes, though he couldn't block out the sound, or the smell. A gut-churning squelch echoed through the tent, blessedly quiet enough not to carry through the open ground. Better if he hadn't watched it with rapt fascination the first time, for his mind to put imagery to the noise. The Blood Claw manifest to consume the body of the slain quartermaster, like raspberry jelly smothered over flesh, dissolving it into the same putrid, gelatinous bile.

He kept his eyes turned outside the flaps. Across the clearing the Dragons were exiting their arrival tent in no particular haste, greeted by salutes of officers wearing the sigil of the Company of the Silver Beetles. He cataloged the position in his mind. Erris d'Arrent's scouts had good maps of the Jun companies situated along the New Sarresant front, and spread out westward across half the continent besides. If they were with the Silver Beetles they were in territory she'd marked *Erhapi Country*, a considerable march from any of Empress d'Arrent's soldiers. Not that it mattered, with the Dragons' gift. Their high command could be in the bloody jungles of the southern Empire, which might serve to explain why the Empress's scouts hadn't been able to find it.

One of the Dragons glanced toward him as he worked the ropes, and he suppressed the instinct to flinch. They'd already procured Jun soldiers' uniforms. Even if he dared not risk another open infiltration after what he'd managed in Gantar Baat, unless the Dragon-*magi* had an unnatural memory for faces and an unnatural paranoia to go with it, he should appear to be no more than an ordinary quartermaster. The Dragon looked away as calmly as he'd glanced over. Tigai's heart still thundered, though he maintained the outward appearance of calmness as he finished the knot, looked once more over the Dragon detachment making its way into the camp, and ducked back inside.

A hissing burp announced Kitian was finished with the body. He winced again. The Blood Claw's work was even less pleasant than seeing the faces of the dead.

"Seven trips now, yes?" Kitian asked, her voice sliding between a metallic scrape and her normal tones as her body shifted back to her Natarii self. "They work their *magi* hard."

"Seven that we've been able to follow," he said. "More, if you count the false starts."

"More than they should be able to manage, no? Isn't that what you said?"

"And they're still not done, unless they don't mean to report to high command," he said. "Yes. I think we may have found..." He quieted his voice by instinct, for all the good it would do if they were being overheard. "A champion. Like me. One who can use the strands at will, without tiring."

Kitian's eyes gleamed. Enough of the Blood Claw remained to have her skin flushed a deep crimson red. Not for the first time he wished Yuli had accompanied him on these trips, rather than her sister. There was something in Kitian's eyes, even after she left the Blood Claw form behind, that looked at him like he was food.

"It speaks well to your discipline, lordling," Kitian said.

"What does?"

"That you keep to your orders," she replied. "In the face of your enemy, so close at hand. I'd be tempted to strike as soon as I sighted the prey."

"If I did that, their Dragons wouldn't go anywhere near high command without a twenty-*magi* escort. They still might not. There will be time enough to plan an attack once we have a target worth attacking."

"As I said, it speaks well of you," Kitian said. "And so will I, when my sister asks. I like your bottom, too, though that much is obvious to anyone with eyes."

This time it was his skin that flushed. Kitian only grinned as she nudged him back from the tent entrance.

"I have the watch, lordling," she said. "I'll shake you if anyone comes."

He nodded and withdrew deeper into the tent, between a row of sealed crates and a barrel of lamp oil. For this to work, he had to keep his eyes shut tight, focused entirely on the starfield, ready to cinch a tether with no more notice than a glimmer of light as the Dragons tethered themselves away. Sitting in an empty tent with his eyes squeezed shut meant an easy mark, if someone stumbled in, hence the need for an escort. Again he wished it had been Yuli.

The starfield around the Silver Beetle camp was as empty and desolate as the flat plain they were camped on. Even the star they'd used to travel here was flimsy at best, a dim, sickly thing made of strand connections only beginning to coalesce into something more permanent. Concentrating on the lines connecting to it, he could feel the thousand or so soldiers in the Beetles' camp, their connections to each other growing stronger every day they spent here. He could also trace the lines connecting eastward, the four Dragons' links to the star they'd left at the Jade Scorpion camp, several weeks' journey into Lakotai land, as it was marked on Empress d'Arrent's maps. He'd done a damned fine job masking his and Kitian's arrival. Their strands were barely detectable, only a faint, reverberating echo between the connections he'd used and the ones the Dragons had. A risky thing, but so far it had worked.

Another jump, perhaps two, and the Dragons would surely go home to roost. Erris d'Arrent had impressed on him already the necessity of reaching the Jun high command. Gathering intelligence there would be well worth the risks, and she'd doubly impressed on him the need to find out who had taken command, now that the Red Lady was dead. He didn't fully understand her need to know her enemy, by name or by reputation, but then, she was the strategist. He was a scout, and he meant to do his duty.

Time seemed to slow as he studied the strands, waiting. No way to know how quickly the Dragons would finish their business here, and depart. But if he wanted to mask their arrivals at the next star, he had to stay on edge, studying the stars for the first signs of new light.

In between bouts of renewed focus on the strands, he missed Yuli. Kitian had said he had a fine bottom; well, Yuli's was twice as fine. He could almost see echoes of her naked body as he studied the starfield. She was taut, more than any woman he'd ever shared a bed with, her muscles firm and hard and lean, but with a tenderness that was still delicate and soft. There was more to her than nakedness, too. She had a fire that reminded him of Mei, the same brazen courage that took action for granted when it was time to act. He could let all his masks vanish when they were together. He wasn't sure what more to make of it, only that she was comfortable, and he wished she were here.

"They're gathering, lordling." Kitian's voice broke through his reverie.

He blinked to clear his sight. "At the marked tent? How many?"

"Nine," Kitian said. "Our four Dragons, plus two more in robes and three without."

"Keep close," he said. This was it. Lucky for him they bothered to gather at the tent they'd marked for travel.

He pressed his eyes shut again, and once more the strands danced to life. Watching so close, and knowing what to expect, made the moment clear as fresh-blown glass.

The star here flickered.

Another would match it, at their destination, though he had no way of knowing yet where that would be. Suddenly a knot of strands twisted out of place. Nine threads picked loose from the tapestry being woven by the Silver Beetles here, growing as they stretched away from the star. Westward. They grew and lengthened, strings stretched taut across a vast, empty space. He traced the lines as fast as he could manage. Losing the threads here meant another day spent like this, starting over and risking being found.

There.

Far, far to the west. The nine threads snapped into place and he mirrored them, placing strands exactly on top of them. Traveling so far meant he had to be precise beyond measure. A slight reverberation was necessary, to keep them from appearing in the same room. But over so vast a distance too great a flutter could put them a hundred leagues away.

He snapped it into place, and the air changed. The late hours before nightfall gave way to dusk. Chirping birds, buzzing insects, and a faint smell of smoke cut through air so humid it thickened in his lungs. He knew before opening his eyes: This was a jungle. A Jun jungle, on the far side of the world.

Kitian was already signaling for quiet, her skin changing to the twisted red of the Blood Claw's form.

He'd hit the mark exactly. Seven thousand leagues and he'd put them on the exact outskirts of the camp. Less than a stone's throw away a perimeter sentry walked between a row of box-shaped tents. No signs of horse-lines or wagons, but that stood to reason: A secret camp supplied by Dragons had no need for other connections to the outside world. High command. They'd found it, and he had no one but Kitian and his ancestors to watch and give him praise.

He stayed in place, ducking beneath the cover of thick overgrowth, waiting for Kitian to do her work. A trickle of blood running toward the sentry would be the man's only warning. By the time the blood touched the sentry's leg it was too late for him. In a rush Kitian's Blood Claw form would run viscous liquid up his body, pouring into his open mouth and lungs, snuffing out any chance to raise an alarm.

The sentry collapsed into Kitian's arms; as quick as she'd inserted her bloody tendrils into his mouth she re-formed behind him, catching his body as it fell without a sound.

That was his signal to follow. He stayed low, fresh tethers ready around his and Kitian's forms, even as she skulked—or no, *flowed*—deeper into the camp.

Another sentry met the same fate as the first, but this time Kitian gestured for him to catch up before she continued on. They were already near the heart of the camp, judging by the density of tents and the buzz of messengers weaving between them. A few outlying sentries served at the edges, but if he knew Jun military doctrines—and he did, well enough—the camp would be organized around a single beating heart, with a minimum of wasted space or inefficiency. They were close. But he still had to reach the central tents, and get inside.

"What do you want to do, lordling?" Kitian asked in her metallic half–Blood Claw voice. "Stealth won't serve us any further."

"Risky, to try and talk my way in," he said. "We have to get to where their orders are written, but in a camp this isolated, they'll recognize an unfamiliar face."

Kitian nodded, too sure of herself by half.

"Wait," he said. "What are you going to do?"

"I'll circle around," she said. "Meet me back where we arrived. Two minutes' time enough?"

"Hold on," he said. "What if they have Herons, or Owls? There's no way to know if you're—"

"Leave me to me," Kitian said. "Two minutes. As of now."

He cursed. Kitian was already gone.

In an eyeblink her body was fully transformed into the Blood Claw again, and this time she made no pretense of moving as a trickle of running red. She crashed forward, through a rope-line hung with officers' laundry, to where a pair of messengers stood gawking at her sudden rushing approach. Bars of viscous, sinewy liquid shot out from her limbs and took both of them in the chest, spraying what had been their torsos across the tent canvas in a shower of blood.

Shouts of alarm went up. Drawn steel echoed through the tents as Kitian surged deeper into the camp, quickly out of sight. He cursed again, and moved.

Most reacted to the shouted alarms with discipline, readying weapons and moving toward where the cries were going up. But the two sentries ahead of him stood their ground, perhaps out of fear, or uncertainty, or perhaps duty-bound to guard the ring of tents at the camp's center.

He fell without thinking into the relaxed-but-harried gait of someone important, taking charge during the crisis. They'd know him for an impostor as soon as they saw his face. With good luck, that would be enough.

"Guardsmen," he barked in his best commander's voice, gesturing toward the sound of Kitian turning anything she touched into blood-splatters in the dirt. "Ready arms! With me! We're under attack!"

Both sentries responded to his order as one, without thinking. Good training. Good men. Their poleaxes dipped to a ready stance as they fell in toward him. One of them had enough warning to furrow an eyebrow as he set eyes on Tigai's face, even as his body obeyed.

He shot the wary one first, straight through the left eye. A snap to the tether he'd set a bare instant before he fired reloaded his pistol, and he fired again, another precise shot through the second sentry's throat.

He blinked again, back to the same tether, and froze, waiting.

More pistol shots were going off elsewhere in the camp. Close enough to give him cover. A few heartbeats, to be sure no sentries were coming to investigate, and he was moving again, this time ducking around the tents of what had to be the central pavilion.

Without warning a man in white burst out of the largest tent.

"Lord Isaru!" a junior officer called, trailing after. "Lord Isaru, wait! You cannot risk yourself! What if the enemy attacks in force?"

Isaru. The name rang like bells in his head. Impossible. He'd left Isaru Mattai to die in the middle of the desert.

The man in white made a dismissive gesture, storming through the camp toward Kitian's disturbance.

The dusk light made the sight uncertain, but he could have sworn the face matched the name. Isaru Mattai. Alive. Here. No time for more than the initial shock.

He stayed low, ducking inside the tent from where he'd seen Isaru exit. It had to be the main command tent, and as soon as he went beneath the entry flap he saw that it was. A massive table stood at its center, covered with open journals, ledgers, loose notes, orders, and maps.

He ran to it, wasting no time.

Markers decorated the largest map, a depiction of the New Sarresant continent in surprising detail. Two clumps of colored figures stood near New Sarresant itself, while a score or more were strewn across the land to the west. Some few of those, six in total, had been tied with colored ribbons. The ones near the city were untouched.

He found an open ledger beside the map, and checked the map again.

Nine companies near New Sarresant. He scanned the company names, heraldry, and numbers. D'Arrent knew about them all; what was more worrying were the fifteen companies positioned behind them, like a second line of battle, waiting for the first to fall back into it. A trap, at least four hundred thousand strong, if the ledgers could be believed.

He committed what he could to memory, then scanned the rest of the map. The colored ribbons caught his eye. What did they mean? Six companies marked in total, all among those strewn out across the western countryside. No mention of the colors in the ledger, and none labeled on the map itself, that he could see.

The other maps, then. The table had four: an empty one, showing what d'Arrent's people labeled the *Old World*, and another showing Jun. A far less-detailed map labeled *Tarzal*, a massive island he had never seen before on any globe or map in an Imperial school. And another, larger but almost totally blank outside a few hastily drawn markings for terrain, labeled *Bhakal*.

Six colored markers appeared atop that one. He double-checked. The same colors. The same companies. Marked for deployment to cities labeled Domakar, Abakra, Senesal, Mbatai, Narambi, and Konghom.

He cursed, wishing for a ledger to confirm it. But there was no time. He had what he was going to get from this sortie, and that was well enough for a report: four hundred thousand soldiers massed outside New Sarresant, a trap waiting to be sprung. Isaru Mattai himself in command. And six companies deployed already to cities on the Bhakal continent. He double-checked the numbers and committed them to memory. Good enough. Let Erris d'Arrent puzzle out what to do with what he'd learned.

He closed his eyes, finding the strands he'd used to transport them here, and kept two more at the ready for quick tethers after he arrived. Kitian would be leading the *magi* in this camp on a fool's chase, and the two minutes she'd given were almost up. Whatever he thought of the madness behind Kitian's plan, Yuli would never forgive him if he got her sister killed.

28

ARAK'JUR

2nd Corps Forward Staging Point
Wilderness, Sinari Land

Sarresant soldiers swarmed like insects as he approached their camp. The lines between the Jun and the Sarresanters had been quiet in the weeks since the city's ruin, yet these soldiers moved with purpose, churning the ground to mud, making it hard to find undamaged patches of aster flowers, butterfly weed, anemones, and marigolds on his way to the front. He had Ghella to thank for the idea of bringing a gift; a bouquet of damaged flowers was far from the least he would do to find the way back to Corenna's heart.

He stopped a soldier to ask for directions to their division commander's flag, and gave a nod of thanks as she pointed the way. Word spread around him as he passed through the camp. He ignored it. Corenna was all that mattered. He saw their general first, a woman atop a brown horse.

Then he saw Corenna, on foot, in a white dress with her face painted blue, and his heart soared like a falcon in the sky.

"Here," he said, proffering the flowers as soon as he reached her. "A gift of beauty for beauty. Ghella suggested it would be unwise to come before you empty-handed."

Corenna stared at him, then down at the flowers, then back at him. Her face was lined with Ranasi markings, the paint caked thick enough to add texture to every expression.

"Flowers," she said. "You bring me flowers, here. Now."

He held them by the stems, though she made no move to take them. The rest of the Sarresant general's retinue stayed still atop their horses, whatever conversations or orders they'd been giving dying down as they watched the exchange.

"Can't you see what's happening here?" Corenna asked. "These soldiers are preparing for battle, not for courting and games. As well if you'd brought our son here as bring a gift like that."

"A battle?" he said, lowering the flowers. "The Jun are attacking?"

"We're attacking," Corenna said. "When the sun reaches its apex." She gave him a questioning look. "Did you and the guardians not receive the same order?"

He shook his head. Erris d'Arrent's orders had been to hold his people in reserve against a renewed Jun advance, or, failing that, to prepare for deployment elsewhere via Lord Tigai or Sarine. The same orders he'd had since the battle that led to the city's ruin.

"We've heard nothing of any attack," he said. "Perhaps word was sent while I traveled here."

"The Empress came herself, in person," Corenna said. "Yesterday. She laid out plans for half the morning."

"Shimmash can direct the guardians in my absence, if I missed the order. But if there's to be another battle, Corenna, you should be among us, at my side. That's why I came here. Whatever I've done to drive us apart, I want you with me. I want us together."

Corenna stared at him again. The blue paint on her face contorted as she frowned, though she was still radiant, a vision of ceremony and Ranasi power, from her white dress to the leather cords braided into her hair.

"How dare you?" Corenna snapped in a quiet, hissing voice. "I've told you these people are preparing for battle. How can you come here and ask me to abandon them?"

"I love you," he said, brandishing the flowers again. "That's why I came here."

"And where was that love when our son was born? Where was that love when you left us behind?"

"Our son is with the Alliance, in our village. A place you haven't been in weeks. I saw him and Ghella this morning. Does that mean nothing to you?"

She struck his hand, scattering the flowers into the dirt.

"You have no right," she said. "I love my son, but I have a duty to be here. To fight."

"You have a duty to him, even if you choose to turn your back on me."

"Why? Because of my sex? You can forsake us and leave him in another's keeping to fight your war, but I can't do the same?"

"You're his mother. Ghella is sure your milk has already dried up. She's had to find two new mothers to nurse him. He needs you. I need you. Corenna, I know I've made mistakes, but—"

"I'm a warrior," Corenna cut in sharply. "My calling, deeper than any *Venari* name. I've known it since I was a girl. The Alliance can provide for my son while I fight. My gifts are fire and wind and ice, more potent than any milk from my breasts."

It hurt, knowing even their son wouldn't bring her home, but he hadn't expected any less.

"Fight with me, then," he said. "With the rest of our guardians. Your place is among us, not here with the fair-skins."

"No," she said. "I won't abandon them. They need me. I remember too well how it feels to be left behind."

He took a step toward her and she flinched, halting him in place.

He wanted to reach for her, to wrap her in his arms and remember softer, better times. The guardian's path had always required sacrifice. Perhaps he'd been a fool to think he could have the life of an ordinary man while he wielded the spirits' power. But standing here, with Corenna close enough to touch, he still wanted it. Wanted her. And she might as well have been a thousand days' journey away.

A crashing sound triggered his instincts; *mareh'et* gave his gift as he whirled, and he saw the same aura around Corenna from the corner of his eye.

Two figures suddenly stood atop a nearby wagon, though neither had been there a moment before, knocking aside the crates stacked in its bed. A woman, or a creature with the shape of one, though its skin was burnt red, almost the color of blood. And with her, wearing what appeared to be a Jun officer's uniform...

"Arak'Jur," Tigai said. "Thank the fucking wind spirits that strand was yours. I've been chasing it half the bloody morning."

Corenna took a step forward, unfurling the sleeves of her dress, her eyes shining blue along with *mareh'et*'s gift.

"It's all right," he said to her. Then, louder, "Lord Tigai. How have you come to be here?"

Tigai and his companion stepped to untangle themselves from the wagon's crates and supplies, each hopping down to the ground.

"Not a moment to waste," Tigai said. "They're coming. I've led them on a chase through every star and strand. The hells only know if they'll be mad enough to follow me here, into the middle of an army camp, but if they do, we'd best be ready for a fight."

"Who is coming?" he asked as Corenna calmed nearby soldiers who'd heard the clamor, or seen Tigai's uniform.

"The bloody Dragons," Tigai said. "At least one Crab, a Heron, and I think they picked up another *magi* two jumps back. Can't be sure which house. They should have gotten tired hours ago, but they're following whenever I use the strands. I found a connection I thought led to you and I followed it. So here we are. If they're coming, they'll be here soon."

"Unless they've stopped again to gather reinforcements," the woman with blood-red skin said. Her voice sounded like metal scraped on metal, while her hair was matted and slick, her eyes and teeth both solid black.

"Who is this?" Arak'Jur asked.

"Kitian Blood Claw Clan Hoskar," Tigai said impatiently. "One of Yuli's sisters. Why did you have to be in a bloody army camp? No chance the *magi* will follow another tether from here. Even if they come, they'll stop to kill as many soldiers as they can. I'd hoped to find you, then follow another tether, to gather our champions and bloody ambush them. It's the Dragon champion following me; it has to be. Only way they could have followed me so many times."

"How many fair-skin binders are there with these soldiers?" he asked Corenna.

"Few," Corenna said as the general's retinue drew closer. "As I said, they were relying on me."

"Can you ask for them to be brought here?" he asked. "And for the rest of these soldiers to disperse? Lord Tigai warns an attack is coming, by way of Dragon-*magi*. Soon. Within minutes." Tigai nodded at that.

Corenna moved without further questions, speaking in a rush of the Sarresant tongue to the Sarresant general and her officers.

"Are any of the strands around you tied to Sarine?" Tigai asked him while Corenna delivered the message.

"How do you mean?" he asked.

"We could use her. Her, Yuli, the rest of her sisters, anyone else, really. No way to tell in advance who or what the Dragons are going to bring across the strand."

"I haven't seen her since we buried Reyne d'Agarre."

"Well, fuck. Probably no time anyway. I'm sorry about this. I really didn't know you'd be in the middle of a bloody encampment. I wasn't even sure it was you I was tracking."

Tigai unlimbered his pistols, setting rope matches in place with steel locks as he took a place beside Arak'Jur. He seemed to be glancing around the camp, frowning and nervous, whereas Kitian was relaxed, brandishing forearms that seemed to be more liquid than skin, as though fire had melted her body into a weapon. He set his stance to match Kitian's and Tigai's, facing the wagons.

"Four *magi* coming, then," he said. "You said a Crab, a Heron, a Dragon, and one more?"

"More," Tigai replied. "At least four just among the Dragons. Kitian kicked the hornet's nest to buy me time at high command, and it's the Dragon champion giving chase. The bloody fucker can move without tiring, the same as I can. It has to be a bond, powering it. Plus High Commander Isaru Bloody Mattai himself. He's alive, did I mention? Which makes him likely bound to the Regnant, too."

He almost drew on *mareh'et* early, to have the power coursing through him when they appeared. Tigai's magic was strange and terrible; a waking nightmare for enemies to appear without warning in the middle of their camps. He had to believe the shamans would give warning if it were about to happen in the Alliance village. Yet Tigai had tracked him somehow, following what he called a strand, and Shimmash had given no warning of a battle coming before he'd left the camp today.

Corenna joined them, leaving the Sarresant officers delivering orders in her wake. It seemed she'd been successful in convincing them to disperse: Soldiers near the wagons were already pulling back, reversing their ranks to face the wagons and readying their guns.

"Two of their binders will join us," Corenna said, and Tigai spat.

"Two," Tigai said. "Two, when Isaru and his Dragons will bring a bloody army if they have any sense. They know who they're following. Just make sure all of you stay close to me. I'll get us out of here if we start to lose."

Arak'Jur didn't bother trying to persuade Corenna. She wouldn't agree to leave the soldiers behind, but he wasn't about to let her stay. Instead they readied themselves, Tigai's pistols hot and leveled at the wagon, Kitian's burned and bloody skin seeming ready to drip into the dirt, Corenna's forearms bared and eyes locked in place, and his spirits waiting, ready to answer his call.

The moment stretched on. Nothing came.

They waited, still and ready. After a time, Tigai stood, unlocking the match from one of his pistols, and tossed the discarded rope into the dirt before fitting a new one in its place. Still they kept in position facing the wagons as the sun climbed higher. Eventually the soldiers resumed their preparations without conferring with him or Corenna, the lines re-forming westward, horses and wagons loading supplies as the tents were struck and packed.

"They aren't coming, are they," Tigai said after a quarter hour or more had passed. "Fuck."

The admission cracked the tension between them and the wagons. Kitian's skin drained some of its color, from burnt red to a softer pink. Corenna leaned back, and the spirits seemed to recede from his touch.

"You tracked me here," he said. "Perhaps they knew what they were facing, if they followed you."

"Best hope that isn't true," Tigai said. "If they could track you and the rest of Sarine's champions by your strands, we'd all be dead already. Wind spirits know I can't track theirs that way; I can only recognize strands I know well. More likely they could tell I was too close to a bloody army encampment."

He turned to Corenna. "It seems they aren't coming," he said. "I'm sorry for the distraction."

"I'll tell the general," Corenna said.

"Corenna, wait," he said.

"For what?" she asked.

The threat had brought them together; as quick as it passed, she returned to the ice she'd been ready to put between them.

"Arak'Jur, I have to tell them the danger is passed."

"I know," he said. "But please, if the Sarresanters mean to continue their attack...at least let me join you. I meant what I said about us fighting together."

"An attack?" Tigai said. "Here?"

"No, the fair-skins were planning an attack on the Jun lines," he replied before turning back to Corenna. She hadn't moved toward the New Sarresant officers. "Please," he said to her. "Let me fight at your side."

"Don't you need to see to the guardians?" she asked. "They need your leadership."

"Yes, they do. But I need you more. That's why I came. That's why I'm here. I love you, Corenna. I may be imperfect, and I may have duties that take me away from all the things I love, but I don't love them any less for it. I want to share those duties with you. Please."

For the first time since he'd come, she hesitated.

"Bloody fuck," Tigai said. "This is why they were setting a trap. The Jun know this attack is coming. They're ready for it, and they outnumber her bloody four to one. We have to reach Empress d'Arrent and tell her to call it off."

Corenna nodded slowly. "Yes," she said. "You may fight at my side. After, we will speak of other things. But for today...yes."

He went to her. Prudence dictated caution, since her words were no surety, only a chance. But a chance was more than he'd hoped for today. She'd said yes. For today, at least, they would stand together.

"Arak'Jur?" Tigai said.

"What?" he asked.

"We need to reach the Empress," Tigai said. "I could use your help traveling on foot. It isn't safe to make a connection to her palace, when the Dragons know the strand connected to this spot."

"No," he said. "Go on alone. I mean to stay here, at Corenna's side."

"If there's to be a battle, we need to reach d'Arrent quickly. She has to know—"

"I said no. Go alone. Take a fast horse."

Tigai gave him an incredulous look. He hardly noticed. Corenna's hesitation had been replaced by something else, the hope of forgiveness in her eyes. Duty could wait; whatever urgency there was in Tigai's words paled against his need to stay with her. Shimmash could manage the guardians. Tigai could travel on his own. No one else could repair the rift between him and Corenna. This was where he belonged if a battle was coming, and, for once, this was where he would be.

29

YULI

Blood assaulted the Twin Fangs' senses. Cold, dead blood. It ran ahead of Sarine and the girl, Reed, following the rage curdling under its skin. Summer never truly arrived in Tiansei, not as it did in the South, and a cold wind blew against its hairless hide, chilling the corpses as they lay in the city's market squares. Dozens of dead. A trail leading toward its prey.

Any survivors had long since fled the carnage Yuli saw through the Gods' Seat's map device. Even soldiers and guardsmen knew better than to try and confront a Natarii warrior gone mad. Carts lay abandoned, their goods spilling into the streets. But the Far Sight was close. The Twin Fangs smelled it.

An empty square. Yuli knew the place: a square devoted to a great hero, a woman called Olina Wind Song. A brass statue in her likeness rose from a fountain in the center, a towering woman covered in feathers, her wings outstretched in defiance of the Jun Emperor's grasp.

Her enemy sat alone on a stone rail in front of the statue's base.

Mileva Far Sight Clan Gorin.

Shadows rose from Mileva's skin like heat rising from a fire. The Far Sight's form was black, a pure, inky black covering a woman's shape underneath. No corpses lay near her. The square was empty, save for the Twin Fangs' prey.

Too easy. Yuli's thought. Too obvious. A trap. But no; the Twin Fangs scented nothing else nearby, nothing closer than Sarine and Reed, following its trail from the Dragon star. Perhaps Mileva wanted to be found. To be killed. The Twin Fangs would grant the wish. This was no trap. This was a warrior provoking a warrior with innocent blood.

It stepped into the mouth of the square, where a wide boulevard emptied into what should have been a bustling marketplace on a summer afternoon. Instead it stood alone in the street, a single figure, set against another lone shape, rising from where she sat at the fountain's edge.

No words. Mileva had already surrendered to the Far Sight's form. Yuli had given in to the Twin Fangs. Explanations were for human shapes. *Why. How. For what purpose.* The warrior-forms knew only blood and rage.

The Twin Fangs charged, and the Far Sight met its attack.

Fangs and claws cut the air as the shadow twisted, and their bodies collided, sending both careening down to the cobbled street. The Twin Fangs snapped back instantly, pivoting from the momentum to launch itself toward its enemy. Shadows lanced from the Far Sight's fingertips, scorching black marks onto the stone where they missed and sending shocks of pain through the Twin Fangs where they didn't. Skin melted, twisting around the beams. It reached its enemy again, howling as it struck in a flurry of claws and teeth.

The Far Sight brought up a hand to parry the strikes, and shadow tore loose as easily as it might have ripped skin. The Twin Fangs raked the Far Sight from three directions at once, each claw stabbing and piercing its enemy while it sank both fangs into the Far Sight's right shoulder, tasting a mouthful of acrid foulness as the shadows came free.

Sound deadened as shadows drew into the Far Sight's form. The Twin Fangs had only a moment's warning.

It dove away, hurling itself behind the fountain and statue at the heart of the square.

A nova of pure black erupted from the Far Sight's body. The wave pulsed and shimmered as it expanded through the square, rippling stone like a pebble dropped into a still pond. Glass exploded from windows. The stone itself, cobbled streets and statue plinth and fountain, all surged with energy, heating to a flash of white and yellow before they cooled. The heat seared the Twin Fangs' skin. It tasted the cooking meat of its own flesh as it sprang from its hiding place to renew its attack.

The Far Sight would be weakened, but still dangerous. The Twin Fangs feinted toward it, springing to strike at an unprotected flank. It connected. Claws and teeth plunged into the shadow, knocking it to the ground as the Far Sight tried to bring up a hand to deflect the attacks. They slammed into still-cooling stone, new beams of darkness cutting into its skin as it savaged its enemy. Relentless strikes pummeled the shaded woman as they grappled together. Claws drove into its flesh, were pulled out and driven in again.

The Far Sight managed to grab hold of the Twin Fangs' mouth, wrenching a hand full of death around its lower jaw. They rolled, cracking the fountain's stone, drenching both in water that had been boiled in an instant. Molten slag dripped from the statue's ruined brass. The Twin Fangs snapped and wrenched its neck sideways while its claws continued to rake and stab the shadow. The Far Sight held its grip.

A whine escaped the Twin Fangs' throat.

It burned. The shadows tore into the soft skin of the roof of its mouth. Putrid rot flooded its senses. Its vision blurred.

The Far Sight's free hand grabbed hold of one of the Twin Fangs' wrists. More pain knifed through its limb. It fought back. A claw pierced the Far Sight's rib cage, slicing into where a woman's lungs would be, seeking the soft places of its heart.

Stone cracked and crumbled around them. Water hissed. Glass crunched.

Its claws cut shadows free, its jaw wrenched and writhed as it tried to snap down on the Far Sight's hand.

Shadows engulfed the Twin Fangs' skin, and it whimpered.

It was done.

The Twin Fangs loosed its grip. Yuli had been a fine host. This had been a fine enemy. A champion's strength against a champion's strength. No dishonor or shame in this death. It would drift again on the currents of the sparks, seeking a new host when it found a soul worthy of its gifts. It would leave Yuli to rest, letting her body inherit the weight of their defeat.

The shadows clung tighter.

Now the Twin Fangs snarled. This was wrong. It was defeated. It should be allowed to move on, and leave Yuli to die.

The Far Sight heaved deep breaths, steadying itself as it rose to its feet. Its shadows still wreathed the Twin Fangs' form, holding it down, keeping it pinned like a wild wolf caged and cut away from its pack.

"I knew it would most likely be you, sister, if it wasn't the reborn Veil," the Far Sight said, its shadows dimming into the form of a woman, its voice giving way from grating iron to a softer, human sound. "But I hoped for another outcome. It was never my desire to inflict this on you. I'm sorry."

The Twin Fangs held its grip under a cloak of shadows. But it wavered. It should be gone. Yuli should be dead. Instead they clung to life.

Why. Yuli's thought. The Twin Fangs' mouth bent, to give it sound.

"Why?" Mileva asked. By now the Far Sight form had slipped away, leaving the woman, wreathed in shadows, dripping blood from a half-dozen deep cuts and wounds. "Because the price is worth the cost. Is there ever another answer?"

Yuli cried. Tears in human eyes, from the pain. She didn't want to die. She wasn't ready. The Twin Fangs receded, slipping into her form, leaving the human woman lying on broken, melted stone.

"He's abandoned us," Mileva continued. "Did you know that? He made us his champions, promised greatness and power so long as we defeated you in open battle. And now he's moved on. Treats us as though we're nothing. As though our promised futures are nothing."

"The Regnant." Yuli's voice was a croak through a damaged mouth, a broken windpipe, pierced lungs.

Mileva nodded. The shadows still hung around Yuli's body, obscuring her sight. Mileva was doing something to keep her alive. The Twin Fangs recoiled under the weight. It should be allowed to flee. Yuli was dead, or dying. Mileva should finish her, and let the warrior-bond dissolve. Instead Mileva sat next to Yuli, tucking her legs under her, moving slowly, gingerly, from the wounds the Twin Fangs had inflicted on its enemy.

"He keeps us alive and bids us to protect ourselves," Mileva said. "To stay away from you, and the rest of the reborn Veil's champions. But the Far Sight knows his secrets. He's made promises to the Bhakal Queen. I thought...if I struck, and attracted the reborn Veil herself, captured her, you understand— he might take notice. He might restore what was promised. Only...I'm sorry, sister. I knew what I had to do. But doing it weighs heavy on my soul."

"You mean...to keep me," Yuli managed through the pain.

"To keep you alive, yes," Mileva said. "Part of the champion's bond. Is it different for you, being bound to her? I haven't tried to hide. If the reborn Veil uses the mirrors in the Gods' Seat she'll see us both. Then she'll come. It's my only chance, do you understand? If the Regnant and the Bhakal Queen manage to succeed they won't need any of us. We're relics, past their point of use. That's what he thinks of us. But he'll reward me, if I can bring her to him. I'm certain of that."

Mileva's words blurred in her ears. The Twin Fangs' gifts had already started to heal her, knitting her body together, though she should have been dead. Fire sparked in her belly. If they were bound to live, the Twin Fangs wanted to resume control, to return to their fight. Yuli could feel a dozen broken bones, half again as many patches of burned skin, raw and covered in blood and pus. She held on, letting the Twin Fangs sew them both together.

"Sarine," Yuli tried to say. "She's...strong. Won't...fall..."

"She's dangerous, yes," Mileva said. "I know. But the old Veil took half the reborn Veil's magic before she died. Your Sarine is vulnerable, and I have to try. I won't let the Far Sight or the Natarii people fall into nothingness. A union of Bhakal and Jun would be too much for us to resist. I know we're of different clans, and I know you won't forgive me for what I did here in Tiansei, but we're still sisters. If there's any chance, I have to...to try..."

Mileva's words trailed off, and she snapped her gaze to the broad street Yuli had come down.

"She came with you," Mileva said. "She's here."

Yuli groaned, trying to roll over to glimpse the mouth of the square. Mileva had already returned to the Far Sight's shadow-form. The clinging darkness around Yuli dissipated like clouds scattered on the wind, and she drew a sharp, pained breath. The Twin Fangs held her body together, knitting and sewing muscle, tissue, bone, and blood. She had the strength to roll herself over to see.

Sarine was there. White and red light flashed around her sister's body. Mileva Far Sight charged over open ground, her hands extended, beams of shadow streaking across the square. Then the Nine Tails took over Sarine's flesh, and their forms blurred together, and Yuli's head hurt, trying to make sense of what she saw.

Her pulse pounded in her temple. A building exploded. Timber and thatch and stone sprayed into the mouth of the square where the Nine Tails had thrown the Far Sight, then streaked after it, rays of pure blackness rising through the destruction. Cracking, breaking sounds came from where they fought, more glass shattering, more wood snapping in half. She drew ragged breaths, trying to follow the fight. Her sister was there, without her. She should summon the Twin Fangs and fight at Sarine's side.

Instead she collapsed against the wet stone.

The patter of footsteps opened her eyelids. Reed.

"You look like the Oracle's bleeding cunt," Reed said. "Are you...? Holy shits, you're alive."

Vision blurred from the pain and pulsing blood in her temple. She ached all over. Her mouth was bruised and bloody. Her jaw broken. One eye already swollen shut.

"I'm..." she said, hearing the pain in her own voice. "Alive. Will be fine... but, Sarine."

"You'll be fine?" Reed said. "You look like someone fed you through a sausage grinder. Don't move."

The girl's hands were tender, gently rolling her onto her back. She could feel burns on her skin. Hadn't yet looked down to see how bad it was, but it didn't matter.

"Twin Fangs will...heal," she said. "Long as I'm not dead. I'll live."

"You'll recover from this?" Reed said.

"I will," she said. Already she could feel her skin being knit back together. It might take weeks, if the damage was truly severe, but so long as the Twin Fangs hadn't abandoned her, she would live. "Help me sit up. Need to see where Sarine went."

"That's not fucking fair," Reed said, propping a gentle hand against the small of her back. "Why don't I have any magic? It's not bloody fucking fair."

She leaned into Reed's help, rising enough to see what was left of the mouth of the square.

The exploded building was only the first of what looked like several. Fires rose a street away, belching fresh smoke up into an otherwise clear sky. The Nine Tails was strong, and she'd already wounded the Far Sight, already driven it to expend a good portion of its energy. But there was no way to be sure, with the power of the Regnant's bond amplifying Mileva's gift. Sarine had her *kaas* magic, and the Dragons' starfield and strands, but the Veil had torn away the leylines and spirit bonds. Fatigue washed over her. Her body needed rest, even with the Twin Fangs' help to speed her recovery. But with Sarine out there fighting in her stead, she couldn't—

FOR THIS ONE, IT ENDS.

The voice reverberated through her body, sending echoes of pain across her skin.

Relief followed the pain. She slumped back against the fountain's cracked stone.

"Yuli?" Reed asked, her face suddenly writ with concern. "Are you sure you're okay?"

Happiness came, and with it, renewed fatigue.

"She won," Yuli said. "The voice. It means Sarine won."

"What?" Reed asked. "What voice?"

"We're safe," Yuli said. "Mileva's dead, and my people are avenged."

Reed looked at her as though she'd gone mad. But it was true. No voice had echoed when Sarine had killed Lin. That voice meant a champion was dead. It had to be. She leaned back against the stone, letting her body give itself over to the Twin Fangs' gifts of healing.

She held on to consciousness all the same, until a figure emerged through the rubble.

Sarine had shed the Nine Tails, clutching her arm where the shadows' beams must have scorched her. Her sister's body was burned, her clothes torn and covered in soot and ash. Exhaustion showed on Sarine's face, but victory, too. Victory. Whatever else Mileva had said, one of the Regnant's champions was dead, and her sister was alive.

Her eyes closed before Sarine reached them, and she drifted into a deep, healing sleep.

30

ERRIS

Grand Ballroom
Rasailles Palace

The room stirred with conversation as she sat back in her chair.

Four hours, and nothing to show for it. She'd summoned governors from every province, her secretaries of interior, war, navy, state, and all the other departments of her bureaucracy. At least they had the good sense to avoid her now that it was done. She needed an answer to the Jun, not endless speeches written by junior aides to junior aides. Perhaps a purge and replacement by military officers was overdue. But already time was the enemy.

"Apologies, Your Majesty," Lady Mei said, bowing as she and her husband approached. "May we disturb you?"

"Minister," she said, "and Lady Yanjin." She masked her annoyance as best she could. At least with Tigai's brother and his wife she'd managed to find competence, all too lacking elsewhere in her governments. He'd been in place as Minister of War for only a few weeks and already earned praises from her generals, no matter his sometime reliance on his wife as a translator. "I thought I saw both of you heading for the dining hall."

"Your servants offer their humblest apologies, Majesty," Lady Mei said, bowing again. "My husband and I beg a moment on behalf of his brother, Yanjin Tigai. He bears a message of utmost import."

Annoyance slipped through the façade she'd been trying to hold in place. "Tigai should bring his reports through the chain of command. I know Colonel Marquand has been missing, but he can escalate through the staff office. Anything Essily deems worthy of my attention will have it."

"Of course, Majesty," Mei said. "Only, Lord Tigai has come to the palace directly." Mei leaned in, lowering her voice. "He's waiting outside the ballroom. We had to beg him not to make a scene. For his sake, for ours, and for yours, perhaps Your Majesty might consider hearing him out."

"Are you bloody—" she began, cutting herself short. Whatever her opinions of her governors, the ravens would be watching, even a few paces out of earshot. "Very well. Where is he?" she said, striding toward the door with the Yanjins at her flank. "I warn you, if he thinks he can abuse your husband's appointment for personal access, he's sorely mistaken. I put Marquand in command of him, Sarine, and the others precisely to insulate myself from this kind of distraction."

"He's—" Mei began.

"About bloody fucking time," Tigai said. He was standing close enough to the door to have charged through if she'd waited another moment. And worse, he wore the uniform of a Jun officer, by itself enough to cause uproar among those who recognized their enemies' colors. So far, thank the Exarch, it had not.

"You forget yourself, Yanjin Tigai," she said, managing to keep a cool exterior. "You are addressing an Empress, in case you'd forgotten. Proper decorum is—"

"We don't have time for bloody politics," Tigai said. "This bloody attack you've ordered, it's half-cocked and stupid, and it's going to get your people killed."

"What attack?" she said.

"The attack on the Jun outside New Sarresant. The Dragons have moved six companies—and I know where now, thank you bloody very much—but the bulk are still there, hiding behind their front lines and your people are running headlong into them like tigers toward a spear-pit. I don't know what other intelligence you've gathered, but I know it wasn't from me, and that makes it suspect at best."

She let him speak, keeping calm enough to hope his words would be dismissed as no more than an unseemly outburst by the diplomats and officers of state around them. A snap of her fingers summoned a pair of guardsmen, and she began walking, leading them all in tow while Tigai continued his rant.

"A room," she said to one of the guards. "Something private."

"...spent half the morning dodging Dragons chasing me across the strands," Tigai was saying. "Then rode here to spare the danger of giving them a connection to your palace, and what do I get for it? Bloody nothing but cold stares and bloody bureaucrats in the way. I damn near had to bribe your people to get through the front gates."

One of the guards rushed ahead, holding open a door as they turned a corner. She ushered Dao and Mei inside, each having the good sense to look ashamed of their brother's display. Tigai followed, still ranting.

She made sure the door was closed behind them before she snapped a faint tether of *Body* in place, then raised a hand and struck Tigai in the jaw.

He vanished as the smack of skin on skin reverberated through the meeting room. It gave her a start, until she saw he'd reappeared in the doorway, clutching a hand to his chin and staring at her.

"What the fuck was that for?" Tigai snapped.

"That was a reminder of where you are, and to whom you are speaking," she said coldly. "Start over. What was this about an attack on the Jun front?"

Tigai stared at her, saying nothing. Dao spoke instead.

"No such attack is planned, Your Majesty," Dao said. "Even our sorties and raids have been curtailed of late, awaiting reports from our scouts and spies."

"This wasn't a bloody sortie," Tigai said. "A full brigade at least was spinning up for a charge while we waited for the Dragons. Arak'Jur was with them, and his woman, Corenna."

"The guardians?" she said. "They're attacking without my orders?"

"No, just Arak'Jur," Tigai said. "And they claimed they *had* your orders. Said you were there in person, a day ago, or maybe two. What the fuck is going on here?"

She darted a glance toward Mei and Dao, even as she picked tethers from among the golden lights in the distance.

"*Magi* trickery," Mei said, barely above a whisper.

"I need to see it," Erris said, and snapped a *Need* tether into place. If Corenna was there, it meant Tigai had most likely been with the 9th Division, stationed at the center of the opposing line. A fine place to start, if there was any truth to it.

Her senses lurched.

Smoke flooded her lungs at once, a burning sting, and pain. She was staring up into the trees, long, limbless trunks like a column of pikes aimed toward the sky. Her vessel's body was broken, both legs twisted beneath her torso at angles neither should have allowed. Blood filled her throat, and she coughed.

She fought to lift her vessel's head. Soldiers in New Sarresant uniforms moved through clouds of smoke around her, but she could see no more than a few paces in any direction. A dead horse lay crumpled in a pile of leaves, with its rider and several more soldiers strewn beside it, all covered in blood. In the distance a light shimmered through the fog in the shape of a monstrous cat, accompanied by the dim echo of a snarling roar. She strained to see it clearer, fighting for short gasps of breath. Then her vessel's neck gave way, and her vision slid back up toward the trees and sky as the *Need* tether snapped.

"Well?" Tigai demanded. She ignored him.

A fresh *Need* tether slid into place. Tigai claimed Arak'Jur was there alone, but if the rest of his guardians had been put in the field, too, she had to know.

Her senses cleared in a dark room, filled with smoke. The remnants of a fire smoldered in a hearth, providing the only light. She recoiled by instinct as the smoke's tang hit the back of her vessel's throat, but there was no sulfur and saltpeter here. Only tobacco, with the sour taste of liquor in her mouth and a bottle in her vessel's hand.

"Empress," a man said, sounding at once both strange and familiar, speaking slurred words in a foreign tongue that her ears translated to Sarresant. She turned and recognized Shimmash, Arak'Jur's second, seated across from her next to the hearth. "A welcome surprise."

"Shimmash," she said, hearing the same slurred drawl in her vessel's voice. "Forgive me, but there isn't time for pleasantries. Where are the guardians now? Where is Arak'Jur?"

Shimmash leaned back, exaggerating the movement, or perhaps only off-balance from the drink. "We are here, among our people. Though our leader is among yours, seeking his woman, fighting for love." He raised his bottle. "A fine thing to celebrate, yes? Though I can speak for him, if there is business for the tribes."

"No," she said quickly. "Not yet. Thank you." She prepared to release the *Need* tether, then hesitated. "Perhaps it would be best to sober up, and prepare the guardians to move."

"Is Arak'Jur in danger?" Shimmash asked, suddenly upright.

"He might be," she said. "I'll send word as soon as I have it."

Shimmash's bottle clinked as it hit the ground, and the shaman rose to his feet. She let the *Need* tether go.

"Wind spirits bloody damn her, I need her attention," Tigai was saying. "She hasn't heard the whole of it yet."

Mei started to say something back, clipped to a halt when she glanced up at Erris.

"You should have made a report through Essily's office," Erris said, preparing the next tether. If the 9th Division was engaged, the rest of the 1st Corps would be close behind. Gods send this disaster was contained in the center of her line.

"Fuck your bloody reports," Tigai snapped. "And will you bloody wait? Like I said, I found out where the Dragons are taking the Jun. Or at least, taking some of them."

She paused, letting the binding hover between her and the golden light. "Where?" she said.

"The Bhakal continent," Tigai said. "Six companies, to six cities, spread across the western half of their empire. And Isaru Mattai is in command." He paused, as though waiting for her to recognize the name. "Isaru Mattai, the *magi* I thought I'd killed by abandoning him in the desert."

She closed her eyes, drawing the *Need* binding closer, not yet snapping it in place. "Lady Mei, will you see to it your brother-in-law is taken somewhere private and debriefed in full. Somewhere far enough away to spare me more distractions."

"Distractions?" Tigai said. "I bring you your enemy's plans, sealed in ribbon and wax, and you call it a distraction?"

"You yourself are a walking distraction, Lord Tigai," she said. "You've brought me critical information, information I must act on at once. Give the rest to your brother and his wife. They'll have sense enough to discern what else requires my immediate attention."

"But if the Jun are being taken to the Bhakal continent, there must be—"

"In good time," she interrupted. "For now, I intend to see to whatever force is trying to destroy my army. The rest will keep. Dismissed."

Mei rose to her feet, laying a hand on Tigai's forearm. Good enough. Whatever else Tigai was, she had to hope his brother and sister-in-law could keep him in check while she worked.

"Have the guards send for Essily, and enough support staff to conduct an operation here, from this room," she said to Mei, barely registering the bow and "yes, Majesty," before she snapped the *Need* tether in place, shifting her senses back to the front.

31

OMERA

Oasis of the Jeweled Falcon
The Sand Sea, West Bhakal

He sagged to his knees, feeling the weight of the sun lifted from his shoulders. Shade. For the first time in two days. Shade. A thick copse of trees grew around the water's edge, and he staggered under the first ones they reached, letting his camel's reins drop where he sat.

Jahi slid off her camel behind him, stumbling under the trees. Two of her thralls did the same, while the other three dutifully gathered waterskins from each saddle, as though the heat were nothing next to the work their mistress had commanded them to perform.

Breath came heavy as he watched the Mindhunter and her thralls. He wanted to stay here, to rest for hours—days, even, as some caravans did. Duty would put him back on his feet as soon as their water stores were refilled.

Jahi uncorked a waterskin, dousing her forehead and drinking what was left. The two thralls she'd commanded to rest did the same, following her movements precisely in a choreographed dance, or, more truthfully, as three marionettes puppeted by the same hand.

"You push your body hard, Your Highness," Jahi said. "Careful you don't wear us all out before we reach the post."

He rubbed a fresh pinch of *ubax aragti* across his gums. His mouth was caked and dry, but the herbs sang in his blood. He'd kept a steady hum going since they'd entered the sand sea. Enough to keep him alert, and let his body ignore the worst of the heat.

"I told you," he managed. His voice was hoarse, coated with dust and sand. "I have to reach the palace at Konghom."

"Your errand," Jahi said.

"My mother's errand," he corrected. "Or do you still doubt it was her who protected my mind?"

Jahi fell quiet, though her eyes bored into him, as they had since leaving Domakar behind. It was as though her eyes were a pick and shovel, probing him for a weak point to begin digging. Or more likely she'd already tried to dig in a dozen places, and found his mother's shield there, rebuffing her at every one.

"Two days to the post," he said, finding renewed strength to rise to his feet. *Ubax aragti* burned hot. His skin was reddened and sore, his eyes aching from the dust. But he could press on.

"Two?" Jahi said. "Most caravans take six days from the Jeweled Falcon."

"I can do it in two," he said.

"You'll kill my thralls, pushing that hard," Jahi said. "Remember these are ordinary men. They don't have your gifts with the herbs, or my sorcery to sustain them."

"Then you'll have killed them, Mindhunter," he said. "Not me. They belong in Domakar, defending their home against the Jun invaders. You should release them and let them find their way back."

She flinched at the suggestion, only the barest movement, like a mother wolf protecting her cubs.

"I never asked you to follow me," he said.

"I don't follow you," Jahi said. "I follow your mother, the Queen. You're being reckless with your own life, and mine, as much as with my men."

"You still don't believe me, do you?" he said. "I swear to you, on my mother's throne, on her blood in my veins: She held my head in her hands and charged me to reach Konghom, to kill Sakhefete, the Queen of the East. Her sister is the betrayer. The reason the Jun were in Domakar, and Queen alone knows how many more of our cities."

"I believe you think that is what happened," Jahi said carefully. "But I know better than you do, Your Highness, the power of magic to influence the mind. Think what you are saying. One sister against the other, using her sons as assassins. I swear to *you*, on your mother's throne, the Queen's Hand was ordered to apprehend her sons and take them into our custody. Why would your mother give such an order, if there was not a chance you had been twisted by our enemies, set to do their bidding believing the order came from the Queen?"

He frowned. He remembered the meeting with his mother: The Jun envoys lay dead at her feet, while she took his head in her hands, repeating the words that would charge him with this duty. Reach Konghom. Kill Sakhefete. His mind had been in a fog, but that had been her weaving the shield that now protected his mind. Hadn't it?

"What of her shield?" he asked. "Don't lie to me and claim you haven't tried to penetrate it, and failed."

"I have," Jahi said. "I don't know how such a barrier was placed on your mind. But then, I don't know what our new enemies are capable of. Prince Omera, I'm only trying to do my duty. At least acknowledge that there is a possibility I am right, and you are being used unwittingly by our enemies."

He glanced between her and her thralls. The two who she'd ordered to rest now moved toward the oasis's waters to refill their skins, while the first three returned, fastening now-full containers to the camels' saddlebags. If Jahi was right, he was no better than one of those poor souls. But she was wrong. She had to be wrong. His mother had touched him, spoken to him, given him a duty as sacred as any of her priests.

"No," he said. "I remember my mother's words. I'd hoped you might help me, if you truly serve her. Can't you ask her yourself? They say Mindhunters can communicate across great distances."

"The Queen's mind cannot be found unless she wishes it to be," Jahi said. "But I will ask for guidance, as you say."

"Then come on, if you're still intent on following," he said, slinging his feet up into his camel's saddle. A pinch of *tisa irinti* calmed his nerves in the face of the renewed heat. He was the traveler, stoic and calm, in the face of the hard road ahead.

He wasn't under anyone's control. He was his mother's hand, swift and sure, aimed at the heart of a dire threat to her and the whole of the Empire. But doubt burned as hot as the sun as they reemerged from under the oasis's shade.

———————

Night came like a balm for open wounds. A dry, hot wind blew across the sands as the sun went down over the horizon. It left the dunes dark, full of treacherous steps for the camels as they trekked up and down the slopes. He tied a lantern to the horn of his camel's saddle, casting a cone of dim light to help the beast find its way.

He hadn't asked the Mindhunter to follow. But still, the sight of her thralls swaying in their seats like corpses lashed in place weighed heavy on him. In his mind he knew they shared their magic with his mother, and while their flame burned like a candle next to Queen Amanishiakne's conflagration of power, he couldn't help but think of what the Mindhunters did as evil. He'd never seen his mother bend the wills of her guards, or his brothers; they served her willingly, out of love and duty, not out of sorcerous compulsion. No few of the men that had traveled at Jahi's side would die for the pace he set. Damn her for a witch, trying to guilt him into slowing, into considering the possibility of truth behind her words. It almost worked. Almost.

Even under the night winds, the heat blasted further thought out of his mind. Jahi would have him seeing phantoms. He was his mother's son. She protected him from their enemies. If the Jun had put visions in his head, set him to killing Sakhefete... but he could doubt anything, any part of who he was, if he followed that logic.

They'd gone another six hours before the first thrall dropped from the saddle.

Passed out, from the look of him. But in the desert heat, unless they stopped to nurse him back from heatstroke, the man was dead. His camel emitted a bleating screech, dragged down in a tangle of lead lines and stirrups. Another of Jahi's thralls slid from his own saddle, running to cut the man free, steady his mount, and lash the beast in place to guide it on a rope.

"You mean to leave him?" Jahi called out. "Do we press on?"

He gave voice to the truth he'd been repeating in his mind. "You killed him, Mindhunter," he said. "Not me."

He made no effort to raise his voice for it to carry across the sand, but he made no effort to slow either. She understood the meaning, whether or not she heard.

They kept riding, leaving a human-shaped lump lying in the crease between two sloping dunes. Sand was already blowing over the body; another victim swallowed by the sand sea.

He hated her for it. He'd killed men before, in honest fights, his *shotel* blade against opposing steel. This felt more like killing a child.

The dunes rose and fell through the night.

He snuffed his lantern when the first rays of sunshine broke the eastern horizon. The camels were hardier than men, yet his animal swayed on its legs by the time the sun rose into full view, sending renewed heat pulsing through his body. *Ubax aragti* kept him in the saddle. Another three hours to the Oasis of the Painted Rhinoceros. They could make it before the sun rose to its killing apex, if they pushed.

"We can sleep here," Jahi called in a voice as hoarse as the dry wind. "This dune is steep. It will shelter us from the heat until evening."

He shook his head. No energy to spare for words.

She stared after him. He felt those eyes, boring into him again. He didn't slow.

One of her thralls dismounted, climbing off his camel in a snap of ropes and saddlebags. Jahi had another thrall grab the beast by its reins. Nothing more was said. She left the dismounted thrall where he stood. The man was haggard, hardly breathing, his skin flushed a burned shade of red and black, but he wasn't like the first that had died. He could have found the strength to press on; or, Jahi could have found it for him.

She left the man to die. A means of conserving the camels' strength, letting them switch riders to give each beast an hour of rest for every three they walked. The dismounted thrall stood there, watching them go with expressionless eyes. She killed him. Not Omera. The blood was on her hands. He closed his eyes, trying not to let the man's vacant expression burn itself in his memory. Yet the sight of him lingered as they crested the steep dune, staring up at them as though it never occurred to the man to cry out, to ask why they would leave him, to protest, to insist he could still walk, still ride, still survive, even only for the few more hours it would take to reach the oasis.

He gripped his sword to still his anger. They pressed on.

The night's heat became a distant memory as the sun rose full into the sky. He could feel blisters forming over top of blisters where his legs rubbed the saddle and the beast's hide, where his fingers gripped the reins and the saddle's horn. His throat burned with every breath through his veil of wetted cloth.

The oasis came into view, shimmering in the distance. Jahi paused her thralls to switch mounts, a precision exercise worthy of his mother's palace guard. Then they drove on, and the green trees became real. Mirages would be a danger if they veered from the eastward path across the sands, but so long as his compass pointed east, directly east, they would travel the caravans' path: from Striped Adder to Golden Hawk to Broken Sword to Fanged Vale to Yawning Lion to Jeweled Falcon and then, finally, to Painted Rhinoceros.

The leafy trees and green brush welcomed them as their camels surged toward the promise of water with renewed strength. The Oasis of the Painted Rhinoceros meant they were less than a day from the sand sea's end. The trading post at Sezama would be waiting, with the promise of cool, fresh water pulled from its wells. And then, from there, two days' hard ride on fresh horses to reach Konghom.

He drove his camel straight to the edge of the oasis's freshwater lake. The beast all but plunged its head into the water, and he did the same, falling to his knees, unwrapping his veil and headscarf, soaking his hands and arms without bothering to remove his traveling cloak. Water sloshed in his ears, drowning the rest of the world as it soaked his skin. It was warm, but clean. The desert's sound faded into a hum. The pain of watching that man staring up at them as they rode away. The pain of the first one, left to die after he'd fallen from his mount.

He wrenched his head up from the water, taking his scarf and veil cloth and wringing them until they were damp. Prudence said they needed a few hours' sleep here at the oasis. No caravan traveled through the noonday heat. But *ubax aragti* could keep him in his saddle. He could reach Sezama post by nightfall, and rest there, while provisioners stocked a pair of good horses for the rest of his journey. If Jahi was fool enough to follow him, the blood was on her conscience, not his.

The sound of drawn steel echoed behind him.

He turned. Jahi should have collapsed, and her three remaining thralls with her, set to finding shade and water for their rest. Instead her thralls faced him with swords in hand, though they hadn't yet moved to attack. Three tired soldiers—and four new faces beside them, fresh, with the look of veteran mercenaries only just crossed to the Painted Rhinoceros from the desert's eastern side.

Jahi stood behind them. Beside her, two veiled women had taken up positions to her left. Both dressed as Jahi had been, back in Domakar: too-fine silks for travelers, wearing jewelry no common woman would dare display on the road.

He wrung his scarf one last time, taking the moment to think.

"Prince Omera," Jahi said. "I know you mean to continue on to Sezama post. My sisters and I urge you to reconsider. There is no need for further violence."

"You didn't reach out to my mother," he said. "You didn't try to confirm my words. You reached out to them."

"Our sister warned us you were well-protected, Your Highness," one of the new sisters said. The voice was deep for a woman, and hard as iron. "And that you were unlikely to listen to reason."

Two of the new mercenaries stepped forward as the Mindhunter spoke, while the other two moved in tandem around his right flank.

"Are these men thralls, too?" he asked. "More innocents to die at your command?"

"Omera, please," Jahi said. "Don't do this. We're trying to help you."

One hand drew his *shotel* while the other smeared a clump of *ubax aragti* inside his lower lip. With so much of the herb already burning in his blood, the new surge gave him a burst of power, but it wouldn't last. He had to end this quickly and escape.

The two soldiers on the right charged, driven by one mind. He lunged, but used it as a feint. Instead of striking at their swords he pushed off his forward foot, springing back toward Jahi's remaining three. They would be exhausted, as heat-scorched as he was. He took one of the men in the bowels before the thrall could raise his sword, spilling hot entrails on the sand. The other two scrambled to meet his steel with theirs, but he was faster. One sword was swatted down, while he maneuvered his blade inside the other's reach. A quick raking cut across the man's chest left a trail of red.

A rush of white-painted armor crashed into him from the side. He'd been too slow. One of the new thralls rushed him without regard for his blade; he met the charge with his *shotel*, whipped around to slice a deep gash in the man's shoulder. The thrall ignored it, reaching to grapple him as though he cared nothing for the wounds Omera would inflict as the price of reaching inside his guard.

Another set of hands grabbed hold of Omera's shirt, pulling him off-balance. Then a third set, then five. He crashed to the ground, flailing his blade, meeting unprotected skin, drenching them all in blood. His sword-arm broke as one of the thralls drove it into the sand. They closed in around him, and he shouted, feeling the coarse desert air still weighing down his lungs. Weight pressed down over his body. A set of arms gripped his left leg, while another man held his right. Two held his sword-arm. The last held his left.

One of the Mindhunters deftly stepped inside the mêlée. Metal clasped around his wrists.

"This is for your protection, Your Highness," Jahi said. "You'll understand, once we can reach your mind."

Ubax aragti still burned in his blood. But so did the desert sun, and the weight of five mindless soldiers, holding him with all their strength. She was wrong. He'd been given a charge by the Queen. He was her son, her messenger, her assassin.

He had to reach Sakhefete. Had to kill her.

Blackness surrounded him as consciousness fled.

32

ERRIS

73rd Regimental Flag
9th Division Front, the Battle of West Verrain

The ground heaved under her feet, the work of the Crab-*magi* charging alongside the macemen rushing toward her position. She crawled in the dirt, latching a hand to the wood pole beneath the blue-white-blue of the 73rd Regiment's flag, a design bearing a roaring lion over top of the Republican colors, and kept her head down to duck the musket shot that would accompany the earthquake and the charge.

It came, whistling overhead in a concentrated volley, and she tucked her legs up and curled her body behind the shelter of a corpse.

Arak'Jur kept his feet, and Corenna beside him. A shield of stone appeared in front of them, though none of the nearby soldiers took cover behind it. The ground still shook in violent spasms. It would stop when the Jun macemen were on top of them, ready to descend into a mêlée. That was the pattern, and it had already produced a tide of dead on both sides, littering the forest.

"Can you hold?" she shouted in her vessel's voice. "I need to know. How much longer can you hold this position?"

"We should attack," Corenna shouted back. "Not hold."

"I need a rallying point, as far forward as I can get," she snapped. "Hold here and Royens's Seventeenth will fall in to attack their flank, with the bulk of the First Corps behind him. But I need to know you'll be standing in an hour."

An explosion shook the ground, and a puff of white smoke appeared around their shield of stone. It cleared as quick as it came, and revealed that the stone still held, undamaged, or at least solid enough to protect them from fire.

"We'll be here," Arak'Jur said. "But fighting like this, we can't protect your soldiers. Our magic will keep us safe. That's all I can promise."

She gritted her vessel's teeth and nodded. Dead bodies littered the ground around them, combatants of both sides shot or stabbed or crushed, ten times as many Jun as Sarresant. But still they came, wave after wave, maces and spears, or pistols and arquebusiers, an endless storm attacking the two guardians' position with the 73rd. It was a testament to her soldiers' discipline that the whole regiment hadn't broken and run.

"Keep your head down, soldier," she ordered in a low voice, meant for her vessel's ears. "Whatever happens, you stay with these guardians, and you keep yourself bloody safe. Am I understood? It's no cowardice to keep yourself alive today, whatever it takes. The rest of this battle depends on you. Do your duty, and do it well."

The earth ceased its heaving abruptly, and a warcry went up in its place, a roar as loud as any musket. She tucked her vessel tighter against the corpses around her, and the pole of the regimental flag. They were coming. Gods send the guardians could hold.

A guttural roar echoed beneath the warcry, and both Arak'Jur and Corenna were surrounded by nimbuses of great cats, facing the macemen as their stone shield crumbled to dust at their feet.

She let *Need* go, weaving another strand before her vision could clear.

Her senses lurched, blinking for a moment to the table-map in front of her in the field command tent before they shifted again, this time at a horse's eye level, galloping in a loose column through the trees.

She wasted no time, heeling her mount forward through the column. This would be the 11th Light Cavalry, freshly returned from the Old World, and General de Montaigne would be riding at their head. The cavalry around her made way at a glance for her golden eyes, and word carried forward, until the general reined her mount to meet her a few horselengths from the front of the column.

"General," she said in her vessel's voice, a woman's this time. "What are you doing on the move? Your orders were to reinforce the Twenty-Second, and now you're riding north?"

"Hopeless chaos there, Your Majesty," de Montaigne said, offering a hasty salute from the saddle. "I opted to preserve my brigade and reinforce Royens at the river crossing."

"Details, General," she said. "Now."

"Three Jun companies were waiting in the trees. The enemy marched around the Twenty-Second's advance in a double envelopment hitting both flanks. My advance scouts saw it and issued a warning to the brigade commander, but there was nothing more I could do. Once the lines were entangled I turned the Eleventh northward to skirmish along the riverfront."

Her mind worked as her vessel's mount kept pace with the general's. The 22nd Brigade had been meant to be the connecting piece between two units caught by the Jun's false orders, the same trap that had ensnared Arak'Jur and the 73rd. Up and down her line it seemed every third or fourth unit had separate orders to attack, and all of them swore to have met with her in person to receive them, two or three days before. Sabotage, on a grand scale, but her people were still her people, whatever games the enemy played. They'd provoked her into action, but if they expected her to roll over and show her belly, they'd sorely underestimated her, and her army.

"Good thinking, General," she said. "Royens needs the help, if we're to secure a crossing this far up the river."

"My thoughts precisely, Your Majesty," de Montaigne said.

"Orders, then. I want you and the Eleventh to take up a position a few leagues inland from Royens's crossing point. Find some good ground, dismount, and dig in."

"Inland, Majesty? Wouldn't we be better served in the saddle, scouting the bank to the west?"

"That's what they'll expect, once they know Royens has cavalry support. They'll try the same maneuver they used on the Twenty-Second, trying to bait him forward. Instead I'll coordinate with one of the First Corps' infantry brigades. When they try their pincer, hit them hard on the eastern push. Royens's people will be there to hit them from the other side."

De Montaigne saluted. "Yes, Majesty."

She returned it, letting *Need* go before her hand fell from her chest.

This time she remained in her own body long enough to catch her breath. The map was all chaos, black figures representing Jun companies interspersed with blue for New Sarresant, light blue for Gand, and pale green for Thellan, with separate markers for cavalry, infantry, artillery, binders, the two guardians with the 73rd and their best guesses for the positions of Jun *magi*. She'd ordered her flag moved from Rasailles into the field; as good as *Need* was to deliver orders, she couldn't gather every scouting report by herself. The map in front of her represented the work of a hundred scouts, the markers changing as fast as her people could ride to deliver their reports.

"The Twenty-Second's position is lost," she said, delivering what she'd seen through *Need* to augment the scouts' work. "De Montaigne has the Eleventh riding north-northwest, shadowing the river to provide support for the First Corps."

Aides scrambled to adjust the figures, nearly colliding with another group moving more figures to the south. She hovered over the table, shifting where she stood to change the angle. Chaos. Half her army had attacked while the rest remained entrenched and fortified. False orders, on a scale she'd never imagined possible. Only now were the rest of her forces committing to the maneuver, and the enemy outnumbered her precisely as Tigai had warned: four to one, or worse, along some stretches of the battle line. But this was salvageable. A desperate hope lit the way through. She'd faced perhaps the greatest general who had ever lived in Paendurion, and bested him. She could match this Jun commander, even with the dice shaved to throw ones on every side.

"How fresh are these reports?" she asked, pointing to a section where two Jun companies held a ridgeline against a Gand infantry brigade. "How many guns already in place on the heights? How many more expected to be up within the hour?"

A senior aide looked at her, wide-eyed, before fumbling with papers. Another scrambled through a different sheaf.

"Now!" she snapped. "I don't have time for incompetence."

"Twenty-nine minutes, Majesty," a third aide said, reading off a roll of parchment. "The report listed seven batteries in place, with six more expected by midday."

"She didn't ask for midday, she said within the hour," another aide corrected him. "And for that, Majesty, perhaps three or four more? The scout's language was imprecise."

She shook her head, letting them argue over what was in the report. Damn but she needed Essily. A fine fucking time for her best aide and chief of staff to have taken a few days' leave. They'd thought it quiet and calm, a fine time for a rest, and so it had been, before the storm.

She scanned the lines, processing each marker, then froze, and pointed.

"I need to know whether this is a mistake," she said. "You have this unit marked as the Jun Company of the Raging Bear. A second company bears the same markings, here in the south."

Another scramble, another report. "Both claim to be accurate, Majesty," one of the aides said. "The southern report is older, forty-nine minutes. Perhaps they stole a march while our scouts rode to field command?"

"They marched twelve leagues and redeployed in forty-nine minutes?" another aide said. "It has to be a mistake. Our apologies, Majesty, we'll make sure it doesn't—"

"Fetch Lord Tigai," she said. "I don't care where he is, I don't care if he's on the front line neck deep in the fighting, you bring him here at once."

An aide saluted and ran from the tent, and she went back to the map. Two copies of the same company could be a simple mistake, or it could mean the Dragons had taken the field. It meant she had to see the battle through the eyes of a commander who could move an entire regiment as easily as she could tether a *Need* binding. With Tigai she could have warnings when they used their starfield—the very reason she'd opted not to make use of his abilities in a similar fashion—but if she understood the battle she wouldn't need them.

That was the key. Every battle had a rhythm, a pulse between one side's objectives, and the other's. She'd already held out longer than her enemy expected, that much was clear from the frenetic deployments, the blunt nature of his attacks. He'd expected the false orders to send her army into chaos, and so they had, but her people were trained well enough to drag his army into the mire alongside them. Now the way through was a decisive action. The Jun commander craved it. She could almost sense the hunger, the desperation. He wanted a hammer blow that would crack her line, let him pour through and convince her army to give in to the uncertainty the false orders had sown.

She swept up and down the map, letting the position of each unit soak in her mind.

The river.

Royens was bringing up the full strength of the 1st Corps to secure a forward crossing. If the Jun cut it off, it would demonstrate that they controlled the field. Her people already held the bridges at Arentaigne and l'Elenne; stopping Royens was a symbolic gesture more than a strategic one. Precisely the sort of victory the Jun needed now. And they already had the units in place to attack.

"Send riders to the Nineteenth, the Second, the Fifty-First and their artillery," she said abruptly. "Orders: Fall back from present engagements, prepare for action in the north. No advance until the enemy begins his maneuver. I'll give the signal through *Need*. Repeat it back."

Two aides began reciting her order in unison, and she nodded when they'd both gotten it right.

"More orders for the Sixth Division," she said, and gave them, then another set for the 9th, and the 13th. The tent came to a standstill as she snapped off the orders in quick succession, aides turning to watch her, or wait for their turn to carry a missive to the front. She stared at the map as she delivered the commands. Her people had to move back, to show weakness in precisely the spot where the enemy wanted them most vulnerable. Riders would lay the powder trails; her *Need* would be the spark to ignite the bomb.

The tent was half-empty when she was done, aides sent running for riders to reach almost every company on the northern side of the field. The movements would have to be precise, a calculated dance to lure their enemy's eye, a temptation too sweet for him to resist the trap.

"Where is Royens now?" she asked.

"With the Fifth Infantry, Majesty," one of the remaining aides said. "According to the last reports."

"On the front line?" she asked. "Or is their flag positioned to the rear of the engagement?"

The aide frowned, shuffling through papers, and she sighed, shaking her head before they could reply. Royens had a general's bad habit of putting himself too far forward. Doubly worse in a field-marshal, but no officer was without their flaws.

She closed her eyes, letting *Need* reach her through the network of the leylines. Her senses shifted, and she braced, expecting powder, smoke, shouts, and gunfire. Instead her nose was filled with the smells of mud and horseshit, her ears heard the bustle of a camp on the move, and her eyes cleared to see four junior officers standing around her, as though each had been hanging on her words a moment before.

Each officer started, and a second lieutenant with a quartermaster's insignia recovered first.

"Majesty," the lieutenant said. "Was there something else? Apologies if we haven't moved quickly enough."

"Royens," she started to say. "I need—wait, what did you say? Moved quickly enough for what?"

"We've got the bulk of the corps pivoting south already, Your Majesty," the lieutenant said. "Captain Vacreuix, ah, that is...you, Your Majesty, or your vessel...well, she deserves the credit. She had contingencies prepared for every order you gave. Now it's only a matter of whipping the soldiers into shape to follow the plan. But if there was something else, I'm sure she, and we, can accommodate...?"

South. If Royens was moving the First Corps' advance divisions south it would unhinge every order she'd spent the last twenty minutes delivering. He was meant to be the fulcrum for her advance, the bait for the trap, and the anvil for the hammer. If his forces weren't in place when the attack came, the enemy would cut through their lines and find her reserve too far overextended for any hope of recovery.

"Who gave that order?" she said.

The four officers shared a look. "You did, Your Majesty," the lieutenant said. "Here, in person. The field-marshal summoned us for logistical review at headquarters not a quarter hour ago. I would have thought you'd still be there, working out the finer points of the southern attack."

Her spine went rigid.

"Take me to Royens's headquarters," she said. "Now."

The order elicited another shared look between the officers. "Now!" she barked again. "Double time, soldier. Move!"

The lieutenant whirled, and they left the other three behind. The 5th Infantry should have been mired neck-deep in the fighting; her latest reports had them hotly engaged with no fewer than four Jun companies. Yet this camp was calm and focused, engaged in precisely the sort of planned withdrawal the lieutenant had promised her they would execute. She thumbed the pistol holstered on her vessel's belt. A six-shot revolver of the same make and model she'd favored in the cavalry. A pity this logistics captain didn't see fit to carry a saber, or to have a horse like Jiri saddled and ready to ride.

"Is there something wrong, Your Majesty?" the lieutenant asked. "If we need to adjust the orders, Captain Vacreuix can manage, I swear it. She's the best logistics officer I've served under. She could plan a rainstorm and not leave out a single drop. You can tell her I said so, too."

"She can hear you, Lieutenant," she replied in her vessel's voice. "How far to Royens's flag?"

The young man's cheeks went red, but he pointed up ahead to a cluster of white tents being struck and taken apart. "There, Majesty," he said. "Looks like the teams are already preparing for the move. Do you need me to fetch him for you?"

She pushed past the lieutenant, running ahead to the tents. Horses and asses hitched to carts already bore the bulk of the field-marshal's effects—she recognized an oaken desk, two matching chairs, and a cabinet—but the 1st Corps' flag was still there, flying behind the bustle of the teams, and that meant Royens would be nearby.

Salutes greeted her, offered belatedly when soldiers saw her vessel's golden eyes. Not a soldier in her army didn't know what the golden light signified, though not all would have seen it in person. She might have been stopped otherwise, a captain storming through the camp toward a field-marshal, and all the more so if they'd noticed her clutching the grip of her revolver.

Instead she emerged through the tents to where Royens was standing, dictating orders to two aides while a woman with six stars pinned to her collar stood beside, nodding along to every word.

It was her.

Her body. Erris d'Arrent, Empress of the Republics of New Sarresant, Gand, and Thellan, and dressed in regalia to match: her usual blue coat, cut from finer cloth than any she'd worn in the field, with white gloves to hide the binders' scars and her hair pulled back tight against her scalp. A mirror's reflection come to life, and she might have gawked if she hadn't already guessed this would be precisely what she would see.

She drew her pistol and fired.

Four shots roared through the tents, and Royens's aides dove for the ground. The field-marshal dove for her, tackling her before she could empty the weapon's chamber. He was head and shoulders taller than her vessel, with a soldier's build, and she felt the wind leave her lungs as they crashed down into the dirt.

"Assassin!" Royens shouted, even as he pinned her down. "The Empress has been shot!"

"Reginald," she managed, gasping underneath the weight of his forearm. "Look at me. Look at my eyes."

He did, seeming to see her for the first time, and he withdrew in confusion.

"That isn't me," she said. "An impostor." Breath rushed in with his weight removed. "You must rescind every order that creature gave, and do it now, before it delivers us into our enemy's hands."

"How can I be sure—?" he began, then glanced back at where her doppelganger had stood and gasped.

She sat up, and joined him in his surprise.

Where her body had been, a perfect copy of Erris d'Arrent, now sat a man's form, clutching his stomach through a weak smile on a familiar face.

Voren.

Fei Zan.

"Impossible," Erris said. "You were dead. Our *Need* bond was severed."

"Severed by the God," Fei Zan said. "When he bound me as champion of the Fox." He smiled again, and somehow she could see all the forms he'd worn at once. Chairwoman Caille, whom he'd replaced before he'd first been exposed. Anselm Voren, her mentor and commander. Fei Zan, the man of the East. "Never expected...this." He gestured toward his stomach and chest, where four red splotches showed through the white shirt beneath his coat. "You were a worthy opponent. A worthy champion."

"You did this," she said, rising to her feet as Royens watched in awe. "You gave the false orders that started this battle."

"I did," Fei Zan said, barking a quick laugh punctuated by blood. "And so many more. You're doomed, Empress. As, it seems, am I."

Dread crept in. "What other skins did you wear?" she asked. "Mine. Who else's?"

He only laughed, a rasping, croaking sound that died halfway through, replaced by a voice surging in her mind.

FOR THIS ONE, IT ENDS.

33

ARAK'JUR

73rd Regimental Flag
9th Division Front, the Battle of West Verrain

Scattered gunfire sounded through the trees, enough to keep him alert, though he and Corenna let their shields of earth drop as the enemy retreated.

"Are you wounded?" he asked Corenna. She shook her head, breathing hard.

"Nothing serious," she said. "You?"

He grunted no. Two punctures in his leg left trails of blood down his calves, and a mace wound on his shoulder was already turning a deep purple. Fragments of stone embedded in his ribs stung when he breathed too deep, but he could already feel the guardian's gift knitting his flesh together.

Corenna bore similar marks: a musket shot through her left arm, leaving her favoring it whenever the enemy withdrew, a gash in her neck that seeped blood, too shallow to be of real concern, and bruises and powder burns streaking across her shoulders and chest. But she stood, and she fought on, and if she said her injuries were nothing serious, then it was so. The spirits would see to her recovery, the same as for him.

He sat atop the stone that had become their rallying point, a boulder almost as large as a small tree. Dried meat, nuts, and fruit were all he'd thought to bring. Enough for a few days away from the Alliance. Corenna sat beside him, and he offered her a handful. She took it, then drank from her waterskin before offering it to him. All along their line the few remaining pockets of soldiers used the reprieve to eat, drink, reload their weapons, and scavenge from the dead. Bodies lay piled deep enough to hide the forest floor on either side of their boulder: macemen, musketeers, pistoliers, infantry, cavalry, and *magi*. The 73rd Regiment had been reduced to a few score soldiers hiding among the dead, and only a shaman could know how many Jun soldiers had broken themselves at his and Corenna's feet. But Erris d'Arrent had asked them to hold, and they'd held, and now the morning sun was high in the sky and the battle, so far as he could tell, continued.

"No more shots," Corenna said, and it took a second look to understand her meaning. The front to the south had been crackling with gunfire all morning, and was quiet now. "Do you think it means the battle might be over soon?"

"Over," he said. "Or moving."

She nodded wearily, letting water slosh over her neck and chest in the heat. "I wish we'd had the rest of your guardians," she said. "I shouldn't have been so stubborn about that."

"No, you shouldn't have," he said. "But Shimmash will have had visions of the fighting. He'll lead them here, even if they don't arrive until tomorrow."

"You think this will continue another day?"

Before he could answer, the soldiers of the 73rd rose from their positions, calling up to their boulder. "Courier coming," one of them said. "Orders, could be."

He slid down the rock, then offered a hand to guide Corenna down beside him. "I think it will," he said. "The Jun wouldn't throw so many lives away unless they meant to purchase something dear. I think this is the fight that will decide their fate in this country."

"Putting everything into one battle," Corenna said. "It seems like madness, doesn't it? I wonder if the same voices that whispered to the Uktani are at work here."

He nodded. Ad-Shi had been the force behind the spirits' corruption, but she was far from the only evil in the world. What mattered now was Corenna held his hand, walking with him through the remains of all the horrors they'd faced today. And it wasn't finished. More would come, and more would die. He saw it happening, almost as if through a premonition of the spirits of things-to-come. A figure, looming in the trees. A single Jun officer, alone, riding toward them from a great distance...

"Corenna," he said. "Do you see that?"

She turned where he pointed. "Yes," she said. "One man, riding fast. An attack?"

"A *magi*, perhaps," he said.

"Guardians," an officer said, coming toward them using his musket as a walking stick. A red stain wrapped with tattered, bloody linen bound the arm he favored. "Courier's arrived. It's orders. We're to march north toward the river, to deploy with the First Corps."

"There's a Jun rider," he said. "Coming from the west. Maybe an attack."

The officer squinted, though the rider was still far enough, and hidden enough by trees and foliage, that the man might not be able to see it without a guardian's gifts.

"Only one?" the officer said. "An emissary, perhaps? Come to treat with us?"

"These orders," Corenna said. "They're putting the Seventy-Third back in the field? Can't they see this unit is finished?"

"I think Her Majesty wants you two, more than the rest of my people," the officer said. "But we can still fight, and we'll do our duty to the last. With a lull in the fighting, it might be best to move now, if the two of you are up for it."

"Yes," Corenna said. "Have the rest of your people assemble and we'll join you."

"The rider, first," Arak'Jur said. "We should stay and face them, in case it's a threat."

"My people are pulling back," the officer said. "The colonel is dead, and both captains with her. Near as I can tell, I'm in charge. If you think this rider could be a *magi*, I'll leave you two to handle it. Then we form and march north together."

Corenna nodded. "That's fine, Lieutenant. Keep your people safe."

The man saluted, and winced for the effort. Arak'Jur had already focused his attention on the rider, tracking the figure as it wove through trees. Better to hope it was an emissary sent to treat with them. They'd faced enough *magi* during the assaults that he wondered what sort of creature could face them alone. The man who had destroyed New Sarresant, perhaps, and that thought was better off dismissed. Fear had no place on the front line of a battle.

"It's one of theirs," Corenna said. "The uniform. A man, I think, and an officer."

"All your gifts ready?" he asked.

"Yes. You?"

"I expended *una're* to aid in recovery. The rest, yes."

The rider drew near, to where the soldiers would be able to see him with unaided eyes. Then the figure raised its hands, both of them, and waved.

He relaxed his hold on the spirits.

"It's Tigai," he said.

Corenna seemed to relax, too, and showed some of the relief he felt. It could too easily have been another battle.

Tigai closed the distance swiftly, guiding his horse with deft precision, riding hard until he reined it to a walk to navigate the sea of dead around their boulder.

"Arak'Jur," Tigai said. "Corenna. What in the hells happened here?"

"A war," he said. "Why did you come on horseback, and not...?" He pantomimed appearing from the air.

"Through the strands?" Tigai asked, finally giving up and sliding down to guide the horse on foot. A well-trained animal, not to balk at the sights and smells of battle. "Better luck for you that I didn't. If the Dragons found a strand anchored here they might have dropped their strength on you without warning. And that's why I'm here. Erris kicked me out of the bloody planning rooms before I could set it in motion, but the way I see it, there's no need to wait for her approval." He paused, looking over Arak'Jur and Corenna. "Are you both in a state where you can fight?"

"We have orders from the Empress," he said. "We're to move out and join a northern attack."

"Bugger the Empress," Tigai said. "I know where we can find the enemy's commander, Isaru Mattai, who has to be one of the Regnant's champions to boot, else he'd have died burning in the middle of the sands where I left him. The Jun Dragons have started moving entire companies, and with so much activity they'll have no way to know it's us using the strands. Especially with you two, we could be in and out, with Isaru dead and their command disrupted, before they realize we've arrived."

"You mean for us to be assassins," Arak'Jur said.

"You know where their generals are?" Corenna said. "And you can... appear there?"

"Not just their generals," Tigai said. "Lord Isaru himself. A *magi*, and a bloody dangerous one. He has the command, and with their Dragons he can be on the far side of the world and still be at their head during this battle."

"Could it be a trap?" he asked.

"It won't matter, if we're fast," Tigai said. "I've seen you fight. You can kill him, and I can get us out, before the Dragons can even read the strands to know we're there."

Corenna paused, glancing back toward the 73rd's flag. She'd refused to leave before, but the regiment was in tatters now. Still, he'd pledged to fight at her side. It meant deferring, if he wanted to keep his word, and so he deferred.

"What sort of *magi* is he?" Corenna asked. "And what powers will he have gained, as one of the Regnant's champions?"

"I'm not certain," Tigai said. "Crab, maybe. He made the ground shake

once, before I rescued Mei. As to what power they gain when they're bound..."
Tigai shrugged. "He's dangerous, but so are the both of you. The goal is to kill
him before he knows we're there."

"What do you think?" Arak'Jur asked Corenna. "It could be an
opportunity, but the Empress gave us orders."

"Striking their commanders seems more valuable to me," Corenna said.
"Do you trust Tigai?"

Tigai gaped at her for the audacity to ask the question in front of him,
but she was right. Everything hinged on the Dragon gift. And he'd come to
know Yanjin Tigai during the weeks they'd spent in the Gods' Seat. He was
a foreigner, but then, so were Sarine, Erris, and Yuli. Tigai fought against his
own people for the sake of what he believed was right: Sarine's vision for the
conflict between her and the Regnant. Tigai was brash and foul-mouthed, but
his heart had never wavered toward that cause.

"Yes," he said. "I do."

"Then we go," Corenna said. "You may take us there as soon as you're ready."

It surprised him, after all the fight she'd shown before. But then, perhaps
she'd taken up the 73rd's cause in addition to pledging to fight with its people.

"All right," Tigai said. "Good. I've scouted their high command already.
When we get there, follow my lead. I'll get us to Isaru with a minimum of
interference from their sentries."

Corenna nodded. He did the same.

"No time to wait, then," Tigai said. "Get close."

He drew a breath and it was done. They'd been standing among the dead at
their boulder, and then foreign vegetation surrounded them, trees grown thick
together, undergrowth so thick he could hardly step through it. But he hardly
had to. A bare ten paces in front of him swirls of color rose through the jungle,
tents of red, yellow, purple, and more, like a painter's canvas come to life.

Tigai made a sharp gesture, pointing forward to indicate a rally point
between a green-striped tent and a purple one, then blinked out of existence,
as fast as he'd first appeared.

Corenna moved, and he tracked behind her.

Almost as quick, shouts of alarm went up through the camp. *Juna'ren* gave
his camouflage, and together he and Corenna blended in beside the tents. A
pistol shot went off in the distance, then another. Then as suddenly as he'd
first vanished, Tigai stood in front of them, impatient as though he'd been
waiting between the tents all along.

"I had anchors on the far side of the camp," Tigai said. "The sentries will be heading that way. Follow."

They ducked between a tent painted deep red, then around one striped orange and green before Tigai froze, gesturing them to take up positions behind him.

"That's the main tent," Tigai said, indicating a pure white one in the center of a clearing. "Isaru should be inside."

"Will he have *magi* with him?" Corenna asked.

"He didn't when I was here before, but they're in the middle of a battle now, so who can say. Are you both ready?"

They nodded, and Tigai drew his pistols, gesturing for them to advance. He understood the plan without speaking it aloud: The attack would fall to him and Corenna, with Tigai in reserve, waiting to get them out if an escape was needed, or the deed was done.

They moved.

Whatever Tigai had done managed to clear the sentries away; the clearing outside the main tents was empty. They crossed in front of the tents quickly, threw open the flap, and were greeted by a full circle of Jun in uniforms of various colors and insignia. Six of them stood around a table, while one man in white-dyed leather stood at their head, and a second figure, an advisor perhaps, an old man in ragged black robes, sat, eyes closed, at the back of the tent.

He and Corenna moved with one mind. He went left, she went right. A habit born of practice in their time together, honed and made sharp by the morning's fighting. *Kirighra* granted his blessing, a shroud of stealth and shadow. Corenna embraced Wind, and *munat'ap*, a snarling growl emitting from her as the spirits surrounded her with their glowing forms. Then she struck.

Two of the six flew apart before they could turn to face her, a blast of wind whipping through them in a rain of blood across the tabletop. Shouts went up, and two more dove in her path as the eyes of the old man in black shot open. Their leader, the man in white, which had to be Isaru, took a halting step as Corenna struck again, another blade of wind spilling entrails as she threw it into the tent, cutting men in half, leaving legs still standing as their torsos tumbled to their feet.

Arak'Jur slid around them into place, the flickering shade of *kirighra's* blessing shifting his vision into gray, black, and white. *Valak'ar* beckoned, the wraith-snake, there to grant its blessing as soon as their quarry was distracted by Corenna's attack.

A third gust of wind cleared the bodies, hurling them into the back of the canvas as a child might hurl sticks, and Corenna advanced on Isaru. Isaru met her, only instead of the man in white, in an eyeblink his form changed. An insect, taller than any man, with great gossamer wings, racks of spiked bone down its spine, and twin scything claws for arms. Before he could call a warning the insect-creature charged.

Wind met it, scraping against the insect's armored hide like chalk on stone, but it leapt into her, fluttering its wings, snapping its jaw, and shearing through the left half of Corenna's torso in a single blow of its claws.

Corenna twisted with the force of it, spinning around as her arm and shoulder detached from her body.

Arak'Jur's heart dropped with her to the ground. But he moved.

Valak'ar granted its blessing, and he traded *kirighra's* cloak of shadows for *mareh'et's* claws without thinking. A twin nimbus of cat and snake surrounded him. The insect screeched and struck again, pounding its claws down into where Corenna fell, now obscured from his sight by the creature's towering form. He wove behind it, ducking the fluttering wings, and grabbed the creature by the abdomen with both hands, roaring as he lifted it off the ground. *Valak'ar* injected its poison through his fingers, blessed by *mareh'et's* claws to slice through the exoskeleton as he picked the creature up, twisting to get it away from Corenna's slumping body. He screamed as it screamed, channeling every gift as the creature writhed, and they both fell.

The weight knocked air from his lungs, but he kept his grip tight, sinking *valak'ar's* poison under the creature's skin. Spikes punctured his chest as the insect wrenched its back into him. He ignored the pain. The creature was already dead, as soon as the poison reached its heart. He had to keep it away from Corenna. He had to keep her alive. The cuts he'd seen could be regenerated, so long as she didn't die. He had to—

"No more."

The old man in rags spoke the words, and suddenly all his rage, all his fear over Corenna, all the fury of *mareh'et* and *valak'ar* dimmed to a distant hum.

He let go of the insect, felt it roll out of his grasp and crunch against the dirt. Corenna had picked herself up on her one remaining arm, propping herself up, though her chest and lower jaw were marred by deep gashes. She froze, looking at him, at the insect, as though they were strangers to her, as though she couldn't recall how she'd come to be here, wounded on the ground.

The old man in rags shambled toward him, bringing a walking stick to rest beside his head. A coughing sound accompanied it, coming from where the insect had lain beside him. Only now the insect was gone and the man had returned: Isaru, dressed in white save for where his shirt had been cut open, revealing a bloody mess of blackened veins pulsing under his skin.

"My lord," Isaru said, a croaking wheeze. "Can you...?"

The old man prodded a toe into Arak'Jur's ribs.

"A champion of the Wild," the old man said. "Another wild mage, unbonded. And the lost Dragon, who should have been mine."

"Please, my lord," Isaru said. "Save me."

He followed the old man's gaze to where Tigai stood frozen, having dropped his pistol to the ground. He should have called on *ipek'a* to leap and crush the old man's skull. Yet instead he was calm. His body lay on the ground, unable to move.

"I'm afraid I cannot," the old man said. "You served me well, champion of Lotus, but *valak'ar*'s poison is beyond even my gift to heal."

Another cough, and this time Isaru spat blackened blood as the veins crept up his chest.

"Almost," the old man said. "Almost you make it worth the risk. Two of her champions, foolish enough to come to die at my feet. Almost I might think her aware of my plans. Do you think the Veil would send you both to die, to bait me into settling this in the old way, and not the new?"

Isaru screamed, then convulsed as the poison worked its way to his heart. For a moment the insect appeared again, then flashed back to the man, rolling over to cough one last time into the dirt.

A voice echoed in Arak'Jur's head. *FOR THIS ONE, IT ENDS.*

The old man clicked his teeth.

"A sad thing," the old man said. "But tell her no. Her time is finished. Tell her I let you live. Remind her that mercy, not vengeance, was ever at the heart of our alliance."

The old man turned and walked. Arak'Jur should have moved to charge after him, to attack, to retrieve Corenna and see to her wounds, to flee, to run, to stand. Instead he did nothing, lying on the ground beside Isaru's body until the old man in rags was out of sight.

34

SARINE

Field Command
The Battle of West Verrain

The Watcher loomed in front of her, shimmering like heat in the distance. Couriers and aides ran around them, seemingly oblivious to the human shape standing between her and the Empress. Erris's consciousness was elsewhere, delivering orders through *Need*, but her body stood hovering over a table at the center of the tent. Sarine should have been with her at the front, weaving *Yellow* and *Green* to disrupt the enemy. Instead the Watcher blocked her path, silent but unmoving, keeping her here when she should have been fighting.

I don't understand, Anati thought to her. *It demanded you come here to the Empress's tent, and now it won't let you leave. But it isn't saying what it wants.*

She tested it, stepping to the side, and the Watcher followed, moving to block her way.

"It's never done this before," she said. "Can you ask it directly? Why did it want us here?"

Anati bobbed her head up and down from her perch on the edge of the table, then vanished. The Watcher made no move to acknowledge her *kaas*, standing still while the tent was a flurry of activity around them. They'd taken Yuli to the palace-turned-medical-ward at Rasailles, and then the Watcher had guided her here. Now the damned thing wouldn't move, and for all it appeared translucent, little more than vibrations in the air, its physical form was solid, and all too effective at keeping her penned in if it didn't want her to leave.

"You're bloody annoying, you know that?" she said. It earned a queer look from one of the nearby aides, which she ignored. "I never asked you to follow me from the Seat. You were supposed to be helping me, not getting in my way."

The Watcher didn't move. She tested it again, this time feinting left before darting the other way. It crashed into her, or she crashed into it, somehow finding it directly in her path before she made it two bloody steps from her chair.

This time more of the aides took notice as she sprawled to the ground.

"Are you quite well, madame?" one of them asked.

She mumbled a curse, shaking her head as she rose back to her seat. "I'm fine, thank you," she said. "And in a second I'm going to use the starfield to get out of here whether you like it or not."

That would be bad, Anati thought, reappearing on the table's edge as she spoke. *You'd give the Dragons an anchor right beside the Empress while she's away with her vessels.*

"I know," she said. "That's why I haven't done it yet. Did you get anything from him?"

Not really. He keeps saying "meet the Queen" over and over. I tried to ask him why we needed to meet Erris. It just made him start yelling "THE QUEEN" at me. Eleven times in a row, I think.

She sighed, slumping back in her chair. Her body ached, sore and stiff where Mileva Far Sight had landed blows with her shadows. What were they doing here, if not meeting the Queen? Maybe it wanted Erris to come back to her body before it would let her leave.

Hm, Anati thought. *Now it's saying something different.*

She sat forward. Different was good. Different was something other than being penned in her chair.

"The lines," it says. "Use the lines to see the Queen." What could that mean?

"The leylines, maybe?" she asked. She studied the Watcher's form, searching it for clues. It hadn't moved, still standing, silent and passive, between her and the tent's exit. "That could have something to do with Erris. But why would we need to use the lines to see Erris if she's the Queen he's talking about?"

I'm not sure, Anati thought. *I think, maybe...*

"I need runners to the Twelfth and Sixth Division artillery," Erris snapped. The order came suddenly, without warning, and where the Empress's body had stood rigid, propped against the table, now she was active, scanning the maps and barking for the nearest aides. "Royens needs fire support, now. I'll coordinate with the southern flanks. The Jun have three fresh companies moving through the valley behind these hills. We need fire, coordinated fire from as many batteries as we can put in range."

The aides swarmed around her, scribbling notes, pushing figures into place on her maps, running from the tent as soon as she finished giving a command.

"Erris!" she called, rising from her chair.

Erris turned, surprise writ in her eyes that turned instantly to determination. "You!" the Empress said, then paused. "Yuli isn't with you. Should I assume one of those '*FOR THIS ONE, IT ENDS*' heralded the worst?"

"No," she said. "She's fine. She and Reed are at the palace. She took a wound, but she'll recover. One of those voices was my doing—one of the Regnant's champions, Mileva Far Sight, is dead. What about the other two?"

Erris shot a glance back toward the map, studying it as she listened. "Fei Zan was one of them, dead at my hand. That's two. Can you not sense if... what are you doing in that chair?"

"The bloody Watcher has me trapped here," she said. "I came to see if I could help with the battle, but he's making it bloody difficult."

"Yes," Erris said. "Yes, Gods yes. Here." She turned to an aide. "Send runners forward to the Sixth Division. Have them feint an attack at the center of the enemy line. Sarine can get in place faster—it's safe to use the stars, the bloody Jun Dragons are using them enough to mask it, and you won't stay there long. I'll connect to Royens and coordinate the counterattack when they take the bait. How many can you affect with your *Yellow*? A full company? Ten thousand?"

"With the sparks I can, but—"

The Watcher grabbed her by the wrist and yanked her to her feet.

It doesn't like that idea, Anati thought. *It says it can "make her use the lines," if it has to, but what does—?*

She only had time to yelp as the Watcher pulled her up from the chair, dragging her toward the Empress. Erris whirled, a hand going to her saber, but the Watcher reached her in an eyeblink, laying another of its incorporeal hands on the Empress's arm.

The world shifted.

She felt it through the blue sparks. A golden light, threading between the leylines, manifest as tight coils of energy surging beneath the Infinite Plane. She felt the torrent of the Watcher's energy mingled with hers, and with a tangle of sparks she somehow knew was Erris, too. Together the three of them leapt across the world, traversing oceans in an instant. Yet only a piece of her made the trip, alongside a piece of the Watcher, and the Empress. Their physical bodies stayed behind in the tent, while the rest traveled through the golden light of *Need*.

They opened their eyes.

The sensation assaulted her senses. It was like three pairs of eyes opening at once. Three hearts beat quickly in her chest. Three pairs of hands, three sets of ears, everything repeated in triplicate. She was here. Erris was here, and the Watcher, too, all sharing the same skin. It churned her stomach. The world blurred, and she could feel Erris fighting her, though she couldn't say how. Sparks surged on the Infinite Plane. Indignation shone through, and a thought—this was *her* gift; she was the mistress of her vessels, the one who commanded *Need*. But it wasn't her thought. It was Erris's, repeated in her head.

Another thought warred with it, this one from the Watcher: *Let the reborn Veil speak. Let Sarine have this body, for now.*

Sarine felt only fear, on her own account. This wasn't what she'd expected. Somehow the Watcher had tethered all three of them together using Erris's gift. Somehow they'd been sent to a vessel's body on the far side of the world.

The Watcher's thought: *Stop fighting her. Let it be what it will be.*

The world calmed.

She could feel Erris receding, drifting into the background of this vessel's body, with the Watcher's touch on the Empress's mind. He'd done something to pacify her. Or perhaps, to subdue her? Before she could puzzle out what had happened her eyes cleared, and she saw the chamber in front of them.

She was in a dark room, lit by torchlight. Her vessel—the body was hers now—knelt alongside six others in a half circle, all facing a woman sitting at their center. Her vessel wore strange jewelry, shining gold rings clamped around her wrists leading all the way to her elbows on both arms, and a white silk dress mirrored by the six other kneelers. The walls were painted with intricate designs, soft colors that dulled to gray in the torchlight. Yet all of it faded against the radiance of the woman at the center of the circle. She'd been mistaken, to believe the Watcher had meant Erris when he said "the Queen." This woman was the Queen, if any woman had ever held the title.

The Queen sat cross-legged, while the other six supplicants held their kneeling pose. Her skin was pure ebony, a deep lustrous black that seemed to catch the light and drink it in, reflecting a metallic sheen. Her hair had been braided and woven with gold, making the appearance of a crown fitted to her skull. Her eyes were pools of white, here in the room and somehow on the Infinite Plane, too; she could feel those eyes in both dimensions, seeing her body, her vessel's body, and the million sparks that made them.

"You're here," the Queen said, and her voice sounded like thunder, echoing in both planes at once. "That is you, is it not?"

Erris and the Watcher both surged into her awareness, then faded again.

The body was *hers*, as sure as the one she'd always worn, without the lines of *Need*.

"I'm not sure how I came to be here," she said. The sound was strange to her ears; she spoke, but it was another woman's voice, lower-pitched and softer, with an accent used to unfamiliar syllables. "I...the Watcher brought me, using my champion's gifts with the leylines."

"I requested the Masadi reach you on my behalf," the Queen said. "It seems he found a way. Understand, I never imagined welcoming the Veil into my presence, no matter what skin she wore. Yet this is a desperate hour. My sister betrays me, as your partner betrays you. So be welcome, Sarine-who-is-the-Veil-reborn. I am Amanishiakne, Sister-Queen of the Bhakal."

Her mind flashed back to the Watcher's book. Partners, the Queen said—Regnant and Veil. The Queen, Amanishiakne, had the air of something ancient, a slowness to her movement, something in her eyes that spoke of eons. This had to be one of the "others" the book spoke of: a rival to the Regnant and Veil. Power emanated from her, here and on the Infinite Plane. Sparks pulsed in torrents within torrents. A quiet majesty projected outward, so the supplicants kneeling around her felt *right*, like a thing put to its intended use.

"You're one of the others," she said, putting her suspicion to words. "A rival claimant to the Soul of the World."

Amanishiakne said nothing, studying her on both planes. Finally she spoke.

"How much do you know?" Amanishiakne said. "When the Regnant made you, what did he give you of her memories?"

The words stung. The Regnant *made* her? She'd never known parents other than her uncle, but she was no creature of his.

"I don't belong to him," she said. "You called the Regnant and Veil partners, but he's never been a partner of mine. I've been working to defeat him, to bond champions and learn my place in all of this."

"And what place do you imagine that is?" Amanishiakne said. "Do you understand why you were made?"

"I know I was meant to be a vessel for the Veil to be reborn," she said. "But I killed her. Lin is dead, and her power is mine now, mine alone."

Amanishiakne's eyes swept over her, here and on the Infinite Plane. Wonder shone through the Queen's expression, wonder and disbelief.

"It's true, isn't it?" Amanishiakne said. "In all my visions, and my sister's, I never imagined...I was certain you were his creature, his trap, laid for all of us."

"All of who?" she said. "You mean the others?"

"Yes," Amanishiakne said. "Your…former…partner, and your predecessor, have sought our extinction for a great many cycles, since magic returned to the Soul. And yet, I desired to meet you in person, to know the truth. You truly see him as your enemy, don't you?"

"Who are you?" she said. "How many of you are there?"

"My sister and I," Amanishiakne said. "The Tarzali Sun and Moon. The Rabaquim Flesh and Blood. The Skovan Chorus, Demonic and Divine. The Nikkon Spirit-Weavers. All who inherited a link in the great chain of magic in this world, but were left out of the Regnant and Veil's designs of Life and Death."

"And you would fight against him?" she said. "You would be allies to stop what he's trying to do to the Soul?"

Amanishiakne's eyes glistened.

"We have fought to claim what is ours—what should have been ours—for more cycles than you know, Sarine-who-is-the-Veil-reborn. But it may already be too late for this one. I wish I'd known what you were before."

"Before what?"

"My sister's betrayal," Amanishiakne said. "He offered her power, *your* power. Sakhefete means to become the new Veil, such as it will be."

"I don't understand," she said. "I control the Soul, as the Veil. How can he give her what's mine?"

"The Regnant's gift is memory," Amanishiakne said. "He will rebuild the Veil within Sakhefete's mind. Then, with her as his partner, they will turn the keys together. You will be unnecessary, and I will be dead. So we are natural allies, whether we trust each other or not. So long as I live, I can stop him from completing the reconstruction."

Her mind flashed to the map room, to the dead bodies of Erris's scouts and surveyors. The Regnant could have used the map room to find her champions, just as Yuli had used it to find Mileva Far Sight in Tiansei. If he had wanted her champions dead, they would have been.

"The champions," she said. "He never meant for his to win."

"If what you say is true," Amanishiakne said. "Then no. He means to replace you with Sakhefete—a partner he can more readily trust, perhaps, if you are truly set on becoming his enemy."

"And we can stop him by killing your sister?" she asked.

"Some among my sons have already been sent to kill her," Amanishiakne said. "What I need from you, if you intend to forge this alliance, is your protection. I can open one of the Dragon stars for you, here in my sanctum. Come, with your strength, and keep me alive until they succeed. Do that, and we can discuss terms of our future together, when Sakhefete is dead."

She met the Queen's gaze, through her vessel's eyes, and with her own, on the Infinite Plane. Sparks roared and surged between them, a dance of a thousand torrents, as if the truth or lie of what they said had form on its own. The shape of something larger seemed to loom over Amanishiakne's words. The Watcher's book had suggested something more—the Regnant and Veil were allies, not enemies; the Others existed, as rivals, with rival paths to power. After New Sarresant, it was clear enough the Regnant had the means to find and kill her champions, if that had been his plan. Now Amanishiakne had laid it bare, at least in part. Sakhefete had to be stopped, and Amanishiakne protected. She could find more of the truth after it was done.

"Give me time to collect my champions," she said. "Then we'll come to you across the stars."

Amanishiakne bowed her head. A sign of relief, perhaps, or acknowledgment.

"Come soon," Amanishiakne said. "I will open the way only for a short time. Then we will see each other in the flesh, on Bhakal soil. Go in peace, Sarine-who-is-the-Veil-reborn."

The threads of *Need* flashed gold and vanished, and her senses snapped back to the other side of the world.

35

TIGAI

The palace wing stank of death and blood. Piles of soiled linens lay stacked in wheelbarrows yet to be taken from the hall to be cleaned, or burned. He walked ahead of Arak'Jur, stepping between the long rows of beds, clearing a path for the tribesman and the woman he carried in his arms. Not that a bare-chested man head-and-shoulders taller than anyone else in the palace needed a path cleared for him. But it was the part Tigai could play, and so he played it. It had been his fault they were there in the first place. His fault Isaru had carved Corenna nigh in half with whatever those claws had been. His fault they'd come face-to-face with Death himself, and somehow lived to look for a medic after the fact.

"Here," he said. "Lay her here. I'll fetch a priest."

It was the first clean bed they'd seen, on a side of the hall with fewer dead and dying. Arak'Jur and Corenna held each other's eyes—a wonder Arak'Jur was able to walk, staring at his woman like that—and he laid her down gingerly, like a mother with a new baby. Wounds never sat well in his stomach, and Corenna's would have left him pale in the face if he hadn't already been in shock. Isaru's claw had ripped off her left arm and shoulder, leaving a gash behind, deep and pulpy and red. Another red mark sliced down the middle of her chest, splitting the skin and leaving ribs poking through below her breasts. Her face had been cut in half, her nose split, teeth cracked, jaw broken. He had no idea how the fuck she was alive. Their magic had to be responsible. Even for a *magi*, Corenna was well past death's doorstep, yet she held Arak'Jur's eyes as firmly as he held hers, gripping his arm with her one good hand, tight enough for them to be locked in place like statues beside the bed.

He pushed through the chamber in a daze. In better times it would have been decorated with paintings, tapestries, fixtures, and gold; he could see the discolored spots on the walls where the décor had hung. White-painted paneling and gold leaf still adorned the walls, with high-vaulted ceilings looking down on the wounded as they moaned, or lay quietly in their beds. He and Arak'Jur should have been dead. That old man who had somehow frozen them in place had to have been the Regnant himself.

A group of people stood clustered together at the far end of the hall, brown robes and nurses among them. He went toward them, trying not to think.

"You," he said when he arrived. He grabbed one of the brown-robed men by the arm. "You. Come."

The priest tried to shake him off with an angry glare. He redoubled his grip, yanking the man back toward him. He'd just been face-to-face with Death. A priest's annoyance was nothing. The man was coming to see to Corenna, even if he had to tether them both to the strands.

"Tigai?"

He looked up, and didn't register what he saw. A few more priests, exchanging words with a group of women standing around another woman, lying on a bed.

"Took you long enough, lordling," one of the women said. He knew the voice. "I would have thought...wait, Tigai, are you all right?"

He stared at them, still holding tight to the priest's upper arm. Shock dulled his senses, no sharper for knowing what it was. Their clothes were wrong for here, and no New Sarresanter had tattoos on either cheek, joined across the bridge of their nose. Kitian, that was the woman who had spoken. Kitian Blood Claw Clan Hoskar. And the other women standing around the bed were dressed the same, and tattooed. Yuli's sisters.

He let the priest's arm go.

"Yuli," he said, moving toward the bed.

It was her. Fang tattoos marked her cheeks, black lines streaking to connect them under her eyes, an intricate pattern he knew from long nights alone. Her skin was pale, her hair matted with blood and dirt, but she smiled when she saw him, and there was strength there, whatever injury had put her in one of these beds.

"Tigai," Yuli said. "I told them you'd come as soon as word reached you."

He cried.

He never cried. Yet for some reason, tears escaped his eyes, and he found himself kneeling beside her bed, his face buried in her linens as she cradled her hands around his head.

"Shh," Yuli said. "I'm fine. I'm here because my sisters are pigheaded and stubborn, not because I need it."

"Like the hells you're fine," Namkat said, her grin spreading the feather tattoos on either cheek. "This Sarresanter girl says she saw you ripped open, neck to navel. Even the Twin Fangs needs a good week to rest and recover after that."

She gestured toward a girl Tigai hadn't noticed before, a young girl in a white dress, standing protectively over Yuli and frowning at him.

Suddenly he remembered. "A priest," he said. "I need a priest. Arak'Jur and Corenna are here. Corenna is hurt. Badly."

Yuli's sisters rounded at once on the priests who had been standing nearby, and Imyan, the one with leaves and roots tattooed on her cheeks, barked something, provoking what sounded like argument from the priests, met with equal fervor from the Hoskar women.

"They'd been trying to get my sisters to go away," Yuli said. "Just as well, if Corenna needs their attention. It will get them to stop bothering us."

She said it lightheartedly, but it provoked another sob. He felt like a child, weeping over nothing. He was being stupid. He should stand up, take charge, make sure Corenna was seen to and judge Yuli's wounds for himself. Instead he cried, and the tears did nothing to make him feel better.

"Are you hurt?" Yuli asked. "Tigai?"

"No," he managed. "No. I'm fine. It was my fault. I took them to attack Isaru, but the Regnant was there. And now you're hurt, and...I'm..."

"Shh," Yuli said. "I'm fine, like I already said. And, wait, you said you faced the Regnant? In person?"

He nodded, and Yuli's fingers gripped tighter, somehow still gentle, stroking through his hair.

"I was sure I was going to die," he said. "He did something to block the stars. I couldn't leave. Couldn't get them out. Corenna was hurt, and it was my fault they were there. We should have died."

"You didn't die," Yuli said. "And neither did Corenna. She's here now. The Sarresant medics are good; they have their magicks, and so does she. She'll be fine. I'll be fine. Everything will be fine."

"They're seeing to her now," Kitian said, coming to sit beside them on the bed. "Sounds like it was a fight to remember, lordling."

"I heard the voices," Yuli said. "Two times—'for this one, it ends.' Both your doing?"

He shook his head. "Isaru died at our hand. I don't know about the others. But I heard the voice three times, not two."

"Once was us," Yuli said. "Well, Sarine. She killed a Gorin warrior who was attacking our people. But the third… you're here, I'm here, Arak'Jur is here… and I have to imagine if Erris had been killed, her people would have carried word. So it has to be another of theirs."

He sat back, wiping his eyes. He felt a bloody fool for losing control. All the more so here, in front of Yuli and her sisters.

"Did you kill the old man?" the Sarresant girl in white asked.

"Who are you, girl?" he asked. "And no, we didn't. He did something to freeze us in place. It's a bloody miracle we're all still alive."

"This is Reed," Yuli said. "She was with us, when Sarine killed the Gorin champion."

"I shot that ugly old man," Reed said. "Before he killed Reyne. If he can be shot, he can die."

"Well, we weren't ready for him," Tigai said. "I didn't know he'd be there, or I'd never have suggested the attack."

"Brave, lordling," Kitian said. "I'd expected caution, from our time together, but I'm pleased to be surprised. I like him, sister."

"Now's hardly the time," Yuli said. "Let him recover first."

"You're the one meant to be recovering," Kitian said. "And this is a time of war. What we put off may be cut short tomorrow."

"All the same," Yuli said, falling quiet and reaching out a hand for one of his. He took it. She wasn't as cold as her pale skin suggested, though Natarii were much paler than Jun, or even Sarresanters. Wind spirits but it felt good to touch her. The low hum that had clouded his mind since the fight seemed to dissipate, holding her hand, seeing her again. On a proper noble Jun lady, tattooist's inks would never be allowed to come near the face, but Yuli's marks were more than the savage markings he'd thought the first time he'd seen her. They were fierce, but delicate. Subtle lines tracing the curve of her cheekbones, others accentuating the dip in the bridge of her nose, the curvature on either side, outlining her gray-blue eyes with thin trails of smoke.

"Tigai?" a voice shouted from the far side of the hall, carrying too loudly for a hospital, even a makeshift one. "If you came this way, I need you."

He sat up, turning to look toward it. Yuli exchanged glances with Reed, then said, "That's Sarine. What's she doing back from the front?"

"Tigai!" Sarine shouted again.

He rose to his feet. "I'm here," he called back. "How did you know I'd be here?"

"I saw that someone had used the star here in Rasailles," Sarine said. She was out of breath, looking as though she'd run the whole way from the battle to the palace. "It was either you, or Jun assassins."

"It's good to see you again so soon, sister," Yuli said. "You came here to protect me, in case it was the latter? I assure you, the rest of our sisters would have been up to the task."

"No," Sarine said. "Well, yes. I came for them, and for Tigai if he was here. For you, too, if you're up to fighting."

"She's not," Namkat said. "No matter what she says. But we are. Who needs killing today?"

"Does the Wind Song speak for the Twin Fangs now?" Yuli said, glowering. "I'm fine. Is this Erris calling on us?"

"This is something greater," Sarine said. "This is opposing the Regnant, on the far side of the world."

Mention of the name sent chills down his back. "You're a touch too slow," he said. "We just returned from the Jun high command, where a certain black-robed villain was there to meet us."

"What?" Sarine said. "The Regnant? Did you...?"

"Tigai faced him, along with Arak'Jur and Corenna," Yuli said. "They're here, a few beds down. You would have walked past them on your way to me."

"We didn't fight him," he said. "Not really." Sarine looked back as she spoke, appearing to search for Arak'Jur and Corenna. "We were there to kill Isaru, and we did. But the Regnant was there, too. He could have killed us. He should have killed us. Instead he let us go. I don't have the faintest bloody clue why."

"The Queen was right," Sarine said. "He could have killed you. He chose not to, which means he has something else in mind."

"What are you talking about?" he asked.

"Something I learned from...it doesn't matter," she said. "Only, I think Amanishiakne was right. He's coming for her. I need you all to come with me to protect her."

"Amani-who?" he said.

"Yuli isn't going anywhere," Kitian said. "She took a mortal wound, and she needs time to rest."

"I'm *fine*," Yuli said. "I walked here on my own feet and laid myself down."

"And you had their doctors gasping when they saw the marks," Namkat said. "You're staying here. We'll come, though, sister, wherever you need us."

"I'm with you, too," he said. The prospect of facing the Regnant again put ice in his blood. But he'd sworn himself to this cause. He wasn't about to let his fear get in the way of what was right.

"Good," Sarine said. "It won't be just us. We're going to protect Queen Amanishiakne of the Bhakal from her enemies. That means her sister's assassins—Bhakal mind-sorcerers—and there's a good chance the Regnant will bring his champions, too. We'll need all the strength we can bring. So, if there's any chance Yuli can fight..."

"There isn't," Namkat said, at the same time Kitian said, "No," and Yuli said, "Yes."

"No," Kitian said again. "I forbid it, as a warrior."

"I, too, forbid it," Namkat said. "Juni and Imyan will as well."

Yuli scowled, but said nothing.

Sarine rose to her feet. "Settle it, please," she said. "We need to leave at once. Erris has already said she isn't coming, and can't spare any strength to help. I'll go see to Arak'Jur and Corenna."

She left, pushing past the doctors, leaving the rest of them alone.

"No chance Corenna will be able to go," Kitian said. "With those wounds, it's a miracle she's still breathing."

He winced. Even if the Regnant hadn't been there, he'd had no idea Isaru could wield magic like that. *Lotus*, the Regnant had called him, a champion of Lotus. He'd never heard mention of the House. His ignorance had almost gotten them all killed.

"Tigai, are you sure you're up for going with her?" Yuli asked. "You seemed shaken. If my sisters are going to force me to rest, surely they'll think you need it as much as I do."

"Sarine needs my help," he said. There was a numbness in the words, but they were right.

"And?" Yuli said, almost glaring at Kitian and Namkat. "You're going to accept that as reason from him, but not from me?"

"I've already told you what I think of our Jun lordling," Kitian said. "He's strong. A few tears after a battle don't make a man weak. He's the sort to be beaten back a hundred times, and come back for the hundred and first, so long as he believes in what he's doing. He believes in her." She paused, then added, "And he believes in you, sister, even if you think the time is wrong for such things."

Yuli's cheeks flushed.

"What does that mean?" he asked.

"We'll leave you two to it," Kitian said, grinning. "Come. You, too, girl."

Kitian's gesture was enough to move Reed to rise and follow them, even if the Sarresant girl did it with a scowl on her face directed at Tigai.

"Well?" he said after they'd gone.

"Maybe Kitian's right," Yuli said. "This is a war, and in war, sometimes what goes unsaid is said too late. You could die, going with Sarine. I could die here."

"Don't say things like that," he said. "We all know the risks. Nothing's killed me yet, and nothing's killed you either. You're going to be fine."

"I know," Yuli said. "And I am. But, you know I had Kitian go with you for a reason. She's my sister. I trust her with my life."

Yuli's cheeks colored again when she finished.

"What is it?" he asked.

"I don't know how these things are done among the Jun," Yuli said. "But in my clan, a woman has her sister live with a man for a time, to judge him. When...when she wants a mate."

"You want to mate, here...?" he asked. "In a hospital?"

"A husband, you bloody idiot," Yuli said. "I'm afraid I might not get to tell you how I feel, if you go off with Sarine. This way, even if you die, you'll die knowing I loved you. And at least I'll have told you what I want."

"You love me," he said. He heard how stupid he sounded as soon as the words left his mouth.

She nodded, then immediately looked down at the bedsheets. The flush in her cheeks shone around her tattoos, giving the fangs a halo almost like they'd been dipped in blood.

"I love you, too," he said. "I've been with a hundred women and more, and none are like you. But I'm not going to die, and neither are you. I'm going to go with Sarine, and we'll do what needs doing, and I'll come back and you'll be healed and we'll bloody well get married if that's what you want."

"You know, a woman doesn't like hearing that her man has been with a hundred women, no matter how favorably he compares her to them."

"Your man is a bloody idiot, then," he said. "He's still yours."

She laughed, and he drew her close. She smelled like sweat and dirt, but she tasted like comfort, like heat on a cold night. He hadn't thought to look for this, but it was here, and it was right. A small circle drawn against the terrors around them both.

"Dao is going to have a fit when I tell him," he said after they separated.

"Your brother?" Yuli asked. "Why?"

"Until he manages a child, I'm the heir to Yanjin. I always thought I'd end up marrying one of the suitors he brought around for me. Forgive my saying it, but he would never have brought a Hoskar warrior to our court. Now our children will stand to inherit the name, if not the estate."

"Our children? You move quickly, Lord Tigai."

"I mean, I thought..."

She laughed again. "Go and fight. Live. I'll be here waiting."

She kissed him again. It was somehow sweeter now, sweeter than it had ever been before.

36

OMERA

A Holding Cell
Sezama, West Bhakal

Metal clanked as he paced across the back wall of his cell. Both his wrists were clapped in iron, a long chain running through the manacles anchored to a hook embedded in the floor. He'd tried kicking it, scraping his wrists against the irons, grinding the chain against the anchor, tried anything else he could think of whenever the sisters weren't watching. His herb pouches, scabbard, and sword were sitting atop a table on the far side of the room. Taunting him. They hadn't even fixed bars in place; if he could slip the chains and reach his weapon, he was free. But so far the irons held.

He'd expected to be tortured, or at least beaten. But they hadn't touched him since the oasis. He'd woken up here, in some darkened, windowless prison the Queen-alone-knew-where. Pressing his ears to the walls, hoping for some clue, some sound of animals or travelers outside, even the shout or sobs of another prisoner, gave him nothing. He was alone, with only his chains and the sisters in their damnable, maddening chair to keep him company.

One sat in the chair now, a short, stout woman who had kept watch on him twice before. She faced him, five paces out of reach of his chains, wearing a furrowed brow and an otherwise vacant expression, precisely like the rest of her sisters. He'd tried shouting at them, waving manacled arms to elicit an expression of surprise, contempt, an order to be silent—anything at all. None of them spoke to him, not even giving their names. He recognized two from the oasis, where their thralls had beaten him past the point of submission, but there had been no sign of Jahi among them, and he knew none of the others.

One at a time they came, they sat, and they stared at him as though he were some caged animal, some prized specimen worthy of study. He felt naked, though they'd left him his traveling clothes. Without windows to provide cues for day and night, he'd begun to keep time by their changing shifts: one in the morning, one at midday, and finally one more in the evening, before they took a long break that had to be nightfall to sleep and repeat it again the next day.

Today he paced, staring back.

The short, stout one seemed not to care. She stared at him, her forehead creased like paper. Hours would pass, exactly like this. He would pace, he would sit to rest, he would eat whatever they left for him at the farthest reach of his chains, he would grow angry, frustrated, shout at them, stand silently, close his eyes, plead with them to listen; none of it mattered. The Mindhunters were like stones.

He came to a halt at the end of his chains. He could be a stone, too. He stood in place, staring back at her with the same intensity she gave him.

She met his eyes.

It had to have been a mistake. Not one of her sisters had ever given him any acknowledgment at all. He might as well have been made of transparent glass for all the attention they paid him, no matter who it was sitting in the chair. But this one met his eyes, then instantly lowered her face, drawing a deep, calming breath as though she needed to steady herself after looking at him.

"Please," he said. Something new had happened. He had to seize the opportunity. "You must release me. By now you have to have seen I've spoken the truth. The shield on my mind was put there by my mother, the Queen herself. By holding me here you interfere with the sacred duty given me by her hand. If you love her, as I do, you will relent, and let me go free."

The short, stout sister raised her eyes, and met his again.

"Please," he repeated.

She rose to her feet without a word.

"No," he said. "No, damn you. You have to see I've told you the truth! You have to—"

The door shut behind her. No latch, no click of iron.

He sagged against his chains, and an empty chair stared back at him where the sister had been. He'd had a chance, if only he'd been able to convince her to listen. He had to find some way, some means of escape, but he'd panicked, and begged like a fool.

Next time he would do better. If they had slipped once—and he was sure acknowledging his presence had been a mistake—then it was a mistake they would make again. He had to have the right words ready. The Mindhunters called themselves the Queen's Hand. They were loyal to his mother. But mentioning her hadn't worked. Perhaps if he invoked the Jun army they'd seen at Domakar. The Empire was under attack. It stood to reason the Mindhunters should be using their magic against the Queen's enemies, not her sons. He could offer them his sword, perhaps, or a future favor, if—

The room's door swung open. He scrambled back to his feet in time to see Jahi enter the room.

He'd wondered if she'd been somehow reassigned, or taken away. But it was her, the Mindhunter who had traveled with him from Domakar, who'd seen the Jun army firsthand, at his side. She came in without thralls, wearing the same purple silk she'd worn in the city, though it had been cleaned and pressed since their time together on the road.

"Jahi," he said, letting relief show in his voice. "I hoped they would send you, eventually. Please. You have to talk to them. Tell them what we saw in Domakar. Tell them the Empire is under attack. Whatever you think of me, we both fight for the Queen. I could have killed you on the sand sea, or left you behind, but I didn't. You have to speak for my loyalty, and get them to stop this. It's driving me mad. Jahi, please!"

Jahi went to the chair and sat down as though he hadn't spoken. He stared at her. She'd been his one thread of hope. If she looked through him like glass, if she treated him as all the others did, it would rip out his heart. Dread washed over him as she sat and smoothed over her silk skirts, poised and ready to tear his hope to pieces.

Instead she met his eyes, as the short, stout sister had done, only she didn't look away.

"Prince Omera," Jahi said. "My sisters aren't quite certain what to do with you."

"Jahi," he said, feeling her words wash over him like a balm he hadn't known he needed. "Please. You have to help me."

"I want to do just that, Your Highness," Jahi said.

"Then do it," he said. "Loose these chains. Give me my herbs and my sword. Ride with me, if you must. I have to fulfill my mother's mission. Please."

"Have you given thought to what I told you, when we traveled together?" she said. "The possibility that your memory has been altered, and that, while you believe you serve the Queen, perhaps you are working against her?"

"There are Jun soldiers on our lands," he said. "You saw them, as clearly as I did. Maybe it's you and your sisters who have been deceived. Why else would you be set to rounding up my brothers instead of fighting against our enemies?"

Jahi's eye twitched. Then she frowned.

"You persist in these falsehoods," Jahi said. "When only the truth will let us free you."

"Falsehoods?" he demanded. "What falsehoods?"

"I'm willing to believe you have been manipulated, Prince Omera," Jahi said. "And I've convinced my sisters of the same. But you must abandon these claims. Whatever your brothers did to put the shield in place over your mind, its strength is tied to your conviction. If you let your guard down, we can enter your mind, explore your memory—your *true* memory—and you can be exonerated. Until then, my sisters will continue trying to pierce the shield by force."

"I don't understand," he said. "You're claiming you didn't see the Jun army with me, marching up Domakar's streets?"

Jahi sighed.

"As you wish, Your Highness," she said, rising to her feet. "I hope for your sake the shield breaks before your mind does."

"No!"

He shouted it, with more desperation than he thought he felt. Pain laced his voice. The pain of being left alone, of being stared at as though he didn't exist.

"No," he said again. "Jahi, please. Don't leave."

She paused, a few steps from her chair.

"Please," he said again. "I...I don't understand what's happening. I have these memories. They feel real to me. I...I...I can't..."

"Our magic is a powerful, terrible thing," Jahi said. "You must open yourself to the possibility of its power over you."

He closed his eyes. The memories were real. His mother, standing over the bodies of the Jun emissaries. Taking his head in her hands. Speaking the words. Protecting his mind. He traveled to Domakar, fled from Jahi and her thralls until they saw the Jun army storming the city. They'd escaped together, and crossed the sands. Hadn't they?

"You said..." he began, forcing the words. "You said my brothers put the shield in place over my mind. I have no knowledge of any of my brothers learning your Mindhunter gift. So far as I know, such a thing is forbidden. I remember my mother's hands. Her face. Her words."

"No man is permitted to study our magic," Jahi said. "On pain of death for him and all his teachers. Yet that is what has happened, Your Highness. That is why your mother the Queen has instructed her Hand to apprehend all her sons, until this evil can be purged. That is why I chased you across the sands. Your brothers set you against our Queens, implanted false memories to ensure that you did their bidding, thinking it was out of love and duty."

"What about the Jun?" he said. "The foreigners attacking our cities. We saw them together, did we not? That's why we fled together."

Jahi shook her head slowly. "We saw no foreign army, Prince Omera," she said. "This is another phantom, designed to give you strength of purpose. Nothing more. Our Empire is secure. Both Queens rule together from their thrones in Konghom. You will be brought before them, once we can confirm your loyalty."

He sagged against his chains. He'd been so sure. His mother's face. Her words. He had to kill her sister, to save the Empire, to save his mother's life.

A lie.

He doubted it still. Jahi had been at his side when they saw the Empire under attack. He was a prince of the Bhakal. He would never have participated in a plot against the Queen. Never.

"Will you allow me to touch you?" Jahi said. "It might make it easier to pierce the shield."

He recoiled by instinct.

"Your Highness, I know this is painful," Jahi said. "Recovery from this sort of memory alteration can take years. But the first step is allowing us in. If I can pierce the shield on your mind, I can show you the truth, taken from your own memories. They will be a better teacher than any words I can give. Please."

Breath came hard. He felt himself trembling. He had no understanding of Mindhunter magic. His mother had put a shield in place to protect him from their attacks. If he relented, and allowed it to be broken, they could erase him, alter him, compel and bewitch him as they'd done to so many thralls. But if he refused, Jahi would leave. He'd be alone, and no closer to fulfilling his mission. And perhaps, if she was telling the truth...

He closed his eyes and nodded.

Jahi stepped closer. The first time in days anyone had come within reach of his chains.

She laid a hand on either side of his head. Gently. A mother's touch. Her fingers were soft, delicate.

He could feel her eyes on his skin, even while his were closed. White spheres, cutting into him, but there was no pain. For the first time he could sense the shield in place to protect his mind, almost as though he saw it from the outside, through Jahi's eyes. A great fortress wall, and Jahi probed it, searching for any sign of weakness. Whereas the other sisters had been battering rams aiming to crash through the fortress's gate, Jahi's eyes were a needle, prying, probing for a single soft point.

She found it.

He felt a stabbing sensation, but as before, without any pain. A single hole, enough for a mouse to crawl under a mighty barricade of stone. She entered. He felt himself enter with her, part of his mind pulled to meet her, to welcome her. His doubts, swirling against a tide of conviction.

They delved into his memory.

He was a child, standing in a dueling ring. Three taller children faced him, adolescents, almost grown, whereas he was no more than eight. The first time he'd ingested the herbs that were a prince's birthright, while the master-at-arms watched over his training.

He was a grown man, kneeling before his mother to receive a sacred charge. To be sent across the sea. To use *tisa irinti* to pose as a servant, to learn of great secrets in terrible times. To serve the Fox, at the heart of the Empire of Order.

Images swirled as Jahi guided him into his past. He returned to Konghom. Watched the Divide fall. He traveled west with his mother, hiding from a terrible threat.

The Jun emissaries came before them.

His mother struck them down.

Took his head in her arms.

Bid him assassinate her sister.

Put a shield in place to protect his mind.

He raced to Domakar. Fought with Jahi's thralls. Fled the city after they saw a Jun army storming the streets.

They crossed the sands.

The images blurred, until he was standing here, in this chamber, chained to the floor.

Jahi's hands fell from the sides of his head, and his eyes came open. Jahi was shaking, her mouth open, her eyes wide.

His mind reeled. Emotion surged inside him. It was true. All of it. The Mindhunters had him doubting the very core of who he was: what he'd seen, what he remembered, what he knew. And they were wrong. His mother had set the shield. His mother had given him the duty to act as her assassin. To kill her Sister-Queen before corruption threatened the Empire's heart.

"That's enough, sister," a foreign voice said, on the far side of the chamber. "Step away from the prince."

Jahi stared at him, still trembling.

Three other Mindhunters had entered the room. All three wore purple silk, and this time they stared at him, not through him.

"Sister Jahi, step back," another of them said. "Your work is finished. We can handle him from here."

"I told the truth," he said. "Jahi. Don't. You know it was true. You know what you saw."

He felt eyes on him again. White spheres, staring down the fortress wall. This time there was no gentle touch, no mother's caress. They circled the fortress in his mind's eye, and they found the mousehole. They moved toward it.

"They...they altered my memory..." Jahi said. "I was sure it was a lie."

"Sister!" the second one repeated. "Step back! The prince is dangerous."

Jahi flicked a hand.

His chains came loose from the floor.

The two Mindhunters staring at him didn't react. The third's eyes went wide.

He lunged, flinging the chains still attached to his wrists at the closest one. They wrapped around her torso, crushing the purple silk, and he wrenched them back, slamming the Mindhunter into the ground. Jahi ran to the table, grabbing his belt pouches and scabbard and throwing them toward him. He snatched them, fingering the pouches of *calimnus re* and *ubax aragti* as quick as he could move.

The white spheres closed in. If they breached the mousehole, he would be reduced to nothing. A thrall, as sure as any he'd seen them do to the rest.

The middle one, the one who hadn't been staring at him with her Mindhunter eyes, panicked, fleeing for the door. He lashed out with the chains again, tangling her feet. She plunged forward, hitting the door hard enough to serve as an alarm. This time his sword was drawn, and he finished her with a stabbing thrust through the left side of her back, straight into her heart.

He whirled on the last sister.

Too late.

The last white spheres reached the mousehole. He could feel it, in his mind's eye, after Jahi's touch. The towering wall of stone, brought low by the tiniest crack in its foundation. The spheres flew into the crack, racing toward the swirling mists of memory and thought within his mind.

A shining light pulsed, and the crack sealed itself before the spheres could reach the other side.

Jahi stared at him with her Mindhunter empty eyes. The third Mindhunter's face creased with worry, fear, shock, and rage. He felt another set of white spheres, these ones familiar. Jahi's eyes. She'd repaired the crack they'd made together. The shield was whole.

He cut the third sister down with a slash across the face, marring her eyes with split flesh and blood and bone. She tried to scream through a broken mouth and twisted jaw, and he cut her again, driving her to the ground as he split her head in two.

"We have to go," Jahi said, blinking as her eyes returned to focus. "There are swift horses here. We can reach Konghom by morning."

"You saw it," he said. "You saw it all. Thank you."

"I serve the Queen, Your Highness," Jahi said. "Her will is mine."

"Then we'll reach her sister together," he said. "My mother's life, and the fate of the Empire, depends on it."

Jahi bowed her head. They left, leaving three Mindhunter corpses behind.

37

ERRIS

Fishmonger's Street
Harbor District, New Sarresant

Cold air and morning fog clung to the streets so near the harbor. Victory rode with her, warming her atop Jiri's back. Royens's First Corps had broken the Jun, at the height of what her people were already calling the Battle of West Verrain. If she'd won this victory two months before, the people would have welcomed her into the city in a throng, shouting her name, waving the blue-white-blue flag of the Republic. Today lights burned in one window in five. Immigrants had come to rekindle New Sarresant's flame, but the cold suited the city, as it suited her mood. She'd lost almost twenty thousand soldiers pushing the Jun off the river. Their names, and the names of their units, loomed larger in her mind than any victory.

She reined Jiri to a halt in front of a sign depicting a fishing rod and a half woman, half fish. The Snared Siren, her aide had said during the briefing. This had to be it. Jiri snorted as Erris directed her to a post, dropping the reins to the ground. No need to tie her off. Jiri knew her place; better to leave her free to defend herself if thieves managed to be among the few souls in the newly resettled city.

Her aides had tried to protest when they'd heard she intended to make this ride. But with the casualty numbers rattling in her head, she needed a morning away from ledgers and butcher's bills. The news waiting for her inside the tavern had been a perfect excuse. So today she was an Empress riding through the city she'd bled to defend. Twenty thousand souls dead or severely wounded at her word, to say nothing of the Jun casualties left behind when their companies pulled back. The Jun number would be higher, she was certain. And someone else's problem. Someone else's nightmare, rattling through their head no matter what they did, no matter how far they rode to distract them from the costs of war.

A newly kindled fire greeted her as she pushed through into the common room. The warmth was welcome; here by the ocean the night air still lingered in the hours past dawn. The barkeep glanced up from where he'd been knelt down, stocking bottles or glasses below the counter. The rest of the room was empty save for one man, a fisher by the look of him, downing a morning ale in the corner by the fire.

"*Buenos días* to you, ah, *Capitán*, is it?" the barkeep said. Thellan accents. A settler, come all the way from the isles for a chance at running a tavern in New Sarresant. She heard the words in Thellan, even as the Gods' Seat's gift translated them in her mind.

"Captain will do," she said, not bothering to correct him. Six stars on her sleeves and collar named her Empress, a general-of-generals, though she'd have worn civilian's clothes if she truly cared about not being recognized on her ride. "I'm here for one of your guests. I received word he'd taken a room here some time ago."

The barkeep nodded, withdrawing a pitcher and pair of glasses from below the counter. "So he's one of yours, then," he said. "*Un poco borracho.* Hardly leaves his room. My copy of the room key for you, *señora*, if the army means to settle his bill."

"You'll be paid in full," she said. "Show me to his room."

"He'll be sleeping," the barkeep said. "Late night last night. Had one of my girls running between the kitchens and the commons until the fires had all but died out, and then some for an hour besides."

"I don't give a damn if he's sleeping," she said. "The room."

"As you will, *Capitán*," the barkeep said. "This way."

She followed up fresh-polished stairs at the back of the commons. The whole tavern smelled more of lye and soap than sailor's stink, alcohol, or brine. A function of the city's resettlement: too few customers, and the city's businesses were being run by owners new enough to put care and attention into their unexpected inheritance.

They walked past a hall of closed doors until they reached one near the end. The barkeep rapped softly, too softly to wake anyone in the throes of drink-induced sleep.

"*Mi coronel*," the barkeep said. "Time to wake. You have a visitor."

No sound came in reply.

The barkeep shrugged apologetically. "Noontime, perhaps, if you wish to find him on his feet."

"I don't," she said. So much for any hope that this would turn out differently. "Give me the key, and go."

He produced it, bowing. "As you say, *Capitán*. I hope you'll remember the Snared Siren took good care of your man, whatever state he was in when he came to us."

She grunted, waiting for the man to bow again and excuse himself. The locks were oiled, the metal polished and smooth. She turned the key and pushed open the door.

The smell assaulted her before she could step through.

Alcohol, sharp enough it had to have been spilled somewhere, left to pool on the floor or seep into bedsheets. Bottles lay against the furniture, nestled among days' worth of discarded clothes.

She prepared a *Death* tether. A bucket of water would have been her preferred method, but *Need* would serve. She made the connection, though the golden sphere was dim and dark in spite of her standing over her vessel's sleeping form.

Her senses leapt forward, jolting her into the man sleeping in his bed. She held it only for a moment, long enough to see what he would see. Herself, looming over the room in spite of her short stature. The look of disappointment and disgust writ on her face.

She released *Need*, and Marquand started, jerking the blankets as he sat up.

She let the *Death* tether fade, too, when it was clear he wouldn't reach for the leylines.

Marquand said nothing, only groaned.

"I knew this was where I'd find you," she said. "This, or somewhere like it."

He slumped back against the headboard, lowering his eyes. Sunken eyes, above red cheeks.

"Why'd you come, then," Marquand said.

"I trusted you," she said. "I counted on you."

He winced. She noted he'd moved the bed so he wouldn't have to face the window when he woke, but even so, the light seemed to burn his eyes.

"Why?" she said. "Why did you do this?"

He shifted to move his face away from her, even with his eyes lowered. Shame stank as thick as alcohol.

"I fucked up," he said. "I'm weak, and you fucked up trusting me not to be."

"I did trust you," she said. "I needed you. I still do. Do you have any idea what's been happening since you bloody disappeared? We fought a bloody war over the past four days. I put you in command of Sarine and her people, and they're scattered half across the world with no purpose or directive as far as I'm aware. And you're here, drinking until you piss yourself, then sleeping it off and doing it again. So I ask one more time: Why? Why the fuck did you do this, Marquand?"

"Because I'm fucking weak, I already told you," Marquand snapped. His voice burned hot. "Why did you come? You said you fucking *knew* I'd be here. You want to see me like this? You need to be that much better than me, to see it and smell it and stand over me like some fucking lord?"

"Don't you dare insult me," she snapped back. "This is your doing, and you'll bear full responsibility for it."

"I know," he said. "Don't you think I know? Shoot me and have done with it, if that's still the penalty for desertion."

"Are you such a coward, then, to want to die?"

He went quiet again.

She matched him with silence. Rage coursed through her, at every detail in the room. Half-empty bottles of brown liquor lay next to the hearth. Wineglasses lay on a wood tray atop a table. Clothes lay scattered across the furniture, or piled in front of an armoire. She saw no sign of his uniform, though the barkeep had called him *coronel*—Thellan for *colonel*, so he must have known Marquand's rank.

"I wish you hadn't come here," Marquand said. "I knew someone would, when they found me. But I wish it hadn't been you."

"You would have left the city if you didn't want to be found. Taken a ship bound for the Old World, or the Thellan isles."

He nodded, sitting forward with his hands on his temples.

"What triggered this?" she asked. "Was it the city? You vanished after what happened here. Did you have family you never told me about?"

"You never understood," he said. "There isn't a reason. There was never a reason. The drink is the reason. It always was."

"That's not good enough."

"Too fucking bad. It's the truth. I'm a piece of shit, and I'm a drunk and here I am. If you want to haul me in and have me executed, fine. Do it. If not, then leave me in peace."

"That's it? You think you're finished? You decide to drink again, and that's it, no more duty, no more responsibility, no more bloody consequences?"

"I already said if you want to have me shot, then fucking do it."

Righteous anger seethed in her, the same as it ever had when she'd had to wake him from his drink. But he was right. She shouldn't have come here. Shame stung her on his behalf, seeing him like this. He was better than this. He'd tried, at least, to be better.

"I'm stripping you of your rank and responsibilities," she said. "Sarine and her people will have a new commander, and you can forget taking part in any high-level discussions, briefings, or reviews. But your duty isn't finished. I expect you to clean yourself up and report to General de Montaigne with the Eleventh. She can find a use for you as a weapon, if nothing else. Even if you could have been more, you can at least give me that."

She looked him in the eyes. Tears had formed and escaped down his cheeks, and she felt the same stirring in hers.

"I'll . . . I'll try," Marquand said. "And . . . I . . . I'm sorry."

The apology knifed through her. It was more than she'd expected. "You bloody well should be," she said. "Not least for saddling me with Tuyard for a chief of staff."

"What happened to Essily?"

She shook her head. "Not your concern anymore. Just know if things had been different here—if you'd had a reason for vanishing better than being mired in the bloody drink—I might have considered you for the post."

Another silence hung between them. This was a man she'd seen hold his ground against five hundred attackers. This was a man who had faced down binders, beasts, and foreign magicks without blinking, who could go blow for blow against generals, lords, and scholars, and never give up a step if he thought he was in the right. She needed him. And he'd been brought down by a bloody fucking bottle.

"Clean yourself up," she said again. "General de Montaigne will be expecting you."

He might have said something more if she'd stayed, but she couldn't bear to hear it.

She went back down the stairs, pausing to give thanks to the barkeep for his service. With *Body*, Jiri could have her back in Rasailles in time for her morning appointments.

38

TIGAI

A Secret Fortress
Ruhadan, West Bhakal

The strands snapped into place, and the air changed.

The Natarii warriors fell into a loose formation behind Sarine. They were in a torchlit chamber of yellow stone, windowless and arid. Perhaps underground. The strands were hard to read from such a distance, though the star they'd used had been unmistakable. Even as Sarine tethered them all, he'd felt it pulsing golden light across half the bloody world, sending up a beacon for anyone who wanted them dead. But no sooner had they snapped the strands into place than the star had winked out of existence. He'd never seen anything like it. The stars and strands were lingering reminders of what had been done in a place: who had come, who had gone, what they'd seen, what connections they had in common. Stars weren't doors to be open or closed at a whim. Yet this one had been. And now they were here.

"Your weapons," a woman said, wearing leather polished to shine like metal in the torchlight. "Surrender them before you meet the Queen."

Sarine held her hands out, open and empty, a gesture to show she carried no weapon. The Natarii women glanced between themselves.

"Is your Queen aware that any of us naked is worth more than a hundred swords or knives?" Kitian said.

"I'm worth two hundred, surely," Imyan said, grinning.

"None without mind-bond to the Queen may carry weapons in her presence," the leather-clad guard said. "This is royal law."

"Leave them here," Sarine said. "Please. We don't want to give offense."

"I want these back," Juni said, drawing a dagger from each of her boots and letting them clatter to the ground. Kitian slipped loose a leather whip from her belt, alongside a short blade sheathed on her hip. The others followed in kind, dropping various lengths of steel and leather in front of them.

"Tigai?" Sarine said.

He blinked.

The strands were still swirling around the now-vanished star. He'd truly never seen anything like it. It was as though all its connections, all the people who lived near it, or had traveled to it, were suddenly set adrift. As though an entire harbor had winked out of existence, leaving its ships moored to nothing but air. He could still see the six strands they'd used to travel from New Sarresant, stretching out across the seas, but there were six more strands folded over top of them, mirroring them exactly, like a twisted reflection, reaching east instead of west. Ordinarily he'd swear someone else had used the star only moments before they arrived, but there was no one here save the Queen's guards. It was more than a damned sight unsettling. If this was the same trick he'd used with Kitian to mask their arrivals while following the Dragons, the strands would have had a reverberation, a slight dissonance to put the eastward arrivals in a nearby room. There was none. The strands matched exactly, which made it impossible. But the thought tangled in his mind. Something was wrong.

"Tigai?" Sarine said again. "Your pistols?"

He blinked again, returning his vision to the room. The leather-clad guard stared at him with ice in her eyes, and all the rest, too.

"Oh," he said. "Right." Unclasping his belt, he let it drop quickly beside the small pile of weapons on the floor. If he had to, he could snap back here and the pistols would be waiting—he'd already placed an anchor without thinking, at the exact spot where the six strands converged between the lines heading west and those heading east.

The guard seemed to relax as soon as the last weapons dropped.

"I am called Daskha," the guard said. "First Attendant to the Queen. You will not speak in Her Majesty's presence, except to answer her, and you must never meet her eyes. Kneel and press your heads to the floor if she stands. Bow twice before stepping within twenty paces of her, and again at fifteen and ten. If any of the Queen's Hand are present, bow once to them, at the same intervals, after you make obeisance to the Queen. Am I understood?"

"Like bloody fucking—" Kitian started.

"Yes," Sarine interrupted. "We understand, and we'll obey. This is her place, and we're here as Amanishiakne's guests. We need her. We have no wish to offend."

"You told us she needs us, too, sister," Namkat said. "It isn't right. Warriors don't kneel to anyone, not even clan chiefs or Jun lords."

"She's more than an ordinary lord," Sarine said. "She's lived for dozens of cycles, which means thousands of years. If anyone deserves respect, she does. Can you please do it, for my sake?"

"We're not objecting out of pride," Juni said. "If she humiliates us, or debases us, there's a risk of the war-forms seizing control. We don't have Yuli's bond to you, sister. The last thing we want is to accidentally kill this Queen."

The leather-clad guard, Daskha, looked as though she was about to choke on her own tongue.

"All right," Sarine said. "Can you ask Her Majesty if my sisters can refrain from the kneeling, at least? We are coming as allies—maybe it's better if we treat as closer to equals."

"I...I cannot *ask* the Queen any such thing," Daskha said. "And you... you...cannot..."

"Please," Sarine said. "It's for Her Majesty's protection, and that's why we're here. Please take us to her. I promise we'll treat her with dignity and respect."

A green light flashed on the strands. Tigai was only half paying attention to the exchange between the Natarii, Sarine, and the attendant, but the light was bright enough for him to blink to avoid it as he continued to study the vanished star. It was still bloody odd. Something was wrong about the mirroring. It was too close. For any easterly arrivals to have used those strands they would have materialized on top of them, in the same room with Sarine, the Natarii, and the Queen's guards.

"Yes," Daskha said, bowing to all of them for the first time. "Yes, of course. Come with me."

They left. He blinked one last time, studying what was left of the star. Then he followed as the attendant led them through a maze of yellow stone halls.

They were definitely underground; that or whoever made this place hated sunshine. The halls were as windowless as the room they'd arrived in, bereft of decorations, too. It had the look of a fortress, solely concerned with defense. The corners were tight and narrow to obstruct vision, with waist-high barricades built into the stone facing down either hallway. Ten determined crossbowmen could hold these halls against a hundred attackers. Ten *magi* could hold against a bloody legion. None of the rooms had doors, or even beads or cloth draped to obscure their contents. He saw soldiers in the same polished leathers the attendant wore, watching them pass with the same icy expressions, too. Racks of curved swords, poleaxes, knives, and spears were mounted on the far wall of every room. Long guns, similar in kind to the ones used by the New Sarresant army, were mounted next to them. He had the sense that every soul here, every cook and page boy, was trained to kill. And what was it Daskha had said? None could bear arms in the Queen's presence unless they were "mind-bound" to her, whatever the hells that meant. So not only were they all killers, they were loyal, too. These were the people to whom Sarine had offered his and Yuli's sisters' help to keep watch against assassins.

"Wait here," Daskha said as they arrived at another room without a door. He could see inside; it was like any of the others they'd passed, except there were no weapons mounted on the far wall. Inside, a ring of six women in white wearing gold bangles from elbows to wrists knelt in a half circle facing away from the entrance. Another woman knelt opposite them. A woman he knew instantly was their Queen.

The Queen radiated light among the starfield and the strands. When he blinked he saw her lined in gold, an afterimage that stayed around her body. Her hair had been braided into a crown of actual gold, while her skin was too smooth, almost metallic, giving her an air of youth that didn't match her eyes. She rose to her feet, and all of her attendants, including Daskha and the two leather-clad guards stationed in the far corners of the room, all went to their knees, kneeling and pressing their heads to the floor.

"Sarine."

The Queen's voice was hard and delicate, both at once. It almost sounded twice in his ears, or perhaps it did sound twice, like a duet singing to an empty concert hall.

"Amanishiakne," Sarine said, stepping forward. The Queen flowed through her room, stepping over the six kneeling supplicants as though they weren't there. Whatever rituals or deference Daskha had intended them to make were forgotten as the Queen drew close to them in smooth, graceful steps.

"Can we trust each other?" Amanishiakne said. "I put my life in your hands, opening the way for you and your warriors. I hope you understand your life is in my hands, too, here within these walls."

"The Regnant is my enemy," Sarine said. "So long as he's yours, too, then there is trust between us."

"Let it be so," Amanishiakne said. Then without warning, the Queen took Sarine's hand in hers and kissed the tops of her fingers. It elicited gasps from the Bhakal attendants.

"Allies," Amanishiakne said. "So long as we, and our enemies, draw breath."

"Allies," Sarine said. He didn't need to have known her well to see the unease on Sarine's face. Yet Sarine returned the gesture with grace, bowing as low as Amanishiakne had before taking the Queen's hand in hers, and kissing it exactly as the Bhakal Queen had done.

"You will each be given quarters among my guard," Amanishiakne said. "My sons draw near Sakhefete. This will be decided, for good or ill, within the next days. I have sealed the Dragon stars inside this fortress, but my sister's assassins are coming; I've foreseen it. When they approach, it will be through these halls, which should give us time enough to raise alarms, and meet them. There will be Jun *magi* among them; I've foreseen that, too. Be prepared for Crab's quakes, for Mantis's fire, for Crane's swords. You will find my guard trained and ready to assist you in the fight, though you will wish to coordinate with my captains, to ensure that each of us understands the other's tactics. There will be time once you are settled for deeper questions, but I will answer anything pressing now, before we part. What do you wish to know of things to come?"

The Natarii exchanged looks with each other, and with him. But Sarine seemed to already know what she wanted to ask.

"You're sure your sons are up to the task of killing Sakhefete?" Sarine asked. "With the Dragon gift, some of us could join in their attack."

"My sons are skilled," Amanishiakne said. "And my divinations have revealed their path. One has already reached Konghom undetected; another is close, with one of the sorceresses of my Hand as his ally. Perhaps, if they fail, there will be a chance to use your warriors to oppose my sister. But I do not believe they will. I have foreseen that Sakhefete will die by my son Omera's hand. I know this, with such certainty as I know my own name."

"What happens after your sister is dead?" Juni asked. "Sarine told us we'd be coming here to keep you alive against her assassins. Have either of you planned for what comes next?"

Amanishiakne paused, considering the question.

"I meant what I pledged," Amanishiakne said finally. "We are allies. Perhaps, if the Regnant cannot use my sister to cheat your side of his pact, we can find a way to cheat his side together."

"You mean you and I sharing the Soul of the World?" Sarine asked.

"If we can agree on a vision in common," Amanishiakne said. "But we must survive the coming days, first. And even if we do, even if my sister falls while I still draw breath, there will be the matter of the Regnant himself. As all of you no doubt know, he is a cunning enemy. We may need some among the others to oppose him. The Rabaquim. Perhaps the Tarzali."

"We'll see to your survival first," Sarine said. "There will be time after to discuss what we'll do next."

Amanishiakne bowed her head. Coming from her, it seemed as deep a gesture of respect as if an ordinary woman had pressed her head to the floor.

"You are not what I expected, Sarine-who-is-the-Veil-reborn," Amanishiakne said. "I think you'll surprise the rest of us, too."

Sarine retuned the Queen's gesture. As she straightened, Daskha clicked her tongue, and the guards from the corners of the Queen's chamber came forward, taking a place with Tigai and the rest of their company.

"The last watch will show you to your rooms," Daskha said, averting her eyes from both Sarine and Amanishiakne. "There is only one entrance to this fortress; we've placed you in equal groups on either side of the main hall. Follow the Queen's guard and they will show you where."

Sarine nodded her head to Amanishiakne again, and the Natarii fell in behind her. The five guards who had been keeping watch bowed to the Queen, then saluted as five new guards seemed to appear from nowhere, moving to take their places in the Queen's chamber. Tigai had to scramble out of the way, though the Bhakal moved with perfect military precision, saluting, bowing, reaching their places as though none of the rest of them were there.

The others followed the now-relieved guards into the hallway. He offered a bow to Daskha instead.

"What are you doing, foreigner?" Daskha said.

"If it pleases Her Majesty, I wish to share something I've seen on our arrival, and seek Her Majesty's wisdom on the matter." He used his best dignitary voice, full of supplication and respect.

"You have already been dismissed from Her Majesty's—" Daskha began, but Amanishiakne raised a hand to cut her short. The Queen said nothing, pausing to regard him in silence.

"What are you doing?" Kitian asked from the hall.

"Go on ahead," he said. "I saw something on the strands. I need to be sure of it, that's all."

"Yes," Amanishiakne said, her eyes suddenly glassed over, milky white. "The rest of you, be gone. I must hear what this man has to say."

He bowed again, deeply, following Daskha's instructions to press his head all the way to the floor.

"No, champion of Freedom," Amanishiakne said. "There is no need for you to kneel. Rise, and face me."

He complied. Her eyes seemed to cover every part of him at once. He felt like a plucked chicken in a butcher's shop.

"Thank you, Your Majesty," he said, earning a reproachful glare from Daskha. "I wished to alert you to a...dissonance...I saw on the strands when we arrived."

The Queen held up a hand again, this time for his silence as she studied him, pacing across the chamber, studying him from every angle.

"A child of the East," Amanishiakne said finally. "A True Dragon; the first I've seen bound to the Veil. I detect the Regnant's touch on you, but your loyalty is truly with her, isn't it?"

"Yes, Your Majesty," he said.

"What do you know of my people?" Amanishiakne asked. "Of the Bhakal."

"Precious little, Majesty," he said, truthfully. "On the Jun side of the world, your ports are a renowned stop for our trading junks. Your spices, ivory, gold, and rare metals are sought after in every Jun city."

"You are a marker of change," Amanishiakne said. "A sign that the old way erodes, and a new one begins. A Dragon, bound to the Veil. A chance, for those of us long excluded from the reins of control."

He remained silent. His instinct had been to warn this Queen of what he'd seen on the strands, but she seemed uninterested. Perhaps he'd made a mistake.

"You faced the Regnant in person," Amanishiakne said. "He saw you as an enemy, not a tool. He was convinced of your loyalty to the reborn Veil."

Amanishiakne said it with a distant look in her eyes, as though she were seeing the scenes play out in front of her.

"Yes, Your Majesty," he said again.

"You are a beautiful man, Yanjin Tigai," Amanishiakne said. "Without and within."

He suppressed a frown. What was he to say to that?

"Ah, but you are promised to a woman already," Amanishiakne said. "A shame. There is sorcery in your blood, old as it is. One of my Hand might have made a fine daughter from . . ."

The Queen smiled, and the milk seemed to drain from her eyes.

"A shame indeed," Amanishiakne said.

He coughed.

"Your Majesty," he said. "I wanted to speak to you about what I saw when we arrived. The star, and the strands connected here."

"I sealed the star the moment after it was used," Amanishiakne said. "No further travel to this fortress is possible, save by way of foot, and horse, and camel."

"I saw it done," he said. "A great thing. But the strands we used to travel here were mirrored, six for us, six more to the east. It reminded me of a trick I've used in the past to travel alongside Jun Dragons without their notice. These were mirrored too closely—they would have appeared in the same room with us, and your guards—so perhaps it's nothing, but I wanted to be sure you knew of it."

Amanishiakne stood still, turning her eyes back on him. Once again her eyes flooded with white, and he felt her gaze as though something was cutting into his mind.

"You saw the star as I sealed it," Amanishiakne said. "The golden light, vanishing from the field. You traced the strands you, Sarine, and the Natarii arrived across. Six lights, connected to the stars of New Sarresant, far to the west. You saw... something more. You saw six other strands, connecting to the east. You saw the faces of your companions. You saw six more faces, cloaked with Fox magic, to appear as though..."

The Queen's guards moved, faster than he could follow.

Not guards.

Assassins.

Daskha's knife plunged into Amanishiakne's back.

The Queen whirled, her eyes flaring a shining, pure white. Daskha's body crumpled to the floor in a heap of boiled leather and ruined flesh. As soon as the attendant hit the ground her body shifted, changing from a woman's form to a man's. A Jun man, his face still shimmering with the magic of the Great and Noble House of the Fox.

Two more guards struck the Queen from behind, their *shotel* blades carving through her body where the first knife had struck, on the left side of her torso, through her heart. The Queen's eyes flared again, a burst of white, before the light went out, and she slumped forward to the ground.

The other three guards rounded on him, running at him with their swords drawn.

He found the anchor he'd set before they'd made him drop his pistols, and blinked away.

39

OMERA

Sewers
Beneath the Royal Palace, Konghom

Sludge clung to his legs as they pressed forward. He tried not to think about what the chunks and slop within the sewer trench had to be. His sword and herb-belt were both draped over his shoulder to keep them out of the muck, and he kept his hands above his waist, one holding tight to his weapons, the other to the hooded lantern lighting their way.

Stone passages and canals ran under the city in every direction, and they'd spent the morning thigh-deep in thick, viscous liquids, breathing through their mouths to avoid the smell. *Calimnus re* could sharpen his senses, but there was no herb to dull them. A failing of his mother's court herbologists. After this, he'd see to it they were well-funded to make just such a discovery.

Jahi trailed behind him, still wearing her purple silks, though by now her dress would be a vile ruin of its former self.

"I think we're under the palace now," he said, swiveling his lantern to be sure.

"How can you tell?" Jahi asked.

"The stonework," he said. "It's older here. And we've traveled long enough. Straight east, from the gates. Much farther and we'd hit the river."

Jahi followed his glances, though she looked uncertain. He knew little about her, but he doubted Mindhunter training included a childhood spent delving into the Konghom palace's secret places. He'd come down here when he was younger, with his brothers, looking to shirk their duties or their training. Fitting for duty to be the thing that brought him back to the muck.

"We'll need fresh clothes, once we're inside," Jahi said. "I smell like a dead camel."

"Here," he said. A dry passage led up and around the canals. There would be a ladder waiting at the end, leading up to somewhere within the palace walls, if his sense of direction proved correct.

"Will there be guards posted where we come up?" Jahi asked.

"You tell me," he said. "Can you sense anyone up there?"

She shook her head. "No," she said. "The room above us is empty. But that doesn't mean there won't be guards nearby. Your Highness knows the palace better than I."

"I know my way through the halls," he said. "Where the guards are posted depends on whether they expect an attack. You're sure they don't know we're coming?"

"I've done what I can to mask us both since Sezama," Jahi said. "But you'd be a fool to underestimate your mother's sister. She'll know we're coming. If fortune is on our side, she'll have foreseen how we attack, not when."

He nodded, shaking off his sword and herb-belt to be sure they'd stayed dry. This was it. He glanced up the ladder. If Queen Sakhefete had seen the manner of their arrival, she might have posted a dozen sentries on every entrance from the sewers. He had to trust his mother's shield, still fixed in place over his mind, its one crack maintained by Jahi's gift since they'd fled the Mindhunter fortress. And Jahi could take care of hiding herself, so she claimed. If providence was with them, they'd enter the palace undetected, and stay that way until he could find the Queen. For anything else, he could improvise.

He climbed the ladder quickly. It was old, but still sturdy, made of firm, strong wood. A stone block had been set in place at the top, iron rings drilled into its corners to ease lifting it in and out of place. He slid it up a crack, peering underneath the stone. Darkness greeted him, and he gestured for Jahi to pass up the lantern. Light revealed little more. The sewer exit led to a narrow, darkened chamber, behind a closed door. No way to be certain they were in the palace at all. But at least they hadn't come up in the middle of a boulevard, trampled by a merchant's caravan, or instantly spotted by the guard. He hooked the lantern on his belt and pushed the stone the rest of the way, until the way was open.

"Finally. I was wondering when you'd get here."

The voice almost sent him tumbling back down the ladder. He spun around, and found a hand extended to help him up.

The hand steadied him before he could fall, and the lantern's light flickered enough to see who it was.

"Kajan," he said. One of his brothers, three years his senior, and about the last face he expected to be waiting atop the sewer exit.

"Omera." Kajan grinned, hoisting him up into the room. It was exactly what the lamp had revealed: a narrow, dark, windowless room, but the stone walls and flooring suggested he'd been right, and they'd reached the palace.

"And you have help, just as mother foresaw," Kajan said, leaning down the ladder to take Jahi's hand. The Mindhunter grabbed hold, and his brother pulled her up to join them in the room.

"How did you know we'd be here?" Omera asked. "How are *you* here? I thought you'd taken a posting on the western coast."

"We were given the same mission," Kajan said. "I reached the palace two days ago. I've been hiding out here, in the servants' quarters, waiting for you to arrive. You're late, little brother. If mother hadn't foreseen that you'd been the one to kill her sister, I'd have already taken the chance myself."

His heart was still thumping from the surprise of someone waiting for them. But relief crept in. Kajan wore a *shotel* blade and herb-pouches, the same as he did. Two court-trained warrior-princes would be better than one.

"I thought you said the room above the ladder was empty," he said to Jahi.

"I couldn't sense him," Jahi said. "And still can't. His mind has been shielded, as yours was, Your Highness."

"Just so," Kajan said, still grinning. "Mother made sure we wouldn't run afoul of her Hand, or her sister's. If your companion can hide herself from the other Mindhunters, we can make our way to the royal gardens without detection. The morning guard is going to be changed in less than a quarter hour, once the clocks ring noon. I've already cleared the passages of servants, so once the guard are on the move, we should have a clear path to the arboretum. We can get into place as soon as you're ready." He paused. "Though both of you stink like absolute shit, you know this?"

"Did you not notice we came up through the sewers?" he said. "It's good to have you here, brother. You're sure she'll be in the gardens?"

Kajan nodded. "She takes tea in the gazebo, precisely at noon, every day. It's our best chance to strike, if we hurry."

"Then we hurry," he said. "Lead the way."

Jahi fell in behind them as Kajan cracked the door, checking the corridors before waving them both to follow. Kajan had told it true: They'd exited the sewers in the servants' quarters, or more accurately, in the tunnels meant for servicing the latrines where the servants emptied the castle's chamber pots. He kept up breathing through his mouth, trying to suppress the taste of piss and shit that clung to him and Jahi after their jaunt through the sewer. If there had been anyone within a stone's throw of either of them, the smell would have announced their presence like royal trumpets. But the passages were empty, even as they tracked through the sleeping quarters, heading toward the inner courtyards, and the Queen's gardens.

It should have felt like a homecoming. He'd grown up here, in these halls, feasting with courtiers in the main hall as often as he'd dined with his tutors and drillmasters in the commons. The palace's entire eastern wing was a school for the Queen's sons, where they learned to fight, to think, to spy, to master the strategies of war and the necessities of commerce and agriculture. He'd never imagined returning to these halls as an assassin. Kajan led the way, but he could have guided them as easily. Secret passages, or lesser-used ones, twisting behind the halls where Bhakal nobility came to beseech their Queen. All empty. Kajan had done well to clear the path; on an ordinary day, servants would have been coming or going, guards taking up their posts while kitchen staff carried hot meals to be delivered through the grounds.

They'd turned down a long, narrow hallway mirroring one of the Queen's galleries when Jahi came to a halt.

Kajan turned back to her. "What are you doing, Mindhunter?" Kajan said. "The gardens are ahead, two more passages before we reach them."

Jahi said nothing. She stared through both him and Kajan, straight into one of the walls.

"What's wrong with your companion, brother?" Kajan asked.

"Jahi?" he asked. Her distant look reminded him of the sisters who had probed him during his imprisonment. Unthinking, one hand went to his sword hilt, while the other prepared to reach for *matarin* and *ubax aragti*.

Jahi blinked, and refocused on him.

"Go no farther down this path, Your Highness," Jahi said. "They're there. Waiting."

"What?" he asked "Who?" At the same time Kajan snapped, "Of course they're there. We're heading to the gardens *because* she's there."

"Your brother is leading you into a trap," Jahi said. "Six of my sisters— six of the Queen's Hand—await you in the gardens." She turned her eyes on Kajan. "And no sign of the Queen."

"She's been turned," Kajan said. "Brother. This witch has been turned against us. She's too weak to protect her mind like mother protected us. We have to kill her."

Kajan drew his sword, a smooth, practiced motion, while the other hand dabbed a pinch of powder on his gums.

"Kill him," Jahi said, her eyes suddenly wide. "He's been corrupted by a Queen's touch. And something else. Something worse."

Omera mirrored Kajan's gesture, freeing his steel and putting the fire of herbs in his blood.

He weighed them both. Kajan stared cold fire at Jahi, his brother's muscles already tensed, ready to spring. Jahi seemed gripped by fear. Without thralls, no Mindhunter could hope to stand against either of them.

He turned his sword to face Kajan, stepping into a protective stance between his brother and Jahi.

"What are you doing?" Kajan demanded. "We're blood. You can't trust her."

"If she'd been turned, I would have been, too," he said. "There's a crack in mother's shield, a crack she's keeping sealed. If she says this is a trap, then it's a trap. Believe her, brother. Believe me. Whatever thoughts they implanted in your mind, you can resist. You can still help us find the Queen."

"You're both corrupted," Kajan said.

More words might have come; instead Omera saw the change in his brother's posture. He moved his blade first, already parrying before Kajan attacked.

Metal clanged in the hall.

Kajan reset his feet and lunged, trying to sidestep Omera's guard. Omera moved, biting his steel deep in Kajan's torso, severing tendons in his shoulder. A second cut slashed his brother's throat.

Kajan's eyes widened. A scream died through broken vocal cords, and blood spurted as it leaked down his chest.

His brother's body slumped forward, still seeping blood with each pump of his heart.

He turned to meet Jahi's eyes. It had been a sudden, impulsive decision to protect her. But he'd been right. If Jahi was lost, he was lost. There was no other choice to make.

"They'll know he's dead," Jahi said. "We must hurry."

"The residences," he said. "If she's in the throne room and ready for us, we won't be able to reach her anyway. We have to hope she's in her private quarters. This way."

Jahi nodded, and they turned back the way they'd come.

Herbs pounded in his blood now. Sounds of alarm came through the walls; they would have heard the duel, whether they knew what it was or no. And if Jahi was right, the Mindhunters who'd broken Kajan's mind would know their creature was dead. They would be coming. They would alert the Queen.

He kept his sword drawn. *Matarin* herbs turned the blade's edge a sickly green, its acid ready to burn through flesh like fire through kindling. He raced through the narrow passage, taking a right turn that led to a shortcut past the galleries. They spiraled up a servants' narrow staircase, tight and cramped as the stone steps had them hunched over. The throne room would be beneath them, on the ground level, but the residences were just ahead.

He pushed open a thin door to an empty room. Blessedly empty; whatever Kajan had done, or, more likely, Sakhefete's Mindhunters, they hadn't encountered a soul since entering the palace. The sounds of commotion came from downstairs, but so far no shouts or cries to raise the alarm. He led Jahi down a hall of apartments, took a left turn at the far end, and circled around the palace's second floor, toward the royal wings. No sign of guards, no sign of servants, or anyone at all. If Sakhefete was watching, she would know they were coming. They could reach her chambers to find her surrounded by an army of Mindhunters and an equal army of loyal guards. But perhaps they could be swift.

They entered the royal wing.

Instead of quiet, two figures in white silk stood guard outside the Queen's chambers. A man and a woman, each armed with strange swords, only slightly curved, where the Bhakal *shotel* bore a scythe-like crescent near its tip. Yet their clothes and weapons were far from the strangest thing about them. They were Jun, with their too-fair skin covered by veils below their eyes.

He didn't wait to exchange words. *Ubax aragti* flared in his blood, and he attacked.

The Jun man fell before he could draw his blades, a thrust wrenching into the silk covering his upper torso, splattering it red as Omera ripped his *shotel* through the man's neck and jaw in an upward slice. *Matarin* hissed as the flesh he struck dissolved, until what was left of him crumpled to the ground, shock still written in his eyes.

The Jun woman was faster. Too fast. *Ubax aragti* should have made him double the match of the best-trained swordswoman in the world. Yet she whipped both blades from their scabbards, adopting a two-weapon style and rushing toward Jahi before he could jerk his *shotel* free from her partner's corpse.

Jahi dove to the ground, her eyes fixed on the Jun woman as she struck. Whatever Jahi did, it was enough to make the woman falter; she lowered one of her blades mid-stride, her arm trembling as though she were suddenly overcome by doubt, or fear.

Omera seized the opportunity, wrenching his *shotel* free and slicing it into the Jun woman's unprotected back. Or, he should have struck her back. The woman in white seemed to suddenly recover her senses, spinning to parry his strike with the smaller of her two swords while the longer blade delivered an arcing cut aimed toward his head.

Ubax aragti gave him the speed to duck beneath her attack. He parried the next and set into a defensive posture. He had Jahi with him. When she used her magic again, the Jun woman would lower her guard as the Mindhunter invaded and turned her mind. All he had to do was wait, and be ready for a chance to strike the killing blow.

It came. The Jun swordswoman suddenly lowered both her swords, folding her body and blades together into a child's pose, pressing her face to the ground.

He tried to strike.

The door swung open, and all the rage of the herbs burning in his blood stilled to quiet, serene calm.

His muscles ached, driven by reflex to lash out with his sword at the now-defenseless enemy. But he couldn't move.

The fortress his mother had built in his mind should have protected him. Jahi should have protected him. Instead he stood, frozen, while Jahi froze, too, both of them fixed on the doorway to the Queen's rooms.

An old, decrepit-looking Jun man in tattered robes had emerged into the hall. He glanced down at the ruined body of the swordsman in white, then across the hall to where the Jun woman knelt, doubled over, averting her eyes as though she were praying to him. Then the old man turned his gaze to Omera.

It was as though he stared into the depths of a great sea. Power radiated from either iris, a terrible power, like a creature moving in the deep. It washed through him, and suddenly he felt all the protections of his mother's shield, the great stone wall of the fortress protecting his mind, dissolve like wet sand against the tide.

"What is it?" a woman's voice called from within the room. A voice he knew. His mother's voice. "Have her assassins finally arrived?"

No, not his mother's voice. Her twin came into view behind the Jun man, the Queen's perfect beauty written on her face.

Sakhefete.

"It would seem so," the old man said. "They murdered one of my Cranes."

Sakhefete laughed. His mother would never make such a sound. It sounded foul in his ears, a twisted mockery of the Queen's laugh, grating steel where it should have been soft and full of love.

"She sent one of her sons," his mother's twin said. "How fitting, to send her boy to kill me at the moment of her death. So fitting. So like her, to match her portents to mine."

"There are two," the old man said. "The son, and another. An acolyte of the mind."

He tried to look back to Jahi and found he couldn't move.

"One of my sister's Hand," Sakhefete said. "Interesting. We'll have to kill her. But leave the son for me. He'll serve as a reminder, if enough of me is left to appreciate it."

"You will remain yourself after reconstruction," the old man said. "Only part of you will change to become the Veil. Only the part we need to unseal the Soul of the World."

His mother's twin nodded, already turning and retreating back inside the room. "Then we finish it. Erase them and come back to me. Only make sure you leave enough of him that I can piece him back together when I return."

The old man turned toward Jahi, and part of the fire that had blazed in Omera's veins rekindled. He fought to bring it back. He fought to raise the sword he still gripped white-knuckled in his hand. Terror swept through him. He couldn't move, not to fight, and not to turn his head and watch.

A slumping sound echoed from behind him. The sound of a body hitting the floor. Jahi.

The old man turned back to Omera.

He wanted to shout, to rage, to fight, to scream, all at once as he met the old man's eyes. The sea rose within them. A rising tide of fear, drinking everything, all sound, all sight, all touch, all smells, until only the eyes remained.

He tried to writhe, to contort his body from the pain. Suddenly all the world was pain. A razor edge tore through him, ripping something from deep within his body. Memory blurred. He was Omera...and he wasn't. He was the child, the favorite son, dueling and fighting and stealing from the kitchens. He was the young man, beautiful and charming, stealing kisses from the prettiest girls among the palace servants. He was the spy, sent abroad to prove his faith. He was the prince of destiny, following his mother's vision to accession. He was the swordsman. The assassin.

He was nothing.

Memory tore free, drifting on the sea of the old man's terrible eyes. It broke, and he lacked the hands to catch it, to keep it close. He was frozen in place. All he was drained from him in a terrible moment, and he felt it go, lurching away until nothing remained.

Only a name.

Omera.

He hovered there, watching as the old man turned, closing the door behind him.

40

SARINE

Private Chambers
The Queen's Fortress, Ruhadan

The Queen's guard took up positions outside the rooms they'd led her to, while the Natarii went in first, scanning the corners.

"If they meant us harm, they'd hardly have needed to hide in our closets," she said.

"Care never killed anyone, sister," Juni said, finally lowering her guard as she seemed satisfied the room was empty.

"Besides, there aren't any closets here," Kitian said. "There isn't much of anything here. Do these people hate art? I've never seen walls so bare."

"This place is designed for fighting," Namkat said. "Not for beauty. And I'm going to go have a look around. Join me?"

"In a moment," Sarine said. "What was that back there, with Tigai? I saw him stay behind."

"He saw something on the strands, he said," Kitian said. "He wanted to bring it to the Queen himself."

"And you let him stay?" Imyan said.

Kitian shrugged. "I've seen him in a fight. He can handle himself, should our new ally prove an enemy."

"Sure you won't come with us, sister?" Namkat said to her. "I hate being caged. And better for all of us if we know the ground, before the fighting starts."

She shook her head. The Watcher was already with them, shimmering in the air as it loomed over her. It didn't usually make its presence known unless it wanted her attention, and their being here was as much its idea as hers.

"Go, and learn what you can," she said. "The Watcher wants me to stay behind."

"That thing," Juni said. "It makes me feel like I've bathed in oil, sister, whenever I look at it too long. Have a care with it, whatever it says."

"The Nine Tails will keep her safe while we prowl the halls," Kitian said. "That is, if those Bhakal guards let us out of their sight. I've half a mind to see if they'll give chase, were I to lead them on a run."

"Sprinting down the corridors near their Queen would put any guard on edge," she said.

"I didn't mean that kind of chase," Kitian said, grinning.

"Take care of yourself, sister," Namkat said. "We'll be back soon. And Watcher: Any harm that comes to our sister will be revisited on you tenfold, I don't care how invisible you are."

The rest of the Natarii murmured agreement, alternately glaring at the Watcher's shimmering form and making eyes toward the Bhakal guards in the hallway. Then the four of them filed out into the hall, leaving her alone with the Watcher in the bare stone room.

She sat cross-legged, withdrawing the Watcher's book and opening it on her lap.

"So," she said. "We're here. And I think I'm finally starting to understand why. Thank you, for all your help so far."

The Watcher's shape shimmered as it moved to sit in front of her.

It says "soon," Anati thought to her. *"Soon we go back."*

"Go back to where?" she asked. "The Soul?"

Anati materialized perched atop her knees, on the book's edge, facing the Watcher.

He's being vague again, Anati thought. *I thought we'd moved past this.*

"He brought us here to keep Amanishiakne alive," she said. "Once her sister is dead, we have a chance to return to the Soul and challenge the Regnant. That must be what he means."

The Watcher shook its head violently.

He says "no," Anati thought. *Then repeats it half a dozen times. Then he says "back," and repeats that, as if I'm supposed to understand him.*

"Well, going 'back' could mean back to New Sarresant, if not the Gods' Seat," she said. "Or maybe something else. Maybe he means we go back to hunting the Regnant's champions, to trying to win the Soul that way."

The Watcher shimmered, turning its form to Anati.

"What did he say?" she asked.

Anati didn't respond. The Watcher stayed fixed on her *kaas*, both of them seeming to stare at each other, unmoving.

"Anati?" she asked. "What is it?"

Nothing, Anati thought.

"That didn't seem like nothing," she said. "It looked like he was telling you something."

Anati went quiet. It could mean she was listening to the Watcher, trying to parse his words. It could as easily be sullen pouting, and they'd been together long enough for her to recognize it for what it was.

Fine, Anati thought. *He wants you to come with us. To listen to him speak directly.*

"Can I do that?" she asked. Suddenly the Watcher mirrored her for attentiveness, leaning forward.

It would mean breaking our bond, Anati thought. *It would mean casting me aside like… like an old sock. Something brown and gray. But yes, you can do it.*

Her *kaas*'s scales flushed to become the very browns and grays she'd mentioned. Neither Anati or Zi had ever taken on those colors before that she could remember. A sense of pity rose in her at the sight; pity laced with contempt and disdain. Not her emotions, she realized; Anati's.

"Anati, I'm not going to cast you aside," she said. The Watcher drew back, adopting a warning pose. She ignored it. "You mean traveling to the *kaas*-realm, don't you? The place with the shapes, where I saw Zi when you and I were first bonded?"

Yes, Anati thought. *If you go there, our bond would be severed.*

"I'm not going to do that, then," she said, pushing a firm resolve to the forefront of her emotions. Anati would be reading her closely, and there was curiosity there, and enough frustration to bubble them both to the surface if she wasn't careful. But she wasn't going to abandon her *kaas*. Nothing else mattered more.

The Watcher slumped its shoulders, and would likely have been scowling at her if it had a face. Or… no. The thing wasn't angry. It picked up the shadow-book that had been lying in her lap, pointing to a page, then staring at her, waiting for a response.

Anati's head perked up. *The book, it says*, she thought. Her scales had a flush of blue over top of the browns and grays. *There might be a way. Something the Veil did.*

Sarine took the book from the Watcher's hand. She'd read every page at this point, all but committed the important passages to memory. There was nothing about the *kaas*-realm, so far as she'd understood.

The Watcher gestured toward the book again, flickering the air. Then it reached for her, clasping its hands around her forearms in a sudden jolt of motion. She almost started away from it, but it moved for her, using her hands to turn the book's pages until suddenly it let her go, leaving the book open on her lap.

She stared down at the page it had chosen. She'd read it before. A diagram of some kind of sculpture dominated the left page, all concentric circles with tiny orbs fixed on the rings, while a cutaway was labeled on the right: a stack of folds like papers, with each fold given a label and little else to explain its meaning.

What should I tell him? Anati thought to her.

"I don't know," she said. "I've studied this drawing before. I thought it was some sort of art. I'm not sure why he wants me to look at it now."

The Watcher stared at her. Its intent was clear, if not its meaning: It gave an exaggerated look down at the page, then to her, then back to the page, and back to her.

She looked again. The pages within the stack of folds were illustrated with intricate detail, each labeled cutaway bearing a different pattern, almost like bolts of lightning spread across the page. As she looked at them again, the lightning seemed to arc in columns of energy. She hadn't noticed when she'd studied the images before, but now they almost looked like...

"The blue sparks," she said. "That's where I've seen this. The patterns within each column on the Infinite Plane."

The Watcher nodded hard enough that the air shimmered like ripples on a pond.

She leaned closer to the text. Suddenly she recognized it, all the swirling energy that made up each column when she embraced the blue sparks. It had looked like a mass of tangled weeds, interwoven enough that she'd never stopped to question whether the energy took any distinct patterns or shapes. But they did. She saw it now in her memory. The columns weren't a single mass of sparks, they were a mix of these patterns, every one depicted on the right-hand side of the page in front of her.

The Watcher took her hand again, no less a surprise, but gingerly this time, carefully moving her finger to point at one of the patterns, labeled *Shadow and Form*.

"Shadow and Form," she said. "Is this...? The *kaas*-realm was all shapes and washed-out colors. Anati, is this how to visit your place, your people?"

Anati had perked her head up to look over Sarine's lap, and now twisted her neck above her forearms in a sort of shrug. *I don't recognize it. For me, home is home.*

It had to be. Without thinking, she shifted her sight to the Infinite Plane. A roar of sparks sounded in her ears, and where once she'd been sitting in the empty room in Amanishiakne's fortress, now all her surroundings were writ in the columns of the Plane. A small sparking torrent for the stone floor under her, another for the door, the walls, the ceiling. Larger torrents burned for Anati, a twisting mass of energy mirroring her coils and scales, while a bonfire of sparks flew for the Watcher and another, equally intense, burned for her.

She saw the patterns now. It wasn't a mass of formless sparking energy; part of her was a spinning current of red and blue, part was spirals of white enmeshed between the currents. Burned-out wisps and torn-away fragments hung between it all, red like ashes or heated wire, and she recognized the wounds where the Veil had torn away her leyline and spirit-bond magic as part of the patterns woven within the rest of her. She pulled away from the pain of it, turning instead to the subtle threads of black and gray the journal had labeled *Shadow and Form*.

They clung like smoke, hidden among the rest of the sparks, but now, knowing the pattern to look for, she found them.

She reached out, and Anati hissed.

The sound echoed in her mind, a memory but no less sharp for it. Anati's face materialized in her thoughts, as sharp and clear as if her *kaas* stood in front of her on the Plane.

No, Anati thought. *Not all of you. Not all at once.*

Meaning drifted between them. Somehow she understood: Touching the smoke would shift her being to the *kaas*-realm. Instead she drew a line of blue sparks, twisting the smoke until it mixed with the patterns that made up her body, the patterns for sight, for hearing, for taste and smell while leaving the rest of her solidly fixed in the physical world.

Color drained around her.

Grays and tiny dots replaced it. Points of light drew patterns in the air, etching shapes familiar and unfamiliar. Squares. Cubes. Cones, pyramids, spheres, circles, and more. Shapes with twelve sides, and a hundred. Shapes that bent in on themselves, impossible shapes that seemed to distort her eye when she tried to look at them. A sea of gray and shining light.

And Anati.

Her *kaas* clung to a long circular rod, perched like a bird as she gazed down, her neck arched in curiosity. Sarine almost gasped at the sight of her, though she had no breath or lungs here. Color, vivid color, flooded Anati's scales, each one shining like a miniature gemstone, made all the brighter for the lack of colors anywhere else. She shone like a thousand polished mirrors, reflecting light from some hidden source around her, as bright as a vast array of multicolored suns.

Are you…here? Anati thought. The voice was like a song, beautiful and haunting. It was still Anati, but somehow deeper, more resonant, echoing across the shapes and back to her with a hint of greater beauty.

"I think so," she said, and found her voice worked, though it sounded flat compared to her *kaas*'s resonance. "It was different when I came here to bond you. Different, but similar. I remember the shapes, and the points of light. The rest is changed."

We're still bonded, Anati thought. Satisfaction dripped from her words, somehow thunderous and delicate all at once. *You'll see through my eyes here. This is my home. This is what I see. This is how I see myself, and how I see you.*

At that she glanced down, noticing her body here for the first time. She shone as brilliantly as her *kaas* did, as though every patch of her skin, every follicle of hair, every scar and imperfection were made of light. She was glass, pure and perfect, illuminating the shapes around her when she moved.

"Anati…" she said. "This is…" Words failed her. This was how Anati saw her? She looked as though she'd been forged for a stained-glass window in her uncle's chapel.

You are a thing of beauty and wonder, Anati thought.

"Do you see all people like this?" she asked.

I see them as they are, Anati thought. *The same as my father does.*

"Zi!" she said. "He's here. Isn't he?"

A flare of pink shot through Anati's mirrored scales, and she felt it as jealousy touched with hurt.

"Anati, I'm not going to replace you," she said. "We're bonded. But I'd like to see him, if I can."

He decides who he sees, Anati thought. *But he'll know you're here once we leave my home.*

"Once we leave your home? I thought all of this was the *kaas*-plane."

Yes, and not-yes. First, I had to bring you here to be sure our bond held. We can leave and join the others when you're ready.

She paused, looking again at what appeared to be an endless horizon of shapes and light. It was different than where she'd appeared last time. Different shapes, in different concentrations. And before, there had been a multitude of other *kaas*, staring at her, clinging to the shapes. Here it was empty, only her and Anati.

"Your home is beautiful, Anati. Did you design it yourself?"

Pride shone through their bond.

I did. I shaped it after your city. The places you loved. A nervous color reflected from her scales. Emotions flowed more easily here, and suddenly she realized she could read Anati's thoughts as easily as her *kaas* usually read hers. Anati was embarrassed, the sort of tenuous excitement she felt when first unveiling a sketch she'd poured herself into making.

"I love it," she said. "It's strange to me, but familiar. Like a favorite painting I've always known."

Green crept up from Anati's tail. Pleasure.

Thank you.

She let it sit between them. Strange to think her *kaas* could read her so easily in the physical world. Here she felt every nuance, every shift of pride, nerves, humility, jealousy from Anati, radiating as clearly as expressions of disgust or joy if she'd made them elsewhere.

"I'm ready, if you are," she said finally. "Is the Watcher here, like me? Can you take me to him?"

He isn't called that here, Anati thought. *We know him as he knows himself, as he knew himself when he first came to us.*

The shapes twisted, blurring as the points of light seemed to stretch and shift.

They were moving, and she felt a tinge of dread through the bond. Her emotion, or Anati's?

Here he is called the Master. And yes. He is waiting.

41

SARINE

S hapes bent around them.

She stood on solid ground, a flat plane extending outward to the horizon, with pyramids and spheres hanging suspended in the air overhead. Another *kaas* was there, a narrow, stub-nosed creature perched atop one of the shapes, peering down at her and Anati. She only took notice of the *kaas* for a moment; the rest of her attention was directed to a series of thin columns arrayed in an open square with no ceiling, and to the man held within them.

He was her height, dressed in a long white coat that draped to his ankles. His skin was dark, Thellan shades, with black hair and brown eyes. An ordinary man at a glance, save that here in the *kaas*-realm, the sight of him stood in sharp contrast to the floating shapes, the grays and points of light. He was rendered in full color, pink in his lips and white in his teeth as he cracked a disbelieving smile. He shook his head, wrapping his hands around the pale white columns surrounding him as he came to face her and Anati.

The Master, Anati thought. *Such as we can hold him.*

The man's face beamed a mix of surprise and relief.

"You found the way," he said. His voice was cracked and hoarse, as though he hadn't used it in a long time. "I knew you would. I had faith."

"You're the Watcher?" she asked. "What are you doing here? This looks like a prison."

"It is," he said. "It is, so very so. And I am. I've been your guide, these many months. I've guided you here. Let us pray I can guide you farther, while there is still time."

She hesitated in approaching the columns, thin white rods she now couldn't help but see as bars. They were spaced close enough that he couldn't squeeze between them, though she suspected she could. Nothing else appeared to be holding him there.

"Why is he being held?" she asked Anati. "And how long have you imprisoned him?"

He was sealed before I was made, Anati thought. *He was here before any of us, except—*

"There will be time for such questions later," the Watcher interrupted. "The how and why are unimportant. What matters is you are here, and I can give you answers at last. Answers you need to preserve the balance, to maintain the forward momentum of Life and Death. The pact still holds, and so long as it does, there is hope."

"First I want the truth of who you are, and why you're here," she said. Something about him was wrong, the wrongness of charlatans claiming hedge magic and selling cure-alls in the market. His smile was too easy, too eager by half. It suddenly called into question the hours she'd spent poring over the shadow's messages and promptings in their time alone.

"Please," the Watcher said. "You must trust me. There is little time, and I've guided you well thus far, have I not?"

"I trust the *kaas*," she shot back. "And they imprisoned you. I want to know why."

The Watcher's smile slipped a fraction. "I made this," he said. "All of this. They turned on me. The thanks of wayward children, for a father long forgotten by time. But I'm here. I've always been here. You need my help if we're to unravel the knots the Regnant and Veil have tied in my absence."

She glanced to Anati for confirmation.

He is who he claims to be, her *kaas* thought. *The Watcher. The Master. The Maker. The Dreamer. He thinks of himself as many titles, but he is a man, only a man, the same as you and all the other Gods.*

"She's right," the Watcher said. "I'm nothing. Nothing now, where once I was Master of this and all other places. Now, please, will you listen to what I have to say?"

"In the Veil's journal," she said slowly. "She referred to a 'Master,' tied to the Soul of the World."

He nodded furiously. "Yes, yes, that's me. I built it, set it in motion, though I lacked the heart to see it through. My children—your Veil, and my Regnant,

Li Zheng, they run the project now. Only Li has lost faith, and it falls to us to convince him to return to the fold. It isn't time, you see. They're not ready. The world isn't ready. Still too much violence, too much hate. They need more time."

She felt her confusion mirrored through Anati's side of the bond, though her *kaas* was touched with other, fainter emotions. Pity? And worry, worry over something unconnected to the Watcher, or the Master, or whatever he was called.

"What is it?" she asked Anati. "Is he telling the truth?"

"I swear I am!" the Watcher began, though she silenced him with an upraised hand.

Not here, Anati thought. *Something in your world. Your champion, Tigai. He's shaking you, trying to wake you up. He's going to hurt you if he's not careful. I don't like it.*

"Tell him I'll return soon," she said. Strange to think her body was being handled in the physical world; she felt nothing at all to signify it, but then, she'd routed the blue sparks of all her senses here, into Shadow and Form. "I need answers first."

Anati nodded and vanished, blinking into nothing.

"Yes," the Watcher said. "Yes, yes you do. Good. Good."

"Start over, then," she said. "You led us here to protect Amanishiakne, to keep the Regnant from using her sister to gain control of the Soul of the World. Then you said we needed to go 'back.' What does that mean? Back to what?"

The Watcher leaned back, still holding the bars of his cage, grinning as though she'd given him everything he wanted.

"Back to him," the Watcher said. "You understand it now. You've seen the power of the Bhakal Queens. You've tasted their ambition. We need this one's help, to murder her sister and keep Li from this rash course of action. But they aren't to be trusted. And the others are the same. By-products of powers we unleashed, at the core of the Soul. Should any of them come to control the Soul itself, the consequences would be disaster, for the world as much as the people in it. Only the Regnant and Veil understood my work. Li has lost faith, but he can be redeemed. He *must* be redeemed. You must convince him. Once his plan to replace you is disrupted, you must return to him and convince my Regnant you mean to be his ally once more."

She recoiled. The Watcher seemed to sense it as he spoke, staring at her with renewed intensity.

"I'm not going to ally myself with him," she said. "Is that what you've been aiming at from the start?"

"You must," the Watcher said. "You must! Light and dark must be balanced across the Soul. The price of magic. Without its torpor the world will age too quickly, until it threatens to break. One day soon the flow will stop, and all of us—all of us!—will die. We who depend on magic, who thrive on its power, who have preserved ourselves across the eons, we are bound to the flow. Even the others understand this. But their vision is chaos, a remaking according to perverse and foreign orders, instead of our nobility. They cannot be trusted with the full keys of creation."

"I don't understand," she said. "I thought the others were potential allies against the Regnant."

"No," the Watcher said. "No, no, no, no, no, no, no. You mustn't risk it. They lack the patience. They lack the *time*. A hundred million years, for a fish to learn to breathe. A hundred million more for nature to run its course, to teach birds to fly, to make a mammal's heart heat its blood, to teach them to care for their young. And in a blink of a shred of a lifetime, we take humans from stones and caves and teach them the secrets of the atom, the mysteries of the electron, the truths behind the dimensional folds. We enchained *magic* to the Soul of the World, we gave them the fire of the universe, and they will purge themselves with it, without time to become its masters."

She studied him, searching for meaning behind his words. This was the shadow, the Watcher, who had given her the Veil's journal, then given her his own book—the *Meditations*—to try and help her piece together the Regnant's plan. And now he meant for her to return to the Regnant, to work with him. The touch of madness gleamed in his eye as he spoke. Had she been a fool, to trust him, to let him carry her this far?

"Anati, why did the *kaas* imprison him?" she asked.

"No," the Watcher said. "That's the wrong question. The wrong question. The wrong question. The wrong question."

He ended a cycle on his own, Anati thought. *I hadn't been created yet, none of my brothers and sisters had, but my father told me the story.*

"No, no, no," the Watcher said. "I was weak. Arrogant. That's why I needed the Veil and Regnant, why we needed to divide power. I see it now. My mistake. One soul can never carry all the keys."

"What did he do?" she asked.

He made a great flood, Anati thought. *Many, many deaths on his hands. More Black than had ever been made at once.*

"A corrupted strain," the Watcher said. "They had to be purged. Had to be! Could have been handled better. More smoothly, less damage to the genetic legacies. But we had to do it. Had to preserve the growth of humankind, no matter what it cost."

A sickening feeling spread in her stomach. She'd made a mistake, trusting him. But there was still hope. Amanishiakne could still be an ally against the Regnant, and there could be more. Whatever the Watcher's reasons for leading her here, she could act on her own, unbound to his plan, or anyone else's.

He isn't listening, Anati thought.

"I know," she said. "I'm sorry for asking you to bring me here, Anati. I thought we could find answers, where to find these 'others,' but—"

No, not him, Anati thought. *Tigai, back in the Queen's fortress. He's demanding your attention, using the word "fuck" a lot, and yelling. Too much red. I told him you'd return soon, but he wouldn't listen.*

She frowned.

"Please," the Watcher said. "Please, you have to help me. I can tell you. I can tell you where to find them. I can tell you *what they are*."

"The Others?" she asked.

The Watcher nodded sharply.

"You have to plead for me, when he arrives," the Watcher said. "You have to get him to release me. Then I promise, I will tell you all of it. I will let you decide whether to support those...those betrayers, those pretenders, instead of the ultimate glory of our project. You'll see. You'll see I was right, from the start. No matter my methods, no matter my mistakes. He'll listen to you. He'll free me, if you command it."

"Who?" she asked. "The Regnant?"

He means my father, Anati thought.

"Zi," she said.

"He's coming now!" the Watcher gasped, then spoke rapidly. "Please. You must make him release me. I only ever wanted to perfect humanity, to imbue us with magic and science and power and all the gifts of divinity. The division between Regnant and Veil was my idea, don't you remember? I've atoned for what I did. Nature doesn't care about the deaths of thousands, millions, entire species, if it achieves her ends. I was only mimicking the natural force. There is no cruelty, no madness in nature, and none in what we did—what we do! Our project is the next evolution of nature itself, a second-order evolution necessary to transcend to greater heights. Please, Evelynn, go to Li, make him see you are still in alignment with our goals. He cannot trust our power to these barbarians, to these uncivilized fools with no understanding of our greater purpose, of the meaning behind—"

Shame radiated through her.

A light cut through the grays and shapes, through the Watcher's storm of words. Shame, powerful enough to churn bile from her stomach. She gagged, doubling over, though she had no physical body here. It took the slow unknotting of her muscles to realize it wasn't coming from her. It was Anati's shame, not hers.

I'm disappointed in you, daughter.

The voice thundered in her thoughts. Fear and sadness punctuated the shame, and something else shone through it. Love.

"Zi," she said.

He was there. She saw him through Anati's eyes, his scales a polished, perfect gold, a halo of light surrounding him as he stood atop a crescent-shape, looking down on them. To Anati he was a vision of power, terrible power, as regal as any King, his presence alone enough to cow her to submission. But in her eyes, he was the metallic half snake, half lizard who'd bitten her finger the first time she'd tried to sketch him. He was the friend when no one in the world cared whether an orphan girl lived or died. He was the protector who kept the alley cats away while she tried to sleep. He was the guide who led her, starving and near death, to the smell of soup coming from the kitchens of the Sacre-Lin.

You shouldn't have brought her here, Zi thought. *You shouldn't have come here yourself.*

Anati's shame stung deep. *I'm sorry, father.*

"Zi, it's me," she said. "I ... I've missed you."

He turned to look at her, and for an instant, all the stern tension in him melted. He was her Zi again, staring at her with his ruby eyes, the rigid posture that meant she had his full attention. There was still love in him, as tender and sweet as the day he'd died in her arms.

Then, just as quick, he was back to the regal King, full of judgment and wrath.

She needed help, Anati thought. *I didn't have the answers. So I turned to—*

You spread poison, as sure as that creature. You risked infecting her, when she should be allowed to become what she will, without interference.

Anati hung her head low.

I'm sorry.

I should sever your bond, as punishment. See to it a better child is given to her.

"Zi, I love you," she said. "But I love Anati, too. Whatever she did, please, don't take her from me."

Zi turned to her again, his eyes still full of wrath.

Sarine, he thought. *Are you certain? You were given a chance to rise beyond your seeds. To grow, and flourish. My daughter has jeopardized that chance. She has unsealed a sickness that poisons all it touches, a poison that still lingers, even in the Soul of the World. I won't say more. But she should face punishment for it.*

"Leave her with me," she said. "Please."

The wrathful King melted, back to her Zi.

As you wish.

Relief shone through Anati's scales. White and silver and a pale blue-green.

"What's going to happen to him?" she asked, turning back to the columns of the prison.

The Watcher had recoiled from their exchange, cowering at the far side of the gray columns with his back to Zi.

My daughter will not summon him again, Zi thought, with all the force of a command. *He remains here, in his prison, and you shouldn't risk returning.*

"All Anati was trying to do was give me answers," she said. "That's why we came here. I didn't know what he was. I'm sorry. It was a mistake."

You wanted truth, Zi thought, and she nodded.

Truth is powerful, Zi continued. *But truth is power, too. Which truths are revealed, which withheld. Those with truth can control those who seek it. Don't let them control you. Find your own way.*

"I'm trying," she said. "I came here hoping to find allies. It's been hard, going against the Regnant alone, when there's still so much I don't understand."

You were supposed to be dead already, Zi thought. *You were born to be a vessel for a Goddess, a body for her to escape a prison, nothing more. But I saw more in you. I chose to trade my mortal life to give you a chance to grow. Don't squander my sacrifice chasing old lies disguised as truth.*

The words rocked her to her core.

"I . . . I didn't know," she said. "You chose . . . the sickness . . . for me?"

You will find your way. Not as the Veil, not as the Master's puppet. You came here seeking allies. Good. Go. Find them. Choose those whom you will trust, and those whom you will oppose. The world watches. We kaas *watch. Go, and do as you will.*

"Zi, I love you. I miss you."

His eyes flashed red. An emotion and an image rose in her mind, of the same love returned, of a fire burning hot, while a million shadows circled around it, waiting to see where it would burn.

The stitches slipped loose on the Infinite Plane, and the shapes and points of light blurred together as her senses returned home.

42

SARINE

Tears flowed from her eyes, a sign that her body had been crying long before her senses returned. Zi had chosen to die for her. To "trade his mortal life," he'd said. Did it mean he couldn't return to the physical world? She would have sacrificed herself for him, in an instant, without hesitation. But it stung deep to hear he'd already done it for her.

"Sarine?" Tigai's voice, full of fury. "Sarine! Fucking finally! Are you there this time?" He grabbed hold of her shoulders, shaking until her senses rattled in her skull. "Can you hear me?"

"Stop!" she snapped, jerking herself away.

"Fucking thank the fucking wind spirits," Tigai said.

See? Anati thought. *I told you he kept using that word.*

Her head throbbed. "Anati told me you were shouting for me," she said. "Were you bloody shaking me the whole time, too? I feel like my head's been boiled in oil."

"She's dead," Tigai said. "Sarine. She's dead!"

"What?" she asked. Her temples pulsed in time with her heartbeat. Tigai's words almost cut through the fog, but she was still half in a daze. "Who's dead?"

"The Queen," Tigai said. "The bloody fucking Queen. Amanishiakne. I watched it happen. The maidservant, Daskha. A Fox. A bloody skinchanger. Same as all five of the guards that were on duty last. They knifed her in the back."

"The Queen..." she said. "Amanishiakne. No. Are you sure?"

"I just said I watched her take a knife in the back," Tigai said. "I'm pretty fucking sure."

Words bounced like dice in her head. How hard had he shaken her? By instinct she reached for the leylines, for a *Body* tether to refresh her stamina, and snapped herself back as soon as she tried it. Red burning wires gouged her, severed pieces of the sparks where Lin Qishan had torn them free. It made her gasp in pain.

"I know," Tigai said. "I know, we failed. This place is a fucking shitstorm right now. Her guards—grown men, fighting men—fell to the ground wailing like children."

"Anati," she said. "I need *Red*." It came as soon as she asked it, her heartbeat doubling in her chest as blood surged through her. It doubled the pain in her head, too, and she winced from it, but with *Red* she could ignore the rest.

"Where are the Natarii?" she asked. "They went out to walk the halls. Get them here. Now."

Tigai stared at her for a moment before nodding once, then again. "Yes," he said. "Yes, all right."

He scrambled from the room. Amanishiakne was dead. Whatever else the Watcher had tried to tell her, he'd been clear enough on what it meant, should one of the Bhakal Queens fall. Sakhefete's mind could be rebuilt as the Veil. Together, she and the Regnant could turn the keys to control the Soul of the World. And now her one ally, however tentative their pact, was dead. She focused on the *Red* pumping through her veins. She had to find calm. They had to go to the Gods' Seat. They had to face him. Fear coursed through her. They weren't ready for this.

He doesn't handle stress very well, Anati thought.

"Who...?" she began, then, "Oh, Tigai. No, he doesn't."

She paused, gathering the Veil's journal and the Watcher's *Meditations*, tucking both into her bag. "Anati, I want you to know, about what Zi said..."

He was right. I deserved to be punished.

"I don't understand why. All you did was try to help me. I want you to know I forgive you, whatever else you did that was so wrong."

How can you forgive me if you don't know what I did?

"How can you question me when you can read my thoughts?"

Anati snorted, but fell quiet, staring at her with a flash in her eyes.

She rose to her feet, doubly grateful for *Red* to keep them steady. They had to stop him. She drew a deep breath, as much to distract herself as center her mind. She could do this. She could face the Regnant, and defend the Soul. Even if Sakhefete had the Veil's memories, she still had a chance.

Tigai appeared without warning in the doorway, looking as though he'd held his breath since she'd dismissed him.

"I've got them," he said. "That is, they're coming. They're here."

A moment later the Natarii warriors trotted up behind him, crowding the hall until Tigai made way. Juni was in front, signs of the Flame Scale already spreading in black and red lines outward from her tattoos. Namkat and Imyan and Kitian bore similar marks, their tattoos distorting as their gifts manifested themselves in their changing skins.

"Sister," Juni said. "You've heard? We failed in our duty here. The Queen is dead."

She nodded. "I know. The Regnant. He struck at her, but now we know where to find him. He'll be at the Gods' Seat with her sister. With Amanishiakne dead, he can make Sakhefete a Goddess, the same as him, and me."

The Natarii exchanged glances, the marks on their faces spreading faster, their skin changing to orange, blue, green, and red.

"We're with you, sister," Kitian said.

"You're sure?" she asked. "All of you? You know how dangerous this will be."

"We're sure," Kitian said. Her face was thoroughly crimson, signs of the Blood Claw congealing, as though she'd become liquid while still holding her form. "And we're ready. Let's go kill some Gods."

She searched the rest of their faces for agreement, and found it. Even in Tigai, whose nerves had been replaced by a hardened look, with a hand on the grip of one of his pistols. There was comfort in having allies at her back. But it was hard not to feel the absence of Arak'Jur, Erris, Yuli, even Reyne. Erris had an empire on her back; Arak'Jur and Yuli were in the hospital. Reyne was dead. This was what she had. This was what she would use to confront her enemy, and fight to preserve the world.

She flicked her sight to the blue sparks. Five torrents, six with her and Anati. She gathered them all, surging toward the center of the Plane, toward the white columns of the Soul of the World.

———————

The arrival chamber was changed, the smooth stone etched with some sort of runic markings, written in a language even Anati couldn't help her read. Or perhaps it was only that the writing changed as quick as she could glance at it, shifting white chalk on the stone walls. The map table was gone, along with the other gold- and silver-plated instruments. Bare floors led the way from the room, forking into hallways as soon as the chamber ended, more passages at a glance than had existed in the entirety of the Gods' Seat before. But she knew the way to its heart. Two minds pulsed there, in time with the energy permeating this place. Two intruders. Two invaders.

The Natarii sisters fell in behind her, now fully changed to their battle-forms: Namkat was covered in feathers and claws, Kitian dripped a trail of blood where they walked, Juni's skin came alight with orange fire, and Imyan's changed to hardened tree bark almost the color of stone. Tigai glanced down the new passages as though making note of every change. None of them questioned her, or her knowledge of the way. They took a left passage, another left, a right, a left again, spiraling inward through a maze of halls and chambers, a maze designed to delay, to distract and confuse. Someone other than her might have gotten lost, spent hours, maybe days unraveling its secrets. She followed the path, clear in her mind, feeling her enemies' presence as it grew closer, louder, until it roared in her ears with every step.

They reached the heart.

The smooth stone around the Soul's light was gone, replaced by a mosaic of light and dark stone. Swirling patterns covered the floor, as though black paint had been spilled, still flowing and changing its shape as it moved. At the center the column of light burned, a radiant energy crackling louder, hotter than it ever had before.

Amanishiakne's twin stood beside it, her arms spread, palms facing the doorway. A hood covered most of her head, and a deep blue cloak shrouded the rest of her body, but Sarine knew her for the torrent lying beneath the chamber on the Infinite Plane: a bonfire of blue sparks, twisting, spreading, growing, so intense she could see the Plane superimposed over top of the physical world.

And behind her, the Regnant.

Her enemy took the form of an old man, garbed in rags, hunched toward the column at the chamber's heart. His eyes were black, full black, a shade that matched the sparks surrounding him on the Infinite Plane. He held his hand outstretched, dipping his fingers into the column's energy, and where Sakhefete turned to meet them, the Regnant made no move to acknowledge their presence, staring with his jet-black eyes into nothingness.

"You must be her," Sakhefete said. The voice was cool, rich, and beautiful, carried through the room as though the walls themselves spoke her words.

"This is my place," she said, and somehow the room did the same when she spoke, echoing her voice until it rang like a song. "Neither of you belongs here."

"This was your place," Sakhefete said. "It's mine now. And I am you, or you as you were meant to be. Our partner didn't think you would come, but I know you. I know your soul. I knew we would face each other before the cycle's end."

The Regnant hadn't moved during their exchange, keeping his hand frozen where it was, disrupting the current of the energy at the room's center.

"I didn't come here to talk," she said.

"No," Sakhefete said. "I suppose not."

Red flooded her veins, as much as she'd ever had in her blood, making the currents of energy slow so she could see every surge, every crackle and spark, and she charged.

Sakhefete flicked her fingers, and blue-white walls sprang up around the Regnant as she spun to face Sarine's attack. *Shelter.* Apparently Sakhefete had been given the Veil's powers in addition to her memories. No time to worry over it now.

She struck, a *Red*-enhanced blow that would have shattered her enemy's skull, had it landed. Sakhefete stepped out of the way in a single, fluid motion, then dodged again as Namkat screeched toward her, streaking like a bird of prey. Kitian followed Namkat's attack with a whip of blood, cracking once where Sakhefete dodged away from Namkat, and again where she dodged the first whipcrack. The Bhakal Queen moved like flowing water, eddying around each strike as though she knew where they would fall before they were made.

A thundercrack filled the chamber, the deafening boom of pistol shot, amplified by the same echo that had carried her voice. Tigai blinked, snapping back to where he'd been standing, and fired again, then blinked and fired again, all aimed toward the *Shelter* surrounding the Regnant at the chamber's heart.

Sakhefete flicked her fingers again, and this time *Shelter* walls went up around Tigai, and each of the Natarii warriors, enclosing all five of her companions at once in bubbles of blue-white haze.

"This should be between us, don't you agree?" Sakhefete said.

She said nothing, willing Anati to give her *Black* as she attacked again.

This time she got within a hairsbreadth of the Queen, throwing a punch aimed at her chest. Sakhefete sidestepped, then lashed out and grabbed her wrist, twisting it until she was off-balance, tumbling to fall hard into the stone.

"I have as much *Black* as you do," Sakhefete said. "You'll not free them that way."

She wrenched herself around, leaping back to her feet, and saw Anati tangled with another *kaas*, both creatures snapping and clawing at each other in a flurry of metallic colors and scales.

"How...?" she said.

"I told you," Sakhefete said. "I am you as you were meant to be. Remade from the Veil's memories, in the full soul of the Bhakal Goddess. And you are a sad shell of yourself, with so much torn and burned away. Even so, the Regnant should have chosen us from the start, and I mean to prove it to him here, today."

Red still hummed in her veins, but with dips and surges in its power as Anati rolled and bit the other *kaas*. She'd never imagined seeing her *kaas* fight claw-to-claw; it came as a shock, and she could feel every snap of the other *kaas*'s jaws, every scratch of its claws, in the desperation carried through their bond.

Her instinct had been right: If Sakhefete had *Shelter*, and a *kaas*, she would have every one of the Veil's gifts, and the Bhakal Queens' magic besides. But if Sakhefete was a copy of the Veil, she wasn't a copy of *her*, and she'd learned more than the Veil had ever given her.

The Nine Tails stirred as she attacked again, savoring the feeling of its host surrendering some part of her control.

Its prey burned hot as it changed. Magic. The scent of it flared in the Nine Tails' nostrils. But the Nine Tails had the scent surrounding it, too. *Red*, given by the lizard companion. And more. The scent of Dragon.

She balanced their awareness on a knife's edge, flickering between herself and the Nine Tails. Sakhefete's eyes widened as she shifted form midattack, and where the Queen easily sidestepped where her *Red*-empowered strike would have been, the Nine Tails' lashing flurry snapped in her face, narrowly brushing her skin as the Queen bent backward to dodge. Sakhefete twisted, trying to set her feet when she snapped back to an anchor, suddenly appearing at the Queen's side. A second flurry of tail-whips lashed her around the forearm, spinning Sakhefete around in a lurch and sending her staggering off-balance into one of the *Shelter* shields, crackling in a hiss as it sent her to the ground.

Blood trailed from a wound on the Queen's cheek, just below her left eye. Sakhefete gasped in shock, but sprang up with *Body*- and *Red*-fueled speed, suddenly surrounded by a nimbus of the Great Cat moments before the Nine Tails struck again.

Tails whipped between claw strikes, the Queen's blazing speed countered by every anchor she set, blinking her and the Nine Tails to strike from behind, from the side, to strike twice from the same position. A claw cut her through the shoulder, slicing through tissue, skin, and bone; she blinked to an anchor, and was whole again. The Nine Tails wrapped around Sakhefete's leg, yanking to throw her off-balance before whipping its tails into a shield of stone conjured at the last moment, shattering rock and dust as it exploded from the force of the Nine Tails' attack.

Sakhefete rolled to her feet, and the Nine Tails was behind her. The Queen spun, and she attacked from the other side, landing a tail lash that shattered bone, crumpling Sakhefete's form around a broken leg and hip.

A bubble of *Shelter* went up around Sakhefete where she landed, pushing Sarine back. The Nine Tails snarled, full of contempt. Its prey had given a good fight. It should die without resorting to tricks.

It struck, lashing all nine of its whip-tails down hard, ignoring the hissing pain each time it struck the shield.

A howling sound echoed from the walls, and the fight shifted to the Infinite Plane.

She felt the attack before it came, a darting thrust of pure will, picking at a hundred knots at once. She and the Nine Tails both shifted sight, finding the torrent of energy that was *her*, that was *them*, crackling and raging around the red wires that had already been cut free. The new presence attacked where the old cuts had never healed, prying loose the sparks that made her who she was. With the Veil's journal in her mind she understood the nature of the attack: Sakhefete meant to sever her connection to the physical world, setting her mind adrift on the Infinite Plane.

Panic flooded her, and she fought back.

The Queen's will unmade a knot, and she tied it, snapping at the intrusion with all the Nine Tails' fury. She followed it, finding the torrent that was Sakhefete herself, and mirrored the same attacks. Lattices of sparks repeated in both forms: pieces of her, replicated in the torrent that now hovered close, until the two almost merged. Where she had red, severed wires, Sakhefete's form was whole, and where she had the nested tangle of the Nine Tails, the looping coils of Dragon, Sakhefete had something else, something foreign. But they shared the bulk of the pattern of who they were, and that was where she directed her efforts, burning away sparks as quick as Sakhefete could fuse them back together, deflecting the same attacks made on her.

Sparks flew into the void. Behind them, all too close, the tower of white fire at the center of the room burned, mirrored on the Infinite Plane, and the raging mass of black sparks she knew instinctively was the Regnant. The black sparks touched the white, and changed them. But she could spare no more than awareness of what was happening there. Sakhefete struck at the core of who she was, at the bond between her and Anati, and she struck back, defending herself and attacking, until the sparks flared into a bonfire of red, blue, purple, and more.

The Nine Tails shattered the Queen's *Shelter* on the physical plane, howling in triumph as it reached its prey.

Sarine saw both physical and infinite, the furious dance of make and unmake, spark and flame, as the Nine Tails lifted Sakhefete's body up, wrapping a tail under either of her arms while two more closed around her throat.

Sakhefete's face went purple, gasping for breath, meeting her eyes with rage, hate, fear, recognition.

A surge of sparks erupted between them. She countered it, every knot retied before it could be unmade. Another flash of sparks, another counter. Furious strikes, until she was too slow, a hairsbreadth too slow, and the Nine Tails' form flickered, vanishing in an instant from the physical realm.

It screeched, a terrible, hollow sound, before she seized hold of the loose knots, forcing them back in place. The Nine Tails was still there. Still part of her. But for a moment, its form had wavered, and Sakhefete's physical body came loose, falling backward, forcing them apart.

Breath came hard. The Nine Tails itched, burned inside her. It needed control again. Needed to finish the kill.

"You are...more than I expected," Sakhefete said, her voice now hoarse and broken, though it still carried through the walls. "Perhaps we erred, in letting the warrior spirits grow unchecked."

Sarine gave in to the Nine Tails, feeling control once more split between them. It bared its fangs as their body changed, growling as it stepped toward the Queen.

"A thing to be considered later," a new voice said, reverberating through the room with a chilling melody, low and deep. "For now, this cycle is at its end."

The Regnant appeared behind Sakhefete, offering a thin, bony hand to help her stand.

The Nine Tails glared. No creature should interfere in its hunt.

Sarine seized control. Horror flooded her. The white column at the room's heart was black now, a surging darkness extending up past the chamber's ceiling, down through its floor.

"What did you do?" she asked. "What's happening?"

"That which should have happened long ago," the Regnant said. "The cycles of Life are ended. The world's torpor can finally resume."

"No," she said, barely a whisper as it carried through the walls. The white-black swirls on the chamber's floor had been replaced by pure black, spreading under their feet, crawling up the walls, driving outward in a rush to cover the hallways, and the chambers beyond.

"Yes," Sakhefete said, a gloating smile spreading on her face as she rose to her feet. "This is his place now. You have no hold here."

The *Shelter* bubbles around her five companions vanished, all at once, though they were frozen where they stood: Kitian holding a blood-whip poised to strike, Juni's fingers flickering orange and red, Tigai with a pistol leveled where the Regnant had been standing before.

The Nine Tails' rage flared. She met the Regnant's eyes, and found pity, relief, sadness, resignation.

"Go," the Regnant said. The single word echoed through the chamber. She felt the world crack under her feet. It struck and enveloped her, a gale wind on the Infinite Plane, threatening to blow her sparks to dust.

All across the Infinite Plane, the sparks changed. She saw it, an endless series of tremors rippling across the world. Trees fell. Stones crumbled to ash. Rains hissed and pocked the ground where they fell. Grass cried out on the Plane as its roots shriveled and died. Clouds turned black and covered the sun.

The Regnant stared, watching calmly.

She seized hold of the sparks that were Tigai, Kitian, Namkat, Juni, and Imyan, clutching them tight as the black wind screamed around them. She kept them together as they were torn loose, uprooted, cast into the torrents spiraling away from the Gods' Seat. The pillar was there, but black, as it was in the physical world, a surging darkness where once it had been light. The tendrils hanging from the Soul came loose as they drifted, splintering into thousands of filaments, spreading black droplets outward on the wind, mixing and poisoning each torrent they touched.

She reached for them, trying to force her will against the droplets, against the currents, and felt nothing, only empty void.

In her mind, the sound of weeping, sobbing filled her thoughts. Anati's sound. Not hers. She was hollow, an empty shell, fighting against oblivion as they drifted on the wind.

BEFORE

PRELUDE

EVELYNN

Ilon-Stream Linear Collider
Lyon, France

Lights shone in her eyes. She tried to keep still, reviewing the likeliest questions in her mind as the cameras were checked and double-checked, the microphones tested, the background adjusted to perfectly evoke the proper image of "science" for the viewers at home. Never mind that all her life science had been done in front of a computer, waiting for new code to compile, algorithms to run, neural nets to confirm theories she knew in her gut to be true. On today of all days she'd as soon have worn her usual sweatpants and too-large sweatshirt, with her hair tied back and out of the way. Instead they had her in a white lab coat—a lab coat!—with enough cosmetics slathered on her face to trap her hair there if any strands got loose. But then, this was part of the job, when she got it right. And she hoped to God she'd gotten it right today.

An image sprang into life on the monitors, the talking head of the man who'd be interviewing her. His name, Steven Plinkett, scrolled along the bottom of the monitor, and his voice suddenly lurched into her eardrums, speaking clipped, precise English with an American accent.

"...we'll be going live shortly to the collider itself, where I'm told we have a very special guest waiting to speak with us: Dr. Evelynn Lacoursier, theoretician, mathematician, author, one of the youngest Nobel Prize winners in history and a key mind behind the new Ilon-Stream Linear Collider, due to begin operations for the first time later today."

The lights switched from red to green, and the on-site producer gave the signal. She took a deep breath and stared into the camera, trying to pretend the news anchor was sitting there, two meters from her chair, and not a cold, impersonal lens of glass and plastic.

"Dr. Lacoursier," the interviewer said, and suddenly her image appeared on the screen beside him. "It's a pleasure and an honor to have you with us here today."

"My pleasure to be here, Steven," she replied, hearing the thick French accent as she spoke. She'd read online comments that her accent was "sexy," "sultry," "part of her charm"; it did nothing for her self-confidence, hearing herself speak next to a news anchor. God but she should have listened to her PR people and found time for those elocution classes.

"You must be excited to have your theories put to the test today," her interviewer said. "And yet, I'm told by our science division that even you aren't entirely certain what's going to happen when they flip the 'on' switch."

"We know precisely what will happen," she said, adopting her best disarming smile. "Two opposing tracks of leptons—electrons and positrons— will be accelerated over twenty-two kilometers almost to the speed of light. We collide the first pairs, then divert the resulting subatomic particles— quarks and antiquarks—into two new tracks, where they are held in magnetic stasis for a fraction of a second before they are accelerated further, and collided again."

"And after that?" her interviewer asked.

"After that . . . we'll see," she said, holding her smile.

"We've heard from some of our viewers that they're afraid the ISLC could rip a hole in space, even create a black hole. What would you say to those viewers?"

"There is science, and there is science fiction, Steven," she said. "The same fears were voiced before the ISLC's predecessor, the Large Hadron Collider, went online in Geneva. I don't think they found any black holes in Switzerland."

"No, I suppose they didn't," her interviewer said with a forced, fake laugh. "What do you expect to find?"

"This will be a window into the composite fabric of the universe," she said, borrowing from the speech she'd given on her last university book tour. "The best microscope humanity has ever had. We'll be able to see and study particles that exist on planes too small for the traditional laws of physics to apply. We might find particles theoretical physics has predicted for decades—gravitons, strings, superstrings. We might discover something new."

"Bringing us back to science fiction," her interviewer said. "You're speaking of the alternate dimension theories you described in your latest book: *Behind the Atom*."

"Not science fiction, Steven," she said. "Multidimensional theory is what made the ISLC's construction possible."

"And yet there has been significant controversy in the scientific community around your theories, to say nothing of the cost. Some forty-one billion euros to build the ISLC, with projected operating costs in excess of two billion euros per year. And no one can say for sure whether it will even work, isn't that right?"

"It will work," she said. "The best scientists in Europe, in the world, agree with my theories. And as for the cost—the human race spent two hundred forty billion euros on cheeseburgers last year. I think we can afford one-sixth of that cost to unlock the secrets of our universe, don't you?"

"I do indeed," he said, showing another fake grin. "I do indeed. Thank you for joining us today, Dr. Lacoursier."

"My pleasure," she said.

Her image vanished from the monitor, and her interviewer began talking about the latest firefighting efforts in California. She held her poise until the light switched from green to red, and the producer gave her a thumbs-up.

She resisted the urge to tear her hair free, wipe her face clean, and throw her lab coat in the nearest waste bin. Instead she withdrew her journal, flipped to a clean page, and began a quick sketch of the room, cameras, microphones, lights and all.

"That was great," the producer said, speaking the same clipped English as her interviewer. "Really great. I'm sure your—"

Blessedly one of her people shushed the idiot, no doubt explaining that when Dr. Lacoursier was sketching she wasn't to be disturbed for any reason. A longstanding rule, and the single best thing, probably the only truly good thing about her fame: She could afford to hire people to tell other people to fuck off and not waste her time. She finished the drawing quickly, short, sharp strokes to capture the moment, freezing it in her memory. Sometimes she sketched and took notes to relieve her anxiety, nothing more, but some of her best insights had come when she worked in her journals, and she could never predict when inspiration would strike.

She closed the book when she was done, hopping up to her feet. The crew was already disassembling their impromptu studio, and her people were ready to leave.

"Thank you, everyone," she said. "Be sure to wish all of the staff you encounter at the ISLC luck. It's a big day. I appreciate your being here to document it for the public."

The crew seemed surprised she'd talked to them, murmuring thanks and good luck as she turned to exit the room. That had been something her father taught her years and years ago: Graciousness to working people went a long way, whether it was cleaning people, restaurant staff, or anyone else who sold labor for their livelihood. He would have been proud to see her today, trying to blend efforts of the mind with working-class elbow grease. None of this would have been possible if he hadn't taught her to work bloody hard in pursuit of her dreams. Now it was time to find out if those dreams were going to come true.

Her people trailed behind as they left the administrative offices, piling into electric golf carts and heading toward central control. Camera crews would be there, too, but with instructions to stay out of the way, to document without interfering in their work. Knowing the media, they'd be hoping for some flashy light show, some momentous finger of God reaching out to touch them and declare Science Had Been Done Here. In actuality all they'd get was some distant humming as the accelerators powered up, then virtual reams and reams of data for the computers to chug on while the scientists in central control cheered that nothing had broken or gone wrong. Dear God, she hoped nothing would break or go wrong. That alone would be cause for champagne. The initial proof of her theories would come in a few days, after the neural nets had time to sift through the first collisions. Then they'd repeat, and repeat again, for weeks if they had to. Nothing was guaranteed, but she was confident they'd get the results she'd predicted within the first few tests. No cause for panic for a month or two at least.

Central control was a model of scientific efficiency, which was to say the waste bins had been cleared of fast-food wrappers, packets of crisps, and cases' worth of cold-brewed coffee and energy drink cans probably a few hours before the camera crews arrived. Computer terminals lay between rack-mounted server hardware, with a series of giant windowpanes looking out over the nexus where the trenches dug for the colliders met. The view wasn't scientifically necessary, but even she would stand there, gazing at the kilometers and kilometers of concrete after they flipped the proverbial "on" switch.

"All right, everyone," she said, back to the comforts of French. "What did I miss?"

Two PhD students came at her as though they'd coordinated the movement, each holding a tablet for her review. Dr. Arnauld, Dr. Keller, and the rest of her fellows nodded to acknowledge her presence, but only Dr. Sebastian Ziegler, a German physicist, longtime competitor and friend, stirred to rise from his workstation to greet her.

"It was a nice lab coat they gave you," Sebastian said. "Do you suppose they have one in my size?"

"Oh Christ," she said. "Shut up. You're lucky they didn't want us wearing them in here. These look good." She nodded to both tablets the students had presented her. "Everything in order. What's left for the calibration checks?"

"Only your blessing," Sebastian said.

"You're ahead of schedule?"

"We're ready, Dr. Lacoursier," Sebastian said. "We've briefed the camera crews. Yesterday's tests were solid, well within acceptable parameters. Coils are heated, venting chambers are clear. I've even prepared the champagne. All that's left is your speech, if you want to make one. Then we make history."

She glanced at the rest of the team, nervously preoccupied with their work but watching her and Sebastian as they reviewed the data coming in on their monitors. The media teams had been tucked away, perhaps waiting for the very speech Sebastian had mentioned before descending to crowd the main part of the room.

"Fuck it," she said. "Let's go. Give the order. Start powering the first and third accelerators."

"You're sure?" Sebastian said. "The media would love to film a speech."

"They'll get one, after we get some results. This moment is ours."

"As the doctor commands," Sebastian said, grinning like the grad student he'd been when they first met, during her first term at the Sorbonne.

Her order percolated through the room, and suddenly every student, every peer was on edge. A palpable change in the atmosphere, like the charge before a thunderstorm. She resisted the urge to check and recheck the nearest terminals, instead sauntering at a controlled pace to the windowpanes overlooking the complex. Four years to build this, in what had to be a record for any project with as much bureaucratic heft. The cameras would already be rolling; some among the journalists would be able to tell they were doing something, if not precisely what. They probably expected some giant switch, some coil of lightning in a rainstorm. But everything was electric now, digitized and simple. A button on an iPad. Trained neural networks to watch and monitor every aspect of the systems, with humans there as audience, stakeholders, and fail-safes.

"Accelerator one is powered," a grad student said, reading from a monitor. "Accelerator three at ninety-two percent. Two and four on standby."

"Start flooding the lepton chambers," Sebastian said.

Her heart was thundering. She tried to appear calm. Her fingers pressed into her journal's leather binding. It was the wrong time to sketch, no matter how much she needed it. The cameras had to see her composed, regal, surveying the accelerators like a prerevolutionary queen. Right now the first electrons would be cycling, positrons flooding behind them. Faster, faster. Faster than almost any other matter in the universe.

"This is it," Sebastian said. The journalists would hear and understand that, if not the rest of their work. Thankfully, blissfully, they kept quiet. "Are we green for release?"

Three seconds. That was how long they would have before the first collisions, once the order was given to release. Then less than one more second before the subatomic particles left over from the first would be recollided, opening the window into the unknown. She reworked the functions in her head, though the better part of the advanced mathematics had all been done by computers. The safety and monitoring stations checked in. The first accelerator. The third. The central combine. The damping ring monitors. All green. All good. All ready.

Sebastian glanced at her, and she gave the smallest nod. All she could manage without throwing up.

"Go," Sebastian said. Dr. Keller pushed the button, and she started counting.

One. The magnets around the damping chamber would begin rerouting.

Two. Electrons and positrons flooding into the main chamber, beginning to travel the twenty-two kilometers toward central control.

Three. All of them moving. First reactions happening as quick as she could think it.

Now the magnetic stasis. The second and fourth accelerators powering.

One more second...

Data would be coming now. She held her breath.

———

Gray clouds hung in her vision.

She blinked, or tried to. A light flickered in the distance. Coming closer.

Panic set in, then calm. Then panic.

She clutched at her journal and found it there, somehow still indented around her fingers. The rest of central control was gone. She was in an empty void, gray and lifeless save for the torrent of sparks on the horizon. Blue sparks, dancing like a campfire.

Calm. Rational, logical thought. She'd been stressed, nervous, excited. She must have passed out from the exertion. Fucking lovely. Camera crews would be swarming around her like moths, and her unconscious body the flame. She could read the headlines, see the video feeds now: *Lead Scientist Collapses As*

€41bn Project Comes Online. Then they'd show video of the ISLC complex, all concrete, metal, and wires, designed to look impenetrable and as wasteful as possible to the average taxpayer, spliced with the image of her falling over in her chair. *Fuck* her anxiety. It wasn't fucking fair.

The sparks were close now. A strange dream. She tried to stay level, breathing in through her nose, out in a slow stream through her mouth. Did she usually have to breathe in dreams? No sense worrying about it. She'd be revived in a moment, and she could start worrying about damage control and PR. The sparks had no heat, only blue surges like a bonfire made of tiny glowing wires. Behind the approaching torrent she could see a dozen more in the distance, then a hundred, an ever-growing mass of blue flames stretching out on an infinite plane. She framed it like a first-year physics problem: Imagine a frictionless plane with an infinite supply of potential energy... all she needed was a bowling ball and an elevator shaft and she could get to solving equations.

Suddenly the plane was gone.

She was in a cramped room with a cheap IKEA desk, an adjustable lamp, and towers of books piled across every available spot on the floor. A lone window lay to her left, looking out over the rain-soaked streets of Marseilles. The port would be there in the distance, the port where her father had worked double shifts as a stevedore to afford to buy her used college physics and math textbooks instead of dress-up dolls and toy ponies.

"Is it comfortable?"

The voice startled her. The man who'd spoken stood in the doorway, leaning against the frame just the way her father had done when he came home from the port.

"I've been preparing for this moment for sixty thousand years," the man said, smiling a too-familiar smile. The sort she associated with politicians. "I hope my preparations were all in good order. I can't tell you how relieved I am that you found me."

"Who are you?" She felt the fear in her voice. This was a dream. Any moment she'd wake up back in central control.

"I am the First," he said. "The Dreamer. The Watcher. The Maker. The Master. And I suppose that makes you the Second, doesn't it?"

He smiled the same sickly smile, as though he'd made a joke.

"What's going on?" she said. "I'm at the ISLC. None of this is real."

"I assure you, it is. You'll be thankful you have me to guide you, you know. When I woke up here after my experiments there was no one to teach me where I was."

"What the fuck is this?" she snapped.

"This is a chance to do things right. I've failed three times. That is, the world has failed. I was starting to think I was a fluke. But now you're here, you've breached the seals, and we can find the tools we need to do this right."

Panic stung deep. She could feel her anxiety taking over, feel the sickness churning in her stomach. He didn't seem to notice.

"We can do better," he was saying. "The *kaas* can perform a full reset, but that means replacing the seals I unlocked to get here—the same seals you unlocked with your experiments. We need to find a way to reset while leaving the seals broken, giving ourselves the ability to refine and perfect the system. They'll call it magic, and they'll call us Gods, but it's just the new physics—the very sort you predicted in your books."

She glanced down, searching for the mesh-wire wastebasket that should be there, if this was a perfect copy of her childhood study. It was.

"Of course, you'll need a name," he continued. "Something shrouded in mystery. I haven't settled on mine, yet, but I've got the perfect moniker for you. A woman, powerful and mysterious, brilliant and unknowable. They'll remember you for generations, across multiple iterations of the system: The Veil. Do you like it? I almost wish it suited me. The Veil."

She grabbed the bin, feeling bile rushing into her mouth as her gut muscles contorted, before she heaved the contents of her stomach in among the crumpled papers and trash.

PRELUDE

LI

Research Facility #3401-AA
Qinghai Province, China

His monitor flickered on. He dismissed the red warning box, alerting him to yet another high-priority message waiting in his inbox. No time for bureaucracy. Not today.

It took a moment for the camera to boot and begin its feed. He stared at it hungrily, waiting, then stared more intently when the first stream of images began to appear.

Subject 38 appeared unchanged from the night before.

His fingers moved quickly, typing notes as he panned the camera. Blisters on the subject's fingers, nails broken from scratching the walls. Significant hair loss, a foreseeable side effect of the pathogens. Track marks on either forearm. Trace amounts of heroin still in the system even after two weeks of testing. Ink leaks where the subject's tattoos had been damaged. That was as promising a sign as Subject 38 had shown so far. A rewrite of the genetic code, or at least a sign of malleability. But he needed more. If last night's injections showed no further adaptations... He eyed the red warning box, still flashing in the corner of his primary screen. No. His latest configuration was flawless. It would work. It had to.

He thumbed the microphone.

"Good morning, Subject Thirty-Eight," he said. The translation software would alter his voice, make it sound as though he were a woman, speaking flawless, native Korean. Different cultures responded better to certain combinations of accents, gender, and age; a matter for the psychologists and software engineers on a different research team. Not something he needed to worry over.

Subject 38 stirred from his sleep, turning over to show the bruises, still fresh and purple, across his chest. He stood, almost mechanically, rising to his feet for inspection. If only the body responded as easily as the mind to conditioning.

Li moved the camera, slowly tracing the contours of the subject's body. The puncture holes in the left thigh were bruised, now changed to a soft green, but there was no sign of the holes they'd made last night. Li pivoted to his other computer monitor, confirming the notes. There should be puncture holes on the right thigh as well. A mistake by the nurses, perhaps. But if they'd injected the left leg by mistake, those bruises would be fresh, and—he checked the camera again—they weren't.

"I trust you slept well," he said into the microphone.

"Shit on your grandmother's grave, you spineless dog-fucker," Subject 38 said.

He thumbed another button, this time flooding the chamber with red light. Subject 38 flinched, but Li refrained from initiating the punishment sequence. Instead he gave over control to the voice-software AI, only half listening as it taunted Subject 38 with a flirtatious, almost seductive retort. His focus was on the right thigh. He studied his second monitor, then brought up another view on a third. The latest pathogens should have damaged the blood vessels, resulting in bruising of the skin if not outright clotting in the femoral artery.

"Move forward and present your right leg to the camera," he said into the microphone. The AI would take his words and weave them into the banter he'd initiated at the right time, but the waiting made him tap his fingers in frustration. Finally the AI gave the order, and he leaned in close.

The subject sneered at the camera. "You want to fuck me after, is that it?" Subject 38 said. "Making me tease you with it first?"

He pressed the button that indicated the highest priority for his order to the AI, then another to initiate punishment.

Subject 38 screamed. The subdural implants would simulate muscles cramping, though he'd personally worked with their physicians to ensure that the implants wouldn't harm the blood flow the pathogens needed to circulate through the heart.

He mashed the "high priority" button again.

Still the AI took its time, waiting for the subject to pause his screaming before it spoke.

"Move forward and show me what I need to see if you want to have anything left between your legs at all," the AI said. "So far we haven't put an implant near your little friend. That could change, if you aren't careful."

Li shook his head. He wished the software wouldn't make threats he wouldn't order carried out. The penis was far too essential for the pathogens' blood flow; there would be no implants there, now or ever.

Subject 38 complied, moving forward to expose his right leg to the camera. Li moved the lens, changing focus. No marks. Not even the needle-point scabs where the subject had been injected. He'd brought up the footage of last night's procedures, playing it through at 4x speed on his third monitor, to be sure. And there it was. It had been done.

The leg had healed. Or changed. Either way, it was a sign.

His breath quickened.

A new alert appeared atop his monitor, sliding to the front of his queue. He dismissed it, staring at Subject 38's right leg. This was it. This was the beginning of his results.

He slid from his chair, tapping a button for the AI to continue in automatic response mode, then another to lock his workstation. His legs flared pain as he stood on them, shooting pains up his spinal cord. He ignored them. An amplified product of age, that was all. He retrieved his cane, a beautiful antique made of oak with a worn, polished brass topper carved with lotus flowers.

He palmed the pad outside his quarters, securing the locks. His nurses wouldn't have stirred yet; their quarters were on the same level as his, and he could see the doors shut along empty hallways. The rest of the facility was automated, run by AI with no more than a handful of security guards to ensure that his subjects stayed under his control. Decades ago he would have run a lab fifty times this size, with scores of assistants, researchers, soldiers, even party attachés to ensure that his reports reached the ears of people in high places. Most of his friends in the party had died by now, whether of treachery or old age, but he'd had enough favors left to secure this one lab. If he'd had a proper team he would have had results months ago, but at least he was on track to having them now. And once he did, once they saw what his work could accomplish, he'd have resources even the thirty-year-old Li would have envied.

He rode the elevator down a level. Only a single button, though he knew the Subjects' Quarters was tunneled twelve stories beneath the lab. A safety precaution, one he'd insisted on, given the potential for danger if his hypotheses proved correct. It made for a long elevator ride. Time to feel the pain spreading in his back. Time to feel his pulse hammering the excitement of what he'd found in Subject 38's right leg.

The door slid open, and he froze.

Men in dark green camouflaged uniforms filled the corridors. Most stood, observing, their hands resting on the submachine guns holstered on their belts. But some were inside his subjects' rooms, or in the process of overriding the locks on their cells. Some were wheeling gurneys with comatose bodies laid atop them.

"What..." he said, feeling the rush of toxins in his blood, threatening to seize his heart. "What is...why...?"

Several soldiers noticed him, pointing him out for a man bearing the three flowers of a colonel's insignia.

"Dr. Li, I presume," the colonel said.

"What is..." Li said. "What is the...the meaning..."

"This lab is closed," the colonel said. "You will have received the order through government channels four days ago, and again this morning to confirm our arrival. I must say, Dr. Li, I'm disappointed in your lack of preparation for the closure. I'll be noting your lack of compliance in my official report."

"You..." Li said. His breath was short, too short. Vomit was rising in his belly, and a sheen of cold sweat covered his forehead. "You can't. So...so close..."

The colonel handed a tablet to an aide, showing his back to Li as another gurney wheeled by. Subject 11's face was visible above a plastic tarp made to serve as a body bag. Pain struck through his heart at the sight. Subject 11 had shown promise, now wasted. All wasted.

Li took a deep, steadying breath, thumbing the syringe hidden in his trouser pocket. He'd meant it for Subject 38. His research suggested that a subject had to show initial signs of mutation before the catalyst would have its full effect. But Li had taken the pathogens into his own system, as a control. If it would have worked on Subject 38, it had to have some effect, even a minor one, in him.

His hands shook as he slid the needle through his trousers, piercing the skin on his leg.

"We have access to your reports, of course," the colonel said. "But if there are subjects that require special care, any warnings will reflect favorably on you. And you should know I've been instructed to bring you to Beijing in person as part of the closure."

The catalyst's fire flared in his leg. Calm pervaded him as it spread, like an ink stain coursing through his blood.

His breath stabilized as the fire reached his heart.

"Dr. Li?" the colonel said. "Are you listening?"

"Who gave you this order, Colonel?" Li asked. "Are you aware my funding comes from the office of Secretary Pei-Lu? My reports flow to her office directly, through Undersecretary Liao."

The colonel gave him a queer look. "Dr. Li, the order to close this lab comes from Secretary Pei-Lu herself. And there is no man in her service called Liao. You may wish to rethink the names you intend to use as a shield, when you speak to my superiors."

"What?" he said. "No, that's not..." He'd corresponded with Undersecretary Liao yesterday, and again three days prior to that. But if the man wasn't who he claimed to be...

"I ask again, Dr. Li, whether there are any subjects here that require special care and handling from my men. If any of my people are injured, I can make your journey to the capital considerably less pleasant. I suggest you consider how helpful you can be."

The colonel's words washed over him, and the uncertainty over Undersecretary Liao. The catalyst was having an effect. That alone was cause for excitement, whatever madness had descended on his lab. His legs felt weak, trembling, but also strong, as strong as he'd felt in years. He could run a footrace, throw his cane aside. He could ignore the double vision, the black spots superimposed over the sight of the colonel's soldiers dismantling his work.

"Special treatment," he said. "Hm. Yes. Subject Thirty-Eight. The only one of my subjects to show advanced progress. This way. You have men armed with tranquilizers? Shock prods?"

The colonel fell in a step behind as Li suddenly cut across the holding area. "We have schematics, Dr. Li. We can find the cells. There's no need to put yourself in danger."

"He's been moved," Li said. "Quicker if I show you."

Three soldiers responded to a snap of the colonel's fingers. They carried submachine guns, though at least one of them had what looked like a Taser holstered on his belt. Another day or two and those weapons would have proven useless; he'd taken the precautions of sturdy mechanical and magnetic locks, psychological conditioning, and, failing those, drugs in the subjects' food and water to control them. Force was a fickle thing, even under the best conditions, and his experiments were designed to shift those parameters, to shift them beyond anything this colonel could have prepared for.

He switched the monitor on outside Subject 38's cell. Audio came through the speakers, audio of his AI making suggestive comments while Subject 38 sat hunched over in the corner, defecating into the waste tube. Li's fingers shook as he pressed a button for the AI to deliver the code phrases that would immobilize the subject before the door opened. He tried to remain calm, to appear unhurried as they waited for the routine to finish. But he couldn't help staring at Subject 38's right leg. He'd been right. The change was beginning. He silently prayed none of them noticed.

The door hissed as it slid open. Pressured and sealed. Another precaution.

The colonel's men barked an order, one of them roughly grabbing Li by the shoulder and shoving him aside while the other two fanned out, entering the doorway as though they needed to check every corner of a two-meter-by-two-meter cell.

One of the soldiers drew his Taser pistol as soon as he was through the door, firing it without further warning at Subject 38's lower torso.

"You've been a naughty boy," his AI said over the speakers in Korean, trying to find some way of incorporating the soldiers' actions into its protocols. "Take your punishment, Subject Thirty-Eight, and be thankful my compatriots are being so gentle."

Subject 38 looked down at the Taser electrodes protruding from his belly. A clicking noise echoed through the cell, signifying the fifty thousand volts of electricity now coursing through him. Li had tested the pathogens enough in rats to know the charge would produce a mild tingling sensation in an advanced subject's brain. A tickle, perhaps. Nothing more.

Now the soldiers noticed the change. Li stared at it, transfixed. Glass covered Subject 38's right leg, body-fitted as though it had been sculpted to perfectly fit his form. It spread, quickly, coating over the lower torso where the electrodes stuck through the skin. Fascinating. A perfect adaptation of the third pathogen strain, exactly as he'd predicted. And the stress would speed the adaptation; he'd planned to use the catalyst, the syringe he'd stuck into his own leg, but the Taser gun would serve equally well. Now the change was inevitable, whether the subject wanted to control it or no.

The second soldier drew his submachine gun and fired.

A short burst, three bullets, but the roar was deafening. It bellowed from the chamber, drowning the hallway like a thundercrack. It should have split Li's eardrums, leaving a ringing whine in its place, but he heard it as a dull thud.

The bullets impacted Subject 38's glass exoskeleton, shattering and cracking it in spiderwebs along his torso. Subject 38 glanced down at the cracks in confusion, the same reaction he'd had to the Taser's electrodes. The psychological conditioning worked, and the AI repeated its code phrases again as the soldiers seemed as stunned as Subject 38 was: "The wise bear sleeps through the winter," the AI said in its teasing, girlish voice. "Don't you agree, Subject Thirty-Eight? The wise bear sleeps through the winter."

"No," Subject 38 said finally. "No, no I don't agree."

The second soldier fired his submachine gun again, this time emptying the clip as he held the trigger down.

The colonel winced, covering his ears as he ducked behind the wall, while the other soldiers readied their guns. All stared as Subject 38's body was encased in glass, head to toe, repairing the cracks from each bullet as quickly as they struck.

Excitement pulsed in Li's veins. The pathogens worked. His hypotheses were right. They worked in humans precisely the same as they'd worked in rats.

Subject 38 flicked his wrist, and the soldier who'd fired his clip went down, gurgling and clutching his throat. He flicked again, and the second soldier screamed, warding his face with an arm that was torn to shreds. The third soldier backed away, fumbling his gun before he could fire. Li saw the glass this time, a salvo of broken shards flying from Subject 38's fingertips, eviscerating the soldier through his uniform, knifing through Kevlar as though he'd been armored in paper.

The colonel stared in horror, frozen in place, darting sharp glances between Li and Subject 38. Another salvo exploded into the side of the colonel's head as Subject 38 stepped into the hallway, avoiding the trail of gore splattered on the floor.

Subject 38 turned to him.

Li was calm. Centered. The third pathogen would result in the metamorphosis to transmute matter to matter, in this case the glasslike substance now covering Subject 38's body. He called that strain the Ox. But the first pathogen, the Lotus Virus, would have mastery over all the rest. That was the one he'd infected himself with, as a control in case of this very sort of breach, and the catalyst would be awakening its strains in his blood with every beat of his heart.

Subject 38 raised his fingertips, pointing them at Li. It sent a tinge of panic through him. Rats infected with the Ox strain, the Crane strain, the Owl, the Fox, Dragon, Mantis, Crab, and Heron—none had been able to attack a Lotus rat. He hadn't been able to puzzle out precisely how the immunity worked; that analysis was meant to come after the first successful human trials. But if he died here, impaled by the very glass shards he'd struggled so long to see perfected in Subject 38...

The black spots took over his vision.

This was death. He was dead. A starfield shone around him, beautiful but dim, as though he gazed up through the clouds from the heart of Beijing, Shenzhen, or Hong Kong.

But no; he wasn't dead. He saw Subject 38 outlined in the stars, saw the glass surrounding him, felt the pulse of the Ox Virus beating in his heart.

Lotus pulsed in time with Ox, and for a moment they were one.

Then Ox ripped free, and he absorbed it.

This hadn't been part of the rat experiments. Or perhaps it had; he'd had no means of telling what the Lotus rats saw when one of the others was goaded to attack. The aura surrounding Subject 38 came loose, drifting through the starfield to attach itself to him, coating his body with orange light.

His vision flickered. Part of him saw the cells and the hallway, the corpses of the colonel and his three soldiers, the stupefied shock on Subject 38's face now that Li, and not him, was covered in glass. The rest of his vision stayed with the starfield.

Subject 38 shouted something incomprehensible, and attacked.

Desperation showed in Subject 38's eyes. The subject thought himself free, free and powerful, changed by the Ox Virus even if he didn't understand what Li's work had done. How easily Li dispatched him, with a flick of his wrist! Glass flew, impaling Subject 38 through the chest, and Subject 38 crumpled to lie beside the colonel, mixing the streams of their blood. This was all Li had imagined it could be. He'd been the first to discover the changes; in the past two years, something about reality itself had shifted, unsealing his viruses to imbue great power, terrible power. Mystical power. And he was the magician.

He turned back toward the elevators, willing the glass to reinforce his armor. He had no need for this lab now, but perhaps the soldiers here could serve as a different kind of experiment.

An image shimmered into being in the second half of his vision, on the dim black of the starfield, and he almost staggered away from it in shock.

"Dr. Li," the image of Undersecretary Liao said. "I see you've progressed far enough in your experiments to validate your theories."

"Impossible," Li said. "How can you speak to me here?" His shock mixed with a fear of failure; was he not the first to discover the mystical side of his pathogens, after all?

"Perhaps it's time to reveal who I am," Undersecretary Liao said. "You may have guessed I am not, in fact, an aide to the party chairwoman in Beijing."

Li nodded, feeling a renewed cold sweat under his glass. Was he a traitor, unknowing?

"I am something greater," Undersecretary Liao said. "I am the Maker. The Dreamer. The First. The Master. I guided you, secured funding for your experiments because you were the furthest along in your understanding, in glimpsing the future an unsealed physics made possible. If you wish it, you will become part of a greater project, an attempt not only to reveal the possibilities your pathogens unlock within humans, but to perfect the human race itself."

"And if I refuse?" Li said.

"You won't refuse, Dr. Li," the Master said. "I've watched you for decades, preparing for this meeting. I know you. You're too driven by your work, and you've glimpsed the unthinkable, the impossible, now. You can't turn back to a mundane world after tasting this fruit. And besides, if not you, there are others we could groom. You see, my partner, the Veil, and I, are in desperate need of a virologist."

PART 3: RUIN

THE SISTER'S DYING BREATH

43

ERRIS

Rasailles Shelter *Dome*
Aboveground, Near the Ruin of New Sarresant

Fire erupted from the top of the dome.

A ripple shot out from the impact, where another meteor was blasted to nothing as it struck the *Shelter* shield. The flash lit the sky for an instant, etching the outline of black clouds overhead, a canopy thicker than the densest forest. Thick enough to black out the sun.

Torches and campfires served for light, and boiling drinking water. It took *Shelter* and *Entropy* binders working to open and close the barrier at its peak to vent the smoke. A chilling reminder that, if they'd been venting smoke as the meteor struck, the shield might not have held.

She had two candles burning on her desk, a sheaf of papers and reports piled to eye level, and nothing overhead. No roof or ceiling. That had been her order; any existing structure would complicate a *Shelter* barrier's ability to regenerate itself. The barrier had to provide the protection. So they camped beside the palace ruins, where meteor strikes and poison rain had already shattered and stained its walls and tallest towers. Thank the Exarch they were close enough for foragers to loot the palace cellars to bring them food.

"Good news, Your Majesty," Doña Portega said, doing a fine job of pretending she hadn't noticed the meteor strike. Her Minister of State produced a single paper, adding it to the top of the stack. "Our first rangers returned from north of the dome this morning. No contact with the army yet, but they were able to traverse seven leagues, and return without permanent injury. A good sign for northerly exploration, and the second group is due back later today."

She retrieved the report. Two binders, both *Life*, and two others, all mounted, and they'd managed no more than two or two and a half leagues per day. By some twist of fate both binders had fallen ill, whether from some environmental toxin or contaminant in the air her doctors weren't yet able to say.

"We need to switch to paperless reports," she said as she read.

"Your Majesty?" Doña Portega said.

"Just what I said, Minister," she said. "Paper won't be in limitless supply. Something else to conserve."

"Yes, Your Majesty."

She read on, glancing at the ledgers she kept open on the right-hand side of her desk. Two thousand six hundred and four souls under the dome at last count, now two thousand six hundred and eight, with the first group of rangers returned. They'd saved most of those who'd been fortunate enough to be inside the palace walls when the sky had gone black, and a few couriers who staggered beneath the dome's protection in the hours after it went up. None since. Not one survivor from the city, but then, the first group of rangers had been sent north, toward the army. The second group of rangers would be returning soon to report any contact from the east.

"Has there been word from the foragers on recapturing the palace livestock?" she asked.

"More good news, Majesty," Doña Portega said. "Twelve sheep and four cows recovered as of this morning. I was, ah, drafting a report for you this afternoon."

She did figures in her head, approximating grain and grazing requirements between horses, cows, and sheep. They'd erected the *Shelter* dome covering a diameter of two leagues, anticipating the need to protect grasses and trees from the poisons in the sky. But it wouldn't be enough. Already her quartermasters badgered her that they needed to expand the barrier, that they couldn't sustain replacement populations for their animals. Now, with more head added to the herds...

She closed the ledger and rose to her feet.

"Your Majesty?" Doña Portega said.

"Walk with me," she said. "They need to see me, today."

Her Minister of State followed without comment. Tents had been ruled out along with using the palace's buildings, and for the same reason. She hadn't even allowed herself the luxury of privacy, however she missed it when she worked. Desks like hers dotted the landscape where her people slept, with their bedrolls, blankets, and pillows scattered free-form around the camp.

It should have been autumn, seasonal rains and cold weather creeping ever-closer to winter snows. But the air was hot, even under the dome, and *Shelter* protected them from the rain.

They walked toward the horse-lines at the eastern side of the dome. She wore the mask of a general who'd already ordered her soldiers into a fight, a calculated pose of determination, will, and sacrifice, and kept her eyes to the horizon as they passed the campfires where her people sat, looking to her as though she could carry them, even if only for another day. Perhaps she could. Despair threatened behind every meal, every report, every breath of their *Shelter*-filtered air. But her people would look at her and see strength, and if the Gods were good they'd find the same within themselves.

Jiri stood at the end of the horse-line, taller at the withers than most of the couriers' mounts that made up the bulk of the palace stables. Her pristine whiteness shone in the dark, reflecting torchlight as though Jiri herself gave off a glow. Erris cradled her head, leaning her forehead against Jiri's. Her horse had been a source of strength for as long as they'd ridden together, and today she needed everything Jiri could give.

"Your Majesty," the head groom, Reignard, said, knuckling his chest in place of a bow. "If you've come to meet the second ranging party, they've not returned yet."

"I'm here for Jiri," she said. "And for you. How are the animals holding up?"

"Your Jiri's an inspiration to the others, Your Majesty," Reignard said. "Even the dogs and sheep. A few more might've bolted if not for her, I'd swear it to the Oracle. She eats, doesn't shy from drinking the water, and keeps calm even when there's fire atop the barrier."

"Good girl," she said, and Jiri nuzzled against her again.

"Have you, ah, pardon my asking Your Majesty," Reignard said. "But have you, ah ... checked ... with the second rangers?"

"Your boy was with them, wasn't he?" she said.

"Yes, Majesty," Reignard said. "Dolland, my oldest. I suppose ... my only boy, if there isn't word from the city."

"I haven't used *Need* with the eastern rangers," she said. "Not for two days. But I can confirm for you: They reached New Sarresant. They were preparing to turn back when I last tethered a connection."

"Ah," Reignard said. "And ... there hadn't been ...?"

"No sign of survivors yet," she said. "But that doesn't rule out hope."

"Of course, Majesty," Reignard said, this time offering a bow. "Thank you."

She let Jiri go, exchanging looks with Doña Portega. She saw weariness there, even in her minister's eyes, and doubled in the head groom's. Hope had been in short supply under the dome.

"Steady me," she said, offering Doña Portega a hand. "I'll tether a link to the rangers now, for your sake, groomsman."

Reignard's eyes brightened. She closed hers. If fate was kind, she'd find the rangers well, and well on their way. A return from the city, even empty-handed, would be a bright light in the darkness for all of them.

She found *Need*, though it was dimmer, darker in the days since the sky had changed. Glimmers of gold, where once her vessels had burned with shining intensity.

The connection tightened into place, and her senses shifted.

She winced inwardly, even before her senses snapped into her vessel. Every connection risked the brimstone, the burning ash in the air that seemed to infect her lungs with a cough even through the protections of *Need*.

She was inside a building. A boardinghouse, from the look of it, or a barracks. Rows of cots sat against the far wall, piled with blankets, pillows, and supplies. Ropes, wax-sealed packages, hooks, tallow, canvas, crates, nails, and more importantly: people. Her rangers went in teams of four, but there were forty or more here in this hall.

"Your Majesty!" the eastern rangers' leader, a young lieutenant and *Body* binder named Cornaille, said. He'd been injured, on the cusp of recovery in the field hospitals at Rasailles, though he looked the worse for wear here: hair full of soot, his skin red and pocked with sores. Yet in spite of it, his face was flushed in the lamplight.

The exclamation, and her golden eyes, drew attention from the rest of the hall.

"Lieutenant," she said. "Are these survivors? From the city?"

"Yes, Your Majesty," Cornaille said, pausing for a harsh cough that couldn't take away the glow of excitement in his eyes. "Yes. They found us right as we were riding out the western gate. That is, Your Majesty, I regret to report that we will be delayed in returning to Rasailles."

"Understood, Lieutenant," she said. Prudence dictated a calm reserve, but she spoiled it, joining him in beaming. This was the first truly good news since the sky changed. Survivors. And supplies, Veil save them all from ruin. "You said they found you. They're organized? City watch, or army?"

"Neither, Your Majesty," Cornaille said. "A binder, a civilian, put them together, used *Shelter* to protect a watch barracks near the boundary between the Gardens and Southgate. He has them searching the city in teams, gathering resources, and other survivors."

"Now that's some work worthy of a bloody medal and a commendation," she said. "Can you get them moving toward Rasailles? Without a self-sustaining source, their *Shelter* reserves have to be close to running dry."

"It's a long walk, Majesty," Cornaille said. "There are women and children here. I can't be sure..." He paused for another cough, then spoke again, softer. "I can't be sure they'd survive."

"It's that, or risk what happens when the *Shelter* fails. Where's their binder? Bring me to him. He'll have to know his leyline reserves aren't going to last much longer. He'll have to convince them to move."

Cornaille nodded, rising from his cot and guiding her up the barracks hall. She saw the same fears on the survivors' faces as they passed, the same gaunt uncertainty as her people under the dome at Rasailles. But she took note of the whispers, the pointed looks and fingers, calling attention to her vessel's golden eyes. There was hope there, no mistaking. Hope, for the first time in weeks.

They reached the end of the hall, where Cornaille spoke to a woman in blue, and a man in a watchman's yellow hooded cloak.

"He's out, Majesty," Cornaille said finally. "Out scouting with one of the foraging parties."

"He can't have gone far," she said, directing it to the man and woman by the door as well as her lieutenant. "*Shelter* won't hold over a great distance."

"'S'right, mum," the woman said in a thick Gand accent. "'S'why 'e's out looking for priests, an' new sources, so 'e said."

"You mean to move to another barracks when this one runs dry?" she said, and the woman nodded.

"Canna move us all," the woman said. "Not w'out more binders. But when we find 'em, 'e means t' see us moved. Got wagons 'n' coaches ready, 'e does."

She glanced back down the hall. Forty souls at least, maybe fifty. She understood the plan; without her bond with Sarine, it would have taken a half-dozen or more *Shelter* binders to ignite the first sparks of a self-sustaining barrier. Whoever rescued these survivors had settled on the only plan available to them: Build a group large enough to pool *Shelter* in four or five places, and rotate between them. But the woman in blue was right—moving so large a group would be deadly without *Shelter* binders to protect them from the sky.

"Tell him to load those wagons," she said. "Load everything you have, and stay put. I can be here by morning."

"You can...be here, Your Majesty?" Cornaille said. "Do you mean—?"

"I mean I'm already sitting at the horse-lines, Lieutenant," she said. "I'll have Jiri saddled and ready to ride within the quarter hour."

"But, Your Majes—" Cornaille began, drowning it in another cough. "Your Majesty. It isn't safe. You risk...the air, the sickness."

The woman in blue watched her carefully, as though she hadn't believed what she'd heard.

"Have the wagons ready," she said, addressing it to the woman in blue. "And tell your people I'm coming. We move all of you to safety at dawn."

44

ARAK'JUR

Wilderness
Under the Blackened Sky

He laid Corenna down, careful to cradle her back as he set her atop a pile of dead leaves.

"We can rest here," he said, hoping it was true. The trees overhead were dead or dying, but enough of their branches remained to provide cover for a time. A mother raccoon must have thought the same—he saw the nest beside another nearby trunk as he carried Corenna into the trees. He might have killed the animal, and her babies, if they hadn't found a doe and stripped its carcass the night before.

"Mmm," Corenna said. "Mmm."

She stirred, half-awake, and he felt her forehead. Hot. Too hot.

He went through the rest of his routine. He removed the bandages around her left shoulder, the clean cloths wrapped around her chest. Water was already scarce enough to be precious; he could boil the rain, but it took time. He made do with a damp cloth where he would have preferred to soak and wash her skin. Her arm had regrown, her shoulder knitted back together. Her face was pristine, as though the Regnant's champion had never slashed and cut her flesh to pieces. When they'd begun the journey from Erris's dome northward in search of their people she'd been healthy, almost as strong as he was. Yet now she'd taken sick, a resurgence of the fevers that gripped her in the first days of her recovery, and he couldn't understand why.

"Arak'Jur," Corenna said. A lucid moment. Precious.

"I'm here," he said, dropping the bandages atop their packs as soon as she spoke.

She coughed. A weak, fragile sound.

"I'm here," he said again, taking her hand in his.

"I...I love you," she said.

"No," he said. "No, you're not so close to dying as that. We'll reach the Alliance village today, if we push. This is a rest. No more."

She smiled weakly.

"You will see our son again," he said. "You *will*."

She nodded, and he felt a flare of strength grip his hand back. "Water?" she said.

He had a skin in his hands before he could think to grab it, conserving each droplet as he helped her pour it in her mouth, over her lips.

She closed her eyes, breathing slow and steady. He almost thought she'd fallen asleep when she stirred.

"Why?" she said. "Why did this happen?"

His memory flashed to visions. Ad-Shi's memories, his last and greatest teacher. Memories of a world blackened by clouds of ash, where sunlight was never more than a dull gray overhead, where the rain poisoned all it touched, where fire fell from the sky, gas rose on the wind, great crevasses tore wounds and caverns in the earth.

"We failed," he said. "Somehow. The great calling, the ascension, the champions. We failed."

"You didn't," Corenna said. "How could you have, when you're still alive?"

"Rest," he said, still holding her hand tight.

She nodded, closing her eyes again. "You didn't fail," she said. "I love you. This wasn't...wasn't your fault..."

He held her as she slept, and made no move to stop the mother raccoon when she darted to snatch the discarded washcloth to bring it back to her babies.

Corenna was right. He was alive. Every champion's death had been followed by the voice, crashing in his thoughts: *FOR THIS ONE, IT ENDS.* Yet no voice had accompanied the last moment of sunlight. He'd been sitting at Corenna's bedside, imagining what their son was doing in the Alliance village. Then the sky had cracked, peals of thunder from a clear, cloudless blue, and the poison had spread, great clouds of ink spreading like fire across the world.

Sarine had warned him this was the price, if they failed. He'd meant to fight to the last breath to stop it, and never got the chance. It was over.

He let himself drift to sleep, too, holding Corenna slumped against the tree.

All that was left now was to find a way to survive.

He woke to the rains stinging his skin.

It hissed, burning like thorns. He'd hoped the canopy would shield them from the worst of it, and perhaps it had; pools lay standing among nearby leaves, splashing as they dissolved the foliage in tiny wisps of smoke. Their journey had been slow, agonizingly slow, on account of the rains. He could have handled it, trusting the guardians' gift to harden him against the poison. But Corenna...

He called on Earth, and grays and browns flooded into his eyes. A shield of stone snapped into place, hovering in the air and wide enough to shelter them both. More hissing sounded atop the stone, rivulets of mud running off the sides.

Corenna stirred, but didn't wake.

He'd have to remain alert, holding the spirits' gift in place, but even a few hours' sleep was a boon. He gathered a pile of leaves under the stone and called on Mountain, channeling the gift of fire that was the Mountain's blood. Warmth would serve them both, for all the air was too hot for the season. The mother raccoon noticed, poking her head over top of her makeshift nest, watching him with caution as the fire surged into life. She stared as he withdrew strips of doe meat, and rubbed her tiny hands together under her chin as he skewered the meat on sticks before lowering it into the fire.

When it was done he tore off a piece, tossing it halfway between him and the mother raccoon's nest.

The raccoon licked her lips, then stared at him, then back at the meat. But she didn't move.

"Come, little sister," he said gently. "Your children need to eat."

On another day she and her kits might have been his prey, and the raccoon knew it as well as he. But today was a day for shared struggle. The world had changed, had become predator to them all.

Earth's power still flowed in his blood alongside Mountain, as strong as either had ever been. A sign that the spirits approved of him, and blessed his use of their power. He flared Earth again, conjuring a shield above the raccoons' nest, broad enough to stop the drizzling poison. This time the mother raccoon made a short screech of surprise, then a chittering sound, before looking back at him, wary and alert.

He nudged the leaves with his foot, shifting the seared meat toward her.

"Eat," he said, and exaggerated the motion as he bit into another strip.

Finally she moved. He might have blinked and missed it, as she darted up from her nest, seized the meat, and returned it to her kits. There were two of them, neither more than a week or two old, and both hungry enough to bite at the morsel their mother gave them. They snapped and tore it, nestling into the leaves in a ball of fur as they ate.

"Fine for them," he said. "But what of you, little mother? You need to eat, too."

He took another strip from the fire. Prudence said to conserve their food; who could say when another doe might present itself for a hunt? But he saw a light in the mother raccoon. A fire that reminded him of Corenna. Here was a warrior, fighting for her little tribe when she should have surrendered to the meteors, the ash, the poisoned rain. And the mother raccoon had her babies, whereas his and Corenna's son was among the Alliance, in Ghella's care. They all deserved a chance to survive.

He threw a whole strip this time, a chunk half as long as the mother herself. She raced for it, then froze, holding the meat in her claws as she watched him.

"Take it," he said. "Take it, and eat."

He tore another bite of his strip, and the mother backed away toward her nest, this time watching him as she dragged the meat through the leaves. She kept an eye on him as she ate, chittering between bites. He could almost feel the warmth in their bellies, taste the sweetness of an end to long hunger. He lay back under the stone, checking Corenna to be certain she was breathing, testing the heat still burning beneath her skin. The fire would help, and he would cook a fresh strip of meat for her when the rains broke, in case she woke between then and the next downpour.

Nothing more to do until then. He made himself comfortable against the tree trunks and waited.

The rain cleared as the sun set, changing the pale gray clouds to a thin haze of orange and red. The last few drops rolled over his shelter of Earth, but he wasted no time, collecting their packs and kicking dirt and leaves over the fire.

Corenna mumbled as he worked. He knelt at her side, checking her skin again. Still hot, but with enough sweat to give him hope. The fever would break soon. It had to. They were a few hours away from the Alliance, and their son.

He shook her gently, tried to let her know it was time to move, that they'd be home soon. She gave no sign she'd heard.

He hefted her into his arms, cradling her body against his chest. Easier if she'd been lucid enough to wrap her arms around his shoulders and hold on to his back, but he could shift positions when she woke.

He'd gone no more than ten steps from where they'd sheltered when a rustling noise sounded from behind.

The mother raccoon emerged from the leaves, both her kits already clinging to her back. She froze when he turned, looking up at him, but she didn't retreat, holding her ground between two pools of poisoned water.

"Coming with me, little mother?" he asked. The sound of amusement in his voice was almost a surprise, after so many days in darkness.

The raccoon chittered, a mimicry of his words.

He laughed. Still, the raccoon didn't flinch, while her two kits held to her back tight enough to twist her fur.

"Come on, then," he said. "But it's on you to keep my pace."

He went another five paces before the little mother's rustling steps followed.

It brought a smile to his face, and kept it there, as they pressed on the last leg of his journey. The forest was sparse, a bare echo of the beauty and richness of Sinari land. They were still behind where the fair-skins had built their Great Barrier, no more than a day's journey from New Sarresant, after more than a week, with the rains, and Corenna's fever. Each time the rains ceased he hoped the clouds would clear, revealing sunlight and an end to the madness that had descended on the world. Yet they never did, and he went on in shades of darkness or dusk, waiting for the next signs of rain.

The little mother and her kits kept up, trundling a few steps closer, then a few more, until they were hardly more than a few paces behind. Rolling hills and dying trees decorated the landscape, with dead brown grasses growing from soil moistened by poison. The few wild fruits and nuts he could gather, he did, and the little mother joined in, stopping to gnaw around the pockmarks where rain had spoiled the food. He fought down the terrible fear: that nothing could grow in this world, that all stored food would be gone soon, that animals would die, that nothing could survive.

"You need a name, little mother," he said after a few hours. "What should I call you?"

She made a cooing sound, almost as though she was imitating his speech.

"Coo?" he said, imitating her in return. "No. Not quite right. The Sarresanters would call you 'raton-laveur,' their words for 'one who washes,' but that was never right either. You don't wash your food."

She made a squeak, now walking almost close enough to brush his leg.

"The Ranasi word for you is similar to ours: *arakun*," he continued. "Almost like *Arak*. You are a guardian of sorts, aren't you? But then, Corenna wouldn't like it if I named you her word for 'raccoon.' Like naming a horse 'horse.' "

The talking helped settle his nerves, though he couldn't settle on a name for the little mother by the time they reached the last hillside. He recognized it, even under the cover of darkness and the threat of poisoned rain. He'd helped choose the site. A defensible place, in a rich valley. The place for a village of six tribes; more than a village. The first tribal city, with the collected strength of fifty guardians to protect it from the wild. Or at least, it would have grown to be a city. Now dread loomed as he climbed the last stretch, Corenna in his arms and the little mother trailing at his side.

He crested the hill's peak, and saw only darkness.

No reason for panic. He'd hoped to see torches, lights, campfires. He'd imagined a village protected by Earth, the same barriers he'd made during their journey writ large enough to cover buildings and trees. But it meant nothing for the valley to be still. Nothing.

The little mother must have sensed his disquiet, changing her pace as he quickened his. Still she stayed with him, trundling along with her kits clawing into her back. He took care with each footfall; a trip or stumble might mean injuring Corenna. She stirred in his arms, while a rumble in the distance echoed through the valley, promising more rain.

"Arak'Jur," Corenna said after he'd reached the valley floor. His name surprised him, focused as he was on traversing ground in the dark.

She reached to stroke his chest.

"Almost there," he said, slowing but continuing forward.

"This is the valley?" she asked. Her voice seemed solid, stronger than it had in days.

"It is," he said. "The village should be no more than half a league distant."

Her hand tightened atop his shoulder.

"Let me down," she said. "I think I can walk."

"You're sure?"

She nodded, making a show of determination, though wisdom said she would still need rest. But he was neither shaman nor doctor. He helped her down, leaving her arm around his shoulder. She found her footing quickly, leaning on him but standing on her own, and eliciting a chittering squawk from the little mother when the human she'd been following suddenly split into two.

"What in the—?" Corenna said, struggling to twist to look behind them, and he laughed.

"My traveling companion," he said. "I called her 'little mother.' She could use a proper name."

Corenna knelt, leaning in while the little mother backed away.

"Here," Arak'Jur said. "Give her this." He produced a small strip of dried meat from his pouch. Corenna took it, offering it in her hand first, then tossing it a short distance between them.

The little mother eyed her with suspicion that slowly gave way to hunger, then darted forward, grabbing the meat, tearing a tiny piece for herself and offering the rest to her kits.

"This is how you snared her into following?" Corenna asked.

"I suppose so," he said. "She built a nest near where we stopped for the last rains. I shared some of our meat, and she decided to follow when we left."

"Fitting," Corenna said. She smiled as she rose, looking as hearty as she had since the day they'd left the dome.

He offered his shoulder again, and she grasped it.

They covered the last half league in silence. Feeling her next to him was enough, but the darkness where there should have been fires and candlelight stilled his desire to speak. The hope that he'd somehow read the terrain wrong flickered in his thoughts, that somehow this wasn't the valley, that the Alliance village was still distant, another day away. But he hadn't; this was the place. They reached the first structures as the booming came closer, thunderheads flashing to illumine the way.

One of the new houses, constructed in the Sarresant style, stood at the village's edge. Or, it had stood. Fires blackened its walls, its roof collapsed in on itself. He and Corenna separated, surveying the damage. A meteor strike, perhaps; they'd seen enough evidence of them on their journey north. But a fire for certain. No bodies at least, and little left behind in the rubble.

He moved to the next house, another built in the Sarresant style, as Corenna drifted to a different building nearby. A similar story greeted him, though the roof had been burned through by the rain rather than collapsing. Blackened streaks and pools marked the walls and floors, with holes in the ceiling dripping water through the roof. It was empty, devoid of most of its belongings, and—thank the spirits—without any signs of death or injury to its inhabitants.

"Arak'Jur," Corenna called. Her voice was weak, but enough to carry through the ruin. He came at once, finding her outside yet another building.

"What is it?" he asked. "Survivors?"

"There won't be any here," she said. "Look ahead—it's only the Sarresant-style buildings left here. No dead that I could see, and belongings packed and taken with them."

"You think...?" he began, and she finished the thought.

"Yes," she said. "They packed the village tents and fled. Just like our ancestors did, when they faced a great cataclysm, with a shaman to guide them. Our people are alive."

His heart surged, covering over the dread without snuffing it out. He and Corenna had journeyed through the wastes left by the darkened sky. To make such a journey with an entire village—with their son!—would tax them past the point of breaking. But if Shimmash, Ka'Hannat, and the other shamans could see a path to safety, they would have followed it.

"We can follow them," he said. "They'll have left tracks."

Another thundercrack flashed to light the village around them, showing him the determination and the paleness in Corenna's face.

"Rains are coming," she said. "We can wait them out here, and follow as soon as it clears."

"I'll scout and find the way," he said. "You and the little mother find a place to cook food, and sleep."

He knew her enough to know she would have wanted to go ahead, and curse the rains, with their people and their son exposed to danger. It spoke to how weak she was that she nodded, taking the pack with their food and blankets from him as they went toward the village center. He might have made better time, relying on the spirits' gifts to see him through the poison storms, but the thought of leaving her behind never surfaced, even for a moment. They were together now. Even in the face of death and ruin, nothing mattered more.

45

TIGAI

Beneath a Baobab Tree
Tarzali Desert

He cursed, running through the litany of every foul word he'd ever learned.

They were going to die here. Because he was impatient.

He shivered under his coat, rocking back and forth against the twisted trunk of a misbegotten tree, warped and bent like a mockery of an elm, but thick enough, thank the tit-fucking wind spirits, to shelter them from the worst of the acid rain.

"You plan to kiss my sister with that mouth, Lord Tigai?" Namkat said. She lay next to him, curled against the trunk, dripping with fever-sweat but grinning through it as feathers half sprouted from her skin.

"I'd do more than goat-fucking kiss her," he said. "If we ever moon-bloody see her again. I'll fucking make her forget any other eunuch-kissed men exist in this half-bred mongoloid son of a sister-fucking world."

Juni chose that moment to drop from the branches overhead, making a rustling crash as she returned to the earth.

"Breakfast is served," Juni said, producing a pair of pink-eared ducks with their heads twisted around and broken. "No thanks to your mouth, Lord Tigai. If the birds in this tree weren't deathly scared of flying into the rain, every one would have bolted away from your 'fucks' and 'shits.'"

"They're not going anywhere," he said, growling it. "Not going bloody fucking anywhere, and neither are we."

"Still no sign of your stars or strands?" Juni asked.

"None," he said. "It's like the whole bloody starfield was wiped clean when the world went to shit."

Juni's skin charred black at her fingertips as she invoked the Flame Scale, scorching the feathers and outer skin of both ducks faster than he could blink. Her magic still worked, and so would his, he supposed, if there were anywhere to tether to. He could still set anchors, and he could sense new strands being formed here, by himself, by Juni and Namkat. But the whole rest of the field was empty and black, and that gave him nothing to hook them to, no way to escape. They were stuck in a bloody fucking tree in the middle of nowhere with nothing but ducks and poison rain to keep them occupied until they died.

Juni offered him one of the birds and pulled the blackened skin off the leg of the other. "At least there'll be some company soon."

"What?" he said.

"Company. Coming our way. Two. I'd guess one man, one woman. Probably heading to our tree to shelter from the rain."

He looked past her, though he couldn't see a fucking thing in the black that hadn't gone away since he'd torn the three of them from the void.

"I promise, they're there," Juni said. She was quiet, meeker than her sisters, which made her only about tenfold more assertive than a proper Jun lady. "The Flame Scale sees heat, and they're coming."

"Better if you save a leg of that bird," Namkat said to him. "A peace offering, as it were, if we have to share our tree."

Juni smiled at her sister, breaking off a chunk of duck and feeding it to her. Namkat's mouth seemed to work perfectly fine, even if the rest of her had fallen ill within the first hour after they'd arrived, and only gotten worse since.

"How far away are they?" he said. "Are they carrying weapons?"

"Five hundred paces or so," Juni said. "Plenty of time to eat before they arrive. And if they're carrying weapons, well, so are we."

His belly had been growling, but suddenly his hunger dried up. What sort of people would live in this bloody desert waste was well beyond him. He'd as soon have built Yuli a house on the ice of Kregiaw.

"Any sign of who they are?" he asked. "If they're a threat, we need to be ready."

"How am I supposed to know?" Juni said. "It's two people, carrying what looked like a litter between them. That's all I could tell from here."

"Fine," he said. "Just eat, and be ready when they get here."

"Yes, Your Highness," Juni said. "Or is it Your Lordship? I can never remember, with the Jun."

"It's Your Grace, I think," Namkat said. "Or maybe Your Imperial Majesty."

He ignored them as she and Namkat continued with their barbs. It was his fault they were here; they had every right to needle him, though he tried to pretend the stings didn't hurt. He'd tried to get Sarine's attention, yelling in his voice-without-a-mouth as they drifted in the void of blue sparks, surrounded by emptiness and not much else. It felt like they'd drifted for days before the stars started to vanish. He'd latched onto one of the last ones left in a panic, and he hadn't had time to trace its strands before he'd tethered them to it. Now the star he'd used was gone—every fucking star in the field was gone—and that meant they were trapped here, in the middle of this wind-spirits-forsaken storm.

Juni and Namkat ate their bird as he waited, going right on eating when the silhouettes took shape at the far edge of the darkness.

Two figures, a man and a woman, as Juni guessed, though both were wrapped tight enough in their strange dress that he could have been wrong. The man appeared to be wearing a suit made of woven grass, one continuous fabric wrapped like a mask around his head, shoulders, arms, torso, legs, and feet. The woman wore a dress of the same fabric, wrapped just as tightly but with loose folds like a skirt draped from her hips. Holes for their eyes, noses, and mouths made them look like actors in the opera. They carried a litter between them, covered with long-bladed grasses piled to hide its surface.

"Hello," he called out in his best statesman's voice. "Be welcome. Come, shelter with us from the rain."

Both newcomers went rigid at his words, holding still as he spoke. As soon as he finished they dropped their litter and went prostrate on the ground, doubled over toward him as though they'd seen the Emperor.

Juni barked a laugh.

"Heavens help us all if that goes to his head," Namkat said.

He glared at both of them. First contact with an unknown people was a delicate thing, all the more so when he had to pretend to diplomatic weight and station. The last bloody thing he needed was laughter at what appeared to be the sacred.

He kept quiet, waiting for the newcomers to speak. They kept their heads down in the dirt, their arms tucked in, remaining silent as the toxic rains drizzled over them. Those rains had made Namkat sick within what felt like minutes, yet both the man and woman appeared unfazed, perhaps protected by their strange grass costumes.

Finally he spoke again. "Rise, please," he said. "We would know who you are, and share our meat and shelter with you, as friends."

"You will greet the Great Dreamer?" one of them, he thought it was the woman, said, though her voice was as deep as a man's.

"Come," he said. No telling what a Great Dreamer was, but diplomacy stressed repeating offerings of friendship and peace. Time to settle the nuance of their expectations after he'd firmly established himself as a friend. "Be clear of the rain. We will share our names, and our fire, together."

The man and woman shared a look, still prostrate, before they rose, gathered their litter, and approached.

Namkat drew herself into a seated position, her back against the tree, while Juni stood over her sister. No hiding Namkat's feathers; since she'd taken sick, she claimed she couldn't keep the Wind Song from exerting some measure of control, and so she appeared half woman, half bird, her face covered in a soft down while the rest of her sprouted feathers through her clothes. Juni changed herself, too, the brimstone ash and charred skin of the Flame Scale spreading as the newcomers approached. If it had been up to him they'd have kept a leash on their magicks, but then, a show of force backed by words of friendship was a tactic unto itself. It wasn't as though he could control the Natarii anyway. May as well use what they gave him.

He made a smooth, precise bow, the sort a superior would offer to a respected near-equal.

The newcomers set their litter down delicately, then rose, and in an instant their grass suits vanished. Magic. One moment they'd been clothed, almost wrapped in a second skin, like an Ox-*magi* encased in iron or glass. Perhaps they were Ox, though neither had anything resembling a Jun look. Both were naked, the one he'd thought to be a man revealed to be a young woman, firm-muscled and small-breasted, with wide shoulders, short-cropped hair, and arms thick enough for a soldier. The one who'd worn the skirt was a gray-haired man, wrinkled and bearded.

"I am called Miroyah," the graybeard said. "Head Tailor of Palompurraw Town. This is my dream-mother, Tetali. We are honored to say our goodbyes to you, you who will greet the Great Dreamer." He paused, then attempted to mirror Tigai's bow, making it an awkward, stilted gesture. "Though you have not the look of the Tarzali among you."

"I am Tigai, first scion and heir to Yanjin House," he said, putting confidence and the warmth of friendship in his voice. Any cultural awkwardness—like saying "goodbyes" instead of "greetings," or a graybeard calling a young woman his mother—could be addressed later. "These are the sisters of my wife-to-be: Namkat Wind Song Clan Hoskar, and Juni Flame Scale Clan Hoskar, both celebrated warriors of the Natarii clans."

"These are not Tarzali names," the young woman, Tetali, said. "How is it you will come to welcome the Great Dreamer after us?"

"We came here to shelter under this tree," Tigai said. "We were caught in the storm that blackened the sky, as you must have been. Yet we have food, and fire. Will you sit with us, and eat?"

"You are *not* Tarzali," Tetali said. "You are—"

Miroyah touched Tetali's elbow, then pointed upward into the boughs of the tree.

"They have yet to greet her," the older man said, grinning suddenly. "We are meant to say our goodbyes together."

"You're right," he said, resisting the urge to look where Miroyah pointed. "We aren't natives to this land. Yet we are friends, or we mean to be, if you'll have us. We're travelers, from—"

"Oh, Great Dreamer," Tetali and Miroyah said in unison, stepping back to pull the woven grasses and leaves from atop their litter. It revealed a feast of fruits and cooked meats, enough food for twelve people, piled in intricate designs spread across the tray. A pyramid of simmering dark meat, a cube of shaped fruit, an artfully arranged trail of nuts and seeds leading from course to course. "You have been welcomed to this land, with the blessings of Palompurraw Town and its people."

He paused, considering what sort of response was merited by the display. A ritual, for sure, or at least a rehearsed greeting. Something of religious significance, perhaps.

Before he came up with a reply, a small girl dropped out of the tree not ten paces away, crouching and surveying all five of them like a feral monkey.

It was all he could do not to yelp, and Juni failed to hold it back. Juni had been bloody climbing through the tree gathering ducks for their supper; how the *fuck* had she missed a girl hiding in its branches? Yet it was a girl, a waif no more than eight or nine years old, with skin as white as a pale moon and deep red eyes to boot. An albino, though any superstitious villager would have been forgiven for calling her a ghost. Or a demon.

Miroyah and Tetali repeated the gesture they'd first offered to him, kneeling prostrate with their hands tucked close to their chests and their heads pressed in the dirt.

"Why aren't *you* kneeling?" the feral girl said to him. Her voice was harsh, but melodic at the same time. A hissing lullaby cutting through the rain. "Why don't you do as they do?"

He was used to hearing words translated in his mind; since going to the Gods' Seat, the gift of tongues had become second nature, as comfortable as setting anchors on the starfield and the strands. But this was no translation. The girl spoke Jun, as flawless and crisp as any courtier.

"Forgive us our rudeness," Tigai said. "We didn't know you were here first, or we'd have offered to share our food, and our fire."

"Yes, you did!" the girl shouted. It made an echo, ringing through the darkness. "You followed me. I was reborn here, and you followed the star. You're a Dragon, one of *his*, and you followed the star. You know I killed the last Dragons who dared to come here, yes? And yet here you are."

Danger hovered in the air. He could sense it, and he saw the same realization in Juni and Namkat.

"My name is Yanjin Tigai," he said slowly. Carefully. "I am a Dragon, but I am not sworn to their house, nor to...him. I followed your star out of desperation, and brought my sisters-to-be with me."

"Oh," the girl said, her features suddenly softening. "Oh, you're one of *hers*. Yes, I can sense her hold on you. That's strange, isn't it? For you to be alive, when the world is *his* again. Strange, yes, very strange. I wonder what it means."

The girl sauntered to the tray as she spoke, plopping herself down in the dirt and leaves, scooping a handful of nuts and fruit into her mouth. Neither Miroyah or Tetali moved, keeping themselves still, kneeling next to her as she ate.

He, Juni, and Namkat exchanged guarded looks. The danger had passed, if the girl's demeanor was any indicator, but too suddenly for him to trust it. The strange girl ate sloppily, smearing berry paste and melon across her cheeks, while Miroyah and Tetali could have been hewn from stone. Prudence dictated following their lead; whatever the girl-child was, the two who'd called themselves Tarzali had braved a deadly, toxic storm to bring her a tray of food fit for any Emperor or King. Perhaps the girl was the source of the storm itself. No telling where he'd taken them, among what sort of strange peoples and magicks. But the girl had spoken Jun, and recognized his magic, even named him Dragon, and admitted to creating the star he'd used to bring them here. If there was any hope of getting back to Yuli, it started with her.

He approached cautiously, taking a seat cross-legged next to the tray. The girl eyed him with sudden intensity, though she kept up her slurping and chewing, her mouth half-open and leaking food into her lap.

"We didn't get your name," he said. "Though I heard Tetali call you Great Dreamer."

The girl nodded as she ate, not bothering to stop chewing.

"She is Orana," Miroyah said with reverence in his voice, though he kept his face planted on the ground. "The gray sister, in the eldest incarnation. Caretaker of the blue sister's souls. She who will be there when the last soul draws the last breath waking from the last dream. The Sun Maiden's twin. The Shepherdess of Tides. The Keeper. The Moon."

"Orana," Tigai said. "Did I get that right?" A risk, to use the name, after being offered a dozen titles and no clue to the appropriate honorifics, but the girl giggled, pausing as she held a melon in front of her teeth.

"Most of you can't even see me when the blue sister goes to sleep," Orana said. "People like *you*, who see with their eyes, won't remember me when the sister wakes."

"Orana," he said again. Good to stress the name. "My sisters-to-be and I were planning to shelter here until this storm breaks. Do you know whether, after it ends, the…stars you mentioned, the anchors of my Dragon magic, will…?"

He trailed off as Orana laughed.

"You'll be sheltering here a 'bloody-cunt-fucking-long time,' Tigai, scion of Yanjin House," Orana said, grinning at him.

"I'm sorry," he said. "I don't understand. I brought us here because something was interfering with the starfield and strands. With this storm going on I can't sense any connections. But if you know I'm a Dragon, you know I can take us away if it clears, and the stars are still there. I could take you, too, if you know a way through."

Orana tore into another chunk of meat, chewing noisily. "I liked you better when you were cursing," she said between bites. "When you were you. Without the masks."

"Honored mother," Juni said. "Tigai means well. He only seeks to find us a way home, to our sisters. To our people. My sister Namkat is sick, and needs care."

"Yes," Orana said sadly. "So much sickness, each time the blue sister sleeps. When my sister and I ruled this world, it was different. Quite different. Yes."

Tigai watched her eat another bite of nuts and figs. This was clearly a creature of power, or at least religious significance, but death spirits take him if he could puzzle out what she was saying. Sarine had sent them off to Bhakal lands looking for "others." If this strange girl was worth bringing a litter of food to in the middle of a storm, perhaps she was at least connected to the source of power in these lands. He had to press harder, to understand.

"Anyways, it won't break on its own," Orana continued. "The fever, or the storm. Not in her lifetime. With the world's soul freshly transitioned there's little harm in it, though it can't be me to make the bonds. The dead are my charge, you understand. For the living, we'd have to take her to my sister Kalira, the Sun."

Miroyah and Tetali rose in unison, hope writ on their faces.

"Our offerings, Great Dreamer," Tetali said. "All we have, all we will have, are yours."

"Your offerings are delicious," Orana said, smiling as a fresh rivulet of fruit juice trailed from the side of her mouth. "But we'd have to hurry. Kalira will be resting soon, too, just like the blue sister. How many Dreamers are there in your town?"

"Six, Great Dreamer," Miroyah said.

"Six," Orana said. "Yes. It's settled, then. For the price of food, and good company before we leave these bodies behind. Now that the world has changed, Kalira is free to bind your six and save them from the storm."

He didn't understand the half of what had passed between Orana and the Tarzali, but he understood the last. Time for another gamble.

"Us, too," he said, offering another, deeper bow. "If it pleases you, Orana. We would make a bargain as well."

"With what?" Orana said. "Your roast duck? They brought me a whole litter."

"All we have," he said swiftly. "And more. Whatever we can gather, if you can save us from the storm."

"You don't need saving," Orana said. "You're already bound to *her*. Champions don't get the sickness."

"My sisters, then," he said.

Orana stared at him. The danger returned, in the piercing white and red of her eyes.

"You mean to bait us into involving ourselves in your games," she said finally. "You mean to provoke us, to enslave us, but we will not be kept, or made to be less than we are. You may return to your mistress and tell her the games should be at an end, for now."

"I didn't come here because Sarine sent me," he said. "Or with any plot or plan other than to survive. Please. I'm asking for mercy, and help."

Again Orana stared. Then she spoke, toward Juni and Namkat.

"He doesn't wear humility often, does he?" Orana asked.

Juni stifled a laugh, and Namkat didn't bother to hide hers.

"No, Great Dreamer," Juni said. "He does not."

"Very well, Yanjin Tigai, scion of your House," Orana said. "I will tell you what your mistress should have, and did not. You have come to Tarzali land, land that has kept itself apart from the Regnant and Veil and all the turnings and cycles of their games. Once, we ruled creation, Sun and Moon, Earth and Stars, before the whispers of the serpents gave magic to our children and saw them break the world. We fought them, oh yes, and we lost. And now we are in exile, free to enjoy our fruits and nuts and meats and save a few of our Dreamers when the world is covered by the Regnant's purging storms. This is what we have, all we have, and you threaten it by asking me to save that which by rights belongs to *him*. Do you understand now?"

"No," he said. "I'm sorry but I don't. I don't mean to give offense. All I want is to find a way back to Sarine and Yuli, and to keep my sisters alive."

Orana laughed. A soft sound, like the girl she appeared to be, but heavier, with a haunting echo behind her breath.

"Fuck it," Orana said. "I liked your offerings better anyway."

He frowned. "What does that mean?"

"It means we have a bargain, Tigai scion of Yanjin House. Your roast duck, and your curse words, for the protection of the Sun. Let's go and find her and give the Regnant and Veil a reason to gnash their 'bloody-cunt-stained teeth.'"

Without warning Orana bolted to her feet, and just as suddenly the sky cleared. The clouds rolled away over top of the tree's branches, making a circular hole above them, and revealed a pale, full moon directly overhead, as bright as he'd ever seen.

"How the fuck...?" he said.

Orana smiled. "They won't notice if I light our way for a little while," she said. "And if they do, well, the Regnant and Veil can both go and drink from a courtesan's twice-used sheepskin." She paused, considering. "Did I use that one right? I want to make sure I've learned them all by the time we reach the Sun."

46

ERRIS

Western Gates
Southgate District, New Sarresant

Sunrise came as a light gray haze in the east. A flare of orange was almost visible behind the clouds, faint enough she couldn't be sure whether she'd imagined it. The horizon would still be dark even at midday, but she could see the silhouettes of the city's tallest buildings in the distance, Southgate's churches and factories, the Gardens' manor houses and banks. They'd come closer as she'd ridden through the night, and now they were here, looming overhead in twisted abominations of themselves, melted, burned, and broken.

She stopped on the city-side of the western gate, sliding from Jiri's back and tethering a horse-sized dome of *Shelter* overhead.

She lifted the tarp from around her shoulders, and removed her wide-brimmed hat, then saw to Jiri for the same. They'd fashioned her horse a barding of canvas and tarp, loose enough not to restrict movement, though even Jiri bristled at being forced to wear it. *Body* and *Life* served to keep her in the saddle and Jiri on her feet in spite of their injuries, but both had been burned, leaving boils and the reddened skin of chemical burns wherever rainwater leaked through.

They'd reach the survivors soon, if she was lucky. She withdrew Jiri's feedbag from her saddle, letting her chew oats while Erris worked to repair and reaffix their tarps. Outside her *Shelter* dome the rains made soft hisses as they struck the cobblestones and brick. Melted stone ran in trails down the buildings; even the west gate's ironwork had been twisted and ruined. Soon the city would dissolve in the acid, leaving nothing behind. She tried to see it through an Empress's eyes: They would have to elevate the priority of salvage missions, try to secure as many resources and survivors as could be saved. But being here, seeing it as herself, she felt the horror of watching her city melt and burn, of knowing that the same rain, the same terrible storms, raged from the army's northern encampment to the southernmost Thellan isles. This was the end. The end of the world.

She finished her sewing, loosened Jiri's feedbag, reattached their tarps, and climbed back into the saddle.

They turned north along the district boundary. Most of the Gardens wall's gold-leaf and decorative plating had been looted during Reyne d'Agarre's first revolution, and she'd never made it a priority to restore the district to its full glory. A lost opportunity now. There were four guardhouses on the Gardens/Southgate border, and her survivors would be in the second, on Farrier's Street. She passed grand theaters, coach stations, even a glass greenhouse whose windows had somehow withstood the acid pouring from the sky. Manors, townhouses, all the choicest land and buildings the immigrants had claimed during her resettlements: all empty, crumbling. But the binder who had gathered the survivors had done it in the wisest place. There would be more people here in the Gardens than anywhere else.

The ground floor of the Farrier's Street guardhouse had been knocked clean through. She saw it even a block distant: The entryway had been smashed apart with all the subtlety of a sledgehammer, or an *Entropy* binding. Yet there were people there. And coaches. The walls facing the street had been ripped open to house the teams, and they spotted her as soon as she spotted them, raised voices and fingers pointing toward her as Jiri carried her the rest of the way.

"Is it her?" one of the survivors said, a question echoing through the rain. She drew Jiri to a halt at the torn-open mouth of the guardhouse. Five wagons had been crammed inside, and twelve horses. Barrels and crates lay piled in their beds, with blankets, bushels, ropes, and canvas stacked so high there would scarce be room for more than a footman and driver for each team.

"It is," a man replied. "By all the Gods themselves." She recognized Lieutenant Cornaille, of her eastern rangers. He saluted, and she returned it as she ushered Jiri under the ceiling.

"Fine to see you this morning, Lieutenant," she said, removing her hat, careful to let the rain run off outside the guardhouse's cover. Whispers passed through the survivors, though only a handful had gathered here, seeing to their wagons or horses on the ground floor. "Where are the rest?"

"Upstairs, Your M—" Cornaille said, interrupting himself with a violent cough. "Your Majesty. But they're ready. Most of the foragers have returned, or are due soon."

She left Jiri's tarp-barding in place, dropping the reins to signal her mount to stay put as she removed her own tarps. Her uniform was far from its best, but the symbol was worth the effort of redonning her travel gear. The sight of it seemed to spread among the survivors, a truer confirmation that their Empress had come for them than her ranger's word.

"You'll sleep safely tonight," she said to the room. "And we'll move as soon as we're ready. See to your teams."

A better leader might have found a speech, some rousing anthem to stir her people against their fears. But she'd always found that hard work was a better distraction than zeal. She and Cornaille crossed the room, weaving between the wagons toward the stairs, through a somber quiet.

"What of this binder?" she asked. "The one who put this group together. Is he a priest? Military?"

"Ex-military, I'd say, Your Majesty," Cornaille said. "Though he wouldn't con—" He coughed hard enough to pause them both, turning his head and holding to the wall to steady himself. "He...wouldn't confirm it, though he has the demeanor. A deserter, perhaps. Calls himself Anton, though if he's a deserter he might not have—" He coughed again, violently. "...might not have given his true name."

She waited for Cornaille to recover himself before following again. Whatever this binder's name and status, he'd done fine work preparing this group. Five wagonloads of supplies and perhaps fifty survivors, though she'd have to take stock of illness among them. Even with a dome of *Shelter* protecting the guardhouse, some would have been exposed to the toxic rain, the ash and brimstone on the air. They wouldn't move as quickly as she and Jiri could, not by a fraction. But with wagons to carry the sick and her *Shelter* for protection, they could reach Rasailles by nightfall. Exarch knew the comfort that would be, both for these people and the rest under the dome.

They reached the top of the stairs, and she came face-to-face with Marquand.

He wore civilian's clothes, but stood at military attention, waiting for her at the front of the room. Behind him the room bustled with activity, a barracks whose soldiers had been called to march. Though these weren't soldiers—they were laborers, factory workers, farmers, tradesmen, and merchants—they moved with precision and efficiency, waiting beside their beds in smaller groups with rucksacks, parcels, blankets tied with goods at their centers.

And at their head, Marquand faced her as though he were preparing to charge an enemy fortification alone, red-faced and stiff with courage.

"I'll be Gods-damned," she said.

"This is the binder, Your Majesty," Cornaille said. "The survivors' leader. Master Anton, of, ah..."

"Your Majesty," Marquand said. "Your ranger told me you were coming."

"I know this man, Lieutenant," she said. "One of the great disappointments of my career."

"Bloody fine to see you, too," Marquand said.

"Are there liquors among your foraged supplies?" she asked. "Is that why your cheeks are still red?"

"I've been out in the rain," Marquand said. "Looking for people. Making sure my wagons are loaded to the brim."

Hot anger burned at her collar. Marquand had saved these people. He'd saved some of hers, too, if his supplies were as bountiful as they looked from a distance. But she wanted to eviscerate him, to bring him back to the tavern where she'd found him lounging in the smell of his own piss.

"Get them moving," she said. Better to distract them both with the task at hand. "We start our march as soon as your wagons can leave."

"Wait a minute," Marquand said. "I gathered my people and loaded our wagons and teams, because you ordered it. But you can't bloody well mean to move us all the way to Rasailles through this rain. Even you can't tether *Shelter* far enough from the city to protect us all."

He had the sense to say it quietly, but enough heard to sow seeds of doubt through the room. Bloody idiot.

"Yes," she said. "I can. You know with the bond to Sarine I don't use stores on the leylines anymore. I can tether what I need, wherever I need it."

"Wait, that still works?" Marquand said. "Your bond? I'd figured, with the world...like this...I figured she'd...lost it."

"It still works," she said. "Get your people up. We move as soon as you're ready."

"Another quarter hour," Marquand said. "Give my last foragers time to return."

She gave a sharp nod, turning to head back downstairs as Marquand began shouting the orders that would move his people in teams, telling them what to expect, telling them how to move under cover of her *Shelter*. Anger still seethed, hearing his voice. But this was his element, and he'd done well, and for all she would have chosen never to see his face again, it felt more sweet than bitter to know he'd survived.

47

SARINE

Void
The Infinite Plane

The world was ending.

She drifted through the Plane, studying the sparks that made up her body, her self. Soft blue currents flowed to shape her body in the physical world. Black and white sparks flowed alongside those, where the Nine Tails nested within her form. Metallic sparks made eddies in the flow; those were Anati, and their bond. Purple and deep blue sparks shaped her mind, her memories and her thoughts. Orange and gray sparks hummed at the top and bottom of the flow, stretching and reaching for the folded space of the starfield and the strands. Red wires burned, severed through her core, where the leylines and the spirits of the wild had once lived within her. Those still hurt, tender to the touch when her will probed them, whenever she studied them in a desperate search for a chance to heal.

She was broken. Everything was broken. She drifted close to other torrents on the Plane, and saw it, both with her will here and with her physical eyes: Flows of silver, iron, gold, platinum appeared where they didn't belong, and left the torrents changed. Diseased. Sick. Blackened, dead or dying.

She collided with a torrent that represented an old redwood tree, mighty and tall, and felt, for a brief moment, the pain of its existence. Its highest boughs were burned, its trunk rotten and falling in on itself. The soft blue sparks of its form had changed to black, a splotched, stained spiderweb of black, like an ink pen leaking across the redwood tree's soul. She saw the world around the tree as the tree saw itself, filtered through its senses. The sky was black, as it was everywhere in the world. Dark thunderheads promised rain and lightning, or opened themselves to meteor storms or volcanic gouts, ash and rock and brimstone falling from the sky. The tree was dying, and it called to her, to something, to anything, to save it, to restore the warmth of the sun.

At first she'd tried to promise the torrents there would be change. She meant to fight, to push back against the tide the Regnant had unleashed on the world. The torrents trusted her, in their way. Rocks and cupboards and oak trees and steel tools and blades of grass. They knew her. When she touched their torrents, they recognized her, flowed toward her will. They were sick, but she could heal them, if she found the way. Only she hadn't.

She'd failed.

Now, ten thousand torrents later, no change was coming, save for the plague and death brought by the iron, gold, and silver sparks. She drifted, and gave in to horror and despair.

Tears flowed in the endless void, though she had no physical form here to cry. Voices had shouted at her, or maybe just one voice, warning her something about stars vanishing, but she hadn't listened.

Weeks went by.

She cried. She relived the last moments in the Gods' Seat, where she'd faced the creature wearing Amanishiakne's face and wielding all the powers of the Veil. The leylines, the *kaas*, the spirits. If she'd ignored Sakhefete and attacked the Regnant while he dipped his fingers in the stream of power at the center of the room, perhaps she could have stopped the change. If she'd been able to unmake the *Shelter* shields imprisoning Tigai and her Natarii sisters, perhaps they could have turned the fight in her favor. If she'd been able to hold her supposed champions together, to win Erris's loyalty, to keep Arak'Jur at her side, to keep Yuli from injury, perhaps they might have been strong enough.

She heard her name, echoing in the endless sea of the void, and drifted through torrent after torrent, letting the world's disease settle in her mind. This was the price of failure. *Sarine.* She was the one who had failed, the one who'd let it happen. *Sarine.* This was the world now. *Sarine.* This was what her uncle had been spared, lucky enough to die before she'd been able to let the whole world down. *Sarine!*

The last iteration of her name shook her.

It came from within the torrents that made up her body, vibrating the rest of her with its force. A memory? Or just a word, slipped loose from where the sparks of her gifts still ran free. She hadn't yet fallen sick, but she would. Perhaps the name was a sign of madness, something to—

Sarine!

The sound shifted her will. She'd been hearing it for days, but not hearing it. An echo, something unimportant. Something she could ignore while she studied the sparks.

Sarine, I know you're still in there, and I know you can hear me. What's wrong with you?

Thoughts, bouncing in her mind. But this one strayed closer to her sense of self. She should recognize it.

Yes, you bloody well should recognize me! You have to stop this. You have to accept what's happened. It's the only way to change it.

"Who's there?" she said. The first words she'd spoken on the Infinite Plane since her banishment. The sparks gave it form, twisting around her, merging with the metallic sheen at the center of her column.

We have to get you out of here. This place is hurting you.

"Anati," she said. She could see the metallic sparks, the echo of life behind them. A form moving between the dimensional folds of different worlds: a metal lizard-snake on the physical world, a shining beacon of light and energy on the *kaas*-plane. A companion here. The source of her name, the sound that had been repeating for days, for weeks. Anati. Her *kaas*.

Sarine. Please. We have to find a way out. I know you're sad, and you blame yourself, but this isn't over yet. You're still alive, and I'm still bonded to you, and we can still fight, if you'll let us. Will you? Please?

Numbness washed through her as they drew near another torrent on the plane. This one was a man, complex and beautiful, but he'd been changed by the iron sparks—she could see the effect of their work, the sickness tainting his lungs, forcing blood up through his coughs, converting a gift for touching the leylines into poison in his veins.

I know. They're sick. But we aren't finished yet. You can spend lifetimes drifting here, if you aren't careful. Sarine. Can you still hear me? Sarine!

"I can hear you," she said. They passed through the torrent, and for a moment she lived as this man did. He was a soldier, in the deep blue uniform of New Sarresant. He huddled close to other New Sarresant soldiers, and to soldiers in Jun uniforms, former enemies brought together through a struggle greater than the animus that had set them apart. Remnants of two armies, mixed and broken under the blackened sky.

The man had a daughter back home. A little girl named Lisette. He was worried for her, and for her mother. He coughed again, burning pitch in the back of his throat. His commanding officer put her arm around his shoulder, whispered to him it would be okay, that between his *Shelter* and the Jun *magi*'s Heron domes they would survive this storm, no matter how bloody long it lasted. He clung to the leylines, never knowing it was the very gift that poisoned him. He was dying. He would never see his daughter again, and it was her fault. Sarine's fault. Her failure.

You're hurting yourself, Anati thought. *Let me take you away. Please?*

"I..." she said. Another torrent drifted closer. A stuffed toy bear, clutched in a little boy's arms.

I can't move you in this place if you don't want to be moved. You have to trust me.

She let her will move closer to the torrent. The little boy was outside, under the rain, crying. It burned his skin, wherever the droplets touched. He was alone. Without touching the torrent of his memories she couldn't know where his parents were, why they'd let him go out under the open sky, unprotected. All she knew was the toy bear loved the boy. It wanted him to squeeze it closer, to use its patchy fur as a comfort, even if he held it so tight it threatened to rip the bear's seams.

"I did this," she whispered. "I couldn't save them. I couldn't stop him."

You don't deserve to suffer like this, Anati thought. *Please.*

"I do," she said. "If not me, who? It's my fault."

It isn't. And you're not done fighting yet.

Wasn't she? The words echoed in her memory. Anati would hear them, but she couldn't bring herself to say it.

Let me take you,

She let herself go limp. A numb surrender. She deserved the pain, she deserved to watch as every torrent on the plane was poisoned, as they rotted and decayed. Instead the world warped around her. Colors washed through the void.

The sparks were gone.

She crumpled to the ground, crying.

If she'd had a physical body in all the weeks she'd spent in the void, she would have spent it like this. Pain, raw and deep, rippled through her. She cried, sobbing into her arm, not bothering to move, though her legs were bent, her body contorted in pain.

Anati nuzzled her snout against her hand.

Thank you, her *kaas* thought. She felt a wave of emotions behind it: pity, sorrow, concern, resolve. She shouldn't have been able to feel her *kaas's* emotions. Not unless...

She blinked, and wiped her eyes.

A horizon of shapes stretched in front of her, colorless and yet somehow every color at once. She felt them as she had before: through detached eyes, while her body drifted on the Infinite Plane. Pyramids and spheres hung suspended in the air, all seemingly drawn from a million points of light. And two shapes lay near her. Two bodies, contorted as she was, but neither moving, neither making a sound.

The poison took them days ago, Anati thought. *I didn't want to leave their bodies on the Plane.*

Her throat was dry as she rose, and turned one of the shapes to see its face. Both their bodies had been blackened, a sickly, gangrenous rot that covered them in patches from their mouths to their legs and feet. The eyes were open, frozen, above tendrils of black and green pus emanating from their mouths.

Kitian.

Her sister. Kitian Blood Claw Clan Hoskar. Dead.

She went to the other shape in a daze. Imyan Iron Bark. Dead. Rotten and decayed, her mouth frozen in permanent shock, and both had been trapped on the Infinite Plane, their bodies left to die while she floated in her daze.

She screamed, then broke into a sob.

The sound carried here, without echo. It grew dimmer, still faintly audible, making a ripple as it traveled across the plane of shapes and colorless, colored light.

Anati lowered her head, and emotion poured from her: shame, grief, regret, inadequacy.

I'm sorry, Anati thought.

"For what?" she snapped. "For me? For what I've done?"

Anger, defiance mixed with the rest. *Don't you dare get mad at me*, Anati thought. *I've been trying to wake you, trying to get you out of that place for weeks. It's not my fault you waited to listen until Kitian and Imyan were too far gone to save.*

She broke again. It wasn't Anati's fault. It was hers. She'd killed her sisters. Killed the world.

Stop it, Anati thought. *I'm sorry, I didn't mean to let you hear that...I...I couldn't take you anywhere else, but we had to leave that place. It was driving you mad. Don't listen to my stupid thoughts.*

She let go of Imyan's decayed, pus- and blood-covered hand.

"Could I have saved them?" she asked.

No, Anati thought. *Not without taking their gifts, unmaking them with the sparks. And then they wouldn't be Imyan and Kitian anymore. They both died well, they both said goodbye to you, they wished for you to find the next children worthy of the Blood Claw and Iron Bark, to help guide them and to be their sister, just as you were theirs.*

She closed her eyes. Pain filled her. Grief, so much grief. Even her uncle's death, even the death of all the people in New Sarresant, couldn't compare. She'd seen the world as it was now, all ash and fire and black clouds and toxic rain.

"What happened to the others? Tigai and Juni and Namkat?"

Tigai said something about the stars vanishing, Anati thought. *Which makes sense. The change will have erased them all. He tried to take you and Kitian and Imyan, but he only took Juni and Namkat with him before the stars faded.*

"Anati, I . . ." she started to say. Grief welled in her throat, and she retched, dry-heaving food she hadn't eaten.

I know, Anati thought. *I know you blame yourself, but this isn't your fault. The Regnant and Sakhefete cheated. But if they can cheat, so can we. You don't have to let this change stand. You can remake the world, just as he did.*

"How?" she asked.

I don't know. But there has to be a way.

If there was a way, she felt nothing for it. No hope. No fear. Only a silent numbing dread.

Unbidden, a memory surfaced. Her uncle, as angry as she'd ever seen him. She'd stolen a chicken breast before he could use it in his soup. He'd had four whole chickens to cook; he wouldn't miss a choice strip of white meat from one of them. But he did. He came roaring after her, climbing into her loft and tearing the meat from her hands. She'd been a child, not more than six years old, but still new to his keeping, too close to her memories of life on the street. A grown man's anger meant death, if he caught her, and here, cornered in her loft, there was nowhere to run or hide. She'd shaken, and pissed herself, before he realized what his anger had done. Then he cried, too.

They'd huddled together in her loft. He said he was sorry; she felt only numbness. Fear. Pain. But he wept. Grown men weren't supposed to cry. They were forces of nature, monsters to be avoided in the night. He held her close, repeating that he was sorry. He quoted the Oracle: "*Wrath is the easiest of sins, and the cruelest master. What we break in moments of anger may take lifetimes to repair.*"

Then they separated, and he picked up the chicken, and quoted the Veil: "*Love is found in giving of ourselves to those in need.*"

He'd asked her, then, if she needed that chicken more than the starving parishioners who would come to their church. They had abundance here, more food than either of them could eat. He would see to it she lacked for nothing, but they in turn had to give what they could spare to those who needed it more. That was love. Love for their fellows. Love for each other. Love for themselves.

It had made her cry. She hadn't ever thought of loving herself. The memory made her cry again, piercing the numbness of her grief.

"No one else will find a way, will they?" she asked through her tears. "It's up to me."

Up to us, Anati thought, accompanied by fresh emotions: resolve, self-doubt, worry, hope. *If you'll still have me.*

"Up to us," she amended. "You're with me, Anati. To the end."

Love flowed over top of all the rest, and she rose to her feet.

"This place is...emptier than usual," she said. "Last time there were more shapes, and other *kaas*."

The change, Anati thought. *It has my people.*

"Zi?" she said, feeling a tinge of panic.

He'll be away, Anati thought. *With as many as he could gather.*

Safe, then. The landscape stretched as far as she could see in any direction, with a few cylinders, cubes, and other, stranger multisided shapes hanging in the sky. But no other *kaas*. A terrifying thing, to imagine that the world's sickness persisted, even here. But Zi would care for his flock, the same as her uncle had tended to his. That was love. That was duty, for those with the power to care for those in need.

She still had that power, as much as anyone with a will to protect the world.

Amanishiakne was dead. Her sister Sakhefete's mind had been rebuilt with the keys to the Veil's power. But there were still others.

She knew their names, if not where to find them. The Rabaquim Flesh and Blood. The Nikkon Spirit-Weavers. The Skovan God-Touched. The Tarzali Sun and Moon. They were the ones with the power to contest for control over the Soul of the World. The ones who could help her stand against the Regnant and his new Veil.

She closed her eyes, shifting her vision to the starfield and the strands.

And opened them again.

"They're gone," she said. "The stars and strands. It's as though the whole field has been wiped clean."

Part of the cleansing, Anati thought to her. *The world is reset for each new cycle.*

"*All* of the stars?" she said. "But that means, even if I used the blue sparks to bore a hole..."

Every Dragon in the world could find you, Anati thought.

She drew a deep breath. The starfield was pure, empty blackness. If she used the sparks to make a new star, every Dragon still alive—from Tigai, if he still lived, to the Regnant's *magi* to the Regnant himself—they'd all see it, and know where she was. She'd have to be ready to fight, or to run. But she couldn't stay here in the *kaas*-plane. She'd already drifted too long.

Wait, Anati thought.

She blinked, returning her vision back to the *kaas*-plane.

There's another way. Our way.

"What do you mean?" she asked.

The way I return to your world. We kaas *don't have starfields, strands, or sparks. We use love.*

"You use love to move between worlds?"

Yes. We go to the one closest to us, in their own hearts. Physical spaces are all adjacent here. Emotion is what draws us together, what binds us, or keeps us apart. See?

She frowned, looking between the floating pyramids, cylinders, and spheres.

"I don't see anything," she said. "I'm sorry, Anati. This place is beautiful, but it's unfamiliar to me."

Here, Anati thought. *Like this.*

Her *kaas* climbed her leg in a flurry, coiling around her arm, her scales flushed shades of pink and purple. Emotion cascaded through her, a mix of her own confusion, wonderment, and Anati's certainty and pride. Then suddenly, she felt it.

A warm wave. An idle thought, a memory from what felt like lifetimes ago, still burning. Something familiar, but distant; old, but strong.

It connected to her. She felt a jolt of excitement, anticipation, joy. But the feeling came as though she were looking into a mirror, as if it were happening to a reflection, rather than to her.

See? Anati thought. *Love.*

"Whose?" she asked. "I don't think this is my emotion. I don't recognize it."

No, of course not, Anati thought. *We go to wherever emotion is strongest in your world. It wouldn't be yours. Your body is floating on the Plane, and your mind is here.*

"Then whose is it? And where are they?"

I don't know who it belongs to; I don't recognize them. The place it's coming from thinks of itself as "Sztetabzrych." Do you know it?

"Szteta..." she said. "No. I don't. That sounds like a Skovan name."

Skova? Is that somewhere you've been before?

"No," she said. "It's in the Old World, about as far to the east as you can go without falling into the ocean. Why would a Skovan be thinking of me?"

Anati sent her the emotional equivalent of a shrug. Uncertainty, ambivalence, indecision.

Should we try it? Anati thought. *Or risk the stars?*

Skova. She didn't know anyone from Skova. So far as she knew, the Skovan were an insular, unforgiving people. They traded with the great powers of the Old World, but they'd never truly been a part of the societies of Gand, Thellan, or Sarresant. Even the best scholars in the West had done little more than gather folklore when it came to Skovan culture or history. But their name had appeared in her research, and with Amanishiakne: The "God-Touched" among them. Whoever they were, one of them would be a potential ally. One of the others.

If she meant to gather strength to face the Regnant again, Skova was a place she'd need to go eventually. And that made it as good a place as any to start.

"We'll go," she said. The wave of emotion Anati had shown her flared, pink and red surging in her vision.

"Um," she said after a moment. "How do I make it work?"

Oh, I can help with that. You let it pass over you, drink it the same way I've seen your people drink the sour grapes you call wine. Love is similar, don't you think? Bitter, sweet, beautiful, but sometimes foul. Let it in, and then—

Her mind and body dissolved, and the *kaas*-plane twisted away.

48

ARAK'JUR

Ka'Ana'Tyat
Sinari Land

Trails of water leaked through the canopy, making a second forest of toxic rain. But here, where the trees grew the densest, he could avoid the streams. He carried Corenna close, keeping her body pressed against his chest as they maneuvered around the leaks in the foliage overhead. The little mother followed, offering a chittering squawk in warning. Corenna had decided on names: Chempa for the mother raccoon, and Iti and Narit for the kits.

Signs of the Alliance's passage were writ around them, even here, after the rain. Broken branches lay under dry spots in the canopy, near imprinted footsteps in the mud. A novice tracker could follow their trail, and it gave him hope, even as they turned inward and northward through the forest. The first days had been spent moving slowly, confirming sign of the Alliance's passage after each stop for the rain. But once they'd moved deep into Sinari land, he'd known their destination even without following the sign. And now, as the trees grew together, knitting wood ceilings in twisted shapes, the forest seemed to defy the acid falling from the sky. This was the spirits' place still, though the wood smoked and burned and gave way to the falling rain. Ka'Ana'Tyat, birthplace of visions.

The opening appeared suddenly, without warning: a darkened place, where the shadows of the trees bent in on themselves, making a cave hewn from the wood. Chempa squealed at the sight, and he came to a stop where the wood was thickest, providing cover from the miniature waterfalls leaking through the branches.

Corenna stirred in his arms, but didn't wake. Her skin burned through the damp cloth he'd set against her forehead. He removed it, pressing a hand to check. A fever of such strength should have torn through her, running for days on end. But the spirits' bond was strong. Corenna was strong. She clung to life, and he clung to her as he lit a fire with dried tinder and Mountain's gift. Chempa plopped down beside the makeshift firepit and unlatched her kits from her back. In their time together the mother raccoon had grown fearless, knowing fire meant food and boiled water to cleanse the toxins. He prepared two iron pots, laying Corenna down where the canopy was thick enough to shield her from the rain, and set to cooking two strips of venison mixed with herbs he'd been careful to clean and preserve along the way.

"Iti and Narit are hungry," he said as the meat cooked. The kits curled and writhed against their mother, nuzzling her belly, while Chempa rolled on one side, giving them access to her milk.

Chempa squawked at him when the pot of clean water boiled, bubbling and steaming beside the other, filled with broth. "Not yet," he said. "Let it cool."

He dabbed a fresh cloth in the water when it was ready, wringing it before setting it gently in Corenna's mouth. She sucked moisture by instinct, her throat trembling every time she swallowed. The sight wrenched his gut, though he tried to focus on his work. She should have long since been dead. He wouldn't let her die. After it had become clear the Alliance intended to make for Ka'Ana'Tyat, he'd dared to hope the spirits would have answers. They'd rebuffed him, before the world's breaking, when he tried to enter Ka'Ana'Tyat a second time. But the need was too dire not to risk offending them again.

He drank from the pot himself to show Chempa the water was safe, then offered her the rest. She lapped at it as her kits got their moisture from her milk, and he set to readying the meat. One strip for him, one for Chempa and her kits, and the broth for Corenna, delivered through her cloths, one moistened rag at a time. He held her for each one, offering more and more until the second pot was dry. A good sign that she could eat, however tenderly, and keep it down. She shook in his arms, but she ate.

Finally his attention turned to the opening in the trees.

It beckoned, a black chasm torn through the wood. He put enough dry logs on the fire to keep it going through the day, and packed away their pots and waterskins.

"You'll have to wait here, if you mean to continue with us," he said to Chempa. She squeaked and made a lolling growl. He patted the ground beside the fire. "Here. If you wish. I'll return soon. If you're gone, then spirits watch over you, Iti and Narit."

Chempa snorted and chirped, and seemed content to curl beside the fire until he rose, hefting Corenna again in his arms, and turned toward Ka'Ana'Tyat.

"I can't leave her behind," he said after Chempa screeched. "There are dry places here, where the trees grow thick. You'll be safe. But she couldn't move out of the way, if the water burned through."

Chempa screeched again. A warning cry. He laughed in spite of all of it. The little mother had made a good companion. He'd be sad if she chose to make her own way.

"You'll be fine, little mother," he said. "And we'll be back soon."

He turned back toward the opening, holding Corenna in his arms. Each step warped the forest around him, the trees twisting until the earth seemed on its side, then vanished, the wood encircling him as the darkness closed.

Chempa screeched again, then suddenly rushed past, both her kits fixed atop her back, trundling ahead of him.

"What are you doing?" he called, though his words were swallowed by the trees, a distant echo, too far and muddled for him to hear his own voice. "This is a place of the spirits." Again, his words scattered to nothing.

He thought to lunge after her, but the little mother vanished. He took another step, and he and Corenna dissolved into shadow.

ARAK'JUR.

The spirits' voice, too long absent from his thoughts. He almost wept to hear it.

Great Spirit, he thought. *I know I've had your gift, the gift of visions, already. But the hour is late, and this time the need is dire.*

OUR GIFT.

The words shook with meaning, carrying fragments of images that flashed in his sight. The sun in the sky. Rain, pure and clean, falling atop an open field. A woman nursing a child. A soldier in a Sarresanter's blue coat climbing a hillside, shouting and waving their flag. A woman in white standing at the head of an army. Himself at her side, surrounded by the auras of a hundred beasts.

THESE THINGS ARE NOT TO BE. NONE OF IT IS TO BE. ALL WILL BE LOST. THEY ARE HERE. THEY ARE COMING.

He felt despair behind the words, racking him with the pain of a loss he couldn't see. Corenna was here, too. He felt her consciousness, warm but distant, glowing faintly in the void. And another set of lights that had to be Chempa and her kits, pulsing three heartbeats in unison, in time with the spirits' despair.

I've come for aid, he thought. *And answers. Why has the world changed? Can it be undone? And can you save this woman—Corenna of the Ranasi, who has fallen sick with the world's poison?*

SLEEP. AS THE BEAR DOES, AS THE SKUNK AND SNAKE AND SNAIL. IT IS TIME TO SLEEP.

A screech came in response to the spirits' voice. A chittering growl, a snap, that he'd grown to recognize. Chempa.

LITTLE MOTHER, the spirits sounded. YES. YOU MAY SLEEP HERE, FOR AS LONG AS THERE IS A HERE TO SLEEP. BE WITH US. COMFORT US AS ALL IS UNMADE.

Chempa's consciousness, and her kits', seemed to glow in his mind, though he had no eyes to see them here. A flash of gold shone, or a vision of it, and feelings of peace, gratitude, and fear for him and Corenna flowed between them.

Chempa? he thought. *Does this mean you can stay here, with the spirits?*

Affirmation flowed. He recognized it. He'd worn the skins of great beasts, knew what it was to be predator and prey. Thoughts wouldn't form in words, but emotions welled, and instinct. Chempa's emotions, manifest in images, hopes and beliefs, and memories.

A sensation of the rain, toxic and impure, burning through the nest where she'd birthed her kits. There had been four, then. Different sensations for each: a small, curious pair of eyes he recognized as Iti. A long nose and sharp teeth biting her nipple; that was Narit. And two more: a sleek coat and beautiful tail who burned to death in the rain. A fragile, clever-minded kit who had loved to stare at the stars, wondering where they'd gone now the sky was blackened, who had starved to death after Chempa left her nest.

He felt an image of himself, and Corenna. The first time Chempa had seen them, in the woods. Fear, an overpowering fear, washed through her at first, overmatched by her fear of the rain. Then the smell of meat. Curiosity won out, and the desire to care for her last two kits. She snatched the food, felt the delicious juices run down her throat, knew her kits wouldn't die today. She saw him, the towering bare-skinned hairless man, and hope overpowered instinct. She had to follow, for her kits' sake.

And now he'd led her here.

Safety beckoned from the opening in the darkest heart of the forest. An old, ancient instinct, older than the oldest memory of the most ancient tree. She would be safe here. She could take the long sleep, and dream, and emerge when the world grew bright again, setting her paws on solid, untainted ground. Her kits would live. He should live, too, and the sick, hairless woman he'd carried in his arms. They could dream here, together, raccoon, kit, kit, woman, and man, in the company of the voices, while the world grew sick around them. He should stay, and be at peace.

I can't, he thought. *I can't stay here.*

A questioning, doubtful screech echoed in his mind.

He formed an image of their son: Kar'Doren. A naked, squealing boy, almost a year old. He put love into it, love from him, but another source poured emotion into the image. A second, faint strand of love, emanating from Corenna's soft light.

Our son, he thought.

This time understanding came from Chempa. A painful understanding, laced with images of the black sky and toxic rain. But if one of her two dead kits had been alive, she would have gone back out for them.

LOVE, the spirits' voices sounded in unison. YOUR SON LIVES, ARAK'JUR.

The same image he'd formed in his mind appeared again, only this time Kar'Doren had grown in the weeks since the world's change. His son's surroundings shimmered into place, though they were murky and gray; no, he was underground. A cave. Surrounded by sick tribesfolk. Faces he knew. All the guardians, spirit-touched women and shamans they'd assembled to fight the Jun. Most were sick, being tended to by those who weren't, and by the rest: his people, those without the spirits' gifts, gathered underground to escape the storm's corrosive rains.

Great Spirit, he thought, relishing the sight of his son in spite of the sickness and the dark surrounding him. *I would know what has happened, if you can show me.*

THE REGNANT HAS THE SOUL OF THE WORLD.

How? Our champions still draw breath. I still draw breath. He can't have won so long as we're still fighting.

HE HAS THE SOUL, AND THE MAKERS COME TO UNDO. THEY POISON THOSE WHO TOUCH US. THOSE WHO WIELD OUR POWER.

Sudden understanding filled him.

The guardians, the women, and the shamans. They were all sick. Dread filled him at his core as the realization spread. *Corenna.*

CORENNA OF THE RANASI, the spirits' voices sounded. HER, AND A THOUSAND MORE. ALL WHO WIELD OUR GIFTS, ALL WHO WIELD THE GIFTS OF THE OTHERS, UNBOUND TO THE POWERS THAT MIGHT PROTECT THEM. THE MAKERS' SICKNESS SPREADS, AND WILL CLAIM THEM ALL.

She was poisoned by the rain, he thought. *By exposure to the ash in the air.*

NO. HER GIFTS ARE TAINTED NOW. THEY WILL CLAIM HER LIFE.

No! he thought. *Why her, and not me? I wield the same power.*

THE MOTHER'S CHAMPIONS DO NOT DIE EASILY.

Neither does Corenna! he thought feverishly. *I've seen her suffer injuries that would fell any other, even a guardian. She's the strongest of all of us. She'll fight this, and survive. There must be a way, and if there is, she'll find it.*

WITHOUT A BOND TO PROTECT HER FROM THE CHANGE, SHE WILL DIE. THIS IS THE WAY, THE ONLY WAY.

A bond? he thought. *You mean as a champion? I thought they had all been chosen.*

THE MOTHER'S AND FATHER'S, YES. BUT THERE ARE OTHER POWERS IN THIS WORLD.

Others. Sarine had spoken of it. Others who might fight against the world's change, if there was still fight to be had. And now, another, better reason: a chance to save Corenna's life.

Tell me of them, he thought. A blasphemous thing, to make demands of the spirits, but he hardly noticed.

THE MOTHER AND FATHER ARE AS MIGHTY OAKS, OLD AND GROWN STRONG FROM THE FIRST SEEDS PLANTED IN THE SOIL. BUT THERE ARE OTHER TREES IN THE GROVE, OTHERS WHO HAVE FOUGHT, AND BEEN TURNED ASIDE. OTHERS WHO STILL COVET THE HIGHEST BOUGHS.

Will they fight? Can the world be changed back to how it was? Can Corenna be saved?

A chorus of voices responded to all of his questions at once.

THEY WILL SEIZE ANY—

THEY CANNOT BE TRUSTED—

THE WORLD WILL CHANGE, AND CHANGE AGAIN—

NO. CORENNA OF THE RANASI MUST STAY—

YES. THERE IS A WAY.

He focused on the last.

What way? How can she be saved?

AN OLD THING. ALMOST OLDER THAN OUR MEMORY. WATCH. LISTEN. SEE.

His mind filled with a fresh vision. A place far, far to the south, across a narrow isthmus of land. The body of a dead man lay atop a stone altar, as what looked like a feather-dressed shaman raised a bone knife over his chest. The shaman had already plunged it into the skin, letting blood and smoke leak out of the corpse. Two massive serpents coiled at the base of the temple beneath them: one red, dripping blood, the other covered in beautiful feathers of every color. Both turned their snouts upward, inhaling the power emanating from the shaman's sacrifice.

Who are they? he thought.

A quiet emanated through the emptiness. As though the spirits waited on the voice to speak on their behalf.

THEY ARE THE FLESH AND THE BLOOD.

THE RABAQUIM.

Once again the chorus sounded, all at once.

THEY ARE DANGEROUS—

THEY CANNOT BE—

YOU MUST NOT—

IF YOU RETURN, YOU WILL—

SHE CANNOT MAKE THE JOURNEY. IF YOU BRING CORENNA WITH YOU, SHE WILL DIE.

Once again, the other voices settled on the last.

HER SICKNESS WILL SPREAD, the voice continued. SHE LACKS THE STRENGTH TO CROSS THE WORLD. THIS CANNOT BE CORENNA OF THE RANASI'S PATH.

You said these Rabaquim offered a path to save her.

THERE IS HOPE, BUT IT WILL BE IN THEIR WAY, NOT OURS. THIS IS A DANGEROUS TRAIL, ARAK'JUR. ARE YOU CERTAIN THIS IS WHAT YOU DESIRE?

Yes. He thought it without hesitation.

VERY WELL.

The words thundered into the void. Images flashed in his sight, faster than he could understand. But the knowledge of it settled into him, as it always did when the spirits granted their visions. He knew the way now. South. Far, far to the south.

Chempa screeched, and sent emotions with it: Determination. Pride. Love. Exhaustion in her bones as both kits clung to her back fur, knowing she should collapse with another step and finding the strength to take two more.

Thank you, little mother, he thought to Chempa. Then to the spirits: *Thank you. I will honor what you have given. I will cleanse the world, if it is within my power to do it. And I will save Corenna, no matter the cost.*

GO, CHAMPION, the spirits sent back. GO, AND FACE THE WORLD FOR LOVE.

49

OMERA

Dining Hall
The Gods' Seat

He was nothing.

"Pass me the salt and butter," Sakhefete said. She sat forward in her chair, a plate of duck and summer vegetables glistening in front of her.

He was a servant, fit to fetch the salt and butter.

"This was one of her favorites," Sakhefete said. "Dr. Lacoursier would send ahead to the hotel kitchens when she traveled, to make sure it was hot and ready for her as soon as she checked into her rooms."

He was the attentive companion. The servant meant to entertain in the absence of other guests.

"You remember what it was, to be her, Your Highness?" he asked.

"No, not exactly," Sakhefete said between bites. "It's a strange thing. I remember what she felt, but I was never her, so it's more akin to watching an actor on a stage. But then, sometimes, when a color catches the light, perhaps, or I taste her favorite dish..."

"More berries?" he asked after a moment.

"I have her memories, too," Sakhefete said. "Your mother's. I kept you alive to gloat, you understand. And now I'm at war with Dr. Lacoursier and—"

She said a name. He wanted to hear. He strained to hear. It was an important name. Someone who had loved him, once. His...mother? Remembering the name would guide him back to everything he'd lost. But it flowed through his ears; he heard the sounds but couldn't remember, even as he heard it.

She continued as if nothing had happened.

"—and neither of them wants what I thought I did, for you. I wanted you humiliated, debased, reduced to a shell of everything my sister promised. She thought you were meant to be King, after she and I were dead. Did you know that? King. I wanted you smeared with filth, when I had Li save your memory. But now, with both of them swirling in my head...the truth is, I miss her. And she loved you."

He stood over her, filling her wineglass. He was the servant, attentive to his lady without the need for her to ask.

Tears appeared on Sakhefete's cheek as she reached for the wine.

He was nothing. The tears weren't something for a servant to see.

A polite cough sounded from across the room.

Sakhefete dabbed a napkin on her eyes. "Li," she said. "Did you need something?"

"There's a problem," Li said. "When you're...finished here. I need you in the map room."

"We're finished," Sakhefete said, rising from her seat. "Omera, with me."

He was the obedient servant. Li turned and led the way without another word, and Sakhefete followed.

The dining hall was far removed from the main corridors of their world. A good servant made it a point to memorize every passage of their mistress's residence, and Omera had done so. This section was devoted to Sakhefete: a menagerie filled with caged animals who somehow needed no food or exercise; a game room stocked with all manner of ivory and gold miniatures, billiards, darts, and more; her private library, the only room she had forbidden him to enter. Li led them away from Sakhefete's chambers toward the central hall, then through it, past the burning column of black fire at its heart. They turned east toward Li's chambers, and then north.

The map room was empty save for two golden fixtures on either side of the door, statues of a serpent and an ox, and the device at its center: a black stone altar larger than the Queen's dining table. The altar's sides and base were etched with jagged lines he vaguely recognized as the shapes of continents, oceans, lakes, and islands. But its surface was smooth and black, like looking down on swirling storm clouds from above.

"What's the problem?" Sakhefete said. The sadness, the hint of melancholy was gone from her voice. She was clinical, like a trained scholar. "The change appears to be progressing at the normal pace. Storm systems healthy and growing. Even the trade winds near the equator are picking up the new pressure banks and dispersing them through the arctic oscillations."

"Not a problem with the meteorology," Li said. "Nor with the gaiaology of the planet."

"What then?" Sakhefete said. "An adaptation among your viruses?"

"You may not have all of these memories," Li said. "When we chose to bind the manifestations of the dimensional folds along the axes of regeneration and torpor, we did so of a purpose."

"I have enough of Dr. Lacoursier to understand," she said. "If you chose not to give me all of who she was, all the better for having me as a partner instead of her, who betrayed you."

"We did so of a purpose," Li repeated. "Among those allowed to handle the dimensional folds, only the champions of the victorious side were meant to live through a change. Which meant when the world was in this state, the torpor state, the only wielders of our magicks among the survivors would be my champions, bound to my lines. Do you understand what this means?"

"Of course," Sakhefete said. "For this transition, because Sarine is still alive, it means her champions are alive, and unaffected by your virus. So what?"

"So what," Li murmured. "So what indeed."

As he said it the surface of the map table changed. The images magnified, racing upward as their view fell through the clouds. It stirred nausea in Omera's stomach, as though he were falling toward the ground. A glimmer of recognition sparked as he studied the coastlines where Li took the map. A place he should have known. A place he'd traveled, once, with *tisa irinti* in his veins. A place he'd been sent, to prove himself, on a mission given to him by . . . by nothing. By no one.

The map zoomed closer. A forest, surrounding the ruin of a great city. A palace, no more than a half day's journey from its walls. And a blue dome the size of a small town rising from the plain.

"God in heaven," Sakhefete said. "What is *that*?"

"That is our problem," Li said. "*Shelter*, unbound by the reservoirs on the leylines. Which means—"

"Which means one of Sarine's champions is there," Sakhefete said. "Can it hold? Surely it will decay over time, without a custodian to keep the barrier in place."

"And if Sarine imbued her champions with Life energy?" Li said. "If they live as long as we do, maintaining cities like this through the change?"

"Cities?" Sakhefete asked. "Plural?"

"Not yet," Li said. "But this *Shelter* dome is already self-sustaining. No reason to believe this champion couldn't travel to create more."

"Son of a bitch," Sakhefete said. "They'd preserve technology a thousand years longer than they should. If the next change came and they emerged with physics, maths...fucking metallurgy and gunpowder, for Christ's sake..."

"You do have enough of Evelynn's memories to understand, then," Li said.

"We have to kill her," Sakhefete said. "Don't you still have a few of your champions? Send them to New Sarresant at once."

"Already on their way," Li said. "But you forget, Sarine stole the Dragons' gift from me. With the starfield blackened, she'll know at once if they move across it."

"And this isn't worth the risk? You could draw her out, even. Make it a trap and an assassination. Two birds."

"You fought Sarine, here in the Seat," Li said. "You know what she's gained, even after Evelynn tore away half her power. Which of my champions would you risk, confronting her directly?"

"One of us, then," Sakhefete said. "The dimensional folds can take us to and from the Gods' Seat without using the starfield. She wouldn't even know we were there until her champion is dealt with."

"Unless she's the one setting a trap for us," Li said.

"What do you propose, then?" Sakhefete asked. "Do nothing?"

"There are three of us, here in the Seat," Li said, with a subtle glance toward where Omera stood against the wall, making himself unnoticed, unobtrusive, invisible.

He was the prized specimen, submitted for his mistress and her guests to study his physique.

"Out of the question," Sakhefete said. "You barely left him enough to serve at table."

"I can restore some of his skill, without his memories or sense of self," Li said. "And the Masadi can provide his herbs: *ubax aragti*, *tisa irinti*, *calimnus re*, *matarin*, and the swords to coat them with."

"I'm not sending him down there alone," Sakhefete said. "He'd have no way back."

"This problem is more important than your preserving trophies of your sister," Li said. "We already said it could be a trap. If Sarine is there, waiting for you..."

"I'll stay hidden. If she's there, we'll leave. No risk. She won't follow us here, not with you in control of the Soul."

"This is foolish," Li said. "Evelynn would understand. She wouldn't put herself at risk, no matter how dire the need, if there was another way."

"I am not Dr. Lacoursier," Sakhefete said. "I understand you worked with her for a great many years. But I am not her."

Li went quiet, studying her in silence.

"You're certain?" Li asked finally, and Sakhefete nodded.

"Fine, then," Li said. "May I?"

Sakhefete gestured toward Omera. A touch of sadness returned to her eyes. The scholar was gone. In its place he could almost see a familiar face. Someone who loved him...but the name wouldn't come.

He was the obedient patient, submitted by his mistress for treatment. Li turned to face him, staring with hot eyes. Eyes that might have unnerved him, if not for the *tisa irinti* in his veins. He'd seen those eyes before. He'd felt them, heard the slump of a body hitting the floor behind him, with all the weight of death in his ears. He'd had those eyes bore into him, ripping holes in...nothing. He was nothing. He was the subject, probed by those terrible, painful eyes.

He screamed.

Li made no move to show he'd heard, while Sakhefete flinched, casting a doubtful look between him and Li.

The eyes tore into him again.

Wires sizzled and recoiled from the invader's touch. Memories fled the presence, hiding in the deepest shadows of who he was. Hiding. Trembling. Shaking. He was terror. He was pain.

New lattices snapped into some part of him, some unknown part, rediscovered. Old muscles flexed from new use. The eyes fused pieces of his body and mind with another place. He almost remembered the source. A weaponmaster, drilling him in the yard. The woman whose name he needed to remember, watching from a balcony above, full of pride and love for...for nothing. For no one. He was no one.

He was the assassin.

He was the swordmaster, the battle-magus, trained to coat his *shotel* blade in *matarin* leaves, whirling and spinning death like a dervish in the sand.

"It's done," Li said finally. "You'll find his implements waiting in your quarters. Finish it quickly, and hurry home."

"Thank you," Sakhefete said. "Thank you for understanding."

"I understand nothing," Li said. "But I value you as a partner. Good luck, and Godspeed."

With that, Li bowed, a sharp, stiff gesture, before retreating from the room.

"How do you feel, my newborn warrior?" Sakhefete asked.

He was the champion, fit to be sent forth to punish his mistress's enemies.

"I am well, mistress," he said. "Whatever your will. I'm ready."

"We'll be going together," she said. "You understand your task? Find the champion responsible for the *Shelter* dome, and kill her. Then return to me."

"I understand, mistress," he said. "The champion will wield the leylines. It will be Erris d'Arrent. I will find her, kill her, and return to your side."

Sakhefete stared at him, part wonder, part doubt. "The name," Sakhefete said. "You shouldn't remember...but perhaps he gave it to you, for this mission."

He said nothing in reply, holding still. He was the dark knight, ready to shed blood in his mistress's name.

"Very well," Sakhefete said. "We'll retrieve your weapons and go without delay."

He followed behind as they left the room. His quarry's face surfaced in his thoughts. Erris d'Arrent. Champion of the leylines. Empress of New Sarresant, Thellan, and Gand. He latched onto it, holding fast to a steady rock in a torrent of sand. He was no one. He was nothing. But he remembered.

50

TIGAI

Awaiting the Dreamers
Outside Palompurraw Town

Orana held up a hand, and they stopped.

It was all Tigai could do not to collapse. He found the strength to set Namkat's litter down gently, then sank to his knees, breath coming hard and ragged as sweat dripped into the dirt.

Juni coughed beside him, a deep cough, hard enough to draw blood. She had to be twice as exhausted as he was. Namkat slept atop the litter, thank the wind spirits, or she'd have spent the morning berating them for carrying her. But neither he nor Juni was about to leave a sister to die, however she insisted. They were going to reach the Sun, whatever the bloody fucking hells that meant. And apparently Orana meant to drive them like dogs to get there before Namkat died.

"Go," Orana said to Miroyah, the bearded old man who'd brought the litter when it was full of food. "Go and return with your Dreamers."

Miroyah bowed along with his daughter, Tetali, and both went. When they'd first met them the old man had called Tetali his "dream-mother"; Tigai had since learned it meant he was her father, and that when they said they had "yet to say their hellos" to Tetali's actual mother—whom they called Tetali's dream-daughter—it meant her mother had already died. The Tarzali had a strange way of speaking, as though they inverted cause and effect, past and future, but it was simple enough to follow, once he understood the premise.

Orana came to sit beside the litter, running a pale white hand through Namkat's hair.

"I fear for her," Orana said. "The sickness has her like a fresh-docked sailor's first dry-land cunt."

Tigai winced.

"What?" Orana said. "Did I use that one wrong?"

"The wrong bloody time," he said. "You don't curse when a friend is sick, and dying. And you definitely don't fucking curse in front of her sister, or her brother-to-be."

"But you just said 'bloody,'" Orana said. "And 'fucking.'"

Juni managed a weak smile through her haggard breathing. "She'd have appreciated it," Juni said. "Namkat likes you, Great One, and your cursing, when she's lucid enough to hear it."

Orana shifted her hand, reaching to take Juni's in hers.

"The sickness has you, too, fiery one," Orana said. "But you're strong enough to reach the sun."

"Where are we now?" he asked. "How close?"

"This is Palompurraw Town," Orana said. "Once we have their Dreamers we can go straight to it. I can see my twin's perch from here. Not far. A few more days."

He squinted in the direction Miroyah and Tetali had gone. In the distance there might have been silhouettes of buildings, but as best he could tell it was more of the same landscape they'd been crossing. The place had a foreign feel. It was a desert, judging by the dry heat in the air, the dust and sparse grasses that seemed to stretch on and on to the horizon. Yet there were trees, great towering colossi, warped and broken by the acid rain. Orana had kept the clouds open over their heads, enough for moonlight to show their twisted, burned branches and the dried-out husks of their trunks. On another day he might have let curiosity reign and gone into the town. Today he lay still beside Namkat's litter, breathing hard and grateful for the moment's rest.

"You said you can see it, though it's still days away," Juni said. "Does that mean you see from the vantage of the moon?"

Orana nodded sagely. "She is me, and I am she," she said. "The blue sister's magic gifts me these bodies, but my senses are still what they are. Don't worry, Juni. I don't forget to be myself when I come here to walk on the blue sister's back."

Juni gazed up into the sky, and pulled his eyes with hers. Black clouds still billowed around them, darkness prevailing from morning to night. It made no sense, as far as he could tell. Shouldn't the sunlight shine through the bore Orana had made in the clouds? Yet it didn't. Only the moon hung there, suspended directly over their heads, full and shining bright. There weren't even any stars in the sky, an unwelcome reminder of the emptiness waiting if he shifted his sight to the strands. Something was wrong here, in this place Miroyah called Tarzal. Something no storm could explain.

"It must be wonderful," Juni said. "No wonder they call you the Great Dreamer." She coughed, then, the same sickening, deep cough they'd heard from Namkat almost from the moment of their arrival.

"Would you like to see it, too?" Orana asked. "The Palompurraw Dreamers will bring us food. We have time, if you want to join our souls together for a while."

"What does it mean, to join souls together?" Juni asked.

Orana answered by extending her hand, smiling a knowing smile that looked impish on her young girl's face. Then she surprised him by extending another hand to him, keeping both outstretched at once.

"You want me to do it, too?" he asked.

"What better way to learn the rest of your new words?" Orana said. "Especially if it's improper to use them around the sick."

Tigai eyed her hand dubiously, while Juni took the other, grasping firmly.

"You would refuse my gift, Yanjin Tigai?" Orana said.

Bloody hells. He was tired, and if Miroyah and Tetali would be away for a time, he'd as soon have caught up on sleep. But whatever Orana was, she had power, and for the time being they were stuck here. Offending a Tarzali Goddess could lead to complications he could do without.

He took her hand, and for a moment it was only flesh, warmer than usual, tender and soft. He and Juni both held her, and she squeezed their fingers in return.

Then he changed.

They changed.

First he was a girl, a small child, kicking her father's arms as he tried to retrieve her from her hiding place. He screamed and wailed. He didn't want to see the chief. He was picked up, hoisted over her father's shoulder, and he bit and kicked and flailed. Only when they reached the high hall did he stop, and only then because the woman at the chief's side bore tattoos more intricate and beautiful than he had ever seen. Future memory gave the face a name: Alka Nine Tails. A warm memory. A sister, now mourned and lost.

Then he was himself. An old memory. Father had just beaten Dao bloody, left him bruised and whimpering in his bed. The serving boy who'd been lying with Dao had been hauled away, sure to be put to death for laying a finger on his brother's noble skin. Tigai saw it happen from the halls. He stole into his brother's room after father stormed away, and found Dao crying into his hands. He held him. Whispered kind words. Joined his brother in words of hatred for their father, and for what he'd done.

Last, he was the moon. A sensation of being without a body made him dizzy, but then, he had no eyes, no belly to heave up vomit as he spun around the earth. Starlight flooded through him, raking his light side with puncturing heat and radiation, while his dark side was cold, airless... but not lifeless. The souls were there. Beautiful souls, thousands of them—millions!—come to sing to him of the lives they'd led, or the lives to which they were about to be born. They flitted between the stars and planets, and he watched them with joy in his heart, looking down to where the blue sister should have reflected the sun's light. Only the sister had gone dark now. Dark clouds covered her skies and seas, hiding the deep blue of her oceans. Storms crackled thunder on her surface, and he wept, seeing the change.

He gasped as the images faded, sucking in breath and snapping his hand back away from Orana's.

The little albino girl looked different now. There was wisdom behind her eyes, a deep, abiding wisdom betrayed by her elfin features and the mischief in her eyes. He knew what she was. The silver orb gazing down on them through the hole in the clouds was *her*, in the deepest, purest sense. The body was a shell, a mask, an illusion.

"Thank you," Juni said. "That was... that was..."

Juni didn't finish it, and he wasn't sure whether he could have spoken at all. For a brief moment he'd felt Juni's memories, all of them, he'd felt her sense of self, he'd felt the Flame Scale, all of it. He'd felt Orana, and felt both of them *become* him. It made him light-headed. It made him weak and dazed. It made him...

He retched, doubling over and heaving into the dirt.

When he finished, Orana was already on her feet, looking down at him. Only then did he notice they were surrounded by kneelers. Six, with two more bowing their heads from the backs of litters exactly like the one they'd used to transport Namkat. All eight were naked, four men and four women, spread in a half circle with Orana at the center.

"I wondered whether you would submit to the exchange," Orana said. "I might have killed you if you hadn't. But now I see you told it true. You are hers: the Veil's. And you see me. There is no cunning here. We are as we pledged ourselves to be: you, the Dragon, and I, the Moon. And now our Dreamers are here, and we have a long way to go yet. Shall we?"

The rest of them responded to the question as though it were a command, rising from their kneeling positions and dividing up into twos to pull their litters. Juni did the same, stretching before she took up her place behind Namkat. He fell in, too, hefting Namkat's litter with burning muscles that felt like they hadn't rested in days. His mind reeled at what he'd seen. There was memory, old and ancient, behind the moon. It faded quickly, like waking from a dream, but for a fleeting moment he remembered vying for control over the world itself—what the Sun and Moon called the blue sister—and the magic that bound her, like chains wrapped around her soul. He remembered Sarine, or a woman who could be her twin, and the Regnant, closing them off from power, relegating them to these deserts, left to wander alone, with only the souls of the dead for company.

The memories faded, but sadness lingered as he pulled the litter across the grass.

He got names for the rest of the Tarzali on the road. Miroyah and Tetali had returned, this time pulling a wrinkled old woman they called their dream-granddaughter on a litter between them. He took it to mean she was Miroyah's mother, or perhaps his grandmother, since both he and his daughter gave her the same title, and spoke her name, Abindah, with reverence, though she had yet to open her eyes as she trembled atop the litter. Two more pulled a second litter: Kwoori and Kaladooh, apparently twin brothers, with a younger boy, Bamparr, coughing but lucid enough to introduce himself when he asked. The last two Tarzali were women, barely more than girls, Ellin and Allakawari, both young and beautiful and evidently inclined to show him doe eyes and giggle whenever he approached. It stung his ears the first time, and reddened them further when they collapsed into laughter as soon as he left.

Orana found time for all of them, passing between the litters and even helping pull, when one of them slowed or needed rest. On the first day they stopped for water only a handful of times, enough to give him a chance to ask the Tarzali their names. The rest of their hours were spent dragging their litters over the desert's dirt and dead grasses. When they finally stopped for the night Juni used the Flame Scale to make a fire, drawing hooting sounds from the Tarzali as though they were a chorus of owls. They asked her to share a story from her tribe, and she did, weaving an artful narrative of what she called the first war between Gorin and Hoskar between bloody coughs that did nothing to detract from her story. Miroyah spoke for the Tarzali, offering a story called "The Dwellings in the Clouds." He tried to follow it, and mostly failed, weaving as it did between past and future tenses.

Ellin came to sit next to him in the middle of Miroyah's story. She and

Allakawari were younger than he'd thought, he decided. Both had women's bodies, full-figured and curved, but they exchanged the sort of furtive glances he associated with young girls at Imperial courts, punctuated by nervous laughs and private jokes.

"Is it a true sight?" Ellin asked him in a hushed voice after a moment together.

"Is what a what?" he asked.

Ellin exchanged another glance with Allakawari, and both giggled.

"The counting," she said. "The number in your future."

He swallowed, clearing his throat and speaking softly so as not to disturb the story. "I don't know what you mean."

"One hundred fifty-eight," Ellin said. "The number of women you will have sex with, before you're born."

He almost choked, drawing eyes from the others sitting nearby.

"I will never dream again of a man with a number so high," Ellin said. "Neither will Allakawari. Do women not tame men, in the lands of your birth?"

"I...I don't..." he began. What was he supposed to say to that? He'd lost count ages ago, but there had been plenty of willing women at court, almost from the moment he'd been old enough to have blood flowing between his legs. How the fuck could they know how many women he'd taken to bed?

"You must know many secrets in the pleasing of women," Ellin said. "I think, perhaps, I might have tried to tame you. Not a Dreaming. Only..." She blushed then, looking away. "A hope, if you've considered it."

"Is she trying to seduce you?" Orana said. Tigai almost expelled a sigh of relief as the albino girl strode toward them, rising from her place beside the fire.

Ellin bowed her head at once. "I will, Great Dreamer," she said quietly. "At least, I will try. He is pleasing to the eye, and with the things we'll dream of him...I thought..."

"He has greater concerns tonight," Orana said. "And so do you. See to them."

Ellin scrambled away, returning to her perch beside Allakawari with a fresh round of giggles and sidelong looks in his direction, apparently undeterred by Orana's rebuke.

"Thank you," he said to Orana. "I can't say I expected that line of questioning."

"Walk with me," Orana said. Her tone was colder than usual, her curiosity replaced by a detached reserve. "We've disturbed Miroyah's story enough."

He followed as she led them away from the camp. He expected her to stop after a few paces, once they were out of earshot, but she kept going. They climbed small rocks, went past a gnarled tree bent inward on itself, and went still farther, until the fire glimmered, shrinking in the distance.

He was about to ask exactly where they were going when she came to a sudden halt, and spun to face him. Darkness surrounded them, though the moonlight seemed to reflect off her pale white skin, casting shadows across her eyes.

"What is it?" he asked.

"I saw your spirit, when you touched my true form," she said. "I would have seen if you intended to deceive. This I believe, with all the parts of who I am. And yet I am made the fool."

Danger spiked in his blood; he felt it, as sure as a guardsman's spear leveled at his neck.

"I don't understand," he said, as meekly as he could manage. "Did I offend, during the story?"

"No, Yanjin Tigai," Orana said. She studied him for a moment before continuing. "Do you understand what it means, for you and your equals to be named champions, to your Goddess, or your God?"

"We were meant to fight each other for control of the Soul of the World," he said. "The voices that sounded: '*For this one, it ends.*'"

"True enough," Orana said. "Though only part of the way. Let me ask it differently: Do you understand why Kalira and I do not also bond champions, to contest the Soul?"

"I didn't know you could," he said, meaning it. The spear was still there; he sensed it in her tone, the way her body stayed still, waiting, like a coiled spring.

"We did, once," she said. "A bloody, terrible thing. Six lines of magic between the Regnant and Veil, weighed against our one. We are stubborn, my sister and I, but the lesson was learned. In all the cycles since, we have never once bonded a champion prior to the turning of the Soul, nor have we conspired with any others to bind champions together."

He nodded. Even having shared whatever had passed between them when he became the Moon, he couldn't fully understand what she was saying. But he felt the truth behind her words. She meant them, with a heavy sadness that lingered after she spoke.

"So why, then," Orana said, "are we to be punished now? You came with truth in your heart, and true need. Never before has it offended the Regnant and Veil for us to save our few, when the world turns. Does your mistress need us to supplicate ourselves again? Do we need to bow and scrape and lick the plague-tainted piss-holes of our betters to be permitted to hold the power that is and was our birthright? Were you a trap, even unknowing, Yanjin Tigai?"

Here it was. The spear-point, brushed against his neck.

"I don't understand," he said. "Orana. You saw it yourself. I didn't even mean to come here. All I want is to save Juni and Namkat and find a way back home. If there is anything I can do to aid you, all you need to do is ask."

"Very well," Orana said. "That is what I needed to hear. And now you must understand what you have pledged to do. Give me your arm. Look. See."

She reached for him and laid a hand on his forearm. He kept himself from flinching, and stayed still.

They changed.

Once again he was the moon, looking down on the blue sister in her sickened, blackened form. Only this time he saw closer, followed another pair of eyes as they cut down through the clouds. They seemed to be falling, racing toward the earth, toward a hole cut in the clouds. They fell faster, passing through the circular hole, falling toward an empty field in the desert, beside a split, gnarled, and ancient tree. Two figures stood at its center, a pale albino girl reflecting the moonlight, and a Jun man. Himself. He was looking down on himself.

"How...?" he heard himself say. The sound of his own voice jarred his ears. He started again. "How the bloody..."

The world spun underneath their feet, and his moon-sight went with it. They pulled back, climbing altitude faster than a soaring eagle, then dove again, just as fast. He felt their senses lurch together until they were a few leagues away, this time under the cover of a sea of black clouds. They fell toward the base of a hill that became a mountain, toward a series of scorched black marks on the ground.

The vision shattered like a broken mirror.

"You see?" Orana said. "You see? They took her. They took her!"

"Wait," he said. "What did I see? I don't understand."

"The Regnant's surviving champions," Orana said. "They came for my sister. If you meant what you said—*anything*, to help us, to save your dying sisters—then you will go, and bring her back."

"Why would they take your sister?" he asked.

"To punish us," Orana said. "To ensure we mean them no challenge, perhaps. Your being alive, and sworn to her, marks a change in the balance between Regnant and Veil. You being here, swearing to help me, is itself a change, if you mean what you say, and I believe you do."

"I do," he said. "I will, if it means saving them. But how am I supposed to go anywhere? The stars are all blacked out since the world went mad."

"You are still a Starwalker," Orana said. "You can travel on foot to this place, where my sister was taken, and follow their strands. Take those among the Dreamers who can fight; take Juni. I cannot go with you myself without leaving the Dreamers unprotected, but I will be there in my true form, watching from the sky. If you need aid, call for it, and I will hear."

He hesitated; she could sense it, from the way she shifted, watching him. The spear-point, still there. But he meant it. Anything, to save Yuli's sisters. Whether Yuli herself was still alive somewhere else under this cursed storm, getting back to her meant working with Orana, no matter the threat she represented if he refused. Yuli would never forgive him if he let her sisters die. He would never forgive himself.

"All right, then," he said. "Fuck me. But all right. I think I can find the way to where they took her, from what you showed me."

"Then go," Orana said. "Go, and bring me back the Sun."

51

SARINE

I t wasn't like using the strands, or boring holes with the blue sparks. She was with Anati on the *kaas*-plane, then the world seemed to twist around her. Emotion flared, a mix of anger, love, resentment, self-doubt. She felt them all as though they were hers, though somehow she knew they weren't. The *kaas'* shapes became colors, then smells, then textures under her fingers. Then she was somewhere else.

A great hall lit by torches and candles. Descending rows of seats surrounded what looked like a stage, making this a theater, or a lecture hall. Darkness showed outside, and rain poured into the hall through crumbling cracks in the ceiling. But enough of the structure remained intact to shelter what appeared to be a dozen or so souls, people huddled where the rain wasn't leaking through the roof.

Some of them noticed her as she noticed them. She stood alone, precariously near a trickle of falling water that hissed where it touched the carpet. They wore clothes not unlike the fashions favored by the New Sarresant nobility, what seemed like two lifetimes ago: culottes and waistcoats for the men, slim-cut dresses lacking embroidery for the women, both making up for any simplicity with bright colors and ribbons tied in their hair.

"Sarine?"

The voice coming from behind her was incredulous, surprised, and familiar.

"It is you," he said. "Gods preserve us, how is this possible?"

She turned. He hadn't changed at all. Donatien Revellion, son of the Marquis, whom she'd once spent mornings watching as he played darts and charmed the ladies on the palace green. He wore Sarresant styles, looking haggard under the eyes but otherwise composed and perfect. A black ribbon tied his hair back in a knot at the nape of his neck, while a sleek coat accentuated his broad shoulders and his height. Looking at him, seeing the mix of shock and adoration in his eyes reminded her why she'd left him to board the ship alone, what felt like years and years ago.

"Donatien," she said. "I'm...not entirely sure. I left the..." She stopped herself. "That is, I left, and arrived here. I'm not sure how."

It's all right, Anati thought to them. *These people know us.*

"That's right," Donatien said. "I sought them out, once I arrived here in the Old World."

"Sought who out?" she asked.

"People like you," Donatien said, a touch of embarrassment in his voice. "*Kaas*-mages. We came to the Skovan capital, after the war. Then, when the storms came, we took refuge here in the university. We'd been searching for an answer as to the storms' cause, but I never imagined in my wildest dreams you would show up here. I almost think I must still be dreaming."

She scanned the room, suddenly changed for knowing who these people were. Conspirators; cultists if it fit better, of the sort who had once attended salons with Reyne d'Agarre, reading from their holy book, their Codex, and plotting revolutions. They were staring at her, not yet moving but drawn to the commotion Donatien was making at her arrival.

"I still don't know why I'm here," she said, addressing it to Anati.

"A blessing," Donatien said. "An answer to a prayer."

Anati's thoughts sounded in her mind: *I told you. Leaving the plane the way we do takes us to whoever feels the strongest emotions about us in the physical realm. For me, that's you. For you, I think it's him. Who is he? He tastes like yellows and blues. And if he's so important, why do you never think of him?*

Embarrassment reddened her cheeks, but it seemed Anati hadn't made herself heard to anyone but her. Donatien kept beaming at her, as though he expected her to say something equally glowing for him. Well, she couldn't reply to Anati out loud, but then, the *kaas* could read her thoughts. So she thought it: *He might still love me, but I feel nothing for him. He's a relic of a different time. Part of my past. Something I thought I wanted, when I didn't know enough to know better.*

"What's this, Lord Revellion?" a fat man in velvet and fur said, carefully avoiding the dripping rainwater as he approached. He had a long white mustache waxed to thin points, and a bearing that expected deference, apparently even from a Marquis's son.

"A stroke of luck, Your Grace," Donatien said. "This is an old friend—Sarine Thibeaux, somehow come to us in our hour of greatest need. She's one of you, the first *kaas*-mage I met, back in New Sarresant, before their revolution. Sarine, this is His Grace the Duc de Dadenchon, uncle to the Dauphin, and first among the *kaas*-mages of the Old World."

She tried to get Donatien's attention to silence him; who could say what ill meaning Reyne d'Agarre's former conspirators would attach to her name? But the Duc surveyed her with a suddenly changed expression, full of curiosity rather than malice.

"Is this true?" the Duc said. "You were a *kaas*-mage across the sea?"

"Yes, Your Grace," she replied. No sense trying to hide it now. "It seems I journeyed east for the same reasons you did: seeking an answer to the cause of these black storms."

"And your people," the Duc said slowly. "Our peers from across the sea . . . do they share our affliction?"

"Her *kaas* is still with her, Your Grace," Donatien said, beaming as though she might reward him for spilling details about her to people she couldn't trust. "It spoke to me as soon as she arrived."

"It can't be," the Duc said. "Your *kaas* hasn't gone silent? Does Lord Revellion have the right of it?"

"What do you mean?" she asked. "Your *kaas* have 'gone silent'?"

"Not a word from them," the Duc replied. "Not a word or thought since the sky changed. And every page of the Codex has gone blank. Not reverted to unintelligibility, mind. Blank. Empty white paper. But if your *kaas* is still with you . . . do you have your copy of the book?"

Here it was. Axerian's Codex had driven Reyne d'Agarre mad. For all she might have hoped Donatien had found *kaas*-mages without it, she saw the fire in the Duc's eyes. He craved it like a drunkard needed wine.

"I, ah . . ." she began. "I don't—"

"She never had the book, Your Grace," Donatien said. "She was different from the others, even in New Sarresant. It might be why her *kaas* is still with her?"

The Duc nodded, still studying her as though he meant to have her served for dinner.

"Will your *kaas* manifest for me, at least?" the Duc said. "If there's to be trust between us, it starts there."

Before she could come up with a polite way to refuse, Anati appeared perched atop her shoulder. Her *kaas* was already leaning forward, studying the Duc's mustache as intently as the man studied them. It was all she could do not to swat Anati, just as she longed to do to Donatien. She thought: *I don't trust these people. No need to reveal so much.*

We need them, though, Anati thought to her. *I thought you said you wanted to find allies.*

Allies that might have the power to resist the Regnant's changes, she thought back. *Others. The Skovan, the ones they call God-Touched. How much help are* kaas-*mages without their* kaas *going to be?*

"Incredible," the Duc said. "And if you still have your *kaas*, you'll still have *Red* and *Green*, won't you? But of course, you must have, if you traveled here through the rains. This could be the answer we've needed. The Skovan, bloody recluses they are, won't talk to us. Won't come near us. We know they've survived—we've seen their scavenging parties—but they run at first sight of my people."

"And you want me to compel them with *Green*?" she asked.

"Our supplies are low," the Duc said. "We've held out here, raiding the university's stores, but we need help, if you could oblige them to give it. Once, I was a powerful man. I might have offered favors, influence, or coin in return for your service. Now I find myself reduced to begging, but if that is what the Gods require, so be it. These people are my responsibility. They followed me here, on my interpretation of the Codex. I'll not let them starve for my pride."

"Yes," she said. "Of course I'll help."

Anati cocked her head in a gesture of surprise, though Sarine tried to quell it with a thought: *I can carry their message without compelling anyone. And he's just given me a means to leave here gracefully.*

Donatien beamed, though the Duc still regarded her warily.

"You must take care with them," the Duc said. "Use *Green* to make contact, if you must, but they will have their hedge-mages, as Skovan always do. If the mages sense what you are doing, it will end badly, and we need their cooperation."

"I'll go with her, Your Grace," Donatien said. "I know the grounds, and there's still hope we could find Arron and Daphène out among the ruins."

The Duc nodded as though the matter were settled. Inwardly she groaned—she couldn't well find a way to use the stars or the blue sparks to leave here with Donatien attached to her side. But then, if it came to it, she wouldn't have any qualms about using *Green* to compel him back here without her.

"Do you need a rest?" Donatien asked. "Or shall we head out at once?"

"Now," she said. "I'm fine to travel." And eager to get away from *kaas*-mages of the sort that might have followed Reyne d'Agarre into madness, though she left the thought between her and Anati.

"Good fortune for both of you, then," the Duc said. "And Gods be praised for your coming, Lady Sarine. Truly a miracle, in a time when miracles are in short supply."

The lecture hall claimed by the *kaas*-mages was one of seven, arranged at opposite ends of a grand garden that would have been beautiful before the sky turned black. Covered walkways ran from each hall toward a gazebo at the garden's center, though most of the cover had been burned away, the tiles lying in tatters as rain dripped and hissed through the cracks.

"I still can't believe you're here," Donatien said as he led the way. "I can't tell you how I've dreamed of seeing you again, and suddenly, here you are."

He guided them toward the garden's heart, cautiously avoiding the drips and trails of rainwater running along the path. She'd spent the past weeks watching the world change through the torrents on the Infinite Plane; it was different, seeing it in person. She'd felt the agony of a stone chewed through by acid, watched soldiers scream as they were caught in the storms, smelled the rot and decay creeping through the fabric of everything, everywhere. Yet being here, seeing it, twisting her body to make sure she stayed within narrow passages where the rains had yet to strike, was a different experience altogether.

"We've explored most of the university grounds already," Donatien was saying. "And taken most of their stores. We'll want to head east into the city. That's where our last scouting party would have gone, before they went missing. Good chance they ran afoul of the local Skovan, or perhaps found themselves on the wrong side of the rains. The storm hasn't let up, not a break in the clouds nor a dry spell for even an hour, unless it came while we were sleeping. Gods but it's so good to see you. I'd heard news, of course, of goings-on in the colonies, of the Empress's investiture—my old commander, I'd scarce believe it!—and the unifications, and of course I've been imagining what role you played. You'll have to tell me everything; I want to hear it all."

"Donatien," she said.

"Yes?" he asked, suddenly attentive. "What is it?"

"Just…slow down," she said. "I know we haven't seen each other in a long time, but—"

"Say no more," he said. "I can be patient. You'll want to take care here. We need to make a run for it to cross to there, see where that street runs alongside the low building, with the sloped tile roof? There's a good sturdy awning that runs the length of the block."

She followed, trailing behind as he hefted his coat to shield his head. The rain stung her skin; Anati flared *Red* in her blood without being asked, and she ignored what was left of the pain.

He grinned at her after they reached the awning. "You'd think I'd be used to the *kaas'* gifts by now. I've been in their company almost since I arrived here in the Old World. But still—it's something else to see you use them."

She ignored the sap underneath his words. Patience indeed. "Tell me more about the people here," she said. "And about this missing scouting party." Even if the real goal was to contact the Skovan, she could at least make good on helping keep the Duc and his people from starving.

"The Skovan have always been secretive," Donatien said, leading her alongside the building, then to another awning. "They allow foreigners into their cities, but only in designated quarters, and never anywhere near their seats of power. They have their own Gods, and their hedge-magic instead of connections to the leylines. It's made them a strange people, with little in common with the rest of the continent."

"And your scouts?" She said it as they crossed from building to building around a wide fountain square. Once, a great statue had dominated the plaza, of what looked like a winged child holding a trumpet. Half the statue had crumbled into the fountain, leaving cracked stone and wire protruding from the child's face and back.

"A party of two," he said. "Arron and Daphène, gone these past four days, and overdue by three. They would have gone into the town looking for unclaimed stores, food, clothing, oil and tallow, whatever they could find. I've led a few such sorties myself, but then, I never encountered the Skovan. I hope to the Oracle our people are only bogged down by the rain."

"Two scouts?" she said.

"That's right," he said. "Sztetabzrych is a large town, though. We'll have to guess at where they went."

"I can sense two people close by," she said. "Or, Anati can, using *Yellow*. That way." She pointed east. No other signs of life nearby, though Anati usually needed the blue sparks to project her influence more than a half league in any direction. No telling what might be waiting for them farther out than that.

Donatien halted mid-stride, breaking back into his beaming grin. Once, she might have melted to see him show it for her, firm-jawed and rugged, with a few days' stubble adding to his usually perfectly kempt face. "You're a treasure," he said.

They changed course, heading up a street that crossed the others in a diagonal. Pocks had been cut in the street by the rain, holes and crumbled stone that seemed especially wrong so near the heart of the city. Anati's *Yellow* kept her focused and aware of the people nearby, sending back a thin strand of emotions: humility, reverence, grief, determination. No way to tell whether they were Donatien's scouts, or potential contacts among the Skovan, though she hoped for the latter. She'd already learned firsthand the dangers of allying herself with *kaas*-mages. Even with Axerian's corrupting influence removed, the damage would be long done, and impossible to repair.

"There?" Donatien asked.

They'd emerged into a broad clearing between blocks, where a great building rose above its neighbors. Twin spires framed a pair of arched doors beneath a stained-glass window depicting a robed man surrounded by light. Not the Exarch—Donatien had said the Skovan had their own Gods—but she knew a church for a church, no matter the differences. Nearby buildings were built for efficiency; this one was built for splendor. And lights flickered inside it, illuminating the windows from within.

"I think so," she said. "The emotions are close. Coming from inside."

Donatien clicked his teeth. "We've avoided going near the Skovan churches. Foreigners are never allowed anywhere near them. With the locals already prickly, the last thing we wanted to do was disturb something holy."

"Well, there are two people inside," she said. "And no one else nearby. Follow me, if you're coming."

He did, keeping his coat pulled up over his head to shield him from the rain. She ignored the pain as it hissed against her skin, studying the feed of emotions from Anati. It wasn't quite grief, more a sense of purpose in the face of despair. And however she tried to isolate them from each other, she could sense only a single set of emotions, though there were definitely two people inside. *Green* and *Yellow* made a single stream of feeling as it reached her through her *kaas*. She hadn't sensed anything quite like it. Lovers, maybe. Though they'd picked a strange place to consummate a tryst, among the pews of a church.

She pulled the iron bar of the main doors, and they swung open, without creaking from rust.

Light flooded the main hall.

Not candles, lanterns, or torches. It would have taken thousands to light the windows from inside as brilliantly as the light flooding around her. It was as though the sun at noon had descended into the chapel. She squinted, shielding her eyes.

"It's her," a man's voice said. "Not the Veil; but the Veil twice born, and born again. You were right, Rashael. Damn us all, but you were right."

The light shimmered, and became two shapes, or perhaps it always had been, and she only needed time to adjust to the intensity: a woman, wrapped in cloth, standing in front of the altar, and an ordinary man beside her. Light blazed around the woman, and white feathered wings unfurled from her shoulder blades until they reached the length of one of the pews. She stood in a protective stance, wielding a sword of light and fire.

<This woman is our salvation,> the light-woman said, though she heard it more akin to the *kaas*' thoughts, projected directly into her mind. It thundered, as though every word were accompanied with blaring trumpets. <You must have faith, Krzysztof.>

"Who are you?" she called into the chapel. "You're right. I'm not the Veil. But I'm the successor to her power, and I've come in search of allies."

"You've come in search of new wells to poison," the man, Krzysztof, said. "God save us all if the heresies are true."

<Truth is never heresy,> the light-woman said. <But we forget ourselves, living a moment of prophecy. I am called Rashael, servant of the Eleventh Chorus. He is Krzysztof, my bond-partner. And you are a woman foretold, come to us to offer a spark of light in the gloom. If that is why you've come. I would hear it from your mouth, first. Who are you? Why are you here?>

It still took an adjustment to hear the light-woman's thoughts and not want to flinch. Donatien, standing beside her, seemed frozen in shock, a hairsbreadth from bolting back into the square in terror until she laid a steadying hand on his arm. He wouldn't be able to understand them, without the *kaas*' gifts, but there was something here.

"I'm Sarine," she said, keeping her voice clear and firm. "I'm what you said: the Veil reborn. Rightful heir to the Soul of the World, before the Regnant stole what was mine. I come in search of allies to reclaim it."

Krzysztof gasped, while Rashael's eyes seemed to glisten over with tears of pure light.

"Impossible," Krzysztof said. "She must have memorized the scripture."

<It's her,> Rashael said. <Our salvation, come at last. You see it now, you hear it with your own ears. It is no heresy. Soon, we will walk once more in the presence of God. Soon, those who have kept the faith will be rewarded.>

"You forget the accepted interpretation of that prophecy, Rashael," Krzysztof said. "This woman is a harbinger of doom, and a forerunner of hell. To trust her is to coddle the viper from the Garden to our breast."

"I'm a harbinger of no one's doom," Sarine snapped back. "I don't know your prophecies or your scriptures. All I know is I came here to find friends, to help me fight against the darkness that's been poisoning the world. If you don't want to help me, then fine, I'll go on my way. But if you want to fight—"

<*We will,*> Rashael said at once. <*You will have no swords more stalwart than the Skovan. But it will take convincing. My interpretation of the scripture led us here, at this hour, to meet you in this chapel. That alone must count for something.*>

"They won't listen," Krzysztof said. "They will call it coincidence, nothing more."

<*They will hear her words, and their hearts will be opened by the Holy Spirit. I know it to be true.*>

"Who is 'they'?" she asked

"The Council of the Archbishops," Krzysztof said. "High heads of our Church. Rashael would have me take you to them."

"And they can agree to help me retake the Soul?"

"This is folly," Krzysztof said, at the same moment Rashael said, <*Yes. He will take you before them, while I plead to the Seraphim for aid. But my bond-partner speaks the truth: Your words must be chosen with care, and your tongue blessed by God. There is grave danger, if the council prove to be fools who cannot see the truth. If you walk in fear and not in faith, all will falter.*>

"I'm not afraid," she said. "We have a chance to retake the Soul of the World, and I need allies to do it. I'll go to them at once, if you can lead me."

<*Then go, with the blessing of the angels, Veil Reborn,*> Rashael said. <*I have faith you will prevail.*>

52

YULI

Medical Ward
Rasailles Shelter *Dome*

She held the priestess's hand as her body went limp.

Another dead. The Twin Fangs sensed it as soon as the moment arrived, before the eyes rolled up, before the last breath escaped the lungs. Yuli knelt beside her and spoke a prayer. Not a prayer the priestess would have recognized, but then, piety was piety. She leaned close, urging the spirit to stay behind and finish its last business before departing on in peace and comfort to join its ancestors. Calm whispers kept the dead from manifesting as malevolent spirits.

Reed stopped abruptly in front of her. "She's dead, isn't she?" Reed said. The girl's white dress—now four sizes too small, if it had ever fit her—was stained red with blood. She'd taken to wearing a belt with pouches hung from its loops, each one full of gauze, cotton swabs, medicinal herbs, thread and needles for stitches, though she hadn't given up wearing the brace of pistols holstered at her sides.

"She is," Yuli said simply. She let the priestess's hand go, placing it gently against the woman's chest. Sores and bruises covered the skin, the same marks covering every patient in the ward. Impossible to miss the common link: Every binder under the Empress's dome had the sickness, save a bare handful, all of whom were showing the first signs of the cough, all except the Empress herself.

Reed let the tray she'd been carrying fall with a crash. It stirred the Twin Fangs' reflexes, but Reed was already storming away. The food she'd carried lay in the mud, a bowl of oats and honey soft enough to soothe the throats of those in the last stages of the cough.

She watched her go. The girl had missed her calling as a doctor; she'd seen it in the way Reed had stared and studied whenever the nurses came to tend her wounds. Perhaps it wasn't too late for her to find a way to set her pistols down. But then, it wasn't Yuli's place to set her course, nor to calm her anger. She took up a cloth and washed her hands in the basin beside the corpse, then got up and set to telling the gravediggers there would be another to add to their day's work.

One or two had begun to pass each day; soon there would be no binders left. It made her fearful—What if the sickness infected anyone with magic? What of her sisters? What of Tigai?—but those thoughts did nothing for her now. She let them drift past her, practicing the warrior's art of focus on the here and now. Tigai would find his way back. So would Sarine. Both could walk the starfield and the strands. Both would come as soon as they could. Neither was dead. She was sure of that, as sure as she could be of anything.

She left the gravediggers and walked toward the stableyard, through the network of roped-off sections claimed by families in lieu of proper housing, or even tents. Glittering pale blue shone overhead, a faux-sky made by the Empress's dome. It almost seemed to invert itself when she didn't look up at it directly, until the dome became a great eye, lidless, staring at them from on high.

The horse-handlers knew her on sight, and they bowed as she approached. Commotion made the Empress's presence obvious even at a distance. In a Natarii city she might have demurred for a chief, but here she was the Empress's equal, both of them sworn champions to Sarine Thibeaux. Better if Erris didn't forget it.

"You leave today, then, Your Majesty?" she asked.

The conversation Erris had been having with her aides died when Yuli spoke.

"Yes," the Empress said. "Or tomorrow. At the first break in the rains. Have you changed your mind, and decided to do your duty?"

"I'm doing it," she said. "By remaining here. And so should you. Sarine will come for us, and will have need of us when she does."

Erris shook her head. "The girl is none of my concern."

The Twin Fangs growled inside her. She almost mirrored it, but preserved her composure.

"Another of your priests died," she said instead. "Are you sure you'll find anyone alive in the south?"

"If you aren't coming with us, then leave," Erris said. "There are preparations to attend to."

She remained, and went quiet, watching the Empress with as cool a look as she could manage. Erris turned back to her aides.

She wished Tigai were here. He would have known what to say, been able to find the lever to move her. His tongue was silver, in all the ways her sisters teased her for, and more. Leaving was wrong. This was where Sarine and Tigai would return, when they could. The storms and poison rains had come because Sarine needed her champions, and hadn't had them; she was certain of it. It was their fault, hers and Erris's and Arak'Jur's.

"What are you doing?" one of Erris's aides said, approaching her gruffly from the side. She turned and recognized Colonel Marquand, the red-faced drunk whom Erris had tried to put in charge of her and Sarine and the others.

She ignored him, keeping up her stare at the Empress's back, until he grabbed her by the arm.

"I said what the fuck do you think you're—" Marquand continued, until she wrenched free, giving the Twin Fangs control enough for strength, and a white glow behind her eyes. A growl slipped loose, too, and Marquand held up his hands in a gesture of peace.

"You can't come here and berate her," Marquand said, finding a slightly more conciliatory tone now that the Twin Fangs vied with Yuli for control.

"I can call her a fool if she's being a fool," she said. By now Erris had moved on, sparing not so much as a glance backward at her as the aides moved to inspect a wagon.

"No, you bloody well can't," Marquand said. "Not unless you want to start threatening everyone under this dome. These are her people. They'll obey her orders, even if it means being on the wrong side of your anger. You won't convince anyone of anything if you start resorting to violence."

She said nothing, resuming her stare at the Empress's back.

"Why do you think she's being a fool?" Marquand asked. "She's traveling south to set up more cities like this one, more *Shelter* domes that can sustain themselves against the rains. She should have done it weeks ago, once it was clear this dome would stay up. The last thing she needs is thorns in her side telling her to stay here and sacrifice the rest of her people for the sake of her fear."

"I'm not afraid," she said, still lacing her words with the Twin Fangs' heat.

"Aren't you?" Marquand said. "She needs every hand, and from what I can see you're strong enough to travel, even in these rains. There are still beasts out there, and brigands, too. Do you want to let civilization die because one of the damned New World devil-wolves chances upon Her Majesty on the road?"

"I don't care about a thousand deaths, or ten thousand," she said. "Not when Sarine needs us. We need to stay here, so she can come for us. She needs us to fight to change the world. You of all of them should understand. Sarine isn't fighting to save a village, or a city. She's fighting for the world's soul, and we have to stay where she can find us, when she comes."

"Look around," Marquand said. "The fight is over. Sarine lost. In all likelihood she's dead, and so are those who went with her. I'm sorry, but—"

She hit him in the mouth, or the Twin Fangs did, before she knew she'd thrown the punch. A wet smack sounded as his head spun sideways, then another when he fell on his side into the mud.

She started forward to help him up.

"Bloody fuck," Marquand said, rubbing his jaw. "Ow."

"I'm sorry," she said. "I didn't mean to—"

Pops sounded in the distance. Two whipcracks that might have been dropped crates or split wood. The Twin Fangs knew better. If she hadn't just given in and let it have control, she might have held back. Instead her body began to change, and she moved.

"Was that pistol shot?" Marquand said, but the Twin Fangs was already shifting Yuli's body to hairless knots of muscle and bone.

It ran.

Sulfur and black powder stung its nose. It dropped to all fours, racing past the horse-lines, the ropes that divided the camp into this plot and that. Close. A hundred paces at the Twin Fangs' loping gait.

Blood. It tasted it on the air, sweet and pure, taking in the taste with the smell.

A girl lay against a barrel, clutching a wound across her belly. A red line traced through a white dress smeared with soot and dirt. Yuli's horror rose beneath the Twin Fangs' senses. Reed. That was the girl's name. She lay against the barrel, her hand quivering as it held a smoking pistol, breathing too quickly, staring ahead into the bush.

"He wasn't supposed to be here," Reed said. "Intruder. I shot him. That way."

The Twin Fangs wanted to help her die. The girl's wound was already mortal, a deep red gash through her belly. It could speed the death, rip the entrails free with a tug of its claws in an act of mercy and sated hunger, both at once. Yuli fought it down. Not the girl. The man. The man Reed had named intruder. The man who'd killed her friend, though with a stomach wound like that Reed would be hours, maybe days in the dying. Find him.

As quickly as she thought it, the Twin Fangs picked up the scent. Steel coated in blood. Blood and...something else. Something vile. Poison. It snarled and charged into the bush.

Reed was right. She'd shot the intruder. The man was crouched, dabbing fingers in the blood from a gunshot wound in his side. He was tall, thick-muscled, and black-skinned. Yuli knew the Bhakal on sight; no wonder Reed had reacted by drawing her pistol. There were no Bhakal living under the dome. But this man was here, carrying a thin, curved sword wet with blood. And the Twin Fangs sensed another. A woman, hiding farther back in the bushes, with the same Bhakal scent. But first, the man.

It bounded through the bush, swiping with both claws in a furious rush. It should have gored him, smashing his bones and ripping his organs through his skin. But he moved.

He moved, too fast, like a gale wind, springing forward and whipping the Twin Fangs' back with the edge of his blade, all in a smooth, twisting motion. Pain burned like fire across its back. Its skin split and hissed with the poison coating the Bhakal's blade.

It whirled around, ready for its enemy's speed.

The man's sword flicked, darting a strike to the left and another from the top, fast enough that both seemed to happen at once. The Twin Fangs raked one of its claws through the air, clanging metal on bone, parrying the strike while the other claw knifed toward his body and struck home.

It seized the skin where the Bhakal had already been shot, wrenching a chunk of flesh free with a spray of blood.

The Bhakal spun in a whirlwind. His blade took the Twin Fangs across the face, gashing through its snout and breaking its teeth. It sprang into him. Both claws plunged into his belly as it stabbed furiously, piercing with the needle points at the tips of each of its fingers. The Bhakal drove his blade into the Twin Fangs from behind, ripping through its shoulder. Both screamed, the man and the Twin Fangs, until he wrenched the sword upward. The Twin Fangs hurled him forward, ripping the sword from his hand as the Bhakal smashed to the ground. Steel protruded from the Twin Fangs' left shoulder, burning and hissing and poisoning its blood. But for now, its enemy was beaten, crumpled in the grass.

The air heated around it.

It dove by instinct as the air exploded over its head.

The woman.

"Omera!" the woman cried. "My Omera! No!"

It needed to change direction, to strike from unexpected angles. It bounded sideways, keeping low as the air heated again, ripping open in a gout of fire.

The woman had both arms raised, approaching where the Twin Fangs had been with cautious steps. She was Bhakal, too—black-skinned and cold-eyed, surveying the bush where the swordsman had fallen to the Twin Fangs' claws.

Sense dictated patience. Erris's soldiers would be on their way. All it had to do was wait. Lie here in the bush, unseen, and ensure that this woman made no attempt to escape. But those were Yuli's thoughts. The woman was an enemy. She pulsed with blood and heat, ready for the Twin Fangs' claws to split her open and spill it out.

The woman knelt over the swordsman's body, and sparks flashed blue, illuminating the bush.

The body vanished.

Magic. Something to take the swordsman away. The woman would follow.

It sprang at her, baring claws and both elongated fangs. The woman moved, as fast as the swordsman had; faster, even. But where the man had met the Twin Fangs with poison and steel, the woman's eyes were full of shock.

White light flared between them. It gripped the woman around her forearm as the white light burned, trying to throw the Twin Fangs back, hissing and smoking as it threatened to hurl them apart.

The blue sparks flashed again.

For an instant it recognized the plane of infinite sparks and torrents. Sarine's place. It held tight to the woman's body, feeling a rush of energy as it collided with another column, until the streams of sparks and colors ran together, red and black and blue and purple.

They reappeared. A pale moon shone overhead, through a dense canopy of trees and vines.

It was somewhere else. A jungle. But it still held the woman by the forearm, and now the white light was gone. It crushed the woman's muscle in its claws, smashing bone and sinew as it severed her forearm in its grip.

The woman's hand and what was left of her forearm dropped to the jungle floor. It hadn't expected her flesh to give way so easily, not after she had put up such resistance before. It stumbled, for only the barest moment. But it was enough for the woman to jerk away, wearing a look of hatred as the blue sparks flashed again, and she vanished.

The Twin Fangs howled.

Its body had been stabbed, burned, poisoned, cut, nearly torn apart. Pain flooded its senses. Its prey had escaped. It stood alone under a canopy of jungle leaves and vines, its skin charred and smoking. The swordsman was here, crumpled in the undergrowth, rolled on his back, exposing the cuts and gashes the Twin Fangs had torn in his belly. Unconscious. No threat. It had already bested the man. No satisfaction in devouring his blood when the true prey had escaped.

Yuli resumed control. The gashes and pain mirrored themselves on her skin; a savage wound torn in her shoulder, another down her back, a deep cut across her mouth and jaw, burn marks and boils, red skin and heat in her veins where poison traced its way through her blood. It hurt. But she'd recovered from worse.

She hobbled to where the swordsman lay, kneeling to check for signs of life. He was breathing, light and shallow. An enemy, an assassin. She tore away his shirt, folding it and tightening it around his stomach to hold his guts in. He'd used magic, when the Twin Fangs had fought him. If his magic was strong, it would save him, but she would do what she could to aid it in his recovery.

Perhaps he would know something of where they were, and how they'd come to be here. It wasn't like Tigai's gift, with stars and strands. It had been the blue sparks and the torrents, on what she recognized as Sarine's Infinite Plane. Perhaps the swordsman would have the same gift, or some knowledge of how they might return.

Tears fell as she worked. He had to survive. He had to know. How else would she find the way back to Sarine and Tigai?

53

OMERA

Manacambu Highlands
The Southern Continent

A woman knelt nearby, tending the beginnings of a fire.

He smelled it before his eyes opened. No *ubax aragti* burned in his blood, but his senses had been sharpened by years of its use. He tried to keep still, to ignore the lingering pain in his stomach and pretend he was still sleeping. He drew even, slow breaths, keeping his eyes closed and listening for some sign of who she was, and how they came to be here.

"You're awake," the woman said. "That's a good sign, at least. I'm sure you'll be fit for travel by midday."

She said it with irony in her voice. A sign of familiarity with him, perhaps, though he didn't know her. And she spoke perfect Bhakal. The same accent he'd heard every day, growing up in...nowhere. The memory bled away faster than he could grasp it. He was...someone. From somewhere. But he couldn't remember either.

"Omera, right?" the woman said. "That's your name? It's what she called out, during our fight. The woman who brought us here." He said nothing. Was he Omera? It fit like an untailored drape of fabric. And a woman...a fight. Memory blurred, but this time it came back, slowly. He remembered a dome of pale blue light. A dance beneath it. *Shotel* sword and claws. He cut his enemy. Then knifing pains in his stomach, a flash of blue sparks, and...

"You might as well stop pretending to be asleep," the woman said. "I've been nursing you for four days now. If I meant to kill you, you'd have long since been dead."

He opened his eyes.

The woman was no one he knew. Pale white skin, wearing an unfamiliar style of leather shirt and breeches. Hair so light it was almost the color of silver, bound in a thick braid by cords running down the length of her back. But his eyes went to the markings on her face. Intricate patterns traced her cheekbones, up to the bridge of her nose and forehead, ringing her eyes in black lines that evoked the shape of fangs dripping blood down her cheeks. Two fangs. The creature he'd fought. Fear kindled in him, and he flinched back, sending shooting pains through his belly.

"Careful," the woman said. "Don't try to move. I did my best with the stitchwork, but I'm no seamstress. Lurch around over there and you'll rip yourself open."

"Where," he said. It hurt. Instinct wanted him to flinch from the pain, but he kept calm, refraining from flexing his stomach. Better if he didn't pass out again. This woman was his enemy, whatever she claimed about nursing him.

"Where are we?" the woman said. "I don't know. I was hoping you might have an idea. Your friend took us here. It looks like southern Jun, near the Empire's heart, but there are birds here I've not seen in any Jun menagerie."

He closed his eyes again. He should be dead. The pain from his stomach shot through him in waves, in time with his heartbeat.

"Need," he said, wincing and gritting his teeth. "Need herbs."

The word changed her demeanor. "Your herbs," she said. "The ones you used to fight. I took them, in case you had any ideas about resuming what you started, under the dome."

"Not fight," he said. "Heal."

"Not fight?" she repeated. "You hurt my friend, back there. I'm sure you meant to do more. To kill the Empress, perhaps? Or were you there for me? In any case, I'm not a fool. I've done what I can for you, but unless you can demonstrate some value for me I'm not about to re-arm you with your magic."

"Value," he said. "Yes. I know...how to get home."

"Do you?"

"Yes," he said. Even with *calimnus re* for healing he was still days away from fighting form. But he had to survive those days for any hope. If survival required a lie, then he would tell one. "I know how. Give me my herbs. I can show you the way."

The woman watched him carefully. He lay still. His sword was nowhere in sight; if she'd taken his herb pouches, it stood to reason she'd taken his *shotel*, too. Playing along with what she needed to hear meant he might have both again soon. Then he could find the woman he was meant to kill. The Empress...or...his memory blurred. Sakhefete. Was that her name?

"I suppose I don't have much choice, do I?" the woman said finally. She rose, then disappeared from sight behind a looming, crooked tree draped with vines. He counted, trying to judge from her pace how far away his herbs and sword were hidden. Twenty seconds. They were close. But then, he couldn't move yet. Until his stomach healed, his herbs and sword could have been on the far side of the world.

"Here," she said, kneeling beside him. She had his belt in hand, scabbard and pouches attached, though the sword was missing. "Which do you need?"

"*Calimnus re*," he said. "Fine powder. Green."

She tried two pouches before she found it, wetting her fingers with saliva and dipping them to coat both in its contents. "Only a pinch, for now," she said. "Once you can walk, you show me where, then we go together. You get more when I'm satisfied you're telling the truth."

He nodded. Whatever she needed to hear. "Long way," he said. "Through the jungle. Toward the river." There would always be a river. Once he had his strength back, he could evade her if she proved to be too much of a nuisance.

She offered her fingers, and he took both in his mouth, tilting his head to press the herb-coated tips against his gums. She understood what he wanted quick enough, pressing harder. Too hard. And too strong a dose. Her pinch was enough to have him convulsing, spewing his stomach into the gutter like some wine-drunk laborer in the early hours of the morning. It didn't matter. It would heal him all the faster so long as he didn't die. He couldn't die. He had to find someone. The Queen. His memory blurred again. His enemy. Erris d'Arrent. No. He resisted it. Not her. Another woman, and a gray-haired man. Erris d'Arrent. It felt wrong, but that was the woman he was meant to kill. Erris d'Arrent. But even as he remembered the name, a different face surfaced in his mind. He latched onto the memory as *calimnus re* ignited in his veins. His body seized as his mind clung to the face. The silver-haired warrior withdrew her fingers in a snap. He shook, and the world faded away as he collapsed, but he kept the image in his mind: his mother's sister. His mother. His...

He sucked in a sharp breath. His belly itched and burned, but his muscles surged. Memory and mind clawed through the haze as he bolted up from a long sleep.

His movement startled the woman awake. She sprang to her feet beside their fire like a cat, suddenly crouched low and ready, whipping her head toward him. Had her features changed? He remembered her tall and pale-skinned, but suddenly her limbs were longer and thinner, her hands marked by the beginnings of claws, her head narrowed to a feral glare, her eyes burning white like two full moons.

Breath came hard. He ignored the pain, and rose to his feet. Slowly. She watched him like a dog unsure whether he was a danger to her pack. Better to show her he was strong again, without being too strong. No; if they were to resume their fight, he needed more time. He needed the rest of his herbs and his sword. He had to find a way back. He had to find his true enemy. Erris d'Arrent. No. Someone else.

"You heal quickly," the woman said. The feral cast to her features had lessened, or perhaps it had only been a trick of the firelight in the darkness surrounding them.

"You gave me too strong a dose," he said. "But it doesn't matter. I can walk. We can go."

"You can walk?" she asked. "Six hours ago you couldn't cough without passing out."

"I'm fine," he said, making a show of standing firm on both legs. He might keel over if he took a step, but *calimnus re* worked quickly. His body would catch up to his will, if he demanded it.

She straightened to join him on her feet. He saw markings on her he hadn't noticed before: signs of wounds on her neck, red and sore, that looked as though they continued on under her leathers. Places he'd struck with his *shotel* during their duel. He remembered more clearly now. So, she could heal quickly, too. Perhaps more quickly than he could. Good to know. If it came to a fight, he would have to kill her cleanly, and fast.

"Take a moment," she said. "You're acting like a fresh-bonded girl trying to impress her sisters."

His impulse was to insist he was fine; enough of the herb still blazed in his veins to keep him moving. But if she needed to see weakness to trust him, he could show it. He moved to kneel beside her fire, reached for a skin of water and downed it hungrily.

"I'm Yuli," the woman said after a moment. "Twin Fangs Clan Hoskar."

"Omera," he said. "First Prince and Son of..." Who? The name was almost there. Mother. Someone. "...the Bhakal," he finished.

"One of Amanishiakne's sons?" Yuli said. "My husband-to-be and my sisters went to fight alongside her, before the world changed. Perhaps you knew them? Tigai. Sarine. Namkat. Juni. Kitian. Imyan."

He heard nothing she'd said beyond the first name.

Amanishiakne.

It rang like a bell in his ears. He clutched it tighter than anything else he knew. A woman with polished stone skin, bright and regal as any jewel, revered and distant as any mountain, unknowable and terrible and full of wrath. A woman who saw the comings of floods, of tides and storms. A woman who sat astride the web of fate, picking and weaving a path for her children, for all the peoples of the Bhakal. A woman who made him spiced oats and honey with her own hand. A woman who loved him, who let him run free through her palace, laughing when her guards tried to catch him after he'd stolen an extra portion from the kitchens.

His mind was broken. Glass shards hung where memories should be. The name fused them together. He was Omera. Not an ill-fitting garment. That was the name the Queen had spoken, when she'd set him the tasks required for his greatness. Omera. Amanishiakne's son.

"Omera?" Yuli asked. "Are you well? Should you lie down again?"

"Forgive me," he said. Amanishiakne. The name shone through him with a heavy light. And Sakhefete. That was the name of his enemy. His true enemy. "Forgive me for all I did to wrong you. If you and your family are friends of my mother, then we are allies."

She looked uneasy, studying him without moving.

"I mean it," he said. "What happened before…I was under the control of my mother's enemies. Sakhefete." It helped to say that name, too, anchoring it in his memory before it could slip away. "Sakhefete was…is…her sister. Her sister." Memory snapped into place. "She and the…old man did something to me. They forced me to go to the dome, to try and assassinate your Empress. I remember now. They are my enemies, not you."

The feral cast returned to Yuli's features, and this time it was no trick of the light. Her limbs grew longer, thinner, but more muscular. Claws extended from her fingertips. Her eyes widened.

"How can I trust you?" she said. "You said you knew this place, and you knew a way home. Start there. Do you?"

"No," he said quickly. "It was a lie. I intended to mislead you long enough to regain my strength, then to kill you and leave your body in the jungle."

A low growl came from Yuli's throat.

"Would I admit it now, if you were still my enemy?" he asked. "You and I have no quarrel, unless you choose to punish me for what Sakhefete did to my mind. But if you would have me as an ally, we can find her together. We can find a way back together."

She stared at him. Fear blossomed in him from her eyes. Those were wolf's eyes. A predator sighting him on an empty plain, with no room to run or hide. He held his ground. Memory wavered, but it was there. Sakhefete had compelled him to do evil in her name. Amanishiakne was Queen. Amanishiakne had shared a vision with him, a vision of…glass broke and cracked in his mind, leaving all the details and stories of his life in shattered disarray. But the two names held him in place.

Yuli's head whipped around.

"Something," she said. "Something on the wind."

"Sakhefete?" he asked.

"No. Something large. Too large. Moving fast. Coming toward us."

"And? What?"

She darted away, loping on all fours as her limbs stretched even further.

He followed her around the trunk of a great tree draped with vines, and almost fell when a bundle slapped into his chest.

His sword, with its scabbard and his herbs.

"Use them, if you're our ally," Yuli said. Her voice had changed to scraping metal, a deep rumbling that only shared a tone with her normal voice. "Be ready."

He buckled the belt, and left his *shotel* drawn in his hand. His body wasn't ready for a fight, but herbs could do what muscle and bone couldn't. He dabbed a finger in his pouch of *ubax aragti*, then another in the pouch of *tisa irinti*, mixing both as he rubbed them into his gums.

He was the swordsman, born and trained for war.

His senses settled into a rhythm with the jungle around them. Leaves dripped rainwater from the canopy above, hissing and steaming where it landed in the undergrowth. Wind blew through the trees, rattling vines and dead brush. The pattern shifted to the east. The rhythm changed. Insects, birds, raindrops, plants, all gave way for…A crashing sound echoed in the faintest part of his ear. Crashing. Something too large for the jungle, like thunder rolling through the trees. And something else. Smaller. Human-sized. Something close.

"Someone coming," he said.

Yuli hissed for quiet. "Be ready" was all she said, and by now she was fully changed. Her body was hairless, all sign of her clothing gone and replaced by leathery sinew and gray flesh. Claws the length of her forearm protruded from each finger, and her mouth and nose had elongated into a wolfish snout marked by two terrible fangs, curved and dripping black blood from her jaw.

He set his feet, and kept his sword level. A waist-high grip.

"Wait," Yuli said in her metal voice. "We know him. We know his smell."

The crashing was close enough now that he would have heard it without *tisa irinti* sharpening his ears.

Yuli snapped her snout toward him, almost growling: "Wait!"

A man appeared, leaping between the trees like a bounding leopard. A tall, powerful, bronze-skinned man, moving faster than anyone without herbs or some other magic could have managed. He flowed through the jungle as though he'd been born to it, flying between leaps and barely touching down with his feet before he pushed off to leap again.

Blood marred the man's chest. Wounds crisscrossed his rib cage as though he'd been flayed with a knife.

The man saw them, and switched course on his next leap. Too fast to see if Omera hadn't had herbs burning in his veins. But recognition dawned in the man's eyes. Recognition, determination, and fear.

"Arak'Jur!" Yuli half snarled. "What are you doing here?"

"Run," the newcomer called to them. "By the spirits, run!"

The jungle crashed behind him. A deep boom, as though the earth itself moved in his wake. Rolling thunder roared as the newcomer—Arak'Jur—reached them and, without stopping, kept up his leaping flight.

Omera turned as Yuli did. Both followed, and *tisa irinti* erased the urge to look over his shoulder as they ran.

54

ERRIS

Wheat Fields
Outside Villecours

White pearls slid through her. She was a conduit between the physical world and the reserves lurking behind the leylines. They threatened to drown her, to smother and overwhelm her meager body. She was a woman, and the reserves were infinite. She held against their tide, directing the endless waves of *Shelter* with sheer force of will.

Ghostly blue walls sprang into being, but she couldn't open her eyes to look. The work was everything. Mind, memory, thought fled against the tide of white. The engineers who had first erected the Great Barrier around the colonies had worked with teams of thousands, there to believe in the power of what was done. That was the key: belief. She needed every pair of eyes in these fields today. They had to believe they were protected by the barrier in order for the *Shelter* to replenish itself and become self-sustaining. Until their faith took hold, she was there to seal any gaps with fresh reserves.

Sweat beaded on her skin. She held.

A gap threatened to tear in the west, near the first foundations she'd laid when the work began this morning. Attention diverted there, and fresh strands of *Shelter* snapped in place. Another hole ripped open overhead, enough to let a few droplets of toxic rain through. It was almost done. A lattice the size of nine city blocks stood around them, encompassing the whole of this field and two others beneath her dome. Four hundred and sixteen survivors stood at her side, there to put faith in her protection. It was enough now. She'd set the foundations in place. It fell to them to believe.

An hour passed. The strands flew through her, until suddenly they stopped. A jolting halt, as though she'd ridden Jiri into a stone wall.

The pearls settled, groaning and then resting atop each other in one final spasm and release. They were solid.

It was done.

She shivered as the leyline tethers slipped from her hands. The old scars throbbed on the backs of her palms. It would have taken a hundred binders working with a year's worth of reserves to do what she'd managed in a day. Her bond as champion gave access to an infinite pool, where strands of pearls, whorls of *Body*, *Entropy*, *Death*, and all the rest waited for her to summon them from nothing. It violated every principle of science and natural philosophy, but the proof was written here, in the shields she'd conjured around these farms.

Weeping sounds greeted her as her senses returned. The survivors. Some stared up at the new dome shimmering above them. Others wept into the shoulder of a spouse, or held tight to a dear friend. Mothers clutched children close to their breasts; a miracle there were any children left.

"You are more than an Empress," a woman said, a young mother standing close. "You are a Goddess. The Exarch come again."

Tiredness stung behind her eyes as she shook her head. Others took up the sentiment.

"You've saved us today," a man said.

"A miracle," said another. "A wonder."

"Goddess." "Empress." "Savior."

Thank the Gods for Marquand, there to see her as the woman she was, exhausted past the point of breaking. He took her shoulder without a word, supporting her as she walked through the crowd. Their faith had the dome shimmering, a crystalline sheen of pale blue. Voices muddled as Marquand led her to the bedroll she'd prepared. She should have eaten first. Instead she collapsed in her full uniform.

The voices around her dimmed as Marquand shouted, "Give her peace, you bloody animals. Let her sleep. Let her bloody fucking sleep!"

She did.

———————

She blinked awake to the smells of fire, and roasting meat. Sleep weighed heavy behind her eyes, but her soldier's training took over. Once awake, she was awake. She sat up, and Marquand offered a haunch of beef on an iron skewer with a pewter cup of water to wash it down. She took both, grateful he'd been attentive enough to stay by her side.

"They were meant for me," he said as she mumbled thanks around her first bite. "But you look like death. Figure I can wait."

Hot juices warmed her throat as she chewed. The water was warm, but clean. It sent energy through her as surely as if she'd tethered *Body*, though the prospect of any tethers at all recoiled her muscles by instinct. Soreness echoed her every movement, turned to stiffness by sleep.

"How long was I out?" she asked.

"Not long," Marquand replied. "Five, six hours maybe. Hard to tell without the sun for a cue."

She nodded and chewed again. It hurt her jaw, but her stomach's greed overpowered the soreness elsewhere. A day or two here would cure her fatigue, but there was no time. With the barrier in place all that remained here was to make sure the survivors were set up with stores and stocks before they rode for Lorrine. They'd need messengers, too, with swift horses and canvas tarps against the rain. Word would spread, now that Villecours had a dome. More survivors would show themselves, and come.

"Is that what you did at Rasailles?" Marquand asked quietly.

It took a moment to register that he meant the dome. "Yes," she said. "More or less. It took longer."

"Damnedest bloody thing," he said. The last thing she needed was for Marquand to join the chorus of wondering eyes; blessedly he said it looking down at the grass, shaking his head in disbelief instead of reverence.

"I tried to help, you know," he said. "When you were in the thick of it, after the outer walls had been set. So did the priests. Felt like we were fucking pissing in the ocean. Used up the leylines' stores here in less time than we might have spent with the pissing. And you kept going. Somehow."

"You know about the bond," she said. "You know what it does."

"One thing to know, another to see," he said. "You're not careful you're going to kill yourself, handling that much energy. A bloody fucking wonder you even woke up. And you mean to do it again in Lorrine?"

"In Lorrine, in l'Euilliard, in Covendon, all the way to the Thellan isles."

"You're bloody fucking mad," he said.

"This is what it takes," she said. "We're going to survive. This is how."

"You're not going to bloody survive the week, you keep this up," he said.

She took another bite. There was no other course. Talking was wasted energy. She chewed and felt the warmth spread from her belly. *Body* would be there, once she had a firmer foundation, and she'd be back on her feet as soon as she was finished with her meal.

Survivors had noticed she was awake, and began to drift closer, eyeing her with the sort of reverence usually reserved for priests. None approached yet, thank the Gods.

They'd already laid preparations for what would become the Villecours camp: bedrolls, pillows, blankets, stores of food, crates of iron nails, stockpiles of wood, parchments, books, ropes and stakes, livestock, horses, cats and dogs. She'd given the same instructions here as she'd done at Rasailles: no walls or tents, nothing between the survivors and the dome to dilute the protection of its *Shelter*. With only four hundred souls to sustain it she'd had to settle for a smaller area, but given the once-fertile soil of these farms there should be enough to keep these people alive for a season of planting and harvest. After that, babies would be born. Children would grow, and civilization would find itself again. They had to endure a year of nightmares, but they would survive. Somehow.

Her meat was finished too soon; she licked every juice from her fingers, downed every drop of warm water from her cup. Then she blinked, snapping a *Body* tether in place to spread the heat from her belly through her limbs, and she rose to her feet.

That seemed to be the cue for the survivors to descend, and they moved in unison as she strode toward the rope lines.

"Empress," one called. Then another: "Thank you. Thank you."

She muttered acknowledgment with as much grace as she could manage. Most of them deferred, making way and returning to the tasks of establishing the camp. Only a small girl stood directly in her path. A child, still in a white dress, holding up both hands crossed against her chest, displaying the scars of the binder's test across the backside of both palms.

She stopped.

"Thank you, Empress d'Arrent," the girl said with a practiced air. A trail of snot ran from the girl's nose as she said it, and she sniffled.

"What's your name?" she asked.

"Thérèse de Maritain," the girl replied. "I'm seven. But I'm not going to become a priest. I'm going to join the army, like you did."

"Oh?" she said. The girl's father lingered a few paces away, clear from the way he stood that Thérèse belonged to him. He looked at the daughter with tenderness, and to her with something closer to awe.

"I've already learned to ride," Thérèse said proudly, coughing into her hands and continuing on without pause. "Next summer I'm going to learn to shoot. I'm going rabbit hunting. The priest said I could see red, which means *Body*. So I'll be a great fighter."

"I've no doubt you will," she said. "The world always has need for soldiers.

Here under the dome your farmers will need protection while they work to sow seeds for the next harvest. Will you promise me you'll keep them safe?"

Thérèse began a solemn nod before coughing again into the scar on the back of her hand. "I will," she said. "I promise."

"I'll hold you to that duty, soldier," she said. She met the father's eyes, giving him a hard look. In better times the girl might have done precisely as she said. Gifted children taken by the army could be a point of pride for even the lowliest families. But harder times were ahead, and both of them knew it without saying a word.

The girl offered her a salute, clenched fist to chest, and she returned it. Pride beamed in the girl's eyes as she and Marquand continued on toward the horses.

"You know that little girl has it," Marquand said quietly after they were away. "The sickness."

She *tsk*ed for silence. Yes, she knew. The mucus leaking from the girl's nose could be dismissed as childish uncleanliness, but the coughs were a telltale sign. There would be blood in those coughs before the month was through. Then the fever, the long days of sleep, and finally . . . None had survived it yet, though her doctors assured her some might pull through. All but a handful of her priests had at least the cough, though she and Marquand had conscripted the healthiest for this journey.

They were already waiting at the rope-lines. Five of their brown-robed companions attended to their horses or watched as Villecours survivors did it for them; two would remain behind here, Sister Joyeuse and Brother Charyn. Both monks were hale and strong. They aided the others, saying tearful goodbyes interrupted by her and Marquand's approach.

"Jiri is ready, Your Majesty," Sister Joyeuse said with a perfunctory bow. She was young, and bright, with no sign yet of the sickness. Part of why Erris had chosen her for this mission. A sign from New Sarresant that all was well in hand.

"You two are my designates here," she said, going to Jiri's side to check her saddle and stirrups and stroke the side of her neck. "Remember it. You speak with my voice, even when we aren't connected through *Need*."

"Yes, Your Majesty," Sister Joyeuse and Brother Charyn said together. Then Charyn said alone, "We won't let you down, Majesty. Your work here will stand for a hundred years, I swear it."

She nodded at his zeal. That sort of belief and passion would be required to make it through the planting season to come. It stung to leave behind any of her priests, each one skilled with *Shelter* enough to maintain the domes and create entrances for venting smoke, for trade and what meager scavenging and hunting they could manage. But the survivors here at Villecours had no *Shelter* binders of their own. Gods send there would at least be one or two with the survivors in Lorrine.

"Finish the rest of our preparations," she said to the others. "We leave as soon as I've connected to Rasailles."

Marquand took charge, inspecting their saddlebags, their tack and canteens. She left him to it. A tree stump offered a seat beside Jiri's hitching post, all too inviting for her to lie against it and drift off back to sleep. Instead she closed her eyes and found *Need*. What had once been a field of golden light had dimmed to a few scattered sparks. Her vessels. So many dead now, or dying. But she found the ones she needed, to the north under the first of her *Shelter* domes and the protection it offered against the toxic sky. She snapped the tether into place, and her senses lurched across the void between them.

Coughing sounded in her ears. Violent and bloody.

Her vessel's chest burned, and she convulsed, dry-heaving between coughs.

"Majesty," Doña Portega said quietly. "Welcome. The lieutenant and I were just discussing ranging plans to the north."

She withdrew a handkerchief from her vessel's uniform pocket, using it to wipe blood from her chin. When they'd left, Lieutenant Cornaille had been healthy, without sign of the cough. A quick turn, if there was already blood.

She cleared her vessel's throat. "The army?" she said. Her vessel's voice was hoarse and dry.

"Yes, Majesty," her Minister of State said. "We've yet to make direct contact with Royens's Corps, or the remnants of the Jun. But we'll need them, all the more so with so many of our *Shelter* binders gone south with you."

"We took what we needed to ensure the creation of new domes," she said. "We don't need to go over the dangers again."

"Of course, Majesty," Doña Portega said. "But as I'd feared, the sickness is spreading. This is why Lieutenant Cornaille and I were discussing plans to redouble our ranging to the north. We'll need army binders, and soon. Two weeks, perhaps, say the doctors."

She let out a breath, and felt every stinging cut in her vessel's lungs and throat. Another cough bubbled up; she fought it down, and lost, expelling a loud hack as though the sickness was rooted in her own body, and not her vessel's. A spasm of coughing followed, matting the outer parts of her handkerchief with blood.

Doña Portega waited patiently for her to finish, but there was strain there, behind the Thellan noblewoman's eyes. A strain that had grown in the days since she and Marquand rode south.

"Two weeks," she said when the coughing was done. "What do you mean?"

"Forgive me, Majesty," Doña Portega said. "I know you've no wish to retread settled ground, but I did warn that leaving us only two *Shelter* binders was a risk..."

"Get to the point," she said. "What's happened? Brother Gerille is sick? Mother Fabienne?"

"Both," Doña Portega said. "Both, almost at once. And progressing rapidly, along the same course."

She swore.

"We knew this could happen, Majesty," Doña Portega said. "And I've already ordered Lieutenant Cornaille's rangers outfitted with as many supplies as their horses will hold. In a week, if we've heard nothing, there will be cause for alarm. For now, we wait and hope the army will find us."

"I'll make connections among Royens's people," she said. "Four of my vessels are still alive with the First Corps, dug into caves and trenches. I'll get them moving south. You'll find them."

"Yes, Majesty," Doña Portega said. A pause, and then she added: "But, if we don't... perhaps you should consider returning early, or sending one or two—"

"No," she interrupted. "We're riding south to Lorrine within the hour. The dome outside Villecours was a success. Sister Joyeuse can coordinate riders to come repair the dome at Rasailles if it's needed. Gods send it won't be."

"Gods send it will be so. Thank you, Your Majesty."

Another cough bubbled in her throat. She released the tethers before it could take over, and her senses faded just as the spasms rose to seize her vessel's body.

"All's well?" Marquand said. He had Jiri and his own horse both on lead lines, waiting for her to finish.

"No," she said. "But we're riding south anyway. Give word to the others."

He nodded, handed Jiri's reins over, and set to barking orders for the rest. She slid up into Jiri's saddle and nudged them forward with her heels. She could make the connections to Royens and the army while they rode, after she'd had a few more hours to rest. Her body was close to breaking, but she would find the strength, somehow. Civilization itself hung around her neck. Four, maybe five more domes, and her people would survive. There would be trade, and farmland, and people ready to emerge when the storms that blackened the skies finally abated. She had to give them hope, however fate conspired to break hers.

55

TIGAI

Temple of the Dragon
Deep Within Shanshin Jungle

The strands faded away.

The air was different here. Tarzal was hot and dry in the foothills, but they were in the jungle now, following the strands Orana had shown him. Hot, sticky air seeped into his lungs, like trying to breathe through a wet blanket. But he had no time to process the surroundings before Allakawari lunged, driving a short steel knife into a young man's throat.

The young man's eyes bulged. He made a gurgling noise that might have turned into a cry for help, had Allakawari not encircled him in a smooth, swift motion, wrapping one hand around his mouth while the other pushed on the knife hilt, severing arteries and vocal cords as it cut.

Tetali moved to the left, and Kaladooh to the right. They were in a stone ruin, surrounded by four crumbling walls without a ceiling overhead. Jungle consumed the stone, leaving creeping vines running down cracks in the walls, and a thick canopy of leaves and green above them. It was dark, as it had been everywhere since they'd returned from the plane of blue sparks. He'd expected nothing else, though it still stung to see the storm on the Jun continent. The blackness and poison rain truly had enveloped the world, and erased the stars on the starfield as surely as it blotted out the ones in the sky. Yet their erasure hadn't prevented these Jun from making a new path he'd been able to follow. Time later to speculate what it might mean, that the starfield continued to work as it always had, only without any stars in place to travel to. For now, a young man, barely more than a boy, was dying in front of him, and thank the wind spirits there hadn't been more than one guard set to watch the endpoint of the strands.

He gave a hand signal: fingers bladed, in a swiping motion side to side. They'd arranged a few such gestures; this one meant *all clear*, so far as he could see. Tetali gave the same gesture from the left break in the walls. Kaladooh made a different gesture: three fingers, twisted front to back, then two fingers, held steady.

He nodded in return as Allakawari set the young man's body down softly, hanging limp as it slid to the ground.

"We will be able to speak," Allakawari said in a hushed voice. "They will be twenty paces off, and unaware."

"Three touched with great dreamings," Kaladooh whispered to them from the crack in the wall. "Eight more, at least, all gifted with lesser sparks."

"Poor odds," Juni said. Her skin was covered with deep crimson scales, while her voice rumbled like a furnace, for all she made efforts to keep it quiet.

"We have made our strike, and trusted in the Great Dreamer?" Tetali said to him.

He glanced between them. No telling what they faced here. The enemy had at least one Dragon, to have made the journey along the strands. What else would have been required to subdue the girl Orana had called the Sun? What would it have taken to contain Orana? Impossible to say. They had the advantage of surprise, but his gut said it wouldn't be enough. His bloody gut. Remarin would have chided him not to even attempt this attack, without knowing better the capabilities of his enemies and allies alike.

"Give me the body," he said. "Wait for my signal, then attack."

"What are you doing?" Juni rumbled in her furnace-voice.

He hoisted the boy's body under the shoulders. Wind spirits but it was fucking heavy. Allakawari had managed to restrain him with no more effort than she might have carried a stuffed doll. Bloody fucking *magi*.

"Trust me," he said. "Surprise is one thing; better if they're engaged already with something else, even if only for a moment."

They watched him, frowning as he dragged the boy's body to the cracks in the walls. But at least they seemed to be standing ready: Allakawari had her knives drawn, one in either hand, though neither Tetali nor Kaladooh carried any weapons. Both of them wore their grass-armor, though here in the jungle it appeared to be made of leaves and stone instead, a camouflage that blended them into the ruins, and all three stood with their feet set, as though they were preparing to hit something.

"I need help!" he shouted in Jun. He put panic into it, the sort of rushed energy that could sweep bystanders into acting. "Help! Here!"

He dragged the boy's body, placing himself between it and the heart of the ruins. If his attention was focused on a limp body, and he gave no sign of being a threat himself, curiosity and a desire to help would be their first instincts when they saw. It wouldn't last more than a moment, but the moment would be enough.

Two pairs of footsteps came running. He shouted again: "He's hurt. Some kind of fall. We need help here!"

An orange-robed woman knelt beside him, while a black-garbed man came to a more cautious halt, frowning at him through a black silk face mask. Good enough. The woman ran her hands over the boy's chest, lifting the head gently to expose Allakawari's knife wounds. In another moment the man would realize he didn't know Tigai.

He raised his hand, fingers curled inward. The gesture for *attack*.

The jungle ruin itself seemed to come from behind the black-garbed man. A blur of vines and stone, but the man whirled, drawing steel in a quick motion to meet Kaladooh in midair. The woman was less quick, and less fortunate. Allakawari appeared behind her accompanied by the sound of ripping fabric, both her knives sunk into the back of the orange robe, jerked downward to cut along the spine.

Tigai drew both of his pistols, spinning toward the ruin's heart, where the other *magi* would be noticing now. Sure enough, they were scrambling, some diving for cover, others slower to react, rising to their feet, peering toward the commotion where he'd shouted for help. He sighted one, a tall, thick-built man with the look of a soldier, who nonetheless had reacted poorly, staring like a country fool standing right in the open. He fired. Two belching roars lit up the ruins with a flash. But instead of dropping the soldier where he stood, his shots struck glass. Glass armor, conjured in the heartbeat before his shots hit skin. Fuck.

He snapped back to his anchor, behind the first four walls. Ox-*magi*. No time to process what sorts of magic the others might have. He ran back to the edge, this time using it for cover as he drew both pistols again.

Juni had transformed entirely; her skin was all scales, her hands and forearms wreathed in fire as she dove into the fight. Two more black-garbed fighters had joined the first soldier, each slashing with curved steel swords where Kaladooh stood, parrying and kicking with his jungle-armored bare fists and feet. Juni took one of them with a flame-covered fist, sending the man sprawling. Those five were too close, too risky for him to shoot into their mêlée. Instead he trained his sights on the Ox-*magi*, now fully armored in glass, charging toward the others. He fired again, this time aiming for the knee joints to slow the man or send him off-balance. His shots struck home, careening the Ox's left leg out from underneath him mid-stride. A crunch of shattering glass on stone sounded in the wake of his pistol shot as the Ox fell.

He snapped back to an anchor again, instantly reloading both pistols for another shot. This time he'd put himself at the wall, barely a half step from where he'd been. More *magi* moved in the distance. He needed to get closer. If they killed the Sun-girl before he could get to her . . .

He fired a shot toward the *magi*'s end of the complex to cover his movement, blinked again, then ducked low and ran toward another building, setting new anchors without thinking along the way. He saw Allakawari appear behind a woman in white, plunging both knives into her throat and vanishing before the body could slump toward the ground. Kaladooh and Juni held against the three black-garbed swordsmen, a spinning tempest of blades, kicks, and fire. No sign of Tetali, and the rest of the *magi* were hidden, having taken cover behind the ruins. He had to get closer. He had to find the girl.

Another shot covered another move, but this time he juked back, darting toward an opening that might have been a doorway.

Instinct snapped him back to an anchor as the ruins exploded.

Right where he'd been standing, a dome of force now consumed the building, shimmering as the rubble, dirt, and grass within it erupted into the air and froze, suspended in place. He darted a look around the wall and snapped again, blinking away as a second dome consumed the last building in the same display of violence and fire.

Juni and Kaladooh were nowhere in sight; he had to hope they'd run once the Force-*magi* began their attack. The three black-garbed swordsmen were gone, too. In their place four domes of shimmering force appeared, heaving the ground and buildings where it seemed gravity held no sway: Dirt and stone and plants floated, whirling and bouncing into one another as though every bond of structure or form had been broken within the domes. If he'd been caught in one of those his body might have joined the chaos, contributing blood and bone to join the rest of the debris. As it was he darted out again, racing across the complex and setting anchors on the way. He needed places to leap to, if this kept up. Blessedly he made it to another building, falling back from the main fight, setting three anchors and running for a second structure, little more than two crumbling walls with vines between them, where he stopped to catch his breath.

A woman in an orange robe with a black mesh face mask stood at the center of the path, both hands aloft, gesticulating toward the four shimmering domes. No other *magi* were in sight, though one of the domes now contained a thousand spinning shards of glass, placed over top of where he'd shot out the

Ox-*magi*'s leg. The woman had murdered her own soldier, consumed the man, glass armor and all, in one of her domes. Bloody fucking madness. Bloody fucking *magi*.

He leveled his right-hand pistol, bracing it against the wall and preparing to revert to one of his anchors. One clean shot she didn't see coming and—

Tetali appeared from between two of the domes, a blur of leaves and grass leaping toward the Force-*magi*, the Heron, as though the jungle itself had been given form.

"No, wait!" he cried. Too late. Too far away. The Heron-*magi* whipped her hands up toward Tetali at the last moment, and all the force of Tetali's leap, all the strength of whatever the Tarzali magic let her do, was channeled back into her. Tetali's body exploded in a rain of gore and blood, splattering the ground red.

He lowered his pistol.

He'd faced a Heron before, in their Tower when he went to rescue Remarin and Mei. It had taken Sarine at the height of her power to bring the Heron down, and they'd taken half the tower down with them. He had to assume the others were dead, the same as Tetali. Yuli would never forgive him if Juni died here, but Namkat was still alive. He had to reach the Sun and get her out of here.

He kept low, darting to another ruined wall, taking a path that led away from the carnage at the temple's heart. The ground shook violently, whether from the Heron's domes or some other magic he had no idea. It threatened to topple the ruins; stone pebbles and chunks rained where the walls trembled and fell. The Sun would be where the *magi* had been when they started this fight. He'd seen her through Orana's eyes, sleeping, or unconscious, in a building with no ceiling or roof.

Jun voices shouted something unintelligible. He ran, careful to keep out of sight. He was close. They'd built a fire in a square between two long buildings, left unattended now as the fight raged elsewhere. The Sun wouldn't be here. Maybe the smaller building off to the other side, across the open space.

"Stop." A woman's voice rang out. "Stop there."

His stomach lurched. A woman in *magi* robes, white with blue trim and the sigil of an Owl, stood between him and the smaller building. He'd missed her, somehow, when scanning the square. He brought up his right-hand pistol, and suddenly the lurch in his stomach became a violent spasm. His pistol clattered to the ground as he pitched forward to his knees, vomiting a torrent of bile onto the stone.

He reverted to his last anchor, and his pistol reverted with him, standing at the edge of the wall overlooking the square. The woman in white dove for cover as he took the shot, ringing out a cloud of black smoke.

"Dragon!" the Owl woman shouted. "Their Dragon! He's here!"

He cursed, snapping back to the same anchor to reload his gun. He had to move. He sprinted forward, racing between a pillar and another wall. His gut seized again as soon as he came to a halt, and he vomited, a stream of pure yellow liquid drenching his pistols and snuffing the matches in their firing locks.

He snapped back, blinking as the residue of the sudden sickness vanished from his body. Wind spirits but that was fucking annoying. This time he'd chosen an anchor on the opposite side of the square. He'd have to move around her in a direction she didn't expect, and stay well clear of the orange-robed Heron at the center of her domes.

"I can't contain him," the Owl woman shouted. "Sisi, I need you!"

Another anchor blinked him away as the Heron-*magi* turned, a precious second away from her having spotted him mid-stride. He waited a moment and ran again. They couldn't see him. Couldn't know where he was moving, or he'd end up with another Force-dome on top of him before he could blink. He'd managed to snap away once, but no telling if he could do it again, even knowing it was coming.

"He's going for the girl," another woman, presumably the Heron, said in an accented voice. "Fall back and keep her safe."

Fuck.

He froze, pressing up against a wall that seemed on the edge of teetering over as the ground shook. At least he could watch and see where the Owl and Heron went to protect the girl. The small building on the opposite side of their fire. He'd been right, curse his luck, for all the good it did him now. Maybe if he waited, Kaladooh and Juni and Allakawari could regroup and renew their attack, pulling the Force-*magi*'s attention away. And maybe all three of his companions were already dead. Fuck fuck fuck. If he waited too long, the *magi*'s Dragon would take the girl away. He could follow again, but this time they'd be even more prepared. There might be a hundred of them waiting, instead of ten. There might—

A figure shrouded in purple and blue appeared beside him.

It was all he could do not to cry out in alarm and go for one of his pistols. The figure snapped out a hand to grab his wrist, shaking it in an approximation of their sign for *no*.

"They will be thirty paces off, across their square," the figure—whom the flood of adrenaline in his heart finally recognized as Allakawari—said in hushed tones. "What have we done?"

It took another moment to realize she meant she wanted a plan for what they were *going* to do, rather than a philosophical pause to consider their actions. Bloody fucking Tarzali.

"The others?" he asked.

Allakawari shook her head. "I will not see them. We will be separated, by the orange-woman in the mask."

"The Heron," he said. "It's her, at least, and the Owl, guarding the Sun. There."

"The smaller building?"

He nodded. They needed a plan. The *magi* were already on high alert; no way he could distract them. Maybe if he surrendered, or made a show of dropping his pistols... maybe they wouldn't know he could blink to an anchor and get them back. A quick shot at the right moment might take out the Heron, if her attention was divided.

"Hey, what are you doing?" he snapped, too late. Allakawari was already gone, as suddenly as she'd appeared. Shadows swirled around her, silent and dark, masking her as she sped into the ruin, moving toward the square.

No sense staying behind. He snapped to an anchor on an opposite wall, checking to make sure both pistols were lit and hot before he ran after her from the other direction.

The Owl-*magi* was standing guard, and saw him as soon as he cleared the long hall. Immediately his skin burned, his stomach seized, his throat caught in a hacking cough. He squeezed a trigger and missed wildly, the pistol discharging over the Owl's head as his body convulsed. He blinked back and fired again, this time with his shot braced against the wall.

The Owl screamed as a red spray appeared where her left arm had been. Blood and sinew and cloth tore away, and her body spun involuntarily from the force of his shot. Suddenly the square was lit from above, and Allakawari appeared in a rush, leaping for the now-shocked Owl. Both her knives were out, a mere armslength from the Owl, when Allakawari froze and slumped forward, hacking and vomiting in the middle of the square.

He shouted something unintelligible, blinking back to his anchor to reload and fire another shot.

This one took the Owl in the head. Her neck snapped as her skull exploded, the body flung down violently in a heap of blood. He saw it clearly, as clear as he'd seen anything since the sky had gone dark. Moonlight shone down on the square, bright and clear, illuminating the bright red splatters through the black powder of his pistol shots. A whistling noise accompanied the light, like a steaming teakettle suddenly set off in the middle of the square. He ignored it, moving to a safer vantage, and willing Allakawari to do the same.

Instead Allakawari gathered herself, collecting the knives she'd dropped, moving slowly, without any grace, in a daze of sickness. If Tigai hadn't been able to blink to an anchor to reset the Owl's work he might have done the same. As it was he called out to get to cover. She was exposed, lying in the center of the square, and the Heron was out there, still unaccounted for.

Allakawari was still dazed, coughing as she rose to her feet. He tried to yell another warning, cutting himself off midword with a blink to reload his pistols, when the woman in orange robes and a black veil appeared, both hands extended as though they were weapons, with one of the black-garbed swordsmen at her side.

A Force-bubble expanded from the Heron's hands, launching itself toward Allakawari as Tigai pulled both triggers at once.

Allakawari recovered some part of her agility, dodging backward as the Force-bubble latched to the ground and became a dome, expanding in all directions in a violent heave. Tigai's shots were swallowed in its shimmering haze as soon as they entered the dome. The whistling noise was still there, growing louder, loud enough to drown out the cracks of his pistols, but he ignored it, turning his attention to the swordsman.

It had to be a Crane. The black-garbed *magi* ran toward Tigai's anchors at the edge of the wall, his steel drawn and held above his head. He would have to snap to a different anchor, one close enough to help Allakawari if—

The swordsman exploded.

He'd been mere moments from snapping away to another set of anchors. Instead he froze, stunned. Something had crashed into the swordsman from above, splattering his body like paste. Those Cranes had moved like whirlwinds, dancing away from Kaladooh's and Juni's attacks, and this one had been caught where he stood, by something falling from the sky.

He stared upward and saw the moon looking down, only instead of the usual pale white, a blood-red orb hung at the center of a break in the clouds, paired with a hailstorm of streaks of crimson fire. Comets.

No. Meteors.

Another explosion shook the ruins, then another, and another, and another. Whistling rain came down, faster than he could brace himself. The Force-domes were gone, along with any sign of the Heron, though a stone had crashed into where the Owl's body had slumped over, leaving nothing but a smoking, fiery crater in the dirt.

He took a risk and raced across the square without looking up.

The smaller building was empty save for a stone bed in the corner. A bed where the sun-haired girl lay sleeping, taking shallow breaths without any sign she'd stirred or even noticed the upheaval rocking the temple around her.

He ran to her side. This was her. The girl from Orana's vision. The Sun.

He spun around as the light from the outside dimmed, and found a figure standing in the doorway. Allakawari. Dazed, moving with a fraction of her usual grace, but it was her, both knives dripping blood in her hands.

"Thank the fucking wind spirits," he said. "Get close."

"What of the others?" Allakawari said. "They could still live."

"They could," he said. "But we came for her."

It stung, even as he said it. This was his mission. His call. He'd left people behind before. Part of him wanted to run back into the ruins, to find Juni if there was any hope at all for him bringing both of Yuli's sisters back to her, healthy and whole. But four more lives, and maybe the way back home through the storm's black haze, rested on his safe return of this girl Orana called the Sun.

He blinked, and touched the strands connecting the three of them to the Tarzali foothills.

56

YULI

Deep Jungle
Manacambu Highlands

Trees cracked and fell together, sending leaves and vines crashing to the ground. Yuli wanted to stare, to freeze and let awe control her. But the Twin Fangs moved. It kept moving. It had to study the creature, to stay clear until it learned enough to find a weakness, to turn the predator to prey. Until it found one, the Twin Fangs ran to save itself, to avoid the jungle crashing down around them, to play its part in this stage of the hunt.

Another mighty tree crashed behind them, dwarfed by the size of a single one of the creature's forelegs, and the Twin Fangs sprang up the face of a cliff, loping up the stone as it jammed its claws into cracks in the wall. Arak'Jur launched himself behind, leaping, almost flying up the cliffside. It had lost Omera in the trees, but the Twin Fangs still smelled him, trailing behind, wafting his clouds of herbs and poison and steel.

The predator slammed the full size of its body into the cliffside, rattling stone and earth as the Twin Fangs and Arak'Jur reached the top together. They vaulted over the stone, sliding down a trench of dirt and leaves, and then the Twin Fangs broke for a thick nest of trees with broad, flat leaves and colorful flowers. Arak'Jur went the other way, and the Twin Fangs lost him as stone cracked behind them. The creature's great claws powered it over the cliff as it leapt into the air. Impossible, for such bulk to move so fast. But it did, thundering as it landed, smashing the hillside in a cloud of dust and springing forward, away from the Twin Fangs, toward Arak'Jur.

The Twin Fangs circled around, running in parallel to the creature, careful to keep enough distance to be able to react if it pivoted.

The creature ran, and the Twin Fangs ran with it.

Trees that must have stood for a hundred years snapped beneath the creature's limbs like twigs. In the dusky light of the overcast, poisoned sky it could see only shadows of the creature's size. It was a mountain, piercing the sky with every step. Four legs, each tipped with claws and thorns like barbs running the length of each foreleg to the joints, which seemed reversed, like a bird of prey. Its mouth was a long snout, a sea of metallic teeth glinting in the dim light, ringed by long, flowing antennae, but the creature was no insect. Leathery hide covered thick muscles, and fur, capped by a great mane, surrounded its shoulders and head like a lion. But this creature could swallow a pride of lions in a single gnash from its jaws.

The creature's scent flooded the Twin Fangs' nose. A scent of wrongness. As though a monstrous cloud had descended into the jungle, the sort of storm cloud that swallowed half the sky. It smelled of tainted water, of blood and rot. Enough to overpower the rest of the jungle's smells. Arak'Jur ran ahead, for now the creature's primary prey. Omera trailed farther behind but still kept close. And two more. Two strangers. One that smelled of fury, whose scent intermingled with the creature's until it seemed as though it came from atop its back. And the other...older...more distant...carried the smell of aged flesh, somehow moving fast enough to keep up with their frenzied chase.

Fire blasted through the jungle, illuminating the trees in a flash of light.

Arak'Jur leapt from atop a tree-covered hillside, surrounded in a wreath of flame. Gouts of fire flew from his hands before he disappeared behind the hill and struck the creature between its forelegs, sending up another flash as the flames licked across its fur. Burning smells stank in the Twin Fangs' nose, but the creature gave no sign of slowing, stampeding through the trees atop Arak'Jur's hill and vanishing down its back side just as quickly, snapping its teeth as though in anger as it bit the cloud of fire.

The Twin Fangs pivoted, daring to get closer to the creature as it ran. It snaked across a ridgeline, leaping over a chasm in the earth, careful to stay above the mulch of broken trees in the creature's wake. The creature's hind legs worked in powerful strides, the inverted joints and musculature giving it the capacity for great leaps and bounding steps in equal measure. Perhaps if it could strike the ligaments, the creature could be slowed. It trailed after, waiting for a stretch of level ground. Then it leapt, when the stride was even enough to be predicted, and landed, all ten of the Twin Fangs' claws sunk deep into the leathery hide of the creature's left hind leg.

It grasped tight, clinging to the creature's skin as it thrashed. A roar sounded, loud enough to split Yuli's eardrums if she'd been in control. But the Twin Fangs' claws held. It rose the height of a small hillside when the creature lifted its hind legs to take a step. Rocks and tree trunks split around it, each step a minor earthquake, rattling the Twin Fangs' bones, but its claws stayed firm, embedded deep in the creature's hide, enough to draw rivulets of blood to soak its hands and forearms.

Withdrawing a claw would have shaken the Twin Fangs loose; it needed all ten finger points sunk deep to keep it steady and attached. Instead it struck with its teeth. Both its long fangs tore into the creature's joint in a savage fury, ripping and slashing as fast as it could work its jaws. The creature would whirl, would fling its leg to knock the Twin Fangs loose, as soon as it felt the damage. It had to sever tendons quickly, if it could reach them. And it did. Blood flowed into the Twin Fangs' mouth, hot and red and touched with iron. No tooth or claw in nature could have broken the creature's muscled hide, nor cut into the soft tissues between its bones. But the Twin Fangs was no creature of the natural world. It cut, and severed, ripping and snapping until the creature reared up, rising to the height of a mountain as it blared another roar into the sky.

The Twin Fangs dropped, rolling into the leaves as the creature crashed backward, narrowly missing crushing it as the creature fell atop itself. Bloody ruin trailed down the creature's left hind leg, leaving a trail of gore mixed with the leaves and trees smashed under its weight.

The Twin Fangs bounded away as the creature howled, swiping behind it. The wind shifted. Now the Twin Fangs was the prey. It sensed it, as surely as an elk knew when the steppe lions had marked it for death.

It ran.

It ducked below a copse of thick trees, and heard them smash and rip apart when the creature trampled them. It bounded over a river, taking the full length from bank to bank in a single leap. Water crashed where the creature dipped one of its thundering limbs in the river's depths. It reached a grassy clearing, pivoting and shifting direction quickly, and felt the ground shake and crack as the creature shifted its massive bulk to follow.

Another gout of fire scorched the air, lighting the jungle in a flash. Ice cracked. Thunder rained from the sky. Arak'Jur's smell filled the Twin Fangs' nose, and another roar bellowed out as the creature slowed and whirled, smashing through a dozen trees at once as it spun its claws in a rearward swipe.

Frustration. Predatory instincts flared as the Twin Fangs slowed, rounding on the beast. The balance of which of them was prey hung in the air, thick as any scent on the wind. Now the creature was at its most dangerous. Now it would try a desperate strike.

The Twin Fangs skulked into the creature's view, ready to spring away if the beast lunged. It had finally stopped moving, the ruin of its left hind leg tucked under its girth while the right hind leg showed scorch and burn marks, the fur still kindling where the muscle burned away. It sat back on its haunches, the rest of its massive height blocking out the overcast clouds, ringed by displaced earth and broken trees and grass, and it roared.

The thundering bellows shook the earth, as sure as its footfalls had, and even the Twin Fangs' ears rattled in pain. The Twin Fangs saw Arak'Jur moving cautiously, on the far side of the grassy clearing, clearly aware of the danger. If they could bait it now, provoke it to extend itself, the other one could strike. But until it moved, there was no way to tell which of them it would attack. Whatever else the creature was, it was a wounded, desperate animal. Both of them had to stay vigilant, reading the wind for any sign of what it meant to do.

Omera charged into the clearing.

It was wrong. A mistake. The Twin Fangs took a step, hesitating, and felt Arak'Jur do the same. If they sparked the creature's ire now, it might bolt again, and renew the chase with a surge of adrenaline. But there was no way to call out and be heard. The creature continued its roar, lowering its head in a silhouette against the dusk-lit clouds in the sky. Omera was a miniature in comparison. A tiny man-sized shape charging across the field with his curved sword bared, reeking of the poison rubbed across its steel.

The creature snapped its head and foreclaws around toward Omera in a lightning rush. Yuli's heart sank underneath the Twin Fangs' control. He was dead. The creature lunged, the full force of its bulk suddenly uncoiled. It moved, impossibly fast.

Omera moved with it.

The Bhakal man threw himself into the air the instant before the creature's claw struck the ground. It tore into the earth, rending dirt and undergrowth in a tempest surge, but Omera was above it, a flying leap taking him over the creature's claw to land on its wrist, and then he sprinted up its forearm without missing a step.

It was all the Twin Fangs needed to see. The creature was distracted by the swordsman running up its arm toward its mouth. If Omera was to live, they had to strike now.

The Twin Fangs charged on all fours, covering the distance before Omera reached its shoulder. The creature twisted its torso upward, raking its other arm across the first, trying to rid itself of the invader who moved like a whirlwind. Its attention was focused upward, on itself, and the Twin Fangs leapt into its belly. Ten claws sank deep into its hide, and this time it needed only one hand to keep itself in place. The other claws plunged in and out of the creature's skin while its teeth ripped, alternating grips as it moved across the stomach, leaving hide torn open, drenching the Twin Fangs in thick, crimson blood.

Thundershocks rippled across the surface of the beast's skin as Arak'Jur landed at the same instant, tearing and ripping with spectral claws engulfing him in images of bears, cats, birds, and fire.

The creature crashed onto its side, threatening to throw them both. Earth rumbled outward in a shock wave where it landed, thrashing its broken legs and arms to try and cover its belly. The Twin Fangs expected it, was already moving as the creature convulsed, using its claws to scale the stomach like a crag wall. Only this wall could be torn and ripped, with new handholds dug into its surface by breaking through its hide. Arak'Jur fell, opting to dodge the flailing limbs by going under, rather than over, and the Twin Fangs lost sight of him, though it smelled his spectral attacks raking the beast's hindquarters without pause as the creature went down.

The Twin Fangs reached its back, and nearly took a spear thrust to its face.

It sprang back, and Omera rushed forward, hooking their enemy's spear with the edge of his curved sword. A heartbeat later the Twin Fangs recognized the scent: one of the unknown men who it had thought was following along, the younger, furious one. But no. Not following. Riding. Somehow the spearman had been standing atop the creature's back as it ran. In the dim light it could see only outlines and shadows, naked from the waist up, a single long braid of hair adorned with gold and precious stones. The rider's spear bore the same ornamentation, plated with gold and gems, though no less deadly for it. He jabbed as quick as Omera stepped and cut, a flurry of strikes and parries too fast for the Twin Fangs to see, almost too fast for it to smell and sense their movements. But no matter how evenly Omera and the spearman were matched, it was enough for the Bhakal to have distracted his opponent. The Twin Fangs left them behind, loping up the creature's side as it wrenched itself on the ground, rumbling beneath their feet. It went for the creature's head, lolled to one side as it made a sound a mountain-sized beast might have made for whimpering pain.

The creature's eyes were open, burning with fury and each one the size of a covered wagon.

It dove for one of the eyes, plunging its claws deep and raking them as it leapt for the bridge of its snout. The beast howled, bringing a claw up to shield itself. The Twin Fangs was ready, racing up the bridge to the crown of the creature's forehead, then sliding across, grabbing hold of one of the antennae as it lashed and quivered around its face.

It cut on instinct, severing the antenna to a bloody stump, then leaping to another and doing it again.

Blood leaked out, soaking the Twin Fangs' body before it rained down on the earth. Quaking howls and screams escaped the creature's snout, sputtered by dry crackles that might have been coughs. Blood poured from its mouth, and white foam like the spray of tides. The Twin Fangs cut and leapt, dodging around the massive claws by instinct alone, never staying in one place for longer than it took to drive its claws and fangs into the creature's hide. It smelled Arak'Jur maintaining the attack on the creature's belly and loins, and the duel between the strange half-naked spearman and Omera atop its back. The onslaught seemed to continue for too long, longer than any creature should have been able to endure, even one so massive as this. Until finally, the creature's claw slumped away, pounding against the ground hard enough to rattle the trees and undergrowth around them.

The Twin Fangs kept up its attacks. The creature was still alive, the blood hot and pumping everywhere it had been cut. But with the claw collapsed, it made no attempt to defend itself. It lay on the broken ground, being torn to strips of bloodied meat and hide. Relenting might have let the creature recover, might have provoked it to try one last time to rid itself of its miniature attackers. The Twin Fangs stayed alert, smelling and sensing any shifts in posture or muscles that might betray an attack. But it felt nothing. The beast had collapsed, and lay dying, savaged by raking claws, ripping teeth, and Arak'Jur's spectral fire.

The creature vanished.

Suddenly there was nothing where the Twin Fangs' claws had steadied itself. Nothing where the clearing had been pounded to churned earth and stone.

The Twin Fangs fell, and the ground rushed up toward it.

Impact shook the Twin Fangs and Yuli together, each feeling the force of striking the ground, each set of instincts vying for control.

The Twin Fangs won out, and rose, the world spinning beneath its feet. It smelled nothing where the creature's scent had been. Where it should have been, still. It was as though the beast had been no more than an illusion, a trick of light and shadow, though the destruction it had wrought on the jungle was plain enough to see.

"He's dead," Omera said. "The beast died with him."

The Twin Fangs snarled, steadying itself as it approached. Omera smelled of victory along with his poison and steel. As he'd claimed, the bare-chested spearman lay at his feet, shorn through the torso by the curved blade in

Omera's hands. A pool of blood and entrails ran into the ruined earth, and surprise was writ on the spearman's face. Surprise, and contentment.

"Powerful magic," Arak'Jur said. The guardian was favoring his left leg, clutching a gash in the right thigh, but otherwise he appeared unharmed. "The spirits granted me a vision of this beast, and I saw you, waiting, if I arrived in time. Thank the spirits I did."

Yuli fought for control. The Twin Fangs pushed her down. Danger was here, still. Danger in its nose, danger flooding through its nostrils. She shouldn't be allowed to wrest control, not with—

"There's another nearby," Yuli said. "That way." Memory of the Twin Fangs' senses lingered even after she forced the change. Her body reeled from the shock of the chase, bruises covering her chest, her back, her belly, both legs, where bones would be broken and ligaments torn. But she would heal.

"Another?" Arak'Jur said. "Another one with the power to summon...one of those things?"

"A man," she said. "I can't know for sure whether he has the same powers. But I'll say what you said: Thank the fucking spirits and all the Gods you came when you did. If that thing had surprised us, I don't know if we could have evaded it alone."

Omera took up his sword. "I sense him, too. Coming this way."

Fatigue washed over her. Neither she nor the Twin Fangs had the stamina for another chase. But she turned to face it, holding the Twin Fangs on the cusp of renewing its control over their body. If they had to fight, then there was no other choice.

A figure appeared in the distance. The newcomer moved slowly, but with sharp jerks for movement and a walking stick it seemed to lean on with each step. It trundled toward them, too quickly, too energetically for her comfort, until the Twin Fangs almost wrested control.

"You gave it to him," the figure said. The voice was high-pitched, too soft to be masculine, but too deeply resonant for a woman. A strange mix. "You did it. You fulfilled the promise."

"Come no closer," Arak'Jur called out. "We meant no harm here—the man we've killed threatened us. We acted in our defense."

"Yes, yes, of course," the figure said. "You did as was expected. Great warriors. Great warriors all. A great honor. The greatest in some years. Many years."

Arak'Jur's warning went unheeded; the figure scrambled closer, but seemingly with all their focus on the body of the spearman Omera had slain. The newcomer went to their knees, reaching out to lay a hand on the brow of the dead man while fumbling with pouches on one of several belts wrapped around their waist.

Silence hung for a moment as the newcomer worked, performing some sort of ritual over the body of the dead. They worked without seeming to notice Arak'Jur, Omera, or Yuli. The Twin Fangs stirred in her belly, but she kept it down. This person wasn't a threat, at least not on the surface. And however she and Omera—and Arak'Jur, for that matter—had come to be here, they were in the presence of a person of power. Staying quiet, observing and reacting to what came was the wisest course.

"I came here following a vision," Arak'Jur said finally. "A vision of great danger, but power, too. The power to heal the mother of my child. I seek a great power. A power the spirits called Rabaquim."

The newcomer chuckled softly as they worked. "Always impatient, you scattered seeds. Always eager to know more than the mother is ready to reveal."

"If you are a shaman of your people," Arak'Jur said, "I'll say again: We came here in peace, seeking aid."

"Aid!" the newcomer laughed. "And a shaman! Yes, yes. Why not. Your aid will come, once the rest is finished. Now come on, don't just stand there. Help me carry Chi'tu'aya's body. We've a long way to go before we can burn him."

The newcomer tried to hoist the dead man's leg and failed; the spearman was four times as thick and muscled as their frail, thin frame. But the newcomer gestured toward the other limbs expectantly, even impatiently, waiting for them to move.

Arak'Jur hesitated. So did Omera.

"We'll help you," she said. "But clearly you have some power here, among your people. We're trying to get home, and to find some way to deal with the blackness in the sky. Can you agree to listen to our stories, if we agree to hear yours, after we help?"

The newcomer smiled.

"Of course, fanged one," the newcomer said. "But it is not Sini'ti'naya's place to help you. For that, you need a God of the Blood, and to summon one of those, you must burn the dead. So helping me is helping you, do you see? Now cease this talking and grab a leg."

She shrugged toward the others. Apparently they'd said as much as would be said here. Caution dictated learning more, perhaps, but she knew enough to know when the time for talking was done. More would come in time. All that was left for now was finding a spot to get a firm hold on the corpse.

57

SARINE

The tunnels were dark, lit by torches instead of lamps or oil. Flickering fire cast shadows around her, and the halls smelled of moistened dirt and incense. Most were empty. The Skovan would have had to spend decades digging out and provisioning these tunnels, somehow knowing they would be needed when the Regnant poisoned the sky. And yet where she might have expected survivors, the tunnels were mostly barren—only a priest or two every dozen rooms, the men in black robes with white collars, with no sign of women at all. Perhaps they were kept hidden from outsiders.

She waited outside a carved oak door, sitting on what felt like a pew bench taken from a church. Darkness beckoned in either direction, but what she could see under the torchlight was beautiful: colorful tapestries, woven with scenes she recognized from the stained-glass windows at the Skovan church. A man preaching to many others, feeding them from a single basket; a man covered with arrows, looking up to the sky; a wise woman with a child in her arms; another man nailed to a cross while onlookers wept. Beautiful scenes, though she knew nothing of the theology behind them. It still gave her some comfort, being surrounded by imagery similar in kind to what she could have found in her uncle's church.

The door creaked open slowly, and she straightened. Finally.

The man—no, the boy who emerged wasn't Krzysztof, and there was no sign of Rashael. They'd gone inside what felt like hours ago, and Donatien had gone to a different chamber, asking after his friends. She'd been here alone, anticipating this summons.

"They're ready for you," the boy said. He was young, no more than ten or twelve, though it was difficult to tell beneath the bright red robe and cowl he wore. Different garb than she'd seen elsewhere in these tunnels. He said nothing else, holding the door for her in one hand while a torch burned in the other. She followed him inside.

Immediately it was clear the chamber was massive; the boy's torchlight touched no walls in any direction other than the door behind them. The floors sloped down; a narrow aisle pointed toward lights in the distance, with empty benches arrayed to look toward what had to be a stage, or a dais where the lights flickered on the far side.

Figures sat in those lights, figures that appeared to be dressed in the same bright red colors the boy wore. Otherwise the room was covered in darkness. No torches or lamps burned on the walls, nor anywhere else. As they walked down the aisle a sense of shadow enveloped her. It was clear the chamber was enormous, and while the benches she could see appeared empty and silence hung in the air, there could have been a thousand people watching silently from the shadows.

There aren't, Anati thought to her. *Only twelve here, on their stage. Two more if you count yourself, and the boy.*

"What about Rashael, or Krzysztof?" she whispered. It earned a reproachful look from the boy, which she ignored.

Not here. It's just you and them.

So much for having an advocate. Not that she knew either Rashael or her bond-partner well enough to trust them to advocate for her, but both had seemed intent on bringing her here, on the promise of what an alliance between them might mean. It would have felt good to have a familiar face in any case, in light of the strangeness in the hall.

They walked at least two hundred paces from the door, and proved Anati right: It was empty. Rows and rows of benches and darkness surrounded them. It almost unnerved her, but then, that was probably the point. Better to remember she was in fact a Goddess, or at least that she had champions bonded, with ties to Life magic and the Soul of the World. She was here seeking allies. This sort of theater was little better than what a gang of Maw thugs might do to intimidate an envoy from a rival gang. The realization put steel in her back. She was above being intimidated by petty parlor tricks, however important these twelve thought they were. She was still the heir to the Veil.

They reached the stage, and she could see clearly the twelve men seated in a half circle around her. They were men, all men, some clean-shaven, some bearded, most with iron-gray hair and all of them wrinkled and aged. They sat atop gold chairs more akin to thrones, elevated so they looked down on her from shoulder height and above. The lights that shone on each seemed to come from above, though she couldn't see the source. It appeared twelve cones of light came down from the heavens, encircling each of them with darkness in between their seats.

The boy snuffed his torch and backed away as soon as she was placed on the center of the stage. She gave no sign of surprise, carefully looking over each of the men in turn, for all she was cloaked in darkness. If they wanted their theater, she would let them have it, and let them speak first.

"Sarine Thibeaux of New Sarresant," the farthest-left voice intoned. "You come before us at a time of great tribulations."

Still she waited. The inequality of the chamber stung her pride. It made her want to drag them all to a tavern somewhere, to get a table and a round of drinks and speak like ordinary people.

"We were warned against your coming," another voice said, almost chanting. "We were warned by scripture, old and true."

"Not scripture," yet a different voice said. "Prophecy. Our oldest, and truest."

"That remains to be seen!" the first voice almost shouted, leaving a silence that itself seemed to echo through the empty hall.

"I came here looking for allies," she said. The temptation was to posture for the scene they'd placed her in, to use the voice her uncle used when delivering his most impassioned sermons. Instead she tried to remain calm. "I don't know why you need to dress yourselves in robes and try to judge me from on high. I'm not here to be judged. I came seeking those with the gifts of magic beyond the reach of Regnant or Veil, to fight against their great evil. Either you'll help me or you won't, but I'm not going to be made to feel less because I don't have a velvet robe and golden chair."

She turned and began to walk from the chamber. Her attempts to calm her nerves failed: Anger bubbled up, anger at the sort of pomp that had kept her walled away behind *Faith* from the courtiers at Rasailles, from the wealth and privilege of the Gardens.

"Wait," one of the men said, one of the two in the direct center. "Wait."

The light that engulfed his chair spread, a widening beam that expanded to cover the forward half of the stage. As it did, he slid from the chair, gingerly setting his feet on the ground.

"Father Wicek, what are you—?" one of the voices intoned.

The man the voice had named Father Wicek hissed a loud *shh*. He then pulled back his red cowl to reveal an aged, weathered face, beardless and balding, with unkempt eyebrows atop piercing blue eyes. He set down a gold scepter she hadn't noticed he carried, moved to kneel in front of her, and reached for her feet.

She almost pulled away, but he grasped her boot gingerly, softly, and leaned forward to kiss the toe.

"What are you doing?" she asked, suddenly feeling more than half a fool. The rest of the stage was lit now by some beam from above, and she saw similar shock and surprise writ on the faces of the other archbishops.

"I do as the Lord's son would have done, for those who hated him," Father Wicek said. "But know that we do not adorn ourselves this way out of pride. We do so because it is a sacred thing, to hold audience with one who claims the heritage you claim, who holds the keys you claim to hold. If our display has given offense, we beg your forgiveness, and hope we can begin again."

"Yes," she murmured, then said again, more firmly, "Yes. We can. It's just... you don't need to kiss my feet. I need friends and allies, not masters or servants."

Wicek smiled and pulled back to sit cross-legged in front of her, gesturing for her to join him. "Let us speak, then, as friends. Or at least, those who might become friends."

The other eleven archbishops seemed suddenly out of place atop their golden chairs, now that the chamber's center was lit. And it was the center— the rows of seats encircled the stage on all sides, making this an amphitheater from all directions. Still, the other eleven stayed where they were.

She sat.

"Your name is Wicek," she said.

"It is," he replied. "I have the honor of leading our council. You're Sarine?"

"Yes," she said. It was possible this newfound humility, too, was an affectation designed to put her off her footing. But this time it worked, and she had to fight to keep her center. "I was born to be a new body for the Goddess called the Veil. But she's dead now, and I've inherited her power. I'm not her. But I'm still fighting against the Regnant, against what he's done to the world."

Eleven voices all sucked in breath at once, making a loud hiss in concert.

"Understand," Wicek said. "This is an old thing, to us. A thing long foretold. *'The veiled sister comes to you, shed her skin and twice reborn, to reopen the path to heaven.'* Some among us have named this an old heresy, a mistranslation of ancient tongues. You will gain many allies among our bishops, claiming what you claim, but many enemies as well."

"I don't know your theology," she said. "But I know the Trithetic scriptures. *'Need sets aside what it must, when the hour is late.'*"

"Wise words," Wicek said. "But our faith has ever stood apart from the bonds of the other nations. We've chosen that separation, and paid the price for it. Many martyrs, both men and angels, have shed their blood in opposition to the one called the Veil. So you might understand how we view your coming with suspicion."

"I know," she said. "But I'm not her."

"And yet your key was turned, to put the world into its sleep. You named the Regnant as the Veil's enemy, but this is not our teaching. The change takes two. Both False Gods, working together. They are both two sides of Satan, in our teachings, Lucifer and Lilith. The God and Goddess of this world. What say you to this?"

"The Regnant used one of the Bhakal Queens," she said. "Sakhefete. He rebuilt the Veil's mind inside hers, and gave her access to the Veil's keys. They bypassed the older way, with their champions, and cheated control of the Soul. I had nothing to do with it."

"He gave the Bhakal passage to the World's Soul?" Wicek said, sounding genuinely surprised.

She nodded. "I fought them both there, with some of my champions. We failed, and the world changed. But I still have the Veil's power. I can find a way back. If we bring more champions, more strength, perhaps we can overcome him and find a way to set things right."

"Ah," Wicek said. "So this is an attempt to bond us, to put us beneath you as your champions."

"I don't care about bonding anyone, or putting anyone beneath me," she said. "I want to find a way to heal this. As I said, I need allies, not servants."

"And you would take our oathsworn to the Soul of the World, to set us against the Regnant himself, and fight alongside us, as equals?"

"I need allies," she repeated. "Who are your oathsworn? You mean bond-pairs, like Krzysztof and Rashael?"

Wicek looked thoughtful for a moment, studying her face. Then he bowed his head, and a figure appeared behind him.

Like Rashael in the chapel, the figure was made of dazzling light, but with six pairs of wings each outstretched to fill the length of the stage. It wore golden armor decorated with what appeared to be steel and ivory designs, far more intricate and detailed than what Rashael had worn. A flaming sword burned in its hands, long enough to need two hands to wield it, its hilt etched with the same steel and ivory, its blade made of pure gold. And where Rashael had been young and smooth-skinned, this figure was old, as aged as Wicek himself, wrinkled with long, flowing gray hair set against the radiance of its sword and armor.

"We swear oaths to heaven," Wicek said softly. "In some ages, when the light of magic burns dimly, the answers to these oaths are metaphorical. In others...well. This is the Archangel Leorain, who is bound to my service, as I am bound to his."

<This is her, then,> a voice intoned in her head, in the same manner she'd heard Rashael, as though a choir of trumpets and voices echoed his every word. *<The one who claims the mantle of the devil.>*

"I'm not a devil," she said hotly. "And I'm tired of answering for crimes I had nothing to do with. I'm not her, no matter how I look or what you think."

<Implying that the Lord and Lady of Lies are above deception,> the archangel said. *<The flocks look to us for shelter, with the Great Shepherd cut off by your foul servants, and we judge you for the viper you are, little Queen.>*

"She hasn't come before us as a Queen," Wicek said. "She presents us an offer to fight evil, and offers power to help our cause. It bears consideration, my friend."

<No,> the archangel said. *<Rashael, our servant, spoke of her at our councils. The Veil wears many masks. We see through this one. The time for listening, and speaking to her, is over.>*

Wicek frowned, and opened his mouth to speak, but the Archangel Leorain was already moving. A swift, flowing motion. The greatsword of light rose in his hands, as fluid as if the blade were made of running water.

The Nine Tails surged in her blood, and she scrambled where she'd been seated. Too slow.

The angel's sword crashed down toward her head, and struck a dome of white.

Anati appeared in front of her, her scales flushed deep red.

You pompous, arrogant, small-minded stupid bastard, Anati thought to them. *You weren't even listening to her, were you? Whatever you think you see, you're lucky you can even recognize your own nose on your own face.*

The white shield flared around them both, and the men behind them on the stage let out a chorus of gasps.

The archangel withdrew his sword and readied it again without looking down.

Anati snarled, and the archangel howled in pain, dropping his sword in a puff of light as it vanished from his hands.

"Stop it! Both of you!" she snapped. "I came here as a friend, offering peace."

They can't see anything but their own distorted version of the truth, Anati thought to them all.

<You see?> the archangel announced to the stage. *<She brings one of these demons, one of the plague-bearers here. She means to befoul our holiest sanctums with disease.>*

Stop it, you idiot, Anati thought. *Stop it and look at her. She isn't what you want to see.*

"I'm not the Veil," she said. "I'm trying to stop her—her and the Regnant both. But if you won't accept that, then I can leave and find allies elsewhere."

"No!" Wicek said. "No. Please. There's no need for violence. Leorain— please. Heresy it may be, but I am prepared to consider her words. A chance to break through the seals, to hold the keys to the World's Soul and see the face of God again, to hear his voice and bathe in his light; isn't this what we have been charged with, since the first breaking of the first seals? Isn't that worth the risk?"

<She already meets with others,> the archangel said. *<Her champions scatter across the world. One is with the Tarzali as we speak, two more with the Rabaquim, in the company of a scion of the Bhakal, all intent on making the same sorts of promises. Do you deny it?>*

Wicek turned to her with something like horror in his eyes.

"I haven't seen my champions since the world was put to ruin," she said. "I came here first, after the world was changed. But my champions knew about all of you. They knew we needed allies, the same as I did. Yes, we need help. Isn't that logical, to gather as much strength as we can before we face the Regnant again?"

"You mean to let them all through to the World's Soul, to confront the Regnant together?" Wicek said. "Bhakal, Tarzali, Rabaquim? And the Nikkon, too?"

"Any who will fight," she said. "I'm going back regardless, with as much strength as I can gather. We're going to set the world right."

"Then we're with you," Wicek said. Murmurs rose from behind him, and a sharp look of disapproval from the archangel at his back. "We're with you! The council has spoken. The Skovan Church will not be left behind in this great hour. God will look on and see his children fight for his name, with the power of his hosts at your side."

"I don't know your prophecies," she said. "And I know nothing of your God, or of finding a way back to him. All I know is we have a chance to set the world right again, if we defeat the Regnant, together."

"Together," Wicek said, nodding. "I will accompany you, and Leorain, as highest of the angelic choir. If you are truly a minion of the devil, then I will offer us both as a sacrifice for falling victim to your deception. But I don't believe it. I have looked in your eyes, and I see truth, and passion, and a chance—a real chance—to fight for what is right. The others will see it, too, and join us in this cause."

"Others?" she said. "Other bishops?"

"No, no," he said. "The others. The Bhakal, the Tarzali. You mean to go to them next, yes? I will join you for the deliberations. Together we will forge a mighty army, the true hammer of God. You'll see. You were right to come to Skova first. When the door opens, you will have us at your side in the Soul of the World. We will purify it together, and restore the world as it was meant to be. I swear it, in your service, Lady Sarine."

"Friends, then," she said, and Wicek smiled. It unnerved her, all the more so in light of the archangel standing at his back, the one who'd intended to murder her not a minute before. But then, allies were allies. The murmurs behind Wicek died down to calm as he'd spoken, and he'd said he was the leader of their council. "Only...I'm not certain how to reach my champions. If they—"

The same way we went to Donatien, Anati thought. *They'll be thinking of you. From my plane, from my home, we can reach them all.*

"Give me time to set affairs in order?" Wicek said. "I must issue a call to the Chorus of the Fallen, too, to procure their highest, and see to it our sanctum is prepared against what's to come. Then we can away, and I will prove our devotion in service at your side."

"All right," she said. Suddenly the reality of what was in front of her took shape. The Skovan would help. It meant there would be more. More allies, or at least more chances to persuade others to fight at her side. She should have done it this way from the start: Bring as much strength to bear as she could find against the Regnant's shadows. It sparked hope. Dim and flickering, but for the first time since she'd been adrift among the columns of the Infinite Plane, it seemed there was a way to undo her failure and set things right.

"Excellent," Wicek said. "We'll be ready to depart within the hour."

58

TIGAI

In the Presence of Sun and Moon
Tarzal

Allakawari knelt as soon as the air changed. He lay on his back next to her, his lungs still stinging from the ash and fire. The network of anchors he'd made by reflex in the jungle ruins seemed to vibrate in his skull. They would fade in moments; none of the anchors had been driven deep into the starfield. But for now, it was like part of him was still there, an eyeblink away from returning to the chaos and ruin. They'd escaped. Five had gone, and three come home.

Orana pushed past him before his eyes could focus. Allakawari was prostrate beside them, bowed in their direction. Orana, and the Sun. The pale-skinned girl with fiery red hair, unconscious beside him. The reason Tetali had died, the reason Kaladooh and Juni had been left behind.

"She lives," Orana said. Both her hands rested on the Sun's head, cupping her ears while Orana stared into her still-closed eyes. "You did it."

"Take care," Tigai said. "The *magi* have a Dragon with them. They could follow the strands and trace us here."

"They wouldn't dare," Orana said.

It wasn't worth arguing. They most assuredly *would* dare, if he knew *magi* at all. But then, Orana had opened the clouds above the jungle and rained fucking meteors on the ruins. Wind spirits only knew if she was precise enough to have avoided him, Allakawari, and her sister. It certainly hadn't felt like it with rocks exploding in every bloody direction. Maybe the *magi*'s Dragon, if they'd survived, would think twice about chasing that kind of destruction to its source.

He blinked a few times, and rose to his feet. It was almost too peaceful here on the steppes. Too sudden a change. But he oriented quickly, and went toward the fire.

Namkat was sleeping, her body fully covered in feathers. He'd seen her fly, soaring above an army, and now she was like a damaged bird, a broken-winged creature doomed to stay bound to the earth. Her breathing was rasped, the indrawn air catching on fluid in her lungs.

"I'm sorry," he said. "I didn't know where to find Juni. We couldn't reach her before we had to go. Forgive me."

Namkat stirred, and immediately coughed. Violent spasms shook her body. He cupped a hand under her neck, steadying her head as the coughs rocked her and she winced, curling toward him.

"What—?" was all Namkat managed to say before another cough racked through her, this time steadied before it could seize her. "What happened?"

"It's Juni," he said. "I... I'm sorry."

Namkat's expression softened. "If she died, she died well." Another cough stirred, and she raised a limp hand to cover her mouth. "If she died, it was her time."

"I'm not certain she's dead," he said. "We had to go. There was chaos, and a Heron-*magi*. I didn't have a chance to find her."

"You found the Sun?"

"Yes."

"Then Juni did as she wished. She was a free woman. A warrior."

He saw the pain he felt mirrored on Namkat's face in spite of her words. Tears rose in his eyes; the same in Namkat's.

"I'm sorry," he said again.

"I'll... I'll miss her," Namkat said. "This bloody fucking sickness. I should have been there, too."

"You would have been, if it had been her who'd gotten sick."

"She *was* sick," Namkat said. "She hid it from you, from Orana. She couldn't hide it from me."

Quiet settled between them. The others lying near the fire had taken notice of his return, but held back. Soon he'd have to be the one to tell them, too. He'd have to tell Miroyah his granddaughter was dead, exploded into a thousand ribbons by the Heron's Force. He'd have to tell Kwoori his twin brother had been left behind. Maybe he'd get lucky and Allakawari would bear that news. At least Allakawari's sister would be spared the same pain.

"I'm going to find a way to get us home," he said.

"Home," Namkat said. "Where is home, for you, Yanjin Tigai? Under these clouds, where is home for any of us?"

"Back to Yuli."

Namkat smiled bitterly. "Yes," she said. "Sisters. Yuli. And Sarine. That's our fight now. The Nine Tails did well, choosing her. I hope the Flame Scale will choose as worthy a new host, if Juni really is gone. And the Wind Song."

It took a moment to realize she'd invoked her own surname.

"You're not going to die," he said.

"Of course I'm going to die," she replied. "We're all going to die, one day."

"I mean—"

"He means you're going to shelter here, and be repaid for your sacrifice."

He turned. The voice was unfamiliar. But as it spoke, a ray of sunshine fell over them from above. Not the pale light of a full moon, the full light of a noonday sun. The clouds broke overhead, revealing a clear blue sky, and a burning, swollen sun. A sight he'd missed more than he'd known, in days and weeks of dim-lit darkness.

The pale-skinned red-haired girl stood near the edge of the camp. Miroyah, Kwoori, and Ellin had all gone prostrate, the same as Allakawari had, bowed with their faces in the dirt toward the girl. Orana stood at her side, beaming and bright as he'd ever seen her.

"You're awake," he said lamely. The red-haired girl appeared vibrant and full of life. If he hadn't known better he'd never have believed she'd been comatose and barely breathing no more than a handful of minutes before.

"This is Kalira," Orana said. "My sister. The Sun."

"And I have you to thank for my rescue, Dragon," Kalira said. "Orana showed me everything. But if you'll permit me a moment, I have important work to do, while there is still fire in my blood. The Regnant may have poisoned our world, but he hasn't stolen everything from me yet."

She closed her eyes, and before he could ask what she meant the world around them changed.

A beam of light flashed across his eyes, with a high-pitched whine that faded as quick as the light.

The ground gave a single, violent heave, then came to rest.

Kalira sagged to her knees.

Orana caught her, holding the other girl's body gently as they both lowered to be seated on the grass.

Words were dry in his throat. It was as though all the moisture had been sapped from his body, as though he'd eaten nothing but sand for a year. He gagged and dry-heaved.

"There," Kalira said weakly. As suddenly as the vigor had returned to her body, it was diminished, though at least she was still awake. "They'll last now. They'll survive."

"What did you do, Great One?" Namkat asked. She was sitting now, too, her eyes full of wonder. "I feel...I feel..."

"Changed," Kalira said. "But healthy. All of you. Each of you. My gift, while it remains to be given. Champions, all, save the one who was already bound to another."

Namkat glanced at her own arm as though it were foreign, but for the first time since she'd fallen sick the feathers retracted in full, leaving only unbroken human skin.

Tigai's stomach still roiled, and he doubled over again, trying to vomit food that wasn't there into the grass.

Orana came to kneel beside him, grinning. "You look like a court-maid who just finished sucking her first cock," she said. The absurdity of it redoubled the sickness, and he gagged again.

"I'm sorry," Orana said. "I should have told her you were already bound to the Veil. It wouldn't be pleasant to have someone try and bind you again."

A hacking cough rose from his throat, and he spit, trying to clear mucus from the back of his tongue. He could taste it, spittle mixed with bile and snot, and it made him gag again.

"No," he managed to say through the convulsions. "Not...bloody..." He almost heaved again. "Not bloody pleasant."

"Better than what the makers did to our friends," Orana said, smiling and sitting beside him as though he weren't in the process of trying to regurgitate a lung. "You did well to bring Kalira home. Better by far for she and I to die here in Tarzal than secreted away to play whatever game the Regnant had in store. We owe you a debt of service, Yanjin Tigai."

"Wait," he said. "Wait. What...she's going to die?"

"We're all going to die, Yanjin Tigai," Orana said.

"Fucking...you know..." He spat again, trying to settle his stomach. "You know what I mean."

"Well, yes," Orana said. "Of course. These bodies perish when the makers do their bloody work. It is as it has always been, since the Regnant and Veil stole the keys to the World's Soul. But now we can sleep, and remember, and save what we can between seasons, between night and day. Thanks to you, Kalira had time to save a few of the Dreamers, and your sister-to-be, and now she can lie down and rest in the comforts of the Tarzali desert and that is as good an end as any of us could hope for, don't you think?"

He sat against a rock, his stomach still grumbling but without any vomit or coughs threatening to rise again. Kalira passed among the Tarzali, laying a hand on their heads or shoulders as they touched her feet. She seemed to shine, all the more so with the richness of the colors around them, bright and under sunlight for the first time in weeks. Her hands were weak, her body seemed unstable on her legs, but she stood, and smiled, and touched them as the Tarzali and Namkat ringed her with thanks and attention.

"What exactly does it mean for the sun to die?" he asked.

"A change, the same as it means for any of us," Orana said.

"And what the fuck does that mean?" he asked. "Is this why the storm is here, why it's going to be overcast night and day? Are there even going to be days anymore?"

"Of course," Orana said. "She's not going away, she's just going to die. The makers do their work to change us all, when they're set loose. It's the way it's always been. There will be another child of the Sun, when the blue sister—your world—is ready to let her walk on its back again. This is only the end of a dream. There will be others, as there are always other nights to sleep."

He looked at her, showing as much confusion as he felt, and she laughed.

"Think of it this way," she said. "When you imagine yourself winning a great fortune, fighting a terrible enemy, bedding a beautiful woman...these dreams are lovely, yes? When they end, do you vanish with them? No. You remain, and the dreams become memories of things hoped for, or desired. This is what life is. A dream within a dream. The thing that is you will remain, long after blood and meat and bone are rotted away."

"You sound like a fucking priest," he said. "That's not helpful, if my goal is getting back to the woman I love."

Orana shrugged. "You can ask Kalira. She might have enough strength to read the torrents and find the way. But I think the end will come soon. See the way she..."

"Yes?" he asked, but Orana had frozen, staring across the grass. He followed her eyes and found Kalira staring back at her, some understanding passing between them.

"What is it?" he asked. "Something's wrong?"

"She's coming," Orana said. "She's coming here."

"What?" he said. "Who's coming?"

Orana turned to him, her eyes suddenly full of fire.

"Your mistress," Orana said. "And if she intends to treat with us as her partner, the Regnant, did, then I'm afraid we are about to become enemies, you and I."

"Wait, *what*?" he said. "My mistress...? You mean Sarine?"

"The Veil," Orana said absently. She rose to her feet. "The sealbreaker. I never dreamed she would dare come to Tarzal."

"Hold on a bloody minute," he said. "If Sarine managed to find a way to come here, that's a bloody good thing. She's not anyone's enemy, not if they're already enemies of the Regnant. I'm her champion and I just saved your Sun's life. You said you owe me a debt, right? A debt of service, you said. I'm calling it in now. Don't attack her!"

Orana hesitated. "You did well. But the sealbreaker has been our enemy since—"

"Sarine isn't your enemy," he cut in. "She's not even the bloody Veil. Promise me you'll listen to her? Don't fucking throw meteors or . . . or . . . do whatever it is the Sun does to people she doesn't like."

"It could be a trick," Orana said. "*You* could be a trick, sent to keep us both from a peaceful death."

"If that were true, wouldn't I have left Kalira behind? Wouldn't I have worked with the *magi* to smash her fucking brains in?"

A light flashed.

Before Orana could reply, a dome of pure light appeared in front of them.

Where before the plain had been nothing more than grass stretching toward the foothills, now there were three figures standing there, underneath the dome. A man in a red robe and cowl stood beside a winged creature Tigai had never seen before: It appeared to be a man made of pure light, wearing golden armor holding aloft a burning sword. And the third was Sarine.

It came as a shock to see her again. Last they'd been together she was floating in delirium among the crackling energy of the Infinite Plane. Now she looked alert, determined, full of life and vigor as she hadn't been since before the sky went black.

<Stay your hands, pagan Gods,> a voice thundered in his head. Somehow he knew it came from the winged man made of light. *<We come as allies, to speak of things to come.>*

Kalira's face burned hot with fury; whatever the winged light-creature said, she had to be a heartbeat away from scorching the plain. But Orana held up a hand, urging her to calm.

"What business does a Skovan oathpair have here?" Orana said clearly. "And how dare you bring the Veil, the sealbreaker, to us?"

"I'm not her," Sarine said, at the same time Tigai said, "She's not the bloody Veil."

"Great Dreamers," the third man, the one in the red cowl, said. "Leorain and I came to kneel before you in honor, to bear a message with our new ally. I am Wicek, first and highest among the bishops of Skova. This is the Lady Sarine, who bears the mantle of the Veil's power, but Sarine is not she.

Through her, we can return to the World's Soul. We can loosen the Regnant's grip, and restore the world as it was meant to be. Treat with us, listen, and you will see."

Orana turned to him. Kalira still looked as though she meant to cook them all to cinders.

"You speak for these Skovan?" Orana asked.

"I don't have a bloody fucking clue what a Skovan is," Tigai said. "But I'll speak for Sarine. If she trusts them, then you can, too."

"I came here seeking allies," Sarine said. "The same reason I went to the archbishop in his council. The Regnant has poisoned the world. We can heal it, together."

"The blue sister is beyond saving," Kalira said. "This is a trick, meant to hasten the effects of your makers' poisons. You carry one of his creatures with you, even now."

<No trick, pagan Goddess,> the winged light-creature, Leorain, said. <We thought the same. But the Bhakal have already been granted a seat beside the Regnant's throne. The order is shifting, and we may have a chance to cleanse the decay, if God wills it.>

"A lie!" Kalira hissed.

"Archangels do not lie," Wicek said. "Forgive us, Great Dreamer, but the time is now, if you will but listen. There is an opportunity here, such as our peoples have not seen in a thousand generations. Not in a thousand thousand."

"We'll listen," Orana said. Kalira glared at her, but she continued. "I remember the Veil's last champions. Boorish. Cruel. Arrogant. This one, Yanjin Tigai, has a good heart. He claims she's different now, too. Lower your shield, and we will speak as friends do, and listen to whatever offer you came to make."

Sarine nodded quickly, though it took a second look between Wicek and Leorain before the dome's light dimmed, then vanished back into the flaming sword.

"It starts with the Soul of the World," Sarine said. "Last time I faced him, I brought only two of my champions, and a handful of other warriors. This time I mean to bring as many as I can. This time I mean to purify the world, no matter the cost."

Orana went to sit beside her, wearing a thoughtful look as Sarine spoke. But he couldn't miss the anger on Kalira's face, nor the sudden shifts as Sarine continued, first from rage to curiosity, then to hunger.

59

ARAK'JUR

Ceremony of the Honored Dead
Manacambu Highlands

Chanting filled his ears. Not unlike the sounds from shamans' tents during their holiest rituals. He, Omera, and Yuli sat on open ground atop a level plateau, and their fourth companion sat with them, the shaman Sini'ti'naya, and not one of them had their mouths open to make a sound. Still chanting filled the air, haunting and deep, echoing down the canyon walls as though the earth itself sang a lament for the dead.

He sat, holding Omera's hand on his right and Sini'ti'naya's on his left. The corpse lay between them. These were the Rabaquim. He knew it, with the deep certainty of the spirits' visions. He'd arrived where he set out to go, though the chanting put fear in him, pulsing in time with the song.

Memory stirred as the melody rose. A creature, too great to be called great, its legs the size of mountains, claws the size of rivers, a jaw that could snap a copse of mighty trees to dust between its teeth. The images seemed almost real in his head, and for a moment he felt again the terror of first looking on the thing that chased him.

It changed. Terror became determination. The vision spirits had shown him this beast. Relief coursed over him like water, the relief of knowledge. He'd come here seeking to slay a great beast. But the memory didn't fit. He hadn't come to kill the animal. He'd come for...a woman? He saw Corenna's face as though he were another man, one unfamiliar with her beauty. Who was she?

Arak'Jur pulled back. He tried to let go of Omera's and Sini'ti'naya's hands. The shaman held him firm.

These weren't his thoughts.

No, of course not. These are the thoughts of the dead. Sini'ti'naya met his eyes as the words came together, as though the shaman were speaking directly into his mind.

Laughter rang in his ears.

Do I offend you, warrior? I forget you must be unaware of our customs. I sat for my first ceremony of the honored dead before I was two. It's different, on this side, but I know it for what it is. I wish to know the man who killed me. I wish to know why, and how our meeting came to be.

The thoughts hammered his skull. Madness. He panicked, but couldn't move. *Una're* wouldn't answer his call.

No. Not like this. You deserve much honor. You lead the three that killed me. You came to us seeking a way to save your woman. And more... to fight the darkness, perhaps? Yes. I see it in your thoughts. But first you must listen. Listen.

His breath came quick and short. Sweat went cold on his skin.

No. Listen.

This. Can you hear?

The earth's melody thrummed inside his chest. A beating drum, in time with the wind.

The laughter echoed in his thoughts. Then, rising from stillness, he heard it in his ears.

His body froze. The hands held in his were gone; Omera was gone. Sini'ti'naya was gone. Even Yuli, who had been seated across from him, was gone. Only he and the corpse remained.

The corpse sat up.

He tried to spring to his feet, but the dirt was gone. Empty blackness stretched around them, emptiness like the void of speaking to the spirits. Only here he had a body, had hands, feet, and eyes. And the corpse was here, placing the spear beside him until he sat across from Arak'Jur, face-to-face among a sea of emptiness.

"This is better, I think," the corpse said. "An easier way. An older way."

"Where are we?" he asked. His voice worked as it always did. Another difference from the spirits' void.

"I am dead, and for a time you sit with me, until Sini gives me to the Blood," the corpse said, smiling. "I am... I was... called Chi'tu'aya. What is your name, warrior? I would carry it with me into the stars, if you are willing to give it."

"Arak'Jur," he said. Panic left him, slowly. This was a ritual. A strange one, and foreign, but no less sacred. He'd witnessed a thousand rites before. He could participate in this one without giving in to fear.

"Guardian," Chi'tu'aya said. "That is what '*Arak*' means among my people. And '*Jur*'...hope. But you have no tribe?"

"I am Guardian of the Sinari," he said. "A tribe from far north of here."

"Ah," Chi'tu'aya said. "Forgive me. Our names are in three parts, not two. '*Chi*' means change...or, maybe better, one who hopes for change. '*Tu*' is love. '*Aya*' is my family, among my people. We are an old line, and proud. The people of these highlands, and these jungles."

"I will honor them, when I meet them," he said. It seemed to fit, as the corpse smiled more broadly when he heard it.

"Will you speak of why you came to our jungles, Guardian of Hope?" Chi'tu'aya asked. "I saw the dying woman in your thoughts. Does she, too, have a name?"

"'*Jur*' is only a name, among the Sinari," he said. "It doesn't mean anything more than who I am."

"Ah," Chi'tu'aya said. "I meant no offense."

He waved a hand dismissively. "My woman's name is Corenna of the Ranasi," he said. "You spoke the truth: I came for her, and for the power to stand against the poison of the world's change. The spirits spoke of old powers, powers that may be able to save her from death, and aid us in our fight. That's why I came."

"The Blood," Chi'tu'aya said. "You seek the powers of the Blood."

"The name I was given was Rabaquim," he said. "Is this another name for your 'Blood'?"

"It is," Chi'tu'aya said solemnly. "We are all Rabaquim, blood and body, but the Blood are our heart, as the beasts are our skin."

"And they can save her?" he asked. "They can protect Corenna from this sickness?"

"You will see it for yourself, my friend, when Sini burns my body," Chi'tu'aya said.

"Please," he said. "I would know what you know."

"We are brothers, aren't we?" Chi'tu'aya said. "Long-lost brothers. Stems from the same seed, with different roots."

He frowned. "Is this part of the 'Blood'?"

"No, no," Chi'tu'aya said. "Only the musings of a dead man. How different the world looks, when my time in it comes near its end! How slight the differences between us. I wish I could have known you, Arak'Jur. I wish I could have known your people, your traditions, your customs, as I wish I could have shared all of mine with you. But in this, yes. I can help. For the sake of your courage, and for your woman."

The dead man picked up his spear, using its point to trace a line in the void between them.

"This world is split in two parts," Chi'tu'aya continued. "Our half is writ in Flesh, like the skin you wear atop your bones. And underneath your skin is blood. So it is with the world: Blood rests underneath. Until the dying time approaches, and the flesh gives way. We were fortunate to live through such a change, watching the skies grow dark, the rains come down with biting fire. Soon the Blood Gods will hold sway, and demand their sacrifices. It is to them you must speak your prayers. The Flesh did me great honors, allowing me to wear the skin I did, before I died. Such a beast walks the earth but once or twice each turning. Giving such a creature's body to the Blood is a powerful omen. They will surely listen, after such an offering, and grant whatever your heart desires."

He tried to contemplate the image Chi'tu'aya had shared. The dead man seemed to feel such joy in the world's transformation, where it had held only death and decay as he'd walked among his people. To see it as part of a natural cycle... like a forest burning down to its seeds, maybe, or a river overflowed to deposit new life farther inland than it had ever reached before. There was peace in such thoughts, though he struggled to hold it among his memories of death and rot.

"Remind them of the service you did, when they come," Chi'tu'aya said. "They are arrogant, if you let them have their pride. If you show weakness, they will leave you with nothing. But remaking a sick woman from your memory? Returning her to you as you remember, healthy and strong, loving you as you wish to be loved? This is within their power, if you demand it of them."

"What does it mean, to 'remake her from memory'?" he asked slowly. "I want Corenna, as she is. I don't want anything done to her."

"The Blood will give all you seek," Chi'tu'aya said. "If the price is paid, and you have done so already, ten times over, with the felling of the beast. Stand firm, make your demand, and they will relent. Hah! Imagine showing Gods such disrespect. But I'm dead now. The cares of the world are nothing to me anymore."

"The creature we killed," he said slowly. "That was you."

"It was," Chi'tu'aya said. "And it was a great honor for my spirit to wear her skin. Her name was *hata'chiya*." He grinned. "I wasn't supposed to tell you that. There is power in names, isn't there? My people believe it to be so."

A foul smell suddenly filled his nose. Smoke, and meat. He almost coughed, though there was no sign of fire here.

"Did you have children?" Chi'tu'aya asked, without seeming to notice the smell. "With this woman of yours?"

"Yes," he said. "A son. He lives still. And another son, who died by the bite of the *valak'ar*, with another woman who died the same way."

"*Valak'ar*," Chi'tu'aya said. "The warrior-serpent." His skin suddenly seemed more pale, though his smile didn't waver. "A coveted end, for powerful servants of the Flesh. I might have worn such a skin, if *hata'chiya* hadn't granted me her blessing."

"Wait," he said. "Your servants of the Flesh...you said they might have worn *valak'ar*'s skin?"

"Different roots," Chi'tu'aya said. "But the same seeds."

Burning meat filled his senses now, and the tang of acrid smoke. He could taste it in his throat.

"Your people...you can become as the great beasts? *Una're, mareh'et, ipek'a?*"

"The thunder-bear," Chi'tu'aya said. His smile finally dimmed as his skin seemed to change to ash. "The hell-cat. The birds of prey. Yes, Arak'Jur. My people do not become *as* your great beasts. We become them. The Flesh Gods put parts of our spirits into new bodies, and that part wanders the wilds in search of deaths as fitting as the one you gave to me. That is the circle of our lives. Flesh to Blood, then back to Flesh again in the cycle of death and rebirth. I hope your death will be as fine, when it comes for you. I hope your son...ah! But they are here. My body is almost gone. My time is finished."

"Wait," he said. "Wait! What do you mean...?"

But it was done. Chi'tu'aya's eyes rolled up in his head, and his body broke.

Flakes of skin crumbled from his chest, slowly at first, then all at once, as though the body had been made of sand and ash, struck by a gale wind. His smile held as the wind blew his body into the void. He vanished to nothing before Arak'Jur's eyes.

He was left alone, kneeling in the emptiness, feeling the shock of what Chi'tu'aya had revealed.

Impossible. The shamans would have seen it. The vision spirits would have shown them the great beasts' source. All the guardians of every tribe would have been called to war, to take *valak* names and run south, to travel to Chi'tu'aya's people and expunge them from the earth. And yet...Chi'tu'aya had welcomed death. He'd said the great beasts sought it out, to die in a manner that gave honor to their strange Gods. He'd said they were different roots of the same plant. All of what the Sinari were, all his people were, they owed to the spirits. Shamans and guardians acted together to keep the people safe from the beasts. Were they no more than the instruments of the deaths Chi'tu'aya's people sought? Different halves of the same whole. A means to shed blood...all his gifts, all his people's magicks...

The void around him deepened.

A darker black, first, so pure it stung his eyes to look on it. Thoughts of Chi'tu'aya's revelations distracted him until the black became so deep it seemed to swallow all hope of light.

Then it changed to red.

Fear returned. He was alone, still. A crimson haze crept inward, toward him, from the edges of his vision. And suddenly he felt a presence. Something was here.

SLAYER.

The thought overpowered him.

KILLER. MURDERER. WARRIOR.

The haze seemed to coalesce into a cloud of vapor, like blood hanging in the air. It took form over top of where Chi'tu'aya's corpse had been. He remained frozen. The thoughts echoed in his mind, repeating a hundred times every moment. SLAYER. KILLER. MURDERER. WARRIOR.

It twisted, the haze moving cautiously, like a snake. It grew with each repetition of the words, until it seemed to encompass all his sight, slowly settling into an unchanging form.

When he could move again, an enormous feathered serpent lay in front of him, a serpent made of blood, making pools beneath itself as droplets ran down its sides. It stretched to the horizon, and beyond, a mass of coils and loops, feathers and scales.

The words echoed one final time, as though every repetition came back to sound again, all at once. SLAYER. KILLER. MURDERER. WARRIOR. Then another word sounded at the end: CHAMPION?

He rose to his feet. The serpent appeared unconcerned. Curious. It cocked its head, a massive snake's head with a mane of feathers, all made of blood.

"I am Arak'Jur," he said. "Champion of the Wild. Bound to Sarine Thibeaux, scion of the Veil, at the Soul of the World."

CHAMPION. The word echoed again, a dozen times, all at once.

YOU FEAR US.

Only a single voice. A few more repeated it in whispers.

No sense trying to pretend to false pride. "I do," he said. "I fear and respect your power. I was guided here by vision spirits. They, too, held you in great respect. I followed their guidance to find a being with the power to cure the sickness that has descended on the world."

NO. NO. NO.

YOU HAVE NO NEED OF OUR BOND. YOU ARE ALREADY CHAMPION. THE MAKERS CANNOT CHANGE YOU.

"Not a cure for me. For my woman. Corenna of the Ranasi. The mother of my son."

The blood-serpent coiled itself to move closer. He held his ground.

A CURE?

"I wish her returned to me, healthy. Strong. As she was, before the storm."

WE SEE. WE SEE HER AS YOU DO. WE SEE YOUR MEMORY. YES. A POWERFUL WOMAN. WE SEE. WE SEE HOW YOU CRAVE HER. WE CAN DO THIS THING.

BRING HER BACK.

GIVE HER BACK.

AS SHE WAS.

AS SHE IS.

FOR AN OFFERING. A PRICE.

WILL YOU OFFER HER TO THE BLOOD?

"I have made an offering already," he said. "The body of Chi'tu'aya."

MMMMMMMM.

DELICIOUS.

NOT ENOUGH.

NO. NOT ENOUGH.

"It is enough," he said. "Chi'tu'aya said such a beast as he ... was ... came no more than once or twice in each turning of the world. *Hata'chiya*, he said the beast was named."

HATA'CHIYA.

WORLD-BREAKER.

The voices swarmed in a chorus, each repeating a thousand different words in a dissonant strain.

"Accept this offering, and grant me what I wish," he said. As soon as he spoke, the chorus silenced.

OR? OR? OR?

OR ELSE WHAT?

What could he say? Threats here, in their place, seemed empty. But he had faced the spirits before, in their places, and held firm. Chi'tu'aya had cautioned him against this creature's pride. Whatever this blood-serpent was, it held the key to saving Corenna. For that, he could face this thing, and hold his ground.

"You are a great power," he said. "But so am I. And I am sworn to one greater. Grant me a fair return for the offering I've given."

OR WE BECOME YOUR ENEMIES?

He had to stand firm. "You *will* grant me what I am owed."

SARINE. SARINE.

SHE SAYS SHE WILL OPEN THE DOOR FOR US.

THE DOOR. THE DOOR. THE DOOR.

SHE SAYS WE ARE TO RELEASE YOU. TO LET YOU GO FREE. TO RETURN YOU TO HER. PERHAPS THAT IS PAYMENT ENOUGH, FOR WHAT HAS BEEN GIVEN?

"You speak with Sarine now?" he asked.

SHE IS HERE. SHE IS WAITING. SHE TOUCHES YOUR BODY WITH CARE, CONCERNED THAT YOU DO NOT MOVE.

"Sarine is far from here," he said.

NO. NO. NO. SHE IS WITH YOUR FLESH. SHE TELLS US WE MUST RELEASE YOU, BEFORE SHE WILL OPEN THE DOOR.

"No!" he shouted. The sound echoed across the void, and a shimmer of color rippled along the blood-serpent's hide. Greens, yellows, purples, blues shone through among the red.

NO?

"I won't speak for her, then, only for myself. Whatever bargain you strike, our debt is not paid until Corenna of the Ranasi is safe. Do you hear me?"

IGNORANT CREATURE.

The serpent flashed its colors again, a brilliant display of rainbow colors up and down its feathered hide.

DO YOU IMAGINE YOU KNOW THE PRICES PAID HERE? THIS WORLD IS OURS, SOON, AFTER SO LONG WAITING. WAITING, FOR WHAT IS OURS. YOU DARE INSULT US SO? YOU DARE THREATEN US? YOU DARE SEEK TO HAVE US AS YOUR ENEMY?

"I don't know what you are," he snapped back. "I know you have the power to heal Corenna. And I know there is a debt between us, for the body of Chi'tu'aya."

NOT THE BODY, IGNORANT THING. THE SPIRIT. THE CHANGE FROM LIFE, TO DEATH.

YES. THE CHANGE. YES.

"Whatever the cause," he said. "You know what I seek."

GIVE IT.

One voice rang through the chorus, with a hundred more shouting it down. WE CANNOT. WE CANNOT. HER BODY IS HERS. HE HAS NO STANDING TO ASK FOR THIS.

The chorus thundered over top: GIVE IT. GIVE HIM WHAT HE DESIRES.

Blood pooled at his feet, bubbling as it rose, and took a different shape.

The serpent coiled away, and he took a step back as the blood pooled.

A SMALL THING, NEXT TO WHAT SARINE PROMISES US. THE VEIL. SHE PROMISES GREATNESS. THE VEIL. THE VEIL. GREATNESS. YOUR PRICE IS NOTHING. NOTHING. NOTHING.

Suddenly he recognized the shape within the blood. Corenna. Sleeping upright, as though she were suspended in the void.

He could trace the pattern of her face, of her hair, bound in its long, thick braid. Exactly as he'd left her, sleeping with the vision spirits at Ka'Ana'Tyat.

WE GIVE YOU THIS WOMAN'S BODY, HEALED AND WHOLE, AND OUR DEBT IS PAID. YES?

The lone voice had become its own chorus, still saddled by others saying NO.

"Yes," he said. "Cure her, restore her to her strength, and there is nothing more between us."

The serpent stared at him, passing between him and Corenna's sleeping form. Then it nodded.

WE WILL MAKE A NEW CHAMPION. The voice sounded. ONE OF OURS.

ONE OF OURS.

The crimson void shattered.

He stood atop the plateau, where he'd sat with Omera, Yuli, and Sini'ti'naya. Dirt and grass replaced endless redness. A fire burned in front of him, where Chi'tu'aya's corpse had been. The flames seemed to burn without kindling, no wood or leaves, yet they towered over him, belching a great column of smoke into the sky.

Omera sat at his side. Yuli sat across from him, on the opposite side of the fire. Sini'ti'naya stood a few paces back, exchanging heated words with Sarine. He might have marveled that Sarine was indeed there, somehow, just as the blood-serpent had claimed. Only there was another, standing in front of him.

Corenna.

She blinked, turning a look of surprise on the others, before finally noticing him.

Corenna was whole. Her skin shone in the firelight, with none of the sickness that had ravaged her in the weeks before he'd left her behind. She stood, strong and firm.

"Arak'Jur," was all she could say before he enveloped her in his arms.

Her skin felt soft, and smooth as it ever had. None of the pale gauntness of her disease. None of the weakness, the fragile shakes that had robbed her of walking, or standing on her own.

"You're here," he said.

Corenna held him back. Sarine said something to him; he didn't hear it.

"I feel... different," Corenna said. "Did you find a way to heal the sickness? From the clouds it looks as though the world is still changed."

"Not for long," Sarine said. "That's what we're doing here. Sini'ti'naya promises me their Blood and Flesh Gods will support us, when we return to reclaim the Soul."

"They will, if you are holding true to your word, Lady Veil," Sini'ti'naya said.

"I've told you a dozen times already," Sarine said. "I'm *not* the Veil."

He and Corenna separated. He still marveled at the feel of her. Corenna was here. Alive, and healed.

"How long was I with them?" he asked.

"Four days," Sarine said. "I've been here for two. You didn't move or even blink the whole time I was negotiating with Sini."

"Bloody unnatural," Yuli said, smiling. "Half again as strange as the corpse-burning ritual was to begin with. And Omera is still out. Have a look at him, if you want to see what you looked like."

He glanced down and found the Bhakal man just as Yuli had said: staring straight ahead, unmoving, gazing into the fire.

"He will be finished with the Blood when the Blood is finished with him," Sini'ti'naya said. "If they wish to bond him as theirs, he will survive. I will tend him until then, and be certain no flesh-bonds come to taste his meat for supper."

"Yuli, will you stay with him?" Sarine asked. "I have one more champion to collect, once Anati is ready."

"Exciting," Yuli said. "Of course I will, sister. But you're not leaving me behind this time, when we return to the Soul."

"Of course. I'll be back once I've set an anchor in New Sarresant, and we'll all gather there."

Their exchange could have passed in a cloud, for all the notice he gave it. Corenna was here. She flexed her hands, and smiled at him, and he held her again.

"What happened?" Corenna asked. "I remember you taking me into Ka'Ana'Tyat... then... blood? A river of it. Like something out of a shaman's visions."

"I don't know," he said. "I'm not sure how it healed you, how it brought you here, or even what it was. The vision spirits saw a chance that something could restore you, if I traveled south. I followed the path they showed, and it led us here."

"I feel like my head has been dipped in boiling water," Corenna said.

"But the rest of you is whole?" he asked.

"As far as I can tell," she said. "There's no urge to cough, at least."

"It's a beginning, then," he said. "I was...scared. Scared I'd lost you."

"A beginning," she said, patting his hand gently. It felt good to have her touch him again, though for a fleeting moment he felt a slight wetness where her fingers left his skin.

60

ERRIS

A Battered, Well-Used Road
Lorrine Province

Halt." Marquand's voice sounded over distant thunder. "We break here. Two hours."

Jiri obeyed without needing Erris's commands. She slumped forward in the saddle, letting her legs slide down from her stirrups. Fatigue ached in her bones. She might have staggered forward into the bushes if Marquand hadn't gotten there first. He held her up, gently lowering her to a dirt patch beside the road. Rain poured over them, crackling as it struck the tarps they'd draped over the horses, hissing and burning where it slid into the grass.

"They should be close," Marquand said, wiping a trail of snot from his nose as he reached for a canteen. "Shouldn't they? Another hour along this road, you said."

"Yes," she said. "We should keep on."

"You're in no state to keep on anywhere," Marquand said. "You need a bloody break. You need a bloody week to rest, after Villecours. And if I know you, you're going to start on another dome as soon as we reach the survivors here."

"Leave it," she said. She reached for her own canteen, hoisting it to drain it dry. Rainwater slipped in as she lifted her hood; she felt it burning her skin. There would be red marks, maybe blisters. Right now she didn't care.

Marquand fished for two apples, handing her one as she finished the last of her water. She bit into its skin, relishing the crispness and the juice. It felt wrong, for an apple to be whole and untainted by the sky. It seemed as though everything should be rotten, down to the last piece of fruit.

She blinked, shifting her sight to the golden sparks.

The leylines were dimmer now. Dimmer every day, except a few scattered points of light. The bright spots represented her vessels, always there, at the far edges of her vision. Those that remained burned strong, calling for her, reaching to her through their bond of *Need*. Only they didn't need her. They needed a God. They needed a savior, come to set the world aright. Two vessels blazed like suns, somewhere far to the north that had to be Rasailles. Another burned on the far side of the sea, in the Old World. Another handful in the south. She'd had thousands, once. Now her connections numbered barely more than a score, a few dozen at best. All of them called out to her for help, through the intensity of their *Need*.

She searched for the nearest, the vessel that had guided her here to Lorrine. A farmer, if she remembered it right, who had once served under her in the 1st Division, gone home to his family after the Gand campaign.

He was gone.

She searched again. If he was sleeping the *Need* connection would be dimmer than usual, but still there. She traced the leylines in her mind, feeling the distant threads that connected her to the far corners of the world. All of her vessels were linked to her, somewhere, even if they weren't always precisely where she expected.

Nothing.

She blinked again, returning her vision to normal, and rose to her feet.

"What are you doing?" Marquand asked.

She went to Jiri, picking up the reins where she'd folded and dropped them, undoing the signal that her mount was free to roam and graze.

"What the bloody fuck are you doing?" Marquand asked again. "You need rest, and so do the priests. I called for two hours."

The others had turned their attention to her, whether because they noticed her or because of Marquand's haranguing.

"Stay here," she called to the priests. "He's right—all of you need rest. But you—mount up. You're coming with me."

The last she said to Marquand, who looked at her as though she'd ordered him to run his face through a sausage grinder. Thankfully he had the sense to approach as she swung herself back into Jiri's saddle, and to speak quietly for once.

"What's going on?" he asked. "What did you see?"

"Nothing," she said. "That's why we need to ride ahead."

"Nothing?" he said. "But you said..."

He took her meaning, finally. Nothing meant her vessel was dead, or otherwise unconscious. The sickness, perhaps, though she'd connected to this farmer the last time they'd taken a rest, no more than a few hours ago. The man had been healthy enough then. An accident, maybe. Gods knew there were too many reasons for injury or death with the world changed. But he was her only link to the survivors here. More than a hundred had come together, at last head count, huddling on the ruins of their farms.

Marquand remounted as quickly as she had. The priests knew better than to question them, thank the Exarch for small mercies. She turned Jiri southeast, channeled *Body* into her and Marquand's mount together, and they rode.

A quarter hour passed, with both mounts running at a gallop. *Body* gave their legs the strength to maintain the pace, each horse breathing no harder than they might from a sustained trot through a field. Marquand's piebald stallion was skittish, new to the strength *Body* gave, but he looked to Jiri for the lead, and Jiri gave it, thundering down the country roads with the same singular purpose as her rider. Her vessel's light going dark might be an accident, and it might mean something worse. The quicker they arrived, the quicker they would know.

They reached sight of the first plantation, and she turned Jiri inward through its fields.

Once, a great crop might have come from this land. Acres of golden wheat and barley, or snow-white cotton plants ready for harvest. The rains had ruined it all. Dead stalks and leaves lay twisted in the dirt, offering no resistance as the horses cut a new path straight across. Their destination stood at the edge of the fields, a grand manor house in the oldest aristocratic style, pale gray in the afternoon haze. They knifed toward it, and she tethered *Life* to sharpen her eyes. If anything moved here, she would see.

Nothing did.

They rode into the clearing around the manor, a dirt road between the house and the field hands' quarters. It was quiet. A stone well stood in front of the house, tools stacked against it: shovels, two hoes, and a horse-drawn harrow, as though the workers had abandoned their duty midway through the day. She slid from Jiri's back and dropped her reins.

"Check the other buildings," she said to Marquand. He nodded and heeled his stallion across the clearing, leaving her and Jiri behind.

"Is anyone here?" she called out as she turned toward the manor house. "You can come out now. It's safe."

The rains answered her, a drumming hiss where they struck what was left of the roof. She went up the steps in front of the front door, a grand carved double doorway under a balcony supported by ivory-painted columns, and pushed her way inside.

Looters had already been at the manor. Glass crunched underfoot from where the chandelier had fallen in the main foyer, but where she might have expected paintings hung on the walls there were only bare discolored spots. The carpets had been torn up, or burned from leaks in the ceiling. A quick walk from the foyer to a conservatory, then a study, revealed the same treatment throughout: missing books, missing art and statues. A wonder how long it took before the fools who'd stolen the valuables came back for the stores of food.

"Come out, if you're in hiding," she shouted. "I'm here to protect you."

Nothing more than the rains replied.

She found the kitchen ransacked. Knives were missing along with the silver, with only a few cast-iron pots and pans remaining on the walls. A torn-open sack of grain lay on the pantry floor under empty shelves, with a rat noisily feasting, too busy gorging itself to notice her standing in the doorway. She rapped on the cellar door, repeating her call to come out, that she could keep them safe. Hefting it up revealed only wine bottles, apparently having escaped the notice of whoever looted the rest of the house. Just as well to leave them. Other survivors might stumble in here and find the sustenance, and she could do without Marquand taking notice of the wine. They hadn't spoken of his drinking since being reunited under the Rasailles dome. Better to leave the past in the past.

She closed the cellar and went back to the main foyer. The staircase leading upstairs had collapsed; there were rooms up there, of a certainty, but without stairs to climb there was no sense looking them over. If anyone was here and wanted to be found, they would have answered her calls.

She emerged through the front door and found Marquand, still mounted, riding toward the house. Too quick. Too much urgency for him to have found nothing.

"Your Majesty," he called, pausing to grab Jiri's reins as he rode by the well. "Mount up. You need to see this for yourself."

His tone put a pit in her stomach. His eyes confirmed what she would find, without needing to say another word.

She followed, and they rounded the first of the field hands' houses.

At first she strained to place it. A painter had come to visit the plantation, staining the houses' outer walls, the dirt paths between them, what remained of the grass. Red. All red. No battle she'd ever witnessed had so thoroughly left its mark on the earth. Because there had been no battle here. Only killing. Only death.

Jiri came to a halt, staring as wordlessly as she did.

Blood seeped from half-torn bodies lying on the ground. Pieces of skin and organs soaked in it. Hands, legs torn from bodies lay scattered between the houses. Not a single corpse remained intact. A woman's torso and head lay under a wagon, while the rest of her had been torn away. An arm in a man's waistcoat still hung from one of the doors, a death grip on the knob keeping it swinging in the wind. A child's head lay in a tangle of hair and grass, severed at the neck, its eyes frozen open in fear. Burned meat left its stink in the air as the rain dissolved what was left of the corpses, hissing and bubbling as it mixed with the blood.

Vomit came up from her guts. She dismounted, kneeling away from the slaughter.

"I know," Marquand said. "I can't...I don't..."

If he'd managed to keep himself together between finding the scene and showing her, he lost composure as she emptied her stomach. Soon the sounds of Marquand heaving out his insides joined hers.

Tears came up as her stomach seized.

This was her legacy. This was what was left of her people. She knelt forward, touching her head to the ground as she wept. It was too much. She couldn't save them. Couldn't protect them.

The smells mixed and threatened to set off another wave of nausea. Blood, meat, her own vomit. She wiped her mouth, sitting back on her heels. Vision seemed to blur. All of it was surreal, like walking in a painting. These people had been alive this morning. They'd clung to life with vigor, clawing survival from nothing, gathering food, gathering together, finding her vessel, waiting for her to save them. She was late, by a matter of hours. It wasn't *fucking* fair. She was no child, to demand fairness and justice from a world that had none. But would some small amount be too much to ask? Something. Something that spared these people the death that had come for them. Something that spared her the pain of another failure.

Jiri brought her back to her senses.

Her horse whickered, backing away from the scene, her ears tucked against her neck, her tail whipping twice, left, then right.

Alarm. It meant something was here.

She was on her feet without thinking, her pistol in hand. "Marquand" was all she needed to say to him. Tone carried her meaning.

The beast trotted out from around the last fieldhouse. A corpse dangled from its teeth, part of a severed leg that dropped to the ground as it noticed her, Jiri, and Marquand. The thing was a cat. From a distance, if she'd misjudged the size, it might have been any calico stray, only it was larger than Jiri, with a lazy, curious look, burning in eyes that blazed like fire.

"Oh mother fuck me," Marquand said.

The cat cocked its head at them, as though it were amazed there were still living creatures here, when it thought it had murdered everything in sight.

"*Mareh'et*," Marquand said. "I've fought one before. Spread. Distract and cover each other. And watch out. The fucker is bloody fucking fast."

She whistled for Jiri to fall back as she put distance between her and Marquand, wheeling around to the left around the edges of the blood. The cat watched their movements lazily. It must have been gorging itself on the dead, wondering whether the two newcomers were worth expending more effort. They'd give the thing reason soon enough.

A pop of *Entropy* sounded in front of Marquand, with an accompanying hiss and puff of smoke. Distract and cover, he'd said. She readied tethers of her own, *Body* for herself, *Shelter* woven but not yet bound in place, and two spears of *Entropy* ready to be made into cannon shot as soon as she snapped the tethers to the lines. The cat rose halfway to the roof of the buildings beside them, its claws the size of wheat threshers. Easy to see how it could have butchered the survivors here, but two binders should make short work of—

It moved.

Even with *Body*, she had to snap her *Shelter* tethers by reflex, out of fear. The cat streaked across the clearing in a blur of blood-soaked fur and claws. Her *Shelter* was useless; it hadn't attacked her. Instead the thing appeared in front of Marquand, as though it had teleported there, already savaging a second *Shelter* barrier he'd managed to get up before it arrived. Thundercracks roared between the buildings as his *Shelter* broke and tore, all in the span of less than a heartbeat from when it had been standing still, considering whether it should attack.

She fired a ball of *Entropy* in one hand and shots from her pistol from the other. The cat was already gone. Her fire exploded in empty air; her pistol shots struck the wood of one of the fieldhouses.

"Behind you!" Marquand shouted.

She ducked, dropping into a roll as a savage swipe of claws cut the air where she'd been standing. *Shelter* tethers came again, this time forming a bubble around her on the ground. The cat snarled and hissed, slamming its massive forepaws against her shield. Blood splashed as she and the *Shelter* both were driven down into the mud. Another explosion sounded. More *Entropy*, this time from Marquand. Six more thumps drummed over top of her in quick succession. Then it was gone.

She released the *Shelter* tethers and sprang to her feet, pivoting to search for the cat. Marquand was moving, sprinting at *Body*-enhanced speed toward the far end of the farmhouses. Trying to draw it away, to give her more time to strike. The cat was following him, almost on top of him before her eyes could even track the blur of its movement. Mud and blood drenched her coat and trousers, and she let go her pistol, letting it drop to the ground. Another *Entropy* blast fixed itself where the cat had been, and then she let go another, and another, trying to lead its movement like she would firing a rifle at extreme range. Each time the cat wove, as though the beast were in her head, dancing with impossible agility to avoid her attacks.

Marquand hollered, then screamed.

One of its claws had raked him along the leg, putting him in the mud.

She charged, raining double blasts of *Entropy*, one set of tethers in each hand. The thing whirled, springing to the side as she blasted the air around it, careful to place her fire over Marquand's head. It sprang away, racing into the fields.

She kept her back to a fieldhouse and went to Marquand, keeping one eye toward where the cat had fled while she tore his pant leg open around the wound.

"No, no, no," Marquand said. "It will come back."

His skin was split down the bone, from his thigh to his ankle, slicing open every artery on the way. He'd need *Life*; nothing else could stop that kind of bleeding. But he was right. A silhouette of fur moved in the fields, racing in the distance. Turning. If the cat meant to flee at those speeds, it would already be gone. Without *Life* to sharpen her senses and *Body* to speed her movements she could never have tracked it. But it was here. Coming again.

A wall of *Shelter* sprang up as the silhouette converged into a solid shape: burning eyes, bared fangs, suddenly rushing them, leaping at them through the air. Her shield groaned as the creature impacted it, rattling the ground, threatening to throw her off her feet. But the *Shelter* held. And just as quick the cat raced around the side, to where she hadn't formed *Shelter* to protect them. A swiping claw reached around her barrier wall, and she blasted it with *Entropy*. It snarled, whined, and retreated, then attacked from the other side, almost at the same instant. This time Marquand was ready. A second blast of *Entropy* exploded on the opposite side of the shield, and this time the creature howled. She whirled, a second too late, as it attacked again.

A lightning-quick jab of its claws tore into her left arm. Pain burned her skin. She yelled something, a wordless roar, and snapped another *Entropy* tether into its chest. It retreated before the tether could take hold, leaving empty air exploding in a ball of fire. This time she spun back to the other side of her *Shelter*, ready for another attack.

It came. The cat was fast, too fast, already there, already striking with its claws before she could pivot around. Only this time it jerked back, as though something had yanked the animal off its feet. It yowled, hissing as it was dragged splashing through the blood.

She let her *Shelter* go, and readied another round of *Entropy* before she could make sense of what she was seeing.

An equally massive shape seemed tangled with the cat, standing on two legs but seeming to have half a dozen fur-lined tails wrapping around the cat's limbs and lashing it across its skin. One of the tails wrapped around either of the *mareh'et*'s hind legs, crushing its bones like coiled serpents. The cat tried to twist itself, to bring its jaws and foreclaws to bear, and found tails there, too, snapping at it, raking it where it tried to attack. Then, in the span of an instant, one of the tails wrapped itself around the cat's throat, squeezing until the neck snapped, leaving its massive head lolling to the side as all the tails let go at once, letting the cat's body thud into the bloody dirt.

She was still holding in her breath, her heart thundering in her ears.

"You're hurt," the massive creature said. Only it wasn't the creature: All of its tails retracted, its hide changed from fox fur to pink human skin. Sarine. "Both of you."

Sarine went to Marquand first, tearing his pant leg open further. Soldier's training pushed away her fear, and her shock. Sarine was right: There were wounded to attend to.

"What are you doing here, girl?" she snapped, taking a place beside Marquand. *Life* came easily, tethered strands finding their way into Marquand's wounds, sealing the arteries shut first before she went to binding the flesh.

At least Sarine had the sense not to get in the way. She backed off, pausing as though noticing for the first time the scene she'd somehow stumbled into. Blood still soaked the ground, mixing an iron smell with the gas-fueled smoke of *Entropy*'s explosions, and now the corpse of the giant cat lay among the bodies of its victims.

"My Gods," Sarine said. "This was . . . the *mareh'et* did this?"

"Might have added two more to the dead, if you hadn't shown up when you did," Marquand said. "That's twice you rescued me from one of these bloody fucking things."

Marquand's body seemed to recognize the leyline tethers as she wove them, and well it ought to. She'd knit him together more than once, and from closer to death than this. It took the bulk of her attention, but not too much to notice the pain stinging in her arm, or the girl suddenly lingering on the edge of the bloody scene that had damn near claimed them both.

"I'll ask again—what are you doing here?" she said to Sarine. "How did you come to be in the middle of farming country right as we were attacked by that thing? Did you have something to do with it being here?"

"What?" Sarine said. "No! I came here the same way I went to Arak'Jur, Yuli, and Tigai. To all my champions."

She shook her head, returning to knitting Marquand's upper thigh around the wound.

"Erris, you are one of my champions, whether you want to be or not," Sarine said. "I need you, and there are more important things at stake right now than your pride."

This time she gave a soft laugh. The girl was a fool, simple and plain.

"I've gathered all of them," Sarine said. "All but you. And we have new allies. The Sun and Moon. The Skovan. The Rabaquim. All of them are waiting on the Tarzali plain. It's enough for a strike at the Gods' Seat. Enough to put the world back as it should be, to end the blackened skies and restore some sanity in all this madness."

"What do you mean?" Marquand said. "You think it's possible to find a way to end whatever is causing this storm?"

"I know what's causing it," Sarine said. "The Regnant. We confronted him, and we lost. He infused the Veil's memories into Sakhefete, one of the Bhakal Queens. I still don't know exactly how he did it, but it doesn't matter. We can undo it. We can untaint the Soul of the World. I need as much strength as we can gather, and I need your help to plan the attack. Please. I know we haven't always agreed on what to do, but you have to see it. The world is dying. We have to try to set it right."

Quiet fell between them. She had the thigh repaired; now she set to ensuring that the wound hadn't damaged Marquand's tendons around his knee.

"Your Majesty?" Marquand said. "Should we go with her?"

"Go with her?" she said. "We're not going anywhere, except farther south. Lorrine's survivors may be dead, but there are more in l'Euilliard. More at Covendon. More at Sadobal and Catalle. We have to put domes in place in time to plant a harvest. We have to protect what can be saved."

"You can save them all," Sarine said. "If you come with me. If you help me lead this attack. I can do this without you, but we'll be stronger with your bindings, with your skill at tactics and planning. Please. We have a chance, a real chance, to set the world aright. How could you see the opportunity to fix this, to heal this…all of this…and let it pass you by?"

Sarine said it with an eye toward the carnage around them.

And Sarine was wrong. Nothing they did would save the dead. But then, with the skies blackened, the disease spreading among every binder, perhaps the dead were the most fortunate of all. There were survivors still out there, counting on her, ones she'd spoken to through her vessels. If she didn't reach them to set up *Shelter* domes they would die, whether to exposure, starvation, or violence as foul as what had happened here.

"How long?" she asked. "How long before your attack?"

"That depends on you," Sarine said. "We're ready to follow your lead. I can take you to Tarzal by way of the *kaas*-plane. You can meet with them, the Skovan oathsworn, the Tarzali Sun and Moon, the Rabaquim, take stock of everything, and help me plan our attack. If you say we attack the Soul tomorrow, we go tomorrow. If you say a month, we take a month. All I know is we can't afford to fail. When we strike, we have to succeed. If we can reclaim the Soul, everything will go back to how it was before."

"I know you don't trust her," Marquand said. "But she's offering you the command. It has to be a better chance than running yourself ragged trying to repeat what you did at Rasailles and Villecours. It has to be—"

"Shut up," she said to Marquand, fixing the last stitches of *Life* in place around his knee. "And rest." She turned to Sarine. "Fine. Take us to your people." She whistled for Jiri, and Marquand's stallion. "Our horses, too. But I make no promises, girl. I'll see what you have assembled and listen to what you know of our enemy. But if I decide it's hopeless, you take me to l'Euillard without a word of question or complaint. Is that understood?"

"Yes," Sarine said. "And you'll see. We have the strength to face him, and win."

"I don't have a damned clue what you're talking about," she said. "But I'll listen. Damn me for a fool, but I'll listen and decide for myself. If there's truly a chance to fix this…mess…then I agree, we have to take it. But I'll be the one to judge our chances, not you."

"Agreed," Sarine said. By now both horses had come closer, Jiri unflinching at the carnage around them, and Marquand's stallion following Jiri's lead.

"So, how does this work?" Marquand said. "You taking us away. Is it like your…stars, or…?"

Before she could voice the same question, Sarine's metallic lizard appeared on her shoulder, its eyes glistening red, the same color as its scales.

No, the thing thought to them all. *Like this.*

The world twisted, wrenching itself sideways, and the darkness, and the blood and death around them, all faded together. She felt the sensation of Marquand, of Sarine, of a creature that called itself Anati, another called the Nine Tails, of Jiri and Marquand's horse, and suddenly all were one, and then apart, and then elsewhere, somewhere without blood or pain, and then they were under the sun again, shining down with light and heat from an unfamiliar sky.

ELSEWHERE

INTERLUDE

DAPHÈNE

A Prison Cell
Sztetabzrych

If she lay still, the pain subsided to a dull, throbbing hum in the back of her
mind.

Dried blood caked her lips, the only moisture she'd tasted in two days. It
might have been more. There was no light here in the tunnels, to help gauge
when the sun might have risen, or set. She'd slept twice since the last meal,
that was certain, and she longed for sleep again, an endless sleep. But her body
wouldn't give it. Even as she found a way to lie so her broken legs wouldn't send
stabbing pains up her spine, she couldn't find the means to let herself drift away.

She wanted to cry. But it would only convulse her, only disturb the quiet
peace she'd found after an hour of shifting to find a way to minimize the pain.

Instead she called out for her *kaas*.

You're still there, she thought. *I know it. You wouldn't abandon me. Never.
Karaxaal. Please. Karaxaal. Come back to me.*

Nothing came in reply.

It had been the great joy of her life, the moment they'd been bonded.
She remembered the curiosity, the questioning look, what she only later
recognized as the *kaas*'s emotions bleeding into hers. His metallic eyes had
appeared first, glistening red, as dazzling, brilliant a red as she'd ever seen, a
pair of tiny gemstones penetrating to the core of her soul. Then the rest of him
shimmered into existence. His tiny legs. His scales, so soft when she stroked
them the right way, from neck to tail. She'd always known she was different.
She was destined for greatness. And he was the proof. Karaxaal. His name

was a treasure she would keep locked in her heart for as long as she still drew breath. A few more days, at least.

Karaxaal, she called to him in her mind. *Please. Please come back.*

Nothing.

Arron's corpse stank in her nose. His body had been hurled into the cell four sleeps ago. Most of the time she could ignore it, but the smell suddenly caught in her throat, and she gagged. The movement sent rocking spasms through her legs. Vomit came up, from pain and stink. Her legs shook, sending violent shocks through her body as she coughed and spat up on the stone floor. The sounds of her knees cracking echoed from the walls. Smaller, miniature cracks compared to what she'd endured the morning before, but the memory brought back the pain. She would never walk again. The priest had promised her, taunted her with the knowledge as both her knees shattered under his machine. He swore this was only a taste of the torment that awaited her in the place the Skovan called hell. The place the priest swore she was bound to go, for consorting with demons, devils, and witches. If she'd had the choice she would go now. Go anywhere, do anything to escape this pain.

Stillness came again, after the hurt subsided. It wasn't supposed to be like this. Karaxaal was supposed to come, to show himself to her and her alone, a private secret she could keep from the world, or not, as she chose. She was meant to wear silk, to be doted over by lords and ladies alike. A world of sex and wine, of fine music and dancing and philosophy, of education, art, passion, and intent. That was her world, the one she'd inherited when Karaxaal had answered the prayers she'd made nightly, poring over the Codex until he became hers, and she became the woman she was born to be. She was never meant to endure this.

Karaxaal could have used *Green* to turn them all to blabbering apes. Or *Yellow* to have them pissing themselves, quivering and shaking at the mere thought that she might turn her attention toward them. That she might strap *them* to their hooks and belts, with *Red* to boost her muscles so she could hold them down alone, with no need for the black-robed, black-hooded men to keep them in place. She could be the one turning the screws, clamping spiked metal around their joints. She could hear their howls as bones broke, ligaments tore, as despair set in after their tears were gone.

"Confess," the priest had said. Only the one word, during the pain. "Confess."

She had already. Yes, she had a bond with the *kaas*, and if she'd submitted and called him a devil at the priest's prompting, she would never renounce him in her heart. Karaxaal was no devil. She'd screamed obscenities at her torturers. She'd offered to do anything, threatened to murder them all in revenge, promised to help them reach the Duc de l'Arraignon. But she hadn't truly broken. She was going to die like Arron had. Proud. Her bond was everything. Even if the *kaas* had gone silent since the skies went dark. Either Karaxaal would come back, shield her with *White* and give her the means to escape, or she was going to die. There was no middle way. The thought brought peace, here in her prison of stone and hurt and stink. She was Daphène Malmont, a lady born to nothing, who would die having tasted the best the world had to offer. There was nothing more to confess. Karaxaal was no devil, and she was no witch, and death would come no matter what else she said.

Footsteps sounded in the hall.

She flinched, sparking another cascade of hurt from her legs. Fear had her quivering, and she pissed herself with what little water was left in her bladder.

They were coming again.

She tried to heft herself up, to push herself away from the door. Footsteps. Not an imagining. Not another nightmare born of pain. Two sets—three. Four? Every step became a phantom of what she'd endured already. Two men in black to hold her down. The priest, in red. The smiling, wicked, evil priest. "Confess." She heard it already, ringing in her ears. "Confess." Then the twisting of the metal, the snapping of her bones. The pain. The wash of pain until her nerves melted into white, and the world became the time between now and the next utterance of his vile word: "Confess."

A key found the cell door's keyhole, rattling like shards of metal in her skull. She began to cry. The pain was already here with her, but she pushed her back against the wall, ignoring the searing hurt from her legs. She had to move. Had to get as far away from them as she could.

The latch clicked. The door opened.

Light from the hall poured in. Two men hurled a body into the dark, just as they had with Arron, only this man whimpered and groaned as he hit the stone, where Arron had been silent, already a corpse.

"No," the man was whining. "No, no, no. I won't. I won't."

But there were others in the hall. Two more men.

"This is where you'll stay, Brother," one man said. A voice she recognized too well. *Confess.* The red priest. "Unless you relent in your heresy."

"How can it be heresy when yesterday it was truth!" the other shouted back. "I brought her to the council out of a duty to my oath-partner. I never imagined they would agree to aid her! This is folly, I swear it on my soul, and it will be the doom of our faith. If you would only listen—"

"I've listened to you enough, Krzysztof," the red priest said. "Tomorrow we will see if the touch of God will make you recant."

The other one, Krzysztof, bowed his head and stepped into the cell. He stepped inside. Of his own volition, he stepped inside.

The others retreated, giving him a wide berth, then shut the door, and turned the key.

Krzysztof went to the other one, the one they had to throw inside.

"Be comforted, my son," Krzysztof said. "They're gone, for now. They won't hurt you any further today. Whatever they did, it's over."

The other one cried, whimpering tears. She stayed pressed against the back wall. It had to be a trick. The red priest would be back, smiling his smile, demanding confessions. "Have to…" the whimpering man said, speaking Skovan with a familiar Sarresant accent. "Have to warn her. Sarine. Not to trust…"

"Donatien?" she said. For once, the shock of seeing him dispelled the pain.

"Daphène?" he said. "Is it…are you…?"

It was him. Somehow. The Marquis's son, and her lover this past year. Seeing him here, with her broken, and him breaking, overcame her senses all at once. Tears returned. She slumped back against the wall, her legs burning with renewed pain. He wasn't supposed to be here. He was supposed to be safe, with the Duc. Anywhere but here.

"Ah," Krzysztof said. "We have another companion, and it seems you two are acquainted. I'm sorry for both of you. But there is comfort in those we know, and love."

"You're one of them," she snarled, sudden heat coming into her voice. "He called you Brother."

"I'm hardly one of them if I'm in here," Krzysztof said. "And who are you? One of the scouts Donatien and Sarine went looking for, I presume?"

"Yes," Donatien replied. "Yes…and…"

"Arron is dead," she said, feeling another wave of nausea and grief. "He's… his body is here, in this cell."

"We're all dead, I'm afraid," Krzysztof said. "The inquisitors believe the innocent will reveal themselves in heaven. Being here, it's best we resign ourselves to the inevitable."

"No," Donatien said. "We have to reach her. Have to warn her."

<You should have kept faith.> The voice came with a blinding flash, as though the hall door had been flung open from every side of the room. She squinted, raising a hand to shield her eyes. And suddenly there was a fourth person in the room: a person made of light, with white feathered wings tucked against her shoulders. Her body radiated enough light to brighten the room, and reveal Krzysztof wearing a brown version of the red priest's tunic, while Donatien was covered in blood from the waist down, the same as she was.

"Rashael," Krzysztof said. "I can't support this. I've studied the scripture, the same as you. Falsely aiding the Veil reborn will break us, as it broke the Children of Israel when they worshipped the calf of gold."

<Don't be a fool,> the light-woman said, somehow thundering it into her head. <Recant. The bishops will allow you to repent.>

"God sees my heart," Krzysztof said. "He knows I think the bishops' intent is evil. We will not win the kingdom through deceit and trickery. Those are the tools of the Father of Lies."

Nausea turned in her stomach. Whatever the light-woman was, she cast enough brightness to illuminate the filth and vileness the darkness had allowed Daphène to ignore. Puke sat in puddles, mixed with piss and blood. Streaks of filth marred the floor, and Arron's naked corpse lay against the far wall, both eyes open, staring at them. His left arm was missing, his body stretched, broken, distended, rib bones broken and protruding through his chest. He'd been a good man. A brilliant political philosopher, intent on finding a way to bring about a world of liberty and justice, and now he was broken and dead. The same as she would be, the next time the red priest came to demand his confessions.

"I'm sorry," Donatien said to her. "I'm sorry you came to be here. But we can fight this. We can find a way to escape."

"We can't," she said. "The…Krzysztof has it right. We're already dead."

"Sarine has to know they mean to betray her," Donatien said. "If we can't reach her, then—"

"Then God's will be done," Krzysztof said. "In whatever form he takes to you, with your Sarresanter virtues. God's will. I put myself in his hands."

<Then you truly are a fool,> the light-woman said. <And I was wrong to choose you, for our bonding.>

"So be it," Krzysztof said. "But when God returns to hear our prayers, he will sit in judgment of us all. I will greet him with a smile, whatever they do to my body here on this earth, before it breaks. He will see me as the man I was, spreading his gospels, serving those in need, seeking his forgiveness and his mercy when I fell to sin. I've lived a life I can put before him, without reserve. I hope you feel the same. I hope you all do."

Daphène nodded along with his words, though it hurt to move her neck. She'd never studied Skovan philosophies, but this one fit well enough for this cell, in this terrible place. She'd tasted a life of privilege, and tried to use her power to do good, to spread revolutionary ideals. Some God sitting in judgment of that would suit her fine. So long as he would know her as she lived: adorned in finery, burning with life, sitting in salons speaking of change among those born to better station than she should have hoped to dream of. That was who she was, not the broken wretch sitting here, waiting to die. Donatien, too. It was sad that they would die here, under a Skovan torturer's machines, but both of them had lived lives they would be proud to have judged by whatever God was there to greet them when they finally left this place behind.

INTERLUDE

THE REGNANT

The Celestial Throne
The Realm of Shadow and Form

He sat alone, waiting. It was always waiting, with the *kaas*. Whether one was a commoner, a noble, King or God, the serpents did things on their own time, in their own way. The Veil had always been the one to deal with this place. It rankled for it to be his duty now. But duty had to be done by someone; that was why it was duty. What had to be done, would be done, even if it dirtied a God's hands to do it.

He thought of a bowl of roast watermelon seeds, and one appeared in front of him atop a low table of beautiful carved ebony wood. The caramel taste was a comfort as he chewed.

The rest of the chamber took on the appearance he subconsciously thought it should. Even being aware of how this place worked—that he could force it to appear as a circus tent, replete with dancing elephants and lions, should he so choose—he still let it speak to his inner visions of power and authority. A grand golden throne stood thirty paces away, elevated on long steps five paces apart, at the center of what appeared to be an endless chamber, extending outward in every direction supported by ivory columns adorned with jade. It was bare save for the throne and columns, the sort of opulence in asceticism that appealed to his personal aesthetic, and always had. A chamber such as this said: *I am wealthy enough to display all the riches of the world, and I choose simplicity.*

His seeds cracked under his teeth, the only sound in the chamber. Maybe the only sound on their plane, if its denizens were still away, seeing to the remaking of the world. Then again, the Master would be somewhere, in his prison, ranting and howling about justice, purpose, purity, and reason. They should let the world progress to the sciences again, one of these cycles. An evolutionary psychologist properly trained might be able to replace him, but then, it risked too much to try and produce one. He'd considered it a hundred times and decided no. Let this be the hundred and first.

Zi appeared atop the throne.

The Lord of *kaas*. He understood that much; most of the *kaas*' hierarchy was beyond him. But when they came to treat with the creatures, it was the one called Zi who answered, and spoke for their kind.

He rose in a simple motion, turning it into a deep bow of respect.

Why are you here, Zi thought to him. *You distract from important work.*

The creature was like the rest of his kind: a common lizard, by appearance, with an elongated body and tail that made it appear more akin to a snake with legs. He'd never been allowed to handle one to learn more of their anatomy. He'd never seen one dead.

"Forgive the intrusion, noble one," he said, remaining bowed low in spite of the pains it caused his joints and back.

Why are you here, Zi repeated.

"War," he said, finally straightening. "War is coming."

You have fought a thousand wars. You don't need us for killing.

"This will be another sort of war. One that hasn't been risked in generations, even as you reckon time. One that deserves your notice, if you'll permit me to share my guesses as to what is coming."

The *kaas* stared at him, its eyes turned bright green, like cut emeralds.

It stung, to put himself under that gaze. These creatures were the source of a thousand fables, of dragons, elves, demons, devils, and all manner of evil spirits. Because they were evil, as humans understood it. The other. The thing which should not be.

"We foresaw this could happen, when we allowed her to be born," he continued. "She doesn't understand what she risks, opening the gates of heaven to foreign Gods with no restrictions or safeguards in place. The Sun. The Moon. The Blood and Flesh. The Devils and Angels. More. She intends to let them all vie for a piece of this world. But we reforged our seals for a reason. If they are broken, all creation, life itself, may cease."

It may, the *kaas* thought to him. *It may not.*

"A truth," he replied. "But a fragile one."

Why are you here? Zi asked a third time.

"You know her, noble one," he said. "We made sure of it. Go to her. Convince her to stand down, before she opens the way to the Soul of the World."

Out of the question.

"Consider it," he said. "Please. My time is running out. Your poisons are killing off my *magi*. Soon I won't be able to stand against her."

Hers will die, too. We kaas *are thorough.*

"Not thorough enough," he said. "She's encouraged the other Gods to bond champions, to insulate them from your work. You must have detected it. Souls your venoms can't touch. She means to bring them all to the Seat. The Masadi already work to fortify it against her attack, but without the *kaas* to weaken them, we risk defeat. Do you wish to see what happens when the Blood Gods taste the world's life? Do you? Can you imagine what the Moon would do, if given reign to unleash the souls in her keeping?"

My imagination goes further than yours. And if this is the reason you are here, then our audience is at an end.

"No," he said. "Zi." He paused, then added, "Please."

We were never allies, the *kaas* thought to him, rearing up on its hind legs as its body uncoiled like a cobra. *Nor should you make the mistake of thinking we were ever your tool.*

"We can release the seals," he said, panic creeping into his voice in spite of his efforts to control it. "A full remaking. No hindrances. We begin the project again, and call it evolution along evolution's path."

Zi's eyes flashed to gold, then white as polished pearls.

You would undo what has been done?

"If we had to," he said slowly. "If there were no other choice."

Did it occur to you that we, too, have evolved?

The words twisted in his stomach.

"What does that mean?" he asked.

You see us as we were, Zi thought to him. *When first you breached the limits of our existence. You see us as viruses given form on your plane. Mindless. Devoid of life. You harnessed our power to purge impurities without considering that we, too, can study the things we kill. We, too, can learn.*

"If you can learn, then you must see the danger of her ignorance."

Hers, or yours? Zi asked. *You allowed her to be reborn. You let that power wander free in your world.*

"Only out of necessity, to fix an error that had grown beyond our control. She was never supposed to survive."

Life survives. That is what we've learned. Change comes, and control is never more than an illusion.

"If that's true, then—" he began, but the plane had already shifted. The throne vanished, and the columns with it. He sat alone on an endless expanse of multicolored, flashing shapes. Only the ebony table and the bowl of watermelon seeds remained.

"No," he said, hearing it echo into the void. "No! Come back! Zi! Come back!"

His heart thundered. Hope was gone. If the *kaas* truly meant to abandon the very thing that had given them life and purpose, if the world's torpor was interrupted, the cycles unraveled to produce the sort of chaos...

But no. The dignity of a God returned.

They'd claimed the Soul once. They could do it again. So long as he and the Veil survived, in whatever form the world would allow.

Defeat would come. He saw its inevitability. But even defeat could be woven into a plan. Even death.

He closed his eyes, letting the *kaas'* realm fade into infinity. Memories and thoughts mattered more than flesh and bone. He found his, a whirling torrent of sparks and shadows. Then he reached out, to a place Sarine had yet to touch, and found hers, too. The *kaas* may have betrayed them both. Sakhefete may have proven treacherous, more loyal to the Bhakal than to the Veil's memories, but Sarine had known nothing else. Together they could endure. Together they could be reborn.

He set the Masadi to making new bodies. All he had to do was find a way to kill her, and then to die. He had been wrong, and Zi, too. There was always hope. And there was always a means to find control.

PART 4: REBIRTH

THE SISTER'S PARTING GIFT

61

YULI

Training Grounds
Near the Ruins of Palompurraw Town, Tarzal

Without the Twin Fangs in control, the attacks landed almost too fast for her to see.

Tigai appeared at the far end of the field, and as quick as she could blink he moved, appearing almost in front of her, beside a split tree trunk. He pivoted around, sighting the purple-and-blue-colored blur charging toward him, then vanished again. She lost sight of where he must have reappeared, but followed the blur as it surged through the long grass, changing direction twice before she saw Tigai again. He'd made a mistake. The anchor he'd used was too close, in the path of where the blur rushed toward him. Then it was on him, and the fight was over.

Allakawari held her wooden knife to Tigai's throat, grinning with obvious satisfaction.

"You will be dying," the Tarzali girl said, holding the training knife close enough to shave him. "You are seeing it, yes?"

"Enough," Tigai said, pulling himself free. "It's not a fair match if you don't give me time to set new anchors. You already knew where this one was."

"I won't know such a thing," Allakawari said. "But if you have taken time before we fight again, then you should have taken it."

Yuli rose to her feet, a skin of water already in hand. In the distance, beyond their field, an explosion lit up the already sun-filled sky. Smoke rose, a billowing column as wide as a house, and the Twin Fangs stirred inside her, making a low growl, barely audible at the far edge of her hearing. Marquand was working with the Skovan archangels again. A faint scent of wrongness lingered in her nose whenever they were near. She ignored it for now, as Tigai crossed the field toward her.

"Not a bloody fair fight," Tigai said, taking the waterskin as she offered it, and plopping himself down beside her on top of her rock.

She kissed the side of his head as he drank. Sweat beaded on his skin, putting the taste of salt on her lips. His sweat. His smell. It was enough to drown out the smell of wrongness, and replace it with scents of comfort and love.

"When you whine you sound like a little boy," she said.

"What?" he said. "She bloody cheated. You saw. I used the anchor by the cleared path, and she'd already turned toward it."

"At least you're my whiny little boy," she said. "Though I like it better when you sound like a man."

He scowled and spat into the dirt. Allakawari probably had cheated, or at least taken advantage of knowledge she wouldn't have had during a real fight. But in a real fight, all the whining in the world wouldn't make a difference after the result was known. Better to learn what one could from failure.

"Your reflexes are getting faster," she said. "Maybe soon you can spar against Sarine instead of the Tarzali girl."

"Would you want me to risk that?" Tigai asked. "Isn't that why you're sitting here as . . . as you, instead of the Twin Fangs? Isn't it dangerous to let the other side have control?"

"I am both Yuli and the Twin Fangs," she said. "If you love me you love us both. And yes, it's dangerous. But if you're fast enough, she won't get close to you. That's what's going to make sure you stay alive."

"You've never let me spar with you," he said. "I haven't even seen you change to the Twin Fangs since we got here."

The low growl resumed at the edge of her hearing, and she forced it down again. Better if he didn't know the Twin Fangs desperately wanted to be in control. Better if he didn't know she'd been fighting to keep it in check since they'd arrived.

"I'll keep sparring with Allakawari, I think," Tigai continued. "I'd as soon not risk having my insides crushed. At least with those wood knives, all Allakawari is going to cut is my pride."

"Be sure she doesn't cut any deeper than she has to, then," she said. "I like your pride."

He handed back the waterskin, scooting down the rock to get back on his feet. He'd be another half hour traversing the field to set his anchors, wanting to be certain he covered every pace, to be sure he gave away no weak points if she saw he hadn't walked over a given area. Not exactly the conditions of a real battle, but the point was for him to practice his reflexes—how quickly he could blink away before danger reached him—and for Allakawari to practice fighting a Dragon.

It was her signal to go. She wasn't about to leave him alone with Allakawari or her sister, Ellin, who conferred on the opposite side of the field. The Twin Fangs wasn't responsible for the distrust she felt for those two; simply noticing the looks they gave Tigai, the girlish giggles when his back was turned, was enough for that. But neither of them would go near him while he set his anchors, and Sarine had promised her time after Tigai was finished with his sparring. The Twin Fangs snarled again in her ears as she set off.

Cloudless blue skies shone down on the training fields, and the roads cut between them. She'd been afraid the darkness would stay forever, during her time under Erris's dome. The storm still lingered on the horizon, beyond the boundary of the fields: black thunderheads crackling with lightning, promising their poisoned rain. But a circle had been cut over top of their training yards, where one of the Tarzali gods had bored a hole in the sky, making way for sunshine in the daytime and a glowing moon and starlit sky at night. A return to normalcy, or it should have been. Noticing it set off the Twin Fangs' growling again, and she tried to mute it, keeping hold on her skin as she walked.

On her right, Arak'Jur sparred with what looked like a herd of horse-sized birds, conjuring shields of stone that cracked and shattered as the beasts dove and pecked and swiped with a scything claw on their feet. That would be one of the Flesh Gods' champions; they'd kept to themselves, mostly, since coming to Tarzal. Ahead Omera used a different field to spar in a more traditional style: sword against spear, both combatants using live steel, and evidently skilled enough to avoid dealing mortal blows when a parry was missed or a step misplaced. She avoided them, too, continuing on the roads that marked the boundary line between sections Erris had ordered cordoned off for each training yard.

One of the two Tarzali Gods was sitting in front of the farmhouse that had become the main meeting hall. Orana, the one they called the Moon. The Twin Fangs surged inside her, almost lengthening her fingertips to claws. Almost making her grow taller, thinner, hairless, as it changed her form. She held it in check.

"Is Sarine inside?" she asked.

"Yes," Orana said. "Are you still trying to warn her about me, and my champions?"

The bluntness took her aback.

"I haven't . . ." she began, but Orana cut in, smiling. By appearances Orana was an eight- or nine-year-old girl, but she'd seen through that façade almost at once, when she'd arrived here. Neither Orana nor her sister were children, or even human, no more so than Natarii warriors were when they changed their skins.

"I'm only joking," Orana said. "You don't need to worry about Allakawari, though. She's never even had sex; she's not likely to know how to seduce your husband-to-be, unless he wants to be seduced, which is really more a problem between you and him than you and her, and certainly not a problem between you and me. I'd rather you and I find a way to be friends, if we can. Your tattoos are fascinating. I'd love to know more about what they mean."

"Another time," she said. "I came to see Sarine."

"Another time," Orana agreed. "You'll find her upstairs. Meeting with the newcomers."

"Newcomers?" she said. The Twin Fangs snarled audibly; it rang in her ears, though blessedly, unless she gave it control no one else would hear.

"The last of us to arrive," Orana said. "The Spirit-Weavers of Nikkon. I spoke with their leader in this age, a woman who called herself She Who Gazes into the Deepest Seas. Can you imagine having such a name? A mouthful for a mother to call a child like that in at supper time. Her own fault, though, I suppose, for giving a newborn girl that name in the first place."

"Mm-hmm," she said, glancing up toward the farmhouse as though it had suddenly changed its shape, or its smell. Something was different. Orana was right; newcomers were inside. The Twin Fangs would have noticed, if it hadn't been distracted by Orana's presence.

"Make time for me, Yuli Twin Fangs," Orana said. "You'll find I'm not your enemy."

Again, the bluntness pulled her out of her thoughts.

"I didn't say you were," she said. "Tigai speaks well of you, and your sister."

"He does," Orana said. "But he isn't you. And he isn't your other half. Kalira tells me both sides are equally important with you Natarii. I don't mean to take either of yours for granted."

"Fine," she said. The Twin Fangs stirred, but made no further attempt to gain control. Its focus was on the farmhouse now, and the smells within.

Those smells had been strong outside the house; they overpowered her nose as soon as she stepped inside. The Twin Fangs itched inside her. Five new, unique scents, not including Sarine. One smelled like coal long-buried in the earth, one smelled of water and brine. One stank of ash and sulfur, another smelled of poignant spices and fish, and the last reeked of cherry blossom perfume, ordinarily a lovely smell, but here, condensed as this was, it flooded her nose, almost enough to make her gag.

She forced them all down. Sarine had promised her time. Besides, whatever was going on here, she was a champion. It was her place to be more than a soldier, if she wished it.

She climbed the circular steps to the upper floor, needing no guide to find the smells' source. In the largest room at the end of the hall the door stood open. There were no chairs or table; all six sat on the floor, the five newcomers ringing Sarine in a half circle with their backs to the doorway.

"Yuli," Sarine called. "All of you, I'm proud to introduce one of my champions, and my adoptive sister. This is Yuli Twin Fangs Clan Hoskar, of the Natarii. Yuli, this is a delegation from the Nikkon isles. I think it's safe to say they intend to join our cause?"

Sarine made the last a question to the room. Heads nodded stiffly. Yuli hardly noticed. As one, the five Nikkon turned to stare at her. For an instant the air shimmered. She was Yuli, and the Twin Fangs, both at once. Images danced around each of the five seated in front of her. She saw the Twin Fangs locked in combat against a man in red armor wielding a spear. She saw the Twin Fangs hefting a dead man, a drowned man, from the water. She saw the Twin Fangs standing atop a great mountain, a smoking volcano, at the head of an army descending on a small village surrounded by autumn leaves. She saw the Twin Fangs fight beside commonfolk wielding pikes and scythes against armored soldiers. She saw a shadow prowling through a sleeping city at night, its claws wet with fresh blood.

"She is known to us," one of them, an ancient, wrinkled woman—the one who reeked of salt and brine—said. "Though she has not landed on our isles in many lifetimes. This time, we come to you. Great Warrior. Woman of the north."

"She Who Gazes into the Deepest Seas?" she said. It fit, and seemed to take her aback.

"You remember us?" the woman asked, full of surprise.

"Orana told me your name," she replied. "If you intend to fight alongside us, then be welcome. I came to speak with Sarine, but I can wait if you're still occupied."

"We're almost finished," Sarine said. "Join us?"

She shook her head. The images of the Twin Fangs still swirled around all five of them. Confusion settled in the deepest parts of her, where the Twin Fangs had been growling and snarling almost unabated for days. A small relief, for the Twin Fangs' rancor to subside, but the confusion felt no better.

"I'll wait downstairs," she said. "Find me when you're done?"

Sarine nodded, and the other five bowed where they were seated. She retreated from the room. It felt like waking from a dream. She went down the stairs, to a small room adjoining the kitchens. A wonder that, in a farmhouse filled with Gods, Empresses, priests, and generals, no one had thought to bring a cook. She set a kettle over the already burning stove, and had tea steeping by the time the bustle of footsteps upstairs indicated Sarine and the Nikkon were finished. To her and the Twin Fangs' relief, the Nikkon smells faded through the front door. Only Sarine's drew closer.

"Sister," Sarine said, and she set her tea down for a quick embrace. The Twin Fangs recognized the Nine Tails, and for the second time today its snarling subsided. Natarii warriors were sisters first, above all other concerns.

"You're happy with how your meeting went?" she asked. "I wasn't expecting any new arrivals. Orana surprised me, when she told me they were here."

"Anati told me they found their way to the *kaas*-plane on their own," Sarine said. "I went to see what they wanted, and they came with me. They'll be strong allies, I think. Their people have lived on the Regnant's side of the world for dozens of cycles, and never submitted to his control. They're eager for a chance to strike at him, and reverse what he's done."

"Well, good," she said. "Did they...did they recognize the Nine Tails, like they did for me?"

"They did," Sarine said. "Apparently your people have a long history with the Nikkon islanders."

She shrugged. Her knowledge was her own, but the Twin Fangs—as with all the other Natarii war-forms—had lived long, long years on its own, with new hosts and new bonds in every age. Its confusion didn't mean the Nikkon were wrong in the visions they'd shared. Only, perhaps, that the memories were old. Very old.

"It's nothing I was taught," she said. "But I'm not particularly wise, or well-learned. It's possible the Twin Fangs visited them, long ago. It didn't seem to know them now."

"What did you want to see me about?" Sarine asked. "We haven't had enough time for each other since coming here. I'm glad you asked to meet."

"It's...ah..." She sipped her tea to gather her thoughts. She wasn't even certain what her thoughts were. But sisters could speak freely. "The Twin Fangs has been uneasy since coming here. I thought at first it was just the change, the return to blue skies, the unfamiliar magicks...even seeing Tigai and Namkat again. And you."

"You miss the rest of our sisters," Sarine said. "Juni, Imyan, Kitian."

"Yes, of course," she said, "But no. Whenever I go near one of these new... allies...the Twin Fangs starts snarling in my ear. Like it wants to seize control of our body and attack them. It's made me suspicious. It doesn't trust Orana or Kalira. It sees Wicek and his angels as enemies. And it *hates* the Rabaquim. I don't know. My emotions are a mess. Are you feeling something similar from the Nine Tails? Or on your own?"

"Yes," Sarine said. "Every day."

The admission was a powerful relief. It went through her like heat from her tea.

"Trust isn't easy," Sarine continued. "We only just met most of our new allies. They might be planning all sorts of things to further their ends, and hinder mine. The Nine Tails wants to strangle shadows lately, with all the suspicion and second-guessing. But one thing I know for sure: We all share a common enemy. Our alliance might be made of sand and twigs after that. We might turn on each other and rip all of this apart. But at least the enemy will be gone, and there will be a chance to set the world aright. I have to do something, and this seemed like my—our—best chance. Do you think I'm being a fool?"

"No," she said quickly. "No, I don't. And thank you. I needed to hear that. I thought I was alone in feeling this distrust. I thought...well, I was worried you were being foolish, if I'm being honest. But if you see the danger I'll trust you to navigate our way through. And I'll watch your back on the way."

"Thank you, sister," Sarine said. "We'll get through this, somehow. And I really do miss the others. So does the Nine Tails. How does it work, for their forms to choose new hosts and be reborn?"

"There will already be girls marked to help them find their way," she said, brushing a finger over the tattoos on her left cheekbone. "But we can speak more on Natarii traditions later. I should get back to Tigai."

"He's still sparring with the Tarzali?" Sarine said. "I don't like the way they look at him. Like he's a cat they brought in from an alley, wondering when he'll let them pet him."

She smiled. "Don't worry about that," she said. "I'll be his claws if he's forgotten he has his own."

Sarine smiled back. The Twin Fangs seemed to settle under her skin. Its suspicions and snarling would return soon, but this time in service to their sister. It helped both halves feel at ease, knowing she and the Twin Fangs weren't alone.

They kissed each other's cheeks, and she emptied the rest of her mug into the basin before returning to the training yard, once more enjoying the unexpected heat of the summer sky.

62

ARAK'JUR

Training Grounds
Near the Ruins of Palompurraw Town, Tarzal

Stone shattered as two *ipek'a* slammed their bodies into his shield. He had already retreated, falling into a crouching stance. *Ama'illa* granted his blessing, changing Arak'Jur's skin to metal plates as the birds attacked again. Wings flapped to distract; the source of their lift was their powerful inverted joints and musculature in their legs. A female struck him with its scything claw as it landed atop him. *Una're* gave him the strength to brush it aside, and a thundering squelch of mud sprayed the area where its body impacted the ground. The rest of the herd renewed its attack a step slower than the alpha female. It gave him time to reconjure a shield, this time of Ice. When they struck, they cracked and shattered pieces like broken glass, peppering the field.

"Good," Corenna shouted from where the observers stood, fifty paces off. "Perfectly done."

"He was slow," Seh'sa'raya, the Flesh-Caller, said. "My female struck him before the second shield."

"He wasn't slow," Corenna said. "Your bird was too fast for the rest of her pack. He didn't need to defend against all of them, and the *Ama'illa* skin was enough protection for the one attack. What did you think, my love?"

He was still catching his breath. All the *ipek'a* instantly retreated, as though one mind controlled the whole herd. Which it did. Seh'sa'raya *was* the birds, just as he was also the man standing by the split-wood fence, conversing with Corenna and watching them spar. The revelation still shocked him to his core, when he paused to reflect on it. No time for such reflections now.

"I can be faster," he said. "Not worth expending *lakiri'in* or *mareh'et* for it. But maybe—"

"*Axatl?*" Corenna suggested. "Or *lu'raki?*"

He nodded.

"Set yourself again, guardian," Seh'sa'raya said. "My birds are ready."

The alpha female snorted, already back on its feet. It pranced away, back to the opposite end of the field. The others followed, trailing after its blood-red feathers with sniffs and chirps, making sounds halfway between lizards and birds. They seemed to be their own animals, each one moving and considering its surroundings with its own mind. Yes, they moved together as a herd, but so did elk, or geese in flight. And yet they were all connected, all sharing part of Seh'sa'raya's mind, or perhaps his soul. Sharing his arrogance, too. He saw it in the way they moved, as though the world and all its inhabitants were somehow beneath their notice. They sauntered into place at the alpha female's behest, and turned as one toward where he stood.

He would try *lu'raki* this time, the vulpine trickster, and pair it with *astahg*. See if the Rabaquim Flesh-Caller was ready for him to vanish and reappear, already disguised as one of his own birds. Neither he nor Seh'sa'raya would strike to kill, but it would be well to test the limits of the Flesh-Caller's coordination between his beasts. And it would hurt neither of them for him to deal a wound to Seh'sa'raya's pride.

He called on Earth, weaving his shield of stone as the alpha female screeched the call to attack.

"Did you see his eyes?" Corenna asked. She laughed, mimicking with her hands. "Wide as water jugs, when he set his birds to attack themselves. And then, after, when he realized what you'd done...Ah, but he needed that, and so did I."

He grinned. His body still groaned from the morning's exertion, raw soreness and a score of cuts and gashes in his skin. But Corenna's laughter was a sound too long missing from his life.

"Is he always like that?" he asked. "He seems either arrogant and aloof, or furious. I don't think I've seen him display another emotion since we came here."

"Seh'sa'raya?" Corenna said. "I hardly know him better than you do. He certainly seems like a cloud in need of rain, though. More at home over there than here with us."

He glanced in the direction she'd indicated, out beyond the boundary of their fields. Storm clouds waited in a ring, thundering and black, kept at bay by the Tarzali Sun Goddess, Kalira, to afford them a temporary summertime. The memory of what those storm clouds meant for the land beneath their rains ached in his skin. He'd slept too many nights huddled under a tree canopy, fighting to ignore the burns and blisters where the rains had leaked through to disturb his sleep. Forests had been scorched, rolling plains turned to fields of mud and fire, and his people and all the others that knew what was best for their survival crawled underground like worms, wriggling and tunneling away from the rain.

"Here," he said. "This seems a fine place to eat."

Corenna unrolled the blanket she'd carried from the farmhouse. The Tarzali patterns were a strange mix of colors and shapes that never quite seemed to repeat or fit into each other. A reminder of how far they'd come to be here. She laid the blanket gently atop the grass and unpacked her basket, withdrawing a pair of burnt, crispy breads, and set to topping them with bean and meat paste and leafy greens. Even the vegetables were foreign here, though he enjoyed the food well enough. He reached inside the basket as she worked, retrieving a bottle of sap-cider the Tarzali called *a-linah*, pouring them each a cup full.

"An incredible thing, isn't it?" Corenna said.

"What is?" he asked.

"That," she said, indicating the ring of storms beyond the fields. "The work of Gods. Who could have imagined we could stand against it."

"We didn't," he said, taking the flatbread as she offered it. "That was Kalira's doing."

"You know what I mean," Corenna said. "We're going to fight to change it all. All of it, all the mysteries of creation, the fabric of spirits and people and Gods and beasts. It's...it's what I've fought for my whole life. I thought my calling would mean fighting other tribes, maybe fighting fair-skins for our land. Now that it's here, and it's becoming clearer what we're meant to do, it all seems so...vast. Like the skies. Too much for one person to hold or understand. Does that make sense? I feel small. But I'm ready, all the same."

He bit into his lunch, enjoying the mix of softness and crunch between the bean paste and the crispy greens. He tried to ignore the wetness. The soft tang of iron. Whatever Corenna touched had carried those sensations, those smells since she'd been brought back to him atop the Rabaquim plateau. Examining his food would show no contamination, no source for the wetness or the smell, but he still noticed it, as though everything she touched had been tainted with blood.

"When I was a boy I thought there were two great challenges in the world," he said. "Pleasing Valak'Innim on a hunt, and trying to get girls to notice me the way they noticed Kar'Emet. Much has changed since then."

Corenna laughed. "Ghella told me stories of you as a boy," she said. "The way she tells it, you had no trouble attracting interest from Sinari girls. She said once you hit your man's growth, even a few of the women who should have known better were watching you across the cookfires."

"I remember," he said. "My mother kept them away. She was never one to yell, or need to raise her voice. She spoke, and they listened. And I was so furious with her. I wanted those attentions, you understand, and she kept them all away."

Corenna finished her bite of food, then spoke quietly.

"You've never spoken of your mother," she said.

"She was a weaver," he said. "The best in any northern tribe. She had delicate hands. A soft voice. She went to Ka'Ana'Tyat before I was born. Now that I know what passes there, I think she asked the spirits for a vision of who her son would marry. She never let any of the Sinari women come near me. I didn't begin with Rhealla until after she'd died. I think...perhaps she saw you. Perhaps she knew the woman I was meant for wasn't Sinari at all."

Corenna smiled gently. "She never told you this, did she?"

"No," he said. "What passes between women and the spirits belongs between them."

"How did she die?" Corenna asked.

"Sickness," he said. "A burning fever. During a hard, cold winter."

"Too much sickness, lately," Corenna said, turning her attention from him to stare off into the clouds. "I'm sorry, Arak'Jur," she said. "That must have been a heavy burden."

"It is," he said. "It was. What of your mother? Did Ka'Hinari tell you how she passed?"

"I was too young to remember," Corenna said. "But she was like me. A Ranasi woman, blessed by Wind. My father told me she was killed by a great beast. The tribe celebrated her, gave her a great burial ceremony. But it was... it was a lie. I know now. They tried to hide the truth out of shame."

He looked to her questioningly, but said nothing.

"You weren't wrong," Corenna continued. "We aren't supposed to speak of what we see at Ka'Ana'Tyat. But I asked about her when I went there, and I saw. She was like me. Truly like me. She rode to war with the men, against the Hurusi. She died from a musket wound, shot in the chest, but not before she took twenty of their warriors with her into death. I think maybe...maybe her memory is why my father allowed me to..."

She trailed off, and he let her words hang in the air. A shocking thing, if it had been known. The sort of blasphemy that might have encouraged the neighboring tribes to unite and take up arms against the Ranasi. How meaningless the politics and tradition all felt now, though the memories still had weight, of how things had been, and could be, and might be again. Yet women fought against great beasts, fought to protect what was left of the tribes. Guardians rode to war, and Corenna was as much a warrior as any man. As much a guardian as he was.

"You honor her memory," he said. "Her true memory. The memory of the spirits."

She wiped her eyes. "Yes," she said. "Yes, I do. If she'd survived, maybe she might have been able to teach me, to better prepare me for this fate. Who can say what might have been different, if things had happened other than they did? Maybe your mother would have kept me away, too. Maybe we'd all be farmers, or trappers, or war-chiefs, in another life. What matters is where we are now. What we're preparing to do. And that we're together, finally. Both champions. Fighting side by side."

He reached to grab her hand, and she took it in a firm grasp. He tried to ignore the faint sensation of wetness, the tang of blood in his nose as soon as their skin touched.

"I love you," he said.

"I love you, too," Corenna said. "Whatever happens. Whatever's coming. We're together, no matter what, until the end."

A hot breeze blew as she said it, and it warmed him deep within his bones. And elsewhere.

He set down his cup of *a-linah* and reached for her.

"I'm sorry," she said, and pulled away. "I can't. I want to. I do. Believe me, I'd hoped, when we found an hour to steal away...but..."

"They're calling," he said.

She was already packing up her food in the basket, her demeanor changed as swiftly as the wind. "Yes," she said. "I'm...I'm sorry. I didn't think they'd summon us again so soon."

Now he saw the signs: a telltale flush in her cheeks, what might have been a rash atop her arm. Marks of what had been done to her, though it stung to think of it that way. Marks of the Rabaquim Blood Gods. She was their champion now, just as he was bound to Sarine. Corenna worked in a flurry, rising, ready to leave, leaning down to peck her lips against his cheek.

"Soon," she said. "Tonight. I promise."

And before he could reply, she was gone. He watched her bound across the fields, toward the stones that had been set up on its northern edge. Two, three times a day she received their summons, and he'd learned nothing of what transpired while she was away. At first it had been enough for her to be back with him, healed and whole, full of life. Now...now it was still enough. She was still here. Finishing his lunch alone, left to carry the blanket and baskets back to the farmhouse, was a small price to pay for Corenna healthy and alive. But it still stung. And the food tasted more bland, the cider somehow duller without her laugh, her tears, her stories to share it at his side.

He finished the meal, turning back to watch the clouds thunder on the horizon. Soon. They were ready to fight the monster behind the world's sickness, as soon as Erris called for their attack. And Corenna was right. Whatever was coming, they would face it together.

63

OMERA

A Stone Altar
Northern Edge of the Palompurraw Fields

He was the obedient supplicant, here to kneel before Gods.
Tisa irinti burned in his blood. They seemed to enjoy the taste, or at least hadn't told him to stop using it. So he used the herbs whenever he felt the burning, the heat rising in his cheeks, the flush creeping across the rest of his skin that meant he'd been summoned here, to kneel. *Tisa irinti* made it easier to sit and watch, to observe without flinching when the blood-priests unsheathed their knives.

All four of the Blood's champions knelt around the altar. Him, the obedient supplicant, perfectly still, his head bowed, his sword and herb-pouches belted at his side. Ta'ta'ichin, the hairless old man, shaved clean, with red patches permanently emblazoned on his skin where the Blood Gods' summons made their marks. Nin'ti'dana, the girl, barely a woman, if she was even flowered, who stared at him the same way she stared at everyone: as though she dreamed of eating them before they were dead and burnt. Corenna, the other of the Blood Gods' champions not born to Rabaquim lands, who knelt in her white dress that somehow managed to never stain.

They waited.

It might have galled, and triggered his princely instincts. He was Omera again. They'd restored his memory, shattered the Mindhunter magic that Sakhefete had used to control his mind; that was the price they'd paid, for him to acquiesce to be bound as one of the Blood Gods' champions, to fight in their service. He owed a debt, and it would not be paid with impatience or irritation. He was the obedient supplicant, and if the Gods summoned him and asked him to wait, he could do it, kneeling without moving for hours, if that was what they required.

Today the waiting would be short. One of the masked priests appeared behind them, escorting a young man by the arm. A low chant sounded in his ears, made by voices he wouldn't be able to see, no matter how he strained to find them. The priest stepped between the champions, helping the youth climb atop the stone. The boy was Rabaquim-born, with their light brown skin, hazel eyes, and curled brown hair, following the priest's instructions in a laggard daze, a step slower than he would have, had he not been drugged. Omera had recognized it the first time he'd been summoned here, before he'd thought to use *tisa irinti* to dull his reactions to what would follow. He'd offended the Gods, then, and been rebuked. He wouldn't offend them now.

The boy lay down atop the stone. A white cloth was tied around his loins, and he was naked everywhere else. The boy's breathing came quickly in spite of the drugs, and he stared up at the sun. His limbs trembled. Yet the boy made no move to rise from the altar, lying still as the masked priest fastened cords around his wrists and ankles. Two more masked priests arrived when it was done, each rotating between the limbs to check the ties. Omera said nothing as they worked. He was the obedient supplicant.

The chanting continued, but now a higher chorus added harmonies atop the droning bass. Dissonant strains sounded fluidly between perfect chords.

The priests drew their daggers together in one motion.

The youth made a sound. A gagging, panicked sound that cut through the drugs that would be flowing in his system. He lurched against the bonds.

The daggers fell. Precise, clean strikes. Two of the masked priests stabbed the neck, the shoulders, the abdomen and lower torso, the loins. One focused on the heart. Repeated strikes with each blade.

Blood flowed down the side of the stone. Blood splattered where arteries were cut, flying from the blades as the masked priests plunged their daggers in and out. The youth cried out in pain, screaming a dulled, drugged cry of alarm that mixed with the chanting. The screams were the melody over top of the harmony twisting underneath.

The screaming continued past the point where the youth's heart should have been dead. Somehow air found its way into the ruined lungs, then back through the pulp left of his throat.

The daggers fell to the ground, clattering against the stone and splattering more blood on the champions. Omera felt the taste of it on his tongue, felt it sting as it splashed across his skin. He was the obedient supplicant. He gave no sign of horror, or revulsion. It was almost finished. One of the masked priests produced a jug of oil, splashing it atop the screaming, bloodied mass that had been the boy's body. The others rubbed it over his skin, covering the young man as thoroughly as they'd cut into him before. Then as one the masked priests stepped back.

Ta'ta'ichin rose to his feet. A slow climb, with arthritic limbs and old, aching bones. The champion took a torch from one of the masked priests and lowered it to the boy's feet. Nin'ti'dana stared at the flames hungrily as they leapt up the youth's legs, engulfing the body in a sudden inferno. Corenna looked at it curiously, detached, as though she were studying it, like a scholar poring over a book. He felt nothing. *Tisa irinti* smothered whatever emotion was there. The flames covered the boy's head, all of him burning, belching smoke up toward the sun. Somehow the screaming continued. Only now there was a second melody, enjoined and harmonizing the first. It grew louder in his ears. Louder, louder, until it threatened to consume the chant entirely, growing still louder as whatever sang the second song approached.

Then it was here.

Redness engulfed his vision. Blood coated the landscape as far as he could see. The others were gone. He was left here, alone, as the serpent manifested itself, rearing on its coils, towering over him as blood changed to brightly colored feathers and scales.

CHAMPION, the serpent hissed and sang, both at once. MY CHAMPION.

"I serve," he said automatically. *Tisa irinti* burned strong, even here. He was the obedient supplicant.

WE HAVE LEARNED, the serpent sang. WE HAVE LEARNED PART OF WHAT YOU WISHED TO KNOW.

He kept his head bowed. If the Blood God intended to share knowledge, it would. Even *tisa irinti* gave him no need to beg.

The serpent relaxed its coils, lowering its head to his level, staring at him with curiosity.

WE WILL FIGHT WITH YOU, the serpent said. YOU KNOW THIS? OUR BOND. WE FIGHT AT YOUR SIDE, AND YOU AT OURS. WE WILL HAVE WHAT WAS PROMISED.

"And so will I," Omera said. The words escaped before *tisa irinti* could snuff them. Those were not the words of the obedient supplicant. Those were the words of a prince.

The serpent's mouth drew back in a smile. The rest of its body had changed from dripping blood to dazzling-colored feathers, brilliant blues and yellows, oranges, reds and greens. The teeth were still made from blood.

KING OMERA, the serpent hissed. KING OMERA, OF THE UNITED BHAKAL.

The herbs flared in his blood. He wouldn't provoke his master. The debt between them was real, however it chafed. He fell back to silence, bowing his head, waiting.

WE DO NOT HAVE POWER OVER YOUR MOTHER'S LEGACY, the serpent sang, a chorus of a dozen voices. HER MAGIC DIED WITH HER. BUT WE'VE FOUND SOMETHING. SOMETHING YOU WISHED TO KNOW.

His vision blurred, and suddenly he saw another image transposed over top of the serpent's coils.

A woman.

Underground, in a pitch-black cave.

Somehow he saw her clearly.

She tended a small fire, shivering.

Meat cooked in a pot.

She cradled her forearm, a severed mash of blood and bone, slowly regrowing, but not fully formed yet.

"Sakhefete," he said. "You found her."

WE FOUND HER, the serpent said, and the image vanished, shimmering back to the plane of blood and scales.

"Take me there," he said, and his fingers were somehow already gripped around the hilt of his sword.

NO. YOU FIGHT FOR US FIRST, THEN WE FIGHT FOR YOU. ONCE WE OWN OUR PART OF THE WORLD.

He tried to relax his grip. His fingers wouldn't budge.

Sakhefete. The reason his mother was dead. The reason her empire had burned. The reason he had been forced to humiliate himself, to beg the aid of this serpent monstrosity of blood. His captor, his mistress, half his people's rightful Queen. She had to die.

PATIENCE, PRINCE. THIS WILL COME TO YOU SOON.

His vision blurred again, and he saw himself.

Wearing a golden crown.

Standing atop the balcony of the palace at Konghom.

Waving.

An adoring crowd cheering.

The Empire's glory restored.

A King.

"Stop," he said. "You've shown me this enough."

YES. BUT YOU MUST BELIEVE WE CAN GRANT THIS. WE CAN MAKE THIS TRUTH. THE BHAKAL, IN UNION WITH VORDU AND RABAQUIM. A GREAT POWER, AS GREAT AS THE UNION OF AMAROS AND JUN, OF REGNANT AND VEIL. YOU SEE? WE ARE NOT GREEDY FOR POWER. WE WILL SHARE. THE FLESH, THE SPIRIT, THE SORCERER. THEY RULE THE LIVING. SO LONG AS WE RULE THE DEAD.

"Is this why you summoned me?" he asked.

NO, most of the voices sounded, while others sounded YES.

WE WISHED TO KNOW OF YOUR PREPARATIONS. WE HAVE SHOWN THE AMAROS EMPRESS ENOUGH. SHE SHOULD BE READY TO STRIKE. THE TIME SHOULD BE NOW.

"I'm not privy to their planning," he said. "When they're ready, they'll call for the attack."

OUR CHAMPIONS ARE NOT TO BE EXCLUDED. WE HUNGER. WE HUNGER.

"I know," he said. "You've told me already. I'm ready. The others are ready. When the call comes, we will go."

WE HUNGER, the serpent said again, this time thundering and cruel, resounding over the plane of blood.

THE WORLD MUST CHANGE. IT HUNGERS, TOO. FOR AN END. AN END TO REGNANT AND VEIL.

"It will," he said. The vision echoed in his memory. He was born to be King, and he would have it. With his mother dead, it would fall to him, if he had to execute every brother, every vestige of her seed. Ambition burned in his chest. What were the dead, to a King? The Blood Gods had restored his memory, inured him against the visions of sickness and death the *kaas* had already wrought inside his body. He remembered who he was. Prince Omera. He remembered everything.

TELL THEM. OUR ENEMY IS WEAK. HE IS WITHOUT ALLIES. EVEN HIS QUEEN. SAKHEFETE. SHE ABANDONS HIM. SHE HIDES IN HER CAVE, THINKING SHE CAN ESCAPE OUR NOTICE. THINKING SHE CAN ESCAPE HER FATE.

"You want me to relay this to Empress d'Arrent?" he asked.

TELL HER. TELL THEM ALL. IT'S TIME.

"Then release me, and I will."

The serpent smiled, revealing its blood-wrought teeth.

The redness vanished.

Burned meat stank in his nose.

Night had fallen on the altar. The others were gone. The other champions, the masked priests. Pieces of the burned corpse remained atop the stone.

His joints were stiff, from kneeling so long. He forced himself up, stretching his legs.

Sakhefete was in hiding. It was good to know, and bittersweet. He'd hoped she would be there, defending the Soul of the World, when Erris gave the order to attack. He would have looked for her during the battle, made sure it was his poisons, his steel that ended her life. Instead he would hunt her down like a mad dog after they'd claimed the world. After he was King.

For a fleeting moment it seemed wrong.

The blood-smell in his nose. The burning ambition, gnawing at his mind. The thirst and hunger for power. The Blood Gods had repaired his memory, filled in every gap, every missing moment, as payment for the debt he swore to pay. Had he always wanted to be King? Had he always burned for revenge, for the chance to murder his enemies: his mother's sister, his brothers, whoever else tried to stand in his way?

Yes. Of course. It was the herb confusing his memory, his sense of self. He dabbed a finger in his pouch of *ubax aragti* to help counteract whatever *tisa irinti* was left in his blood.

The others would already have gone to the Empress, to plead the Blood Gods' demand for action. But Erris d'Arrent would have ignored them. An old man, a flesh-crazed girl, and a foreign tribeswoman. Champions they may be, but they were less than a pale reflection of his shadow. He was a King. When he spoke, the Empress would listen.

64

ERRIS

An Empty Field
Near Rasailles Palace

The wind blew cold, without rain. The dome should have shielded them from it, from toxic rains and wind together. Instead gashes hung in the air, broken flaps of white and blue suspended as though frozen in glass. Half the *Shelter* had collapsed and vanished into nothing. The rest lingered as a monument to her decision to abandon her people. She was Empress of nothing now. The Rasailles dome was broken, and she was to blame.

"It couldn't have degraded so fast," Captain Perain said, the commander of this detachment of scouts. "Never in all my years have I seen such a thing."

He said it for her ears. He knew she was here, watching behind her vessel's golden eyes. Instead of responding she stared at the ruins. This was the right place: The lingering *Shelter* would have confirmed it, if the bedrolls, wagons, food stores, crates, and barrels hadn't. Toxic mud sizzled from the rain, and scorch marks marred the newly planted grains where they'd intended to make fields for harvest. But there were no bodies she could see. That meant there was still hope.

"There are survivors," she said. "We had contingency plans to flee nearby, to a cave network in the foothills to the west. Five leagues, on a direct line. Can you find it, Captain?"

"Yes, Majesty," Captain Perain said. "We'll pick up their trail and report."

"Good," she said. "I'll return on the half hour. Don't waste time foraging here, or gathering supplies. We can come back later to figure out what happened. For now, the people are the only priority. Am I understood?"

"Perfectly, Majesty," Captain Perain said. "We'll find them."

She passed another look over where the dome had once stood, and nodded, as stoically as she could manage.

She let *Need* go.

Tears came almost before her senses returned to her body.

She was alone in her private chambers, what had once been the master and mistress's bedroom, the lord and lady of this manor, or whatever they were, as the Tarzali reckoned such things. The status mattered nothing for her claiming the rooms. She'd needed the space for planning. Writings and drawings lay scattered across every surface, every table, armoire, and half the couches and chairs. Guesswork, mostly, theories and ideas of what they might face when Sarine opened the way to the Gods' Seat. This was why she'd left the Rasailles dome, and all the other domes she'd meant to make, behind. This was what she'd chosen over the people who had looked to her to save them.

She cried. Emotion surged in her belly, making knots in her throat. In public, or in others' company, she might have held it in, presented the face of the leader they needed to see. Here, alone, she could let it out. The people at Rasailles had depended on her. They trusted her, put faith in her, and she'd abandoned them on a fool's dream of making new cities to stand against the storm. Then she abandoned them again to come here, to lead this impossible army against a figment of an impossible nightmare. It weighed too much. At least they hadn't seen any bodies, torn and twisted and ripped apart, burned by the acid from the storm. The people must have gotten away from whatever collapsed the shield. Her binders had been sick, yes, but they weren't so close to death that they would have let it fall to disrepair. Something must have happened to force them away from the dome.

She took up a sheaf of papers she'd been reviewing, leafing through them to find her place. Drawings, facsimiles illustrating ideas that Sarine, Kalira, and Marquand had worked on that morning. Guesses, mostly, of what sort of defensive fortifications the Regnant would use what Kalira had called Masadi to put in place at the Gods' Seat. The whole exercise was madness, simple and plain, like a carnival game made real. But this was what was in front of her. For an officer who had made her career in studying the ground, in knowing her soldiers and her enemies better than any of them knew themselves, it seemed impossible, like waging war in someone else's dream, with faerie tales for weapons and nursery rhymes for enemies.

The image of the broken dome fought through her concentration, and she ignored it. She had eighteen Gods and champions here at the farm, twenty-three if the five late-arriving Nikkon Spirit-Weavers would be fully integrated into their attack. Reports suggested the Regnant could have anywhere between five and fifty, depending on whether he'd gathered allies as Sarine had, whether he was bringing *magi* that hadn't been bonded as champions. So much she didn't understand. She could plan an attack of one squad of elite soldiers against an enemy fortification anywhere in the world, only this fortification wasn't in this world, and every one of her elite was worth an army unto themselves. So were her enemies. Not a strike of eighteen, or twenty-three, against five, or ten, or fifty; she was planning a clash of powers too terrible to consider, a fight between men who could shatter earth at their feet, women who could turn any force against itself and amplify its destruction, between the avatars of the Sun and Moon, between shadow-limned assassins and spearmen who wielded animals as though they were extra limbs in combat.

She needed a drink.

She rose from her couch, crossing the room to find another sheaf, this one documenting the abilities of what the Skovan called their "archangels." Two champions had come from their race: an old wrinkled man, Wicek, and a younger, sharp-eyed priest called Kacper. Leorain was the archangel bound to the first, a winged warrior of pure light, while the other's angel, one they called "fallen," was named Baael, a creature of shadow and fire, with the sort of wicked curving horns mothers might conjure to frighten their children into behaving and eating their suppers. She thumbed through Marquand's notes. Her mind had made a connection by intuition, even if she didn't fully understand it. Something here connected with what she'd been reading before about the Tarzali.

A rap sounded on her door, startling away the conclusion that had been almost there, almost in her grasp.

"Come in," she said, annoyed.

Sarine entered with Kalira behind her. Two girls, one hardly an adult no matter how much power rested in her hands, and the other a literal child, by appearances no more than nine or ten years old.

"I don't have time for more debate," she said before Sarine could speak. "I'm due for a scout's report in less than ten minutes' time."

"I'm not here for that," Sarine said. "We'll attack when you're ready. Kalira and I were working on something, with the blue sparks. I think... it might give you what you've been asking for. Part of it, at least."

"Part of what?" she said.

"A way to see what we're up against," Sarine said. "You're always saying how you can't go into battle without knowing the ground, how you'd never order infantry to charge without cavalry support. I think we may have found a way."

She set down her papers. Kalira came and sat across from her, as cavalierly as a true nine-year-old might have done. Never mind Sarine butchering military aphorisms; if there was a chance, any chance at all, to scout before their attack...

"Tell me what you have," she said.

"These are excellent drawings," Kalira said, picking up one of her papers, the illustrations of the Skovan archangels. "Did you do these?"

"No," Sarine said. "I did. And Marquand. Tell her, though. Tell her what we found on the Infinite Plane."

"I always hated the Sathenine," Kalira said. "They're really nothing like the Cherubim, all teeth and horns. And they have no music at all. Hard to imagine, isn't it? No music, no songs."

"What do you have?" Erris said. In a matter of minutes she'd find out whether Captain Perain's scouts had found the survivors' trail. Whatever well of patience she had for nonsense had long since run dry.

"A window," Kalira said. "I'm no master among the sparks, you understand; that was never my domain. But we may have succeeded in forging a connection between our world and his. A way to look, to see without touching."

"See what?" she said. "Be specific. No time for cryptic or obscure language."

"We found a way to look into the Gods' Seat on the Infinite Plane," Sarine said. "At least I think we did. If we're right, then we can see the columns of sparks that represent the people there. I know some of what their sparks will represent, and Kalira knows more. It's possible the others...Leorain, or the Rabaquim, might recognize even more. It would give us a way to scout what we're up against."

"Explain this further," she said. "What exactly can you tell from these 'sparks'?"

"The gifts of this world," Kalira said. "I know you as an order binder from the patterns of your sparks. A gray net of *Faith* to trap the others: red *Body*, green *Life*, and so forth."

"You can see the colors and patterns of the leylines?" she asked.

"Of course," Kalira replied. "And the same for some of the others. I recognized the bond the Nikkon girl has with the dweller of the deep, the one called She Who Gazes into the Deepest Seas. On the Infinite Plane, their bond shows as two columns, one for her, one for her whale-serpent, both linked by a crackling chain of white and purple. If I saw her in the Gods' Seat, I would know she had joined our enemy instead of us. Do you understand what I'm saying? If we're careful, we can observe the properties of the souls he has with him in the Seat."

"To say it differently: We can tell how many champions he has, and with what gifts," Sarine said.

"Well, no," Kalira said. "Not precisely. 'Champion' means a bond with the apex of a line—I think, judging from the numbers we saw, he's risking bringing them in without that protection. But the point remains. We can scout, as Sarine put it. We thought you'd want to know as soon as possible."

"I thought the bond as a champion was what kept us from falling sick," Erris said. "Are you telling me he's brought *magi* with the sickness to fight on his side?"

Kalira shrugged. "It seems likely. We'll have to do our scouting in more detail to know for sure. I don't know the *kaas'* patterns, but Sarine will, given her bond with them."

"Wait, what do you mean?" Sarine said. "What do the *kaas* have to do with this?"

"Enough," Erris said. "Don't bring me speculation or disharmony. You two go and work out whatever disagreements you have, then bring me firm information and courses of action. For now, if you have a way to scout and ascertain the numbers and abilities of our enemy, then I need you to do it, immediately, and bring me a report. How long will it take to gather the information?"

Sarine and Kalira exchanged glances. "A few hours, maybe?" Sarine said. "Or maybe a few days. I can't be sure until we've spoken with the others."

"Then do it," she said. "Give it your highest attention. Start now, and return to me the instant you have something workable."

Kalira rose, offering an almost mockingly sweet curtsey, the sort a child would practice before their first showing at court.

They left, and left her mind turning.

It would be a start, knowing the numbers she faced. Until now her notes and papers were speculation, culled from Tigai and the others' recollections of which *magi* houses' champions had been faced, which defeated, and which were likely to still be in the field. She had a good accounting of what the *magi* sworn to the Regnant could do—the swordsmanship of Crane, the force manipulation of Heron, the rapid-onset disease and sickness of Owl, and a half-dozen others—but Sarine and Yuli had reported facing another champion, similar in kind to Yuli and her sisters, a woman who had wielded a shadow-form of the Natarii. Scouting the precise composition of her enemy's forces would change and tighten all her plans. Contingencies could be scrapped and replaced with solid preparations.

She gathered the papers she had prepared on the Flesh Gods' champions—

Seh'sa'raya, Wata'si'tin, and Nalai'ti'turu—and moved them beside the newly drafted notes on the Nikkon Spirit-Weavers. Seh'sa'raya commanded an *ipek'a* pack alongside his personal use of whip and sword. Perhaps his birds could be paired well with what Marquand had described from the woman called She Who Shakes the Trees with Thunder: a blinding flash when her spirit manifested itself, followed by ball lightning and gusts of wind. Or perhaps that would pair better with Corenna or Arak'Jur, both of whom could shape the wind and direct it, and maybe the lightning with it. It bore testing, during the day. A sparring session, if she could organize it, or—

Another rap sounded at her door, only this time they didn't wait for her call to enter. Omera came in, striding as though the chambers belonged to him.

"Your Majesty," Omera said, offering a crisp bow. "Forgive the late hour."

Hard to believe she'd known the man as a servant. He stood now more like a lion, surveying her chambers as though he were looking for something to eat.

"It isn't a good time," she said, returning her attention to her papers. "Return in the morning and I'll hear whatever you have to say."

"I passed Sarine and Kalira on the way upstairs," he said. "I expect they'll have told you of their efforts to open a window to scout the Gods' Seat."

She paused, glancing up from her work. "What do you know of that?" she asked.

"I know they made a terrible mistake," Omera said. "The Blood Gods watched them do it. Kalira and Sarine peered through the window, yes, but, Your Majesty, while they were looking in on our enemy, something peered back at us."

The earlier excitement froze in her veins.

"What do you mean?" she asked. "The Regnant?"

"It had to be," Omera said. "Their window went both ways. He can watch us now, the same as they're watching him."

"Call them back," she said. "Go. Now. Get them. No, I will." She was already on her feet, following where Sarine and Kalira had left.

65

SARINE

On the Porch Steps
Manor House, the Tarzali Farm

W hat did you mean, about the *kaas* sparks being present in the infected?" she asked. Anati's emotions had spiked when Kalira said it, though Kalira herself seemed calm, as calm and collected as she ever was.

"They won't be there long," Kalira replied. "It would be delicate, to catch the serpents in the act of poisoning their victims. But then, they're almost done. A few more months, at most, before all traces of the *kaas* will be gone."

They went down the manor house steps, heading toward one of the empty barns they'd claimed for their work on the Infinite Plane. Livestock would have lived there, if they hadn't been frightened away or killed in the rains. But the space was open and clean enough, once she and Kalira had shoveled away the manure. Best of all, it stood apart from the manor house and field hands' quarters where the rest of the champions and Gods had taken up residence. Privacy was in short supply on the farm.

"But what do the *kaas* have to do with binders, and all the other magic-users, getting sick?" she asked.

I'm sorry, Anati thought to her. *I . . . I wasn't sure you wanted to know.*

"I'm not certain what you mean," Kalira said. "The *kaas* aren't making them sick. The *kaas* are the disease."

She felt as though she walked on unsteady ground, though the dirt and grass hadn't changed or been rained on to turn them to mud.

"Anati, what is she saying?" she said.

We're the agents of change in this world, Anati thought. *It falls to us, when the time is right, to sever and change... to revert things to how they were, when the seals were broken, but to allow for growth. We... kill. We harvest* Black. *We've tried to learn and grow ourselves, but the unmaking always falls to us.*

"They were made by granting intelligence and memory to what your people knew as viruses," Kalira said. "One of Li's first experiments, before he became known as the Regnant. Their bodies came later, as did their plane."

That's a lie, Anati thought. *We always existed there. We've always had souls.*

"Not souls I ever recognized, little snake," Kalira said. "Not souls that come to me or my sisters when you die. *Can* your kind even die?"

I'm not a fucking snake, Anati thought.

"Wait," she said. The ground was spinning now, not just made of mud. "You mean to tell me the *kaas* are what is making people sick?"

"Not only the people," Kalira said. "Take a look around, past the edge of my sunlight. The *kaas* are responsible for every poison the Regnant unleashed on the world. Not just responsible, either—they *are* the poison. Disease given life."

"Then..." she said. "Then they can change it back. Right, Anati? You can change it back?"

"They're only tools," Kalira said. "They have no will, when it comes to control over the Soul of the World. Isn't that right? You are good tools, who do as you are instructed. Win control over the Soul and they will happily remake the world in whatever form you desire. Why do you think my sister and I and all the others were so receptive to your offers of alliance? We all have our vision of how things ought to be, and the *kaas* are good slaves, fit to bring those visions about however we see fit."

Anati said nothing. Without seeing her, she couldn't say for sure, but she had the image of her *kaas*'s scales flushed red, her neck low, her body hunched forward on all four legs. Signs a *kaas* was furious.

"I..." she said. "I don't know what to say."

"Sarine!" a voice interrupted from behind.

She turned with Kalira to find Erris all but bounding out the front door. They'd just left the Empress's rooms, where she'd seemed at least interested in the prospect they'd brought to her, if more than a little tired and overworked. All traces of the latter were gone now.

"What—?" was all she managed to say before Erris all but trampled her and Kalira together.

"The window you opened to look into the Gods' Seat," Erris said. "Omera claims it can be used in both directions. He claims the Regnant is using it to watch us, to count our numbers and abilities, as we speak. Is it true?"

The Bhakal prince emerged from the house, and approached at a measured pace, wearing a stoic, unreadable look. He and the others sworn to the Rabaquim Blood Gods had unnerved her since their arrival, and the prince's detached air only reinforced it now.

"Of course," Kalira said. "Li Zheng is no fool. We were never going to be able to watch him without being watched ourselves."

"Wait," she said. "What? You didn't say anything about the Regnant being able to reverse what we did."

"Not reverse," Kalira said. "Just a consequence of observation: What we see can see us back. Simple physics."

Erris cursed.

"You have one hour," Erris said. "Understand? Gather every scrap of information you can bring me on what we're facing."

"One hour?" Kalira said. "Didn't you hear Sarine before? It could take days to properly read the sparks on the Plane. We have to work with the others to even begin to understand everything we're seeing."

"One hour," Erris repeated. "Your instructions are clear. Get to it, and report as quick as you can."

"What happens in an hour?" she asked.

"We attack," Erris said. "You two managed to botch whatever hope we had of surprise. Our best chance now is to catch him when he's still gathering information, before he's had time to put it to use. A hasty attack is better than being where and when the enemy expects. Omera and I will gather the others. You two scout as many of their numbers and capabilities as you can before we go. Meet here, on this spot, in one hour and not a hair's turn of the clock over. Understood?"

"I understand what you want, but—" she began, but Erris had already wheeled around, marching back to the house.

"Well," Kalira said. "That was sudden."

"Why didn't you say anything?" she asked. "If the Regnant could be watching us the whole time we worked, couldn't he have attacked us, too? Weren't we in danger the whole time?"

"When are we ever not in danger?" Kalira said. "You are the Goddess of Life, and I the Goddess of the Sun. There are always poisoned knives lurking in the dark. Always. I trust you to handle it, or I wouldn't be your ally. Now, shall we get to work before that woman comes shouting again?"

"I still want to talk about what you said before," she said. "About the *kaas*."

I thought you'd be angry, if I told you, Anati thought. *I'm sorry.*

"Later," Kalira said. "Time enough after we win, and if we lose, then what does it matter? First, let's get the Empress what she wants, and see to readying ourselves for a fight."

"Fine," she said. Emotion stewed like a bubbling kettle, but Kalira was right. It stung, all of it, thinking their success at watching the Gods' Seat carried a hidden failure, that they might be forced to attack before Erris was ready, that they risked everything and it was going to be her fault if they failed. Thinking that Anati lied to her, that she'd concealed the truth of what had been happening since the Regnant poisoned the Soul.

I didn't lie to you, Anati thought. *I just didn't want you to hate me.*

"Later," she said. "I need to focus."

The *kaas* retreated into her thoughts by the time they reached the barn. Her mind was still spinning, jumping from failures to blame, but the sparks came easily enough as she sat atop the hay piles at the center of the room. Kalira sat opposite her, meeting her eyes, staring with her bright red pupils, and the world shifted between them.

"Together," Kalira said, her voice already disembodied, seeming to come from all around. "Like we practiced. You lead, and I follow."

———————

Sparks shifted and flowed on the Plane. She felt Kalira with her, yet also distant and separate, a second column intertwined with hers. Watching. Attached. Seeing what she saw. She was in control of movement, of where they looked and what they observed, but she shared her eyes with the second column. Her torrent was blues and blacks, with the platinum sheen of Anati's form nestled inside hers. Kalira was all red and orange.

"There," Kalira said, her voice echoing in thought as though she'd spoken aloud. Or perhaps she was speaking aloud, sitting on the floor of the barn, and she only heard it through her body on the physical plane. "That's our window."

She recognized it, and guided them in.

The towering spire of the Soul of the World burned on the horizon, a black pillar now, where before it had always been pure white. Continuing on to reach it would have taken mere moments; anything she could see here on the Plane was as good as at her fingertips. The trick to opening the window was to leave the Soul at the farthest edge of her vision, a marker on the road, as it were. Metaphor seemed pointless in a world where sparks defined every shape and form, but she'd grown accustomed to moving here. More and more it felt natural, like learning to swim instead of panicking over drowning. She guided them toward the entrance, and they moved as one.

Sparks flowed and crackled all around them. But the physical world's sparks followed certain rules. Torrents made each shape, each object, in combinations of colors and patterns that repeated and held constant for each form they represented. A chair would always have the pattern of a chair. A cat would always have a cat's patterns, with different colors for its fur, for its claws, its temperament, how hungry it was and how long since it had slept. Near-infinite degrees of complexity, but always an underlying pattern and truth. If she'd had a hundred lifetimes she still wouldn't be able to memorize it all, but it was enough to know it was there, unchanging and constant, that she could have memorized which patterns and colors corresponded to what.

The rules changed in the Gods' Seat.

She felt it, more than saw it. Wherever the Seat was, it existed in different space. Sparks still flowed and burned, but in shifting patterns, ever-changing, as though reality itself bent around the energy of each torrent and column.

They drew close to the window, until the torrents that represented her and Kalira almost pressed flat against its surface. The invisible barrier had been the clue they'd searched for, a demarcation of the line between the physical world and a different kind of space. It had taken a week of searching to find it, then another to learn how to manipulate their energies to straddle the line without physically shifting from one place to another. Now she moved them into place almost without effort. This place was hers, even when it lay beneath the Gods' Seat. Perhaps especially so, then. It belonged to her, and she meant to reclaim it.

"Focus," Kalira said. "We have to find them. As many as we can."

She nodded, or tried to. The gesture had no meaning here, when her body was little more than a shower of sparks.

The Seat had changed.

Without understanding what physical realities the sparks evoked she struggled to see it in physical terms, the way her eyes would process the image if she were standing there in person. But before, the place had always been a stone labyrinth, a network of twisting corridors and chambers. Its sparks should have been...gray. Gray and static, slow-moving, like stone itself. Now, looking through the window, the sparks were fluid. Greens and purples and pale blues, in shifting patterns, billowing like long grass in the wind. What did it mean? Would they arrive in the Seat and find themselves in a grassy field instead of the stone hallways? That could be useful, too, if she could discern exactly what sort of ground awaited them. What sort of traps the Regnant might have set, or built into its design.

"Two," Kalira said. "I recognize an Owl, and a Crab. Both champions. No sign of the *kaas*."

She turned her attention to the space between the sparks for the terrain. Kalira was right to be focused on their task. She practiced what they'd done before, calming her mind, letting the natural rhythms of the space settle around her. Deviations would stand out, no matter how small. She could—

"Another," Kalira said. "Or . . . it could be the same Owl. Damn it. It is. He can't have two champions bound from the same line. Unless he has allies, too, but I don't think Li would—"

"Kalira," she said. "I need to focus."

"Oh," Kalira said. "Of course."

Calm.

The billowing grass sensations returned. Green sparks sizzled and popped, unchanging. Black ones intertwined with the green, and purple seemed to fall between them, as though trying to fill an empty pit between columns of the other colors, only to vanish into nothing when they fell too far. All static. Slow. Until . . .

"I see one," she said. "Red sparks twisting around a silver core. Some blue."

She felt the sensation of Kalira's sparks moving over top of hers. Orange and red haze clouded her vision. The first time she'd done it Sarine had severed the connection at once. It still felt invasive, like a parasite gnawing on the inside of her head.

"Yes," Kalira said. "Yes, that's one of them, for certain. And not a champion. See there? The residue of a *kaas*-pattern. That one is sick. Damn it all. That means we were right. He's going to have a lot more than five or six champions waiting for us. See if you can spot another to confirm it."

The red and orange shimmered as Kalira separated from her space.

They were going to fail. The thought came suddenly, but hit hard. There was no way they could scout every column and torrent in the Gods' Seat. Even if they'd had the days she'd asked for, there was no bloody way. There could be two hundred columns waiting, hiding, moving, confusing one sighting for another. Erris had given them an hour. They weren't going to be ready, and it was her fault.

There will be time for self-pity later, Anati thought.

No need to let Kalira hear her replies. *I'm not pitying myself*, she thought back. *I'm feeling emotion. It's not the same thing.*

It is when the emotion you're feeling is self-pity, Anati thought. *And anyway, you may have put Erris in charge, but if you don't like her decisions you can take control. You can call off the attack.*

No, she thought. *The others trust her. I trust her.*

Then trust her, Anati thought. *You have to believe we can win. Erris does, even if you do end up going in without having taken the time to look individually at all fifty-three souls in the Gods' Seat.*

"Wait," she said out loud. "Fifty-three?"

"Fifty-three what?" Kalira said.

"Anati?" she said.

What? Anati thought. *Aren't you trying to look at all of them one at a time? To tell what magicks are bound up with their souls?*

"You mean to tell me you know exactly how many there are?" she said.

Of course I do. Don't you? They're right in front of you.

"Anati says there are fifty-three people there, beyond the window," she said. "She thought we wanted to look them all over, individually, but she says she can get the count by just looking through the window."

"Fifty-three?" Kalira said. "He couldn't have so many. Most wouldn't be champions, which means better than eight in ten would be sick."

I can't tell you what magic they have, Anati thought. *But yes, she's right. Forty-seven of them are . . . sick. If that's what you call being touched by my race.*

"Leaving six," she said. "Six champions, out of fifty-three. The rest are just *magi*. They won't be as strong, and they'll be infected. I'm sorry, Anati, I know I've offended you but I could kiss you right now. Erris will want to know this right away. Kalira, can you—"

The window shattered.

It felt exactly like glass, except it was made of sparks, hot and burning. A thousand burning wires erupted around her.

Kalira shouted something.

Pain flared in her body in the physical world. A step too late, *White* sprang up around her, severing half the cloud of shattering sparks, leaving the rest burning, embedded in the torrent of blue and red and platinum that was *her* here. Sparks flooded through the tear in the space in front of her, almost twisting reality where they touched the sparks and torrents of the physical plane. She was caught in it. Even surrounded by *White*.

Kalira was still shouting. Finally she recognized the words.

"Get us out!" Kalira screamed. "Get us out! He's here! Get us out now!"

A shadow moved behind the flood of sparks. A backdrop of black instead of emptiness. She fought to clear her head. She could leave the Infinite Plane with a thought, and return them to their bodies in the barn. Pain lanced through her. And something else. A tendril made of ink, darting through the sparks like a knife. It touched her. Connected itself to her. Wrapped around the core of who she was.

She should be dead.

The Regnant's tendril touched her, enveloped her. Death magic tore through her being.

Then it was gone.

The sparks vanished, replaced by bales of hay, dim lamplight, and the smell of manure.

Kalira shot to her feet, gripping both sides of her head and staring at her as though she were a corpse.

"Sarine!" Kalira shouted. "Sarine, are you there?"

She blinked, and pulled back. "I'm fine," she said, or tried to. It came out in a cough, and she tasted blood.

Kalira backed away and let her finish. She wiped a hand across her mouth and cleared her throat. Her stomach heaved, as though the cough might turn to vomit. It didn't. A deep breath, then another. Steady. Calm.

"You look like you went through a wheat thresher," Kalira said. "Are you sure you're all right?"

Her body ached. Another glance at her arm showed why: She was covered in cuts. Her skin burned, pocked by skin-deep gashes everywhere she could see, and, judging from the burning over her whole body, everywhere she couldn't, too.

"Yes," she said, trying to stand and look herself over. "I'm hurt but I'm fine. What in the Gods' name was that? Was that him?"

"It was," Kalira said. "I expect he didn't enjoy being looked at. Naturally, he tried to kill us."

The black tendril shimmered in her mind. It touched her, but hadn't brought any pain that she could remember. That had come from the bursting sparks of the window between worlds shattering in her face.

"Did…did we make it worse?" she asked. "Now he knows we're watching him and his people. We never looked so closely before. Now he'll be expecting us to attack."

"Let's leave that for your tactical genius," Kalira said. "One of the perks of having champions bound to us: We don't have to be experts at everything. Are you sure you're okay to walk?"

"I'd as soon find some water for a hot bath," she said. "You can heat it, right? Being the sun and all?"

Kalira grinned. "You're fine," she said. "Let's go tell Erris what we've learned. With any luck, she'll go ahead with the order to attack. Then your next bath can be in the Gods' Seat, and we can watch the *kaas* remake the world again, together."

66

SARINE

They stood in loose groups, pairs and triads, eyeing each other as much as watching Erris walk among them, giving final commands.

Kalira stood at her side, and one of the Nikkon, a man dressed in red silk called He Who Stands Before the Highest Mountain, whom Erris had only just assigned to their group. Her skin itched. The cuts had been shallow, already healing thanks to the Nine Tails. But Gods if she didn't want to itch through her clothes.

"You look like you have fleas," Kalira said.

"I'm trying not to," she whispered back.

Next to them, Erris was addressing another group of three: Wicek, the Skovan archbishop, with Allakawari, the Tarzali knife-fighter, and Omera, the Bhakal prince. She'd seen those three drilling together. Leorain, the angel bonded to Wicek, would put up a shielding barrier around them, then flash blinding light from his sword to cover while the two close-fighters attacked with knives and curved sword. Devastating at close range, and protected from longer-ranged attacks. So the theory went, anyway. All the rest of the pairs and triads were organized along similar lines. She'd spent most of her time studying the nature of the Gods' Seat and the Infinite Plane, but Erris had been devoting her energy to building them into a miniature army, combining their talents and drilling them on working together for attack and defense.

"Fifty-three," she said. "I wonder if we should have brought more who weren't bound as champions. We could have brought fifty more."

Kalira shook her head. "One of Li's gifts is for memory," she said. "Without the protection of a bond, he could erase their thoughts, make them freeze, perhaps even shatter their minds altogether."

She thought back to her first attack on the Seat. Had the Natarii warriors suffered from that sort of attack? Only Yuli was bound as a champion then. She hadn't been able to see them, hidden behind the *Shelter* barriers Sakhefete had put up around the chambers. An assault on memory, though...that was how New Sarresant had been destroyed. It was the Regnant, not that she'd had any doubts. That was how her uncle had been killed. And...

"Wait," she said. "What about Reyne d'Agarre? He was my champion, and the Regnant killed him during the attack on the city."

"Memory isn't the only gift Li has," Kalira said. "And if he did attack your champion's memories, and you didn't protect him, that's on you."

"You mean I have to do something to shield them?" she asked. "I needed to know this *before* the assault, don't you think?"

"You shouldn't have to think about it," Kalira said. "It's part of the bond. They draw energy from your connection to the Infinite Plane."

Erris had finished with Wicek's three, and now came toward them, forestalling the thousand questions she had burning on her tongue. All of this was too sudden. She never had time to prepare, time to fully understand her place, her gifts, the bonds she had with her champions. Fear bloomed, and a touch of anger. It would have taken a thousand years of study to know everything she needed to know, and if they failed it was going to be on her shoulders.

You're thinking too much, Anati thought to her. *Trust your instincts. You have good ones. My father always said so.*

She shook her head, but Erris arrived in front of them before she could reply.

"Sarine," Erris said. "Kalira. He Who Stands Before the Highest Mountain."

They each nodded, or bowed, in turn.

"Our Nikkon allies are latecomers," Erris said. "But I've had time to consider how their gifts will fit with yours. First, you understand how your abilities pair together?"

"Sarine will use the Nine Tails and the *kaas' Red* and *White* to guard me against any threats that get close," Kalira said. "While I rain fire on their heads."

"More or less," Erris said. "And He Who Stands Before the Highest Mountain fits right into that plan. No time for a demonstration, but his gift, as I understand it, is in a similar vein to yours, Kalira: fire, from a great distance. Your group is intended for long-range support. Think of yourselves as an artillery battery. Try to get to a vantage point for a battle where you can hit their long-range attackers without exposing yourselves to counterfire. Don't under any circumstances close into mêlée. If you do get into trouble at close range, Arak'Jur and his group will be coming. They have orders to shadow you and screen anyone trying to approach, but we can't discount the enemy's ability to use Dragons to appear behind our lines. So stay sharp and always, always, be ready for them to be on top of you without notice. Am I understood?"

"Perfectly," she said. "What do we do when we reach the Soul?"

"That's why I want you and Kalira back from the main fight," Erris said. "From your account of the last time you assaulted it, the Regnant didn't need to wait for the fight to be decided before he put his hand in the stream and changed the Soul of the World from white to black. That's what you saw, yes? I know you say you don't know how he did it, but our battle plan is to try and move you and Kalira toward the Soul. From there, absent a total victory over his people, you're going to try and figure it out. If you can end this and spare us even a moment of bloodshed, you do it. As to the rest, no battle plan survives contact with the enemy. We remain flexible, identify and assist each other in reaching smaller-scale goals, and key off each other for movements. Stay in sight of as many other teams as you can."

All three of them nodded, though Erris continued without waiting for confirmation.

"Kalira is your commander," Erris said. "Obey her orders at once and without question. Your first goal is keeping Sarine safe. Secondary goal is to stay clear of the Regnant. Tigai's team is tasked with dealing with him if he appears. If you see him, you use Sarine's Dragon gift to get out, no matter what else is going on, no matter who else you put at risk. Tertiary goal—and I stress, this is your tertiary goal—is to reach the Soul and work on breaking the Regnant's hold. But even if you're midway through that work, you run if the Regnant appears."

"Wouldn't it be better to use my gifts like you're using Tigai's?" she asked. "I can bring people to where they're needed as easily as he can."

"You're not here to question my orders," Erris snapped. "If you die, we've lost. The only reason I'm bringing you at all is that sitting you out means sitting out all four of your champions. That's all accurate, yes?"

"Yes," Kalira said. "And I understand your orders, Empress. I'll keep Sarine safe whether she wants me to or not."

"Good," Erris said. "Then are there any other questions? He Who Stands Before the Highest Mountain, have you understood all this? You understand your role?"

The Nikkon Spirit-Weaver bowed deep. "I understand, Majesty," he said in crisp, clear tones. "It is a great honor to serve in this battle. It will be remembered forever, whether we win or lose."

"I intend to see to it that we win," Erris said. "I'll be with the vanguard group. Others have orders to key their movements off of mine, but if you see me during the fighting, you defer to following me, so long as it doesn't conflict with the directives I gave you. Good luck to each of you. We'll be ready to move inside the quarter hour."

She saluted, then pivoted away without waiting for a gesture in response.

"Exciting," Kalira said. "It's finally happening. You feel ready? And you?"

He Who Stands Before the Highest Mountain bowed again. "I'm ready, Goddess," he said. "Lord Koryu's spirit is ready with me."

"It's a shame we didn't have a chance to work with you before," she said. Erris was walking to the next group, a duo of Kwoori, a Tarzali champion whom she hadn't had a chance to observe, and Nin'ti'dana, one of the Rabaquim. So many champions whom she didn't know well enough to have a sense of what they could do. At least Erris had studied them all. But they could have used another month at least to prepare.

"It is," He Who Stands Before the Highest Mountain said. "And a shame we haven't had time to get to know each other as warriors. Perhaps your Empress will allow us a tea service before we go?"

"I don't think—" she began, before she noticed the corners of He Who Stands Before the Highest Mountain's mouth turning up in the faintest suggestion of a smile. "Oh. You meant it as a joke."

"We'll come to know each other better in battle than in peace," He Who Stands Before the Highest Mountain said. "I've always believed it to be so. 'To know a man, spill blood together. To know him best, spill his blood.' My father said it, and I hold it as wisdom, near my heart."

"Then we'll all know each other well, by the time today is done," Kalira said.

He Who Stands Before the Highest Mountain's smile turned grim, and he nodded.

"You're ready to take us all to the Seat?" Kalira said.

"That, at least, I've been practicing," she said. "Yes. I'm ready. I could take a hundred, so long as they follow my instructions when we're on the Plane."

"Then all that's left is waiting," Kalira said. "And, I suppose, itching yourself until you bleed again."

She lowered her fingers, glaring at Kalira. Somehow the burning wires hadn't left a scratch on Kalira, while they'd torn her skin in a thousand places.

Well, Gods send that was the worst of her injuries today. It weighed heavy, looking around, knowing many of the champions might not survive this attack. But there was hope, too. Hope for each other, hope for a chance to set the world aright. It was in motion, and whatever happened, everything would be settled within a few hours, for good or ill.

67

ARAK'JUR

Approaching the Gods' Seat
The Infinite Plane

Sparks roared as they flew across the Plane. Corenna held his hand tight, though Sarine had said there was no need for physical contact. She knew them, knew their patterns and forms, and claimed she could transport them all together, so long as they remained calm and gave in to her control. He did, letting his mind drift to simpler things. Readiness for battle. Readiness to receive the spirits' blessings, with the knowledge they were with him now, watching what he did today.

Kacper, one of the Skovan, had been assigned to his command. A wiry, white-haired priest, though he was young and spry, trained and ready for combat, yet the man paled beside the creature he summoned: the archangel called Baael, a cross between a massive goat and a man, wreathed in shadow and flame. Erris had instructed him that he, Corenna, and Kacper were intended to be a reserve, plugging holes and reacting to the enemy's movements, especially if they threatened Sarine. Fine, for a beginning, though circumstances would change as the battle went on. So long as he survived, and kept Corenna at his side.

The sparks shifted as they turned, twisting the long columns away from their movement. Suddenly at the far edge of his vision a black column appeared, towering as far up and down as the rest of the Plane stretched to either side. Space seemed to bend around it. He knew this place. They'd come here before, when the column had blazed white instead of black. It towered above them as Sarine made them move, weaving and dodging through a hundred dangling tendrils made of pure shadow. Touching one meant death;

somehow he knew it, felt it, as one instinctively knew to fear the bite of a snake or spider. Fear threatened his control: Sarine moved for all of them here. One wrong dodge, one misstep and—

She touched the central column, and the world shifted.

He was on solid ground again, with his physical body. Earth obeyed his call; a shield of stone sprang up around him and Corenna before his vision had time to clear and take in his surroundings. He moved. This would be their weakest point, arriving all together as one. They had to spread, and he didn't bother giving the command. Corenna would know. Kacper would follow.

He leapt forward. Behind him the rest scattered in every direction. This wasn't the Gods' Seat as he remembered it. Black and purple skies looked down overhead, full of shimmering stars, painted with greens and blues and oranges. Before, the place had been indoors, a fortress of stone. Now, patches of crystalline grasses stretched out on all sides, growing from perfectly level ground made from what appeared to be transparent glass. Banks of white sand glowed under the glass's surface, tracing contours around rocks and boulders, even trees, all frozen underneath the ground. Ripples of colored light went out from beneath their footsteps, pulsing bioluminescent lights where they touched the rocks and sand. Every footstep became a burst of color, shooting to the horizon almost too quickly for him to follow. A beautiful display. And a warning to their enemies they had arrived.

"Stand ready," Erris shouted behind him, though he was already moving fast enough that her voice had dimmed when it reached him. "They'll know we're coming."

He touched down on the glass, sending a ripple of green and blue to the sand below the surface. In the distance the black column he'd seen on Sarine's Infinite Plane towered over the horizon, stretching up until it blended into the sky. That would be her goal, which made it his. It could be two hundred leagues off, or two; the endless flat glass surface distorted perceptions, all the more so when he had no way of knowing how large the column was. She would be behind him for now, so he, Corenna, and Kacper could move ahead, screening for her as they approached.

Instinct flared in his mind, and he moved before he saw the attack.

Ipek'a's gift still burned in his blood, granting him the strength to leap, but he called on *astahg* to warp him to the surface, behind the *magi* who must have teleported into place using their Dragons' gifts. Pockets of them appeared without warning all across the glass plain. Ripples of color marked their enemies' steps as surely as they signaled Sarine's, Erris's, and the rest of theirs: There were five here, almost on top of the last place his feet had touched before he pushed off the ground. They were distracted, momentarily, whirling around looking for their prey. He would have been there, had he not already taken to the air.

He grabbed hold of a young woman in an orange robe, borrowing *mareh'et*'s claws to rip her in half.

A dome of Force exploded next to him, but he was already moving, bounding away with *lakiri'in*'s speed. Color shot out from under his feet. The other four *magi* rounded on him, barking orders, and he remained visible, running as fast as his gifts could propel him over the open ground.

A terrible roar sounded. Baael crashed down atop their domes of Force, shaking the glass as the archangel whipped at them, his weapon rebounding from the domes' surface. It served to distract, precisely as they'd practiced in their drills. The Heron-*magi* turned their attention to Baael, sending shock waves through the air as they turned the power of the archangel's strikes against him. *Kirighra* granted a cloak of stealth, and he doubled back under cover of the Great Panther's shadow. Corenna got there first. Two copies of her moved to flank the *magi*, one of flesh, the other a mimickry, a pantomime of her shape, made of dripping blood. The blessing of the Rabaquim's champions, and both forms mirrored every gift she called from the spirits.

Wind came, two gales blowing opposite directions, one from the south, one from the north. It conjured a tornado in an instant, the winds spinning into a cyclone as Corenna and her blood-mirror pushed to make them turn. A single Force-dome sprang into place to block the winds, making a pocket of safety where one of the *magi* stood, another desperately diving to take cover behind it. The other two turned too late. The winds seized them, ripping them off their feet, and Baael with them, flinging them up into the sky.

The remaining two, who had managed to shelter behind their dome, vanished before he could arrive. Gone. Teleported away.

"All safe?" he called. "Unhurt?"

"Safe" was all Corenna replied. It came from the mouth of the blood-mirror, while the true Corenna focused on the sky, turning the wind to make sure it tore the *magi* apart. Blood misted down as her tornado rose over their heads, making the ground calm and splattered red, with a puddle leaking from the ruined body of the woman he'd struck first. Chunks of her lay atop the glass, sending small ripples of color where her blood leaked and ran over its surface.

"Safe, God willing," Kacper replied. "Though Baael won't appreciate you tossing him into the heavens."

Behind them, fire bloomed against the night sky, mixing with the greens and purples. Yuli and Namkat grappled with a figure in glass armor some two hundred paces east, while one of the Nikkon avatars, a towering giant made of ice, strode above the horizon line, raining crystalline shards into what appeared to be wreaths of Mantis-fire hurled against it. He scanned farther, calling on *munat'ap* to sharpen his eyes, ears, nose, and tongue. Sarine was unengaged. And moving.

"Come," he said. "Toward the spire."

68

ERRIS

The Fields of Glass
The Gods' Seat

*B*ody surged through her as *Shelter* collapsed, exploding outward as the pearls came undone. A glass-titan barreled through the gap, one of the Regnant's Ox-*magi*, standing a full head and shoulders over even the tallest man she'd ever seen, glaring left and right before it sighted her and charged.

She erected another barrier between them, and ran.

Seh'sa'raya trailed after her, the man, not the animals he commanded. This place betrayed their movements, sending flashes of colored light everywhere they stepped. *Life* tethers sharpened her senses enough to hone a soldier's instinct for danger: The enemy were coming from the other side, flanking her *Shelter* walls with what had to be their Mantis-*magi*, clad in green robes and hurling rings of fire that seared and burst through *Shelter*'s pearls.

"There!" she shouted, half her vision in the physical world and half shifted to the leylines, where she saw the white pearls pale to a soft pink.

Seh'sa'raya closed his eyes at the same moment she leveled her pistol. The *Shelter* wall gave way to a gout of fire erupting from the other side. She fired two shots, as quick as she could set the hammer and squeeze the trigger. A distraction. It worked, inasmuch as there was no Ox-*magi* covered in glass waiting to burst through the wall when they destroyed it. Heat billowed through the gap. She was sweating through her uniform, her skin burned in half a dozen places already, but it had been her choice to charge here, occupying the center of the fight with a maze of *Shelter* while her companions tied up as many as they could. For now, it was working. They'd drawn at least fifteen *magi*, maybe more. Difficult to get a count without a better vantage point, or a scout.

"Back!" she shouted. Seh'sa'raya followed. The man was sluggish, all but worthless in a fight, though he carried a leather whip in one hand and a bulky, oversized iron sword in the other. Perhaps he would focus better if there was immediate danger to their persons; for now his attention was split between the birds of his *ipek'a* pack, attacking in a dozen directions at once on all sides of her *Shelter* walls.

Two of his birds sparred with the first glass-hulk as they retraced their steps, with a third waiting behind, crouched low in a sign that it was ready to pounce as soon as its sisters got the man off-balance. The first two snapped and flapped their wings, screeching cacophonous cries as they pecked or slashed with their scythed claws, retreating before the Ox could reach them, or spray glass to catch them and cut them down. She spared an *Entropy* binding as they raced past the mêlée, exploding the air immediately in front of the Ox-*magi*'s face. It triggered the third *ipek'a* to leap, crashing into him from behind. Ripples of blue and pink erupted where he collapsed forward to the ground, but she and Seh'sa'raya were already moving, ducking behind another *Shelter* wall, building out the maze as they moved toward the center of the fighting.

Area control. That was the most important part of her strategy for this terrain. She'd expected a fight in close quarters, though she'd planned for everything she could imagine, everything she, Kalira, Wicek, and Marquand could come up with that might meet them in this place. Kalira had warned her the Regnant might remake the Gods' Seat as something else entirely: a fortress filled with traps, a network of underground tunnels, a series of defensible bastions and fortifications. Instead he'd made it an open field, barren atop what appeared to be thick glass that flashed color to signal footsteps anywhere between them and the horizon. If she chose to fight on ground like this, she would do it to concentrate her enemy, to draw them into the open and commit them to a fight. Everything about the ground shouted that the Regnant wanted them here, wanted to know where they were. It reeked of confidence, the sort of move a general might make if they knew they had overwhelming numbers and sought to annihilate the enemy without concern for their own losses. It put her on guard for a trap. Until she sprang it, the rule of the day was to obfuscate, to render the open ground meaningless, and *Shelter*, combined with as many bodies as she could put into the chaos, was the best tool she could muster to execute that plan.

Another blast of heat signaled a *Shelter* barrier going down in front of them. She redoubled her tethers without thinking, slamming another wall in place behind the first. She gestured left, and Seh'sa'raya ran alongside her, down temporary corridors forged from *Shelter*'s pearls. One of his birds waited at a corner, cocking its head as they approached, then falling in as though it were one of her soldiers. The three of them raced down the makeshift hallway. She had to loop around, to try and wall more of their *magi* in, letting them think they were the ones with the initiative. She meant to take the Regnant's bait today. The more *magi* he committed here, the fewer would be there to stop Sarine and Arak'Jur.

An explosion tore apart the wall at the long end of the *Shelter* corridor, and before she could remake it two green-robed *magi* stepped through, with a red-robed figure behind them.

Their eyes widened when they saw her. She made to weave another wall, but the air changed, growing hot around them.

Seh'sa'raya's *ipek'a* screeched and leapt over their heads, flying down the hall with a toe-claw extended. Fire took it, a blast engulfing its body, then impacting on the wall she managed to conjure at the last instant, flames licking over the top, leaving searing heat in the hallway even without a ceiling. Before she could steady herself, another explosion rocked the ground behind them. She heard another *ipek'a* screech, piercing through the fire, and pivoted to see a second group of three, the same mix of two green-robes and one red, only these focused their attentions away from her, down the long corridor around the corner they'd just traversed.

She tethered *Entropy* to match them fire for fire, and raised her pistol. The man in red lifted his hands in response, twisting her stomach with them. Vomit flooded her throat, and she gagged, but not before she loosed her *Entropy* cloud into their heads.

Her pistol clattered to the ground as she clutched her stomach. The red-robed *magi*, who had to have been an Owl, was engulfed in a burst of fire, charring all visible skin to a putrid black crisp. He remained on his feet, stunned and dead in an instant. Everything above the man's waist was blackened char, his skin flaking, his blood reduced to thick, sizzling sap. Whatever he'd done to her remained, and she sank to her knees, coughing between gagging knots, her stomach trying to seize. Seh'sa'raya ran past her, but she didn't see more, twisting sideways toward her *Shelter*, coughing and fighting for control.

Fire erupted. The heat of it bathed her skin, though she had her eyes shut, squeezed tight against the pain. Iron clanged on something metal. She fought to still her breathing, to force her stomach to settle. *Life* came quickly, unraveling whatever had been forced on her internal organs. She restored balance as quick as she could, feeling her legs tremble, her eyes water, a hot fever burning alongside the scorched air and smoke that filled her maze.

The sound of bone cracking mixed with a scream, then a snap of teeth, then another scream, then the slump of flesh hitting the ground.

She wrenched her body back into control, turning to see. The Owl-*magi* remained on his feet, what was left of him. Seh'sa'raya stood over the bodies of the two green-robed Mantis, next to a towering, horse-sized white wolf. The creature had blood dripping from its jaws, staining red its otherwise pale white fur, so white it seemed translucent. A black aura surrounded it, as though its shape had been inked and outlined, lending an otherworldly halo to its movements.

She'd managed to drag herself to her hands and knees when the wolf vanished, and its mistress came bounding around the corner.

She Who Howls with Hunters paused to glance at Seh'sa'raya before darting down to grab Erris by the upper arm.

"You're hurt," the Nikkon woman said. Erris shrugged off the help and rose to sit back on her knees.

"I'm fine," she said. "And we have to move. We shouldn't be so close together. Two more Mantis and another Owl, on that side of the wall."

Seh'sa'raya shook his head. "Dead," he said absently. More *ipek'a* screeches echoed the word, as though he'd forgotten and spoken through their mouths as he spoke through his own.

She Who Howls with Hunters bowed, a sharp, stiff movement, then straightened and ran down another corridor.

"Sure you're not hurt?" Seh'sa'raya said.

Her stomach was still twisted, and now it was empty, leaving behind pools of vomit atop this place's strange flat glass.

"I'll manage," she said. "No sign of their Dragons yet. They must have pulled them out immediately, once the fighting started."

Seh'sa'raya grunted.

"Can you cover me here?" she asked. "I'll need thirty seconds, no more. Then we move."

In reply two silhouettes cast shadows overhead, so sudden it almost triggered her reflexes to let loose *Entropy*. She held back at the last moment, and the shadows became two of Seh'sa'raya's birds, landing with a thundering crunch into the glass.

She wasted no time.

Need slid into place. She hadn't been able to bind any of the others— loyalties ran deeper to the champions' masters than to her. But Marquand would be there, watching from as safe a distance as he could manage.

Her vision shifted. He was already looking through a spyglass, thank the

Gods. She took over his movements midway through, panning it across the perfectly level field of glass.

"I'm here," she said through Marquand's mouth, hearing his gravelly speech in place of hers. "The Empress. Report."

Ellin, the Tarzali girl she'd assigned to serve as Marquand's second, spoke quickly.

"He will say your place is worst, in the center," Ellin said. "He will count nine there. Five more where the Natarii are, farther in the direction he calls west. Shifting numbers elsewhere."

She panned the spyglass, seeing for herself. They'd agreed west meant left from wherever they entered the Seat, with the rest of the directions oriented from their original headings at the farm. That side of the fields was frenetic, covered in silhouettes running, flying, fighting in close quarters or dodging away from fire. The eastern side was quieter. Bodies lay still on the glass there, too far for her to tell which ones, whether they were hers or the Regnant's. The spires lay on the horizon, impossible to tell how close. And the center, where she, Seh'sa'raya, and She Who Howls with Hunters held, was a nightmare of smoke, *Shelter* walls, and fire.

"Any sign of the Regnant?" she asked.

"He will not see him," Ellin said. "He is searching, waiting, even now."

"Good," she said, as much for the girl as herself. "Can you reach Wicek's group? You know the ones I mean? Tell them to follow Arak'Jur and Sarine toward the Spire. We're holding enough of the enemy's *magi* here. But if the Regnant hasn't shown himself yet, it means he's waiting for our attack there."

"How can you know this?" Ellin said. "Are you seeing his mind?"

"Make her go, Marquand," she said, this time addressing her vessel directly. No time for insubordinate civilian fools. "Keep yourself back, in position to observe the fields. I'm going to push west to link up with Yuli. That should hold the center for now."

A fine start. She let *Need* go, snapping her senses back into place as she rose to her feet. From the look of things through Marquand's spyglass they were holding their own, more than holding, considering the count of corpses she'd seen already. More robes than anything else, by a factor of three or four to one. Another fifteen minutes here and they'd know whether the Regnant meant to send in more Dragons with his reserves. If he did, it meant this was the fight, and he'd show himself in person before it was done. If not, she would redirect more strength toward the spire.

She turned west, letting a *Shelter* barrier dissipate to clear the path as she and Seh'sa'raya turned back toward the fighting.

69

OMERA

Eastern Flank
The Gods' Seat

Ubax aragti burned in two bloodstreams at once: his, and that of the creature that took his shape. Two Omeras danced atop the glass, one he recognized as himself, while another sent sensory images to his brain, obeying his commands like an old muscle, long forgotten.

The Crane monk danced with both parts of him. The rest of the world faded away. There was only this. Only the steps of this dance.

His blood-self feinted high with its *shotel* while his true-self attacked from the flank. The Crane woman set her feet perfectly, deflecting the blood-self's blow and spinning, using centrifugal force to parry and send his sword off-balance. *Ubax aragti* kept the movement slow enough for him to follow with both sets of hands and feet. Red and purple lights flashed as his blood-self reset its feet for another attack, skittering in a half circle around her guard. His true-self moved the opposite direction, careful to keep the Crane monk pinned between them. He struck again.

Her sword was already there, already moving. It rang out steel against steel in a threefold pattern, blocking his first strike, then a second set as he shifted to strike again. *Din tarain* poison shone from the edge of his blade. It should have bitten through her steel like acid; some force protected the Crane woman's sword. He might have taken a moment to apply *matarin* instead, the poison that bit flesh instead of steel, but there was no time. In the heartbeat it took for her to parry the second threefold set of strikes, she spun, lashing out in her own attack.

His true-self fell back, desperate to keep his sword turned ahead of her blade. She aimed high, then shifted her grip, twisting into a torso strike followed by another rhythmic clang when he raised his *shotel* to block, just in time. She moved a foot forward, and he retreated at the same instant. She shifted again, and he matched, and another flurry of blows came before his blood-self could threaten her from the flank. This time he counterattacked, and she counter-riposted, and he parried again, leaving an opening for the blood-self to engage. It did. She stepped away, leaving him a half beat off-balance, a hairsbreadth from another attack that might have ended him, though it would have cost her life to make it. She shuffled two steps back, and steel clanged as she turned the blood-self's attack. He took a breath. The first he'd been aware of in too long. It burned his lungs, and he stepped forward to renew the dance.

The sounds rang in his ears. Clash, clang, a whistling song in a pulsing rhythm. Artful. Beautiful.

He tried a feint, low this time, and she ignored it. His blood-self had both feet set wide, holding its sword in a middle guard, fighting purely defensively, swatting aside probing strikes without any counterattacks. If he'd had more time to practice the new gifts, if he'd had more time to spar, he might have managed a more precise attack. It came as a strange disappointment in the moment, as though this Crane was owed better. He had dueled with the finest fighters in his mother's Empire—in *his* Empire now—and never fought a better match. In time he could have, should have, been better. Sad to think this woman would never meet him as she deserved, at the true apex of his skill. He moved behind her, flashing lights on the ground warning her, and she spun at the last moment. Her sword met his, then went limp in her hands, and she crumpled forward like paper under a heavy wind.

Allakawari stood behind her, kneeling to retrieve a knife from between the Crane woman's shoulder blades. Anger surged in him, redoubled by *ubax aragti* and mirrored in his blood-self.

"That will be the last of them, here," Allakawari said. "We should—" She froze.

He pulled back the blood-self before it could go through with the strike it had prepared to level at Allakawari's head. It snarled, dripping blood from its mouth like spittle.

"Was there a problem?" Allakawari said instead.

The Crane woman looked peaceful. She was untouched from the front, dressed in gray clothing that fit her body, allowing for perfect movement during their duel. The curvature of a smile marked her eyes above the gray veil covering her mouth. Lifeless eyes now. Blood seeped from her mouth, staining the veil, consequence of her punctured heart. She'd been his equal. Maybe even his superior, without the Rabaquim's gifts. Now she was dead.

"You... interfered," he said. He withdrew a heavy cloth treated to absorb his herbs, following through with the ritual of wiping his blade clean before he sheathed it. A calming ritual. Meant to quell the thirst for blood before *ubax aragti* could spark it again.

"Ahh," Allakawari said. "I will apologize. In the moment, I will be thinking only of your safety."

Bloody corpses lay around them.

Red robes, and white. They'd been attacked without warning; it was one thing to hear Empress d'Arrent tell them the enemy had Dragon-*magi*, that they could appear in an instant, directly in the middle of their groups, or behind them, or above. Another entirely to feel the rush of adrenaline as he suddenly had to sidestep a blade that hadn't been there the instant before. He'd killed two of them, red-robed enemies that had done something to interfere with the way *ubax aragti* burned in his blood, as though they'd been trying to make him sick up his stomach. Fortunately his herbs had protected him from whatever they'd tried. Both had died with surprise writ in their eyes when he approached, his sword rammed through one of their throats while his blood-self's blade did for the other. Then he'd turned his attention to the Crane woman, who had not died so easily.

The archangel knelt with his back to them, his wings tucked in to cover a body on the ground.

"Leorain," Allakawari called to him. "Wicek. We will want to have been moving. The fight has continued elsewhere."

Omera saw it before she did. His blood-self fell in at his flank, its sword vanished when he sheathed his. Both stared at the body beneath the angel's wings.

He went around, stepping cautiously, though every footfall sparked pulses of orange, green, purple, or yellow light atop the glass. It seemed wrong. Like a street magician's light show, performed in the middle of a funeral march.

Wicek lay in front of Leorain. The old man's body had been shredded by shards of glass. Flaps of loose skin lay open under torn robes, stained by blood that had already ceased flowing. The archangel touched two fingers to the bishop's eyes, speaking the words of a prayer in a language Omera couldn't decipher, that he somehow couldn't bear to hear. Every word carried pain, forgiveness, mercy, justice, all at once. As though the angel spoke the tongue of a God.

"Oh," Allakawari said. "Oh no. I will be sorry. Leorain. I will be so sorry."

The angel only turned his head, his eyes closed, though even with his body made from light it was clear tears welled in the corners of his eyes.

<Go on,> Leorain said. His voice was music, as it always was, but made by a choir of somber voices instead of the brass heralds that usually accompanied his words. *<Leave us behind. I will tend to his last rites.>*

"Of course it's regrettable that he's fallen," Omera said. "But we have a duty. There will be time to mourn later."

<You do not understand, heathen,> Leorain said. *<I am bound to him. When his soul departs for heaven, I go with him to the gates. Leave us, and let me prepare a great man for his final journey.>*

Allakawari laid a hand on his arm before he could speak again. It stilled him to quiet. Without Leorain's shielding they would be exposed; he'd listened to Erris d'Arrent's briefings, her drills and planning, and thought her strategy for the three of them a good one. If the angel had fallen himself, somehow, that would be one thing, but the creature was alive, here, ready to fight. Yet perhaps he wasn't. If Wicek was dead, perhaps the angel was finished, too. If he'd known it, perhaps he might have paid closer attention to defending the old man during the fight. Perhaps, if he'd used his blood-self to watch... but no. Battle was never the place for second-guessing. Such thoughts would torment him later. For now, they had to move.

He scanned the horizon. An endless, flat, level plane of glass punctuated by bursts of color wherever any of them moved. *Shelter* walls rose near the center, making a great maze filled with what appeared to be smoke and fire. Further, more smoke rose, and sounds of battle, while in the east, a spire of black rose against the horizon, the only feature that differentiated one place on this plane from another. Tempting to move toward it, but Erris had ordered them to key movements off of her, and *Shelter* meant she was at the center, in the thick of the fighting. A trait he could respect in any commander, for all he'd hate to see her end like Wicek, covered in blood and mourning.

"We should move," he said. "There, toward—" he began, but Allakawari cut him short.

"No," she said, pointing back toward where they'd entered this place. "My sister has been here. You see? She was coming straight toward us."

He turned back in the direction they'd come from. Sure enough, a lone woman was running toward them.

Without waiting for him to confirm it, Allakawari raced toward the woman she'd called her sister. It left him exposed, and annoyed. What if another round of Dragons dropped *magi* on his head? Leorain would be no use, kneeling and weeping over the dead. And he was a King. Command should have fallen to him in the first place, and all the more so now with the Skovan archbishop lying dead atop the glass.

He left the angel and Wicek's body behind, trotting toward the Tarzali women. His blood-self lingered a step behind, scowling to mirror the anger and resentment he felt without showing it.

"You're certain?" Allakawari was asking when he and his blood-self arrived in earshot. "The Empress meant to divide us?"

The other woman—Ellin, he remembered from the farm—nodded fiercely. "Her dream-vessel will shout at me. He will call me a 'pig-faced donkey fucker' when I misspeak the orders he means for me to memorize."

"He will sound like a donkey fucker himself," Allakawari said, eliciting a giggle from both of them.

"What orders?" he asked, trotting up alongside them. Every footfall made him nervous, like they were sending out beacons for the enemy's Dragons to find and attack.

His blood-self mirroring his approach drew uneasy looks from Ellin. She stared at it as she spoke.

"Empress d'Arrent will order you, my sister, and the priest to follow Arak'Jur and Sarine. Into the spire. There. The black tower, that way."

"The priest is dead," Allakawari said. "Does this change the order?"

"The Empress will not say," Ellin said. "I think her vessel would shout at me again when I went back to ask."

His blood-self suddenly spiked emotion into his veins. A sense of anticipation. Jealousy. Hunger. All foreign, as though he'd ingested some unknown herb. Somehow he knew it came from the blood-self. It turned to look at him, a movement he hadn't intended for it to make.

"No time for second-guessing," he said. "If the Empress ordered us to the spire, then that's where we go."

The blood-self relished the words, nodding along as he spoke.

"Take care of yourself, sister," Ellin said, and she and Allakawari exchanged hugs. A strange sight; moments ago Allakawari was an assassin, an instrument of death, reaping enemy *magi* on the points of her knives. "My Dreamings will not touch on what happens here, or before. I've hoped it means the world will change."

"I know," Allakawari said. "I have taken great care not to die, sister. You have done the same."

They separated, both with tears in their eyes.

He didn't bother waiting for Allakawari to follow. He was in command now, as he should be. The spire seemed to burn his eyes when he looked up at it. Something waited there. His emotions blurred where they touched the blood-self's; perhaps some of the hunger was his. The spire would be where they claimed the Soul of the World, which meant glory waited there, for him as much as any of them. Old memories made the sight familiar for the King of the Bhakal. Champions among his people had walked this path before, in ages long past. The Blood Gods had helped to show him his place, and now, finally, he remembered.

Pulses of light reached them from farther ahead, past the set of bodies he, Allakawari, and Wicek had killed, past another set of dead that must have been felled by Arak'Jur or Sarine. They'd have to hurry to catch the others before they entered the spire. Caution still reigned here. He kept a hand on his sword hilt, while the blood-self kept its sword out and drawn. Sarine's and Arak'Jur's groups were well ahead, but every step carried them closer. He'd been content to carry out orders, to ensure they took and held the ground against their enemy. But the moment was close now. And none of them, not Erris d'Arrent, not Arak'Jur or Sarine would stand between him and his destiny.

70

SARINE

A crag of polished black rock rose at the pillar's base. Light shone from it—black light, if such a thing was possible, light that seemed to drink illumination rather than give it off. It defied her expectations, but then, this was the Gods' Seat. She'd come to expect surprises here.

Her steps pulsed a deep blue atop the glass, almost black, like the deepest parts of the New Sarresant Harbor. Kalira's steps matched hers for intensity, though hers were crimson instead of blue, and He Who Stands Before the Highest Mountain's were white, equally brilliant, pulsing across the landscape with their every footfall on the glass. They illuminated the earth trapped underneath its surface: showing blades of grass, trees, the contours of terrain frozen below its surface. When they'd arrived their footsteps flashed a dozen different colors. Now they each had one. A way for the Regnant to identify them, perhaps. To warn him as his enemies drew closer to the spire.

"He's there," Kalira said. "Waiting for us."

"You're certain?" He Who Stands Before the Highest Mountain said. "Your Empress believed he would come out to face the attack."

"He's there," she said. She could sense it. Something about the darkness, the way it twisted, pulsing shadows the way it should have given off light. This was his place. A place of death.

She went forward.

The stone crag had an opening, more akin to a cave than a doorway, large enough to drive a carriage through it. The Nine Tails remained alert under her skin, sensing danger in every direction. If she'd given it control over their body, it would have been pivoting and sniffing the air, whirling to jump at shadows. There were stars here, anchors for Dragon-*magi* to use, so bright they covered her vision when she blinked. One could appear anywhere without warning. She could use them, too, if it came to it, and put them in the spire room in an instant. It was almost certainly a trap, but the awareness was there. Using them would be an act of desperation, but she stored it away, saved it as they walked under the cold black stone.

She'd lived here for months, and only now did she begin to recognize what the Regnant had made of the place. The layout had to be different—there was never an opening onto a great field of glass before—but here, inside, their steps were normal, giving off no light. The stone curved so the hallways were almost circular, cut from hard stone. There would be forked passages spiraling around its center, where the pillar burned. Perhaps there would even be living quarters, the meditation rooms, the library, and the maps.

They came around a corner in the main tunnel, and the first fork opened two new tunnels, left and right. Arak'Jur stood between the passages, bare-chested and cut across the ribs. The guardian gave no sign of any pain; knowing him, he'd be healed within minutes. Still it drew the eyes, a terrible gash reddening his skin, leaking blood down his lower torso.

"Sarine," he said as they approached.

"Arak'Jur," she replied. "You're hurt. Are the others...?" She left the question hanging in the air. Some among her champions wouldn't survive the day, but she knew what he'd endured already to bring Corenna back. Losing her again would cut him to the core.

"They went ahead," Arak'Jur said. "That way." He pointed down the rightward passage. "I stayed to be sure we didn't separate."

"That wasn't necessary," she said, then stopped herself. It *wasn't* necessary, and he should have known it. She could sense her champions here, in the Gods' Seat. She sensed one now, to the west. Down the leftward path, not the right.

"Has there been any sign of the Regnant or his champions here?" Kalira asked.

"None," Arak'Jur replied. "I took this wound approaching the spire. Since we arrived it's been quiet, though I wouldn't make the mistake of assuming it will remain so. It's possible our enemy put all his strength on the fields of glass outside this place, but he is no fool."

"No, he isn't," Kalira said. "We'll want to be on guard for—"

"You said Corenna went on ahead?" she interjected. "And Kacper?"

"That's right," Arak'Jur said. "Both went to scout the passageways. I thought

I might recognize some of the halls, but I didn't. It appears the Regnant reordered this place, or at least, added sections beyond what I remember. The rightward path was a guess. If it forks again, one of my companions will wait to guide us while the other scouts farther ahead."

"Lead on, then," she said, falling in behind him.

He nodded, glancing between her, Kalira, and He Who Stands Before the Highest Mountain as though to confirm they all followed her lead. Then he turned down the rightward path, and she let the Nine Tails rise from beneath her skin.

The transformation began immediately. Sarine receded, and the Nine Tails emerged, her limbs growing longer, thicker, her face narrowing, her skin sprouting a thin coat of white fur, her spine lengthening, splitting from her tailbone first into two, then three, then five, then seven, then nine. In the span of a step it had control. It lashed out, snapping two of its tails around Arak'Jur's legs, another two wrapped around his arms and shoulders, a final one seizing and encircling his neck.

He sputtered, calling out a curse as its tails lifted him from the ground.

"What are you doing?" Kalira exclaimed. "Sarine? What is this?"

It treated him gently at first. That was Sarine's urging. The Nine Tails would have preferred to break the man, to snap his bones and taste his blood. But its host was strong, and it obeyed her pleas. Its host knew this man. He should have summoned his spirits, if only to defend himself. Instead Arak'Jur choked, coughing and gagging as it tightened the tail it had wrapped around his neck. He dangled like a snared bear, mighty and powerful, but caught, reduced to sniveling and whining instead of wielding the power of his frame.

"Sarine!" Kalira shouted. The Nine Tails ignored it.

Its tail tightened, and Arak'Jur's skin bruised. His eyes bulged as his head tilted back, gasping for air that couldn't fit into his throat. Still the Nine Tails squeezed.

A flash of white light rose from Kalira's hands. Blinding light. A threat. Only the transformation was done. It dropped the body to the ground, and changed back to its host's form.

The body wasn't Arak'Jur anymore. It wasn't even a man.

A woman lay curled on the stone, wearing a blue robe, her neck still encircled with bruises where the Nine Tails had choked off her air.

"A Fox-*magi*," she said. "This isn't Arak'Jur, and never was."

Kalira gasped, and the radiance that had shone from her fingers dimmed to a halo around each hand.

"How did you know?" Kalira said.

"I left him an opening to use his gifts, in case I was wrong," she said. "But Arak'Jur would never leave Corenna to go ahead without him during a fight. He all but threatened to hit Erris when she tried to put them in separate groups." She rose from the Fox-*magi*'s side, leaving the woman still breathing, if only barely. "The *magi* wanted us to take the rightward passage, but I can sense my champions here in the Seat. Arak'Jur—or, at least, one of them, is somewhere to the left."

"A trap," He Who Stands Before the Highest Mountain said.

"Definitely," she said. "Which means either the Regnant or some of his champions are going to be here waiting for us. Not that we doubted it. But stay on your guard. I'd as soon follow Arak'Jur and Corenna down the left passage if the Regnant meant us to spring a trap down the right, but there will be others for sure."

He Who Stands Before the Highest Mountain bowed, straightening quickly and moving to follow her down the left passage.

Kalira's hands flashed.

Without warning a flare of sunlight engulfed Kalira, illuminating the corridor's murky light with a dazzling burst. Two focal points shone, then dimmed and vanished as fast as they'd flared into life. When the light receded, Kalira's hands smoked like freshly fired muskets, but her skin was unbroken and unburned. On the ground in front of them the Fox-*magi*'s body was gone, replaced by a pile of cinders, ash, and blackened bone.

"Kalira!" she said. "Why did you do that?"

"She was an enemy," Kalira said simply.

"She was still alive," she said. "She might have survived."

"I know," Kalira said. "That's why I killed her. Do you want a Fox-*magi* trailing behind us, pretending to be the Empress, or worse, Orana or one of the Rabaquim?"

"Time to ponder questions of morality later, I think," He Who Stands Before the Highest Mountain said. "Best if we keep moving."

She closed her eyes, trying to shut out the image of a woman turned to ash and embers in an instant. Bad enough she'd had to violently choke the *magi*, and she'd certainly condone the same or worse against whatever enemies they encountered. Maybe Kalira was right, though it still stung to murder someone lying unconscious on the ground.

The stone curved in familiar ways as they tracked down the leftward path. It was the same construction the Gods' Seat had used before, though the stone was darker, the passageways more dim. Perhaps it was only the light at the Seat's heart having changed from white to black. They took a left passage, and she expected three rooms connected by three archways on the right. Sure enough, they were there, though they were empty, and they passed by to another fork, leading left and right. If her memories were correct the right passage would lead to a meditation room, then farther to the map room showing the eastern side of the world. The left hall would lead to the room that had been Erris's chambers, and farther to Tigai's and Yuli's, before spiraling inward toward the central chamber, and the pillar of light.

They went left again, and immediately she heard shouts, then a piercing crack, then a thundering roar echoing from the stone.

She didn't wait for Kalira and He Who Stands Before the Highest Mountain to follow. Once again her body changed with each step, and this time Anati flooded their veins with *Red*. She raced forward, pivoting around a corner, then charged down a long hallway with no doors.

Corenna fought immediately in front of them when she rounded the next bend in the hall. Or rather, a clone of her did: a mirror image of Corenna, made entirely from blood, long claws protruding from her hands, locked in a contest against a swordsman in tight-fitted gray clothing and a matching gray veil. The true Corenna, made of flesh, stood a few paces farther down the hall, pressed up against a barrier of ice thick enough to block any vision and muffle the sounds of what lay beyond.

The Nine Tails snarled and snapped its jaws at the swordsman, and instantly the blood-Corenna moved to flank what had to be the Crane-*magi* between them. The swordsman ducked and tried to leap back, carving out space around him between his two attackers. He might have moved quickly enough to force her back, had the Nine Tails not had the *kaas*'s *Red* in its blood. It sliced the air with one tail to draw the swordsman's blade, then cut with another from the left. The swordsman pivoted his grip, a quicker reaction than the Nine Tails expected, and swept his sword upward to parry both attacks in one stroke. But the Nine Tails had seven more strikes ready, and cut with three from the opposite side of the swordsman's blade. Two tails grabbed hold of the Crane-*magi*'s left arm while the third fixed itself against his shoulder. They pulled, and flesh and sinew snapped as the swordsman's limb tore free, clattering his blade to the ground while the *magi* howled in pain. In the same moment, the seventh tail wrenched the swordsman's head around to snap his neck, stifling the cry.

The blood-Corenna took a step back, lowering its bloody claws.

"He's here," the true-Corenna said, still pressed against her ice. "The Regnant. With four more *magi*. Up ahead, twenty paces."

The Nine Tails' blood went cold. Him. The host's Great Enemy.

Without prompting, the true-Corenna dropped her ice shield, and the Nine Tails raced forward.

The Skovan archangel, Baael, was drenched in flame, flailing its whip overhead, its massive body shrunken down to fit in the narrow hallway. Gouts of fire met it, billowing smoke and heat, and though the Nine Tails couldn't see the source of the flames, it could smell them. Two *magi*. One pressed against the left wall, another lurking in a doorway a few paces farther back. And another smell, dimmer. The Regnant. He'd been here, though there was no sign of him now.

The Nine Tails charged through the fire.

White flared around its body, and it struck without slowing. Two tails lashed in a whipcrack, taking one of the *magi* in the face, shattering bone and teeth. The other *magi* dove into the chamber, but the Nine Tails caught them by the ankle, slamming down to wrench their body into the stone. Bone cracked. It let go, still racing past.

A familiar scent led to Arak'Jur, shielded by stone. A warrior's form slammed its claws against his shield, shattering the rock into shards as it roared. The Nine Tails knew this one: the White Talon. A war-form that had been its sister, in some lifetimes, and a mortal enemy in others. It smelled of rot, and death, and reeked of tethers to the host's Great Enemy. So they would be enemies, too, in this life. It dove over top of Arak'Jur's stone, grappling the war-form with six tails and lashing out with the other three.

Its body slammed into the White Talon, knocking them off-balance. The Talon's body was slender but hard, covered in armor plating, its hind legs thick and powerful, while its forelegs were little more than joints to swing its massive claws. They crashed together, and the White Talon's back grew spores, launching pustules of burning gas that exploded where they touched the Nine Tails' fur. Rippling explosions went off up and down its body, and against the stone walls where the pustules missed their target. *White* flared again from the *kaas*, and the Nine Tails grappled close, ensnaring both joints to disable the White Talon's claws. It bit the White Talon's hide below its head, and the war-form screeched, writhing and struggling to break free.

Arak'Jur moved, surrounded by images of a crocodile, a cat, a lizard, and a boar, all four at once. The Nine Tails sensed the human's plan, even without knowing it. It wrenched the White Talon to the side, lancing its tails across its joints like tentacles, pulling and entangling to keep it from striking back, or dodging Arak'Jur's attacks. The guardian joined their mêlée, wrapping his hands around the White Talon's midsection, carving through its armor as he cut and slashed, moving almost as fast as it did with *Red*.

A second wave of pustules grew and launched, exploding against the Nine Tails' body, chipping and raining down rock from the ceiling and filling the hall with the stink of smoke and sulfur. But the guardian's attacks cut quickly. Armor chunks fell to the ground, and the White Talon lurched, straining to break free of the Nine Tails' hold. Two of the tails broke their grip, almost freeing one of its claws to swipe at Arak'Jur's head, but the Nine Tails whipped a third tail into place an instant before the claw struck flesh, wrenching its joint back and wrapping it more firmly than it had held before. Then the final armor chunk broke free, and Arak'Jur cut into its belly, opening a gushing vein of blood to drench their legs and soak the floor.

Blood-Corenna leapt over them, vanishing beyond a twist in the hallway. The Nine Tails rose, letting most of the White Talon's broken body crack and fall, careful to keep it suspended enough for Arak'Jur to disentangle himself and get back on his feet.

True-Corenna was there before they both were free.

"Are you hurt?" Corenna asked. "Are there more?"

Arak'Jur shook his head. "The Regnant was here, I saw him before I raised my first shield of Earth. But he appears to have fled."

Sarine resumed control of their form.

"He was," she said before the transition was done. It came out as half snarl, half speech, but both of them seemed to understand. "The Nine Tails could smell him."

"I saw him, too," Corenna said. "He ordered his *magi* to attack, then retreated."

Bodies and smoke decorated the hallway. Kacper and Baael emerged from one of the adjoining rooms, neither apparently wounded.

"Sarine!" Kalira shouted from behind. "You idiot! What did Erris say?" Kalira stormed past the fallen Crane- and Mantis-*magi* as though their broken bodies were no more than clutter in her way.

"I'm fine," she said. "The Regnant was here, but he's retreated."

"You aren't supposed to charge into fights," Kalira said. "*Especially* not if you think the Regnant could be nearby. And he was here. He was here! Do you have any idea what you're risking, getting into a fight with him? You were supposed to use the Dragon's gift to retreat if you even suspected he was nearby."

The Nine Tails stirred inside her, but she forced it down. "You're right," she said. "I was being a fool. I saw Corenna and Arak'Jur in trouble and I let the Nine Tails have control."

"They're both more than capable of defending themselves," Kalira said.

"And even if they're not, how am I supposed to keep you safe if you go charging off as soon as you see anyone in danger?"

"We went this way to try and reach the central chamber," Arak'Jur said. "And the pillar of light. It's likely the Regnant is waiting there. But if you think it best to retreat, we can go ahead to see."

"What do you think?" she asked Kalira. "Should we fall back, and let Arak'Jur go ahead?"

Kalira glanced between Arak'Jur and Corenna, only just seeming to notice the hulking corpse of the White Talon at their feet.

"No," Kalira said finally. "We're close. We should press on. But this time if you see the Regnant anywhere, you fall back and let others take the risk of confronting him."

She nodded. Adrenaline still pumped in her veins, but Kalira was right. She'd found enough allies with enough strength that she didn't have to take the risk personally. It stung, though, leaving others to fight her battles.

"Stay behind us, then," Arak'Jur said. "Unless he's changed the halls ahead more than the ones behind, we're close."

71

TIGAI

Outside the Shelter *Maze*
The Fields of Glass

He fired both pistols at once, both shots striking the glass wall the *magi* put up between them. Shards cracked and shattered, skittering across the ground and sending up a hundred flashing lights where they touched it. But there was no need to blink back to an anchor to reload his guns. The *magi* were retreating, and for now, he welcomed them to it.

Erris d'Arrent holstered her own pistol, favoring her left leg as she approached. Her uniform was burnt in twenty places, and her skin along with it, red and blistering on the side of her face.

"How are your people?" she asked. Strange to hear the words from her voice, and not from Marquand's.

"Good," he said. "Fresh. You wanted me here, so I came. I've kept the rest of them back from the fighting, as you ordered."

Erris nodded, wiping sweat from her forehead as she watched the *magi* falling back behind their wall.

"He's not coming," she said. "Not out here."

"The Regnant?" he asked.

"The Regnant," Erris said. "His people are broken. We've taken losses, but he's taken five times as many. If he was going to arrive and try to turn the tide, he would have done it by now. All that's left is mopping up the rest of them out here."

"Out here," he repeated. "What about the spire?"

"Precisely," Erris said. "That's where I need your people to go. Take Yuli and Namkat. I can link up with Wata'si'tin and Kwoori for another push across the field. That will keep them penned in and prevent their Dragons from reinforcing. We'll push toward the spire once the fields are clear."

He squinted, looking through the white powder haze and the smoke that still lingered near Erris's maze of *Shelter* walls. He couldn't get a count of anything through their glass, but Marquand had said there were twenty or so of the *magi* left on the field. It made no sense. If he'd led an attack where the garrison had lined up for slaughter he would have pulled back, expecting a trap. From everything Sarine and the others had said about the Regnant, he was supposed to be an extraordinary foe, not a dog hiding and sniveling while his soldiers died.

"Forgive me, Majesty," he said. "But doesn't this all seem a little too easy? His *magi* are good, but we have champions and Gods from what, six? seven? lines of magicks. So far we haven't seen anything from him we couldn't have drawn on ourselves attacking a monastery town at the heart of the Empire."

"We don't know what's waiting in the spire," Erris said. "Stay alert and keep your people ready. Sometimes a battle is decided by overwhelming force on one side—but that's the best time for the enemy to lay a trap."

"I'll feel better when we've sprung it," he said. "At least then I'll know what we're facing."

Erris grunted assent, then turned her back on him as three towering bird creatures approached next to a man, one of the Rabaquim whose name escaped him.

It all felt bloody wrong. His instincts screamed to retreat and reassess. *Magi* were too valuable to throw away on delaying tactics, even in a fight of *magi* against *magi*. It would be good to have Yuli by his side again, though. They were a bit farther north; he saw Namkat flying overhead, though he hadn't seen the ice creature that had fought with them since the start of the battle. He closed his eyes, seeking the starfield and the strands. This place was infested with anchors and stars, a carpet draped underneath the physical world, as if someone had walked the length of the entire field setting anchors with every step. It made it easy to guess where a tether would lead; he wouldn't trust it for precision, but he had his choice of any of fifty stars to tether to shift himself north toward Yuli and Namkat's place on the field.

He chose one, and hooked himself to it. He'd almost cinched the tether tight when the starfield dimmed. It was as though something drank the light from a hundred stars at once. A block, all together, flickering and going dark.

He let the tether he'd been about to make dissipate.

"Your Majesty," he called. "Majesty. Something's wrong, on the stars."

"What is it?" Erris said, turning her attention from the Rabaquim and his giant birds.

"I don't know," he said. "It's as though something is tethering itself to multiple stars at once—scores of them. I've never seen..."

He trailed off as the stars flashed.

And then took shape. A monstrous shape: a swirling cloud of darkness, towering up into the colored sky.

"Oh fuck me," he said.

Erris frowned at him, then turned to see.

She started shouting orders at once. He heard her: She wanted him to go back to Marquand, to retrieve the rest of his people and put them in the field. But right now he had to go forward. Yuli was there, right on fucking top of the thing. And he had to get to her first.

72

ARAK'JUR

Approaching the Soul of the World
The Black Spire

He and Corenna moved together at the front of the hallway. Earth and Ice answered his call; both were ready to weave a double shield without delay. Corenna would do the same, in both her blood and flesh forms. Whatever misgivings he had about the Rabaquim's strange gift counted for nothing now. The blood-gift was a magic suited for battle. If it kept her alive, none of the rest mattered.

This place was almost as he remembered it, and he nodded toward a passage turning right. Corenna sent her blood-self ahead by a few paces, then followed at his side. Empty. For now. The Regnant himself had appeared last time, and set his fighters on them. His instincts had full control as they walked. This was a battle, even if there were no enemies in sight. Dragon-*magi* meant there could be fighting in the span of one pace to another. He kept his senses sharp, as sharp as if he were stalking prey in the last moments before striking for a kill.

They took the last passage. A short hallway from where one of the libraries had been, spiraling in toward the center. The stone was blacker, the light dimmer, but the passageways were as he remembered them. If a fight was coming, it would come now.

They emerged into the central chamber, and the Regnant was there.

Stone slammed into place in front of him, while Corenna favored Ice, both shields springing into being to enclose the mouth of the hallway. Her instincts were as sharp as his, but where he'd expected an array of *magi*, the vast central chamber was empty, save for one man. The Regnant. An old, hunched-over man dressed in gray, standing beside the burning column of shadow at the room's center. The Regnant hadn't moved when they appeared, but he and Corenna had acted quickly, putting their shields in place before he could strike.

"He's there," he called behind. "Be ready."

He waited, readying Ice to supplement the barriers between them. Sarine was exchanging words with Kalira; he ignored them. The fight was here. Any moment the attack would come, shattering his and Corenna's stone and ice. He was ready to move. *Kirighra*'s gift was close at hand, and *ipek'a*, and *astahg*.

No strike came.

"He's not moving," Corenna said beside him. Her eyes were half-closed, as they were when she saw through her blood-self's senses. "It's as though he doesn't see us. How can that be?"

"Let me," Kacper, the Skovan, said from behind. The man spoke a word—a vile, evil word. It failed to translate in Arak'Jur's mind, in spite of the Gods' Seat's gift when it came to tongues. It was always so, when the Skovan summoned his companion, but had never failed to stand up the hairs on his skin when he heard it.

Baael, the archangel, appeared on the other side of the stone and ice. He saw the shape through the sections where ice held sway, moving toward the column of black light, and the blurred silhouette of the man beside it. Baael struck with his fiery whip, roaring as it slammed into the Regnant's form. It roared again after, this time in frustration.

"Nothing," Kacper said. "That's...curious."

"It's as though he's there, and not there," Corenna said. "An image of the man. Not the true thing."

"Drop the shield," Sarine said. "Let me see."

Kalira started arguing with her again. He kept his instincts sharp, focused on what had to be a trap to bait them into loosening their guard.

Stone stayed in place, but the Ice that Corenna had summoned thinned and melted, running into puddles on the stone.

She stepped inside the room first, with him a step behind.

Baael hovered over top of the Regnant, snarling as the archangel readied his fiery whip for another strike. Corenna's blood-self had taken up a position opposite them, on the far side of the chamber, stalking around the black column. The Regnant was frozen exactly as he'd been when Arak'Jur first glimpsed him. He noticed now, though, that the old man was shimmering, almost translucent, standing beside the black column. His eyes were closed, his beard frozen to the hair, all of him unmoving in spite of the archangel threatening him, the blood-copy of Corenna stalking through the room, the other five now pouring into the chamber.

The Nikkon man who'd come with Sarine and Kalira gasped.

"He's performing a summoning," the Nikkon, He Who Stands Before the Highest Mountain, said. "Forgive me, Great Ones, but I recognize this. This is how we Spirit-Weavers channel our ancestor spirits."

He stayed alert, putting enough distance between him and others in case the Regnant awoke and moved to strike.

"Is there danger?" Sarine asked.

"I don't know," He Who Stands Before the Highest Mountain said. "I cannot summon Lord Koryu save where I can see. But who can say where the Great Evil One's eye might fall? His gaze is said to stretch farther than the farthest of our isles out into the sea."

"You mean he's summoning one of your spirits?" Kalira said. "Meaning he could dismiss it and he'd wake up here, standing right in front of us? Does he know we're here?"

"No, Great One," He Who Stands Before the Highest Mountain said. "When we summon the spirits, we go away, to a place that is not a place. He will sense nothing from his body."

"It's safe to try the pillar, then," Sarine said. "The rest of you protect me while I work. If he comes back, we can escape if we have to."

"Too dangerous," Kalira said. "What if we can't pull you back from the sparks? Why would he leave this room undefended? It has to be a trap."

"How else am I supposed to cleanse the Soul?" Sarine said. "He's standing right bloody there. He can't spring a trap when you're all standing on top of him. I'm going to try."

"No," Kalira said. "We should fall back. We can engage the spirit he's summoned. He'll die if it dies, right?"

"Yes," He Who Stands Before the Highest Mountain said. The Nikkon man's face had paled. "Though I fear I know the spirit that would answer the Great Evil One's call. A dark, forbidden thing. We should flee."

"We're not going anywhere," Sarine said. "I'm going to try this, and you're going to watch my back while I do."

"Sarine, if you die—" Kalira said.

"I won't," Sarine said. "Not with you to keep me safe. Anati can watch the room, too. She'll reach me no matter where my senses are if there's danger."

Sarine's *kaas* appeared, perched atop her shoulder, as she approached the column.

"I don't like this," Kalira said. "I don't like this at all."

"It's a chance, and I mean to take it," Sarine said. "The rest of you, stay alert. Watch him for any sign of movement."

Arak'Jur kept silent during their exchange, keeping five spirits' gifts at the edge of use. He drew close to the Regnant, which meant drawing close to the towering column of shadow burning at the center of the room. It radiated heat, with a slight tang of sulfur, like a clear mountain spring. It seemed... pure. He'd expected something vile, something tainted and evil. Instead the shadow burned clear, as though beckoning him in, offering him a chance to be cleansed by its pure black fire.

The Regnant still hadn't moved. He stood facing the room's entrance, frozen upright as though he were carved from stone and only painted to look like a man. Easier to imagine their enemy as prey sighted by its predator, frozen, contemplating before it bolted away. It would mean death, swift and sure, as suddenly as the Regnant realized he was surrounded by foes. The Nikkon man was mumbling dire curses, the archangel holding its whip aloft, ready for another strike. Corenna kept as focused as he did, her true self wheeling around to face him from the front while the blood-self circled to take a place at Arak'Jur's side.

"Here goes," Sarine said. "Gods but I wish I knew what I was doing."

A gust of wind blasted through the chamber.

Lakiri'in almost answered his call; but it was only Sarine. She'd approached the column and dipped her hand into the stream of pure blackness. The Regnant hadn't moved.

Darkness flickered. It seemed to leak from the column, then snap back, then leak again. A sheen of jet covered Sarine's body, metallic and glistening, then melted away.

Kalira moved beside her, close enough to touch the shadows, determination written on the girl-child's face. Anati stared at the Regnant. All of them kept still, as unmoving as their enemy. Any moment, death would come, all their enemy's power, or perhaps his Dragons, unleashed into the room to stop whatever Sarine was doing with the column.

Until then, they waited.

73

YULI

On the Fields of Glass
The Gods' Seat

The glass shattered, and she fell.

Blood and bodies sloshed in the water that had apparently been trapped beneath the glass's surface. Her senses reeled, suddenly engulfed by wetness and light. She mistakenly tried to breathe; liquid filled her lungs and she coughed, only welcoming more water into her throat. Fear took hold, and she kicked her legs, trying to swim upward, back toward the surface, stirring a million flashes of bioluminescent lights. Purples, greens, pinks, blues, yellows reacted to her every movement, flashing and dazzling around her, until she couldn't be certain which way was up, which way she needed to swim to escape the sudden deluge. She'd been standing atop the glass, squinting toward Erris's maze of *Shelter*, certain she'd seen Tigai appear there. Then suddenly there was water everywhere, and shattering glass and lights.

The Twin Fangs pushed to take control, and she refused. There was no fight here. Only water. Only the threat of drowning. She kicked, and rose.

Coughs sputtered from her mouth as she broke the surface. The brilliant colors dimmed around her, though her body was still submerged in it.

"Sister!" Namkat's voice called. "Take my hand!"

She blinked, fighting for vision. The colors had all but blinded her, leaving superimposed images that didn't change whether she blinked or kept her eyes open. She flailed her hand forward, and grasped Namkat's. Feathers, soft and downy, covered her sister's skin when the Wind Song had control. Namkat pulled, and water slid from around her, until she was hauled back onto the glass. Namkat's wings beat a thrumming sound, spraying droplets of water.

Coughs stung her throat, but air found its way in as she purged the water in her lungs.

"How?" she managed to say. "What?"

"I don't know," Namkat said, her voice touched by the ethereal pitch of the Wind Song. "One moment you were standing there, then—"

She coughed again. The brilliant lights dazzling her vision subsided in an instant, and though her sight still hadn't returned entirely, it was dark now.

Namkat let go of her hand. The shadows deepened.

"Then what?" she asked between coughs. "Namkat?"

"I...I don't..." Namkat said. "I've never..."

She blinked, trying to clear her sight. This was wrong. It shouldn't be so dark, not after lights had flashed and seared her vision. But whatever was wrong with her eyes, the Twin Fangs' senses wouldn't be so impaired. Reluctantly she gave in, reaching out to let it take control.

"Sister, we have to go," Namkat said. "Now! Grab hold!"

The Twin Fangs wouldn't come.

It washed over her in shock. She blinked again, repeating the exercise of emptying herself, making her body available for the warrior-soul to claim and change. She'd done these exercises since she was a young girl, since her face had been chosen and tattooed. Even when she'd failed, then, there had always been a spark, a stirring, a burning hunger just out of reach. Now there was nothing. Only darkness.

"Sister!" Namkat shouted.

She reached out and took her hand again. This time the feathers and down were gone. Namkat's hand was only skin.

Namkat pulled on her arm, but instead of beating wings taking flight, lifting them both into the sky, she jerked them both forward, collapsing together onto the glass.

"What's going on?" Namkat said. "Why...?" Her voice had changed. The Wind Song's ethereal pitch was gone. "Oh no. No no no."

She glanced over her shoulder. Red and darkness still dominated her vision. But now there was something else. An outline. A shadow, rising high above the skyline. Impossibly large. A column of twisting energy rose from the shattered glass and bioluminescent water where she'd fallen in. It swirled and grew to a humanoid shape, though it was a hundred times larger than any man, wrought of shadow, stretching its limbs upward as it grew.

"I've seen this before," she said. And she had, at the Tower of the Heron.

Somehow she knew it was the same presence. The same evil. Then it had been only a spark, growing from the seed of its champion's death. Here it was greater. More. And still it swelled larger, growing and darkening the sky. "We have to run. Now!"

She scrambled to her feet, picking a direction at random. Her vision cleared rapidly, though redness still seared her eyes.

Tigai appeared in front of her.

Not a mirage. Thank every God in the heavens. He was standing there atop the glass, one of his pistols still smoking in his hand. He stared behind her, up at the growing shadow emerging from the ground.

"Holy motherfucking shit," Tigai said.

"Get us out of here, now!" she shouted, still holding Namkat's hand.

It startled him back to the moment. He reached out to touch her, and closed his eyes. It felt good beyond words to feel his hand on her shoulder. Not least for it being him. But his touch meant an escape, somewhere far away from that thing rising from the glass. His touch was comfort and safety, all at once.

"I...I can't," Tigai said. "Something's wrong with the starfield here. I can't move us. What the fuck is going on?"

Dread replaced comfort as quick as it had come.

"Run, then!" she shouted, or tried to.

Instead a blast of shadow engulfed them all, swallowing her words, obliterating vision as a dark wind carried away their screams.

74

TIGAI

Engulfed in Shadow
The Gods' Seat

The wind roared in his ears, burning his skin, blinding him. Instinct screamed to snap back, to tether to any of the thousand anchors that should have been there when he closed his eyes. He'd faced death in too many forms: shot, stabbed, burned, drowned, poisoned, torn apart, or hung from a noose. Every time he'd escaped through the starfield and the strands. This time he closed his eyes and there was nothing. Only a hand grasping his in the darkness. Yuli. Somehow he'd come to love her, and she him. A poet somewhere might see beauty in them dying together, but he grasped her hand tighter, afraid to let go, and she did the same.

Time stretched with the agony. His body burned, and everything he could see or touch was shadow, apart from Yuli's hand.

A light surrounded him.

He was dead. This was death. And yet Yuli still grasped his fingers, and he grasped hers. Perhaps they'd gone over to join their ancestors together. Now that would be a piece of poetry. But the pain was gone now, and he could see the light for what it was.

An armored figure made of pure radiance stood at the center of the dome, holding aloft a flaming sword. It had wings like an eagle's, outstretched to fill the space, as though its feathers were part of the barrier protecting them from the darkness raging outside.

He wasn't dead. Yuli knelt beside him, holding his hand with one of hers, and Namkat holding the other. All three of them huddled under the dome of light.

<*Go,*> the armored figure said. Its voice seemed touched by trumpets, and harmonies of a thousand other voices singing its words. <*My blessing will protect you, for a time. Go, and get to safety.*>

"What the bloody fuck is this?" he said, words coming to his mouth before he could consider them.

<*I saw your sacrifice,*> the armored figure said. <*You came to save these two with no thought for your life. It pulled me from my grief. This was how Wicek would have wished for me to die. Now go, and leave me to my fate.*>

"Leorain," Yuli called. "That's your name, isn't it? Whatever you mean to do, if you can stop this shadow, then you can retreat with us. There's no reason to die here."

<*No,*> the figure, Leorain, said. <*Don't tempt me, for your sake. My shield is made of zeal. If my resolve falters, so falters your protection. Go. Now.*>

He scrambled to his feet, all but pulling Yuli up to hers. He'd come close enough to death not to want to try it a second time.

"Wait," Yuli said. "We can't just leave him. He saved us."

<*You aren't leaving me,*> Leorain said. <*You're freeing me to act on God's will. Now go! While I still have strength to fight.*>

"Listen to him!" he shouted. "Let's get away from this thing, so I can take us to safety."

Yuli hesitated again, but Namkat pulled her other hand as he pulled the one he held. Leorain nodded as they began to move, whipping his flaming sword around into a battle stance, facing the heart of the shadow that had engulfed them.

They reached the edge of the dome of light. Shadow still raged on the other side, a tempest of wind and lightning. Namkat tried it first, pushing a hand through the barrier. Its protection persisted: Light seemed to cover her skin like armor where she pushed through the dome. Good enough. He glanced back over his shoulder just before he went through, and saw the archangel spread his wings further, until they, too, broke the boundaries of his shield, still covered in a dazzling glow. Then Leorain bounded upward, his sword outstretched, and the angel vanished into the darkness.

He kept Yuli's hand clasped tight as they ran. Shadows and electricity crackled around them, but he saw it through a yellow sheen, as though looking through a pane of stained glass. The same yellow glow surrounded them all, joined where their hands connected, and the roaring wind was muted to a hum in his ears. They ran, as fast as all three could move together, until finally they emerged from the roaring shade.

He blinked immediately, and found the stars. The glorious, beautiful, pure and perfect stars.

He looped tethers around them all, and the glass shifted under their feet.

Suddenly the shadows and wind, the cracking glass and thunder were all gone, or at least, were far in the distance. They were back where they'd begun, still here in the Gods' Seat, but safe. Finally, blessedly safe.

Namkat had already grown her feathers. He understood the feeling. He wanted to tether to two dozen anchors at once, just to reassure himself the shadow hadn't permanently stolen away his gift. Instead he turned to Yuli and wrapped her in a wordless embrace.

She held him back. Neither spoke. He'd almost lost her, and almost lost himself trying to rescue her from that bloody fucking thing. Emotion welled up. He loved her. He'd already lost so much: his people, his estate, his family. He couldn't lose her, too. He'd rather die himself. In the moment he knew it was true: He would rather have died trying to retrieve her than let her fall.

"Where the bloody fuck have you been?" Marquand cursed at them, lowering a spyglass as he turned to glare. "Her Majesty sent your people forward without you, and you show up here as if now's a bloody fine time for romance."

They separated, little as he wanted to let Yuli go, and even less on the prompting of a red-faced drunk with a mouth like a sewer pipe.

"Apologies, Colonel," Yuli said. "Tigai was busy saving me from...whatever that thing is."

"Safe to assume it's him?" Namkat said. "The Regnant?"

"Her Majesty believes it to be," Marquand said, sparing one last glower before he raised his spyglass again and turned back to the battlefield.

It was something quite different, seeing the shadow from a distance. The creature towered to an impossible height, swirling and raging like a whirlwind as it spread across the glass. Deep blue color pulsed away from it, drowning the tiny bursts of color from the champions' footsteps. The shadow pivoted atop its swirling base, and where it pointed, columns of dark wind blasted the ground, or tried to. A wall of pale white *Shelter* stood on one side, protecting a group of champions huddling behind it. That had to be the Empress's position. Seeing it oriented him toward the rest of the fighting. Farther north, a wall of blood had the same effect as the Empress's *Shelter*, staving off a torrent of wind being thrown against it. Explosions and fire leapt through the darkness, bursting inside the creature's body with no other noticeable effect to slow its attacks.

"What's the plan, then?" he asked. "What does Her Majesty intend to do?"

"You were supposed to be the plan," Marquand said. "Transporting Orana, Ta'ta'ichin, and the Nikkon woman, the one who smells like a bloody harbor, to attack the Regnant wherever he showed himself. Or did you forget your duty so quickly?"

"I can't," he said. "Getting close to that...*thing*...snuffed my magic. I couldn't so much as see a star, let alone tether to one."

"Bloody convenient for you, then," Marquand said.

"What about the others?" Namkat said. "If they draw too near..."

"They'll be caught unable to use their gifts," Yuli finished for her. "Do they know?"

"How should I know what they know?" Marquand said. "I know the Empress didn't bloody tell them before they left."

"We have to warn them," Yuli said.

"*I* have to warn them," Tigai said. "You have to stay right here."

"Not a chance," Yuli said. "I'm not sitting out, not while that thing is out there."

"I almost killed myself trying to save you," he snapped back. "And I'm going to bloody marry you, if it kills me. But I'd as soon live, and have you do the same. So stay here. I'll go, warn them, and come back. You won't even notice I'm gone."

"Sister, he's right," Namkat said. "Even the Wind Song can't get close enough to have any effect on that thing. The Twin Fangs would be gone before you got near enough to strike it."

"Don't you fucking die," Yuli said. "Don't you dare."

She wrapped her arms around him. He held her back.

"If you're going, best go now," Marquand said. "That's Orana's group there, running along the western part of the fight. Can your gift get you to them directly, or are you going to have to run after them? I thought you had to have visited a place before you could hop to it."

"There are already anchors here," he said. "Anchors bloody everywhere." He saw the group Marquand pointed to. Still far enough from the shadow that his gift should be working.

He blinked, and found the closest stars.

"Stay safe," he said. It didn't help to have Yuli staring at him as though he were already dead.

He cinched the tether into place, and the roaring returned to flood his ears.

"Here!" one of them shouted. The Nikkon woman, She Who Gazes into the Deepest Seas. "We dare not draw any closer."

"Still too far," Orana shouted back. "I can't strike from—what in a maiden's virtue are you doing here?"

All three noticed him at once. She Who Gazes into the Deepest Seas, Orana, and the third one that had been assigned to him, Ta'ta'ichin, one of the Blood Gods' champions, the young woman with the hungry, too-wide, and too-empty eyes.

"I came to warn you," he shouted. "That thing—the shadow. It stops your magic if you get too close."

"We know," She Who Gazes into the Deepest Seas said. "Its name is Akuryo—an evil spirit of great and terrible power. A forbidden thing, among my people. A secret, evil knowledge."

"Time for a bloody lecture later," Orana said. "We have to get closer than this. Look, the Tarzali are closer. If they can risk it, so can we."

He looked where she pointed, and saw a man launching bolts of light into the shadow-creature from around its northern side.

"Too dangerous," She Who Gazes into the Deepest Seas said. "Akuryo is a living thing, like any other. It isn't bound in place. If it moves, and we're caught, then we're dead."

Orana turned to him. "Tigai can move us faster than that fucker can. If we see that thing turn toward us, he takes us somewhere else. Simple."

"I didn't..." he started to say, then stopped. He'd promised Yuli not to die. Fuck. "All right. Fine. Just stay close."

"And stay behind my shield," Ta'ta'ichin said. "If you stray outside it, then it's not on me when the darkness takes you."

"Stay behind what?" he asked, but in response she closed her eyes, and a wall of dripping blood sprang into being in front of them. Red droplets ran and leaked onto the glass, and the whole thing seemed fixed ten steps in front of her, even when she moved, leaving trails and rivers smeared across the ground.

"Forward, then," Orana said, grinning.

They moved. Toward the shadow.

His stomach turned over, and he blinked too often by reflex, reassuring himself the stars were still there. He should have been by the sea somewhere, with a cup of liquor strong enough to sear his nose and throat before he sipped it. He and Yuli could be swimming naked in the waves, spreading out blankets and making love on the sand. He'd made the mistake of trying that without the blankets before, and found it was more sand than love. But he'd sooner fuck a sea turtle than walk back into this shadow. Yet here he was, playing the bloody fool again.

Ta'ta'ichin's blood-wall towered over them, and still couldn't block the shadow entirely. He stared at it, watching for the first sign of movement, or another blasting wind.

"Here," Orana said, and they stopped. "This is close enough for me."

Her eyes rolled up into her head, leaving only the whites of her pupils. She Who Gazes into the Deepest Seas froze next to her, her body shifting to an ethereal, misting state. Suddenly the sky seemed to open above them, though it had all been empty colors before. Now there was a moon, a shining full moon overhead. Behind them at the same moment the glass surface seemed to change to water, a raging sea in the middle of a storm. And something moved underneath its waves.

Both struck at once. Meteors fell from the sky, burning chunks of rock appearing first as tiny sparks accompanied by a whistling whine, both growing as they fell toward the shadow. At the same moment, a beast emerged from the sea behind them, a massive, coiling serpent breaking the water's surface in a seemingly endless leap as it rose over their heads. He gaped, forgetting for a moment to watch the shadow. The water-snake was more a water-leviathan, each segmented chunk of its body the size of a watchtower, flying through the air as it surged above the waves.

The shadow snapped around, toward them, and suddenly the dark winds returned.

Two torrents at once met and blasted into Ta'ta'ichin's blood-wall. Howling wind screeched in his ears. Orana's meteors crashed into the shadow, a thousand explosions shattering glass, sending spheres of smoke, ash, fire, and stone into the sky. The leviathan collided with the shadow, emitting a brilliant light where the two towering figures touched.

He anchored all four of them to another star, and snapped it into place.

They were on the opposite side of the field, near Erris d'Arrent's *Shelter* wall. The shadow had moved, surging toward where they'd stood before in less than a heartbeat's time. It stood atop where they would have been, had he not hooked them away. Impossible for a creature of such size to move so fast. But it had. He was going to die. Fuck.

Orana closed her eyes again, as quick as she'd appeared beside him, and the moon flickered overhead, another cascade of meteors whistling high in the sky. She Who Gazes into the Deepest Seas did the same, shifting her body to mist as a second ocean appeared behind them. The first had vanished when he'd tethered them here, but the same leviathan-snake leapt from the water as soon as it appeared. They were farther from the shadow this time, but evidently close enough to strike. And the shadow turned again, seeming to stare right at him, and sending a rippling flash across the starfield and the strands.

"He can follow me," he said. Horror crept into his voice. "That thing. It moves through the starfield, and it can sense which anchors I've used."

"Then move us again!" Orana shouted. "We can keep up our attacks. Just take us away!"

He hooked to another anchor, tightening the tether as he felt a hundred new strands hook on top of where they now stood.

They shifted across the glass. New meteors fell; a new ocean arose instantly, and the shadow appeared on top of where they'd been moments before.

He hooked them again. They moved. It followed.

His breath caught with every step across the strands. Whatever Orana and She Who Gazes into the Deepest Seas were doing, they seemed to draw the creature's ire instantly. The thing had ignored the lights and explosions from the others, but it reacted at once, as soon as the meteors appeared, as soon as the leviathan emerged from the waves. Meteors summoned to where the thing had been crashed into the glass, sending gouts of fire and bioluminescent water into the sky a thousand explosions at a time. The massive leviathan vanished each time he shifted them, but appeared without fail each time, surging from a new ocean's surface, hurtling toward the shadow in a stream of endless coiling scales.

He tried to avoid the other champions on the glass, but the shadow appeared atop a pair of them, the ones Orana had identified as the Tarzali, snuffing them both in a violent fury, leaving nothing behind when it vanished. He made sure to stay as far from Marquand, Yuli, and Namkat's observation point as he could, veering them across the open glass plain. Twice he tried to predict where the meteors would fall, shifting the four of them into place so the shadow would appear just in time to be pelted with a thousand flaming daggers from above. It worked. Screeching winds rose across the glass when Orana's meteors struck the creature, but the thing still pursued them, shifting across the glass each time he hooked to a new anchor, each time snapping into place a bare instant behind his escape.

Once he put the shadow atop She Who Gazes into the Deepest Seas's ocean, and the leviathan entangled itself in the winds, flashing a bursting light like a hundred suns where they collided. Yet the shadow still pursued. If they'd hurt the thing, it gave no outward sign.

Until he hooked to what had to have been his hundredth anchor, and the shadow didn't follow.

He expelled the breath he'd held for what felt like a half hour. Orana's eyes went white again, the moon shifted overhead, and a fresh round of meteors came falling. She Who Gazes into the Deepest Seas turned incorporeal, and the sea opened behind them.

The shadow stayed still at the last anchor point. Darkness swirled at its base, lit by flashes of thunder, but it remained frozen as the meteors fell. He held a new set of anchors ready. It had to be a trick. A change in their rhythm to throw him off, to make him stumble. He stayed focused on the strands, watching for any sign of new tethers, any sign of movement, any sign at all.

The shadow vanished.

He gasped, and Orana's meteors struck nothing, colliding all at once into a flaming crash atop the glass, breaking it and splashing colored water high above the smoke and fire. The leviathan dove into the empty space, then as quickly it, too, vanished, and She Who Gazes into the Deepest Seas turned corporeal again, pivoting around in what looked like confusion.

"It's gone," he said. He was out of breath, riding on a knife's edge, keeping his senses focused on the strands. Nothing there, too.

"It can't be," Orana said. "We hardly struck the thing. Can you follow it on the strands? It has to be here somewhere."

"I saw it fucking vanish," he said. "Could you have killed it?"

"No chance the Regnant would die so easily," Orana said. "His shadow can't be gone. Find it. Take us there."

"Not gone," She Who Gazes into the Deepest Seas said. "Look."

He followed where she pointed. Toward the spire on the horizon, the only discernible landmark atop the empty glass plane. It had been a towering black light, cutting from the skyline to the ground, radiating shadow. Erris had said that was Sarine's objective, and the champions that had gone with her. It wasn't black any longer. The light had changed. Now it flickered from black to white, the shade changing a hundred times a second, balanced on the edge between both sides.

"He can't fight two battles at once," She Who Gazes into the Deepest Seas said. Her voice was touched with reverence, as though she spoke a prayer.

"Then he's inside the spire?" Orana said. "If he's summoned the shadow there, then everyone inside could already be dead. We have to—"

The spire flashed again.

This time the darkness was gone. All that remained was a pure, brilliant white light.

75

SARINE

Remaking the Soul of the World
The Infinite Plane

Darkness flowed around her, mixing with the sparks wherever they touched. The colors that made her were blurred, connected to lines of pure black that covered her like oil. She was still herself underneath the stains, but here, closest to the source, the world was drenched in shadow. It should have stunk like rot; instead it reminded her of the smell of a hospital, or a sick ward—rot and decay, yes, but cleanliness, too. Purity, an almost noxious, medicine smell. And it seemed reversed: The rotting smells came from everything else, while the black oil was the cleansing draught that clung like soap, fighting to purify whatever it touched.

An illusion. It had to be. The black fire that replaced the white had changed the world from healthy and natural to sickly and weak, covered in unending acid storms and fire. Now it fell to her to fix it.

She tried pulling on the web of ink that stained the sparks. It came free, obeying her will as though she were dredging seaweed out of a shallow point in the harbor. For a moment her heart surged, watching the blackness lift from the sparks that made *her*, the reds and whites and platinums, untainted. Free. She pulled the oil away, ripping it and setting it aside into the void. She was clean again. It felt no different, but then, what manifested here on the Infinite Plane wasn't always what manifested in the physical world. She swept through herself, finding a few last vestiges of darkness and purging them away with a thought. Knowing they were there was the key: Recognizing it, naming the shadow for what it was, seemed to dislodge their hold, and she set them adrift, left to burn away in the void that persisted between sparks on the Plane.

For a moment she felt a thrill of victory. She'd separated oil from sparks, even here, touching the fires of the Soul of the World. But it was nothing. She was one torrent, and the world was a trillion trillion of the same. She could as soon have dredged all the seaweed in all the world's oceans by hand.

She turned back to the column of shadow.

It burned hot here, where it wasn't even warm in the physical world. It warped the Plane around it, creating an infinite vertical space only here, where the column burned, while the rest of the Plane stretched horizontally. Touching it before had burned at the core of who she was, threatened to warp memory and time and self at the slightest brush of its tendrils. Maybe that was part of the answer? With the light turned black instead of white she could touch it freely. It had sparked nausea and revulsion at first, but that had to be in her mind, drawn from her expectations more than reality. She could stand in it now, and feel only a warmth, like coming too near a burning hearth.

All of this was too vast. The Plane truly was infinite, or massive enough to make no difference, where one person, one will could touch. When the Regnant had dipped his hand in the shadow it had taken him mere moments to change it. Another clue: Whatever she had to do could be accomplished quickly, once she found the answer. Unless she found a way to stop time with it, there was no chance of siphoning off the black oil from each torrent one by one. But hadn't the *kaas* helped him change the world, after the light itself had gone from white to black? He *hadn't* changed the torrents—the *kaas* had. Or something else had, at least. So all she needed to do was change the column itself.

I think that's right, Anati thought to her. *We didn't touch the light. We can't touch it. Only the sparks.*

"What do you mean?" she asked. "Is there something particular about the column?"

Something other than it being the world's soul?

"Okay," she said. "But you said the *kaas* can't touch it. You mean that literally, don't you?"

I mean we can't touch it, Anati thought. *I don't know why.*

She stared up at it again, then down. It stretched both directions, on to infinity. It still seemed to give off light, as though it could be made of shadows and still illuminate the Plane, brighter than any torrent of sparks.

"What happens when you try?" she asked.

We can't, Anati thought.

"You can't even try?"

Do you need to have tried to touch molten iron to know it would kill you? It's like that. We would die.

That had to be a clue, too, though to what she still had no idea. Something about the column would kill a *kaas*. Hadn't Kalira mocked Anati by asking if her kind could even die? So something as old and powerful as the Sun didn't know the true nature of the Soul. It was truly ancient, then. And the *kaas* would have been made not to be able to touch it. A safeguard, maybe. Maybe the Soul itself had some kind of protections built in. Something that clearly didn't apply to her now—though perhaps they had before. Perhaps that was why the tendrils of light had jarred her, threatened to shatter her mind at even the slightest accidental brush.

She probed toward the column gently, the same way she'd handled the oil where it touched her torrent, only lightly touching it with her will, not forcing it to move, yet.

NO, Anati thought.

A shock wave rippled from the Soul. It caught her in a violent fury, spinning her will around in a hundred directions at once. It poured into her, around her, through her, filling every part of her and draining her empty and dry. For an instant pure energy lanced through her, though there was no pain. Then as quickly the shock wave moved on, traveling vertically, where there were no other torrents or sparks.

Sarine! Anati thought. *Are you hurt? Why would you do that! I told you it would kill you if you touched it!*

"I didn't..." she said. She felt empty, somehow. Exhausted, as though she'd run through half the city. "I thought I was touching it already. See?" She moved part of her sparks into the path of the shadow, and felt nothing more than the same dull heat.

Being present with a thing isn't the same as touching it, Anati thought. *Space is layered beyond counting. Consciousness isn't. Please don't try to do that again. I don't want you to die.*

"Well, how am I supposed to affect the damned thing, then?" she asked.

You don't have to kill yourself to change it, Anati thought. *The Regnant didn't, did he?*

Another clue. Anati was right. She didn't have to observe it in the same manner she observed the sparks. Just as well not try to go down that road. Her senses were still spinning, every part of her reeling from the pulse. But if she couldn't try to change it directly, it meant she had to change something around it. What was the bloody thing, then, if not the column of burning light, whether bright or dark? It had heat now, but it hadn't before. Was that part of the answer? The light, too, shone from the column. But maybe the color wasn't part of the Soul itself, or at least, maybe the light it gave off wasn't. If she was wrong and tried to push her will into some forbidden attribute it could well end with another energy spike. What else was she missing?

She studied the column again. She needed something more detached, something that affected the column without being part of what it was, what made it itself. The light was too inextricably tied to the object: She couldn't conceive of the Soul without thinking of the light. If she tried to change its color directly it would be like trying to change the color of her own sparks. She wouldn't be *her* anymore, if the sparks were that different. Would she? But the sparks swirled and flowed in all directions, making whorls and patterns without pause. Maybe the Soul did the same.

This time she watched the light without trying to force her will to exist alongside it. She kept her will detached. Only noticing what it was. Not even the lightest touch, or attempt to change.

It was black. Pure black. Clean. A tide of flowing ichor, flowing like molasses down a stick.

Wait.

A white spark. Only the faintest stray, but she caught it. A single flash showed amid the river of black. It leapt upward, while the rest of the column flowed down.

She saw another. Now that she noticed, she saw a dozen. All tiny, single sparks. They would have been lost in the tide if she hadn't taken care to notice each one. They flashed and were gone, as fast as she could spot them. Each one leaping upward, against the flow of the rest of the light.

"I wonder," she said. "If I changed my perspective...would it...?"

This time she thought of changing herself, rather than the column.

Would it what? Anati thought.

She hardly heard.

The column was white again. She spun her will...upside down, was the only way she could think of it. Now the light flowed upward, rather than down. It glittered like sunlight, shining directly in her eyes. Pure white light flooded around her. And this time the sparks leaping against the grain were black, scattered wisps of darkness flowing down instead of up.

She snapped back to her first orientation. The column changed back to black.

"I know what I have to do," she said. "When the light flows down, it's black. When it flows up, it's white. That's all the Regnant did. He changed the polarity, like magnetic iron."

Oh good! Anati thought. *How do you do that?*

"I don't have a clue," she said. But she was close now. The Regnant had done it quickly, in a matter of moments, and he'd done it without changing the nature of the column itself. In fact, the column contained both sides already, dark and light, as part of its nature. Something about it had required her hand; Kalira had said she couldn't help, didn't know how to effect the sort of change they needed. So it had to be within her power to change it.

She fixated on the light sparks, the ones flying against the flow. She'd seen only a few strays at first, then more as she'd noticed them, as she'd known what to look for. She wanted to touch the column with her will, to help guide the sparks along, but held back. Maybe it was enough to notice them.

It was.

A dozen light sparks showed at first. Then a score. Then a hundred. The flow was black, a million parts shadow to one part light. But the flow of strays leaping against the grain seemed to double with each moment she spent noticing them. A hundred. Two hundred. Four. Eight. Sixteen. Thousands. Enough to change the pure black to a flickering white whenever the sparks surged.

Sarine, Anati thought.

The surges came more often. But something seemed to be fighting against them. The sparks were still only a rebellion, a current fighting against the dominant force of the river. They needed to change the flow. They needed her help. They needed her to notice them, to believe it was possible. She held the key, teetering on the knife edge between white and black. It was in her power to change it. But something was in the way.

Sarine, Anati thought again. *I need you.*

"I...I can't," she said, barely able to spare thought for the words. She had to focus. Noticing every spark. Doubling every light she believed in.

He's awake, Anati thought. *He's here. I need you now!*

Fear tore through her. Him. The Regnant. Did the black lights double when he noticed them, too? They seemed to be multiplying as fast as her white sparks. Almost as fast. She was winning. The white light was growing.

Sarine!

She relented.

Her focus split, and suddenly she could see in two worlds at once. Her white sparks begged for her, groaned as some part of her focus ceased to notice their growth.

The rest of her senses returned to the Gods' Seat's central chamber.

The Regnant stood across from her, facing her, no longer frozen in the stasis in which they'd found him. Determination filled his eyes as he advanced toward her. A Force-sphere surrounded him, shimmering like heat in the distance, and a stream of energy lanced from his shell toward her.

Corenna stood between them. Her Ice had conjured a barrier, replenishing it as fast as the Regnant's Force could rip it apart. It sent shards scattering through the room, scorched to droplets of water and hissing steam where Force struck her shield.

Kalira was shouting at her. "Leave! Sarine! Use the Dragons' gift! Run! Flee!"

Arak'Jur, Omera, and Allakawari all struck at the Regnant's sphere of Force. Claws, sword, knives all rained in a flurry, to no effect, only fueling the bursts of power and energy lancing between the Regnant and her, with Corenna and her Ice in between.

She should have used the Dragon's gift. Kalira was right. No barrier Corenna could conjure with the war-spirits' gifts could stand against the Force her allies were pouring into the Regnant's Heron-shield. Anati surged *Red* into her blood, and the Nine Tails screamed for control, for the strength and speed it would take to escape.

She should have run. Instead she pushed against the tide.

She noticed the sparks, ten thousand at once, twenty thousand, forty.

The light flickered.

The Regnant let loose a yell. A howl of battle. A surge of strength.

Force erupted from his shield, blasting Corenna's Ice to nothing.

Blasting Corenna to nothing.

Her body exploded, her flesh scattering under the power of the Regnant's assault. Anati's determination flared in her thoughts, and Arak'Jur screamed death in her ears.

White shone around her. All of Anati's strength poured into defending her body from the Regnant's blast of Force.

The light changed.

The Regnant's eyes filled with panic.

Suddenly ten thousand shadow sparks flew against the new tide. Twenty thousand. She pushed back. The light changed again. Again. Again. A thousand times in a second, balanced on the edge between light and shadow, flickering between black and white.

Please, Anati thought to her. *I can't keep up this much* White. *Please. Sarine. Go. Save yourself.*

The Regnant's Force stream poured into her, dissipating against Anati's shield.

His barrier broke first.

Arak'Jur cleaved him in half with a roar loud enough to echo through the halls of the Gods' Seat. Spectral claws knifed into his guts, spilling blood and gore onto the stone. Omera's blade took him in the back of the head, splitting the Regnant's skull in a hiss of acid. Allakawari's blades cut the rest of him down, flinging the corpse to the ground.

The Soul changed for the last time.

Pure white light illuminated the chamber.

Blood shone against the stone, reflecting her champions like a still pool. The Regnant's face was torn and twisted, broken in half by Omera's sword, while his body was ragged, bone poking through split flesh. Corenna's blood ran into his, pieces of her body scattered and cast across the room.

Arak'Jur sank to his knees, weeping.

She blinked, noticing the last of the sparks as they redoubled for a final time, drinking all of the shadow, flowing the column upward, until the black was gone, and only white remained.

"It's..." Kalira said from behind her. "He's dead. The light is changed. You...you did it. It's over."

Exhaustion tore through her. She stared between the column, as pure and white as it had ever been, and the Regnant's broken body.

"Thank you," she said. "To all of you. You kept me alive. We did this together."

Corenna's blood-self approached from the opposite side of the room, its head cocked in a mockery of Corenna's form. Somehow it was still alive, still present, despite the true-Corenna being torn apart. It looked over Corenna's body quizzically, coming to stand behind Arak'Jur. The sight reviled her; the last thing he needed to see was a blood-effigy of the woman he loved. But he seemed to give it no notice, tears streaming down his face as he squeezed his eyes shut in·pain.

Blood appeared on Arak'Jur's chest.

He looked down in disbelief. She did the same, only belatedly noticing the claw protruding from the left side of his ribs, puncturing his heart. A claw made of blood. He slumped forward, revealing Corenna's blood-self kneeling behind him, a *mareh'et*'s claws grown from its fingertips.

"I'm sorry," Kalira said. "But it has to be this way. Cleaner if your champions are dead. Easier if your keys all pass to us."

Sarine spun in time to see Kalira's hand flash.

Sunlight illuminated the chamber, a brilliant bloom of pure fire. For a moment *White* flared around her. Anati screamed in her thoughts.

Then her body was incinerated, her skin and bones and muscle all charred to ash.

76

ERRIS

Broken Glass
The Gods' Seat

The Regnant's shadow had carved a path of destruction atop the glass. This place had enjoyed a purity, the sort of beauty she could only appreciate after a battle was decided. But the fighting destroyed it. Massive swaths of glass were broken, leaving fires, molten slag, and colored water behind. What little blood had been shed was washed away in the breakage, leaving ankle-high floods as the water trapped beneath the glass's surface was allowed to rise.

She began her trek back to Marquand alone, as soon as the pillar changed from black to white. Others made the same journey; she saw them pulling back across the plain. Her ankle was broken, making her among the slower walkers, but they'd covered a great distance in the opening charge and subsequent fighting. A few scattered souls, pulling back to celebrate their victory. The light changing had to mean they'd won: The Regnant's shadow had vanished just before the change. He had to have been defeated. And yet, the aftermath of any battle was never more than bittersweet. Now was the time to regroup, to assess the last remainder of the enemy's force, and to count the dead.

She had no accounting of those who had ventured inside the spire with Sarine; those would come later. But among those fighting on the glass, she counted heavy losses. Wicek, and his archangel, Leorain. Kaladooh and Nin'ti'dana. She Who Shakes the Trees with Thunder, and He Who Delves into Secret Places. She hadn't seen Wata'si'tin since the shadow's initial appearance, and Yuli and Namkat had been underneath the thing when it first showed itself on the field. So many dead. Always too many.

But some had lived. Marquand. His *Need* spark still shone on the leylines every time she closed her eyes. She saw Nalai'ti'turu and his spectral bears limping back from where the shadow had shattered a field the size of ten city blocks, to the north of her position. Seh'sa'raya and his birds were heading straight for her, rather than vectoring toward Marquand and the rallying point. She Who Howls with Hunters was farther ahead. Tigai must have returned during the fighting; how else were Orana and She Who Gazes into the Deepest Seas able to maintain their assault on the shadow as it warped around the field? So they would be alive, some of them at least.

She paused to open the buttons on her coat. It was hot, too bloody hot. Sweat covered her skin, but then, she'd been burned over what felt like half her body. *Life* would fix it, and *Body* would keep her standing until it did. Gods send she had enough strength to finish the day. Perhaps ten or fifteen of the Regnant's *magi* remained on the field; she could see them, too, in their colored robes, gathering behind a smoking ruin where one of Orana's meteor barrages had torn apart the glass. With the light changed and the Soul reclaimed they had to see that the fighting should be over. But that didn't mean they would give up easily.

She sighed, squinting to try and make our their numbers more clearly. Marquand would have a count. Already her mind was turning, considering whether it was wiser to wait for an accounting of who'd survived the spire before reengaging the enemy or demanding their surrender. Even if only half her force had survived, the numbers alone might cow the *magi* into accepting defeat. But it would depend on how many of them remained alive as much as how many had the will to fight.

Need came, tightening the connection between her and Marquand, and her senses shifted across the field.

Pain shot through her. Superficial. A knife wound. A blade was still stuck in Marquand's upper thigh. He was hanging back, behind what looked like Yuli's Twin Fangs form. A dead girl lay on the glass next to him. Ellin— Allakawari's sister. The Tarzali girl been scorched by what looked like *Entropy*, half her side charred and burned, covered in deep red blood and flaking skin.

Yuli stood in front of him, facing off against her sister. Namkat stood twenty paces off, her body covered in her Wind Song feathers. Neither moved, until Namkat glanced to meet Marquand's eyes—which now were *her* eyes, illuminated by the golden light of *Need*. Then without word Namkat bolted, leaping up into the sky to fly toward the spire.

"What's going on here?" she asked with Marquand's voice.

Yuli's Twin Fangs form glared at her, sparing a second look as Namkat flew away. Then it changed, its snout shortening, muscles receding, limbs falling back into place, and within two heartbeats Yuli was there, her face full of confusion and doubt.

"Empress," Yuli said. "I don't have a bloody clue. Marquand was watching the field, trying to find signs of Tigai, when the spire changed colors. Then Ellin bloody stabbed him, he killed her, and the Twin Fangs sensed danger—danger, from my own sister! Namkat tried to spear me with her feathers. I'm fine, only a few cuts but...now you're here."

"Both Ellin and Namkat attacked, at the moment the spire changed?" she asked.

"That's right. I thought the light going from black to white meant we'd won. Isn't that was Sarine was trying to do?"

Dread threatened to snuff out clear thinking. She forced it down.

"Does Tigai know you're alive?" she asked.

"Yes," Yuli said. "He saved us, me and Namkat both, and took us here. What does that have to do with this?"

"He'll come for you, then," she said. "Can you see me there, on the glass?"

She pointed toward where her body was standing. Suddenly Seh'sa'raya's direct approach toward her instead of the rallying point took on a new meaning. She wanted to be running in spite of her broken ankle. And She Who Howls with Hunters was almost here, almost to Marquand and Yuli.

"I don't understand," Yuli said. "What's going on?"

"Betrayal," she said. It tasted bitter. But she'd guessed this was a possibility, for all there hadn't been time to plan enough contingencies against it.

"From who?" Yuli asked. "All of them?"

"If your sister is with them, we have to assume so," she said. "Every champion, and every God not bound to Sarine. When Tigai comes for you, have him move you and Marquand to me. Then we escape."

"Escape," Yuli repeated. "What about Sarine, Arak'Jur, and the others? They're still inside the spire."

"We'll see," she said. "If Tigai can move us there with minimal danger, we'll go. Otherwise, we leave this place and regroup. Clear?"

Yuli nodded.

She let go of *Need*, returning to the pain in her ankle and the burns on her skin.

She withdrew her pistol, checking the cylinder. Four shots left. She had fresh munitions on her belt, and *Entropy* to char the glass if it came to it. Tethers came, for *Entropy*, *Shelter*, *Body*, *Mind*, and *Life*, woven into her or held at the ready. Better if she looked weak. Like she was wounded, resting, exhausted from the fight. All true, but she needed to look the part.

Seh'sa'raya and his birds were a hundred paces off, closing at a leisurely pace. Hunters, sated from a kill. At a quick count, perhaps fifteen of his creatures had survived the fighting. All of them had blood-red feathers, where only perhaps two or three had been crimson when the day began.

She waved toward him when he crossed seventy-five paces. He returned the gesture in his way, almost mocking.

When he reached fifty paces, she drew her pistol in a smooth motion, sighted, and fired.

The sound rang across the field. Followed quickly by the wet smack of his body falling backward to strike the glass, his ruined face bent and twisted while the rest of him fell like a stone.

His birds howled, and then the lead one, the largest of them, pivoted its neck to stare at her and screech.

Too much to hope the birds would scatter, or better still fall dead with their master. Four leapt at once, sailing toward her while the others ran.

Shelter slammed into place at the last instant before impact, sending the birds careening off across the glass, while *Mind* sent out six copies of her in either direction. Her foot would slow her, but *Body* let her ignore the pain. She made a second *Shelter* wall with a narrow gap between, huddling against it as she might have done with a choice piece of rock wall or farmer's fence on a battlefield. The birds closed the distance, racing with their powerful hind legs, their jaws opened to reveal rows of teeth more like a lizard's than a bird. Two darted in toward the gap in her *Shelter*, and she loosed *Entropy*, cooking them where they stood. The others wove, some snapping toward her *Mind* copies, while others raced around her flank.

She found another three with a second blast of *Entropy*, but two more leapt through the resulting smoke cloud, slamming into her and knocking her against her own *Shelter* from behind. Searing pain went down her left side as one of them raked a claw along her skin. She blasted its leg to cinders, then fired two more pistol shots at its partner, taking the beast in the neck and the eye, exploding its flesh as surely as if she'd struck with *Entropy*. She tried to scramble to her feet, putting up a ring of *Shelter* around her on all sides, and found her left leg unresponsive. Broken, or the tendons had been cut. A massive gash showed through her uniform, with blood leaking out on the backside of her leg. Adrenaline kept her from feeling the pain. *Life* knit together what could be knit in the moment, as she found her footing, balanced on unsteady feet, when the remaining birds slammed against her *Shelter*, changing its color from a deep blue to a paler white with every charge.

She waited. The rhythm of their attacks kept up, the birds throwing themselves into her barrier to break it down with raw force. She let it drop just before a strike hit, dodging to the side as the bird sailed past, unsteady on its feet. *Entropy* seared its feathers black, and she ducked, falling prone as its partners leapt toward her now that her forward shield was down. She rolled, letting them hit the far wall, then slammed another barrier into place, caging them inside. Simple, then, to let a thin sliver of *Shelter* dissipate and cook the inside of the cage with *Entropy*. Flame roared in the confined space, and the birds' shrieks died down as the smell of burned meat rose on the air.

She spun as quick as it was done. Fourteen were dead, by her count. One remained.

It stood twenty paces back. The largest of them, the one that had screeched when Seh'sa'raya fell. It stared at her, ignoring the movement of her *Mind* copies, as though it could sense her true self as she stared back at it.

It made a chittering noise, then a snapping growl, then what sounded like a whine.

She held *Entropy* at the ready, her heart thundering, waiting for the beast to move. It backed away, a few steps at first, before it turned and ran.

She sank to the ground, favoring her left side. More *Life* tethers sprang into place, as quick as she could stitch them. Blood still seeped from the wound, and she pressed her hands to it as she worked with the tethers. She'd seen soldiers survive worse, but without constant aid from a binder she'd lose the leg, and risk bleeding out. She had to stay conscious, at least until Marquand could tend to her. Breathing came hoarse and ragged from her already burned lungs. In the distance, figures moved. She squinted to see, droplets of cold sweat leaking into her eyes.

Three shapes appeared without warning.

Yuli immediately went to her side. Marquand joined her, probing with *Body* and *Life* even before he finished kneeling. Tigai wrinkled his nose at the pile of charred birds.

"You were right," Yuli said. "The Nikkon woman—She Who Howls with Hunters—set her wolf on us as soon as she came close. They're all turned against us."

"I'll bloody say," Tigai said. "Orana tried to claw my arm to keep me from getting away. Tried to hold me and her bloody self in the path of her own bloody fucking meteors. Fucking insane."

"We need to get away," she said, hearing the weakness in her own voice. "Can you take us from here, Tigai?"

He nodded, as Marquand said, "She needs a doctor to go with my bindings. I'm not skilled enough for this. Can you take us to Rasailles?"

"What about Sarine?" Yuli said. "She's inside the spire."

"Sarine has the Dragon's gift, same as Tigai," she said. "If she recognizes the treachery, she'll escape on her own. If not, then she's already dead. We have to survive."

"I don't understand why they did this," Yuli said. "We were allies. Sarine did it. She cleansed the Soul. We won."

"Wouldn't be the first time allies turned on each other to divide the spoils," Marquand said.

Tigai closed his eyes, then opened them. They hadn't moved.

"Something's wrong with the stars," he said. "They're there—the ones in the real bloody world, I mean, not this place. But they're in the wrong places. And they're moving. The stars are moving. What the bloody fuck...I've never seen them behave like this. It's like the world is changing as I'm watching it."

"Can you take us to one?" she asked. "We can sort out the where later. For now we need to get away from here."

"She needs a doctor," Marquand said gruffly.

"No telling where it will be," Tigai said. "Don't hold it against me if we end up in the middle of an ocean, or inside a bloody volcano, or worse, if you don't give me time to trace the strands."

"Just do your best and get us out," she said. "Now."

He muttered something.

The glass vanished.

77

ANATI

Adrift in the Void
The Plane of Shadow and Form

The emptiness hurt most.

Since the moment of the bond, part of her had awakened, and been aware. All her life until then that part had lain dormant, like a limb or a muscle she hadn't known was there. Then in a glorious moment she'd been *alive*. Suddenly all her senses were attuned to another's. Every thought, every feeling, every memory, every touch or interaction had been coupled with Sarine's. Her father had been right. Sarine was more than an ordinary woman, more than even the luckiest bondholders could ever have hoped to find when they came into the physical world. She was powerful, and she was kind. She couldn't see suffering without fighting to end it. She was *more*. More than humans were supposed to be able to be. But now she was dead.

The loss echoed through her, finding new parts of her to inflict with pain. Even the pain itself should have been shared. She should have been able to tell Sarine, to share in her feeling, to watch Sarine care for her, love her, try to fix whatever hurt her. The hardest part of death was not having Sarine there to share her grief.

And the failure had been hers.

White sprang from hope. Her hope. Sarine's. She'd burned it all away trying to stop the Regnant's attack. But he was a True God—an old one. She'd expected to need everything, every reserve of hope she'd stored away, and she'd used it all. Almost every drop. Then when Kalira turned, when the Sun flared in her hands, for a long, eternal moment she'd watched and been powerless to shield Sarine from its fury. The memory of the death burned deep. She'd never forget it, not in a thousand remakings of the world. Not if her bond passed to a thousand new humans.

Her scales flashed blue, for sadness. Black, for death. Purple, for loss and pain. She was drifting in her place, the place Sarine had said she'd loved. The first thing she'd done after the bond was severed was come here and destroy it. Her home was no home anymore. It was nothing now, the same as she was. A void, where before she'd placed blocks and shapes as perfectly as she knew how, hoping it would impress Sarine. And it had! That moment was among her most treasured. But she didn't deserve it. She didn't deserve anything more than an empty void to call her own, and so she'd torn the blocks apart, displaced the shapes and scattered the pieces. There was no aesthetic here anymore, no beauty in nothingness. Only hurt.

She wanted a thousand years to mourn for every day she'd spent bound to Sarine. But another presence appeared in her void. A green shape. She wanted to snap at it, to unmake it as violently as she'd ever unmade stones and mountains. Nothing else belonged here, only her and her grief. But *kaas* did not unmake each other. Courtesy demanded she come and greet the visitor, and even in the depths of her pain she was still her father's daughter.

She appeared beside the green shape, bowing her head in greeting.

The visitor flared its scales emerald in a rude display, showing contempt, anger, jealousy, disdain.

Arix, she thought. *Elder brother. Be welcome in my home.*

This is no home, he returned. *Is this how you've spent your time since returning to us? Practicing unmaking your own things?*

Her scales flashed red, only for the barest moment. But Arix was old. He would have noticed.

My bond was cut, she thought back delicately. *To grieve is proper.*

Not when you have yet to present yourself before the throne.

My father will understand, she thought, this time indelicately. *He knows what I've lost.*

The subtlety of what she'd said wouldn't go unnoticed either. She and her father alone of those *kaas* still living had been bonded to a True Goddess. None of her siblings could hope to understand. She knew it, and Arix knew it as well. If there were princes and princesses among her father's brood, holding the bond she'd held would elevate her, and all of them knew it, though it was not a thing to be spoken of.

Your extravagance has been noted, Arix thought to her. *And your work is being passed to others while you wallow in your human emotions.*

This time she snapped at him, putting her will to his and banishing him from her place. Not an unmaking, but he vanished as surely as if she'd scattered his parts to the void. She was *not* wallowing in human emotions.

Her scales turned deep red now that no one was watching. She almost wanted to create a sphere or a cube just to smash it, to have the pleasure of rending something to its core, of watching its form linger and beg her for a continued existence she alone could deny. But there was nothing left to smash here.

Arix was right, and it stung her to the underside of every one of her scales.

She didn't want to face her father. Not now, not ever.

He'd trusted her. He'd put Sarine's life in her hands, when he couldn't continue holding the bond without risking his death. She hadn't been ready. All of them knew it. All her brothers and sisters. She'd thought at the time that father had chosen her because she was special, because she nurtured a hidden promise none of her siblings could see. *Those* were human emotions, the sins of ego and pride, but hadn't father chosen her, after all? Hadn't she been right? She was special. But all the specialness in the Shadow and Form couldn't bring Sarine back to life.

She had to go. It hurt, but Arix was right. She wasn't special. She wasn't anything but a stupid *kaas* that harbored human emotions, a stupid failure who let a True Goddess die when she should have jumped in front of Kalira's sunfire first, let it annihilate her pathetic body before even a single drop touched Sarine's skin. She was a coward, and a wretch, and hiding here was only going to make it hurt more when she finally summoned the courage to go before her father's throne.

She closed her eyes.

They would be waiting. All the chorus, all the siblings and other lords and ladies and their broods. All of them would be there, watching her, silently pleased at her failure, vindicating them for believing that father had sent her in error.

Her scales softened from red to pink, then yellow, then finally white. If she was a princess among the *kaas*, then let her be judged as one. She straightened her tail, stiffened each of her legs. Then she made a sphere. Only one, hovering in the air near the center of her void. It wasn't placed where any shapes had been before; the pain of replacing anything Sarine had said she'd loved cut too near, even with her scales in white. She spun being from nothingness, letting it grow until it was a perfect size for the space. It balanced the rest of her void, and she hadn't made any mistakes crafting it. It helped. Making things always centered the emotions; even humans knew that. Then, when it was done, she was ready.

She drew a deep, cleansing breath, then left her void.

The throne was close. It was close to everything in the Shadow and Form, at the center of all connections. Never more than a simple making away. She made herself there, standing upright, her scales pristine uncolored white. She summoned courage. She prepared for the thousand eyes that would greet her, relishing her fall.

Daughter. You come at last.

She kept her back stiff, with her head bowed. Her father sat above her, coiled in a relaxed position atop the elevated block of white gold that was his throne. But then suddenly he was next to her, his neck craning to examine her, like a human mother checking a child who cried over a skinned knee.

It embarrassed her. It wasn't proper for her father to show such concern here, in front of the chorus's watching eyes. Only there were no watching eyes. There was no chorus. They were alone.

I sent them away, Zi thought to her. *When I sensed you were preparing to come. A severed bond is not to be paraded for the envy of those who know nothing of what you've lost.*

Blue and purple broke the veneer of white in her scales. Childish. Even more embarrassing. She should have maintained her pride. But she couldn't fight the colors, and they soaked like ink deep into her scales, and her body trembled, and she hid her eyes.

My daughter, Zi thought. *My Anati.*

He curled around her. The touch sent a jolt through her; *kaas* did not touch. That was a human thing. Yet Zi enveloped her coils in his, letting the blue and purple bleed from her scales over onto him, mirroring her emotion and redoubling it, until the colors burned too brilliantly for eyes to see.

I'm sorry, father, she finally thought, and with the words came more trembling. *I'm so sorry.*

I know, he thought back. *I know what you feel.*

For a great length of time she trembled, and he held her, and their emotions bled together as one. Blues and purples, for sadness. Red for anger at herself. Black for death, remembering the moment of loss. Green for memories of better times. Pinks and yellows for love, and for fear of what grief lay ahead. Then finally a flicker of white, for hope.

When white flashed, they separated, and she bowed her head again.

You see, Zi thought. *Even in this, there is life. Even in the darkest despair, there is a way forward.*

Yes, she thought back. *I see it. Thank you, father.*

I mean it, he thought. *At its worst, the pain will tempt you to unmake yourself.*

Don't do it. Don't think it. There is hope, there is always hope. Remember this. Remember love.

His words shocked her. Unmaking herself? No *kaas* would even think it. Yet among all her siblings, all the living lords and ladies and their broods, he alone had been bonded to a True Goddess. He alone knew the pain of living without her in his thoughts.

Father, she thought. *Did you ever consider...?*

I felt the pain you now feel, he thought, interrupting her before she could voice the shocking words. His scales were white again, colorless and pure. *I still feel it, sometimes. I don't believe it will ever go away. But we live with it. We live, and go on.*

I will, she thought. *I didn't know what I wanted, coming here. But I will. I'll do my duty.*

You may take time to grieve, my daughter, he thought. *I only wish to remind you that you aren't alone. Even without Sarine, there are still ways forward for us. Ways we can grow.*

I know, she thought. *But I don't need more time. I need to work.*

He paused, cocking his head to look at her.

She unsealed the Soul again, didn't she? she thought. *That means we have work to do, remaking the world. I can be of use.*

My daughter, Zi thought. *You know who holds the keys now? The Sun. The Moon. The Blood. The Flesh. The Angelic Host. The Spirits of the Dead. All of them together, warring over who will have final control. All those who betrayed you. Those who killed Sarine.*

Her scales flushed blue and red, only for an instant.

I don't care, she thought. *The world still needs to be remade. Send me there to do my duty.*

You're certain? he thought.

This is how I'll find my hope, she thought. *This is how I stay alive.*

Now his veneer of white slipped. A flash of yellow, but only a flash, and then it was gone.

Then go, he thought. *Work, and remember my words.*

She bowed her head. She'd come here expecting ridicule, and found something more. Her father had struggled for many *kaas'* lifetimes to produce Sarine, to protect and guide her until she could remake the world. Now she was dead, but he still went on. He found hope. She could do the same.

Somehow, she could do the same.

Thank you, father, she thought.

His eyes flashed a metallic white, the color of steel. Pride. In her?

The Shadow and Form slipped away before she knew the answer. In its place she descended to the physical world, and the fabric behind it. A familiar place. Around her a thousand siblings and cousins tore and reshaped the contours of the earth. They would see her here and know she had presented herself to Zi. They would know her as one of them, and not question her place. But none among them had known what it was to be bound to a Goddess. None among them knew the depth of her loss.

There was still work. She felt the will emanating from the Soul of the World, the power of the instructions contained within. She tore apart a raincloud, scattering the acid and darkness into nothing, and reshaped something else in its place: a storm, full of ice and sleet. She watched the snowflakes whirl and blow on the wind. On *her* wind. Soon they would fall atop the ground below, covering this part of the world in a beautiful sheen of pure white. Other voices pushed at her from the Soul while she worked, some demanding sunlight in place of snow, others a deep jungle, others a rolling, open plain. She ignored them. A snowstorm suited her mood, so that was the will she listened to. Gods and Goddesses never knew the precise details of what they wanted, anyway. There was artistry in interpreting their demands. That was her life now, without Sarine.

78

YULI

The Twin Fangs ran across the snow. Ice stung its nose, mixing with the familiar scent of water deer. The beast had no business being out in a blizzard. It must have been caught; the sudden onset had surprised Yuli underneath the Twin Fangs' skin. Without warning the sky had changed, replacing the twilight darkness and acid rain with overcast skies, sleet, and snow. The Twin Fangs raced toward it, ignoring the cold. Broken trees scarred by acid stood next to trees as pristine and perfect as if they'd grown untouched for a hundred years. The water deer would be there, sheltering in the copse of new-grown trees. It switched direction, and raced ahead.

The water deer caught the Twin Fangs' scent. Unmistakable. Its prey changed direction, too, and ran. Snow pounded on the wind, biting cold.

Then suddenly, it changed.

The Twin Fangs stumbled out of the blizzard into sweltering heat.

Sand stretched in front of it, as far as it could see. A desert? It hadn't scented the change. Behind it, the blizzard still raged. It had to glance twice to be sure. Wind and ice swirled in the air, leaving fresh snowbanks as fast as they could cover the ground. Then suddenly, sand. Dry air, devoid of moisture, choked life from the land around it.

The water deer stood there, too, snapping quick looks in all directions, full of the same confusion. A few bounding steps. The water deer scrambled to pivot in the sand, the loose footing costing it precious seconds before it could change direction. The Twin Fangs didn't stumble.

A claw through the throat brought the beast down with a soft bleat. Blood ran into the Twin Fangs' hand. Sweet blood. It was hungry. It should eat. A need hummed underneath its thoughts. A command, a request. Once, it had been unable to ignore those sensations, when their bond with Sarine still held. Now it hesitated. But no—the thought came from Yuli. It should restrain itself. The rest of her companions needed to eat; that was why the Twin Fangs had gone out in search of food.

Instead of devouring the water deer where it stood, the Twin Fangs hoisted it by the legs, draping the carcass over its shoulder to let the blood run down its back. It spared one last look of wonder for the sand. Then it turned back, carrying the water deer through the blizzard back toward home.

Their cave was already blocked by snow. The Twin Fangs pushed through it, and soft firelight greeted it on the other side. It relinquished control grudgingly, leaving Yuli's muscles to carry the water deer's body as it approached the fire.

Erris was sleeping, curled under the one blanket Marquand had managed to find since they left the Gods' Seat. Both Marquand and Tigai went to their feet as soon as she emerged from the snow.

"You're back," Tigai said, moving to help her set the water deer's carcass down against the cave wall. He withdrew a knife immediately, setting to the work of skinning it and preparing its meat. Always a pleasant surprise, when her courtly Jun man demonstrated wilderness skills. She let him do it, grateful for the respite after running through the cold.

"It's strange out there," she said. "I'm surprised there was any wildlife at all, between the acid and now the blizzard."

"A good sign, though, isn't it?" Tigai said. "A sign something has changed."

"Hold still," Marquand said gruffly.

She did, letting him close his eyes, sweeping his hands near her as though he were performing a prayer.

"Not much of a struggle, was there?" Marquand said. "I need more *Body* than this, girl. She needs more."

She shrugged. She still knew little to nothing about how their leylines worked.

"More than just the snow," she said while Marquand harvested whatever he was harvesting. "About a league and a half from here, the blizzard stopped. It was sand. As sudden as the snow."

"Sand?" Tigai said. "The coastline, then?"

"No," she said. "Not a beach. A desert. Arid. Dry. Right next to a bloody snowstorm. Hot and sweltering. A cloudless sky."

Marquand retreated swiftly, kneeling next to the Empress's sleeping body.

"A desert," Tigai said. "Bloody strange."

"I know," she said. "It has to be part of the change. Maybe Sarine is still figuring out how to repair the world."

"Should we move, then?" Tigai asked. "I don't like the idea of staying put in this snowstorm."

Erris coughed, stirring from under her blanket.

"I don't know," she said. "The sun was shining there, but it was as harsh a desert as I've seen. I think Sarine is still learning control. That has to be part of it, right? She's remaking the world, but she ends up putting a blizzard next to a desert. There might be more terrain close by, maybe somewhere safer for us. I can go out scouting after we've eaten."

"Sarine is dead, girl," Erris said. "Better for all of us if we accept it."

The words stung deep. Too many sisters had died already.

"You don't know that," she said.

"I know when Sarine was alive, I could draw as deeply on the leylines as I wished," Erris said. "And now I can't. I know Tigai was exhausted to the bone, bringing us here, and he could use the Dragon gift as often as he wished, before. I see the struggles you've had, controlling your other half."

"The Soul of the World has changed," she said. "You don't know what that means. Maybe champions aren't needed anymore."

"We were betrayed," Erris said. "There's no point in pretending otherwise. We took a fool's risk, and paid a fool's price. At least we're alive. But Sarine isn't. The sooner we accept it, the sooner we can find our place in what's to come."

Rage boiled inside her. Inside it. The Twin Fangs stirred, hearing the words of an enemy. Muscles began to lengthen, fingernails sharpened to tiny points.

"Your Majesty," Marquand said. "Please. You need to rest."

"She needs to accept the truth," Erris said. "Until we find more survivors, we have to rely on us. Fantasies and delusions of secret victories will only get in our way."

She rose to her feet, and went back out through the collapsed snow, leaving the fire behind.

Cold stung her skin.

"Yuli!" Tigai called after her. She ignored it, fighting to control her breathing. Calm thoughts floated on the surface, with darker ones underneath. So many sisters dead. Alka. Juni. Kitian. Imyan. They were more than fellow warriors. Of all the souls in the world, only a bare handful knew what it was to wear the tattoos, to welcome another spirit to share their skin. If Sarine was dead, she was alone. Namkat might have survived, but as a twisted thing, a hideous mockery of the Natarii spirit. How else could a sister raise a hand against another sister? She must have been perverted by the Sun, when it had offered to save her.

Snow flaked in her hair, on her eyelids. She felt the winds battering her, felt the power of the Twin Fangs to ignore the cold. She could give in. She could let the war-form take control, rage back inside the cave and rip the Empress apart for her words. Who else but a sister could understand the temptation, the power, the humiliation when the other self took control.

"Yuli, stop," Tigai said, stepping through the fallen snowpile at the mouth of the cave. "You're going to fucking freeze out here. Come back inside."

"I'm fine," she said. She needed to run away. She couldn't risk the Twin Fangs injuring Tigai in its anger. She could feel it, rising in her, her limbs growing longer, her eyes changing.

"Erris is being a jackass," Tigai said. "She's angry at herself for her failure, and she's been in pain. You don't have to listen to her."

"I know," she said. "I . . ." The anger burned, too hot to control now. "Tigai, I love you, but you need to understand. Without a champion's bond . . . there are going to be times when you can't be near me."

He looked hurt. He looked sad. He looked as though he wanted to find the right words, the words that could calm her down. He didn't understand. Couldn't understand.

The Twin Fangs bloomed inside her, and she turned and ran into the snow.

She remembered the first time, when Alka had forced her to leave her family, to run into the wilderness for fear of hurting them, to leave and not come back for days.

Shame bit at her insides as they changed. Her skin grew tougher. Her legs hardened, her fingertips extending outward into five claws on each hand. Her mouth elongated, accommodating the two massive fangs that gave the form its name. She didn't want this. But she wasn't in control anymore.

The Twin Fangs burned with anger. And hunger. Its water deer was lying in the cave, with Tigai's knife protruding from its hide. That had been its kill. It was well within its rights to return, to slaughter those who dared to steal its food.

Yuli begged it not to. It listened. For now.

Instead it ran. Snow fell harder, cutting its skin on the wind. There would be other creatures here. Others emerging from the acid and shadow that had prevailed, now giving way to snow and sleet. Its senses projected outward across the countryside, hungering for the slightest change, the smallest disturbance, that would signify the presence of something for it to kill.

Something else caught its notice.

A change on the wind. A change to the wind itself. A boundary, a place where the snowstorm stopped abruptly, to the north. The direction from which they'd come, when Tigai had set them down here, following the stars he'd claimed were changing, moving. It had been a short journey to find their cave. And now their cave was covered in snow and ice. Perhaps there was something better, to the north, if the blizzard wasn't blowing there. Something more hospitable than ice, or sand.

It changed direction, racing northward. The hills here sloped and fell steeply, still low enough in altitude to be covered in trees. It saw the same mix of old and new, of decayed, desiccated husks alongside pristine oaks and pines. Sarine had to be alive. That was Yuli's thought, but it surfaced with enough force for the Twin Fangs to listen. But even as the thought came, the truth of Erris's words sank under its skin. There was chaos here. The sort of chaos that would manifest with too many designers, too many artists sharing a canvas for their paint. It ran toward the boundary, now sure there was a boundary between the blizzard and something else.

It reached a hilltop, and looked down over a golden plain.

Impossible. There were supposed to be mountains here. Ten steps ago it could see the peaks and crags from within the blizzard, great silhouettes cast against the clouds. But now that it had reached the hilltop, it saw nothing on the horizon, only a sea of amber grasses blowing on a light breeze. No snow or ice. And the only clouds in the sky were red, a shade of deep crimson, as though they were full with blood about to rain down on the grain.

Its senses snapped into the moment. Hunters. It smelled them on the wind. Four shapes, gathered around a place near where Tigai had brought them. Instantly it fell prone, flattening its body against the hilltop. Snow still blew behind it, less than a pace separating the world of golden grain and the world of ice and sleet. The noise was a distraction as it surveyed the hunters.

They reeked of blood. No—they *were* blood. All four shapes. No flesh among them. Three men and one woman, each made like the Blood Gods' champions had been during the attack. Corenna, Omera, Nin'ti'dana, and Ta'ta'ichin. But two of those were women, not one. New champions, then, or at least new *magi*. Here following their trail. Here to hunt them.

The hunters hadn't noticed the Twin Fangs yet. It sensed it in the way they carried themselves, each one scanning the plain, seeking sign to use for tracking. They wouldn't find it here. The world had been remade since their arrival.

It wanted to kill them. It wanted to taste its enemies' deaths in its jaws. It wanted to race down the hillside, to cut through the golden grass and fight. Four against one, but a Natarii warrior would accept longer odds, expecting victory, even against the unknown. It longed to feel the exertion of its muscles well-used, its claws soaked in carnage and ruin.

Yuli urged caution. The sense made it want to snap its jaws in frustration. Yuli didn't know these creatures. These blood-*magi*. She wanted to return to the cave, to warn the others, to scout, perhaps to flee. Where four could come seeking them, more would be ready. They needed to be prudent if they wanted to survive. And it did. The Twin Fangs paired with human souls to give it wisdom, to elevate it from animals and beasts. It craved blood, but Yuli's sense was wiser than its hunger.

It watched to be sure the hunters hadn't spotted it. Then it slinked back, slowly crawling in reverse, retreating into the snow.

No helping it: The hunters would find tracks here as soon as they reached the edge of the storm. An hour, perhaps, if they were thorough in searching their surroundings on the plain. Less if they were lucky.

It raced back toward the cave. Yuli would need control again, to tell the others what they'd seen. But for now both enjoyed the freedom of running in the wind. It craved killing, to sate the anger at being mocked, to sate its hunger for blood and meat, but it had patience, too. It could always kill the Empress later, if Erris continued goading them into rage. The thought pleased the Twin Fangs and Yuli both, a salve for the pain of knowing Erris's terrible words were true, and her sisters were all dead, or dead to her.

79

OMERA

Volcanic Basin
Eastern Sarresant

He opened his eyes, and the world shifted. Sulfur and ash filled his nose, enough to make a lesser man gag and choke. He ignored it. Travel from the Gods' Seat was a simple thing now, a reflex triggered through his blood-self, as champion of one of the key-holders bound to the Soul of the World. But finding this place had cost him everything. And now he was here.

He stepped gingerly over an exposed lava flow, hugging the rock wall to his left. His blood-self traversed the same incline a few paces ahead, showing him the way. He'd seen it already during a vision, though it had been dark, blanketed by the storm clouds that covered the world during the Regnant's brief accession. Now molten rock swirled and bled from the mountainside, belching smoke and hissing steam. But the terrain was the same. The pathway was still here, leading up the twisting rock face toward a man-made cave, or better, a woman-made one. Fate waited there, along with the last drops of royal Bhakal blood outside his veins.

The blood-self waited at the opening until he came around the last bend. It watched him, then vanished inside. Beckoning him. He pressed himself close against the rock, edging forward, taking proper care with every step. *Ubax aragti* focused his attention, giving him enough balance and strength to dance on a pebble before it slipped and fell. Still he trod carefully. It wouldn't do to have the southern continent's true King die by slipping into a flow of molten rock.

He reached the entrance, and went inside.

The cave walls were smooth, cut by magic. Perfect square hallways made an indent in the side of the mountain, lit by a soft glow without any apparent source. The halls forked ahead, but his blood-self waited, meeting his eyes before it took the rightward passage. Deep within the mountain a rumbling sound accompanied the volcanic activity outside the cave. Soon this place would be swallowed by the earth, another casualty of the fall of Regnant and Veil. But she was here. The blood-self was sure, and so he was sure. He followed another fork in the passageways, until a room opened at the end, a room without a door. His blood-self waited, unmoving, standing guard at the entrance as he approached.

She sat inside behind a lacquered desk. The same soft light shone here, without an apparent source. It illuminated a workspace filled with rows of books on bookshelves lining every wall. It shone on two chest-height plants situated behind the desk. And it shone on her.

Sakhefete. His mother's sister, her features too close to look on her without remembering the face that had borne him, the face he'd loved and feared in equal measure.

She closed her book atop the desk as he entered the room.

"Omera," she said. Her voice was steadier than he'd expected. "I wondered how long it would take you to come."

His blood-self sneered, reflecting the hate he felt burning in his belly, though he showed no sign of it, keeping his face calm and smooth.

"Majesty," he said, affording her the barest nod. Whatever contempt he felt for her, she was still a Queen.

"What did the Blood Gods offer you, for my death?" she asked. "Not that, surely?" She said it nodding toward his blood-self.

His hand went to his sword hilt by reflex, but he didn't draw.

"You have it wrong," he said. "I bargained with them to learn the location of this place."

"You paid them with their own coin, then," Sakhefete said. "The Rabaquim have been trying to kill me since before your mother bore her first son."

"You're ready to die, then," he said.

"No!" she said, almost shouting it. "Omera," she said, softer. "Sakhefete is already dead. She lives inside me, and I share her memories, but the Queen as she was, the woman who betrayed your mother, who stole your memories—she is gone. If you listen, I can explain it further, and tell you what the Rabaquim mean to do here today."

His blood-self bared its teeth, reflecting his anger.

"You're a coward and a liar," he said. "The Blood warned me of this. That you would say anything to live."

"No," she said. "If you mean to kill me, and if you can, then so be it. But what I say is true. The Blood Gods are using you to do what they alone cannot. Think. Haven't they, too, changed your memories, as Sakhefete did? Haven't they given you this purpose, this ambition that drives you here?"

"They restored my memories," he said. "I'm whole. Or I will be, once your blood is shed."

"They lied to you," she said. "They manipulate you, even now. I have Sakhefete's memories of who you were before she changed you. These emotions you feel: arrogance, hatred, pride, the denial of your birthright. None of those were there before she made you her creature. You once were an uncertain boy on the cusp of manhood, a man who was told he bore a great destiny, yet struggled to see how he was meant to fulfill it. Duty, love, compassion— these are who you are, who you were, before she destroyed you. And now the Rabaquim have made you something worse. Something more terrible."

He hesitated, still gripping his sword hilt.

"You remember your mother's love," she continued. "That was too strong for them to have erased completely. Even Sakhefete knew she couldn't uproot those seeds, not even with Li's help. Tell me, Omera, would your mother have loved the ambitious, prideful man who came here to kill me? Would she have comforted you, kept you at her side, shared her secrets and her trust with a man so bent on becoming King? Or would she have had you eliminated, as she so ruthlessly dealt with any of your brothers who had designs on her throne?"

"How can you know this?" he asked.

"I told you," she said. "I am not Sakhefete, taken as she was with her own ambitions. I have her memories, all the memories of all the exchanges with Amanishiakne before she died. But I see what she could not. I can show you, if you'll let me. I can restore you to the man you were meant to be, the man your mother loved. The man she trusted as custodian of her Empire. The man she chose as her successor, when she foresaw her own death."

Doubt bloomed inside him. He was King. He was meant to be King. Any who bore royal blood had to die. But she was right. If all royal blood had to be erased for him to rule, that meant he would have had to kill his mother. He would have needed her dead, had Sakhefete not already done it for him. But that thought wouldn't stick in his mind. The face that loved him, that held him when he cried, that whispered legends of great heroes, that promised him fate would make him one of them, that stories of his deeds would ripple through generations of young Bhakal . . . he couldn't have wanted her to die.

"You are Sakhefete," he said finally. "I see you in front of me. How could I trust a woman who murdered her sister?"

"Li put my memories into Sakhefete," she said. "He wasn't desperate enough to remake my body on its own. Or perhaps he hoped for a vessel he could control. But he had to have known I would conquer her, eventually. Her mind was weak, and I've had thousands of years to know myself far better than she could have ever hoped to."

"Then," he said. "If you aren't her...Who?"

"I'm Li's partner," she said. "Or, his former partner, I suppose. Li—the Regnant, as he calls himself. You can call me Evelynn, if you wish. Or the Veil. I've been a Goddess long enough the name has stuck, even in the way I think of myself sometimes."

"Tricks and lies," he said, feeling a rush of anger. "We killed the Veil. I watched her die. Kalira blasted her to nothing after she changed the light from black to white."

"I gathered as much," she said. "Was the girl Sarine really foolish enough to bring the heads of so many lines of magic to the Soul, and then unseal it while they watched? It sounds like something I might have done, when I was young and stupid."

"You can't be her," he said. "I remember you, tormenting me. I remember..." But his mind blurred. He remembered a woman, a woman he'd fought beside, struck down and killed. He remembered being erased, made to eat *tisa irinti* and serve at the table of a different woman, a woman who hated him. He remembered wanting to be King. Deserving to be King. He remembered training in the fighting yards, while...someone watched over him from the balconies above. He remembered looking up, desiring her approval more than anything in the world. But no. He wanted to be King. That was what he desired most. Wasn't it?

"I can't promise my restoration will be perfect," she said. "I've never had Li's gift for memory. But I can do my best. You'll be closer to the man you were, at least. Free of the Blood Gods' trickery."

His blood-self seethed. He felt the anger, this time running in the opposite direction, from the blood-self to him. He should have mirrored it. He should have been enraged at her obvious lies. He should have drawn his sword and cut her down.

"Yes," he said instead. "Change me."

The blood-self would have howled, if it had a voice. But it obeyed his will. This woman, the Veil, if she spoke the truth, was right. Something in him was wrong. If she could repair it, if there was any hope at all, he could finally be free of others' yoke on his will. Both parts of him—the would-be King and the uncertain man and everything between—demanded freedom first. The rest would follow.

She rose from her desk, eyeing the blood-self as she approached, both hands held open, as though to show she held no weapon. He wasn't fool enough to believe her harmless, but he submitted, dropping to kneel in front of her as she placed both hands on his head.

Memory warped.

He was a boy, hollering and holding a wooden sword aloft while the yardmaster looked on in approval. He was a young man, repeating the words of a sacred oath. He ran a footrace through the streets of his city. He feasted, dressed in the finest court attire. He was a spy, a servant, filled with herbs and sent across the sea. He came before his mother in confidence, and she spoke the truth to him, the truth as he had never imagined it could be. He was a prince, and a warrior, running from his enemies, seeking his mother's protection. He grieved her death. He was...nothing.

The pain of reliving the moment seared through him like fire. He watched the Regnant rip apart his mind. He was a servant. He was an assassin. He was awakened, and restored, promised life and healing with the fumes of a burning corpse in his nose. He was suddenly full of pride, sure in his desire to do anything to become King. It wasn't him. It had never been. He was his mother's son, her finest son. The jewel in her eye. His only ambition was to please her, to fulfill his duty, to do right by his people, to fulfill his mother's vision of who he was meant to be.

He was an empty husk, written on by false Gods who sought to remake him into a tool to further their will, not to honor his mother's memory.

It hurt. He sagged under the weight of the Veil's hands. The pain awakened in every part of his body as she kept her hands in place. He wanted to cry. He wanted to weep for the boy he had been, for the love of the mother he had lost.

She held him upright, and the memories continued.

He was a warrior-prince, a champion. He was there at the farm, watching Sarine and Erris train the rest. He counted them, weighed their talents in his mind. He made note of every type of magic, every gift, every pairing and strategy they'd devised for the assault.

The blood-self growled. Pain receded.

He was a supplicant, paying homage to the Rabaquim Blood Gods at their altar covered in blood. He paid careful attention to what they said, to the slightest cues that might betray a meaning.

He had no wish to relive these memories. They were his, but another mind was invading his, using what he had done. He tried to pull back, and found his head fixed firmly under the Veil's hands.

He was a fighter at the Soul of the World. He rewatched the battle, keeping careful note of which champions had fallen, which magicks were used, and how. Time slowed as he watched every step again. Their entrance into the spire. The path they took through the halls. The central chamber where the light burned black. The silhouetted shape of the Regnant, standing beside the light. Sarine. Sarine. Sarine. His memory fixated on her, staring, studying, watching as she dipped her hand into the lightstream. The Regnant, waking from his stasis, suddenly attacking Sarine. Corenna shielding her. Himself, his blood-self, Arak'Jur, Allakawari diving to strike at the Regnant's shield.

He watched as Corenna's body exploded in a torrent of blood; far too much blood for an ordinary human body. Then the Regnant's shield faded, and Arak'Jur sliced into him with his claws. Omera was a step behind, slashing into the Regnant's body with his poisoned steel. Allakawari stabbed him, shoving the broken pieces of the Regnant's body to the floor.

The Veil gasped, resetting her hands atop his skull.

The scene played again. The Regnant's shield faded, and Arak'Jur sliced into him with his claws. Omera was a step behind, slashing into the Regnant's body with his poisoned steel. Allakawari stabbed him, shoving the broken pieces of the Regnant's body to the floor.

"He's dead," the Veil said in a whisper. "They . . . you killed him. No. It can't be true."

He tried to jerk his head away. She kept him held firm. His blood-self burned with rage, circling around the chamber. Its hand went to its sword. His anger mirrored it. He was no one's puppet. Not Sakhefete's. Not the Blood Gods'. Not the Veil's. But she kept him in place.

The Regnant's shield faded, and Arak'Jur sliced into him with his claws. Omera was a step behind, slashing into the Regnant's body with his poisoned steel. Allakawari stabbed him, shoving the broken pieces of the Regnant's body to the floor. The Regnant's shield faded, and Arak'Jur sliced into him with his claws. Omera was a step behind, slashing into the Regnant's body with his poisoned steel. Allakawari stabbed him, shoving the broken pieces of the Regnant's body to the floor.

The scene played again. And again. He stared at the Regnant, studying his every movement. Again. Again.

Then suddenly the Veil laughed.

"He isn't dead," she said. "See? His soul, the moment before the Heron-shield fades, he leaves his body b—"

She choked. Her hands slipped. He yanked away from her touch, whirling to find his blood-self standing behind her, its sword jammed through her neck.

The Veil's eyes bulged, her hands going to the gaping wound. His blood-self withdrew the blade, and her head collapsed forward, leaving the rest of her suddenly lifeless flesh to slump into a bloody heap on the floor.

His breath came hard.

The blood-self lowered its sword, resheathing it.

"You're mine, you understand?" he said to the blood-self. "You tell no one what happened here. You report nothing."

The blood-self stared at him.

He was himself again. No one's puppet. Part of him had been sworn to the Rabaquim, the price of restoring what he thought were his memories. But they'd played him false, and he owed them nothing. He could control the blood-self, so long as he concentrated on bending it to his will.

And he'd heard the Veil's final words.

The Regnant was still alive. Somewhere.

The clue was hidden in his memory. The Veil had seen it, before she died. He could replay it, find the answer, use his blood-self to track it down.

His burning ambition had been stilled. But he was still his mother's son, and the Bhakal still had a role to play in this. The Gods now in control of the Soul were tearing the world apart, knowingly or not. For the first time in a long time his destiny was clear. He meant to find a way to put it all back together. Being a King meant nothing if he had no people, no land to rule. His mother would have understood. He had her blessing, even from beyond the grave.

He sat down, quieting his mind, focusing again on the moments before the Regnant's death.

80

SARINE

The Tomb of Emperor Sun Qiang
The Jun Empire

Her eyes came open.

Her body hurt. Her muscles ached. A carved ceiling loomed over her, depicting scenes in wrought gold. Soldiers fought each other with spears and maces, a great horde on either side, each led by a man on horseback. One wore a demon-mask. One was surrounded by a brilliant light.

The light.

Sunlight.

She gasped and sat up.

A Jun woman in a blue-and-white hooded robe bowed to her, then set the tray she'd been carrying down atop a table beside her bed.

"Where...what is this place?" she asked. Her voice was hoarse, dry.

"Shh," the Jun woman said. "Try not to speak. You need food, rest, and healing. You will have all three, by the grace of the Great Lord."

She looked down at herself. She was naked. She should have been dead. She remembered the sunlight flashing from Kalira's hand. She remembered the dread at realizing what she'd done. How she'd failed. The light touched her, flashing against the shield of *White*. Then it broke. Her skin burned. She'd died. Yet her body here was untouched, pristine and perfect, without bruises, scars, even dirt or sweat.

"Who?" she managed to say through the dryness. "Where?"

"I am Diaolong, of the Great and Noble House of the Owl," the Jun woman said, bowing again as she said it. "This is the Tomb of the Emperor Sun Qiang. Our instructions were to prepare your bodies to awaken here. Forgive us if it displeases."

Coldness rose on her skin, though the air inside the chamber was warm. The Great and Noble House of the Owl. That meant...

"The Regnant," she said, forcing the words out. "I...I saw him die."

Diaolong bowed again. "The Great Lord is already awake, Great Lady. He will wish to attend you as soon as you have eaten, I am sure, and had time to dress. May I have the honor of assisting you?"

She wanted to shake her head no. But her body was sore and stiff. Moving caused pain. And her stomach was empty, growling hunger and exhaustion from sitting up.

She tried to ask Anati for *Red*.

Nothing.

She thought her *kaas*'s name, a summons if ever there had been need for one. Nothing there. An emptiness where there should have been eyes watching over her, emotions sharing and exchanging everything she felt and saw. The Nine Tails was gone, too. No awareness, no hunger, and she blinked and saw no starfield, no strands, only empty blackness.

Tears came at the corners of her eyes.

Diaolong lowered her head. "I have displeased you, Great Lady," she said. "Whatever penance you require will be administered swiftly."

"No," she said. "I...I didn't expect this. You've done nothing wrong."

She tried to steady herself, sitting atop a stone bed covered in blankets and pillows. The rest of the chamber was decorated as finely as the ceiling. For twenty spans on either side of her the walls ran carved with scenes of fighting, or finely dressed lords and ladies kneeling before the same figure she'd seen on the ceiling, the man surrounded by brilliant light. Emperor Sun Qiang, Diaolong had said. This place must have told the story of his rule. A Jun place. And the Regnant was here, awakening from his death, as she was. Fear bloomed inside her. But if he'd meant her harm, he could have left her dead. Whatever followed, she needed the strength to meet it, no matter her pride and her fear.

"Help me eat," she said. "And dress."

Diaolong went at once to the porcelain bowl and silver spoon on her tray. The soup was spiced and hot, full of soft meats and tender noodles. Her jaw hurt with every bite, but the soup spread warmth in her belly, and soon her exhaustion had become a dull ache rather than a suffocating pain. Diaolong held the bowl up as she drank the last dregs, barely resisting the urge to lick the porcelain clean. It was as though she hadn't eaten in weeks, though if she ate much more her stomach would surely empty itself, knotted as it was with hunger. A cup of tea was waiting, too, and Diaolong held it to her lips as she sipped until it was gone.

A pile of silks waited at the foot of the bed, and she surprised herself by having the strength to stand as Diaolong dressed her. Linen undergarments first, then the beautiful silk. It was white with red and gold trim, stitched in intricate designs around every seam. Padded slippers covered her feet, though she shook her head no when Diaolong offered a tray of cosmetic powders and gold and gemstone-encrusted jewelry. Already she felt out of place in the billowing silk robes. If the Regnant intended to meet her dressed as a Queen, he would have to settle for her as she was: her hair bound in the sort of quick knot she usually tied behind her head, her skin untouched by powders or cosmetics, though if her face was like the rest of her in this body, there would be no blemishes, no marks of any kind. It was as though her body had been remade without any marks of age, any of the scars life had given her, any of the wear she'd earned along the way.

"The Great Lady looks radiant, if she will permit me the compliment," Diaolong said. "May I endow you with what gifts I have, to give you strength before you meet our Lord?"

She nodded, the exertion of standing and being dressed already draining what little energy she'd gotten from the soup. Anati should have been there. Or the Nine Tails. Neither was. The emptiness tore at her. But if an Owl-*magi* could offer her some strength, she wouldn't refuse.

Diaolong closed her eyes, and fire suddenly burned inside her.

It should have been a searing pain, so much heat at once. Instead it was the warmth of a hearthfire on a winter night. A hot bath poured to melt away the city's dirt. It spread through her limbs in a slow wave, reverberating through each of her muscles, one at a time. Exhaustion fled under its heat and pressure, leaving her renewed and strong, full of life and energy.

"That's incredible," she said, finding her voice solid and firm. "I've never felt anything like it."

Diaolong lowered her eyes. "Thank you, Great Lady," she said. "Many of my House train our gifts for war, hoping to be chosen by the Great Lord for service as his champion. I chose another path, of healing and comfort. I am pleased to hear you find my service to your liking."

"Is it…permanent?" she asked. *Body* could offer the facsimile of strength, but one had to be careful leaning too hard on muscles supported by its power. Perhaps the Owl's gift was similar.

"The Great Lady will need time to rest," Diaolong said. "And more food, when her stomach is ready for it."

"Agreed," she said. "If I ate another bowl I'd burst. But I want more as soon as it settles."

"Of course," Diaolong said with a smile. "Anything the Great Lady requires."

She swallowed, looking toward the gilded doors on the far side of the chamber. He was there. Waiting for her.

"It's time, isn't it," she said.

Diaolong bowed, saying nothing.

"Diaolong, do you know why he did this?" she asked. "Why he brought me here, saved me from death?"

"This one is only a servant," Diaolong said. "The workings of Great Lords and Ladies are not for one such as me to fathom."

She nodded. Failure stung deep, the foolishness of the alliances she'd made, all to oppose the man who now waited for her outside the chamber door. He'd been her greatest enemy, as long as she'd known her place in the world. Bringing her back to life, saving her, made no sense as she understood him. He'd poisoned the world, and she'd risked everything to find a way to cleanse it, to restore it to beauty and life. And now he'd restored her. She was terrified, but she was here. Alone. With none of her gifts. But she was alive.

"Let's go, then," she said.

Diaolong bowed and led the way. The chamber door swung open easily, though it looked to be made of heavy, gilded stone, revealing a massive expanse beyond. Ten more doors equally beautiful and carved ringed the central chamber. More *magi* in blue-and-white robes stood along the opposite walls, where colorful carpets, tapestries, and carvings adorned the floors, walls, and ceiling. Gold and porcelain jars and statues filled every plinth and surface, all surrounding an elevated stone tomb at the center.

She hardly noticed any of it.

Her eyes were fixed on the man standing in front of the tomb. He wore a white robe trimmed with red and gold, a perfect match to hers. Gold jewelry hung around his wrists and neck, with rubies pierced in either ear and his long black hair tied back in golden cords. She'd known the Regnant as an ancient old man, but somehow she knew him here, too. Not a youth, but not old. She recognized his face as he turned to look at her. Li Zheng, as he had been in the prime of his career. His hair was black, with only the faintest suggestion of gray at his temples. He had a thin beard, neatly trimmed, and his skin was as perfect and unblemished as hers was now.

A ringing thud echoed through the chamber, and every blue-and-white-robed Owl-*magi* bowed at once, including Diaolong at her side. Then they retreated, closing the nearest chamber doors and vanishing from sight, leaving her alone with the Regnant in the Emperor's Tomb.

81

SARINE

Central Chamber
The Tomb of Emperor Sun Qiang

He stared at her, as she must have been staring at him. He was a figure from a painting, decorated in silk and gold. A figure from a nightmare.

"Sarine," he said. The word echoed across the chamber.

"Regnant," she replied, trying to make her voice confident and sure.

"Call me Zheng," he said. "Or Li, until you're comfortable."

"Li, then," she said. He nodded. "Why am I here?"

"You invited wolves to our holiest place," Li said. "They killed you. They killed me. I anticipated both."

She glanced down at her hands. Perfect skin, remade without crease or blemish. And yet, coming from him, the gift was tainted.

"You're my enemy," she said. "Why bring me back to life?"

"No," he replied quickly. "I was never your enemy, Sarine. What you say, you say from ignorance. An ignorance that was my doing. Mine and Evelynn's. And the *kaas*. Will you listen, if I explain now what I should have told you from the beginning?"

"You poisoned the Soul of the World," she said.

"Yes," he replied.

"You murdered my uncle, and all the citizens of New Sarresant," she said. "You caused the poison storms that killed millions, ruined every city in the world."

"Yes," he said again.

"Then you're my enemy," she said.

"No," he said again. "But I understand why you would say it."

The room fell quiet. Without the Nine Tails, without Anati, she felt naked, despite the silk. Was he similarly powerless? If he had all his gifts, and she had nothing, she was no more than a housefly buzzing in his ear. Yet he'd brought her back for a reason. She was still herself, even without the *kaas* or the Natarii soulbond. She wasn't going to break for anyone. If he wanted her dead, he would have left her that way.

"I made a mistake," he said quietly, though it carried through the room. "When you were first created. I never imagined you would prove stronger than Evelynn. I never imagined it would be you standing here today. If I'd suspected it was even possible, I would have told you more. I would have instructed the *kaas* to keep nothing from you, instead of sheltering you from the truth."

"Don't," she said. "Don't tell lies about Zi."

"Zi is my servant, and has ever been," he said.

"Don't you fucking dare," she said.

"My words cause you pain," he said. "For that I grieve. But you are here to learn the truth. No more. If you can face it, and accept its burden, we may have a chance to set the world aright, in time. If not, then you may leave, and we will face the end on our own, in our own ways."

"You'd let me go?" she asked.

"You aren't a prisoner," he said. "If you won't work with me willingly, then you are free to leave of your own will, as you choose."

"Then I choose to leave," she said. "Now."

He stared at her.

Slowly he pointed toward one of the doors, the most ostentatious of them all, a carved double door covered in gems and gold. "That way," he said. "Take the right passage, then another right. From the main foyer take the center path toward the surface."

"We're underground?" she said.

"This is a tomb," he replied. "Though aboveground is being remade by the wolves you let into the Soul of the World. It might be jungle, floodplain, an ice storm, a lava flow, or a raging sea. I suggest you face it with appropriate caution."

She didn't move.

She saw coldness in his eyes. And pain. If she went toward the door and left the tomb behind, she had to believe he'd make a move to stop her. But why? She was powerless now. Yet clearly he saw something in her. Something he believed would give them a chance to undo the damage she'd inflicted with her desperation.

"What makes you think we can stop them?" she asked.

"It won't be easy," he said. "The Soul is sealed now. But it will open again, and when it does, both of us, together, at our full strength, can stand against any army. We've done it before. We can do it again. Even if it means sacrificing our work. Even if it means starting over."

Once more the emptiness where Anati should have been stung. Did he not know her gifts were gone? It seemed unlikely—whatever strangeness she felt here, this was his place. His magic that kept her from death.

"I can't imagine us finding common ground," she said. "You mean to poison the world. I mean to save it."

"At times, they're one and the same," he said. "Don't you remember?"

"Remember what?" she said. "I—" But suddenly, she did.

She remembered the flow of magic into the Soul of the World. The light and darkness—a finite coating that flowed from one end of the world's spirit to the other, like sand in an hourglass. She remembered the experiments they'd performed, together, to determine the coating's properties. Her, the physicist, him, the biologist. She remembered proving that it could unmake the world entirely if they ever allowed the coating to run all to one side, or to the other. How they needed a balance. A time of torpor, Li called it, a time when the world ran black, to counterbalance the times when it ran light. That was the price of magic. The price of—

"Get out of my head!" she shouted. "Those aren't my memories. Those have nothing to do with me!"

"No," Li said. "They aren't yours. They were hers. I apologize, if my gift is unwelcome."

"Don't do that again," she said. The images still lingered in her thoughts, but were already fading, like waking up from a dream. Yet like a dream, they remained in some part, deep under her conscious mind.

"That, I cannot promise," he said. "There is too much for you to relearn. Better if you understand, as she did, and judge truth for yourself."

"I don't want them," she said. "I don't need your versions of truth. I don't—"

Once again, memory surfaced.

She remembered evolutionary biology. Never her field of expertise, but she'd learned enough to follow along with Li's theories. He'd proven the concept of cycles before she'd breached the seals: how the rapidity of change in observed species differentiation didn't match the periodicity required for genetic drift and propagation of mutations; in layperson's terms, that there hadn't been enough time since the genesis of life to produce the wide variety of species they saw in the world. He'd proven something the religious pseudoscientists had been clamoring for, which they explained as the need for the hand of God. But, combined with her work on subatomic particle theory, and the revelations of the "seal" she'd somehow broken, producing particles smaller than the Planck length at the ISLC labs, they'd pointed toward the discovery of the place Li had jokingly named the Soul of the World. Together, they'd proven it was possible to remake the world itself. A terraformer's dream. And, not only that it was possible, but they'd learned it had been done.

Cycles. A rebirth and resetting of the world's flora and fauna, to give time for evolution to take its course. Yet in their day, the resettings had been crude. Artifacts and fossils of earlier times were left behind, unexplained: dinosaur bones, megafauna, fossilized creatures none could imagine walking the earth today. Even humans. Prior iterations explained the *Australopithecus*, *Paranthropus afarensis*, *Homo erectus*, Neanderthals, even early cultures of *Homo sapiens*.

They'd learned the one that called himself Master was nothing of the kind. A charlatan, having found the abandoned tools of those who came before him. A child, having stumbled onto its parent's gun. But the gun had power. Great power, for those inclined to learn the discipline of its use.

And without it, humanity was doomed.

The infusion of magic, with the seals broken, was more than a species of tribal nomad hunter-gatherers had evolved to handle. Even technology had progressed beyond what human brains could be entrusted with. The morality of sun-worshippers resulted in genocides and ethnic cleansings in an interconnected, multicultural world. Tribal posturing and warmongering meant a handful of young men dead when tribes clashed over the steppe's choicest watering holes; with mechanized armies at the scale of nations, wars erupted to cover the globe, destroying untold millions of lives for the instincts of a few leaders drunk on power and political games. And now, in the modern world, armed with nuclear fire, they threatened the end of life itself.

Humans needed new instincts. And for that, they needed time.

They needed time for evolution to take its course. For the instincts of war and power to soften the worst aspects of humanity: the brutality of primitive religion, of sexual dimorphism and patriarchy, of oppression, imperialism, exploitation, and greed. A hunter enriching themselves by stockpiling food in a cold season and doling it out for favors and power harmed few, and may even have proven an advantage for the survival of their genes; the same instinct writ on the scale of corporations monopolizing water supplies and medicines threatened to eradicate entire cultures and ways of life.

For humanity to survive, evolution without threat of self-annihilation would be required. Already, humans had evolved brains capable of rapid technological progress. Whereas a hunter-gatherer society had existed unchanged for hundreds of thousands of years, modern humans could bring society from farming to quantum processing and miniaturization in a matter of centuries. But they needed more time. They needed new cycles. Enough for the hundreds of thousands, maybe even the millions of years it would take to evolve to handle the power of industry, and now, with the seals broken and the sparks of light coating the Soul of the World, the power of magic along with it. They needed gatekeepers: brave souls willing to oversee the beginnings of new cycles, to exterminate humanity and all of its progress, keeping only a minimum viable population of survivors as breeding stock for the new succession of generations.

She and Li had stepped into those roles. They'd become Gods, the Regnant and the Veil, and mastered the new disciplines of magic that the seals had unleashed into the world. They'd had to defend themselves against challengers who had also mastered those weapons. They'd harnessed the *kaas* to work with them, to remake the world with greater efficiency than even the Master, or his progenitors, would have believed possible. They'd created the system of champions and ascensions to give the world's people something to strive for, and to ensure the eventual rebalancing between light and dark states, to maintain the balance of magic in the world. Everything they'd done had been to preserve humanity, to empower and enable humans to rise to greater heights than they could possibly imagine on their own.

She remembered all of this, as though she'd lived it.

Tears came to her eyes.

It faded, the same as before, like waking from a dream. Enough stayed with her that she sank to her knees, and sobbed.

She didn't hear Li cross the chamber, but she noticed as he knelt in front of her, close enough for the silks of their white and red-gold embroidered robes to touch at the hems.

"I'm sorry," he said. "I know you aren't her. I don't expect you to make the same decision she did. If you still wish to go, I understand."

"How?" she said. "How could you make that choice? Millions died, every time you reset a cycle."

"Without it, all would die," he said. "A great evil, to prevent the greatest evil, of a permanent extinction."

"I...I can't..." she said. The words wouldn't come. She felt horror, and sadness. Shock, and pity.

He bowed his head in silence.

"Why?" she said finally. "Why me? What's so special about me that you need me to carry this? To help you?"

"I could find another, perhaps," he said. "I tried most recently with the Bhakal Queen, before she fled and vanished. Both of us have tried with others before. Would you prefer I show you...?"

"No!" she said. "Enough of the memories. I don't want you to do that ever again."

"I understand," he said, then paused. "I suppose I need you because there are such things as goodness, and talent. Evelynn had both. Your talent is unquestionable; you couldn't have bested her without it. Some have the gift of working with the sparks of Life. None have it as deeply, as powerfully, as she did. As to your goodness, I don't know you yet. But Zi speaks more highly of you than he has of anything, or anyone."

The reminder of the loss of her *kaas*, both Zi and Anati, threatened to bring new tears.

He stayed quiet as she turned away, covering her face with her hands.

"They aren't gone, you know," Li said finally. "Your bond with the *kaas*. Your other gifts."

"What do you mean?" she asked, wiping away her tears.

"When we're reborn like this, our patterns are incomplete. But you'll still have your affinity for Life, and I for the magic we named Death. A result of time spent studying them, perhaps. Neither of us was sure. But you can use your sparks to remake your pattern. It should restore all the other affinities you developed. Your *kaas*-bond. Your leylines, and spirit-magicks. Even the ones you stole from me: the Dragon gift, and the Natarii soulbond. All of it, so long as you remember the patterns."

"The leylines, and the spirits," she said. "When we fought, the Veil tore them away."

He smiled sadly. "She was always gifted with the sparks. But your gift is at least equal to hers, if not stronger. You should be able to remake what she unmade."

"How?" she said. "How do I do it?"

"You'll want more rest, and food, before you try," he said. "Take the night to consider what I've shown you? I need rest, too. We can speak tomorrow, after you've had a chance to sleep on what you've seen."

She nodded, and he rose quickly, offering her a bow before he left her sitting in front of her door.

82

SARINE

The Infinite Plane
The Tomb of Emperor Sun Qiang

The pattern held in place, and red and blue sparks swirled around her. They intertwined and raced in eddies, turning and convulsing, wrapping themselves around the core of her, then spiraling away, threatening to pull the shapes apart. She held them. They pulled against her control, leaking light into the void. First a few, then more, then finally too few remained to evoke the pattern. The light dimmed as red sparks dissipated into nothing, leaving only the blue behind.

She blinked, shifting her vision away from the Infinite Plane.

Diaolong was there, already waiting with a fresh cup of tea.

She took it without a word, sipping and feeling the liquid sear the back of her throat.

"Another success, Great Lady?" Diaolong said.

"No," she said. "Close, though. Is there any food ready? My stomach feels like it's eating itself."

"I will retrieve what I can from the kitchen," Diaolong said. "Though, perhaps the Great Lady should rest?"

"I've slept already," she said. "Can you give me the Owl's gift again, please?"

Diaolong frowned. "The Great Lady slept two hours," she said. "And has been working for five. Relying on magic to animate the bones is unwise, if you will forgive me for saying so. There are stories among my House of soldiers blessed by our gifts who fought without rest until they dropped dead, without warning. The Great Lord would not forgive me if you shared their fate."

"I'm close to unlocking another one," she said. "Another attempt, maybe two or three at most. Did your soldiers die after a single morning refreshed by your gift?"

"No, Great Lady," Diaolong said. "But they swung halberds and maces. You wield a higher power."

"Please," she said.

Diaolong hesitated, maintaining a smooth expression, but before she could nod, a knock sounded against their door.

Her attendant scrambled to her feet, bowing apologetically as she went, instead of giving the Owl magic needed to refresh her strength. Fatigue burned in her limbs, a heavy dryness behind her eyes. She would have preferred to stand as Diaolong swung the door inward, but lacked the strength to rise.

Diaolong bowed at once, as soon as the door was open, a deeper bow than she'd given Sarine, pressing her forehead almost to the floor.

The Regnant—Li—entered the room.

He wore the same white robe trimmed with red and gold he'd worn yesterday. As soon as he stepped within her chamber his eyes darted between her and the Owl-*magi*.

"What are you doing?" he asked. "Have you worked all night? You were supposed to sleep."

"I have slept," she said. "I slept enough."

He rounded on Diaolong. "Did you fuel this?" he snapped. "Your gifts were meant to keep her alive, not push her to the brink of death!"

Anger rose in her, though when she tried to stand her limbs were too weak, like brittle sticks meant to support a heavy stone.

"Don't yell at her," she said. "Diaolong has been a faithful attendant. She did nothing I didn't ask of her."

Diaolong said nothing, quivering as she kept her face pressed to the stone floor.

"Sarine," Li said. "What you are doing is dangerous, and foolish. Please do not risk your life. You need time to eat, to rest, to let this body heal and grow strong."

"I'm already growing stronger," she said. "See?"

She called on *mareh'et*, feeling the Great Cat spirit fill her body with power. It was like an old memory, and a perfect fit. The spirits had rejoiced, hearing her voice again. The pattern had been a mix of black, white, purple, and gold, spinning around the core of her like a tempest. The trick had been to stop trying to control it, to let the sparks flow like a river, with her guiding them between the banks of who she was rather than forcing the current. And now the nimbus of the Great Cat enveloped her like a blanket, radiating warmth and power through her. She'd used it for the last several attempts, and hadn't expected it to be ready again so soon; evidently the Spirits wished to show themselves to Li.

He looked taken aback, and quickly composed himself. "A great success," he said. "But you must pace yourself."

"I have," she said. "I haven't been working with the sparks without pause. Diaolong has kept me fed and full of tea. And between *mareh'et* and Owl I've had enough strength for each attempt. It's only the times in between when I feel weak."

"I see," Li said. "And you have the full use of the Vordu gift again? The spirits of war, and beasts?"

"As though they never left," she said. "Now, if you'll excuse me, I don't want to waste the cat spirit's blessing."

"Even with their strength, you're still taking a great risk," he said. "There's no need to push so hard. With time, you can master each pattern safely."

Her physical body heard his words, but she was already moving, already shifting back to the Plane. With *mareh'et*'s power coursing through her, she had the strength to focus, to hold the entire pattern of *her* in her mind. Whatever delays Li thought prudent, she had the energy to do the work now, and besides, if she could recover the leylines, for *Body*, or the *kaas*-bond, for *Red*, it would only redouble her efforts and quicken her pace. She could be the judge of when her body needed rest. And yes, it did. Badly. She could sleep a full day already. But she could make another attempt or two at least before she did.

The pattern swirled in front of her, matching the idea in her mind.

Blue sparks formed the core of who she was, with flashes of other colors running along them. Millions upon millions of sparks flowed and jumped into existence, flashed, and vanished. The new pattern, for the spirits' gifts, flowed inside them, and she held it in place. Whites and purples and golds swirled inside the blue, nestled within her, flowing outside and then back in, a wild rush of currents and whorls. She could hold it all, mirroring everything she saw with the image in her mind of who she was, who she was meant to be. A thousand times more complex than the patterns of the room around her, of the carpets, carvings, urns, and stone. Diaolong's pattern was there, too, lingering in the distance, all blues and whites, while Li's threatened to overwhelm her, flooded with uncountable threads of black, white, blue, red, gold, silver, jade. But they were distractions. She had to focus. Focus on herself. Focus on the differences between the image in her mind and the reality in front of her.

At first there were no differences. Then she added them. Red sparks, interwoven with the blue. Gray sparks, then white, then paler shades, mirroring the first. Shades for every leyline, every energy within their patterns. *Life*, *Body*, *Shelter*, *Entropy*, *Death*, *Mind*, *Need*, and *Faith*. She hadn't planned a sequence for her gifts, only followed what her memory demanded, what fit best, seemed most out of place when it was missing. A subtle feeling; her conscious mind would have demanded the *kaas* first. But contemplating why was a distraction, too. She had to focus. She had to keep the sparks in place.

They surged against her. A thousand leyline-sparks jumped into being, and vanished, then repeated, vanishing faster than she could find room for them within her core. She maintained the dissonance between her mind and reality.

They vanished again. Again. Then the latticework swirled inside the blue. A perfect foundation, an arch supporting a greater weight, and another arch, and a greater weight. The leyline sparks settled in atop each other, threatening to collapse if even a single spark slipped out of place.

They didn't.

It held.

It held.

She opened her eyes.

Li knelt in front of her, with Diaolong at his side. This time he held the tray with tea.

"You are as stubborn as Evelynn ever was," Li said. "And as foolish."

Body tethered into her. Red motes, pulled from the leylines running beneath the tomb. Strength filled her muscles, though she could still feel the crippling fatigue lurking underneath. She probed herself with *Life*, feeling the wonder of her pristine, new body. No scar tissue, no damage, no impurities. She resisted the urge to tether *Death*, *Entropy*, *Shelter*, or *Mind*. But they were all there. All waiting for her. She could touch them again. For a brief moment she gave in and touched *Faith*, her oldest, greatest ally. Only for a moment. Diaolong gasped as she held it, and released it, blinking in and out of view as *Faith* rendered her invisible to sight.

She reached for Li's tray and took a fresh cup of tea.

"*Faith*," Li said. "You succeeded."

"Twice," she said, smiling as the tea warmed her tongue. "Three to go."

"I understand your desire to have these gifts back," he said. "But is there truly a rush for the others? You risk doing permanent damage to yourself."

"I have *Body* now, to help," she said. "Besides, isn't this body new, and strong? I'm tired, yes, but I've been tired before."

"Working with the sparks isn't like keeping late hours studying," Li said. "You're remaking your form, the very essence of who you are. A mistake and you could injure yourself. Severely."

"Then I won't make mistakes," she said.

"How simple you make it sound," he said.

"Isn't it important that I restore my gifts?" she said. "You said we had a chance to return to the Gods' Seat, to confront Kalira and the others. Isn't it worth a risk to be ready quickly?"

"No," he said. "When did I say our chance required reckless haste? We can't return, short of a champion bound to one of them being foolish enough to take us. Neither of us possesses the keys, until a cycle turns and the seals open on their own. They defeated us, in this cycle. We can challenge them again, but not until the way to the Seat is open."

"What are you saying?" she said. "We should just accept that they're in control?"

"They *are* in control," he said. "For now. We engineered it that way. Once the Soul has been remade, it takes a new cycle to turn it again. Fortunately for us, the torpor state lasted only a few months, leaving the world in desperate need of healing. The next cycle, whatever hellish nightmare they design, will be short."

"But that's not possible," she said. "After you changed the Soul, I was able to return and change it back."

"Because I cheated," he said. "I didn't follow our protocol of champions and keys. You were left with both of yours, even after the turning. You could return at will."

"Then why not cheat again?"

"We can't even get to the Gods' Seat, without the keys. If we could reach it, we could undo what they've done. But we can't."

Her mind reeled, made worse by the fatigue settling deep in her bones.

"How long?" she said finally. "You said the next cycle will be short. How long?"

"A thousand years, perhaps," he said. "Possibly less. Not even enough time for the beginnings of industrialization."

"A thousand...?" she said. "But... how will we even be alive for that?"

"How do you think we've lived all this time?" he said. "We use Life and Death to prolong our life spans, and long sleeps to cover vast distances in time. Once the world has settled and we can plan for what we expect to face, we can sleep. Our next confrontation could feel like a week from now, once we're satisfied we know what Kalira and the rest will make of this world."

"I don't know what to say," she said. Suddenly hope felt drained. A thousand years. Everything she knew of the world would be gone, if it wasn't already. Hundreds of new generations, born and grown and dead. It amplified the failure. Her failure. She'd let Kalira deceive her. As though she'd thrown open the doors of her uncle's chapel and let rioters loot their stores.

"I apologize," Li said. "I should have taken more care, revealing this. I forget there are differences between what you know, and what Evelynn knew." He rose to his feet, and offered her a bow. "I'll leave you to rest, and consider. But please, do take the time to rest. There is time enough to do your work at full strength."

He left, and she hardly noticed him going. A thousand years. She felt adrift, as though time were a relentless current, washing her away from the shore. As though she could see the harbor slowly vanishing as she was pulled out to sea.

"I should see to fetching the Great Lady some food," Diaolong said.

"No," she said. "Not yet. I need Owl's gift. For one more try."

"One more...?" Diaolong said. "But Great Lady! The Great Lord's instructions were clear. You require rest."

"I'll rest soon," she said. "But the Regnant...Li...doesn't give me instructions. I can face what he told me. I can handle it. And I'm not going to do it alone."

"I don't understand, Great Lady," Diaolong said.

"Will you give me strength, or not?" she said.

Her attendant looked between her and the door, as though she meant to run out and bring Li back to shame her into sleeping. Instead Diaolong bowed her head, and Owl's fire returned. A searing heat coursed through her muscles. *Body* magnified it, drawing red motes into her limbs. And finally *mareh'et*'s nimbus shimmered into being around her.

She surged with strength, near to bursting. Enough to run a hundred footraces. Enough to climb to the top of a cathedral spire. Gods send it was enough for this.

She closed her eyes, and shifted herself to the Infinite Plane.

This time the pattern was easy. She should have done it first. She had no sense of self without the metallic sparks entwined with who she was, from her earliest memories, clinging to life on the streets of New Sarresant. The first times Zi had shooed away the feral cats come to poke and claw at her when she tried to sleep. The first times would-be predators ran away in fear from the alleyway she'd claimed as her own. The sweet, caring face of the man who had taken her in, who had become her uncle, whose church had become her home. The way Zi had bent his will to want to love and protect her, though it hadn't required much in the way of bending.

There had always been part of her attuned to the *kaas*. Now that she knew how to restore it, the sparks came effortlessly, snapping into place one at a time, but quickly enough it seemed like ten thousand at once. They rushed to greet her, like old friends, long away, now come home.

It was done, as quick as she'd begun. But there was still emptiness, a void in her thoughts, all the more pronounced for lacking someone there to hear. She'd rebuilt the capacity, and now needed something to step in and fill the space.

She opened her eyes. And closed them again immediately, shifting her awareness far from her physical body, far from the physical plane.

83

ANATI

A Jungle, Drenched in Blood
Rabaquim Highlands

She held herself close to the bark, trying to feel what it was to be the *huacrapona* tree. Its trunk rose to the top of the canopy, branching into leaves that thirsted for sunlight. She tried to rejoice as it did when light fought through the clouds to touch its boughs. She tried to feel its thirst slaked by the blood left over from the storm.

She didn't care.

A million trees stood here in the jungle. All the same, or near enough not to matter. One bent left, one bent right. One nestled its branches under the highest canopy, fighting to keep light from bleeding any lower. Their forms were distinct, unique, and utterly, pointlessly boring. When did they laugh? When did they surprise her, doing something rash and foolish, risking their lives for some ideal, some thought that had occurred to them, some fight that hadn't mattered an hour before they'd noticed it existed? A tree was a tree. It stood there. Growing. Growing. At a glacial pace. It fought for light. It fought for water, or, since she and her siblings had adapted this forest, for blood. It grew leaves. They fell off. It grew more. It grew bark.

It was so boring she wanted to gnash the thing in half with her teeth just to watch it fall over and crash into the others and die.

Her siblings would notice, if she did. She almost didn't care. Almost.

One of her sisters was working above her head, changing the sky red. It was nighttime here in Rabaquim, in the southern and western part of the world. A crimson orb hung where the moon was supposed to be. Her brothers would mock her if they knew she thought of it that way—as though the moon, or the trees, or the clouds, had any *inherent* form, unmutable, unchangeable. That was a human idea. *Kaas* were meant to see the true forms behind the shadows cast on the material plane. There was no elemental reason the moon couldn't be a giant orb of blood hanging in the night sky, even if it wasn't made of blood anywhere but Rabaquim, or at least, anywhere the Rabaquim Gods didn't hold sway. There was no reason the clouds had to store water or ice, raining down in storms or blizzards. If the Blood Gods wanted it to rain blood, the *kaas* could make it rain blood. But why not make it rain sugar candies or lampposts or giant rocks to crush all of this stupid jungle and flatten all of these stupid trees into dust?

At the thought, a single rock came crashing down from the sky.

Her scales flared pink. She had to unmake it. Frantically she abandoned her *huacrapona*, shifting her will to the rock as it hurdled from the clouds. Granite. She knew granite. She could—

Too late. It crashed into the trees, splintering them and sending cracked wood flying into the others, breaking still more, sending more shards hurtling through the air. Animals and birds screeched and howled in pain and surprise. Dust and blood still soaking in the dirt and undergrowth was hurled into the air as the rock struck the ground, breaking apart, smashing the trees' roots and sending a cloud into the reddening sky.

Questioning emotions ran from *kaas* to *kaas*. Half-formed thoughts from which she couldn't hide.

Did you...?

What was...?

Was that...?

Why did...?

It was me.

Her guilt radiated through the chorus. They rounded on her as one will.

Perhaps you need some time to rest and sleep, sister, one of her sisters thought to her. A human idea. Sleep. It stung under her scales.

Amusement echoed between the rest of her siblings.

We have work to do here, a brother thought. *The Rabaquim have given us instructions. Rocks falling to crush the trees were not among them.*

I... She tried to think back. She should have thought she was sorry. But she wasn't. She wanted more rocks. She wanted rocks to come crack every tree in half.

Perhaps remaking trees with blood is beneath our princess, the same sister thought. *Perhaps she should go back to father's throne.*

Her scales were bright pink. The others were looking now. The sky had stopped reddening. The blood-clouds brewing on the horizon held in place. The trees stopped swaying. All of them had paused their duties to stare at her.

She left.

She ran.

Anger ripped through her. Human emotions. She was so *mad*. She wanted to find the sister who'd taunted her and scream in her thoughts. Or make ten more rocks and have them plummet on top of whatever that sister was doing, to make her start again, then do it over and over until she wasted a hundred years of futile, fruitless efforts. She wanted to scratch her scales with her claws, to rip one off and hang it as a trophy.

She tucked her neck low, under her coils, to hide her face.

She was in her place. The sphere she'd made hung overhead, but another block was there, too. Challenging it. It sparked her anger. She hadn't made that block! And...the block was precisely, exactly, perfectly, down to the smallest particle, right where Sarine had said she loved it.

It broke her. She was a human creature. Crying. If she'd had tear ducts she would have had a wet face.

She hadn't made that block. Except she must have. Subconsciously. Like a human. She was a *kaas* that made things without thinking about them, without knowing their forms, their purpose, their place. She abused the power of creation because she was *lonely*. Because she was *sad*. Because she *missed someone*. She might as well shed her scales and grow hair and skin. She might as well put on a dress and go dancing and meet a nice boy and fall in love and move away from her parents and have adventures and go sailing on a boat on the water because she'd always wondered what it would feel like to float on top of things in a body that had to obey gravity as though she were made of rocks or something equally weighty like wood or cheese or feathers or iron.

But she wasn't. She was a *kaas*. It helped, to remember it. Her scales dimmed, the pink bleeding into the void.

She stared up at the block. Sarine's block. It hung next to her sphere, the one she'd made when she decided to try and heal. She hadn't made the new block, not on purpose. It should go away. She tried to think it, to let it be reality. This was her place. It shouldn't be there, if it displeased her. But the block didn't move. It hung, suspended in the air, defying her, aesthetically perfect, with a perfect four sides, perfect sharpened corners, balancing the space exactly, as perfectly as she'd made it the first time. It was as though another will had anchored it, setting itself against hers. Vying for control of her space. A strong will, stronger than it had any right to be here in her place.

Father.

He must have done it. Who else?

She attuned herself to his emotions. A rude thing. A terribly rude thing. But she knew how to do it, and if he was going to defile her space, he had to expect her to try and find out why.

Father was here, on his throne. He was...Shocked. Surprised. Fearful. Intrigued. Questioning. Doubting. Planning. Thinking. Considering. Full of love. Full of memory. Full of hope.

None of those emotions touched on her. She felt them again, sifting through them for the thread that would have led him to remake the block. A lesson, perhaps. Maybe he'd been watching her in the Rabaquim blood-jungle. Maybe he put the block there to shame her along with her siblings. But no. The desire to shame and punish wasn't there. He was overwhelmed with something, some presence in his throne room. He was listening to a plan, an idea, something dangerous and foolish, something that terrified him, but that he nonetheless wanted to try. He was feeling guilty, but proud, too. He was—

He was aware of her watching.

Shame pulled her awareness back inside her place. He followed.

Anati, Zi thought. She expected him to be angry, scolding, shaming, disappointed. But he wasn't. He was...full of joy. Fear. Worry. Hope. *Come to me. My daughter. Come to me now.*

She hesitated. Maybe he was only masking his true emotions. A difficult thing, for a *kaas*. But who was her father, if not capable of difficult things? She wouldn't be the first to try and spy on him, and she wouldn't be the most skillful to do it. She felt like a child. But she was *his* child. She owed him obedience.

Yes, father, she thought back, and his mind was gone from her place as quick as she could think it.

She closed her eyes. It was going to hurt, being rebuked again. But she deserved it. She deserved it as much as she'd deserved her sister's mocking in the jungle.

Her place shifted away, and she was in her father's throne room. His blocks and spheres hung in their usual places, and he sat atop his platform, and Sarine stood in front of him, and there weren't any other *kaas* there, and she—

She stared.

Sarine was there.

Tears were at the corners of Sarine's eyes. The happy tears still touched with sadness, the ones Sarine had felt when she said goodbye to her uncle sitting at his gravestone in New Sarresant. She'd memorized the patterns of those emotions, deep and full of life. She'd been in awe, watching Sarine feel all the things she'd felt, then. The pain of saying goodbye. The hope and love and memory. The tears in Sarine's eyes now were the same ones, the exact same ones.

No, she thought. *No. You're dead. I failed, and I let you die.*

"Anati," Sarine said. "I'm not dead. I'm here."

You didn't tell me the Regnant had tethered her soul, father thought to them both. *Didn't you notice? When he touched her consciousness, on the Infinite Plane. Before your attack.*

She hardly heard father's words. Sarine was there. Standing there. Wearing what looked like an Empress's dress. White, for pride. Red, for anger, will, determination. Gold for nobility, and perfection.

Our custom is not to bond the same pair twice, father was thinking. *But I think, considering the circumstances of your separation, it would be acceptable to—*

I will, she thought. *I do. I want to be bonded to her again. I want it more than anything.* Then she remembered her failure—the shield, sputtering out under the heat of Kalira's attack. *If... if she'll have me. If she wants me back.*

Sarine smiled, a perfect, beautiful, hopeful look that flooded her with white and green and red, all at once. "I do," she said. "Of course I do. And bonding her won't cause any problems with the Soul, will it?"

No, Zi thought. *We can answer your call, once you have control.*

What do you mean? she thought. *What call?*

"Something we're going to do, together," Sarine said. "Working with the Regnant, though I never imagined I'd say anything like that. I think I finally know how to heal all of this. With his help, and Zi's. And yours. Anati. I missed you. Even though it's only been a few hours, for me. Has it been longer, for you?"

Ages, she thought. *Too long.*

"May I, then?" she asked father, and he bowed his head at the base of his neck.

Light crept into her.

At first she didn't trust it. It couldn't be hers. Couldn't be real.

Sarine closed her eyes, and sparks lashed between them. Last time she'd been too new, too young to understand what was happening. This time she felt part of her pattern, part of the form of who she was being rewritten, shaped into a form that fit a place inside Sarine's sparks. Gold light radiated everywhere. Everything seemed to melt, and re-form itself through a different set of eyes.

She wasn't just a *kaas* anymore. *Red* flowed through them both. *Green, Yellow, White, Gold, Black.* She was everything Sarine was, and Sarine was her. Emotions flowed between them. Human emotions. Sarine was the one who was crying. Not her. Not her little body, shaking with unshed tears of joy.

84

ERRIS

A Ruined Temple, Under the Moonlight
Sardia

Her leg burned as Marquand carried her over his shoulder. The world seemed to roil with every step, as though they walked on the deck of a man-of-war, bending and dipping in the waves. She fought for clear vision, through the haze. Or perhaps she was dreaming. They were climbing a hill, in rocky, mountainous country. Pillars of white stone stood ahead of them, white columns like lights descended from the black, star-filled sky. She blinked, and nearly passed out from the pain. Marquand grunted and held her tighter, but there was no *Body* to spare. There had been almost none, and no *Life*, since Sarine had died.

Pistol shots went off in the night. A blinding flash illuminated the hilltop, showing the contours of a temple in the distance. The white stone columns led to it, marking the path they followed. She recognized the architecture: a Sardian place, in the Old World, a temple to the Gods worshipped on the islands of the inland seas. The Sardians had a vast army, but they were mired in the adoption of old technologies and military disciplines. Sluggish in the field, prone to using war elephants mixed in with their cavalry, as though the poor beasts were anything more than targets for muskets and artillery. Their officers were nobles, which made them arrogant and slow to adapt and improvise. She could beat them. These hills would make for an excellent defensive fortification. All she needed was a good infantry line, and engineers to dig trenches and build stone walls. Royens could bring up the 1st Corps and entrench here. This temple would be her headquarters.

"Artillery," she said. The words sounded muffled, distant. She tried to shout, to make them clearer. "I need the Nineteenth Battery in place on that hill over there. Order the Eleventh Cavalry in place to screen while they deploy. Do it now!"

The man-of-war suddenly lurched to a halt, as Marquand lowered her to the ground beside one of the stone columns.

"No," she tried to say. "No time for my wounds. Order the Ninth Division forward! Forward, for the Exarch's sake!"

He rolled up her pant leg, and touched where her wounds had gone septic. She recognized the smell, even without looking down. It hurt, but she could bear it. Her soldiers would be fighting through worse than she'd gotten, today. She had to focus on the battle at hand.

Body lanced through her. Her vision shook, as though she'd been hit in the head. Only a small trickle, but the red motes latched onto her leg, spreading through her blood, to her heart, to her head.

Another pistol flashed. Tigai came trotting up the hilltop, holstering both of his guns.

"We're safe, for now," he said. "Yuli's chasing the last one to make sure it can't report."

"For all the good that's seemed to do," Marquand said, then pressed his hands to her temples. "Majesty, are you there? Can you hear me?"

The world seemed to spin. Fever fought with *Body*, but she saw clearly. She was here, in a ruined temple, atop a hill. Marquand was with her, and Tigai. Yuli was nearby. No one else. No Royens. No 1st Corps.

"I'm here," she replied, hearing the pain in her own voice. "It's gotten worse, hasn't it?"

Marquand didn't say anything. He focused on her leg, where he was already changing her dressings. She couldn't bear to look.

"There were five this time," Tigai said. "They picked up our trail almost immediately. Bloody fucking annoying. If we're lucky we'll have another few hours before they try again."

"She meant the wound," Marquand said. "And yes, Your Majesty. It's gotten worse. You need a surgeon, or a bloody trove of *Life* and *Body*. I'm giving you all I can."

"I know, Colonel," she said.

She closed her eyes. Pain came in with every breath. She was close to the end. A great irony, that she'd only survived this long because of the blood-creatures chasing them. Tigai and Yuli produced *Body* every time they fought, even if only trace amounts. And Marquand was right. She needed more than a single fight's worth of *Body*. She needed a clash of armies. The *ipek'a* birds had raked her left side to the bone, and her flesh was pink and brown where it wasn't black and rotting. So far they'd had to escape to new stars, to keep moving, one step ahead of their blood-pursuers. They hadn't yet found any sign of civilization, and the leylines everywhere were bone-dry, as if they'd been freshly created. Not even any *Life*, growing wild where plants and trees lay undisturbed. It was as though the world had been wiped clean, intent on making sure she was denied any hope of survival.

"Have you recognized any of them?" she asked. "The blood-things? Have any of the same ones attacked us twice?"

"I have no bloody idea," Tigai said. "Yuli might know. She's the one getting close. I try to stay as far back as I can."

"Shh, Majesty," Marquand said. "You need rest."

"I need a miracle," she said. "Rest isn't going to help anymore."

"Yuli's coming," Tigai said.

"You know, I never forgave you, for drinking again," she said. "I'd hoped for more from you. You could have been so much more."

"Don't do this now," Marquand said. "Whatever you think, you need rest."

"You could have been a general," she said. "Not a staff officer, either. A field-general. You have the mind for it, and the courage. Soldiers would have followed you into fire if you ordered them to."

Redness appeared on his cheeks. Emotion, maybe, but too similar to all the times she'd watched him drink himself into a stupor.

"You saved those people, in New Sarresant," she said. "Even while you were a fucking drunk. Imagine what we might have done, if you'd been able to stay sober."

"We can't all be you," he said. "No matter how disappointing that is for you to hear."

"I had maybe, maybe a half-dozen officers as capable as you," she continued. The fever was burning again; she could feel the sweat, but she didn't care. "In the whole bloody army. You're the only one who washed his talent down with a barrel of wine."

"And you drove us all too damned hard!" he snapped. "How many units went into the field ragged and tired, marching forty leagues to fight a battle, just because you could do it?"

"I never asked more of my soldiers than they could give," she said. "I made them better than they knew they could be. I made *you* better."

"And now they're all gone," he said. "All dead. What was the point of your *empire* if it was going to end this way? Dead and gone because you couldn't see the potential in Sarine's power, couldn't work with *anyone* who refused to be inferior to you."

"You don't have a damned clue what you're talking about," she said. Anger mixed with the fever, making her skin hot, bringing a cold sweat on her forehead.

"I know if Sarine had your mind behind her from the beginning, we might not be here. The world might not be a broken, misshapen husk of itself. She tried to rely on you, tried to come to you, tried to put you in command, over and over, because she saw your genius. You saw nothing in her. And it's your fault as much as anyone's."

"*You* were the one I put in command of her and her *champions*!" she shouted, though her body was weakening, her voice straining for volume. "And what did you do? You vanished into your fucking wine!"

"I failed!" he shouted back. "There? Is that what you needed to hear? I'm a fucking failure. But it should have been you. You should never have put that weight on me. It was yours to carry, and you bloody fucking dropped it."

Exhaustion knifed through her, and she slumped back against the stone.

Her head was full of cotton, her breathing hoarse and ragged. The *Body* was running dry, and her vision was starting to blur again.

"Marquand," she said. "Marquand."

"What?" he snapped. But she couldn't feel any more anger; the heat from the fever had burned it through.

"Make sure they survive," she said. "Tigai and Yuli. Make sure they have children."

"No," he said, shaking his head. Tears appeared at the corners of his eyes. "You can't die."

"Yes, I can," she said.

"No," he said again, but the sound was distant, quieter than it had been. She needed to sleep. Her body was so tired. The weight of empire fell on her shoulders, all the decisions, all the missteps, all the dead who had looked to her for protection. There was nothing left anymore. She'd carried all she could, and fallen short.

Footsteps drew near. Someone approaching. Someone she should know. It didn't matter now. Her battle would be over soon. Command would fall to someone else.

Marquand scrambled to his feet, going to the newcomer. Yuli. She'd been fighting. That meant—

Another wave of *Body* jolted through her. She stirred, but her eyelids felt heavier than they had before. The fever simmered on her skin, everywhere.

"No," Marquand was saying. "No. I don't bloody care right now! Can't you see she's dying?"

"We have to go," Yuli said. "They're coming, in force this time. They know we're here."

"I can't," Tigai said. "Not yet. I need time before I can use the strands again."

"Then we fight," Yuli said.

A fight. She should order the reserve to come up. And where was Jiri? She needed to order Jiri saddled, so she could ride to the front herself. She could lead the charge, her banners flying in the wind, her saber raised high, leading her people to victory. But first she needed sleep. A short rest, to give her body strength to fight through the pain.

85

TIGAI

A Ruined Temple, Under the Moonlight
Sardia

He checked his ammunition pouch and powder. Not a thing he'd had to do often, when he'd been bound to Sarine. Without being able to snap back to his anchors and to reload his weapons, every shot had to count.

Yuli stood out in the open, exposed under the moonlight. Her hair looked silver instead of its usual gold, while the tattoos on her face blended with the shadows, making her more a demon than a woman. No matter which way the blood-creatures took to climb the hill, they would see them long before they reached the top. Good, open ground, with fixtures and fortifications to hide behind. The sort of place Remarin would have picked to hole up and set an ambush for an enemy they knew was coming this way.

Marquand kept back, fool that he was. The Empress was going to die, it was clear as glass. Having him in the thick of the fighting would have been useful. Instead Marquand was going to protect her, with all the *Shelter* and *Entropy* he could find among these ruins. Little chance Erris was going to do anything more than mumble and moan through the fighting. Maybe she'd prove to be a distraction, if they were lucky. He'd already tried tethering them all away; his body couldn't handle it, but perhaps, if they could buy even a few minutes, he could get them out of here. The stars were there, moving, re-arranging themselves. All he had to do was hook to one and the chase would start again. Another few hours of sleep before the next blood-creature scouting party came to investigate.

"There," Yuli said, pointing down the left side of the hill. "They're coming."

He set the match on one of his pistols, bracing his firing arm against the column he was hiding behind. Nothing for it now but to survive. The scouting parties had never been more than four or five of the creatures. But then, they'd never let one escape before. Who knew how many the Blood Gods would send after them, now that they knew where they were.

A blood-creature's head came into view, cresting the hillside. He fired.

Splattering blood flew in all directions.

For a brief moment the pistol-flash illuminated the ruins. Yuli's hair was gold again, though it was already shrinking into her skull, her body growing into the hairless muscle of the Twin Fangs. The blood-creature's headless body collapsed. But in the flash he saw what was behind it. Not three or four companions. A fucking army. A bloody fucking army. A hundred of the blood-creatures, shambling in unison. All given pause by his first shot, while the sight of them sank his heart into his chest.

They were going to die.

He cracked the pistol in a flurry, fitting another ball into the chamber. His other hand raised his second pistol and fired. Then he ran.

Yuli dove into their front line, a whirl of claws and howls and teeth. He finished reloading both guns as he ran back toward the ruins, where Marquand and Erris were holed up against the stones. He had anchors set here, if he needed them, but every time he snapped back it would delay the energy he needed to get them the fuck out of here. He had to be cautious. He had to stay alive. He had to—

A blood-creature appeared in front of him, wielding a spear. He raised his pistol, fired, and exploded half the creature's upper torso in a spatter of blood. It flailed backward, but threw its spear, narrowly missing as he dodged to the side.

Three more blood-creatures ran at him. He fired his second gun, clipping one of them in the foot, blasting it clean off and sending the creature sprawling to the ground. The other two dove at him, one wielding a long, curved sword and the other a spiked club. He raced between the columns, ducking and pivoting around. No time to reload the pistols. He drew the long knife from his belt and sliced the air, missing one of them while the other jabbed with its sword and the first recovered its footing, leaping at him with its club.

Fuck. No choice.

He snapped to a nearby anchor, firing both freshly loaded guns at once. Both blood-creatures were in the middle of swiping at where he'd been standing before he'd blinked away. His shots took them both in the head. Both exploded, their bodies collapsing backward. The exhaustion from using the strands settled over him, masked by the adrenaline of the fight. He had to get to a safer vantage, where he could reload and fire into the mêlée. He and

Yuli had planned to face another squad, another four or five at most. Not a bloody fucking hundred. He had to move.

The hilltop swarmed with blood-creatures already. Luckily for him, the greater mass circled around Yuli, trying to entrap her as she moved them away from the ruins. *Shelter* walls had sprung up where they'd left Marquand and Erris, but the colonel and the Empress had drawn only a handful of the creatures. He reloaded both guns on the run, keeping the matches set and burning. An *Entropy* blast shook the ground near the *Shelter*, putting four or five of the blood-things down, smoking and charred. But with these numbers, Marquand would run out of leyline energy. He would exhaust himself snapping to new anchors, never getting close to being able to tether them all away. And Yuli would be overwhelmed, fighting fifty-to-one.

All that mattered for now was each shot, each kill. Like Remarin had taught him: If he had to die, he'd take as many of these fucking things as he could with him into the grave.

He stopped near another column. None were chasing him now, thank the wind spirits. He took the time to line up his shot, and fired, taking one of the creatures swarming Yuli in the back, sending it careening into one of its fellows. A second shot quickly followed the first, and this time a group of the creatures pivoted toward him, toward the flash of his guns.

He broke from cover and ran again, trying to reload at least one of his pistols as he sprang over the crumbling outer wall of the temple courtyard. A glance over his shoulder counted five. Five creatures racing toward him.

The ball he'd been trying to load dropped from his fingers. He cursed and fished out another one from his pouch. Yuli broke free of the swarm, howling as she raced along the hilltop, her arms and face drenched in blood. She saw him and howled again, turning toward the blood-creatures closing on him in the outer ruin.

He tried to scramble backward, but they reached him, one of them spearing him in the leg while another sailed over top of the crumbled wall, bringing its sword down toward his head.

He blinked away.

The exhaustion rocked him in a wave of nausea. But both guns were reloaded again. He moved out from behind the column and fired both shots, striking the now-shocked swordsman in its chest, and missing with the other, exploding a rock formation next to one of the other blood-creatures' heads. Yuli descended on the rest, carving them in half with swipes of her claws and teeth. The mass following her had sighted him. Fifty of the fucking things. All racing toward the ruins.

He didn't bother to try and reload on the move. He ran.

Yuli, wind spirits bless her, tried to meet them.

She charged into the fray, cutting and slicing and dodging around their frenzied attacks. Too many ignored her this time. Twenty came running and leaping over the walls and ruined stone building frames of the temple's heart. He wove through what was left of the buildings, climbing over fallen stones, staying a few steps ahead. He sprang over top of a pile of fallen marble and gold, and crashed into one of the blood-creatures who must have moved around to flank him.

They went down together. He punched, striking the thing in the side of the head. It hit back. If it had a weapon it must have dropped it, but it traded blows, keeping him entangled in the debris while the dozen creatures who had been chasing him arrived. They rolled to the side, but the blood-creature grappling him wrenched him toward the others, exposing him to their spears.

They stabbed, relentlessly, with no care for puncturing through his body and injuring their companion holding him in place.

Pain knifed through him.

He blinked away.

He gagged, vomiting as he knelt beside the column. He was near the *Shelter* walls, where another group of four were trying to attack Marquand. This time no *Entropy* met them, only the colonel, on his feet with a saber in his hand, standing over the Empress's body.

He raised his pistols, firing twice and blasting two of Marquand's attackers square in the chest. His hands shook as he fumbled for more balls to reload.

The shock of being fired at turned the blood-creatures' attention long enough for Marquand to lunge, swiping one of them dead and clanging steel with the other. His sight blurred as they fought, trading parry for parry. The world seemed to spin. He was on the verge of collapse. But he managed to finish reloading the guns, and staggered to his feet in time to see Marquand deliver a killing blow, ramming his saber into the blood-creature's guts.

In the distance near the ruin the better part of the blood-creatures were still swarming, fighting around Yuli. A few scattered creatures skulked near the columns, turning toward the *Shelter* wall, and toward him.

He tried to lift his pistol and fire. It went off wildly, shooting a ball into the night sky.

He blinked, trying to focus. The shot had drawn the attention of the creatures nearby. They kept low as they turned to him. Perhaps by now they knew his shots tended to come in twos.

He held the second shot. He'd need to fire at close range, if his hands were unsteady. Another blink and he'd pass out. Six of the creatures were approaching him, and three more drew toward Marquand. His legs trembled from exhaustion, but he kept his back to the column, leaning against it to keep him upright.

He had to make his shot count. One more enemy would die before he did. He held the gun, propping his right arm in his left.

The six moved toward him.

He fired.

Blood exploded in a wrenching torrent, spraying among the columns.

That wasn't from his shot.

He squinted.

Lightning surged everywhere he looked, illuminating the ruins in a dazzling flash. It leapt from blood-creature to blood-creature, a brilliant arc of energy that exploded everything it touched, then forked and seemed to search for more.

He had to cover his eyes to shield them from the light.

When it cleared, blood soaked the hilltop everywhere he looked. Pools lay where the blood-creatures had been. Trickles ran down the sides of columns, down the crumbling stone walls and buildings. Chunks of blood-flesh lay among the pools, pieces of their enemies decorating the ruin, and a sudden, thundering quiet in place of the sounds of fighting.

It took another moment to notice the figure in white, moving to kneel at Erris's side.

An impossible thing. The woman wore a white silk dress, the sort a high courtier, maybe even an Empress would wear, embroidered with red and gold. A metallic, crystalline lizard perched on the woman's shoulder. He'd seen her before, and seen the lizard before. He knew them both. The shock reverberated through his skull along with the afterimages from her lightning.

"Sister," Yuli said. She'd returned to her human form, clutching at her skin to cover what looked like a dozen slashing and piercing wounds, leaking blood through her shirt. "Can it really be you?"

The woman in white glanced up at Yuli, but kept her attention fixed on Erris's body, lying prone in front of her.

"Yes, it's me," the woman said. "I'm sorry it took me this long to find you. The stars are a mess, but there haven't been many using them. Thank the Gods Tigai was with you."

"We thought you were dead, girl," Marquand said, hovering over her as she worked with Erris.

"I was," the woman said. "I'll explain everything, once I can get you all to safety."

He staggered forward. Somehow his legs had the strength to stand, though walking seemed to be a challenge.

Sarine.

That was her name. And her *kaas*, Anati.

It seemed important, to remember those names. Nothing else mattered at that moment. They were safe. He wasn't going to die. Yuli wasn't going to die. He just needed to sleep for a few thousand years and he'd be ready for anything.

"Tigai?" Yuli said. "Are you—?"

He didn't hear the rest, over the sound of his body collapsing to take a nap under the stars.

86

YULI

The Tomb of Emperor Sun Qiang
The Jun Empire

She sat cross-legged, dabbing the cloth against her wounds. It stung, as only medicine could. The *magi* claimed the herbs soaked in the cloth would speed her healing, but so far they only served to redden and irritate her skin.

"So, this is his place," she said. "The Regnant's."

Sarine nodded. "I awakened here after I died."

She looked around, taking it all in. Their arrival had been sudden, first with Erris being laid out atop a bed, where Marquand was still glued in place. They'd taken Tigai to the next chamber, where a *magi* called Diaolong brought tinctures and ointments for her, and nothing more than a pillow for him. It seemed unfair that Tigai could be speared, cut, knifed, and smashed a dozen times and blink away, leaving him with nothing but a headache and the need for a few hours' sleep. Her skin was torn in twenty places, bite marks, claws, bruises, spear-point wounds, and slashing cuts marking her legs and upper body. She sat stripped naked, dabbing herself, while hot towels soaked in the medicinal liquid lay draped over both of her thighs. Diaolong swore she'd be restored in full in a matter of days; with the Twin Fangs' rapid healing, it would likely be a fraction of that. But it still stung like a swarm of bees let loose in her trousers. And Tigai slept like a newborn child, pristine and beautiful, his skin untouched but for a few powder burns on his hands and forearms. Unfair.

"It's..." She searched for the right word. "Resplendent. I've never been in a room like this. And the whole place is decorated the same way?"

"I know," Sarine said. "I felt like an impostor when Diaolong dressed me to match these chambers."

"No," she said. "It suits you. You more than any of us. You'd look better with some proper tattoos for the Nine Tails, though."

Sarine smiled. "Maybe after this is all over," she said.

She returned the smile. It felt good, even if they were in a place that looked like it was all carved from a single block of gold. Murals depicted Jun heroes on the walls and ceiling, great armies and generals fighting their enemies with spears. Not that Jun generals ever did their fighting themselves, when there were armies of conscripted peasants and mercenary soldiers to throw at their problems. Still, whatever the Jun did, it clearly earned them enough gold and wealth to make a place like this to rest their dead. The decorations here could feed every family on the northern steppes and tundra for ten years, with gold and jewels to spare.

"Do you..." she began. "Do you think... this is a Jun place. This is the sort of thing they're accustomed to, right?"

"It's an Emperor's tomb," Sarine said. "Not exactly fare for common people."

"I know," she said. "But Tigai is a lord. I never saw his estates. Do you think he'll want to live like this?"

"I think he'll want to live with you," she said. "And I can't imagine you or the Twin Fangs being comfortable in jewels."

"I want him to be comfortable, too, though," she said. "It's just... I met him when we were adventuring, living where we were and sleeping wherever we could." She looked up at him, resting atop the stone bed at the chamber's heart. He was a beautiful man, even if he did drool in his sleep. "I don't want him to have to settle for less than he wants, because of me."

"From what I've seen of Tigai, he's happy whenever he's near his family," Sarine said. "I don't think he gives a damn whether that means he's sleeping in a stable or a palace."

She raised an eyebrow, and Sarine laughed.

"All right, fine," Sarine said. "Maybe he enjoys palaces more than most. But you'll find what works for both of you, together."

"I love him," she said. "I never imagined it would be like this. Natarii warriors don't marry. But I thought, because of..."

"Because of what?" Sarine said. "And why don't you marry?"

"What if the Twin Fangs is hungry one night, and I can't control it?" she said. "No more husband. No more children. But I thought, with your bond, with the control it gave me, I could let myself be with him. I let myself feel more than I was supposed to."

"I had no idea," Sarine said. "But that's good, isn't it? Good for both of you."

"I suppose you're right," she said. "It's not going to matter much, if we don't win."

"What do you mean?" Sarine asked.

"The Soul of the World," she said. "You need it to restore our bond, right?"

"Oh Gods," Sarine said. "You mean...your bond was severed, when I died. Not just yours. All of them. That's why Erris was almost dead from a leg wound, why Tigai couldn't just blink you all away...I'm such an idiot."

"It's fine," she said. "I learned discipline from the moment they put the first tattoos on my face. I can control the Twin Fangs, most of the time."

"No," Sarine said. "I have some of the Veil's memories now, courtesy of the Regnant invading my head. Bonding you at the Soul of the World was only for the ascension rituals. A thing they did to...never mind. It doesn't matter. Hold still."

She cocked her head; it hurt, straining the cuts on her neck and shoulders.

A light flashed.

She felt part of her bleeding into something else, as though a piece of her soul had been cut out and fused back together.

Suddenly her body was whole.

All her cuts were gone. All the stinging pain, the medicine seeping into her blood.

The Twin Fangs growled inside her, by instinct. Something was attacking them. Changing them. It wanted control, to defend them from the threat.

It had no hold on her.

It was part of her, as it always was. But she was its master again. The bond pulsed in her soul, connecting Yuli and Sarine. Sarine and Yuli. The Twin Fangs served her, and she could summon and dismiss its power at will. She was a champion once more.

"Sister," she said. It came out in a broken whisper.

"I'm *such* an idiot," Sarine said. "I should have realized this would happen."

Sarine was already rising to her feet, going to where Tigai lay sleeping atop the stone.

"You mean you can bond us all again, without the Soul?" she asked.

"Yes," Sarine said. "Of course. A champion's bond is just a bridge between the magic you use and the magic I do, letting you tap into the same reservoirs I use on the Infinite Plane. Kalira and the others bonded champions the same way; instead of Life, she let her champions use the Sun. It's all the same fundamental source, even if it expresses in different ways, and for the most part the rules are the same, too. Just as well for the memories the Regnant gave me to do some good, I suppose. Even if—"

Tigai gasped and sat up.

"Bloody *fuck*," he shouted.

"Good to see you, too, Tigai," Sarine said, stepping back.

Yuli went to him and wrapped her arms around his chest.

"Careful," Tigai said, eyeing her. "Aren't you all cut and bruised?"

"I'm not," she said. "I'm whole. Really whole. Sarine bonded us. I'm in control of the Twin Fangs again."

"And you're naked," he said.

"I was applying a tincture, before Sarine healed me," she said.

"It's fine, I don't mind," Tigai said. "Though I'd like it better if Sarine excused us for a moment to be alone...wherever we are."

Yuli laughed. They were healed. Both of them.

"Fine by me," Sarine said. "I need to see to Erris anyway."

"No, sister," she said. "He doesn't need that right now. We need to hear more about where we are, how you came to be alive. And why you...why we, are suddenly working with the Regnant."

Tigai's hands slid down to her hips. "Excuse me, he'll be the judge of what he needs right now," he said.

"We'll speak soon," Sarine said. "After Erris is bonded again. I promise. I'll tell you everything."

Sarine was already on her way out, opening and closing the heavy stone door.

Even before she was gone, Tigai's hands moved. It felt good to feel his touch again, without the threat of stirring the Twin Fangs. Knowing he would be safe with her, always. He kissed her, and she kissed back, and even here, in a strange, foreign place, surrounded by gold carvings and murals of unfamiliar heroes on the walls, love was welcome, a temporary escape, a rekindling of why the world was worth fighting for, a strength for both of them to draw on, together.

87

ERRIS

The Tomb of Emperor Sun Qiang
The Jun Empire

White heat poured into her lungs. She breathed fire. Light flashed in her eyes, in all the colors of the leylines at once. This was death. She was dead.

A poisonous, noxious taste filled her mouth. She sat up, coughing and spitting. A hand was on her back, propping her up, pulling her hair out of the way.

Marquand stood at her side. She coughed, clearing her throat of spit and bile. Sarine stood in front of her.

Sarine. She'd been wrong, somehow. Sarine had lived.

"I'm sorry," Sarine said. "I know there can be pain, when the bond heals an infection. Cough it out of your system and you'll be well again."

She did, hacking and tasting foulness on her tongue, not that she had any choice. Her lungs rumbled and her throat cracked and twisted, like gargling sewer water. She spat it out and another wave came up as fast. She was in a room covered in gold and paint, full of foreign designs whose objects she recognized well enough: soldiers, fighting, conquests, war, even if the costumes were alien and the style of the art was like nothing she'd seen on either side of the oceans.

"Thank every God for you," Marquand said. "She was never going to last another night."

"I should have realized sooner my champions' bonds were severed," Sarine said. "And I'm sorry I can't bond you, too, Colonel. It only works for one: one conduit between Life and the leylines, or the others."

"Where are...?" Erris tried to say, smothering the rest of the words beneath another cough. "Where are we? And where did you learn this?" She coughed again. "You speak as though..." Another hack. "As though you know more than you did."

"I do," Sarine said. "And it won't be easy to hear, or understand. It wasn't for me either."

She waited for more, clearing her throat with another wave of noxious bile she spat over the side of her bed.

"I was...wrong," Sarine said. "In opposing the Regnant. Or at least, in opposing him the way I did. He wants to heal the world, too, in his way. He gave me some of her memories. The Veil's. He showed me why they organized this system."

"He's been your enemy from the start," Marquand said.

"He's the one..." She held in a cough this time. "He's the one who poisoned the skies, is he not?"

"Yes, and yes," Sarine said. "But he did it for a purpose, to heal and rebuild the world's stores of magic. Kalira, Orana, the archangels, the Nikkon and Rabaquim are tearing the world apart, for ignorance as much as greed. I think... I know it sounds like he's controlling me somehow. But he's not. I've learned sometimes one evil has to be accepted, to fight against another, greater one."

"That doesn't sound like the girl I knew," she said.

"Maybe not," Sarine said. "But it's true. Isn't it?"

She cleared her throat again, spitting a ball of black tar to the ground. She'd marred the carpets with the leavings from her lungs and stomach, smearing black paste and bile across the kingly décor.

"It is," she said. "And...thank you. You saved my life."

Sarine bowed her head. "The least I would do, for one of my champions."

She blinked by reflex. Sarine had said something about the bond, while she coughed. She didn't dare to think it, to hope the champion's bond might somehow be restored...

But it was. The leylines poured their stores out to her again. *Need* shone from Marquand, as bright as it ever had, and from scattered survivors, far to the west. *Body*, and *Life*, and *Mind*, and all the rest pulsed to greet her with vast stores of energy. More than her leg, somehow repaired and healthy at her side when it had been bandaged and rotting for days, the leylines meant she was whole.

"So, we're working with the Regnant now," she said. "Where is he?"

"He's gone to find survivors among his people, the same as I did," Sarine said. "He'll return soon."

She nodded, still feeling raw in her throat and empty in her belly. She'd spent months—years, even—ignoring this girl, when she should have been listening. Marquand had been right, smug and arrogant as he was. It was time to fight her war in truth, not as a last resort. Not because there was no better option, no other matter pressing for her attention.

"All right, then," she said. "No need to wait for him. Start from the beginning. What are our next steps?"

"What do you mean?" Sarine asked.

"Kalira and the rest control the Soul of the World," she said. "But without a clear hierarchy in place, or a mechanism for them to share power. That's why the world is going mad, why there are deserts next to blizzards, lakes of fire and jungles covered in blood. Right? They control the Soul, and we mean to take it from them."

Sarine nodded slowly. "Yes," she said. "But I should warn you: We can't just go back and claim it. There are seals in place. They won't open again for another cycle. A thousand years, maybe. Maybe more."

"Tell me everything you know," she said. "From the beginning."

Sarine started talking, and she listened. She'd been right; something about the girl had changed, but it wasn't only foreign memories, terminology, and ideas she'd never heard Sarine mention before. Perhaps it was their failure at the Gods' Seat, at having the world rest on her shoulders, and letting it slip. She recognized it. She'd seen it in her commanders, even in herself. Giving orders and watching people die for it changed you. It was easy to criticize, to sit back and be certain you knew what was best, when nothing depended on your word. Sarine had tasted failure, tasted it for the greatest stakes she knew. Some broke under that strain. Others found steel inside themselves, and fought on.

Midway through Sarine's explanations, Tigai and Yuli rejoined them, entering quietly through the chamber's great stone door. Tigai wore the same clothes he'd had on before, while Yuli had changed hers for a blue-and-white silk robe. Both appeared disheveled, and Yuli had the beginnings of a walnut-sized bruise on her neck, though she showed no other signs of injury. Good. It was a great relief seeing them both alive, and neither interrupted as Sarine continued her account of what had happened, and why, and what would follow.

"We'll have another chance to fight," Sarine was saying. "When the next cycle opens, perhaps a thousand years from now. We may even find new allies among the people alive then, those who have mastered our lines of magic."

"A thousand years," Yuli said. "I don't like it, sister."

"I know," Sarine said. "I don't like it either. But this place, this tomb, has been prepared as a place for us to rest. We can sleep until the end of the cycle is near. Then, when we awaken, we can find survivors and take stock of what Kalira and the others have done to the world, and how we can undo it."

"What if there are no survivors?" Erris asked.

"That's never happened before," Sarine said. "Those in control of the Soul of the World remake it according to their vision of how the world should be. Even Kalira isn't trying to murder everyone."

"But six designers at once might inadvertently destroy what they design," she said. "We've seen it. The world is going mad out there. Changing on a whim, from fire to ice to calm to blood and thunder. Not a place for life to flourish, or even survive."

"I can't do anything about it," Sarine said. "We had our chance, and failed. All we can do now is plan to endure."

"A thousand years is a long time," Yuli said. "Our people, our families... they'll all be gone."

Tigai squeezed an arm around her shoulder.

She wasn't ready to accept it so easily. If Sarine didn't know another way, then perhaps the Regnant would, when he returned. If the girl—if Sarine said their allegiances had shifted, so be it. She was no stranger to changing colors in wartime. But they needed reconnaissance and a deeper understanding of what forces were in play before she resigned herself to sleeping away the years until the seals on the Gods' Seat opened again. She'd already failed once; the first assault on the Gods' Seat belonged to her as much as to Sarine. She could do better. Already her mind spun, working on plans to leverage Tigai's gifts alongside the others. This time she knew Kalira, Orana, the Rabaquim, the Nikkon, all of their strengths and weaknesses far better than she'd known the Regnant, or his champions.

She swung her legs down from the stone bed. Both healthy, where her left had been rotten to the bone not a half hour before. A miracle unto itself.

She touched her bare feet to the chamber floor, and a crashing thump sounded from the hall outside.

She immediately withdrew her feet. Had she somehow—?

But no. Sarine and the others pivoted immediately toward the door.

It swung open. *Entropy* sprang to her hand like an old, well-used pistol.

She almost loosed her *Entropy* when a woman in a blue-and-white silk robe stepped inside. But the others relaxed when they saw her.

"Diaolong," Sarine said. "What was that?"

"An intruder, Great Lady," the woman—Diaolong—said, bowing as she spoke. "Please forgive us. This place was meant to be a secret. I don't know how we were discovered. But there is no need to trouble yourself. My brothers and sisters will handle—Great Lady, please! Stay here!"

Sarine was already on her feet and moving, with Marquand and Yuli at her side. Only Tigai and she were a step behind, weighing each other for a moment before they followed. Damn fool of a girl. Marquand may have been right that she and Sarine should have worked together from the start, but Sarine still had the instincts of a bravo with something to prove to the world, as though she were drunk on liquor and zeal.

They emerged into a grand chamber as finely decorated as the room where she'd awakened. She ignored the opulence and splendor, scanning the room with a soldier's eyes. Other *magi* in blue-and-white robes stood around its edge, all facing toward the room's far wall, where a man-shaped creature of blood stood, sword in hand, while its flesh-duplicate clutched his stomach, kneeling and fighting through choking spasms in his throat.

"Stop," the flesh-form was trying to say, coughing and raising a hand as though to ward them away. The voice was familiar, though it was difficult to place through the gagging and coughs. "I'm not...not...your enemy...Need the Regnant. Need..."

"Omera?" Sarine said. It was. The young, smooth-faced Bhakal man, whom she'd known first as her mentor's one-eyed servant, before he was restored and then bonded as a champion of the Rabaquim Blood.

Omera glanced up through the pain writ on his face, his eyes widening as he saw Sarine. He nodded, and tried to speak. "I...you...tell them..." was all he managed.

"Stop whatever you're doing," Sarine called to the *magi* in white and blue. "He's not a threat. Let him stand."

"You don't know he's not a threat," Erris said. "He's bound to the same blood-creatures that have been hunting us since the Seat."

Sarine glanced back at her, but held firm. "Let him up," she said, and two of the *magi* bowed to her in unison. At least there was still the distance of the grand chamber between them. Time enough to react, if he moved to attack. She tethered a strand of *Body*, to be sure her reflexes could match, and held *Shelter* at the ready.

Omera coughed a final time, wiping his mouth as he rose from his knees. "Thank...thank you," he said. "I had no...no idea you'd survived, too."

"I did," Sarine said. "But Erris is right. Your people have been hunting my champions since the Seat. Why have you come here? How did you find out about this place?"

"Not...not my people," Omera said. His voice was rough and cracked, still raw from whatever the *magi* had done to him. "I'm...Bhakal. My mother's son. The Rabaquim...tricked me. Paid me in fool's gold to restore what the Regnant took from my memory. I'm myself now. If...if you and the Regnant live, then I mean to offer both of you my sword."

"How can you pledge yourself to another master, when that... *thing* fights beside you?" she called out across the room. The memory of the blood-creatures hunting them was too close, too punctuated by the sight of them, chasing no matter how many they cut down.

"I can't disperse the Blood," Omera said. "But it fights for me. I am its master, not the other way round. I can shut the Rabaquim out of my thoughts, and give them the same thing they offered me: nothing."

"But why would you turn on them?" Sarine asked. "They control the Seat. They control the Soul."

"They and five others," Omera said. "I've seen what they're doing to the world, fighting among each other for control. What point is there in being a King if my land and people are destroyed before I can claim my throne?"

"He can take us back," Yuli said. "He's one of their champions. That means the way is open for him, isn't it? The same as it was for Tigai, when you held the Seat. No need to wait a thousand years to attack. With him, we can go now."

Sarine wavered; so did she. She saw it now: This tomb had been prepared as a place for Sarine and her champions to sleep, with the Regnant's *magi* in attendance. She saw in Sarine's face that Yuli's words were true, if Omera's were. But the girl would never be able to make that sort of judgment on her own. Sarine was too driven by hope. If she'd learned anything about Sarine at all, it was that. But then, that was why she needed allies. Why she needed champions.

"Give him to me, for interrogation," she said. "Me and Marquand. We'll find out the truth of what he claims. Until we do, don't let him within a hundred paces of you, or of the Regnant. Both of you must be kept safe, if we're going to have any chance at making this world right again."

"Will you submit to questioning?" Sarine called out across the room. "We need to be sure of what you say, before we consider you a friend."

Omera bowed his head. "Yes, of course," he said. "Anything."

Sarine turned to her. "Thank you," she said. "Yuli's right: With one of the Rabaquim's champions among us, we could reach the Soul even with the seals in place. But if he's playing us as false as they did...if it's a trap..."

"I'll find out," she said. "Until I do, stay alert, and keep those *magi* on guard. If he can find us, more could be behind him."

Sarine, Yuli, and Tigai went back toward the room, leaving her and Marquand alone with the *magi* and Omera in the great chamber. The girl could be trusting to a fault, a symptom of the hope that all but sustained her. She had no such delusions. A potential ally in an enemy's colors could turn a battle, and just as easily collapse the ground under their feet, if they were betrayed again. Her methods would be as ungentle as they needed to be to find the truth.

88

SARINE

Embalming Chamber
The Tomb of Emperor Sun Qiang

She paced the length of the room, pivoting to pace again when she reached the end.

"The Great Lord won't like this, Great Lady," Diaolong said. The Owl had escorted them all here, to a room with stone basins filled with pools of strong-smelling liquids. "Forgive my saying it, but you should have let us fulfill our duty. Our orders are to kill any intruders."

"Does it mean you'll have to move?" Tigai asked. "If one hunter found you, another could."

"It won't matter," she said, continuing her pacing. "Yuli was right: If Omera is telling the truth, we'll be able to return to the Seat."

"Are we ready, if he is?" Yuli asked. She and Tigai sat together on a wooden bench beside one of the pools. Both were close, as though they looked for any excuse to touch, and both were healthy and strong, all the signs of their wounds erased by her bond.

"I don't know," she said. The sting of failure lurked inside her, when she thought of returning to the Seat. The Regnant claimed they needed to sleep a thousand years, and she'd rejected the thought. Now, with the possibility of a return hanging over her, the memory of Kalira's outstretched hand, of sunfire and betrayal, bit into her stomach with guilt and fear.

"We could take the time to prepare," Tigai said. "The Regnant has resources here, and between my gifts and his, we could find *magi* to bring with us to the Seat."

She shook her head. "We saw how well his *magi* fared during our first attack," she said. "More won't matter. We'll need to rely on stealth to get as far as we can."

"Stealth?" Tigai said. "Won't they know the moment we arrive?"

"They might," she said. "But I've...rediscovered...certain gifts. *Faith* can shield us while we move. If we attack them directly, it should be as a distraction. I'll settle it with Erris, once she's satisfied Omera will help us. All I need to do is reach the Soul. Once I do, I can finish this."

"We believe in you, sister," Yuli said. "Whether we can return or not, we're with you to the end."

She resumed her pacing, leaving Yuli and Tigai to share whatever passed between them without words.

Possibility stretched in front of her, and fear. This was all a second chance she didn't deserve. She'd made the mistake of trusting Kalira and the others, believing any ally was preferable to the horrors the Regnant had unleashed on the world. Now she understood, though the knowledge was fouler than any rotten meat, any rancid fruit or drink. The Regnant's torpor was the price of magic. While the coating of sparks covering the Soul of the World ran along its spine, wonders flowed onto the physical plane. Those black and white sparks were conductors of power between the world that *was*, the world of form and potential, and the world that reflected that reality in the physical space around them. Magic flowed from one source: the ability to change the true forms and let the shadows dance when you did, like making puppet-shapes on the wall by holding up fingers in front of a torch. When the sparks ran dry, the world had to be upended, letting the sand of magic flow against its grain. Life energy had to be subsumed by Death. White to Black. Sunshine to Poison rain.

The truth behind all of it was simple: For magic to exist in the world, a regenerative stage was required to replenish its power, like rainstorms watering the seeds of a new harvest. A time of darkness, poison, horror, and death, before a rebirth into light, beauty, growth, and life.

And all of it counted for nothing if she couldn't return to claim the Soul.

It frightened her, to imagine the horrors she'd unleashed on the world. Kalira wanted all creation to bow before the Sun's power, while Orana wanted to nurture the oceans, to cradle the dead before they journeyed onward to the stars. The archangels sought to make the world as a reflection of their God's will, balanced between paradise and damnation. The Flesh hungered for new life, new forms and shapes for creatures, plants, and all other living things, and the Blood demanded payment for it all, souls and death as the price of life. The Spirit-Weavers wanted to please their ancestors, though none of them could have said what whims those long dead would unleash on their descendants.

Somehow she knew all this about her former allies, and now she knew the source: the Veil's memories, still lingering in her head, this time muted and quiet instead of fighting her for control, but they were still there. She'd been such a fool. Such a bloody fool. The Others weren't benign powers, content to be set aside or used as pawns when it suited the Regnant and Veil. They had designs of their own, ambitions and dreams for what they might do with the power of the Soul of the World. Six of them all vying for control at once only made it worse, and chaos and destruction were the inevitable result.

It was her fault. All her fault. She'd only ever wanted to do what was right, but she'd let it trick her into believing others shared her dreams, that she could use them without consequences, and she'd paid a terrible price for her hubris.

I think you deserve a second chance, Anati thought to her. *I think we all do.*

It paused her midstep. Instead of continuing, she sat beside the stone basins, on the far side of the room from Diaolong, Tigai, and Yuli.

"Thank you, Anati," she said. "I hope I won't waste it."

What are these liquids? Anati thought to her. *They smell like* Black.

"This is an embalming chamber, I think," she said. "A place where they preserve the dead."

They would have had to preserve you, to let you sleep?

"I hope not," she said. "I think that's a trick of the sparks, of Life and Death magic. The fluids here are for corpses, before they're interred."

Oh, Anati thought. She'd appeared midway through the last thought, dipping one of her foreclaws in the basin without appearing to disrupt the liquid inside. *I don't want you to be a corpse again. I promise I won't let them do it. I'll keep you safe, no matter what.*

"I don't mean for either of us to die," she said.

Is that a trick of Life and Death magic, too? Anati thought. *Everything dies, doesn't it?*

"Well, yes," she said. "I guess I mean I don't mean for us to die yet. We have too much to do, first."

Anati looked up at her, her eyes shining like sapphires, reflecting the lamplight in the room.

Saving the world, Anati thought.

It almost made her laugh. She held it back.

"Yes, I suppose so," she said. "You, me, Yuli, Tigai, Erris, Marquand, Omera, and all the *magi* of my ancient enemy."

I thought he was your friend now?

"Is he?" she said. "I don't know. What do you think?"

I don't think you can trust him, Anati thought. *He's been in power so long I think he defines rightness as whatever he wants. That's dangerous.*

"That was my mistake, too," she said. "Though after all this, I can't help but second-guess myself. How do I know that what I want is right?"

Because what you want is peace, Anati thought. *And hope. That's all you've ever wanted.*

"Is that so?" she asked. "How do you know that?"

That's what loving someone is, Anati thought. *Knowing what they want more than anything in the world.*

She smiled. "You're magnificent, Anati," she said. "As much as Zi ever was."

Her *kaas*'s scales colored a deep pink, enough to bleed off her foreclaw into the embalming fluid, leaving a tiny trail of ink in the pool.

Before Anati could reply, a chime sounded, loud enough that it seemed to come from everywhere, yet with no particular source she could discern. The lamplight throughout the room changed color with the sound, in a moment going from a cool yellow to a deep blue, before it flashed back to its usual flame.

She rose to her feet as Diaolong did.

"What was that?" she said. Diaolong bowed before answering her.

"He has returned," Diaolong said. "The Great Lord, along with his new champions. With the Great Lady's permission, we must go to him at once, and inform him of the intruder."

89

OMERA

Pain lanced through him. Searing heat drew sweat from his skin. Anger simmered underneath, while his blood-self boiled over, hurling itself against the pale blue *Shelter* separating it from the rest of the room.

A loud crack sounded as his blood-self struck the wall and rebounded, collapsing to the floor.

"He's yours," his tormentor said. Sakhefete. No, that was someone else. His mind blurred from the pain. Erris. Erris d'Arrent. "Clean him up. I'll return once he's caught his breath."

His skin ached. He knelt on the floor, his upper body stripped bare and scorched by her magic. *Entropy*, she'd called it. Decay. The breaking down of order; in this case, the order of his unblemished skin and the blood vessels underneath.

"Why?" he said, forcing words through the pain. "Why do this?"

The other tormentor knelt at his side. A man. Large, brutish, red-faced. Colonel Marquand. He dabbed a wet cloth against Omera's shoulder. It stung. It felt like he was wiping skin away with the sweat and smoke.

"Why?" he repeated. "I'll tell you everything. There's no need for this."

"Shh," Marquand said. "Take the time to rest."

"But *why*?" He said it fiercely this time. "I was your ally before. Why…this?"

"Empress d'Arrent needs to be sure of what you say," Marquand said. "Think of how much depends on her trust. Would you risk as much, without being sure?"

He fell quiet, letting Marquand dab the cloth along his torso.

They'd taken his herb-pouch and his sword after they'd knocked him down without warning. He'd thought they meant to sit, perhaps to break bread or share tea or wine, to ask him questions of all that had happened since the Seat. Instead they'd walled away his blood-self and set to hurting him at once. She hadn't even asked him any questions.

The blood-self hurled itself at the *Shelter* again, crashing to the floor in a thud that rattled the walls.

"Why does it struggle?" Marquand said. "Doesn't that…thing…obey your commands?"

He shook his head. Finally, a question.

"It's part of me," he said. "Like an arm, or a leg. It does what I want, but if you're injured and your arm twitches, you don't control it."

"I see," Marquand said. "What about reporting back to its masters? We were chased by dozens of those things. They seemed to know what the others before them had seen."

"*I* am its master," he said. The strain sent another wave of pain across his skin, and he winced. "Yes, it wants to report back to the Blood. I've told it not to."

"You've 'told' it?" Marquand said. "I thought it was like an arm, or a leg."

"It is," he said. "It won't do what I don't want it to."

"I see," Marquand said, stepping back and withdrawing his cloth. It was covered in grime, stained with blood that had seeped through his skin.

"Tell her," he said. "There's no need for this. I will answer any question you have. I came here to offer my sword to the Regnant, for a chance to fight for my people."

"I'll tell her," Marquand said.

He left the room.

Pain returned, now that he was alone with it. His blood-self had regained its footing, walking the length of the room enclosed by their *Shelter* walls. His anger poured out into the blood-self, leaving a dull awareness in his true body. Minutes passed. Not hours. Not yet, he didn't think.

He flinched when the door opened again, and Erris stepped back into the room.

The blood-self stared at her through the *Shelter*, though its walls were opaque. She came in with purpose, striding toward him. His warrior's instincts called out for *ubax aragti*. He should rise, meet her on his feet, try to strike her when she came close. But he was here as an ally, whatever evil she intended to make him prove it. He would comply with her methods. He would endure.

She came to a stop in front of him, then knelt so they were eye to eye.

He almost flinched again, but forced himself to meet her stare.

"You're lying to me," Erris said.

"What?" he said. "I haven't said anything—!"

Pain returned.

He screamed, writhing backward as her *Entropy* settled over him, cooking his skin in a flash of heat and fire.

"You claim you can control your blood...thing," Erris said. "Yet you also claim it wants to report back to its masters. How can both be true?"

He lay on the floor. His blood-self had charged the *Shelter* again, and now lay dazed and prostrate on the other side of the chamber. The world seemed to spin.

"How!" Erris shouted. She'd asked a question. He searched his brain for the words.

"I..." he tried to say. "I don't..."

"How, unless *you* want to report back and betray us?" she said. "Or perhaps you aren't as in control as you claim?"

"No!" he shouted as she took a step toward him. "No. It has...it has desires. Instincts. Separate from mine. But I control it."

"Do the Blood know where we are?" she demanded.

He shook his head. "No," he said. "I haven't told them. I don't serve them anymore."

Once more his warrior's training came to the fore. He could cower, lure her into thinking he was vulnerable. She was approaching now. He could wait, and strike. A leg-tackle would bring her to the ground where he could reach her windpipe. Once it was crushed her magic might sear him again, might even kill him, but she would be dead, and he would have a chance to survive, to escape.

He fought it down. He wasn't her enemy. He was here to fight against the monsters poisoning the world.

"Go on," Erris said. She was close. Close enough for him to strike. "Do you think I don't see you want to?"

He darted up to look in her eyes. She was cold. Stoic. And she had a warrior's training, too, for all she was less than half his size.

"I'm not here as your enemy," he said.

She stared down at him. Waiting. Her feet were set as though she expected an attack. A subtle change from the way she'd stood before.

"I don't believe you," she said finally.

He searched for words. The right words could calm the situation, could make her see.

Instead fire surrounded him, and he screamed.

———————

He awoke to the sound of chimes in his ears.

He still had ears. Still had eyes. Still had a body.

Fire had left its mark on his skin. He was sore, and raw. He needed his herbs. He could heal quickly, in a matter of hours. Less, if he risked consuming more than a few pinches. He'd seen a vision during the pain. His mother, watching over him. Sad. He wasn't supposed to die like this. She'd seen it. He had to find survivors among the Bhakal, had to lead them to safety in the aftermath of all this chaos. That was his place. Not here. Not like this.

"Up," a voice said. "Carefully now. Slow."

His blood-self was asleep. Or unconscious. He still felt the duality of its senses superimposed over his. A dull emptiness cloaking the world. Waking and being comatose, both at once.

"Are you awake in there?" the voice said. Marquand. He blinked, and saw the colonel's face.

He nodded, and Marquand looked relieved.

"These are the ones she says you take, to heal yourself," Marquand said, and held out a handful of azure dust mixed with red.

Ubax aragti. Calimnus re.

His eyes opened wider.

He glanced back at Marquand, distrustful.

With a small pinch of either he could restore himself. With the blue, his body would begin to heal. With the red, he could ignore the pain in his body and fight. He could murder Marquand before the colonel suspected Omera was more than the broken, tortured shell in front of him. He was a weapon, a firearm loaded and waiting to kill; all he needed was the powder to set the explosion.

"Take them," Marquand said. "She doesn't mean to kill you. She's worried she went too far. I asked her to let you have these, and she agreed."

He tried to move. His body didn't respond. Sluggish. Too much pain. Instead he opened his mouth.

Marquand raised the hand to his lips, the taste and smell of the powders mixing into an alluring, intoxicating scent as they filled his throat. The smells of power, and freedom.

The powders worked better if he inhaled them through his nose, or, more commonly, rubbed them into his gums. But he could breathe them through his mouth, too. He did. Marquand upended his palm onto his tongue, and Omera left them there as he inhaled, slowly, carefully, drawing the particles of the crushed herbs into his lungs.

In an instant he was transformed.

His body was already healing; the itching spread on his skin, a cleansing fire as the azure *calimnus re* powder worked its way through the network of his blood vessels, filling every limb, every muscle, every patch of broken skin. *Ubax aragti* blazed in his blood alongside the blue. It gave him control. It gave him strength to ignore the pain still present in his body, in spite of the healing. It let him ignore the noxious dose of *calimnus re* he'd consumed. It kept him still, unmoving in spite of the miracles pulsing through him. To Marquand's eye he was still the invalid, the prisoner tortured ten steps farther than a body should be able to take. He hadn't flinched, hadn't given any sign of the change. Yet now he was a warrior again. Even without his sword. He could kill Marquand before the colonel had any idea he was a threat.

He closed his eyes, and breathed deep.

"Tell her," he said. His voice was caught halfway between scorched pain and healing. "Tell her there's no need for this. I came here as a friend."

Marquand seemed to relax when he said it. A tension Omera hadn't noticed was there melted away.

"I will," the colonel said, resting back on his heels as he looked Omera over one more time.

In the back of his mind his blood-self stirred. It blinked awake, smelling Marquand, though it was still too weak to rise. It had to go. It had to return to its masters, to warn them it had found one of the survivors, one of the Goddess's companions who had fled the Seat after their attack. He willed it to stay where it was, and to be silent.

Part of him longed to feed off the blood-self's anger. He could channel it, could fly to his feet in a frenzied rage, ignoring the damage they'd done to his body while he savaged Marquand to pulpy, ruined flesh. They had no right. He'd come here as a friend, as an ally, prepared to betray the Blood who had first betrayed him with their lies.

He was still that. He drew deep, calming breaths, letting the herbs course through his system.

Marquand rose, and left.

In the distance the chimes sounded again. The colonel hadn't mentioned what they were. A herald of something? He had no way to know. He tested his arms and legs, stretching them one at a time. His skin was still raw and red in spots, but his strength was there. A shame the colonel hadn't seen fit to return his *shotel* blade along with the herbs. A warrior felt naked without it. But he was a prince, too, and a prince could meet his tormentors with strength and courage, on his feet.

He rose slowly, carefully. The blood-self was aware now. It scrambled up as he did, staring at the swirling blue haze of its *Shelter* prison. He saw it from the other side, where part of him was walled away in the corner of the room. His body ached even through the *calimnus re*, though *ubax aragti* gave him the strength to force it to respond. He stood upright, as he'd seen his mother stand. Regal. Aware of everything around him while paying no particular attention to any one thing.

He waited.

Footsteps sounded outside the room. *Ubax aragti* sharpened his hearing enough to discern it. More than one pair. More than two. Five . . . ten, perhaps. A gathering. Had Erris summoned all her allies to aid his torture, or perhaps to witness? He straightened, setting his feet and facing the door.

It opened. Erris came in first, with Marquand at her flank. Sarine followed behind, and Tigai and Yuli. They were speaking, though their voices had been muted in the chambers beyond, muted even past what his herb-enhanced senses could hear. He heard them now, addressing the others with them: a man in white and red and gold, matching what Sarine wore. Another in a red robe, another in black, another in yellow-gold, and one more in white.

"We aren't finished," Erris was saying. "We need more time with him, to be certain it's safe."

The man in white and red and gold went to the swirling haze of *Shelter* cordoning off the left side of the chamber. He ignored Omera, sweeping a gaze across him before turning his attention to the barrier.

His blood-self stirred. A scent had entered the room. The scent of the man studying the *Shelter* wall. The scent of power. Terrible, terrible power. The blood-self was afraid. Deathly afraid. It recoiled from the *Shelter* where the man in yellow and red and gold stared at it, as though he could see through its haze, as though his eyes were on the blood-self's body, piercing through to its soul.

"Is he hearing me?" Erris demanded. "We've made progress, but we need more time."

"What did you do here?" Sarine asked, her eyes fixated on the blood- and soot-stains on the chamber floor.

"Omera," the man in yellow and red and gold said.

His name.

It filled the room as the man said it, finally turning his attention from the *Shelter* haze to him, standing firm, as a prince should, facing the newcomers to his chamber.

He knew that voice. He knew those eyes. The man was younger, all trace of wrinkles and age somehow shed. But he knew the man. The God. The Regnant.

He resisted the urge to bow, to kneel, or to cower. The last time he'd faced those eyes his memories had been invaded, purged, destroyed.

"Regnant," he said, keeping his voice pure and strong. "I came to offer you my sword."

"This is foolish," Erris said. "Neither of you are immortal. Keep your distance until we're finished with him."

The Regnant ignored her. He stepped away from the *Shelter*, toward where Omera stood.

"Prince Omera," the Regnant said. "Nine thousand, four hundred and nineteenth son of Queen Amanishiakne of the Bhakal." Their eyes met as he spoke. His words seemed to fill the air. His gaze seemed to penetrate into Omera's soul. He had nothing to hide. He'd come here to risk everything for his people. This was death, come for him. He would meet it.

The Regnant took another step toward him.

"Can you tell him?" Erris asked Sarine. "This is bloody foolish. We gave the prisoner his herbs, to test what he would do. Neither of you should be anywhere near him."

The blood-self howled.

It pushed its back against the *Shelter*, as far from the Regnant as it could move.

Death saw it. Saw to its core. Saw what it was. Saw who it served. It had to hide. It had to escape. It had to return to its masters.

The Regnant broke their mutual stare, and whirled to face the others.

"He tells the truth," the Regnant said. "He came here to betray the Blood. We have a chance. Now. Before they notice his betrayal, and sever their bond."

"Now?" Sarine said. "How long do we have?"

"If his concentration slips, and his blood-mirror is allowed to return to their fold alone, they will sever him at once," the Regnant said. "I said now. I meant it."

"But we need time to plan," Sarine said. "Time for Erris to work out the details of our attack, to coordinate my champions with yours. We can't go now. Can we?"

She said the last to Erris, who shook her head slowly.

"Sometimes the enemy's back is exposed," Erris said. "When the moment is on you, you don't waste time questioning whether you're ready for it. You either strike, or retreat."

Sarine swept a look across the room, weighing her people—Erris, Marquand, Yuli, Tigai—and the newcomers, the four *magi* dressed in their colored robes and garments, and finally the Regnant himself.

"Then we strike," Sarine said. "Can he take us all?"

The Regnant turned to him.

"He can," the Regnant said. "Though he doesn't know he can. His blood-mirror can do it, if his will is strong enough."

The words ignited pain in his blood-self, writhing and scrambling to get as far from the Regnant as it could.

"What is it you want me to do?" he asked.

"Drop your *Shelter* walls on my command," the Regnant said to Erris and Marquand. "Let his mirror free." He turned to Omera. "You must control it. Subdue its will. Then give it what it wants: Let it return to its master. Let it return to the Seat, and the Soul of the World. I can attach the rest of us before it moves. Can you do it?"

Trust was fleeting. Last time he faced those eyes, they'd scourged his mind. He'd come here seeking allies against the Blood, against the others in control of the Soul. Now they were here, facing him. If he was wrong, if he'd chosen the wrong side again, it could mean his people's ruin. But now he was himself. His mother's son. He had to do as she would have done.

"I can," he said. Suddenly the blood-self's movement stilled. It froze, awaiting his will to move again. "Give the order, set it free, and I can do it."

The Regnant nodded.

Erris looked to Sarine first, who made the same gesture.

The *Shelter* vanished, and his blood-self lurched to try and escape.

He held it in place.

He projected his will outward, the same as he'd done to leave the Soul, to hunt down Sakhefete, to find this tomb. The blood-self delved into the veins of what the world was, then moved beyond. Its master was elsewhere now. Somewhere close to the source of the world's blood, close to its pulsing, beating heart.

He released it, and suddenly another will covered them all. Sarine. The Regnant. Erris. Marquand. Yuli. Tigai. The *magi* in red. The *magi* in black. The *magi* in yellow. The *magi* in white.

Space folded, and they moved.

90

TIGAI

The Fields of Broken Glass
The Gods' Seat

Dust crunched under his foot. He was no stranger to suddenly appearing somewhere else, but if it had been his tether that took them here, he might have sent them back at once.

"Wait," Sarine said to all of them. "No one move."

They stood together atop a broken nightmare of metal and glass. The landscape stretched in all directions, marred by misshapen chaos everywhere he looked. Twisted towers of iron erupted through shattered glass, while the ground seemed to be leaking fluids everywhere: flashing, colored water, or thick, viscous blood running between the hulks of metal in miniature rivers and streams. They were supposed to be in the Gods' Seat, but this was the third time he'd visited it and it looked nothing like the other two. Two orbs hung in the sky overhead, one blazing fire and one cold and gray. But other than the broken glass and flashing lights in the water, the place seemed to have been transformed into a sculpture of death or some other macabre art. Only the spire on the horizon was familiar, sending a pillar of white light up into the sky.

"There," Sarine said. "I've shrouded everyone with *Faith*. It will hold on its own, until you start pairing it with other magicks, so delay using them as long as you can."

"Do they know we're here?" Erris said, speaking as quietly as Sarine had, but still enough to carry through the group.

"They might," the Regnant said. "Be ready."

Erris nodded, then quickly pointed between them. "Three teams," she said. "You, in black, you're a Dragon?"

The *magi* she'd indicated nodded. They hadn't even had time to get the newcomers' names. All four looked like Jun monks, more than a touch wide-eyed, not that he could blame them. They'd survived a cataclysm that wrecked cities and countryside, then had their God show up, call them chosen, and whisk them away to fight to save the bloody world. If it were him, he'd have tethered away as soon as the Regnant's back was turned.

"You're with me," Erris said. "Marquand, me, our Dragon, and Omera." The names she'd spoken shuffled toward her. "Next team. Tigai. Yuli. Yellow—a Heron?" The *magi*, a woman barely more than a girl, nodded and bowed as she confirmed it. "And red—Mantis?" Another woman, this one much older, with iron in her hair and lines around her eyes and mouth, nodded and bowed precisely as the Heron had. "Good. That's two teams of four. And finally: Sarine, the Regnant, and the one in white, a Crane to keep you both safe from close attack. That's as balanced as I can come up with on short notice."

A wrenching noise sounded in the distance, drawing all their eyes toward it. Glass crunched and cracked as a fresh spire of metal punctured the ground, sending distorted ripples of color and sparks into the sky. For a moment they hung on the sound of twisting metal. But nothing more came, and Erris continued her whispers.

"Each team has at least one defensive presence, one close attacker, and one ranged, with a Dragon-*magi* to move them from place to place. No time for more than simple orders, but if we keep together and stay aware of our enemies, we can get this done."

He weighed the two newcomers Erris had assigned to him and Yuli, blinking to memorize their patterns on the strands. The Yellow looked frightened out of her bloody mind, eyeing him as though he were a creature from her nightmares. The Red was stoic, calm, and collected. He made a note to rely on her, if it came to it, over the Yellow. Bloody strange to be fighting alongside a Heron and Mantis now, when they'd been the enemy last time.

"Tigai's group will strike in the open, to draw them out," Erris said. "Run if you have to, stay mobile, and stay together. They know the strategy we used last time, and they'll be expecting an attack in force inside the spire. My group will feint that attack, then retreat to meet up with Tigai. We'll hold them outside the spire while Sarine sneaks in with her *Faith*. Once she's reached the Soul, we redeploy via the Dragons' strands to defend the central chamber inside the spire until she and the Regnant can regain control. Any questions?"

"How does this *Faith* work?" he asked. "Sarine said we're invisible, but I can see the rest of you just fine."

"You'll be able to see each other," Sarine said. "And it will last until you start tethering other types of magicks."

"But if I can see everyone else, how will I know when the shroud is gone?" he asked.

"You won't be able to see the others if you break the shroud," Sarine said. "I know it's not the best indicator. Don't rely on it more than you have to."

"We'll roam around to set some anchors first, then," he said. "Wait for us to start sending up fireworks before you provoke them inside the spire."

"Last time you said there were anchors already set here," Erris said. "Has that changed?"

"That was my doing," the Regnant said. "This place's new masters will have erased them."

"My team is ready, then," he said. Yuli hadn't yet transformed, but he saw echoes of the Twin Fangs in the tattoos on her face. She was ready. She was always ready, for anything. Wind spirits but if he'd known her in his pirating days they would have conquered half the bloody Empire by now.

"And mine," Erris said. "Sarine?"

She looked toward the Regnant, both of them wearing looks more suited to a funeral than the cusp of a battle.

"We know what we need to do," Sarine said finally. "But I don't like the rest of you putting yourselves in so much danger. You know what Kalira, Orana, and the others are capable of. Don't take them lightly."

"You take care of yourself, too, sister," Yuli said. "I expect you to be first maid at my wedding when this is finished."

"Move out, then," Erris said. "Exarch bless all of us today. Stay sharp, and stay alive."

———

He scrambled over top of what appeared to be a pile of slagged iron. It gave a vantage to see out over the rest of the plain, though if there was anyone hiding they were doing a bloody good job of it. The glass floor remained from the Regnant's time in control of the Seat, but it had been pierced and punctured by so many towers of metal he could hardly recognize the serenity of the glass and bioluminescent liquids that had been there before.

He blinked, hooking an anchor to the strands, satisfied with this place for a potential retreat. Light pulsed on the starfield, a miniature map of where they'd traversed the field so far. A few other anchors had appeared elsewhere, closer to the spire, the work of the Regnant's new Dragon, or of Sarine or the Regnant himself. So far there wasn't any sign they'd been noticed.

"That way for the next one," he said, pointing east toward the crimson light on the horizon. "Make them think we're going for the spire."

Yuli glared, or rather, the Twin Fangs did. She'd transformed as soon as they'd started walking, loping across the metal-twisted landscape as effortlessly as he might have strolled through an open field. She shot ahead at once, gliding down the iron hulk and leaping across a narrow stream of flashing water onto the next heap of metal, this one made of steel.

The Mantis found her own footing as they jumped the stream, and he extended a hand for the Heron, helping guide her across. Blood marred his legs and boots, and stained the hem of the Heron's robes, too, though the Mantis's deep crimson hid it better and Yuli's hairless skin seemed to be immune to any of it sticking to her. Blood ran everywhere here, as thick as the flashing, colored water.

"Careful," he said as the Heron scrambled up the side of the steel heap.

"Thank you," the Heron said.

"We can take a moment to rest, if you need it," he said. They'd already covered at least a few leagues, though it was hard to tell when the landscape appeared the same everywhere he looked that wasn't the spire.

"No, thank you," she said. "I can manage."

"Well, I could use a few moments to catch my breath," he said, gesturing toward the Mantis to hold position. Yuli would be aware of him without needing to think; if they held here, she would scout ahead and make sure the next stretch of the field was safe.

"Bloody strange place, isn't it?" he asked. "Last time I was here it was all glass; the time before, smooth stone. Now it looks as though someone hired an Ujibari decorator and shorted them for payment."

"Is it wise for us to be speaking?" the Heron said.

"If Yuli can't find any threats, there aren't any listening," he said. "And I never did get either of your names."

"I am called Peizhi," the Mantis said. "She is Song Xiu."

He nodded to both. "I'm Yanjin Tigai," he said. "Our companion is my bride-to-be, Yuli Twin Fangs. Were either of you here before?"

"Here?" the Heron, Song Xiu, said. "In this place?"

"I was," Peizhi said. "I survived, and the Great Lord chose me again. But we should keep moving. This is no time for rest."

"We will," he said. "You both know what to do in a fight?"

"Of course, Lord Yanjin," Peizhi said. "The Great Lord would not have chosen either of us, were we not prepared to do his will."

Song Xiu looked uneasy, as she had since first coming here.

"Stay close to me, and keep me safe," he said. "I'm not saying it out of arrogance. I'm our way out, if things get too hot. Make sure you know where I am at all times, and get to me first, if you hear me order us to move."

"If we need to keep you safe, I can shield you, with the Heron's gift," Song Xiu said.

"That's why Erris put you with us," he said. "Keep me alive, and I'll keep you alive. We're not even here to inflict damage on them; that will be up to Erris and Sarine. We're here to distract and pull their attention. So whatever you do—"

A twisting screech sounded from ahead.

He shot to his feet. Yuli had gone that direction.

A new spire pierced through the ground, rumbling and sending shards of glass and iron out of its way. Not two hundred paces off, though Yuli wasn't near it, thank the wind spirits. She stood atop what looked like a pile of misshapen brass and copper, watching it, the same as he was.

"This bloody place," he said. "Peizhi is right. We should keep moving."

They traversed the rest of their pile of steel, crossing another channel of flashing water to a heap of rusted iron. Jagged edges coated in blood threatened every step, as though the whole place had been made from discarded weapons, or from farm tools that had first been involved in some sort of savage accident. At least the glass and water that had announced their every step last time he'd been here had been broken and marred. Now the water flashed with bright colors almost every instant, running as it was between the hulks of metals.

When the spire was close, perhaps a quarter league away, though it was difficult to tell given the scale of a plane that seemed to go on infinitely in every other direction, he called another halt. An anchor here would serve as a perfect misdirection, suggesting they intended to assault the hulking stone of the only structure in sight. Shifting here might cause their enemies to scramble, to abandon an attack elsewhere if they correctly read his intent.

He blinked, setting another anchor in place.

Something on the starfield was wrong. Out of place.

He blinked again.

His last five anchors were there, shining beacons spread across the field of blood and twisted metal. But he'd set twice that many. His first anchors, the ones near where they'd come in, were gone.

"Well, fuck," he said.

"What is it, Lord Yanjin?" Song Xiu said.

He squinted, scanning back across the field, retracing their steps. The next anchor in sequence, if they were following in sequence, was there, the one he'd set at the base of a mountain of scrapped gold and silver.

"Yuli," he said. "There. Is there something I can't see?"

He pointed, and the Twin Fangs took up a place beside him, staring out across the field.

Suddenly she growled. Then just as quick, the Twin Fangs shifted into Yuli.

"Two of them," Yuli said. "Right where you pointed. One small, one larger. Can't see more at this distance."

"Shit on a plate," he said. "So much for setting anchors."

"I don't understand, Lord Yanjin," Peizhi said. "Our enemies are out there?"

"Oh yes," he said. "And 'one small, one larger' means Orana, or Kalira, perhaps, and a bodyguard...one of their champions, if I have to guess. Out there unmaking our work."

"They know we're here," Song Xiu said.

"A safe bet they do," he said. "But we're here to attract their notice anyway. So that's what we're going to do."

Yuli shifted back to the Twin Fangs without a word, letting loose a low, snarling growl as she took up a place beside him.

"Get ready," he said. "If what Sarine said is true, as soon as I tether us to the strands her shield of *Faith* or whatever it was is going to drop, and they'll know exactly where we are. Get your Heron-shields ready, and get some Mantis-fire ready to dump on their fucking heads."

"Ready, Lord Yanjin," Peizhi said, and Song Xiu nodded, her face suddenly paler than it had been before.

"All right," he said, preparing a tether for the next anchor, the one near the heap of scrapped silver and gold. "Let's go pick a fight with the bloody moon."

91

ERRIS

The Spire
The Gods' Seat

Four oversized leopards moved between them, their padded feet tapping the stone floor.

The hall was narrow, filled with so many bodies. She and Marquand pressed themselves against the left wall, while Omera, his blood-mirror, and Longzhu—their Dragon-*magi*—pressed themselves against the right. *Entropy* almost sizzled in her hand, with *Mind* and *Shelter* ready to answer her call. The leopards tracked between them in a line, lazily trotting one after the other. None of the beasts gave any sign they'd noticed the would-be predators lining the walls. They trundled forward until they turned a corner, out of sight.

She held up a hand, with all five fingers extended. A gesture to hold. To wait.

The leopards' master would be coming.

They heard his footsteps in the hall. Wata'si'tin. He'd survived the first battle at the Gods' Seat, along with his leopards—his *guarajin*, if she recalled the name correctly. Those beasts should have scented the four of them two leagues away. Evidently Sarine's *Faith* was bloody good for concealment, from noses as well as eyes. Imagining what she might have done, had the girl revealed that talent while she was in place to order scouts or raiders to pair with her in the field...but she had to focus now. Their prey was coming around the corner. He stepped lightly, as relaxed and careless as his leopards, with their bearing reflected in his step. He moved like a cat, graceful and aloof. A champion of the Flesh.

She waited until he passed. He gave no sign he noticed any of them.

Entropy snapped into place in front of her. Light flashed, and flame.

Suddenly the air filled with the smell of charred skin. Wata'si'tin hadn't flinched, hadn't jumped or dodged or moved. He crumpled forward, a singed husk of a man, his blackened skull and spine protruding where the back of him had been burned away. He crunched with flakes of ash as he fell forward, leaking blood from charred red and black skin onto the stone floor.

She slammed a *Shelter* wall between them and the leopards.

Immediately howling growls sounded, and rushing claws.

"Move," she said, pointing up the hallway, the direction Wata'si'tin had come from. Suddenly she was alone; with her shroud of *Faith* gone, she couldn't see or hear the others. But the *guarajin* were screeching, throwing themselves against her *Shelter*, filling the halls with their yowling and crashing thuds.

She turned a corner into an empty room, decorated wall to wall with scrolls and books.

"Hold here," she said quietly. "More will come to check on the noise. We strike when they do. Is there still activity outside the spire?"

Longzhu, the black-robed Dragon-*magi* replied, though he was still invisible to her eyes. "Yes," he said in a crisp tone, as quietly as she had. "Another Dragon using the strands."

"Good," she said. "We'll join Tigai soon enough, once we've made our mark here. Everyone stand ready. If what Sarine said is true, you'll all still be hidden. They'll only be able to see me."

It was more than a little unnerving, deploying alone when she knew the others were there, around her, still unseen. Marquand would watch her back, if Omera or his blood-mirror thought to exact revenge for what she'd done to him in the tomb. She'd assigned the Bhakal prince to her group precisely because she didn't trust him. But she'd intended to keep him in front of her, not leave him cloaked in *Faith* while she was exposed. At least he'd reveal himself if he attacked. And she'd placed her life in Marquand's hands too many times to worry over it now.

The *guarajin*'s howls continued, echoing through the halls. Her *Shelter* still held, though it would fold soon, given the thuds and crashes accompanying the leopards' grief.

More footsteps echoed down the hall. Her heart thumped in her chest. No way of knowing what they faced until it was on them.

A figure emerged around the corner.

Entropy slammed into place.

The figure glanced sideways, only a glance, enough to reveal her standing, uncloaked by Sarine's *Faith*, in the center of the room.

Fire from her leyline tethers erupted out of the doorframe and into the hall. The newcomer should have been incinerated, reduced to bones and ash, as Wata'si'tin had been. But in the split second between when the figure had come around the corner and when she'd loosed her *Entropy*, she saw who— and what—it was.

She Who Howls with Hunters. A Nikkon Spirit-Weaver.

In the instant before her *Entropy* cooked everything in the hallway alive, the Nikkon woman shifted her body, her skin turning ghostly and ethereal, shrouded in mist. The fires washed over her without touching or burning even the smallest hair on her limbs or head. A bare moment was her only warning of what would follow.

She dove to the side as a white wolf crashed into the room.

The wolf shimmered with ethereal mist, the same shrouded covering as She Who Howls with Hunters. It shone pure white, its fur made of shining light, though it was limned in shadow, with a dark, black outline around the edges of its otherwise shimmering white form. It was five times the size of an ordinary wolf, almost too large to fit in the confines of the hall.

Shelter sprang up between her and the ghost wolf as it pivoted, snapping and crunching its massive jaws against her shield. A burst of energy and noise erupted as it ripped a hole in the *Shelter*, smoke pouring from its muzzle as it wrenched and bored a way through.

Then suddenly the wolf whined and growled, both at once, snapping its jaws back as it withdrew from the hole and spun to face the room.

Omera. The Bhakal prince had appeared, attacking from its flank, throwing off his cloak of *Faith*, as she had. Marquand and Longzhu had orders to keep theirs running as long as they could.

She let her *Shelter* dissipate, weaving *Body* into both herself and her saber. The wolf spun, facing down both Omera and his blood-copy as they darted their curved swords in and out of range of its claws. It snapped its jaws at the blood-copy, and the blood shifted back, keeping its blade between them as it tried to find room to retreat. Omera danced around it and struck, just as she did, both their swords cutting across the shadow-outline to plunge into the wolf's hide of light.

It howled, then vanished.

She immediately raced for the door.

Sure enough, She Who Howls with Hunters had shifted out of her ethereal state, now running at full speed down the hall.

She prepared another blast of *Entropy*, loosing billowing flame down the cold stone.

Once again, the Nikkon woman went ethereal just as the blast of heat and fire reached her. Once again, the wolf appeared, midcharge as it sprang toward her.

She tethered *Mind*, six copies of her suddenly rushing toward the wolf.

It snapped and struck, jaws wrenching back and forth into nothing as one of her copies dissipated to harmless light. Her true-self blasted the wolf with fire.

The creature gave a piteous whine as she cooked its backside. It vanished before it could die.

"So, you found a way to return," She Who Howls with Hunters said. "I accept my fate, even if you have defied yours."

Omera only now emerged into the hall, both he and his blood-copy surveying the now-scorched stone.

She let loose a final blast of *Entropy*, and She Who Howls with Hunters died, crumpling forward into a pile of ash and bloody, singed meat.

"Follow me," she said to the others. They had to get close to the central chamber, where the light of the Soul burned. Two champions dead was a beginning, but they needed to draw out as much strength as they could, if their feint was to be a success. Gods only knew what Tigai was facing down outside the spire.

She and Omera spread, covering both sides of the hall while Marquand and Longzhu would be following behind.

The layout of the hallways here had changed, with new passages where she'd expected none. But the core tunnels remained the same, or at least so she hoped. They spiraled inward, ignoring the chambers attached to the hall, and the forks leading off into new parts of the spire. A good sign, that the only enemies they'd encountered here had been champions she knew from their time together at the Tarzali farm. There weren't more than a dozen survivors of the first attack, and while it was possible Kalira, the Blood, and the rest had brought in scores more of their *magi* and allies, Omera was living proof that that sort of trust bred weakness. More champions meant exposing themselves to more potential betrayals. If luck was on their side, there would be no more than a handful of enemies here, and two were already dead.

She hadn't intended for them to reach the central chamber itself, only to be seen close to it, threatening it. Perhaps she'd blundered. If Sarine and the Regnant had been here instead of her feinted attack, they might have reached it in the first push of surprise. She'd meant to use the feint to divide their enemies, but perhaps they hadn't been as ready as she would have been. They reached the last spiraling, curved passage, winding their way inward toward the Soul.

The last hall was empty. Until Kalira stepped out of the central chamber.

The Sun Goddess appeared exactly as she had before: a tiny, red-haired girl no more than seven or eight years old, her pale white skin covered in freckles. Kalira's eyes shone with recognition as she stared across the gap between them. Fifty paces. Fifty paces between them and the room that housed the Soul.

She slammed a barrier of *Shelter* between them, and shouted a warning as she dove aside.

Sunlight blasted into her wall.

A burning spot appeared where Kalira's energy struck, and for a moment the whole *Shelter* wall went pink, then white, and then it shattered, sending pieces of leyline energy flying like shards of glass.

"What is she doing here?" Kalira shouted as her sunlight carved its way across the hall. "Erris d'Arrent? Bound to the Blood?"

Omera had followed her lead, diving into a side chamber, but Kalira seemed to be addressing him. Perhaps it could give her an opening, but Kalira's attacks continued unabated, her beams of light slicing across the open air.

Damn it all. She had no way of knowing where Longzhu was, or Marquand. They needed to reach Omera and get out. Facing Kalira alone was never in her plan.

"The Blood has betrayed you," Omera called back. "We mean to take what is rightfully ours."

"No," Kalira said. "That can't be true." But her beams ceased for a moment.

A thundering blast sounded in the hall. For a moment Kalira was engulfed in smoke and fire. It should have been enough to melt her where she stood, the same as the *Entropy* loosed on Wata'si'tin and She Who Howls with Hunters. Instead the Sun Goddess's body was surrounded by pulsing light, shimmering like the sun at high noon.

Marquand stood in front of her. The bloody, fucking idiot. He'd used his cloak of *Faith* and dodged the sunbeams Kalira had used to scorch the whole hallway, getting close enough to unleash *Entropy* at point-blank range.

"Run, you damned fool!" she shouted at the same moment he must have realized his *Entropy* had done nothing more than test her defenses.

She charged into the hallway, and two *Shelter* barriers at once slammed into place between Marquand and Kalira, hers and his. Only one chance. She had to trust Longzhu not to have turned and run the moment those sunbeams started flying.

She ran toward Marquand, vectoring toward the side hall where Omera and his blood-copy had taken refuge. Sunlight pierced through both her and Marquand's *Shelter* walls as though both had been made of candlewax, dripping and melting as Kalira's beams cut and seared through the rest of the hall.

She jammed a third *Shelter* wall into place as the first two went pink and exploded, sending fragments of the leylines ricocheting against the stone. Marquand reached her, ducking around the corner where Omera and his blood-copy huddled against the walls. She couldn't see Longzhu. He had to be there, too, or all three of them were dead. She had to believe *Faith* wouldn't continue to hide a corpse, if he'd been taken by one of those sunbeams.

"Liars!" Kalira shouted. "Petty fools, loyal to a dead woman and a dead cause. And now you die, as she did."

"Get us out of here!" she yelled over Kalira's renewed attack. A second wave of sunbeams cut into her last line of *Shelter*, warping and twisting it from pale blue to white and pink.

The world shifted around her.

92

YULI

Atop the Metal Hulks
The Gods' Seat

Whistling noise came from overhead. The Twin Fangs kept its senses focused, but the whistling droned in its ears, growing louder with every step. The figure in front of it blurred, engulfed in shadows as it danced atop the twisted metal, moving almost too fast to be seen. It had time. But it had to move quickly.

The Twin Fangs leapt across a stream of blood, cutting off the shadow-dancer before she could threaten a move toward the Heron-shield that cloaked Tigai. It couldn't reach Tigai before the whistling stopped. But so long as the Twin Fangs kept the shadow-dancer's knives at bay, it could survive after Tigai warped the Mantis, the Heron, and himself away on the strands. He would know the Twin Fangs could look after itself. He wouldn't be stupid enough to wait.

It leapt again, this time setting itself in the shadow-dancer's path.

The girl grunted in frustration. Yuli had watched her and her sister making eyes at Tigai. Now satisfaction poured over them both, Yuli and the Twin Fangs, at their ability to match the dancer's moves. The girl, Allakawari, wasn't used to encountering anything that could keep up with her steps.

Both daggers flashed. A high stroke. The Twin Fangs swatted them away, roaring and snarling as it flicked its claws in a blistering sequence of attacks. Allakawari spun and parried, shadows whirling and smoking as steel clanged against claw. The girl set her feet as if to spring away, and the Twin Fangs matched, kicking where the girl meant to put her weight, forcing a shift into an off-balance stance. They tangled together, a second too long. An instant too late. Panic flooded the girl's eyes. The Twin Fangs could die here. It would be a good death, a worthy sacrifice to take down a worthy enemy.

But Yuli didn't want to die.

They separated, and the whistling was almost deafening now. It bounded backward, arching its back to spring off a shard of twisted steel and push to get away. It kept enough of its senses focused on the shadow-dancer to watch her move just as fast in the opposite direction. Away from Tigai. Good.

The whistling stopped as Orana's meteors crashed into the ground.

A rippling shock wave erupted from the glass and metal. Stone, iron, glass, water, blood all flew together into the air. Heat and fire from the friction exploded outward, and the Twin Fangs felt the blast wave waft over its body, searing its skin as it raced away.

The meteors pounded into the ground, one after another, sending more metal and fire up in a cloud of smoke and dust. The Twin Fangs kept moving, already clear of the explosions. The closest anchor was five hundred paces off, atop a hulk of platinum and silver. But it saw no sign of Tigai there. It kept scanning as it raced away from the meteor shards. No sign. He must have taken a tether on the opposite side of the impact. But that would put Allakawari closer. He wouldn't be so foolish...

Except he was. A new Heron-shield shimmered into place where the fourth anchor had been set, across the now-smoking field of ruin between them.

It would take the shadow-dancer a few extra moments to locate them and begin moving. It had to. But the Twin Fangs could spare no time for misdirection. It ran toward the shield.

A full-strength Heron-shield might repel the shadow-dancer's knives for a few moments. The girl, Song Xiu, was far from the strongest Heron either Yuli or the Twin Fangs had seen. But it had to be enough.

It leapt through the now-settling debris, doubling back on its path. Heat and fire wafted from the meteors' impacts, smoke and dust billowing through the air. Yuli might have choked and coughed; the Twin Fangs only ran. It lost sight of the shadow-dancer in the smoke. But it knew the path Allakawari would take: the straightest, most direct route to her prey.

Other figures decorated the field now. Spectral bears raced toward the Heron-shield, kept at bay by the popping gouts of flame from the Mantis's gift. Other human-sized shapes moved toward them, their gifts not yet manifest. Larger silhouettes moved in the distance. Orana was out there somewhere, calling down her meteors, if she hadn't obliterated herself in the first strike. The Twin Fangs kept its senses focused on the assassin. All that mattered was keeping Tigai alive. The rest came second.

Without warning, Tigai and the Heron-shield warped away again.

Allakawari stood on top of where they'd been, a bare moment before.

Her daggers were red.

Tigai's blood.

The Twin Fangs howled.

It slammed into her, ripping and slashing its claws in a flurry. Their bodies crashed together, careening down the side of an iron hulk, the metal tearing into its side where its skin caught on a jagged edge. Shadows flared around them, cloaking Allakawari's movements. A hand darted left, cutting with one of her daggers, and her body twisted, leaving only shadow behind. The Twin Fangs sank one of its teeth into what should have been her shoulder, and tasted only darkness. Its claws raked against her right-hand dagger's blade, shifting and parrying as quick as either of them could move.

Blood drenched them both as they rolled down into a stream, splashing as the shadows flooded between them. Suddenly Allakawari was on her feet, scanning the field. The Twin Fangs snapped and lunged, but the girl danced away.

A sword clanged against her knives. A sword made of blood.

The Twin Fangs was on its feet, bounding after her. But another figure was there. Two figures.

Omera. And his blood-copy. Both locking their swords with Allakawari's daggers. The shadow-dancer knelt between them, turning both blades at once with either of her knives. The Twin Fangs snarled and leapt into her. A claw tore into her back, below her left shoulder blade, and the girl screamed.

Blood and shadow leaked from the wound, but Allakawari darted forward, rolling between Omera and his blood-copy as both prepared to lunge toward where she had been a moment before.

The shadows flickered, and the girl raced away.

Yuli coughed, clutching at her side. The Twin Fangs had suffered the wound from the scraping iron, but it cut her body just as deep.

Omera and his blood-copy both looked startled, whirling around as though he could track the shadow-dancer's escape. Erris d'Arrent and Colonel Marquand had already erected *Shelter* walls around them, while the black-robed Dragon-*magi* stood behind.

"Tigai was here, was he not?" Erris called to her.

"He was, a moment ago," she replied. Her transformation seemed to have caught the Sarresanters off-guard, but they recovered quickly. "Did everything go smoothly in the spire?"

"As smooth as it needed to," Erris said. "It looks like we have their attention."

"Tigai is there, across the field," she said, pointing to the anchor beside the platinum and silver where he should have gone the first time. "Take us there and we can regroup."

Erris shook her head. "No need," Erris said. "He has his orders and he knows what to do. We need to be spread out for now."

"I'm gone, then," she said. "I need to be by his side."

Erris nodded. "Go," she said.

The Twin Fangs resumed control. Her body shifted as easily as breathing, with the benefit of Sarine's bond.

Allakawari had retreated in the other direction. Its claws had wounded the girl, but she would return to the hunt soon enough. It scanned the field, searching for threats around the shimmering Heron-shield. None so far. But more would come.

It ran toward Tigai, loping across the metal hulks, leaving Erris and her people behind.

93

SARINE

Approaching the Soul of the World
The Spire, the Gods' Seat

The spire was empty and cold. It hadn't felt like this before. Even when the Regnant had control, the place had been full of life, a sensation in the air, something she hadn't noticed until it was gone. She should have been able to sense comfort, safety, familiarity, and something had intruded to spoil it all, as though she'd entered her uncle's church to find vandals come to break the windows and steal the cookware.

Faith held around her, Li, and their Crane, a young woman named Katsuri. The other eight had thrown off their shrouds, somewhere out across the fields. It had to mean they were fighting in earnest, following through on Erris's plan to draw attention away from the spire.

Katsuri had gone ahead, and returned to wave them forward down the next hall.

She and Li stepped together, both still wearing their red and white and gold Emperor's and Empress's garb. Hard to trust him, even now, even with the kernel of the Veil's memories settling like sand at the bottom of a stream. Today they fought together. But she had to hope there would be no fighting until they reached the Soul.

They rounded the corner and saw death.

One of the Rabaquim Flesh champions, Wata'si'tin. His back had been burned away, leaving the front of his face pristine, frozen in surprise. His corpse lay twisted in the middle of the hall. Katsuri stepped around it, trotting lightly on her feet, her two-handed Nikkon blade held to point where she meant to go.

Another bloody corpse greeted them as they rounded the next hallway, this one too badly burnt to tell who it had been.

She stepped gingerly over the bodies, avoiding the blood and charred ash that had been their skin. Even in passing them by, the dead still weighed on her shoulders.

Katsuri jerked her sword to the side, huddling against the wall.

She followed by instinct; Li did the same. Both pressed themselves against the side of the hall as footsteps sounded, coming this way.

"No," a voice sounded, muddled before it came around the corner. "I won't. You're not injured enough to have brought you here in the first place."

The voice was small and high-pitched. A girl's. Kalira's. The sound caught in her blood.

"Great Lady," another voice said. "You will know best, of course. But I haven't been able to match the two-fanged thing without your blessing."

The speakers came around the corner ahead of them. Kalira. The Sun, housed in the body of an eight-year-old girl. The hand that had flashed and killed her. One of the Tarzali was at her side, the assassin; Allakawari, who clutched her shoulder where blood and shadow seeped out between her fingers. A third figure strolled behind them: a Nikkon woman, leader of their Spirit-Weavers, She Who Gazes into the Deepest Seas.

"You'll get back out there, find their Dragons and kill them," Kalira said. "Leave us to our business. You get a new body when you've sustained a mortal injury and not before. Am I clear?"

Allakawari bowed and hurried away, all in the same fluid motion. It took her past where Katsuri, she, and Li huddled against the wall.

Li met her eyes as Kalira and She Who Gazes into the Deepest Seas approached. It would be so simple. A strike from the cover of *Faith*'s shroud: *Red*, *Body*, the Nine Tails' gift paired with *valak'ar* and *mareh'et*. She could attack before Kalira knew she was there. They were close, so close. And if she failed, the advantage of surprise would be gone. The new Gods' defenses would rally around the Soul. They might never reach it, and certainly not without drenching themselves in blood.

She let Kalira and She Who Gazes into the Deepest Seas continue on past them.

"The Blood have betrayed us," Kalira was saying. "It's the only way the Veil's former champions could be here. The Rabaquim must have thought it could use them to surprise us. But we're ready. Gather your people here before—"

The words faded as Kalira and She Who Gazes into the Deepest Seas rounded the corner, heading deeper into the spire.

She and Li both exhaled at once.

Katsuri bowed her head sharply, then raised her sword and continued on.

No more bodies greeted them as they followed the twisting passages. She hadn't expected *Faith* to make their approach so swift. There would be defenses near the light of the Soul, but with Kalira and She Who Gazes into the Deepest Seas heading elsewhere in the compound, they might be able to reach it without being noticed.

The ground lurched midthought.

Shelter came to hand, and she felt Anati readying their *White*. The rumbling grew.

"Go," Li said quietly. "Swiftly."

They ran toward the central chamber. A quick turn, down a hallway scorched and marked by black streaks. No more blood, or bodies. But a battle had taken place here. The spire shook harder, sharper, the earth quaking beneath their feet as they ran.

The sound and shaking grew with every step. Had Kalira somehow detected them? She'd given no sign, when they passed in the halls.

"Together!" Li shouted. "Around me, now!"

She almost ran into him as he stopped mid-stride. A shimmering bubble of Force appeared around them, and Li turned his back. Katsuri pressed her sword close against her body, tucking herself against him.

Then the spire exploded.

She felt herself lifted from her feet, as though the ground itself had rejected her, somehow pushed her away. Stone and fire erupted around them, washing over the Force-bubble, rippling against its surface as the three of them were thrown, together, away from the burning light of the Soul of the World. She couldn't see anything but the light through the chaos. Li's bubble shimmered, and they were surrounded by smoke, fire, flying rubble, a violent burst of energy that should have incinerated them. Sound rushed in her ears, and the smell of molten rock, like a blacksmith's foundry, full of sulfur and slagged iron.

They hit the ground in a violent crash, the edge of Li's bubble humming with heat and steam. Rocks pounded the ground around them, peppering and pelting the earth in hisses of molten earth and smoke.

The light of the Soul was still there, burning white, reaching into the sky. But the rest of the spire was gone.

A smoking crater stood where it had been. They'd been inside it. They should have been reduced to rubble and ash along with the rest of the stone. The shock of it washed over her eyes. She should be dead again. A towering column of smoke rose over where the spire had stood, engulfing the sky in a billowing cloud. Rocks continued to fly away from the explosion, raining down overhead, shimmering against Li's shield where they struck his dome of Force. Whoever had been inside it had to be dead. But no. Two massive figures moved in silhouette against the smoke.

A giant serpent rose, coiling around and through the haze, its scales a deep azure blue like the darkest part of the sea. It lashed out in a spinning dive, striking into a second serpent, this one a rich crimson red, the color of blood. Both serpents wrapped and entangled each other, darting into the smoke as they fought. And between them, columns of pure sunlight exploded, arcing beams cutting through the ruins in dazzling bursts of color and fire.

Kalira. She Who Gazes into the Deepest Seas. And the Rabaquim Blood Gods.

She scanned across the field for sign of Erris's or Tigai's teams, finding nothing more than the wreckage of the spire. Silhouettes and bursts of energy shone through its haze, but without apparent source.

"They've turned on each other," Li said. "We can use this. We can reach the Soul now."

"No," she said. "Look."

The sunlight bursts were moving, falling back away from the blue and red serpents, toward the burning column of the Soul.

"Kalira is going to try and claim it for herself," she said. "Or at least to defend it from whatever's going on out there."

Li grimaced. An unusual expression on his normally stoic face.

The two serpents were rising up, becoming clearer as the smoke spread out above the ruin. Both towered over the field, biting and snapping at each other in lightning-quick strikes, too fast for creatures of such size. But she was right. Kalira was striking from farther back each time, moving in the direction of the column of light where the spire had been.

"You have to go," Li said. "*Faith* can shroud you as you approach. I can draw them away, at least to distract her long enough for you to reach the Soul." He said it with hesitation, his eyes lingering on the column of light.

"All right," she said. Her head had cleared enough to see the way. The world still spun, but her purpose shone through. This was her place. For once, her path was clear.

"Can I trust you?" Li said.

The question struck like another wave of rocks. In a way, it was good to know that distrust still ran between them.

"You gave me enough of her memories," she said. "I know the price of magic in the world. And I know we can't leave Kalira, or any of them, in control of what you and Evelynn built. I may not like it, but I'll do the right thing."

He held on to her, studying her face.

"Go, then," he said. "Reclaim the Soul. I'll keep them away."

He closed his eyes, then vanished, snapping away through the starfield and the strands, leaving her and Katsuri alone amid the rubble and ruin.

94

OMERA

Standing in Two Worlds | The Gods' Seat
Standing in Two Worlds | The Realm of Blood

His vision fractured as he took a step. In one world he planted his feet, raising his *shotel* blade to ward off the *gahaman*'s claws. He and his blood-self stood amid a pack of the creatures, massive bearlike ghosts conjured by one of the Rabaquim Flesh champions, spinning and dancing between them while Erris, Marquand, and Longzhu attacked from the flanks.

But his step carried him elsewhere, too.

A place of red. A sea of running blood and viscera. A thousand other faces stood around him, all gazing upward at the serpent hovering in the blood-red sky.

In the physical world he wove between a pair of rushing *gahaman*, whipping his blade in a frenzy that sent one of the beasts rearing on its hind legs while the other drew too close, its ghostly flesh hissing as the poison on his blade sliced it along its torso. Fire erupted nearby, *Entropy* bursts from Erris or Marquand. He kept moving, aware of his blood-self mirroring his attacks, spinning and dodging away from the *gahaman*'s claws. And the rest of him, the part of him suddenly shifted against his will into the presence of the Blood, stared upward, enraptured, listening.

MY CHILDREN. WE ARE BETRAYED.

The voice thundered through him. Others standing near him shuddered in ecstasy. The words rattled in his head. Betrayal. The Blood had sensed what he'd done. It knew he'd opened the way to the Gods' Seat. It meant to kill him. It meant to call the others to—

A *gahaman* roared, and he slashed his *shotel* into its foreclaws, severing one at the paw and rolling with the momentum of the beast's attack. *Ubax aragti* sang in his veins, giving him the speed to duck as another *gahaman* struck from behind. The two bears crashed together and he rolled aside.

ANSWER MY CALL. RETURN TO THE SEAT OF GODS. WE FIGHT. WE FIGHT HERE NOW.

The winged blood-serpent writhed as it spoke, moving languidly through the air as though it were swimming in water. It swiveled its gaze to each of the thousand blood-figures in attendance, one at a time, though the gesture took no more than a fraction of a moment.

Erris had conjured a *Shelter* wall nearby; he ran for it, with two *gahaman* close on his heels. They snapped and followed, running headlong into the Sarresant Empress's trap.

He dove, and rolled, and *Entropy* exploded behind him.

He quaked under the feathered serpent's eyes.

He stood frozen in fear. The Blood knew. It had to know what he'd done. The serpent's gaze lingered on him, longer than it had on any of the others. It saw into him. His blood-self longed to betray him, longed to report to its master. But he held it back, even so close to the serpent's form, burning the herbs in his blood to give him strength, here and in the physical world. He was its master. Whatever lies the Blood had told him, whatever gifts it had given him in return for his false loyalty, he was himself again. His mother's son. He wouldn't break under the serpent's gaze.

The serpent cocked its head, the smallest gesture of curiosity. It knew. It would cry out any moment, and alert the others.

Instead it broke away.

KALIRA HAS BETRAYED US. RETURN, MY CHILDREN. KILL HER. WE TAKE THE SOUL OF THE WORLD FOR OURSELVES.

His presence on the blood-plane shattered like glass.

Suddenly he was one man, standing in one place: on the fields of glass and iron, behind Erris d'Arrent's *Shelter* shield, standing next to her as she hurled sheets of exploding fire. His blood-self ached to follow the feathered serpent's command: to find the Sun Goddess and kill her and claim the light that should have been theirs alone from the start.

"Omera!" Erris shouted. "The left flank!"

He spun without thinking. One of the *gahaman* was charging around the edge of the shield, roaring and swiping at them with its claws.

He whirled his sword, raking the beast twice across its chest and right shoulder.

He was still a champion of the Blood, while the thousand blood-creatures had been only its children. He was above them. More was expected. He fought to clear his head, to keep his senses in the moment. He was here with Sarine and her counterpart. The Blood's commands held no sway over him. The thirst he felt, the enmity and rage at the Sun Goddess's betrayal, were illusions born of a false bond. But he could feel the others, the Blood Gods' children, answering the call. Hundreds. Thousands. Blood-images that once had been human beings, twisted into shells of their former selves, appearing on the fields of glass and iron.

The Blood was in danger. He knew it subconsciously, even as he struggled to retain himself under the yoke of the feathered serpent's commands. Kalira had come into the Blood's presence. He saw the scene, superimposed over his vision: Kalira, and the Nikkon woman, She Who Gazes into the Deepest Seas, in the heart of the spire.

He felt its energy building.

Exploding.

"*Shelter!*" he shouted. "*Shelter*, now! From behind!"

Erris reacted as fast as any *ubax aragti*–trained warrior. She slammed a barrier into place without hesitation, and they huddled against it together.

The spire erupted.

Through *Shelter*'s blue haze the spire was no more than a gray and black silhouette, but he saw what the Blood had done. A shock wave emanated from its heart, an expanding dome racing across the field. Rubble and stone flew into the sky in an outward burst. Heat and fire and smoke exploded upward, then outward.

It caught them. Passed them by. The world warped around them in seconds. Dead *gahaman* were swept aside as the shock wave ripped through the hulks of metal and glass, flattening them, warping them further, heating and melting the landscape as the spire's destruction surged across the plain. Pressed against the *Shelter*, he still felt the burning heat, the howling winds, and the impact of a thousand rocks pelting against their wall.

He saw no sign of Longzhu or Marquand. The world was engulfed in the shadows of smoke and winds carrying the rubble from the explosion.

Erris was shouting at him. He couldn't hear her words.

The Blood was here.

He felt it before he saw its shape manifest. Two silhouettes merged together through the *Shelter*'s now-pink haze. Two serpents, tangling in the sky. Beams of light danced between them, and he recognized both: the first, the serpent conjured by She Who Gazes into the Deepest Seas, a massive azure wyrm rising from churning waters that hadn't been there moments before. And the feathered coils of the Blood, a titan larger than any cloud, hovering and biting at its enemies as a rain of crimson droplets let loose over the field.

"What is this!" Erris shouted. He finally understood. "What's going on?"

"They've turned on each other!" he shouted back.

She shook her head. She didn't understand. He mimed it, the two serpents attacking each other.

She shook her head again. "Spire!" she shouted. "Sarine inside?"

He took her meaning. If Sarine had been in there when it exploded, she was as good as dead. No way of knowing. But if Sarine and the Regnant were dead, their attack had failed. They had to continue on toward whatever sliver of victory they could see.

"If she's out here, she'll move toward the Soul now," he said. "While they're distracted fighting each other."

Erris nodded, seeming to understand. The roaring continued around them, rocks and rubble from the spire continuing to impact the ground and explode into thousands more shards and fragments.

"We draw their attention," Erris said. "Move away. Give Sarine a clear path."

"No," he said. "The Blood's champions are here. Moving toward the Soul. We fight there if we want to distract them."

Erris paused, as though trying to look through the *Shelter* for a clearer view of what lay across the field.

"How can you be sure?" she asked.

The lingering command of the Blood rattled in his head. He felt them. He'd thought he was free of their control, that he'd turned his back on the pact they'd made when it was clear they'd betrayed him, laid him a false trail of memories to deceive and manipulate him. But they were still in his head. He felt hundreds of the Blood's children still arriving, the blood-monstrosities warping themselves toward the Soul. They were here, on the fields of glass and iron. And Kalira was there, too. Their enemy. His enemy. His blood-self strained to obey, to charge across the devastation and fight to clear the way toward the Soul of the World. He was going to do it anyway. Kalira *was* his enemy. Yet it felt tainted, obeying any command that came from the Blood.

"The Blood is calling its champions," he said. "Demanding they fight for the Soul. Sarine won't be able to reach it alone. If she's there, if she's coming… we have to draw their attention. Give her a chance to claim it before they know she's there."

The haze of dust and rubble was lighter now. Erris dared a look around the edge of the *Shelter* wall, and nodded.

"Marquand has a barrier set up that way," she said. "No sign of those bears. You ready to move?"

"Ready," he said. He was doing this of his own will. He meant to help Sarine and the Regnant. To remake the world and undo the corruption inflicted by the Blood, by Kalira and the rest of them. He fought for a world free of their evil, a place for the Bhakal people to grow and flourish. Not because he was sworn to the Blood. Not because the Blood had ordered him toward the Soul, to put down its enemies, to let it claim the power for itself. His blood-self quivered with anticipation, huddled against the *Shelter* wall and ready to spring forward as soon as he unleashed it.

"Then follow me," Erris said. "Straight on toward the Soul."

95

TIGAI

On the Far Side of the Field
The Gods' Seat

He cinched the strand-tethers into place, and they moved.

He hadn't had time to suss out the right pairs. Instinct demanded he grab hold of every nearby tether and yank them together, like grasping a handful of yarn and thread from the sewing box. Without an anchor they could have ended up smashed together, buried in the hulks of metal and glass that made up the ground in this place. Blessedly they appeared atop it, as far away as he could bloody take them.

Peizhi and Yuli squared off against the archangel he'd accidentally dragged along. The creature was one of the light ones, a female, with towering white wings, a flaming sword, and a halo of light over its head. But even the angel turned to stare when the spire exploded.

He'd carried them far enough away that the explosion was distant, but they still heard the thundering boom, saw the shock wave erupt from the pillar of light that stretched into the sky. The ground shook as a million shards of stone and gouts of fire flew into the sky in every direction. Smoke engulfed the horizon in a mushroom-shaped cloud, expanding outward the higher it grew.

For a moment he stared in shock. Song Xiu gaped. Peizhi recovered herself quicker, and Yuli barely seemed to register the explosion before she dove around the archangel's sword.

The angel parried the Twin Fangs' rushing attack, clanging its fiery metal against her claws.

Yuli spun, savaging the angel faster than he could see. He was still staring at the explosion, trying to piece together what it could mean. Yuli leapt at the angel's helmet, landing a savage blow that clanked and snapped its head sideways, ripping loose a chunk of the metal and exposing its long, free-flowing hair. It buffeted her with its wings, knocking her loose as it desperately shuffled back to get away from her attacks. Peizhi maintained her Mantis-fire, a stream of it blasting at the angel and scoring its armor black. Finally the angel leapt upward into the sky, unfurling its wings and clearing the ground as Yuli sprang up after it.

It deflected her leap with its sword, and Yuli came crashing back to the ground. Then the angel flew away, bolting toward the ruins of the spire.

"Take us back," Yuli said, half growling it as her form shifted back to her human shape. "Take us back into the fight."

"Into that?" he said.

"It's all gone," Song Xiu said. "Anything near that explosion will be flattened and burned."

They all stared together, again. The smoke was still rising, and the shock wave had dissipated, though metal and rock were still flying in a cloud around the base of the explosion.

"What could cause an explosion so large?" Peizhi said. "No Mantis, nor any Heron could summon a fire that size. Perhaps the Great Lord himself?"

"If the Regnant could do that, we'd never have beaten him," he said. "Maybe Kalira. I don't know the tenth part of what she can do."

"The Sun Goddess is growing in strength, then," Peizhi said. "She couldn't do that when we abducted her. But perhaps, now that she is in control of the World's Soul."

"Wait, *you* were one of the ones who abducted her?" he said. "The ones we fought, in the jungle?"

Peizhi bowed her head.

"What should we do now?" Song Xiu said. "If the Great Ones are willing to destroy the Soul of the World instead of see it fall to us..."

"It isn't destroyed," Yuli said. "See? The light is still there, behind the smoke."

The pillar was dimmed, darkened by the column of black around it, but it still glimmered, rising up into the sky of this place, for all the smoke seemed to blot it out.

"I see it," he said. "But what the fuck are those?"

Something he hadn't noticed before, that now drew all their attention. Two serpents, massive creatures, writhing together on the far side of the smoke. Beams of light shot between them as they smashed into each other. At this distance, anything smaller than a mountain should have been no more than a speck, yet these two wyrms were crashing into each other with lightning-quick bits and snaps of their long necks.

"The fight continues," Peizhi said. "Perhaps Yuli Twin Fangs is right, and we should rejoin it."

"How do we know any of our people are alive?" he said. "I'd as soon not take us back there unless we have a fucking clue what we're up against."

"They have to be alive," Yuli said. "Or we're all dead, and none of this matters. Sarine has to be out there."

He shook his head. "I can still get us out of here," he said. "I'm not throwing my life or yours away on hope. We can use the strands to get back to the real world, and we can hide."

"If you take us away, you can't bring us back," Yuli said. "Don't."

"What then?" he said. "Did you see what just happened to the spire?"

"Can we get closer?" Song Xiu said. "If the Great Lord and Lady are still alive, perhaps they're responsible for one of those serpents. We can rejoin them and see."

"That's not anything I've seen Sarine do..." he began, then stopped. "Wait. I know one of them at least. The sea-snake. Orana and I helped her use it to fight the Regnant. That's the Nikkon woman, She Who Gazes into the Deepest Seas."

"The other one, then," Peizhi said. "The red dragon. Who can say what the Great Lord is capable of? None of us know his mysteries."

"Song Xiu is right," Yuli said. "We need to get closer. If hope is lost, we can run. But not until we're sure."

He wanted to take them away anyway, a simple tether to some beach somewhere. Not that he knew of any beaches anymore, none that weren't marred by the chaotic mess the world had become. Determination showed like fire on Yuli's face, the sort of expression that had made him fall in love with her in the first place.

"Fine," he said. "Bloody fine. Stay alert and get the Heron-shield up as soon as we move. My farthest anchor from the ruins is still too bloody fucking close for safety."

Yuli's body changed, shifting in an instant back into the Twin Fangs' hairless muscle and claws. Peizhi raised both hands, and Song Xiu mirrored her gesture. All four of them were bloody fools for going back into the fire. But as always, it fell to him to take them.

He closed his eyes, and blinked, and they moved again.

Crackling cinders greeted them as he stepped away from the anchor. Molten gold dripped from the twisted metal fixtures that pierced through the ground, mixing with hissing steam rising from pools of blood and water. Heat washed over him, enough to have him raising a hand to his face to ward against it. Yuli immediately moved away, searching the landscape in all directions. The Heron-shield shimmered into place, vibrating as rocks and pebbles struck its outer edge. So far as he could tell, it was quiet in their immediate surroundings, not that that was any bloody surprise. Anything fool enough to have been standing here when the spire exploded would have exploded with it.

"The red serpent," Peizhi said. "It's made of…blood?"

He reoriented, turning to find the two serpents tangling in the clouds. Now, closer, both loomed over the field like titans, darting and pecking each other in a fury.

"It can't be," he said, though it was. Droplets of blood sprayed from the crimson wyrm, pelting the ground around it with a haze of rain. The azure one bit into it, writhing and towering over all of them, a thousand times taller than any person or building he'd ever seen. The creatures battled against each other where the clouds would be, if there were clouds here.

"If the Rabaquim are fighting the Nikkon, we might have an opening," he said. "Maybe they've all gone as fucking mad as the world has, under their control."

As he spoke, Yuli entered the shimmering dome of Force, and just as quick the Twin Fangs' muscles condensed, her body shifting back to her human form.

"A host is gathering out there," she said. "Blood-creatures, like the ones that have been chasing us, the ones we fought in the temple ruin. Dozens are appearing between us and the Soul."

"Have our enemies made enemies of each other?" Peizhi said.

He squinted, trying to make out anything in the direction of the Soul's light. It was all dust and smoke.

"Any sign of Erris?" he asked. "Or Sarine?"

Yuli shook her head.

Bloody wind spirits. If Sarine was alive, she'd be hidden by her *Faith*, and the Regnant with her. Much as he wanted to take them all to a beach somewhere, everything was finished if Sarine and the Regnant were dead. They had to be alive. And if Sarine had any sense she'd wait to show herself until her opening was certain. But he could have used a dose of Erris's tactical brilliance right about now. If the blood-things were appearing on the field, the Rabaquim were here in force, making a move on the Soul. Combined with the blood-serpent tangling with the water one in the sky, it had to mean at least that the Rabaquim and the Nikkon had turned on each other. But what did that mean for the Flesh half of the Rabaquim Gods, for Orana, Kalira, and the angels? No way of knowing where the battle lines were, which meant no way of knowing whether he was retreating to safety or diving into the thickest part of the coming fight.

"We're here to distract," he said. "To pull attention away from the Soul."

"Well, we've failed at that," Yuli said. "Those blood-things are massing toward the light."

"Right," he said. "But the blood-serpent seems like the greater manifestation of the Rabaquim's strength. Maybe we'd do better trying to attack them there."

"You want us to attack those...*things*?" Peizhi said, staring up at the wyrms.

"Maybe?" he said. "I don't know. I mean to cause chaos. If you three can protect me as we get close to them, maybe I can hook one of them away to opposite sides of the field. That might pull their attention away from the Soul, at least."

"Is he mad?" Song Xiu said.

Yuli laughed. "Oh yes," she said. "Yes he is."

"What?" he said. "I can't do a bloody damned thing about dozens of those blood-creatures, and besides, a bunch of foot soldiers are never going to claim the Soul. *They're* a distraction, the same as us. The real powers are over there, throwing dragons at each other in the sky. That's where we have to strike, if we're going to..."

"Yes?" Song Xiu said. "If we're going to what?" He didn't hear.

"He's there," he said. "The Regnant."

It turned all of their eyes at once.

A swirl of shadow had appeared behind the haze of smoke and dust. It was growing, still a formless shape of swirling shadows and thunder. But he recognized it on sight. He'd clung to the barest thread of life, tethering himself, Orana, and She Who Gazes into the Deepest Seas to fifty different anchors trying to stay a step ahead of that thing. This time it was supposed to be on his side, but the thought did little to quell the fear prickling his skin, seeing it again. The Regnant's shadow. The nightmare that drank magic, snuffing it like sand on fire.

"The Great Lord," Peizhi said, her voice touched with awe.

"If he's fighting them, should we go to help?" Song Xiu said.

"He had the same thought I did," he said. "Bloody fucker. He's trying to draw them away from the Soul for Sarine."

Wind spirits but attacking the Nikkon and the Blood was going to be a thousand times harder if he had to dodge the outer ring of the shadow-creature's aura. But then, they'd be trying to flee, too. With some good anchors and strands he might be able to chase them down when they tried to escape, to pen them in and force them to fight the Regnant head-on. Like bloody feeding crocodiles to lions. And himself caught in the middle.

"We move on your word," Yuli said.

He nodded. "Sarine can handle the blood-creatures. She destroyed fifty at once, on the hilltop. If we can keep the serpents away, we can give her a chance. And if we have to work with the Regnant to do it, bloody fuck me but we'll do it."

The other three tensed. Yuli's body changed again, in an eyeblink. He shook his head.

"No anchors this time," he said. "None set over there, anyway. This time we go on foot. Let's move. And keep your distance from that shadow; we get too close, and suddenly my tethers stop working, and your Heron-shield with them."

They signaled understanding. Good enough. He should have chanced a tether to a bloody beach. Somewhere hot, with clear water and white sands. Yuli was fucking right, but if he died here he'd never forgive her for it.

96

ERRIS

In the Thick of the Fight
Approaching the Soul of the World

*E*ntropy exploded in bursts of blood and heat. She moved, keeping *Shelter* deployed in front of her and to both sides, with six *Mind* copies ranging around her on the field. The blood-creatures battered themselves against her defenses, then collapsed when she released the tethers, letting them fall inward as she cooked them and remade the *Shelter* again.

Marquand hovered behind her, hurling bursts of fire into anything that made it around the edge of her walls. Omera and his blood-copy prowled around Marquand, flicking their swords and killing anything left standing. They had to keep moving. She'd made a fortress of *Shelter* and *Entropy*, slaughtering the blood-creatures by the score. If she could get close enough to the Soul, then move away, she could draw them into giving chase. So long as they recognized her *Shelter* as their enemy, she could control the flow of battle, moving her enemy each time she deployed a new set of walls. It gave her the initiative, so long as she could keep her squad alive.

She signaled another move, snapping three new *Shelter* tethers into place and charging across the suddenly open field.

She took the moment to orient to their position. The Soul was close. Maybe a hundred paces off, the well of light extended upward through the haze of dust and smoke. No sign yet of Kalira, or Sarine.

Three of the blood-creatures howled and charged before she could reach the new barriers. She put one down with her saber, feeling it squelch as she dug her steel into its shoulder. *Entropy* took another, exploding in its face and scattering its upper torso to the dust and wind. The third bit into one of her *Mind* copies, until Omera collided with it, hooking the spear-head in the curve of his *shotel* before slamming it aside.

Ten more steps to reach the new *Shelter*. Across the field it seemed twenty more of the blood-creatures took notice of her movements, rounding on her as they appeared. They came from nothing, materializing here in the Gods' Seat like Tigai using his strands. Not for the first time she wondered whether attacking them here had been an error, and dismissed the thought as quickly as it came. They were committed. All that mattered was pressing on, pulling as many of them down as they could manage until the battle turned away from the Soul.

She hurled another blast of *Entropy* into a pair of freshly materialized blood-creatures, scattering burnt blood into smoke. *Shelter* strands snapped into place on the run, and she took cover again behind the next set of walls. The blood-creatures were appearing by the hundreds now, swarming around her *Shelter* as they moved toward the Soul. But she had their attention. A mass of them were gathering in the east. If she hit them there, and pulled them away, there might be a chance to—

Her *Shelter* went pink. The center wall, situated between her and the light of the Soul.

"Down!" she shouted. "Get down!"

No time to wait for Marquand and the others to drop. She hurled herself to the ground, what had been twisted metal once and was now slagged, smoothed-out melted iron.

The center wall exploded, scattering shards of leyline energy into the air. A beam of sunlight pierced through where it had stood, sweeping across to the other walls in her fortress.

"Take us back," she shouted. "To the approach. Now!"

The left and right walls went pink, superheated past the point of breaking. Two new sunbeams lanced through both in turn.

The ground shifted.

She sprang to her feet. Longzhu had put them precisely where she wanted them: five hundred paces back from the Soul. Through the dusky haze she saw the remnants of Kalira's work, as beams of sunlight scorched and burned the ground, bursting through the pieces of her last leyline tethers.

Immediately three new *Shelter* walls sprang into place, in the same formations she'd used during their first assault. Omera and Marquand fell in, with Longzhu at her side.

"Advance, again, on my mark," she said. "This time to the east."

She waited.

The blood-creatures would see the new *Shelter*, and recognize the pattern as the same mobile fortress that had carved through their lines. Behind them, this time, but she had to hope they would turn toward it, and recognize her *Shelter* for the threat it represented. Toward her, and away from the Soul. Gods only knew what Kalira would do, now that she had entered the fight.

"Move!" she shouted, and let the tethers fade.

Three new walls slammed into place forty steps east. She made them taller this time. Surer to draw the enemy's eyes.

The blood-things were stirring. The new arrivals surged together; she saw shapes, silhouettes moving through the smoke. But enough had turned, enough were moving toward her. She knew the moment, all too well: when infantry pinned down an enemy, only to hear the thunder of cavalry hooves behind them. Who could say what emotions creatures made of blood possessed? But if they were human at all, there would be chaos, fear, confusion, dread. It fell to her to be the nightmare. To break them with their own fear.

Mind sent out fresh copies of her, and of Marquand as they advanced. The first two *Shelter* fortresses went untouched, without combat. The next was closer, close enough to see shapes moving with clarity for their swords, their pikes and poleaxes. Thank the Gods the blood-things seemed incapable of manifesting pistols or carbines.

"Set anchor here," she shouted, not bothering to be sure Longzhu had followed the order. He was a good man; he would see it done. A commander had to make snap judgments on a battlefield.

"Charge!"

She and her *Mind*-copies led the attack, swooping across the field of smoothed-over stone and iron. A wall of blood-spears had been set against her; she blasted five of them with a single burst of *Entropy*, unmaking them with fire. Two more of the creatures, a man-shape and a woman-shape both wielding swords, dodged around the fire, bounding toward her with their blades extended forward. She feinted with one of her copies, sending it to meet them with its saber drawn and whirling over its head.

The woman-shape tried to parry and riposte, finding its blade connecting only with a *Mind*-copy, a trick of the light. It sent the blood-woman down, off-balance, and her true saber was there to punish the misstep. She rammed her blade into the blood-creature's back, pivoting to greet the man-shape with a fresh burst of *Entropy*.

Marquand and Omera replicated her dance, pushing to arrive behind her *Shelter* at almost the same moment. Blood drenched them all, with only tufts of black hair, patches of color in their jackets and boots to signal they weren't made of the same stuff as their enemies.

She gestured with the point of her saber for the next move. A longer one this time. Fifty paces south and east, closing the gap toward the Soul.

She let *Shelter* fade, and slammed the new walls into place.

Twenty blood-creatures stood between them, and the attack renewed. Fire erupted in the dust. Steel met blood-tinted steel.

They'd covered half the ground when sunbeams sliced the air between them.

Kalira stood in the middle of the field, surrounded by blood-creatures exploding as fast as they could approach her. She swept sunlight around like a torch, burning a ring of fire at her feet. She'd sighted them through the mêlée, advancing to cut them off before they could reach the new fortress of *Shelter* in the distance.

"Back," she shouted, as she tethered a fresh set of *Shelter* walls between them and Kalira. "To the anchor."

Longzhu came to a halt behind her, as another wave of sunlight pierced the *Shelter* almost as fast as she could set it into place.

Marquand came scurrying toward them, and Omera turned from farther back, both sprinting to close the gap. Blood-creatures hounded them, racing after both men with their false steel weapons swinging and piercing through the dust.

Another sunbeam lanced wide of their position. Almost as though Kalira had missed on purpose. It cut through the air well clear of her *Shelter*, passing north and west, precisely where—

"Wait!" she shouted. "Don't tether us to—!"

They moved. Directly into the path of Kalira's beam.

She dove before they materialized. Light exploded around them, a brilliant flash erasing everything nearby in pure white light. She hit the ground, seared and burned, coughing. Marquand landed beside her. Neither Omera nor his blood-copy was there. Incinerated, or they hadn't reached her before Longzhu made his tether.

Longzhu collapsed backward, engulfed in fire.

The Dragon's eyes were wide. The rest of him was scorched and black. She'd seen Tigai take mortal wounds a dozen times and blink away. But this attack had been waiting for them, as if Kalira had known precisely where they would appear.

Longzhu's body crunched as it struck the iron. Pieces of him flaked away as ash.

"Move!" she shouted, though with Marquand at her side no orders were necessary. He was already scrambling at her side, already tethering *Shelter* to go with hers, screening their movements as fresh sunbeams turned it pink.

On any other day, any other battlefield, she would have given the order to retreat. But they had Kalira on their hook, and the eyes of every blood-creature within a thousand paces of the Soul. Without their Dragon, the slightest misstep would be their end. All she had to do was be perfect in her attack, perfect in her movements. She and Marquand. A feint forward, into a calculated retreat, and another attack. She could do this. They could do this, together.

Shelter shimmered into place, and they moved with one mind. East, and south. Toward Kalira and her sunbeams. Away from the Soul.

97

SARINE

Shrouded by Faith
Approaching the Soul of the World

Blood soaked the ground as she drew near the light. The world had
been redrawn in red, in the orange haze of the dust still settling from
the spire's eruption, in the silhouetted shapes that appeared here, conjured
from nothing, made to resemble people etched from blood. No, not made to
resemble them. Evelynn's memories came to the surface: They *were* people,
changed by the Rabaquim Blood Gods. Their champions retained the use of
their flesh forms, and the rest were monsters, creatures of nightmare, onetime
sacrifices driven mad by obedience to the blood-serpent's demands.

They swarmed, and Kalira disintegrated them with the power of the Sun.

She watched, careful to keep her distance, under cover of her shroud of
Faith. Kalira swung her hands in circles around the battlefield, sweeping the
ground with blasts of pure sunlight.

Katsuri, the Crane swordswoman, kept in front of her, stepping as carefully
as she did. Kalira gave no sign her senses penetrated the shield of *Faith*, but
that was no guarantee. The memory of being under one of those piercing
beams shot to the surface. She had no intention of dying again. *Shelter* held
at the ready, and she could feel Anati clutching hold of *White*. The Nine Tails
lingered near the surface, aching for control. But for now, her defense was
Faith, moving quietly, carefully, and unseen. They stepped together around
the pools of blood soaking the ruined earth. The Soul was close. It burned
with white fire, stretching up into the sky. Always before there had been stone
around it, the stone of the place she'd thought of as the Gods' Seat. Now it was

uncontained, stretching to infinity, upward and down, the same infinity she saw reflected through the blue sparks of the Infinite Plane.

The first *Shelter* walls took her by surprise.

At first she snapped to check her *Faith*, certain she'd loosed the walls she'd held at the ready by mistake. But no. Her shroud held, as did Katsuri's. Three conjoined walls of *Shelter* appeared across the battlefield, punctuated by fire erupting around them. She turned to stare as the Rabaquim's blood-servants did, and only after the second salvo of *Entropy* did she understand. Erris. And Marquand. They were attacking to pull attention away from the Soul. She gestured to Katsuri, and they hurried to move out of the blood-servants' path. Footing was unsure here, the iron and stone only recently cooled from the explosion that leveled the spire, but *Body* and *Red* sufficed where her feet might have faltered. They scurried aside as the blood-servants turned, drawn toward the *Shelter* walls like flies to a decaying corpse.

Another hundred paces to the Soul.

Blood-servants appeared by the score, everywhere they thought to go. More than once, she or Katsuri almost fell, almost collided with their enemies. They wove through the press of blood-servants, each hefting their spears, swords, maces, polearms, and mauls and immediately seeking out some means of fighting. The Blood had called them here to die. She lost sight of Kalira in the press, darting and weaving around each new group of soldiers called to the battlefield. Only the *Shelter* walls conjured in the distance were visible in the haze. Moving. New walls conjured first to the north, then the east. Moving away from the Soul.

She broke through the line of blood-servants a step behind Katsuri. Forty paces now, over empty ground. But something had joined the pale blue haze of *Shelter*, glittering through the fog.

Sunbeams.

Kalira shot her energy directly into one of the *Shelter* walls, ripping it apart. The wall turned pink first, then white, then erupted in a spray of sharded leyline energy. More beams followed, and more *Shelter* appeared. Another fortress of three conjoined walls, farther across the field, where a Dragon anchor had been set into the firmament of their starfield. Kalira's energy discharges illuminated the earth, scorching the blood-servants fool enough to wander into her path, or more foolish, those who tried to attack her, disintegrated without so much as slowing her down.

She could sense the next-nearest Dragon anchors. Erris was there, fighting for her life. Even at the apex of their power, no champion of the leylines could match Kalira's strength. She could snap a strand connection into place and appear beside them, bolstering their defenses. Without her, Erris and Marquand would last no more than a minute, two at best. With her *Shelter*, her *Black*, *Red*, *White*, and the storm spirits' gift, they would have a fighting chance, at least to retreat while she faced the Sun Goddess herself.

But it wasn't her place.

She turned back toward the Soul of the World.

The blood-servants had shied away from the light burning here. For forty paces in a ring surrounding it, the blood-servants kept back, aimlessly colliding with each other when they didn't sense danger, or something the Rabaquim Blood Gods had named their enemy. And Kalira was away, hurling sunbeams into Erris's *Shelter* walls.

She stepped carefully toward the light. Cautiously. It wasn't above Kalira to set a trap.

Her consciousness shifted as she walked, mirroring her approach on the Infinite Plane.

A thousand vortices swirled red and black, the forms behind the blood-servants as they swarmed around the light. *Faith* cloaked her sparks in gray mist, and Katsuri's, too, as they drifted toward the energy at the Infinite Plane's heart. Nearby she saw Erris's form, laced with the leylines' patterns and golden threads. Marquand stood beside her, and one other. Kalira approached. Omera was close, too, tied as he was to the twin pattern of red swirling around him. None were in place to stop her approach to the Soul.

She reached it.

Faith would insulate her, and bar her from touching its light. For a bare moment, she had to cast it off. Had to be vulnerable. If a trap was set, it would be here.

She prepared her defenses. *Shelter* strands set in place. *Body* coursing through her. *Red* pounding in her heart. *Mareh'et* ready to answer her call, and *lakiri'in*, and the power of the Storm.

Ready? she thought to Anati.

Her *kaas* was there. Materialized coiled around her arm, her snout perked toward the fight, where Kalira still tangled with Erris and the blood-servants across the field.

I'm here for you, Anati thought. *I'll die before I let them touch your skin.*

The Nine Tails quaked inside her, desperate for control. It would have it soon enough, once she shifted her consciousness in full to the Infinite Plane.

Ready? she thought to Zi.

The *kaas* thundered back in response, the full chorus replying as one. A sensation, more than any words. A feeling. Readiness. Anticipation. Hope. Fear.

On the Plane, she could sense the titans struggling together, here close to the Soul and farther away, where the great wyrms clashed together in the sky. Where the Regnant had only now begun to manifest his shadow-form, set to tilt a conflict between Gods into one between pantheons, unleashing the full power of memory, thunder, and devastation.

As soon as she began, they'd know she was here.

Soon after, they would know what she meant to do.

Faith dissipated for the last time. No hiding now. She appeared, and plunged her hand into the light. Her consciousness surged forward on the Infinite Plane. Her sparks were swallowed in the river flowing up and down the Soul, and far away she heard the beginnings of a scream.

Hers. Kalira's. The Blood. The Angels. The Moon. The Flesh. The Ancestors. All together, all at once.

She let the sound and the energy flow around her, washing over her without touching her skin. She wasn't here to worry over her enemies, over what they might think or do. She was here to face them all, to remake the world, or die before she could.

A pulse of light raced across the Soul. Neither black, nor white. A colorless burst, silver and gray and all the other colors at once.

A signal, to the other Gods. A beginning of the end.

98

YULI

On the Edge of the Conjured Ocean
The Field of Iron and Broken Glass

Whistling thundered in the Twin Fangs' ears.

It sprang from the top of a mound of melted steel, leaping into the air. The archangel saw it coming. Deflected. Moved at the last moment, snapping the tips of its wings to ward off the attack.

Claws sank deep into the angel's back, piercing through its golden plate armor, through the fleshy base of its wings, clanging claw against spine.

The angel rocked in midair, sent spiraling off-balance by the weight of the Twin Fangs' claws now impaled into its back. It flailed both wings, and the Twin Fangs tasted its blood, sparkling and divine. It sank both fangs into the creature's neck, and together they plummeted back to the earth.

They landed in the water, with a thundering splash. Suddenly the world moved slower, engulfed in brine. Waves pounded overhead as they sank together, enveloped in currents spiraling outward from the thrashing leviathan that rose from its depths. The Twin Fangs held its prey, severing and snapping tendons and muscle with its teeth while claws pinned its wings in place. The angel lashed and writhed against its hold, swinging its fiery sword, somehow still burning here, under water. It grazed against the Twin Fangs' flesh. Burned. Pain spread from the wounds, but still it held, snapping, biting, until it was done.

The angel's head came loose from its neck, and its body went limp. Glittering light poured from the wound, leaking dazzling blood into the water. The Twin Fangs shook it one more time, to be sure, before it let go.

The meteors were coming. But Tigai had already shown he understood;

he would wait until the last moment, to be sure she wasn't coming to him for escape.

The Twin Fangs kicked to plunge deeper in the pool. Far in the distance the massive coils of the leviathan moved under the ocean where the floor should have been. It churned the water as it moved, bending and twisting to support ten thousand spans of mass protruding above the waves. Far overhead it would be snapping and biting the blood-serpent that matched it. They continued their fight, even now, even with the shadow swirling on the far bank of the ocean's shores. The whistling was louder now. It could hear them coming, even here, under the water.

The meteors struck, and the waves exploded.

The Twin Fangs' body was twisted, tossed by violent currents. Meteors became rocks, superheated enough to instantly convert their surroundings to steam. A rain of them plunged into the water's surface, a dozen massive rocks and a thousand smaller ones, all pelting the ocean in hissing columns of steam and fire. Overhead the sky turned black and red, swirling colors distorted by the waves. The leviathan shifted its coils away from the explosions, sending another surging current up to meet the Twin Fangs as it fought to hold its place.

Finally the steam cooled. The meteors slowed, plunging slowly into the deep instead of hurtling with the force of their fall from the sky. Black and red still churned above the water's edge, but it could navigate the aftermath of the destruction. It kicked and rose, swimming for the shore.

Smoke greeted it when it tried to fill its lungs, and it snorted, hefting its body up out of the water.

Yuli demanded it look for Tigai. It scanned the surface, toward where he'd set his anchors. He'd be reappearing there, with Peizhi and Song Xiu at his side, once he was satisfied Orana's meteors had finished their work. But he wasn't there yet.

The Twin Fangs ran through the meteors' wake, leaping atop newly formed craters filled with smoke and fire. The wyrms continued their clash, biting and snapping at each other far overhead, blood raining down to hiss and become steam where it met the heat. On the ocean's far bank the Regnant's swirling column of shadow and thunder roiled, growing in size. The angels and beasts of the Flesh champions were gathering there, silhouettes and shapes already fighting. It should be there, too, fighting against them. But Yuli demanded it first make contact with Tigai. It loped toward the anchor, frustration seething under its skin.

It leapt across a chasm where a boulder had split the ground, landing atop a mass of copper and iron. Then it pivoted and leapt again. Tigai had set his anchor near where the Nikkon woman channeled her spirit. The ocean was still there, and the azure wyrm with it; he hadn't reached her, or been able to affect what she did. But he would try again. That was where the Twin Fangs would meet him. It pushed off the next mass, leaping over a second chasm, and almost collided with a tiny child.

Fear spiked through it, and through Yuli, as they landed.

That was no child.

Orana stood at the chasm's edge. Her body was small, no more than eight or nine years old. Her skin was pale, eyes red, hair white. And both Yuli and the Twin Fangs knew what she could do, what she had done already.

For a moment the Twin Fangs locked eyes with the girl. With the Moon.

Prudence said to run. It was here to protect Tigai from the champions and soldiers of the Gods, the angels, the assassins, the flesh-creatures and blood-copies. It was never meant to face a God alone. Yet it was here. She was here. Orana must have known where Tigai had set his anchor, and been moving toward it, too, just as they were. He was in danger. It fell to her—to it—to protect him. Yuli made the decision, and the Twin Fangs obeyed.

Orana's eyes narrowed as the Twin Fangs bounded off the crater's lip. She darted sideways as it landed, swiping where she'd been standing with both claws and tasting only air. The Twin Fangs snarled and rushed to follow.

"Are you sure?" Orana said, dancing out of the way again, her movements lined in tufts of shadow, too fast for any mortal eyes to follow. "Are you sure this is how you want to die?"

Claws swiped at nothing. The child bounded backward, seeming to leave afterimages shimmering where she'd stood.

Whistling sounded overhead.

Close. Closer than the others had been, and smaller. Still the Twin Fangs' ears picked it up.

It rounded on the child. Orana stood atop a hulk of iron, showing it a half smile, full of pity. The Twin Fangs leapt, slashing and biting into shadows as it landed. Orana was behind it. Standing between metal hulks, in one of the streams of blood.

"They give me new bodies, when mine die," the child said. "Mortals don't mind it. They enjoy seeing what's on my other side, before they venture into the unknown. But you won't be reborn, if you stay here. When my rocks land, you'll die, and I'll die, and I'll go on living, and you'll be a memory."

It leapt after her as she spoke, clawing and swiping and finding nothing, only empty air. Panic rose on its skin, hairless as it was. The whistling was growing louder. It surged toward the girl, ravaging shadows with its claws, biting air with both fangs. The girl seemed to sidestep with effortless grace, leaving shadows in her wake. It tried a feinting attack, doubling back with both claws after contorting its body in a false leap. Orana slid sideways.

"Run, fanged thing," Orana said, grinning like a child. "See if it isn't too late. See if—"

A white light flashed in the distance, at the column of the Soul of the World.

Whatever it was pulled Orana's attention. The girl's eyes went wide, and she stopped to stare.

The Twin Fangs impaled her through the gut.

Intestines wrapped around its claws. Brown slime mixed with blood. It lifted the girl off the ground, hoisting her tiny body above the hulks of iron. Orana seemed not to notice. Both the girl's hands went to her midsection, but her eyes were locked in the distance. Toward the Soul of the World.

"No," Orana whispered. "No, it can't be. Sarine was dead."

It had to move. The whistling was louder now. Almost on them. But what had Orana said? The Twin Fangs longed to bite into her body, to turn the Moon Goddess into a corpse. It thirsted for flesh, for the blood of the elusive creature who had dodged so many of its strikes. Yuli remembered. Orana would get a new body when this one died. So this one needed to stay alive.

It held Orana aloft, pressing the Moon-girl's body close to its chest, holding her in place with both claws, and it ran.

It bounded from the iron hulk to a copper one, then to a gold, ignoring the tiny body struggling against its strength. Whatever blessings Orana had for movement through her shadows, she could do no more than an actual eight-year-old girl might have managed in resisting being carried.

"Let me go, you fucking ugly shit-stain," Orana said. "Or cut my head off and let me die. Do you have any idea what's happening over there? What your mistress is trying to do?"

The whistling stopped. The meteors struck behind it, erupting into fire and stone. They were well clear of the impact, and still it felt the ground tremble, slipping its footing as it bounded across the plain.

It sighted the spot where Tigai had placed his anchor. Near the shimmering form of the Nikkon woman, She Who Gazes into the Deepest Seas, on the edge of the ocean she'd created to conjure her wyrm. Rocks and pebbles pelted the ground, remnants of the meteors' impact. It let them strike its back, protecting the cradled form of the wounded girl in its arms.

"No, you stupid, stupid fucking monster," Orana said. "She's going to erase *you*, too, you addle-brained asslick. Let me go. Let me die. Now!"

It wanted to oblige the girl, to dash her head on the iron and drink her blood. Carrying her was Yuli's idea. The great wyrms colliding in the sky had stopped, both turned toward the pillar of light in the distance, as though even the serpents were frozen in shock. The shadow vortex across the waters had turned, too, and half the figures she could see, the angels, blood-copies, and beasts, all rounded to stare at the pulsing, soft gray light now running along the Soul of the World. That was strange. It had been all black, or all white before. It needed Tigai here to make sense of it. It needed Yuli to tell it what to do. If it left the girl here, Orana would find a way to die, smashing her forehead into the jagged metal, or opening the wound the Twin Fangs' claws had made in the girl's stomach.

Have to make her unable to kill herself. Have to take away her ability to walk, or to strike herself with iron or stone. The thoughts came from Yuli. The Twin Fangs had no reservations; if the girl needed to be mangled, the girl would be mangled, and kept alive. It had already cut her belly, but that was the sort of wound that would bleed for hours and not let her die. It had to embrace the delay. Let Orana linger on, to give Sarine the time she needed, to conquer the Soul.

"What are you doing?" Orana asked. "What are you—?"

It seized Orana's head in its other hand and snapped her neck.

The bone cracked loud enough to echo across the metal. Orana choked, and spat something brown and viscous onto the Twin Fangs' feet. The rest of her lay still and unmoving, lifeless and limp, while her head whimpered and shook from the pain.

"No," Orana whispered. Her head was wrenched sideways. The rest of her was still. Calm. Paralyzed. "Don't. You don't understand."

"What in the Great Lord's name...?"

The Twin Fangs whirled to find Song Xiu at Tigai's anchor, her eyes wide, her mouth gaping as she stared at the girl-child's form, twisted on the ground. Tigai had appeared beside her, and Peizhi.

Yuli seized control, shifting their form to hers.

"Is that...Orana?" Tigai said.

"It is," she said. "She gets a new body whenever she dies. That's how she kept the meteors raining down on her own head."

Orana's head twitched on the ground, weeping, though the rest of her was limp and dead.

"Her neck is broken?" Tigai asked, and she nodded. "You think she'll live like that for a while?"

"Yes," she said. "But I only caught her because she was distracted by whatever's going on at the Soul. Did you see what happened there?"

Tigai shook his head, while Peizhi stared out across the waters.

"It has their attention, too," Peizhi said. "Look."

They all turned to see movement, on the far side of the azure serpent's lake. The Regnant's shadow-vortex seemed to be moving with the beasts, with the angels and the rest. All toward the Soul. Even the Blood and the leviathan seemed to be abandoning the fight between each other and rounding on the pulsing gray light.

"What is it?" Song Xiu asked. "What's going on there?"

"I don't have a damn clue," Tigai said. "But it has to be Sarine doing it. And if they're moving to stop her, I mean to keep them as far away as I can."

"Tethering them away on the strands?" she asked.

"Precisely. Let's go. I have anchors in their path. We can delay them at least, so long as we keep our distance from that fucking shadow thing."

"No," Orana croaked, her face angled downward into the ground. "You have to stop her. Can't let her do this."

The Twin Fangs took control again, relishing the smell of Orana's blood and guts in its nose. It was easy to ignore her, though Song Xiu and Peizhi eyed her with unease until Tigai gathered them together.

Then Tigai closed his eyes, and they moved, leaving Orana's writhing form behind.

99

OMERA

In the Shadow of the Gray Light
The Soul of the World

He was alone in a sea of blood-soldiers, the only flesh among a thousand human forms. He set both feet on a firm patch of ground, and caught a spear in the curve of his sword. A careful movement wrenched the point away, and his blood-self dismembered the soldier carrying it. The thing hadn't moved, hadn't reacted as his blood-self slashed it apart. Around him the blood-soldiers stared up at the light of the Soul of the World. All shambled forward, all dazed, in awe, uncaring as he cut them down.

He was a tempest raging in a field of madness. He sliced a woman-shape open, spilling a rain of blood from her belly. He dismembered a maceman, shoving off its corpse as it fell, while his blood-self chopped the legs out from under a pair of young men, knocking them over in the path of their fellows. Each had been human, once. Memory burned through the haze of slaughter. He knew how these creatures were made. Each one a sacrifice, willing or not, brought before the blood-priests' altars. Their bodies burned as their souls were torn away, reaped by the blood-serpent's thirst. Now the serpent had summoned them all here, thousands of the blood-forged, all gathered around the Soul of the World. All watching, enraptured, seeming not to care what happened to them, what happened around them.

He gave over to his instincts, letting his sword have free rein. *Ubax aragti* gave him speed, while *matarin* burned away the blood of anything touched by his steel.

In the distance he saw Erris d'Arrent's *Shelter* flicker and go pink. New walls went up, dissolved, vanished, and were created again, twenty paces distant. Always away from the Soul. He should have stayed with her. But the blood was here. His enemies were here. A reminder of what the Rabaquim had tried to make him: a mindless soldier, obeying the serpent's every whim.

He let his body and blood-self go, dancing a path of destruction through the blood. He cut them down, and they offered no resistance. Every eye stared at the light, bathing their faces in pulsing gray.

Then suddenly, as one, the blood-soldiers dissolved.

Every figure, all at once. Everywhere around him. For an instant their faces lit up, overcome with... joy, perhaps, or relief. The moment passed, and every one of them reverted to the blood from which they'd been forged. Masses of congealed blood suddenly gushed into pools, disintegrated like liquid poured from human-shaped containers.

Unmade. Broken. Only he remained, and his blood-self, while around him every figure melted into thick, viscous blood.

A pool of it rose at his feet, enough to soak him to the ankles.

Suddenly the plain was clear. He swept around in a rush. Everywhere the blood-soldiers had melted. Two hundred paces off, Erris and Marquand dashed behind a wall of pale blue *Shelter*, while a small girl ran away from them, howling something as she charged toward the Soul. The rest of the plain was empty, changed from a sea of soldiers to a pool of blood.

Panic rose from his blood-self. He mirrored the emotion, struggling to keep the feeling under control, until he dabbed a finger in his pouch of *tisi irinti*, smearing a mix of blood and herbs into his gums, and all emotion receded. He was the warrior-prince. He was here to face Gods, to redeem himself and secure a future for his people. He was no coward. He was not afraid.

NO.

The voice thundered in his thoughts. The unwanted voice. His captor. His enemy.

MY CHILDREN. NOOOOOOOOO.

He turned, and faced its source.

The great red serpent flew toward the Soul. It had been wounded in a hundred places, fighting with the blue leviathan arcing up from the distant waves. Now both creatures had turned toward the column of light behind him. Both were rushing forward, howling.

The blue was nothing to him. A figment of another power, the ancestor-spirits of the Nikkon Spirit-Weavers.

The red was everything.

He raised his sword, now standing alone on a field of empty blood. As though he'd been transported against his will to the Plane of the serpent's making, the world drenched in red. He faced the serpent, and his blood-self cowered, overcome with fear and panic. None of those emotions touched him. He was the King. The True King. The hero, ready to face evil.

A host of other creatures had turned toward the Soul. All were coming. The blue serpent, arcing up from the ocean as its waves cascaded toward the light. The Regnant's towering shadow, pulsing with thunder and lightning as it surged across the field. The Skovan angels, leaping into the sky on white wings, crowned in halos and wielding fiery swords, or sprouting horns with tridents of fire. Rabaquim beasts of the Flesh, spirit-bears and leopards, cats and titans of the forest.

They had been fighting among each other, and now turned, all as one, racing toward the light.

Come, he thought to them all. *Come, and see what I've brought you.*

YOU. The serpent's thoughts thundered in his skull. *YOU BROUGHT HER HERE. YOU LET HER UNMAKE MY CHILDREN.*

The red wyrm had rounded on him; even from afar, he could feel its eyes boring into him, piercing through the core of what he was.

I repaid your betrayal, he thought to it. *You should never have treated Bhakal as Rabaquim. My people do not bend to your lies.*

YOUR PEOPLE ARE NOTHING, the serpent thought. *YOU ARE NOTHING.*

I am Omera, son of Amanishiakne, he thought back. *I reject your gifts. I reject your promises. You've failed. Sarine has reached the Soul of the World, and reclaimed it. And now there is a future for me, and for my people, free of your control.*

The serpent arched its back, contorting itself in the air. It loomed larger than a mountain, its coils unfurling as it stretched across the sky. Terror flared in his blood-self, a cowering horror as the serpent approached. He felt nothing. Only the moment. His feet set steady on the ground.

KILL HIM, the serpent thought. *KILL HIM AND I WILL PROTECT YOU FROM THE FATE OF YOUR BROTHERS AND SISTERS. I WILL RETURN YOU TO YOUR FLESH, AND YOU WILL HAVE EVERLASTING LIFE, FIRST AMONG A NEW BREED OF MY CHILDREN.*

For a moment the words washed through him, and he struggled to understand. Kill him? Kill who?

Then he knew: the words were meant for Omera's blood-self, not for him.

Its fear was strong: the fear of being unmade, as it had watched thousands of its kind dissolve into blood. Hope burned inside it, the hope of somehow surviving its master's betrayal. Shame, the shame of being bound to such an unworthy vessel. The blood-self wasn't him, though it had been forged to mirror him. Once, it had been its own man. Not Omera. Something else. Something offered as a sacrifice. Something it now knew could be reclaimed.

The blood-self turned to him, and raised its sword.

It should obey. He willed it to quell its rising fury, to step back, and lower its blade.

Instead it settled into a fighting stance. The stance his mother's masters-at-arms had taught him to use when facing a warrior of great skill.

Blood flowed around their feet, and they attacked.

Both blades surged forward at the same moment, clanging blood against steel. A snap cut rang out against a counterparry, and they shuffled into each other, his leftward step matched by the blood-self's right. Two jabbing thrusts struck against a swift parry into a riposte. He turned his body, shifting his balance, and the blood-self mirrored it, returning strikes at an identical tempo. *Ubax aragti* flared, and his movements became a blur, too fast to calculate his next move. Instinct was everything. Their swords struck, and he shifted his feet again, carefully, deliberately, relying on his herbs to keep his footing in the rising tide of blood. Liquid sloshed as they fought, sending ripples outward across the pool. In the distance a host of monsters approached. Angels, demons, flesh-beasts, the blue wyrm, and the terrible red. He ignored them all. Only the moment was here. The strike. The parry. The step. The turn. The block. The thrust. The lunge. The retreat. The renewed attack.

He could feel the blood-self in his head. Reading his mind. Inheriting his thoughts. He felt the same. He knew when its grip shifted, presaging a downward swipe. He could feel its right foot lift, moving its center of balance for a lunging strike. Instinct governed all, instinct and *tisa irinti*. He was the perfect swordsman. Emotion faded before it could find any hold. He was the warrior. He was the fight. He was the perfect duelist, fighting the perfect duel.

Light flared behind him. He ignored it.

The beasts closed the distance across the plain. He ignored them.

The red serpent gnashed its teeth, writhing as it swept closer through the sky. It was nothing to him. There was only the steps. Only the blood. Only the steel.

He tried a low attack, sweeping a cut up under his blood-self's guard. It moved, twisting its body away before his blade could land. It stepped closer, snapping its sword down toward his knees. He leaned into it, turning them both in a half circle as he parried with an inverse grip, rotating to flip the stopped swords into a strike of his own. The blood-self matched him, struck, parried, struck again. He parried, struck, parried with it.

A low whine sounded in his head. In the blood-self's, too.

It rose with each movement, each attack, each moment the red serpent drew closer as it approached across the field.

IGNORE HIM!, the serpent's thoughts came. *IGNORE THE BETRAYER. REACH THE GIRL. STOP HER, AND I PROMISE YOU IMMORTALITY.*

The blood-self hesitated.

Tisa irinti smothered the sudden burst of anticipation. He felt nothing. There was only the moment. Only the steel.

The quarter-step difference delayed the blood-self's parry. Only a hair. It raised its blade to block; instead Omera's sword sliced through its face, splitting a crevasse between the blood-self's eyes, down the bridge of its nose, past its teeth, through its tongue, to the back of its throat.

The blood-self was gone from his thoughts. It slumped backward, instantly a lifeless run of blood dissolving down to join its brothers and sisters in their pool.

Howling sounded in his mind.

His heart thundered. "It's done," he said. "I've beaten you. I'm free."

The howling grew, past the confines of his skull. A wave of sound blared from the red serpent as it gnashed and writhed in the heavens, rolling down over the fields of glass and iron and blood.

STOP HER, the serpent screamed. *I WILL FORGET YOUR TREACHERY. I WILL FORGIVE. YOU WILL BE MADE MY EQUAL, A KING OF KINGS. ANYTHING. STOP HER! STOP HER NOW!*

He kept his feet set. The beasts and wyrms would arrive any moment. But now even they turned to watch as the red serpent screamed. The thundering approach halted as every eye turned to the source of the terrible sound. The Rabaquim Blood Gods, manifest in the feathered serpent's form.

For an instant something materialized across the red serpent's body. Shapes. Like small, crystalline four-legged snakes. Then they vanished.

The serpent dissolved.

Just as the host of blood-soldiers had melted, disintegrated into the pool now soaking his feet, the whole of the red serpent's enormous body became liquid, all at once. A gray light flashed behind him, and the Rabaquim Blood God was nothing more than a storm of crimson rain. It sloshed down, soaking the fields a thousandfold heavier than the dissolution of its children.

A thousand screams erupted across the plain, from the mouths of every being, every beast close enough to make a noise he could hear. He heard anguish in them all, but to his ears the only sound was peace.

100

SARINE

The Soul of the World
The Infinite Plane

One of the chains broke, untethered to the Soul's light. It unwrapped itself as fast as she could pry it loose, as fast as the *kaas* could aid her fingers. Light spilled out like blood leaking from a wound. It shone, and flashed, and came free, slipping away from the column of light, drifting into the void.

Blood magic. The Rabaquim Blood Gods.

They were gone. Dead. Unmade.

A tide of despair rippled across the Gods' Seat, and the Infinite Plane. She was in both places. Her fingers and her will worked together, absorbed in the light. Emotion answered her work, and the *kaas*, in currents of sparks shared between the columns close to the Soul. The Gods, and their champions. They knew what she was doing now. No way to hide it. She had to work quickly, before they could reach her and put it to an end.

She turned her will to another chain. That was how she saw them now. The coating of white and black sparks covering the Soul of the World wasn't a single, monolithic thing. It was twenty things. Fifty. She had to break them all. It was the only way to keep the world whole, to restore it to its beauty, free from the need for the terrible storm clouds and acid rains. The price of magic was death, a torpor that slaughtered millions, that poisoned the ground, the skies, all that was beautiful in the world. Li and Evelynn had seen it as part of the price that had to be paid, to give humanity the time it needed to evolve to handle its own strength. But there was another way. Growth without stasis. Goodness, without the need for evil. Seeds to be planted, without needing to burn the forest to be sure they took root.

If she could purge magic from the world, it would remain pure, without the need for times of horror and death. That was her plan. All she needed was enough time to see it done.

Zi was here. His consciousness swirled around hers, and ten thousand *kaas* at his side, all working at her direction, under her will.

The towering column shimmered, radiating light from its open wound. She bent her sparks around it, careful not to touch its core, as a second coating to pair with the first. The sea of white sparks flowed up the Soul, and her sparks joined them, gray sparks, scraping and grating against their hold. Friction gave off heat, an endless wave of heat, pulsing across the void. The *kaas* scurried along the outer edge, pulling and prying, searching for a foothold to break another chain.

They found one.

Suddenly all her effort, all her will, went into the crack. Zi directed his *kaas*, and ten thousand conscious minds worked to amplify her strength. A white, shimmering mist leaked as they ripped the sparks away from the Soul's light. The void shook. Anguish redoubled on the physical plane. They pulled, and the chain came free.

She handled it gently at first, guiding the line of magic away from the essence of the world. Pain answered her. The pain of all those who used the white mist, all who would have to let it go. She knew the pain of having magic torn from her, knew the deep ache that would never heal. She mourned the pain she inflicted on those whose essences were built around the white mist. But it had to give. For the world to heal, the chains had to be broken, one by one. She pulled gently, and the white mist slipped away from the light, drifting into nothing as it faded from the Soul. Its patterns dissipated, from the Soul and from the columns that contained its power, leaving nothing in their wake.

The Nikkon, Anati thought to her. *Their Spirit-Weavers.*

She saw the image superimposed over top of the Infinite Plane, from the physical world.

The azure leviathan that had risen from the ocean on the Gods' Seat twisted, writhing in midair. All its power, all its strength, suddenly vanished. It burst in a shower of brine. The woman who had been its master, She Who Gazes into the Deepest Seas, suddenly returned to her physical form, standing in a daze, staring up where the creature she had summoned should have been, watching as it became nothing more than salty rain, drizzling over the fields of glass and iron.

She felt the pain as She Who Gazes into the Deepest Seas tried to summon her leviathan again, and nothing answered. She felt the anguish, the grief, the hollow emptiness as she tried again, and again, and again, and nothing was there. Their magic was broken, and the Nikkon people would break with its loss. But the world would heal.

For a moment she was with them, sharing their grief. Zi had already returned his attention to the Soul. The *kaas* swarmed like sparks of their own, flaring and hunting across the chains that bound the light.

Sarine, Anati thought to her. *They're almost here. You have to come back and fight.*

An image came with the thought, once again superimposed over her work on the Infinite Plane. Kalira, running toward the Soul. Erris and Marquand, desperately putting *Shelter* walls in her way. More coming, in the distance. The Rabaquim flesh-beasts, the Skovan angels, the Regnant himself, by now realizing what she was doing, understanding her betrayal.

I can't, she thought. *Too much left to do here.*

I won't let you die, Anati thought. *But you* will *die if you don't defend yourself.*

In answer, the Nine Tails flared its strength in her belly. It knew she meant to kill it, to cast it and its kind into the void. It and all the war-forms of all the clans. But it was prepared to die for her. It was prepared to give itself for her vision of the world, unsullied by the taint of magic. And until it was time to make that sacrifice, it would fight. If she gave it her body, it would fight.

The *kaas* found another break in the chains. She had to pour her will into it, to guide it free and feel the grief she would visit on another people. But Anati was right. The Gods and their champions were coming. She had to protect her physical body, to ensure she had the time to finish the work here with the Soul.

Fight, then, she thought back to Anati. *Help the Nine Tails keep me safe.*

We can't fight them without you, Anati thought back.

You have to, she thought. *Just keep me alive long enough to finish this work. I believe in you, Anati, and in the Nine Tails. Fight, and be strong.*

Uncertainty came back across their bond. But there was no time. She saw the images from her physical form. Kalira was close. The others would follow.

She stepped back from her body, giving the Nine Tails control.

She changed. Her will retreated into the Infinite Plane. She grabbed hold of the *kaas'* loose chain, helping them pry it from the Soul. Vordu magic slipped free, and this time she felt it mirrored in her own form. The spirits of land and beasts, of past and present and things-to-come, the spirits that had spoken to her, at Tanir'Ras'Tyat, at Ka'Ana'Tyat, when she'd slain the *mareh'et*, the *lakiri'in*, and a hundred more from Evelynn's memory. They grieved the loss. They cried out to her in pain. She had loved them, feared them, respected their wisdom. But they had to die, for the world to live. The chain broke, unwrapping itself from the Soul, and drifted into the void.

On the physical plane she could feel the adrenaline rushing in her blood, the power of *Red*, and the Nine Tails' speed and strength. Her body left the Soul behind, joining the fight as Kalira's sunbursts bored holes in Erris's *Shelter* walls.

The rest of her focused on the fight here, to remake the Soul of the World. With three chains broken, the core of its essence shone through, a shimmering, perfect light, reflecting all colors and none. The *kaas* skittered along its length, from top to bottom, searching, prying, hunting for weakness in the chains. When they found one she would help them pull it loose, and cut another strand of magic from the world. A few more chains, and the rest would give easier, accelerating as it drew near the end. The anguish reflected around her, as the Gods and former Gods, champions and former champions, would be able to feel what she was doing. She needed time, to see it through. And Gods send her own champions would be willing to make the sacrifice, to keep her safe until it was done.

101

ERRIS

The Last Line of Defense
The Soul of the World

Ten *Shelter* walls held, in three layers of fortifications. Eight were hers, burning every drop of leyline energy she could channel through her body. Two were Marquand's. They'd kept together, somehow, him running after her, pivoting and dancing away from Kalira's blasts of sunlight. Three figures—her, Marquand, Kalira—moved with the destructive force of three armies. But she was in Kalira's head now, as surely as she'd ever been a step ahead of any enemy commander. She could feel where the next blast would come, where the next *Shelter* wall would collapse and burn. A single misstep and they were dead, and Sarine with them. They hadn't misstepped yet.

"There!" Marquand shouted, pivoting on his feet to reverse course. She'd already seen it.

One of her walls went pink, shimmering white before it exploded, scattering fragments of energy into the others near it. They caught sight of Kalira, aiming both hands forward as she cut a swath of light across the field.

She slammed another wall in place, before Kalira could move forward, and they ran.

"You two are both fools!" Kalira cried after them. "Don't you see what she's doing? Can't you feel it? Don't you see what it will cost you?"

Gray light rippled from the Soul. They ran at an angle, barely twenty paces from where Sarine stood, frozen, her hand plunged into the light. A new bulwark here, four more walls, and Kalira would move around to try another angle of attack. It took time to cut through each layer; so far Kalira had been more interested in moving, in finding less-defended avenues to approach the light. But there was desperation in the Sun Goddess's voice now. Redoubling their defenses here might stall her another thirty seconds, maybe more.

She let some of the eastward- and westward-facing walls dissipate, re-forming their energy into six new walls here, layers upon layers, each ready to be rebuilt when their outer cousins were destroyed. Marquand followed her lead, adding another barrier between them and Sarine.

"She's taking them all," Kalira shouted. "Everything, even her own magicks. *Your* magicks, you bloody idiots. That's how she convinced the *kaas* to do it. You're going to be dead, and your people will be left with nothing."

A new beam blasted an outer wall on the left. Heat and leyline fragments exploded upward, wafting over top of the next line of *Shelter*. Another wall was ready, slammed into place as soon as the first gave way. She'd been right. Kalira had given up maneuvering. Another beam blasted into the replacement wall, drilling it and the layer behind it in a single burst. She couldn't stop Kalira from advancing, but if she deflected, if she delayed to the right, it could mean ten more seconds before she reached Sarine.

"Watch the left!" Marquand shouted.

Kalira appeared, rounding the corner, raising both hands toward them.

Marquand slammed a wall in place, instantly shielding them as the burst struck and turned it pink. She layered a second shield behind it, and they moved together without speaking. Costly. She'd been wrong, for a step. Kalira was still sliding around her fortifications, even if her attack was focused on moving toward the center. She was a cavalry commander again, dancing around a superior force of infantry and artillery, with the advantage of better ground and initiative of movement. But even the most nimble cavalry could be pinned and hammered if they deployed on the wrong ground. She had to stay sharper, two steps ahead of her enemy, not one.

"I'll spare your lives," Kalira shouted. More desperation. "Anything you want, you'll be granted. You'll live as a Queen and a King. As Emperors."

Another explosion wafted over the double wall between them. Kalira was close. No more than thirty paces from the light. They had to fall back, to defend Sarine where she stood.

Marquand sensed it, the same as she did.

They retreated together, rounding the corner where Marquand's last shield still stood.

Nothing.

For a moment panic threatened to shatter her battlefield concentration. There was nothing here. The light burned, a towering column of gray pulsing waves across the battlefield. But where Sarine had been, frozen still, her hand plunged into the column, there was only empty ground.

Marquand's wall exploded, and Kalira stepped through.

For a moment they locked eyes, before Kalira swept a look around the light, finding it as empty as they had. Sarine should have been there. *Entropy* came to hand, and another wave of *Shelter*. They would die in close combat with Kalira, but if Sarine was gone it didn't matter. They'd failed. But perhaps, if Sarine wasn't gone, if she'd only pulled back from the Soul, cloaked herself in *Faith* again, then—

A blur of fur and claws stepped into view, behind Kalira.

The Sun Goddess whirled around at the last moment, as one of the creature's tails wrapped itself around her throat.

She and Marquand moved, each taking a different route around the Soul. From her vantage Kalira raised both hands, sunbursts erupting wildly from her fingers as she tried to scorch her attacker. White light flared around its body where the sunbeams struck, a shimmering shield dissipating the sunlight. She tethered a *Shelter* wall between them as Kalira's flailing lights burned through the area around the Soul, taking cover behind it while the silhouetted shapes of Kalira and her attacker struggled on its far side.

Not this time, a voice thought inside her mind. A familiar voice—Sarine's *kaas*, Anati. *Not again, you fucking bitch.*

White light pulsed bright enough to block her vision.

When it cleared, her *Shelter* wall had collapsed, burned through in five places. She was safe. Marquand was there, too, on the opposite side of the light. The creature stood over Kalira, two of its tails holding down both of the girl-child's arms, two more holding her legs. The girl's throat was crushed, her face red, eyes bugged out of her skull.

It held on a moment longer than it had to before releasing the corpse, letting Kalira's lifeless body thud to the ground.

She hadn't recognized the thing before, but now she saw it for what it was: the Nine Tails. Sarine. The girl had detached herself from the Soul of the World in time to cut Kalira down.

"It's finished, then?" she asked. "Or do you need more time?"

The Nine Tails shook its head, then shot its gaze up toward the sky, over top of the *Shelter* walls still ringing the light.

Not finished, Anati thought to them. *Sarine is still in there, on the Infinite Plane. The Nine Tails and I are going to keep her body safe while she works.*

"Can we move away from the Soul?" she asked.

No time, Anati thought. *They're coming.*

The ground shook in the distance, but instinct drew her eyes upward.

Six Skovan archangels flew over her *Shelter* walls, and she, Marquand, and the Nine Tails moved together.

Two of the angels were of the feathered, golden-armored variety while four were horned and covered in fire. All six landed almost on top of the Soul, but she, Marquand, and the Nine Tails had already taken cover behind the bulwark she'd put up against Kalira's advance. Confusion would reign for a moment. The angels would expect to find Sarine's body there, not changed to the Nine Tails' form and ready for a fight.

"Now!" she shouted, and stepped out from behind the wall.

Entropy snapped into place, engulfing the clearing around the Soul with fire. Marquand matched her step for step, and the two feathered archangels leapt upward at once, their wings scorched and burning. The four brimstone-angels seemed unfazed by the blast, the *Entropy* only serving to inflame the patterns of ash and cinders on their skins. She cut off the flow as they whirled to face her, readying *Shelter* and *Mind* and drawing her saber. The Nine Tails raced ahead, its movements a blurred flash, even with *Body* speeding her up and *Life* magnifying her senses. Two of the angels' fiery whips cracked, and she and Marquand took cover while the Nine Tails charged.

The thing's tails spun, whipping out to meet their tridents, ensnaring hands and hafts in equal measure as it danced between them. *White* flared around it only once, when a spear should have found the Nine Tails' belly. Instead the trident's point turned, as though it had struck heavy armor, and two free tails whipped the angel across the face, snapping one of its horns in two.

She pulled back, taking stock of the ground. The Nine Tails had the four angels well enough in hand, but their *Shelter* fortifications had been erected to deny Kalira's approach, with no thought to what else might be coming. She released some of the outer walls as the ground shook, revealing the landscape beyond. She had to remake the *Shelter* to blunt whatever advance was coming from…the hills? She squinted, trying to make clear what was coming closer from the horizon. Everywhere else here on the Gods' Seat the ground was level and flat, other than the protrusions of metal hulks and boulders from the now-destroyed spire. Yet there were three hills, and they seemed to be…

Moving. The hills were no hills at all. They were beasts the size of mountains. And they were heading straight for the Soul.

"What in the bloody…?" Marquand said, staring at the same moving mountains.

"Rabaquim flesh-beasts," she said. "It has to be."

"Our *Shelter* can't hold against that," Marquand said. "We have to pull back until Sarine can find a way to stop them."

Armor clanked as the remaining two Skovan archangels landed in front of them.

Suddenly she was dodging a flaming sword, the burned feathers of the creature's wings still smoldering in front of her. She leapt backward, bringing her saber up to parry the strike and barely succeeding in deflecting it. The archangel pressed the attack, hammering blows with his flaming sword as she tethered *Entropy*, unleashing a blast of fire as it tried to move toward her.

Both its wings raised to block the flames, the feathers catching fire once more, but it gave her an opening to tether *Mind*, duplicating herself in the narrow confines of her *Shelter* walls. The archangel pushed through the fire, batting its wings to dispel the smoke as it heaved its sword forward in a desperate lunge. The blade impaled one of her *Mind* copies, dispersing it into light, and the angel lost its footing, expecting to meet resistance to its attack. It stumbled forward and she found *Entropy* again, this time directed into its unprotected flank.

The blast singed the creature's left side, fully charring one of its wings to black cinders. It tore off its own half-melted helmet, letting loose a long mane of golden, iridescent hair as it spun to meet her. She knocked its flaming claymore aside and cut it across the chin with her blade. Its one working wing flapped and pulled it away, but only with enough force to collide with her *Shelter*, not to raise it into the air. She loosed *Entropy* one last time, and the creature collapsed, letting its sword clatter to the ground.

She rounded on Marquand, and found him in trouble.

He'd taken a wound from the angel's sword, his right leg cut from thigh to ankle. They had moved during the fight, thirty paces away from the Soul. He'd put a new *Shelter* wall in place, and a cloud of fire, but the angel had sidestepped both, now advancing on him as he fumbled to draw his saber.

She ran to take the creature from behind. She wouldn't get there in time.

The angel flapped its wings to push it forward, lending it a burst of speed as it lunged to avoid a last, desperate cloud of *Entropy* loosed in its way.

Marquand flung his sword from its scabbard, tossing it into the creature's path. The angel deflected the blade in midair, turning it with its own strike before it leveled its two-handed blade again, this time aimed for Marquand's head.

She shouted something indiscriminate, and saw him mouth a curse.

Gray light flashed from behind them.

She was racing toward him. Too late. A step too slow. *Shelter* was ready, to divide them. *Entropy*, to attack. She saw it happening, as though the world had slowed to give her a better view. Marquand's head should have split like a ripened fruit, cooked by the flames licking up the archangel's steel.

Instead the angel changed.

The wings vanished. The flames went out. The golden armor flashed before it changed to ordinary plate and mail. The halo of light above the creature's head diminished to nothing. All of it happened in an instant, leaving only an ordinary man, an ordinary soldier with no touch of light, no fire, no wings, no sign of magic, behind.

It dropped its sword, letting it fall to the ground instead of splitting Marquand's head in two, as its eyes widened in terror.

The soldier had no time for any other expression. Fire engulfed it from Marquand's hand, a renewed blast of *Entropy* turning the man to cinders inside his now-blackened armor.

She reached his side, already tethering waves of *Body* into his leg.

"What the bloody *fuck* just happened?" Marquand snapped, wincing at her lack of delicacy in handling his wound.

That's what Sarine is fighting for, Anati thought inside their heads.

They both turned to find the Nine Tails hovering over the bodies of four ordinary men and women, instead of the demons it had been fighting before. Their tridents had become ordinary spears, their flaming whips no more than leather cords lying on the ground. No sign of the brimstone flesh, no sign of horns or goat's feet or any of the other markings of the divine.

"She's purging our enemies' magic?" she said.

All of it, Anati replied. *One line at a time. She's almost finished. A few last pushes, a few last waves of defense, and it will be done.*

Kalira's warnings echoed in her head. Sarine was purging all of it, the Sun Goddess had said. Even Sarine's own gifts. Which meant her gifts, too. The leylines, and all the rest.

Bloody fool of a girl. It was exactly the sort of impetuous, foolish, rash decision she'd come to expect from her.

But then, magic had tainted the world. The poison skies, the chaos run rampant, the millions who had died and the millions more who would inevitably fall with them. If there had been time to debate it, time to plan the strategy, she might have argued the point. But she was a soldier. She was here on the battlefield, and she'd chosen her side. Leaving the Gods in power meant keeping the world plunged into chaos and ruin. She stood with Sarine, and they could settle what it meant when the battle was over.

"Form with me, then," she said. "We have to stop those flesh-creatures from reaching the Soul."

The Nine Tails nodded, while Marquand gritted his teeth, waving off an offer of her shoulder to lean against. With *Body* coursing through him, he could walk, and even run, though ignoring the pain would risk further damage to his leg. No way to help it now. The ground was still thundering, the moving mountains growing closer in the distance, and all the other beasts that came with them. *Shelter* could at least funnel the creatures away, possibly to give them enough time to evade their attacks. Her mind spun as they moved, trying to plan the rest of this fight. No chance of outright victory, but Anati had assured her it would be over soon. Delaying could be enough, if what Sarine was doing could be finished in time.

102

TIGAI

In the Flesh-Beasts' Path
The Field of Iron and Broken Glass

The ground rattled under his feet as he ran. These creatures were enormous, too massive to be believed. One foot was the size of twenty pine trees bundled together, arcing upward to a leg the size of the hillside the pines would be planted in. Three of the beasts loped forward, galloping toward the pulsing gray light of the Soul. He ran, as fast as his legs could carry him, trying to get close to the first of them, the one in the lead. Song Xiu had her skirts hiked up, matching him stride for stride, while Yuli and Peizhi had broken away, fighting some giant bear or salamander or whatever other horror had tried to waylay them as they closed the gap. This whole thing was a bloody fucking nightmare. But he had no desire to wake up anytime soon, not if waking meant being crushed or trampled or bitten or whatever else these creatures would do if they caught him.

He blinked as he sprinted into the path of one of the beast's forelegs. This was fucking stupid, even for him. The creature's strands were there, but they were massive, each one thicker than the tethers for a bloody army. No way he could handle so many. Even at his strongest he could take maybe eighty, maybe a hundred souls at once across the starfield. This creature's strands were like ten thousand bodies packed together tight enough to form a single thread. As if you'd unraveled all the rugs in the Emperor's palace and bound them into one fucking cord. The thing thundered across the plain, each step covering a quarter league or more. Now or never. He hooked one of the creature's strands, straining to snap it to an anchor on the far side of the field.

Song Xiu was there, too; she got swept up in it as he fought to widen his reach. No chance he could grasp even the hundredth part of the creature's tangled strands, but perhaps if he tethered part of it, he might at least take a chunk of it with him across the field. A key tendon or joint, perhaps. Maybe a slice of its heart or lungs.

It rose its foreleg to take another quarter-league stride, and he cinched the tethers into place.

The beast's foot thundered into the ground, causing another minor earthquake. His feet threatened to shake out from under him, and Song Xiu grabbed his hand to try and keep them both steady.

They were alone. Suddenly the three mountains had become two, rising above the distant horizon. The third one was here with them, in its entirety, still striding toward the Soul, only now it was a hundred leagues away, as far as he could take them, to the anchor he'd set when fleeing from the spire's explosion.

He whooped and ran before the beast's next step could smash him to pulp.

"It worked!" he shouted. "It bloody fucking work—"

The rest of his exclamation was drowned in a thundering blast from the beast's mouth. A roar, a whine, a howl, all mixed together, loud enough to fill his head with pain. Song Xiu winced and covered her ears. He blinked quickly, snapping another tether into place to take them both away.

Suddenly the howling whine was muted, as they appeared across the field. The third beast was still there, trumpeting its rage in the distance. It reared on its hind legs and truly became a mountain, violently shaking the ground even a hundred leagues away.

"You did that?" Song Xiu said, her eyes wide. They were now at one of his first anchors, halfway between where he'd set the third beast and the Soul, where the other two were closing.

"I don't know how, but it worked," he said. "Stay close. We have to try and get to the other two before they reach the Soul."

Song Xiu stepped toward him, her fingers working as she prepared another Heron-shield. Little good that would do if he put them in the path of one of those beasts. He blinked and scanned the field. Most of his anchors were too far. The smaller beasts stampeding with the massive mountains had encircled half the area, meaning he risked being trampled or gored before he knew where they'd appeared, no matter which anchor he chose. Yuli would be among those beasts, and Peizhi. Might as well choose one as far forward as possible, with as much time to close on the mountains as he could give them.

"All right," he said. "Moving in three. Get your shield up as soon as we move. Two. One."

He snapped the tether into place.

The ground heaved under his feet, and this time he fell.

A screech blared in his ears as he scrambled to his feet, and Yuli sailed over top of him, slamming into a bird in midair. Feathers and claws exploded outward in a rain of blood, spattering to outline the dome of the Heron-shield as it shimmered around them.

Song Xiu offered a hand, and he took it, rising quickly to his feet. Peizhi was nowhere to be seen. Yuli had already careened off the giant bird's corpse, spinning and clawing as she dove into a pack of what looked like fucking tigers, if tigers had teeth the size of kitchen knives. He tried to clear his head. They'd appeared where he'd intended, a good half league from the nearest mountain-beast. Yuli must have run here, expecting this was the anchor he'd use. Bloody woman. Bloody amazing woman. He'd never bloody forgive her if she got herself killed.

One of the tigers launched itself into Song Xiu's shield, its mouth opened to bare two rows of metal fangs, and it crunched into the dome, slumping to the ground in a piteous whine as the shield held strong.

"There," he said, pointing toward the nearer of the two mountains. "Let's move."

"Wait," Song Xiu said. "Isn't that...?"

He turned where she pointed. A man ran alongside the packs of beasts, hurling fire and force to sweep them out of his path. The man wore a robe of red and white and gold, same as the Regnant. No, it *was* the bloody Regnant, all sign of his swirling shadows and thunder vanished.

"The Great Lord," Song Xiu finished. "We should help him reach the Soul."

"Wasn't he using his shadow-lightning...thing?" he said. "What's he doing on foot?"

Another tiger struck at their shield, again rebounding off the side as its body was torn by the Force repelling its attack. He still flinched. Bloody fucking animals.

"We should go to help him," Song Xiu said. "Do you have any anchors closer to—"

A tiger leapt onto Song Xiu, its jaws clamping on her throat as it tore her apart.

He stood, stunned.

One moment the shield was there, shimmering around them with reflective Force, strong enough to repel the beasts' attacks. Now it was gone. The tiger gorged itself on Song Xiu's flesh, biting and snapping as it ripped and tore her neck and chest to bloody pulp.

He raised one of his pistols and fired, still only half believing what he saw. His shot struck the tiger's hide in a puff of smoke and blood. It was as though Song Xiu had dropped her shield and let the thing kill her. No chance the tiger could have broken through on its own. She should have had time to give warning, to duck away or do something, anything, rather than standing there and bloody fucking dying in front of his eyes.

The beast ignored the shot, but a second creature nearby sighted him and pounced.

He had the strands cinched in his fingers when Yuli gutted the thing. The Twin Fangs rushed into it at a full run, knocking it sideways in midair while both her claws savaged the tiger's belly, spilling a rain of guts as it spun around and landed, gored open, leaking its insides onto the metal and glass.

"She's dead!" he shouted, as if it wasn't perfectly obvious Song Xiu had fallen to the first creature's attack. The Twin Fangs spun and raced toward him, taking up a position at his flank, pointing toward the nearest mountain-creature. She meant to protect him where Song Xiu had failed.

"No," he said. "Song Xiu was right. We need to help the Regnant."

With that the Twin Fangs leapt on the other tiger from behind, sinking five claws into its neck and wrenching its head sideways, letting it collapse off of what was left of Song Xiu's body as it slumped to the ground.

For a moment, the battle lulled around them. The beasts had run away, but the ground still shook with each of the mountain-beasts' steps.

The Twin Fangs was Yuli in an instant. The transformation was still jarring, even when he'd seen it a hundred times.

"Where?" she said.

"There," he said, pointing toward where Song Xiu had sighted the figure running toward the Soul in white and red and gold. Only, as soon as Tigai pointed, the Regnant's form shifted, changing from the man to a giant insect, flittering wings and massive scything claws knifing through the air as it leapt toward a pair of spectral bears, slashing and cutting at the beasts as they tangled in a mêlée.

"That's a war-form," Yuli said. "Like the Twin Fangs, or one of my sisters. I didn't know the Regnant had one of our bonds."

"Well, if that's the Regnant," he said, "then we're helping him, and he's helping us. Isn't he?"

"I'm not sure," Yuli said. "The Twin Fangs doesn't trust it."

"It's heading straight for Sarine," he said.

"Then we go to her," she said, changing to the Twin Fangs midway through. He snapped back to the same anchor he'd used to get here, blinking a step away and reloading his spent pistol, then drew both, pointing with the left barrel down the path he meant to take. The beasts were swarming away from both him and Yuli; it looked like they were gathering around the Regnant-turned-insect-war-form. If they ran parallel to both, they could intercept the throng before they reached the Soul. He cursed and ran, the Twin Fangs loping along at his side.

103

ERRIS

Shelter *Walls*
Near the Soul of the World

A *guarajin* sprang at her, and she blasted it apart with *Entropy*. Fire and fur exploded at her feet, and she dove behind a *Shelter* wall as two *mareh'et* came running toward the light. Marquand aimed at one of the horse-sized cats with his pistol, firing as though a ball of lead would do anything to slow them. Neither cat appeared interested in him, or in the spatter of blood where his shot struck one of them in the neck. They ran toward the column, coming to an abrupt halt a few paces from the Soul, suddenly peering around as though they were confused, as though they expected to find Sarine there, immobile, holding her fingers in the light.

The Nine Tails met them, snapping three tails each to coil around the cats' necks and slamming their heads together.

She turned her attention to the onrush of beasts. Sarine—or whatever it was controlling her body—could handle herself.

She moved from her *Shelter*, putting two new walls in place to give her protection on the new ground. Marquand would know to stay back and cover her, and he did, laying down three pistol shots and a sheet of *Entropy* on the left flank as she charged into the right. Four *ipek'a* birds rammed her *Shelter* as soon as she reached it, one after another in sequence. She tethered *Entropy* in front of the wall, cooking flesh and feathers in a burst of fire, then ducked behind it. The beasts were still coming. A horde of them, as though the Rabaquim Flesh Gods had emptied their jungles into the Gods' Seat.

A massive wolf with jaws of metal came bounding around her *Shelter*, and she met it with a blast of fire. She moved, and the wolf followed, undeterred. Marquand hollered something behind her, and she ducked on instinct. The wolf sailed overhead and collided with an equally massive bear, letting out a shock wave of thunder as the two met in midair.

She rolled, *Body* surging through her veins. Suddenly the Nine Tails was there, lashing and slapping its tails into the eyes of both beasts. This time she sprang to her feet, supporting Sarine's attacks with bursts of *Entropy* fire. The ground shook under her feet, but she kept steady, searing an arc of flame across the bear's hide as the Nine Tails grappled it into submission.

Three new *Shelter* walls sprang up around them to give Sarine the time she needed to finish the beasts. Others were coming. She huddled against the edge of her defensive line, preparing another weave of *Entropy* to meet them. More *guarajin*, the leopards, with another of the massive thunder-bears behind them.

No, Anati thought inside her mind. *Don't. You have to fall back.*

"What?" she shouted. The *guarajin* were almost on her shields. A running leap and she could step out, blasting them with *Entropy* before they reached Sarine. "Why?"

The leylines, Anati thought. *They're about to go.*

Her stomach twisted. But her soldier's instincts won out. She ran.

The world seemed to speed up around her.

Shelter vanished.

Body left her system.

Life dulled her senses as it went.

Entropy tethers wilted before she could snap them into place.

All her *Need* connections, all the golden threads she was aware of beyond the reach of her conscious mind, winked out like snuffed lanterns in the dark.

Suddenly she was only a woman, running along the smoothed-out ruins of metal and glass. The *guarajin* loped behind her. Where *Body* had given her the speed to keep pace, to evade the predators and turn the fight on her attackers, she was reduced now to an ordinary soldier. But she was still a soldier. She could still fight.

She whipped her saber around, catching the leopard midleap. She struck it hard enough to send it careening to the side with a gash across its face and forepaws. She fired two pistol shots at the next cat, one puncturing its shoulder while the other took it directly in the eye. The first had already rebounded, springing back on its paws and turning on her lightning-quick. Fear pulsed through her. She ignored it. If this was death, so be it. She was ready.

It was. But not for her. The Nine Tails blurred into view, whirling and snapping as it swept like a tempest through the cats.

Go, Anati thought. *Run. Get to safety.*

She scrambled backward, searching for Marquand. He was there, standing in the open amid the rubble and debris from the spire, where her *Shelter* had given him cover only moments ago. Without *Body* he limped, favoring his wounded right leg, but he still held his pistol, cracked open, feeding new bullets into the revolving chambers.

She reached him without saying a word. He raised his pistol to give her time to reload hers. Both knew without speaking it: The leylines were gone. They were dead if the fighting reached them in earnest. But they had a duty, and neither of them feared to pay the price to see it done.

"Fight's moving away," Marquand said as she worked to refill her pistol's chambers. "Move forward or pull back?"

Without her *Shelter* for protection she could see the chaos around them, the massive hulks moving toward the Soul, two mountain-sized beasts close by and another one, rising on the horizon, barely a silhouette. The Nine Tails worked to carve a swath of death and killing through the beasts, but off to the left a second storm of violence swirled in a blur of movement, blood, and claws.

"What's that, there?" she asked, pointing.

"No fucking clue," he said. "Must've started a few moments ago. The beasts fighting something else? I can't tell."

"Forward, then," she said. "Put ourselves in its path."

He followed as she sprinted, though he couldn't keep pace on his leg. She caught glimpses of the second fight: bears and cats and wolves, all snarling and snapping around what looked like a giant insect, when it stopped moving long enough for her to take it in. The thing was tangled in beasts, the same as the Nine Tails was on their end of the fighting. Whatever it was, the flesh-beasts seemed to want to kill it as desperately as they were trying to kill Sarine.

She took cover behind a boulder left over from the spire's explosion, gesturing for Marquand to follow. No way of knowing what the insect-thing was. It sliced a bear clean in half with one of its claws, leaving the back half of a bear corpse skidding along the ground. Less than a hundred paces off now, with the Soul at their backs. She braced her firing arm against the rocks, taking sight into the stampede, aiming for the beasts. Whatever the insect was, it seemed to be on their side for now. She fired into the wolves, emptying six shots as fast as she could sight and pull the trigger. Marquand did the same when he reached the rocks, firing while she reloaded again.

The Soul was humming, pulsing gray light across the field. Then it flashed, and the beasts collapsed.

As one, every creature in sight dropped dead. The massive timber wolves, the bears covered in thundering sparks, the horse-sized cats, the birds, lizards, serpents, and leopards all slumped over, suddenly lifeless and still. Even the mountain-sized monstrosities dissolved to dust.

For a heartbeat she stared. The insect-thing froze as soon as the beasts died, and she caught sight of it without its blurring motion. It stood as tall as any bear rearing on its hind legs, covered in chitinous plating, each of its arms a claw as long as a scythe. It had already surrounded itself with the rended corpses of the beasts, parts of wolves and cats and bears lying strewn at its feet. Now it stood alone among what had been a stampede only moments ago. The beasts were quiet. Still. Dead. But it moved; whatever the insect was, it wasn't one of the Rabaquim's host. The Soul hadn't taken its magic yet.

The Nine Tails turned to face the insect across the gap on the field between them. Sarine, too, was surrounded by a pile of lifeless jaguars and birds and lizards. Neither she nor the insect was more than a hundred paces from the Soul. The Nine Tails moved first. Toward the insect, while it moved toward the Soul.

She weighed whether to fire at the thing. A moment's hesitation. Long enough for a third figure to charge and grapple the insect from behind.

Yuli.

The Twin Fangs launched itself at the insect, and just as suddenly another figure descended from above, this one covered in feathers like an eagle diving from the clouds. Chaos erupted in a blinding rush of motion. Claws swiped against claws; feathers swirled, exploding outward, and the Nine Tails rushed toward them.

"Hold," she said. "We risk hitting Sarine if we fire into that."

Marquand nodded, keeping his pistol ready, the same as her, training their sights on the mêlée. No chance of hitting anything meaningful now. But if the Soul kept up its pulsing gray light, soon their magicks would vanish, the same as the leylines. She meant to be ready when they did.

104

YULI

The Last Stand
The Soul of the World

W hat the fuck are you doing!"
Tigai's words. They washed over the Twin Fangs like clear rain.

It knew. It could sense a sister in danger.

The Regnant-insect pivoted toward the Soul. The insect had murder in its heart, a wolf sighting an unprotected lamb. The Nine Tails called to it for help, without making a sound. Sarine's war-form ran in vain to stop the insect from reaching the Soul. The Nine Tails wasn't close enough to stop it. The Twin Fangs was.

It plowed into the insect-form from behind, jamming a claw under one of the beast's wings. Green and purple ichor leaked over its hand, the insect screeched, and both of them went down in a rush of claw and putrid stink. Noxious gas leaked from pustules on the insect's back, enough to gag the Twin Fangs and sear its throat. Not enough for it to release its claw. They fell together in a tangle, and its other hand struck, stabbing and raking while the insect tried to spin itself around.

An eagle-cry filled its ears as they struck the ground.

A familiar sound.

Namkat's Wind Song form descended from the sky in a flurry of talons and feathers. Yuli's sister, forgotten and lost to the power of the Sun Goddess's bond. It had tasted betrayal from Namkat's hand. It hungered to punish, to kill, to cast the wayward sister out. But today, with the Sun Goddess slain, the Wind Song fought at its side, as it should have from the start.

They crashed together into the Regnant's insect-form, the Twin Fangs' bite and claws paired with the Wind Song's feathers. Both sisters savaged the insect's chitinous hide, tearing chunks of armored plates and flesh as it screeched and writhed.

The smell of gas filled the air as they attacked its back. Liquids seeped from pus-sacs under its wings, until a shock went through them both when they touched it, an electric spike like an eel or fish, and the Twin Fangs knew to roll, to expose its back, and protect its face.

Fire.

The insect's electric spark caught the gas it emitted in a burst of flame. Namkat, too, had leapt away, the Wind Song's feathers erected in a shield to protect its body. The fire scorched the Twin Fangs' back, but it burned away the gas in a mere instant. Enough for the Twin Fangs to roll away, and snap back to its feet. Enough for the insect to do the same, and face them with its pair of massive claws.

This time the Nine Tails was there. It sensed its sisters' presence by instinct. The Twin Fangs would attack first, baiting the insect into striking, letting the Wind Song knock it off-balance while the Nine Tails ensnared its limbs and forced it down into the ground.

It rushed forward.

The moment froze.

It was being torn away.

Somewhere distant, somewhere out of reach, and yet here. Always here. Somewhere it truly *was*, the core of it, its essence, the foundation of its bond with Yuli.

They were being ripped apart.

It loved her. It would remember her always. It was part of her, and she was part of it. It was time to say goodbye.

Yuli stuttered to a halt, the momentum of the Twin Fangs' rushing charge enough to send her down, sprawling to the ground.

Namkat thudded to the ground beside her, all sign of her feathers gone as the wind was knocked from her sister's lungs.

Sarine fell next to them, her body comatose, with no sign of life.

The Regnant stood, in his mortal body once again, surveying them all for a bare moment before he ran toward the Soul.

The shock of it ran through her senses. She needed the Twin Fangs for this. She'd always had the Twin Fangs, since she was a small girl. It *was* her. And it was gone. The ache was a canyon a thousand paces wide, cut through her like a hundred knives boring into her belly.

But she was still a warrior.

Sarine was still her sister.

The Regnant meant to do her sister harm. Something had changed, the Twin Fangs had been sure of it. And even with the Twin Fangs gone from the core of her, she trusted its instincts.

She snapped to her feet and ran toward him.

Shots rang over the plain. One missed. One struck the Regnant in the leg, sending him down in a howl of pain. Erris and Marquand huddled behind a rock, and the Empress raised a hand in a gesture to hold fire.

She closed on the Regnant's fallen form from behind. Erris and Marquand had pistols trained on him. And during the mêlée, Omera had positioned himself between the Regnant and the Soul, his curved Bhakal sword drawn and ready, though he moved slowly now; a man, no longer pushed by herbs and magic, but still ready to fight.

"That's far enough," Omera said. "This fight is finished."

"It isn't," the Regnant said. "I can still stop her. Let me reach the Soul."

Tigai came running behind her, both his guns trained on the Regnant as sure as Erris's and Marquand's.

"What the fuck is happening?" Tigai said. "Is he our enemy now?"

"He always was," she said, feeling the lingering instinct from the Twin Fangs, sure and certain of his intent. "He meant to kill Sarine. To kill us all. To poison the world again."

"Of course I did," the Regnant said, half snarling it through the pain. "She knew it. She betrayed *me*. What she's doing will leave us all powerless, unable to shape the world."

Maybe the world doesn't need shaping, Anati thought to them all. *Maybe that's what she's learned, her and my father.*

"No," the Regnant said. "She's a fool, and all of you with her, if you let this happen. Let me through, and I can still stop her."

"Our magic might be gone," Omera said, leveling the point of his sword toward the Regnant's throat. "But we choose to stand with her. We choose a world free of your poison. We choose—"

Omera froze.

All the rest of them froze with him.

Her muscles went rigid, locked in place. She wanted to move, to run at the Regnant and force him to the ground. Instead she watched as he picked himself up, limping as he favored the leg Erris had shot through.

"I'd hoped to save my strength," the Regnant said. "Too much to count on the wisdom of pawns."

Sarine, Anati thought. *Sarine! He's doing something. He's frozen them all. We need you! We need you now!*

Yuli strained to move, and nothing answered. It was as though her body had forgotten how to respond to her mind's commands.

The Regnant limped toward the Soul.

Sarine! Anati thought.

She stood, frozen in place, as the Regnant reached the light. All of them stared, unmoving, as he plunged a hand into the stream, and the gray light flickered black.

105

SARINE

The Fires of Creation
The Soul of the World

Anati's thoughts echoed in the distance. She could almost hear them through the weight. The terrible weight. It pressed on her, all the power of the earth's chains coming free into her hands. Power surged and flowed around her, rattling and snapping as the sparks came free. They flowed around her in a burning torrent, and she held on, with all the *kaas* at her back.

The column of the Soul of the World burned hotter as it let the sparks come free. Anati cried out again: *He's frozen them all. We need you! We need you now! Sarine!*

The needs of another place. Two chains were left. Only two. The two oldest, the two most deeply embedded into the core of what the world had become, shackled down by magic. They wrapped around the Soul's light in double and triple knots, rusted and ancient. The *kaas* swarmed over them, prying and biting, finding no opening yet. Her will held, steadfast. This was her work. This was her purpose. Her senses reported dull images of the physical world, of the fighting at the Gods' Seat. Her body lay slumped against the stone. Any of her champions could have betrayed her, could have killed her, or let her die. But they'd held. Even without knowing what she'd meant to do, they were with her. That was her strength, in the end: More than Li, more than Evelynn, more than any who came before, she believed in goodness. She believed the world could find its way, that a choice between lesser evils was no choice at all.

The last two chains slipped loose together, both at the same moment.

The first sign of weakness.

Her heart surged, pouring the *kaas'* strength into finishing the work.

Black sparks flared. The chains stopped before they could move. Something was wrong. The *kaas* hovered over the chains, projecting emotion back to her: hesitation, uncertainty, confusion, indecision. Something had changed.

He's here.

Zi's thoughts echoed in her mind.

Suddenly she could feel him. Not Zi. The Regnant.

Li's presence swirled and grew, a torrent of sparks large enough to envelop the Soul, almost infinite. The same as she was now.

"Don't do this," Li called out through the hollow of the void. His words echoed through creation, amplified by the Soul, by the energy flowing between them. "Sarine. Stop, before you can't undo this mistake."

She pushed, and some among the *kaas* obeyed. Sparks flared, striking around the current of the Soul's light. A river of power flowed around the world's energy, cloaking it in a mix of white and black. Both currents surged wildly, leaking torrents of energy into the void. Life and Death. The two strains of magic left clinging to the Soul.

"Sarine!" Li shouted. His words would echo from the skies, on the physical world, and in the Gods' Seat. She heard him through the vibrations in every torrent on the plane.

"No," she said. It took effort to speak. All her consciousness was poured into the light. Her lips moved on the physical plane, and here, and all creation heard her words. "The world has suffered enough. It's time to let it heal."

"That's what I intended to do!" Li shouted. "The torpor of Death is required to balance the power of Life. You know this. You have Evelynn's memories."

"I do," she said. "But I'm not her. I won't make her choice. Balance isn't what the world needs. It needs freedom. The power to grow and change and become what it will be."

"On its own, life will destroy itself," Li said.

"Maybe," she said. "But the Soul of this world was never meant to be controlled by Gods. We can sleep here, if life needs us. We can rekindle the fire if it ever threatens to go out. That's our place. Watchers. Guardians. Not tyrants. Not murderers."

"But why?" Li said. "Why extinguish magic from the world?"

"Because the price is too high," she said. "All of this, the champions, the ascensions, the Gods and all our magicks, were made to protect our place. To ensure we could live, and act, and lead lives of power instead of letting the world progress on its own."

"You mean to die?" he said.

"If I have to," she said. "If that's what it takes to do what's right."

Silence prevailed.

The sparks hung between them. The *kaas* waited. The last two chains hummed and crackled, sparks dancing as they hovered over top of the world's fire.

"I won't," Li said.

Suddenly his will flared against hers.

Sparks raged, where before they had surged and flowed.

The void erupted into a dazzling burst of light.

Their columns merged together. The sparks that were *her*, and the sparks that were *him*, collided on the Plane. With the *kaas'* will behind her, and the power she'd harnessed to unchain the Soul, her torrent had grown to encompass nearly all of creation. But she wielded the power of Life to do it. He wielded Death. His sparks grew as hers had, only his will wasn't directed at anything external. He poured his will into her, into unmaking her being, as she had unmade the chains.

Pain flared through her.

In an instant, swaths of her sparks were snuffed. In the same instant she fought back, directing the full power of her will against him. Black sparks turned white; white turned black.

Everywhere, in the torrents of all things, Life and Death collided.

Sparks flared into being, new lights summoned from the power each of them held through their wills. A sea of sparks raged and flowed into each other, waves of energy crashing into new currents, giving off blinding flashes across the Plane. Where the void had held between torrents, there was only energy, a crackling, unending balance as both powers unleashed themselves against the other.

Her consciousness struggled to hold on.

Pain and exhaustion swept through her in a storm.

"Zi," she whispered. "Help!"

Emotion came back to her. Will. Pain. Struggle. Fear.

He...has us. The same as you.

The *kaas* were caught in the storm. Violent unmaking swept over them, as it swept over all the other torrents on the plane. Life tried to sustain them, her will projected outward to protect all the *kaas* as she protected herself. Death attacked their forms. Crystalline serpents threatened to break where it touched them, tiny mists melting off their scales and drifting into the void. *White* flared around them, each *kaas* fighting to keep itself alive.

"Can you...push back on him?" she said.

Trying, Zi thought. *Fighting. A mistake, to bring all of us...here. Dangerous, to expose ourselves to his magic. Trapped. Dying.*

Not all of us.

Anati's voice. Echoing from within her.

A bloom of *White* flowered inside her, growing as it spiraled outward through the sparks of Life on the Plane.

No! Zi thought. *Daughter, no. Your bond protects Sarine on the physical plane. You can't be here. You can't touch so much Death.*

Yes, I can, Anati thought back.

Anguish washed through her from Zi.

Love, from Anati.

Suddenly all her sparks were enveloped in *White*. A flash, extending everywhere her sparks touched, everywhere on the Infinite Plane. A flare of strength, all of Anati's reserves channeled into a single moment of protection.

But in that moment, all her sparks lashed out at the Black, and the Regnant's attacks dissolved into Anati's shield.

No! Zi thought. A scream. A howling cry. *Don't do this!*

The Regnant screamed, too. A thundering wail of pain.

Death's power struck her again. After the moment of reprieve it stung like a thousand cuts. For a brief moment all of the Regnant's power had been channeled at Anati instead of her. *White* took it all, until there was no more *White* to shield her.

For a moment, Anati's love pulsed through her being. One final time.

Then Anati broke apart, dissolving into the void.

My daughter! Zi cried.

Rage coursed through her, and grief, and pain. She struck at the Regnant's black sparks in a renewed fury, and this time, with the bare moment of shielding Anati had given her, the tide turned.

Black gave way to *White*. A cascading burn swept across the Infinite Plane. The Regnant howled from the pain. Zi wailed for Anati. Her own tears leaked out on the physical plane, where her body lay still.

She watched from both planes, the physical and the Infinite. The *Black* sparks snuffed themselves under the tide of *White*. The Regnant stood beside the Soul, his hand plunged into its column of light.

He stood, shaking from pain, until the last *Black* sparks were consumed, and his physical body was consumed along with them, disintegrating in a gust of ash.

Her champions shook themselves, suddenly free to move.

The *kaas* on the Infinite Plane moved, too. Their shields of *White* dissipated, and they returned to the sparks with lethargic awareness, almost disbelief. The *Black* was gone. Death had spared them.

All but one.

Anati was gone.

Zi, she thought. *I'm sorry, I didn't know Anati would do that. I didn't know—*

My daughter died a hero, Zi thought.

I know, she thought. *But there must be some way we can save her, some way we can return her from the void.*

She died to let you finish this work, Zi thought. *See it done.*

The final chains came free, both Life and Death slipping loose from the column of the Soul.

After the exertion of facing the Regnant's attack, the final push was no more than a light shove, a bending of her will without fighting for her life. Only this time neither chain dissipated into nothing. Life and Death both settled into her. She'd expected it, and still felt a pang of fear when it came. Evelynn had faced this once, when her champions had ensnared her in a prison of glass. The power of Life, turned inward, with Death to make a mockery of what living meant. Stasis. The world needed room to grow, to find itself without magic poisoning its children. She would be the keeper of the power that remained. She was the living seal, ready to return if the world needed her. But that need would come from people, acting as they would, without the burden of death and poison extinguishing them when they knew too much.

Her last act was to put a link between herself and Tigai.

One sliver of magic still touching the world.

It would die when he did. The Dragon gift had no purchase on the Soul of the World. But so long as the thread between them held, his gift would give her champions a way to leave the Gods' Seat, to find the survivors scattered across the earth and bring them together to plant the seeds of life again. Anati had already died for her, and Arak'Jur, and Reyne, and too many more. She had to give the rest a chance to live.

You're sure? Zi thought to her. *It will mean he can still anchor himself, still travel great distances, while all other magic is stripped from the world.*

I'm sure, she thought back. *They deserve to live.*

Zi nodded. Then her prison was sealed. The Soul was cleansed. The chains of the earth were broken. She would remain here, watching, waiting, while the world and all its people grew and changed and lived their lives without the threat of death hanging over them and their descendants. It was right. Even if it cost her the chance to be part of it. Her uncle would be proud. Anati would be proud. And Zi's emotions shone through, even within the crystal seal: Pride. Love. Grief. And hope.

AFTER

EPILOGUE

KAR'DOREN

The Sinari Village
Vordu Continent

He tried to stay still while the shaman decorated him. The paints stunk. The red one smelled like blood, and the yellow smelled like pee. The feathers she'd tied in his hair tickled his skin, and most of all he could hear the other children outside the tent, still playing with the leather ball the shaman had dragged him away from. He wanted to be playing ball, not standing here being painted to look like a turkey. It wasn't fair. It was dumb, and it wasn't fair.

"Hold still," the shaman said, jerking his head toward her roughly.

He made an angry face, furrowing both brows as he stared back at her. He wanted to argue, but that wasn't the right thing to do, so instead he made sure she knew he was angry.

"Don't scowl at me, little guardian," the shaman said. "You've known today was coming for two moons' turns at least."

"I don't want to go," he said, still scowling.

She laughed softly. He hated when adults did that. Like they knew something he didn't know. And she'd called him "little guardian." He hated that name.

The shaman brushed her paints down the side of his left cheek, a mix of red and yellow and black. He could feel her fingers touching him lightly, each one tracing a different color as she made the designs on his skin.

"I shouldn't have to go," he continued. Maybe the shaman would listen, if he tried hard. "It isn't fair."

"You will represent our tribe," the shaman said. "Do you understand what that means?"

"I know you're Sinari," he said. "But I'm not."

The shaman paused, pulling her fingers back.

"Who told you that?" she asked.

"Everyone," he said. It was true. All the children complained when his teams won at ball. They complained he wasn't really Sinari anyway, that he shouldn't be playing with them. That he should find a Ranasi team of Ranasi children, which wasn't possible because all the Ranasi children were dead. What they really wanted was for him to play with the Olessi, or the Vhurasi, and what they really *really* wanted was not to lose, but it wasn't his fault he was bigger and stronger and smarter, even at four years old, than most of them.

"What was your father's name?" the shaman asked him.

He scowled again.

"Have you forgotten it, to shame him so?" the shaman said. "Say his name."

"Arak'Jur," he said.

"And what tribe was your father born to?" the shaman said. "Before he became *Arak*. Before he became the greatest of all *Arak*s, before he belonged to all tribes, to all of our people."

"Sinari," he grumbled.

"I see," the shaman said. "So you haven't forgotten your father's blood."

He went quiet as her fingers returned to his skin. This time she painted designs on his chest, and he could see what she did, even though she'd told him to keep his eyes up, to look straight ahead while she worked. He looked like a cat, covered in stripes.

Suddenly he started to cry.

It wasn't his fault. His eyes filled with water, the same as they always did when the children teased him about not really being Sinari, because his mother was Ranasi and his father belonged to all the tribes. It was wrong to cry now, when the shaman had just painted his face, but he couldn't help it.

The shaman said nothing. She only stopped painting, moving to rinse her hands in her basin and scrub them on a cloth, as though she was ignoring him while he cried. He knew it was wrong to be crying, but she'd mentioned his father, and he'd loved his father before he went away for the last time. He hardly remembered anything from when he was a baby, but he remembered the feel of his father's arms, thick and strong, lifting him farther up than he'd ever been lifted by Ghella or any of the other Sinari. He remembered his father kissing his forehead, the deep voice telling him he loved him. He remembered the scars covering his father's chest. He remembered feeling safe in his arms.

The shaman's cloth took him by surprise, wiping away the paints and tears as they ran together under his eyes.

"Poor child," the shaman said. "Sit, for a moment. We have time to finish after we rest."

He did what she said, folding his legs under him on the shaman's floor. He tried not to keep crying. His body didn't listen, convulsing and letting water run from both his eyes.

"I knew your father, before I became a shaman," she said. "Back when I was only Symara of the Ganherat. I wielded the power of storms, and of the earth. Do you know what that means?"

He nodded. The war-magic. It was all gone now. But he remembered.

"Like mother," he said.

"Yes," she said. "Like your mother. But also not like your mother. Back then, she was the greatest of all the women who wielded the spirits' gifts. I was nothing, compared to her strength. And even she was no match for your father, who had been chosen by the spirits. Do you know what it means, for your father to have been chosen?"

He shook his head. He'd heard the stories, but he didn't really understand.

"It means they needed him, to bring about a better life for all of us. Do you remember our caves, when we were forced underground? And then the wildness, when the world changed from snow to sea to sand and back again? That was the spirits fighting their war against the great powers of chaos and evil in our world. The spirits needed your father to be their champion in that war. Do you know what happened, after he went to fight?"

Tears threatened to come back. "He died," he said.

"Yes," the shaman said. "He died. But the spirits won. Your father sacrificed his life to give birth to a new world without the need for magic to protect us. So when we say Arak'Jur was guardian of all tribes, that he belonged to all tribes, it means he was the greatest among us, in the spirits' eyes. Your father was Sinari by blood, but he was chosen by the spirits who govern us all. You are never less, for being his son. Anyone who says otherwise is a fool, and you need shed no tears for the words of fools, my poor child."

She dabbed her cloth under his eyes again. He sniffled. The tears were still there, but she was right. It wasn't right for him to be crying now. He was still sad, though.

"If only it was so easy," a voice said from the tent's entrance.

Mother's voice.

He got up and ran to her.

The paints on his chest smeared against her white skirts. He didn't care. She didn't seem to care either. Her hands reached around his back, pulling him in closer.

"Corenna, my honored sister," the shaman said, bowing. "I regret that my work now seems to be spread across your dress."

His mother smiled. Streaks of yellow, red, and black now decorated her skirts below the knee. She ignored it, kneeling and keeping both hands on his shoulders.

"I miss him, too," his mother said. "Every day. And sometimes fools' words cut inside me, even when I know better than to listen. I fought alongside your father, too, and part of me died with him, even though the spirits kept my true body safe. And I'm grateful they did, because it means I got to come back to you."

His tears came back again. It was stupid. He shouldn't cry so much. Only, his mother had tears, too, so maybe it was okay.

"I hope we have the rest of the afternoon, to redo the painting before they arrive," the shaman said.

"We don't," Corenna said. "Tigai is here already. Waiting by the cookfires."

Symara grimaced. "Give me a moment, then," she said. "I can at least make him look presentable."

Corenna rose, letting the shaman take his hand and put him back in front of her paints. Her dress was covered in smudges and inks. It made him feel bad, though she didn't seem upset.

The shaman knelt in front of him, working with paint-covered fingers on one hand and her wet cloth in the other.

"Mother," he said while the shaman worked. "What does it mean that 'part of you' died with father? Why didn't all of you die, like he did?"

"Kar'Doren!" Symara said. "That's not a kind question."

"It's all right," his mother said. "I know what he means. In a way, it means my heart died with him. I loved your father. But in another way, I was there, too. I don't know how to explain it fully. When the world first changed, I was very sick, along with all the others who used the spirits' magicks. Your father took me to a sacred place, where I slept until your father won his battle and our magic was taken from the world."

"You slept the whole time?" he asked.

"I did," she said. "I had terrible dreams, nightmares from my fever. I dreamed of a great Blood God, who took the shape of my body and used me to fight, alongside your father and all the rest of the champions. I remember those moments, too, on a Tarzali farm, under a bright sun when the rest of the world was in darkness. I believe those moments were real. But no matter what happened in the dream, my true body slept with our spirits. And so when the fight was won, I awoke, cured, and now I miss your father, the same as you do."

"There," Symara said. "That will have to be good enough. Unless you think, perhaps, Lord Tigai would wait another hour for me to get it right?"

"Delay his wedding, for the sake of our pride?" Corenna asked. "I don't think so. He'll understand, for my dress as much as for Kar'Doren's paint. Sometimes tears make a mess of things. That's just how it is."

That much, at least, he understood. He hated crying. But sometimes tears came. It was better when he had someone to share them with.

"Are you ready, then, my dear?" Corenna asked.

He nodded. His body stank, but it felt good to wear the tribe's designs. His father would have worn the same ones, he realized, whenever he'd attended something important. Since he was Sinari, before he became a member of all the tribes. Maybe he'd gone to a wedding covered in black and red and yellow, too, once. Before he became a legend, when he was still a man.

"Did father wear these designs, too?" he asked.

"Oh yes," mother said. "And the feathers, and cords. Your father was a beautiful man. Just as you are a beautiful boy."

His mother stopped to say something to Symara as he waited at the tent's entrance. The other children were still playing ball on the greens outside. He wanted to run over and join them, but maybe dressing up like his father was all right, too. It made him happy, to think his father might be proud of him. Mother had told him he would meet some of father's old fighting companions today. Maybe he could ask them for stories of what his father had been like. That would be good. He could always play more ball tomorrow.

EPILOGUE

YULI

A Dressing Room
Chagratai Keep

She fought to keep her head still as her sister cinched the laces on the back of her dress. It hurt like a hundred snakes biting her at once. She could hardly breathe with four of the laces tightened, and there were still six to go. But she was determined to be beautiful today. Even if it took enduring a little pain and suffocation.

"I'm...bloody...sorry for this," Namkat said, cinching the fifth lace down across her spine. "I think that dressmaker is a devil in disguise."

"Tricking you into torturing me?" she asked.

"Something like that," Namkat said. "Are you sure you're okay?"

"I'll manage," she said. "Keep going. It's almost time."

Namkat stepped back, eyeing which lace might inflict the least pain. It didn't really matter which she chose; they would all hurt, and she would endure anything their devil-dressmaker had in store. The stand-mirror she'd procured for today showed a reflection of exactly what she'd dreamed of, since she'd dared to hope this day might come. Another woman stared back at her through the mirror-glass. Yet when she moved, the mirror-woman reflected her motions. When she winced, the mirror-woman winced along with her, somehow making even suffering look elegant. Heavens send Tigai saw the same beauty. Half the pain she suffered here was for herself, to fulfill those dreams of what a Natarii warrior's wedding day ought to look like. But the other half was for him.

Gold and silver entwined together wrapping around her legs. A full train hung from the back, eschewing lace for silk and satin, a blend of Natarii and Jun styles. Red took the place of the traditional white; Namkat had found a store of red silk bolts, perfect for a Jun wedding dress, and instead her dressmaker had crafted it into a Natarii gown, embroidered along both shoulders and her left arm with designs of dragons, for Tigai, and with wolves, for her. Thin silk paneling, almost sheer, exposed the top of her chest and her neck, custom-stitched to trace the lines of her tattoos so they ran from her face down her skin, making it look as though the Natarii warrior-spirit was present in all of her, from her breasts to her cheekbones and her forehead. It was bold, almost sacrilege, but the dressmaker had worked with ink-artists to maintain the proper lines. She might even visit the ink-artists to have the tattoos done permanently, when this was finished.

Her appearance was completed by gold jewelry encircling her wrists, embedded with rubies cut small, to accentuate rather than draw the eyes. She wore nothing around her neck, letting the tattoo-lines carry the presentation. That had been her demand, over the dressmaker's strong objection. But the Twin Fangs lived on in her tattoos. It was right for it to be here, in some part. Her hair was bound up with ivory pins in the Jun style, brushed and folded over like a thin sheet of gold. Her mask was pushed up, ready to be drawn down to cover her face before they walked into the festival hall. She'd insisted the mask be painted with the Twin Fangs' lines, in a precise copy of her face, forged in black and gold.

The last laces cinched tight enough to crush her lungs. Namkat made an apology after each one, but she ignored the pain, and kept steady on her feet. Today had been a long time coming, and long overdue. She needed it to be perfect. A few shortened breaths wouldn't stain it. Though, perhaps this was another reason Natarii warriors couldn't marry: fitting the dress would have drawn out the Twin Fangs, if it had still burned inside her. Hardly an auspicious beginning to a marriage, for her warrior-form to have decapitated her attendants.

"And, done," Namkat said. "If you can still breathe at all in there."

"Set the mask," she said. Her voice was only slightly more strained than normal. "Make sure they're ready for us."

Namkat moved swiftly, gently placing the gold and black mask over her face, taking care to preserve the arrangement of her hair and pins. Then she went to check the hall, leaving her alone.

She took the time for one last look in the mirror. The dressmaker had done it. She was the perfect blend of Jun and Natarii, and today she felt it. They'd spent almost two years working to find survivors, to rebuild the communities thrown apart and sundered in the world's devastation. Chagratai was a new city, built from nothing, but she could be proud of its walls, proud of the keep they'd built here. It was no palace, but then, there were no true palaces left in the world, Jun or otherwise. Chagratai was a monument to her people's strength, and she could stand behind that, marrying a Jun lord. Her people rushed to have the hall ready for this day, and they'd done well. Banners had been sewn, for décor, and the first spring flowers had been gathered and hung around the hall. The preparations had been a celebration unto themselves, and the final reward was a marriage fit for the ages. One of the last Natarii warriors, wedding the last Jun *magi* in the world. A story she could tell her grandchildren, a story that would spread across the world, twisted and bent in the telling, but with her and Tigai, always together, at its heart.

"They're ready," Namkat said. "If you haven't passed out, and you can still move?"

"I can move fine," she said, grinning behind her mask.

"Good," Namkat said. "I wouldn't want to have killed you on your wedding day."

"Another day would work better for you?"

"Careful," Namkat said. "Laugh and you might rip a seam."

She felt the weight of the pins and jewelry in her hair, and offered an arm for Namkat to walk beside her. Her sister took it, falling in at her side. If her father had been alive, he would have been there. But without him, a sister would serve better than a man unbound to her by blood. Tradition had to bend as the world did.

They walked together, and she heard the beginnings of the music playing in the great hall. Jun music, with its high-pitched horns and strings. On her first hearings it had sounded like goats fighting in a tinmaker's shop, but its melodies had grown on her. Tigai loved it, and she loved him, and today, that was enough.

They reached the great hall, and stopped before the main doors.

Namkat went to knock, two firm raps, then fell back in at her side. The music would stop, and switch to a proper Natarii wedding march. Then the doors would open. Her breath came quick, as much for the dress as for her nerves. Any moment now, she would face a hundred pairs of eyes, and Tigai, waiting for her at the apex of the room.

"Oh, I almost forgot," Namkat whispered. "You look beautiful, sister. A vision of perfection, on a perfect day."

"Don't patronize me," she whispered back.

"I mean it," Namkat said. "I know all our sisters are watching you right now, as proud as I am, and they're jealous as all the hells that I'm the one who gets to be at your side."

She smiled, feeling water welling up in the corners of her eyes. So much for the powders and dusts she'd spent half the morning applying to her face. But then, a wedding without smudges from tears was no wedding at all.

The great hall's doors cracked open, and swung inward.

As one, the congregation rose to their feet. The left side was nearly all Natarii clansfolk, the men clad in furs trimmed with more furs, while the women wore proper tattoos on their faces, dressed in fine wools trimmed with fox and ermine. Two military uniforms stood out from the others in the front row, both wearing the deep blue of New Sarresant: Erris d'Arrent, holding a fist to her chest, and Anton Marquand, trying to replicate Erris's gesture and having to lean on his crutch to do it. Corenna of the Ranasi stood beside them, and her and Arak'Jur's son, Kar'Doren, along with four other tribesfolk, representatives of the Nanerat, Vhurasi, Olessi, and Ganherat. The right side of the chapel was mostly Jun, ferried in for the ceremony by Tigai. They wore silk, and thick, patterned wool, stitched with house insignia. Again, the outliers stood out: King Omera, and his new wife, surrounded by a squad of Bhakal guards. Allakawari, the assassin who had served Kalira and Orana, stood next to them, with an entourage of Tarzali at her side. Representatives of the Rabaquim were there, too, alongside princes and princesses of Gand, Skova, Hagal, Nikkon, and more. Survivors of every nation they'd recovered, leaders, diplomats, merchants, scholars that she and Tigai had helped bring together in the aftermath of the world's devastation. The great hall was a conclave of fashions and cultures, jewels and paints and fine fabrics in a dozen styles, and she had eyes for none of it.

At the head of the chamber, beside a Natarii priest tattooed with the lines of beasts on her cheeks and forehead, stood Yanjin Tigai.

She almost laughed when she saw him. He'd tried to do the same as she had, adopt dress that reflected her culture as well as his. Only his dressmaker had apparently insisted he clad himself in chieftain's garb, an albino bear's fur draped over both his shoulders, replete with preserved eyes and fangs swallowing his head. Dark lines surrounded his eyes in a reflection of clan tattoos, while his mouth was covered in Jun paints, both his lips stained white. The rest of him was garbed in Jun silk, and he looked all the better for it. White and red, matching her dress, in the same dragon and wolf patterns, spiraled up his coat and sleeves, and he had the same gold bangles she did around his wrists. She could have done without the bearskin, but it didn't matter. He'd worn it for her. And he was beautiful in any clothing, rags or fine silks. He stared at her, and she stared at him, and the rest of the chamber melted away.

She floated forward, gliding past beaming smiles, tearful eyes, and knowing looks. The music thrummed, and she noticed none of it. Namkat made a bow when they reached the altar, offering her a sweet smile with tears in her eyes as she took Yuli's hand and placed it in Tigai's, then vanished to take her seat. Their eyes met through her mask. She changed her mind. The bearskin looked regal. His face was composed and stern, the picture of a Jun lord, but in his eyes sparks danced, the sparks that had made her fall in love with him. He took her hand gently, stopping to face her in front of the priest.

"Honored guests," the priestess intoned as the music came to a stop. "Friends, families, cousins, travelers from distant lands. We come here today to celebrate the love of two souls seeking to be joined as one: Lord Yanjin Tigai, brother of Yanjin Dao, and Yuli Twin Fangs Khansdaughter Clan Hoskar."

The priestess continued speaking, and the words flowed around her like water. She gripped Tigai's fingers, and he gripped hers. Cords were wrapped around their wrists, wine spilled over both their forearms to stain the cloth. She knew all the symbols, all the ritual, every word the priest would speak. None of it mattered. She stared into his eyes, and he stared into hers. When her mask was lifted, and his eyes went wide, seeing the embellishments and cosmetics she'd applied to her tattoos, it stirred her all the more. He loved her. He thought she was beautiful. She could see it reflected in his eyes. She thought the same. He was perfect, with all his flaws. She loved him more than she imagined she could love anything, or anyone.

She broke with ceremony slightly, reaching up to remove the bearskin hood and lay it across his shoulders after he removed her mask. The priestess took it in stride, even improvising a line about her revealing him for all to see and recognize, as he had done for her. He seemed relieved, and she'd as soon kiss him without bear fangs threatening to scrape her skin.

Finally Tigai began repeating the oath they'd written for each other.

"I, Tigai, Lord Yanjin, do solemnly promise to honor Yuli, to love and keep her and face all the chaos of this world at her side."

Simple. But they'd faced enough together to know what it meant. The priestess turned to her.

"I, Yuli Twin Fangs, do solemnly promise to honor Tigai, to love and keep him and face all the chaos of this world at his side."

She went back to staring at him. The priestess said something else, something proclaiming them husband and wife, and the great hall rose to its feet, suddenly cheering. Music began playing again, or perhaps it was only in her head.

Tigai kissed her.

Part of the Natarii style. He'd told her public kissing wasn't done in Jun ceremonies, but then, it seemed perfectly appropriate to kiss her husband wherever and however she pleased. Her husband. He was her husband. She kissed him again, to be sure.

Finally they separated, and turned to face the crowd. Erris and Marquand clapped and beamed in the front row. Corenna cried, while Kar'Doren wrinkled his nose, cupping his hands over his ears at the noise. Omera held his bride by the waist, her belly already swollen and pregnant. She and Tigai bowed to the crowd together, then turned and bowed to each other, then once more, finally, to the priestess.

The hall kept up its cheering, and she went into his arms. He held her, strong and firm, and she kissed him again.

"I love you," he said softly, meant for her ears alone. "All of you. I wish the Twin Fangs were here to be part of this."

"It is," she said. "All my sisters are watching over us. The Twin Fangs, and Sarine, and all the rest. And I love you, too."

"You should know: I have anchors set in our bedchamber. Say the word and we're gone."

She laughed. Of course he would.

"This ceremony is for them, too," she said, nodding toward the hall. "I think they'd be alarmed, if the bride and groom suddenly vanished."

"I think they'd know exactly where we've gone," he said. "And know better than to disturb us."

"Soon," she said, patting his hand as she stepped back. The crowd was coming forward, ready to greet them as husband and wife. Husband and wife. She liked the sound of it. She was his, he was hers, and the world was brighter, now that they would face it all together.

Tigai was swarmed by Jun lords, by King Omera, Allakawari, and the rest. She accepted a firm embrace from Erris, and from Marquand, careful to favor his crippled leg. Corenna wrapped her with both arms, squeezing her tighter than her laces did, and she felt a pang of guilt that Arak'Jur hadn't survived to be here at her side. Namkat greeted her with kisses on both cheeks, and then the new Natarii Khan and his wife took turns to grapple and kiss her and cheer for her and Tigai both. After five or six more greetings, embraces, and celebrations she found herself casting a look through the crowd, meeting Tigai's eyes and wishing for his anchor. But she'd been right. This day was for their guests as much as for them. She saw it in their eyes, a renewed spark of hope and life that the two who'd traveled the world, seeking survivors, had finally made their union official. She and Tigai had shared in the reunions, when husbands and wives, parents and children were brought together by his gift in the wake of the world's sundering. Everyone deserved to be with them now, to share and celebrate their love.

For a while, anyway. Tigai's anchors were still there, beckoning. Perhaps she'd find him and steal away after the first drinks were poured, or during the meal. He was right, too. Their guests would know exactly where they'd vanished to, and hopefully have the good sense not to disturb them once the doors were closed.

EPILOGUE

ZI

A Crystal Prison
The Soul of the World

He willed himself to change, and to move.

A making and an unmaking, both at once. If he wasn't careful, he might not appear. But he was always careful. Movement was second nature to the *kaas* now, though he remembered a time before that was so. So much had changed. His people had grown further than he'd dared imagine, and too often they forgot the miracle that was change, growth, adaptation, survival. The world owed them nothing. They got what they could take; without careful management of possibilities, even the *kaas* could go extinct. A cold reminder, as he appeared on a cold, lifeless plane, covered over in smooth, polished glass.

He moved again, closer. Rude to draw too near without warning. But she felt him coming. She stirred, a seed of light and warmth spreading outward from the heart of her tomb.

Zi, she thought.

Sarine, he thought back.

Magic pulsed between them, and he appeared in front of her.

Crystal encased her body, a diamond prison frozen around her. The clothes she'd been wearing, the Empress's dress of red and white and gold, still clung to her, cleaned and made pristine within the glass. Her eyes were closed, her skin preserved, though he felt her senses on him, her awareness of the sparks that were *him*, on the Infinite Plane.

I was hoping you'd come, she thought.

You were sleeping, he thought back.

I was. But your company is welcome. Always.

Did you see the wedding? he asked.

Yes, she thought. *Yuli looked beautiful. I wished I could have been there in person.*

It will grow easier, with time, he thought. *When you don't know the people of the world. When their blood is diluted over generations. You'll sleep and soon they'll all be your children, and Yuli's, and the rest.*

Quiet fell between them. The crystal flashed with emotion. Green, and gray.

I'm scared, she thought.

I know, he thought back. *That's why I came.*

Life and Death, she thought. *They're part of me now, aren't they? And the others . . . they didn't dissolve into the void. I've been thinking about it. They scattered, but they can't truly be gone. They're just patterns, energy shaped a certain way. Someone else could reshape the magicks, and they would return.*

Yes, he thought, trying to mask his surprise. He hadn't expected her to guess this for a millennium or two at least.

So if magic does return . . . she began, letting the thought trail off into nothing.

That's part of why you're here, he thought. *You carry the seed to restore humanity, but also to unmake, or remake, their magic, if they're ever ready for it. That's for you to decide.*

Well, now I'm even more frightened, she thought. *I wish Anati had survived.*

Pain and grief shot through him. He didn't bother hiding it.

So do I, he thought.

Their grief mixed together. He brushed his scales against the crystal, feeling its cold, smooth surface against his skin. Without his bonds to the chorus, the sensation was his alone. Still unfamiliar, to be the only mind in control of his body.

I had another thought, too, she thought to him. *The Master, he didn't make the Soul, or shape the energies of Life and Death. He found them, intact, when he broke the seal, then Evelynn and Li found them when they ascended. All the tools they needed for creation, ready-made, as though they'd always existed. As though the world demanded there be Gods.*

This one he'd expected her to puzzle out. But he thought nothing back.

It was you, wasn't it? she thought. *The kaas. Li thought he created you, but he was never capable of that kind of making. You existed before. You made the tools, the Soul, the prime magicks, all of it.*

My kind have traveled a long way, he thought. *And we still have far to go.*

You still won't tell me, she thought.

It's not my place, he thought.

Who else? she thought. *Aren't you their King? Or whatever passes for it?*

No, he thought. *I'm alone now. I left the chorus before I came here.*

The hollowness of the thought echoed in his mind. But then, he'd served for long enough. He'd earned peace. Easier, if Anati had been alive.

What does that mean? she thought.

I had thoughts, too, he thought. *I never meant for you to pass the eons alone. My daughter was meant to survive. I stepped down from the chorus, and severed the links between my mind and theirs.*

You retired? she asked. Amusement, a green-yellow mix, flashed across the crystal's edge.

I wanted something else, he thought. *That is, if you will accept me again.*

The green-yellow held for a moment. Then the crystal flashed red, and white.

Wait, she thought. *You want me to . . . ?*

To bond me again, he thought. *If you'll have me.*

Zi! she thought.

It's time for another voice to guide the chorus into our next age. With this cycle finished, my people are leaving this earth behind. But the thought of you, alone, was more than I wished to bear. I let them go on, and stayed behind. To be your companion once again, if you wish it.

Of course I'll have you, she thought. *Zi. You were always part of me, even when we weren't bound together.*

It will be a long sleep, he thought. *Are you certain you won't tire of me?*

Never, she thought. The crystal hummed white now. Hope, and love.

He felt his consciousness fold into hers on the Infinite Plane. He'd worked to engineer her birth and creation for precisely this moment. She was an evolution of human, able to dance along the sparks and strands of creation without being tempted to use them to forge chains for others. Power, with compassion. Strength, with love and sacrifice.

Life flashed between them.

Her feelings settled into his. An old, familiar warmth.

He let his body dissipate, shifting his consciousness to the Infinite Plane. They were both free to move here. Free to watch the world, and look in on her children, and his. They could watch the ages come and go together. If the need arose, they would awaken, her carrying the sparks of this world's magic, and him carrying the wisdom of an old soul, long traveled, but, for now, finally ready to lay his burdens down.

He'd forged the fires of creation. He'd made the world, drawn children here, given them the means to become Gods, to shape themselves, to grow and change as his people had, once. Now he deserved love, of the sort of which only humans were capable. Selfish, perhaps, but that too was an evolution. That, too, was change.

Thank you, Zi, Sarine thought. *I'm glad you came back to me.*

I am, too, he thought back to her.

Now I suppose we wait, she thought.

That's always the best part, he thought. *To see what your children do, to watch them change and grow without your guiding hand.*

So the kaas *were the ones who made all this.*

Red flickered on his scales, even here on the Infinite Plane.

You engineered the world this way, without magic, he thought back. *What happens next belongs to you as much as it ever belonged to me.*

I love you, Zi, she thought.

Warmth pulsed through their bond. Perhaps that was all he'd truly needed to learn from this age. He did his best to send the same emotion back to her. It worked. She was content. And for the first time in a great many ages, so was he.

THE END

ACKNOWLEDGMENTS

It's done!

Thanks to Sam Morgan, my agent. He's since retired and will be missed, but this series never gets made without his vision and willingness to take a chance on a new writer.

Thanks to the entire Orbit staff. Brit Hvide and Angelica Chong, my editors, helped shape and reshape this story until we got it right. Incredible to think how far we've come in the years this trilogy has been in progress. I'm deeply indebted to all of the people at Orbit for giving me a chance to tell this story through to its end.

My family. These have been hard years for most of us, and I would be nothing without their love and support. My parents, Don and Mary. My daughters, Aurie, Jamie, and Evangeline.

My wife, Lindsay.

She's carried me through everything. From the earliest chapters of the first book to the final ideas behind this one, none of this story happens—none of it—without her. I'm proud as hell of her. Watching her grow with me is the great privilege of my life.

Thanks to you, my readers, for sticking with me. I hope you were pleased with how it all ended. At times I was as surprised as anyone—the perils of writing without outlines. But that leads me to the biggest thanks of all.

Early in the process of writing book one, I began to feel an enormous sense of obligation. These characters were trusting me to tell their story. I've spoken to other writers about this, and I find it's a common sentiment—maybe you've experienced it, too, if you've ever sat down to write. At my best moments, it was as though my fingers became a conduit for something else, something greater than my talent could produce alone. After those writing sessions I frantically backed up my work, convinced I could never reproduce it if some terrible accident wiped out my computer.

So now, after almost nine years since I first typed "1" on the first page of the first chapter, I think I can say I was a good custodian of these characters' stories. My biggest thanks go to them.

To Erris, for her arrogant brilliance. To Arak'Jur, for his desperation for love. To Tigai, for his eternal optimism. To Yuli, for her romantic heart. To Reyne, Marquand, Corenna, Revellion, Dao, Mei, Acherre, Llanara, and Father Thibeaux. To Paendurion, Axerian, and Ad-Shi, and to Evelynn and Li.

To Anati, for her fierceness. To Zi, for his wisdom.

To Sarine.

I loved them all. I hope you did, too.

meet the author

Vakker Portraits

DAVID MEALING grew up adoring all things fantasy. He studied philosophy, politics, and economics at the University of Oxford, where he taught himself to write by building worlds and stories for pen-and-paper RPGs. He lives in Kansas with his wife and three daughters.

Find out more about David Mealing and other Orbit authors by registering for the free monthly newsletter at orbitbooks.net.

orbit

Follow us:

:fb: **/orbitbooksUS**

:twitter: **/orbitbooks**

:youtube: **/orbitbooks**

Join our mailing list
to receive alerts on our
latest releases and deals.

orbitbooks.net

Enter our monthly
giveaway for the chance
to win some epic prizes.

orbitloot.com